1983

Last and First Men

&

Star Maker

TWO SCIENCE-FICTION NOVELS BY

OLAF STAPLEDON

DOVER PUBLICATIONS, INC.
NEW YORK

This Dover edition, first published in 1968, is an
unabridged and unaltered republication of *Last and
First Men,* as published in 1931, and *Star Maker,*
as published in 1937.

Standard Book Number: 486-21962-3
Library of Congress Catalog Card Number: 68-19448

Manufactured in the United States of America
Dover Publications, Inc.
180 Varick Street
New York, N.Y. 10014

Contents

Last and First Men

A STORY OF THE NEAR AND FAR FUTURE

BY

OLAF STAPLEDON

DOVER PUBLICATIONS, INC.
NEW YORK

Foreword

TO THE ORIGINAL AMERICAN EDITION

MAN seems to be entering one of the major crises of his career. His whole future, nay the possibility of his having any future at all, depends on the turn which events may take in the next half-century. It is a commonplace that he is coming into possession of new and dangerous instruments for controlling his environment and his own nature. Perhaps it is less obvious that he is also groping toward a new view of his office in the scheme of things, and toward a new and racial purpose. Unfortunately he may possibly take too long to learn what it is that he really wants to do with himself. Before he can gain clear insight, he may lose himself in a vast desert of spiritual aridity, or even blunder into physical self-destruction. Nothing can save him but a new vision, and a consequent new order of sanity, or common sense.

America may play an important part in creating the new vision. But visions, if they are to be permanently helpful, must embody the whole breadth and depth of experience. They must not be crude, extravagant, lopsided. They must be conceived not only with originality but with sanity, even if sanity has to take up a new orientation in consequence of the new vision.

In early chapters of this book America is given a not very attractive part. I have imagined the triumph of the cruder sort of Americanism over all that is best and most promising in American culture. May this not occur in the real world! But since the possibility of such an issue is admitted even by many Americans themselves, I shall, I hope be forgiven for emphasizing it, and using it as an early turning point in the long drama of Man.

Contents

THE CHRONICLE

DIAGRAMS

Preface

TO ENGLISH EDITION

THIS is a work of fiction. I have tried to invent a story which may seem a possible, or at least not wholly impossible, account of the future of man; and I have tried to make that story relevant to the change that is taking place today in man's outlook.

To romance of the future may seem to be indulgence in ungoverned speculation for the sake of the marvellous. Yet controlled imagination in this sphere can be a very valuable exercise for minds bewildered about the present and its potentialities. Today we should welcome, and even study, every serious attempt to envisage the future of our race; not merely in order to grasp the very diverse and often tragic possibilities that confront us, but also that we may familiarize ourselves with the certainty that many of our most cherished ideals would seem puerile to more developed minds. To romance of the far future, then, is to attempt to see the human race in its cosmic setting, and to mould our hearts to entertain new values.

But if such imaginative construction of possible futures is to be at all potent, our imagination must be strictly disciplined. We must endeavour not to go beyond the bounds of possibility set by the particular state of culture within which we live. The merely fantastic has only minor power. Not that we should seek actually to prophesy what will as a matter of fact occur; for in our present state such prophecy is certainly futile, save in the simplest matters. We are not to set up as historians attempting to look ahead instead of backwards. We can only select a certain thread out of the tangle of many equally valid possibilities. But we must select with a purpose. The activity that we are undertaking is not science, but art; and the effect that it should have on the reader is the effect that art should have.

Yet our aim is not merely to create æsthetically admirable fiction. We must achieve neither mere history, nor mere fiction, but myth. A true myth is one which, within the universe of a certain culture (living or dead), expresses richly, and often perhaps tragically, the highest admirations possible within that culture. A false myth is one which either violently transgresses the limits of credibility set by its own cultural matrix, or expresses admirations less developed than those of its culture's best vision. This book can no more claim to be true myth than true prophecy. But it is an essay in myth creation.

The kind of future which is here imagined, should not, I think, seem wholly fantastic, or at any rate not so fantastic as to be without significance,

9

to modern western individuals who are familiar with the outlines of contemporary thought. Had I chosen matter in which there was nothing whatever of the fantastic, its very plausibility would have rendered it
unplausible. For one thing at least is almost certain about the future,
namely, that very much of it will be such as we should call incredible. In
one important respect, indeed, I may perhaps seem to have strayed into
barren extravagance. I have supposed an inhabitant of the remote future
to be communicating with us of today. I have pretended that he has the
power of partially controlling the operations of minds now living, and that
this book is the product of such influence. Yet even this fiction is perhaps
not wholly excluded by our thought. I might, of course, easily have omitted it without more than superficial alteration of the theme. But its introduction was more than a convenience. Only by some such radical and
bewildering device could I embody the possibility that there may be more
in time's nature than is revealed to us. Indeed, only by some such trick
could I do justice to the conviction that our whole present mentality is but
a confused and halting first experiment.

If ever this book should happen to be discovered by some future individual, for instance by a member of the next generation sorting out the
rubbish of his predecessors, it will certainly raise a smile; for very much
is bound to happen of which no hint is yet discoverable. And indeed even
in our generation circumstances may well change so unexpectedly and so
radically that this book may very soon look ridiculous. But no matter. We
of today must conceive our relation to the rest of the universe as best we
can; and even if our images must seem fantastic to future men, they may
none the less serve their purpose today.

Some readers, taking my story to be an attempt at prophecy, may
deem it unwarrantably pessimistic. But it is not prophecy; it is myth, or
an essay in myth. We all desire the future to turn out more happily than
I have figured it. In particular we desire our present civilization to advance
steadily toward some kind of Utopia. The thought that it may decay and
collapse, and that all its spiritual treasure may be lost irrevocably, is repugnant to us. Yet this must be faced as at least a possibility. And this kind
of tragedy, the tragedy of a race, must, I think, be admitted in any adequate myth.

And so, while gladly recognizing that in our time there are strong
seeds of hope as well as of despair, I have imagined for æsthetic purposes
that our race will destroy itself. There is today a very earnest movement
for peace and international unity; and surely with good fortune and intelligent management it may triumph. Most earnestly we must hope that it
will. But I have figured things out in this book in such a manner that this
great movement fails. I suppose it incapable of preventing a succession of
national wars; and I permit it only to achieve the goal of unity and peace
after the mentality of the race has been undermined. May this not happen!

May the League of Nations, or some more strictly cosmopolitan authority, ✓ win through before it is too late! Yet let us find room in our minds and in our hearts for the thought that the whole enterprise of our race may be after all but a minor and unsuccessful episode in a vaster drama, which also perhaps may be tragic.

Any attempt to conceive such a drama must take into account whatever contemporary science has to say about man's own nature and his physical environment. I have tried to supplement my own slight knowledge of natural science by pestering my scientific friends. In particular, I have been very greatly helped by conversation with Professors P. G. H. Boswell, J. Johnstone, and J. Rice, of Liverpool. But they must not be held responsible for the many deliberate extravagances which, though they serve a purpose in the design, may jar upon the scientific ear.

To Dr. L. A. Reid I am much indebted for general comments, and to Mr. E. V. Rieu for many very valuable suggestions. To Professor and Mrs. L. C. Martin, who read the whole book in manuscript, I cannot properly express my gratitude for constant encouragement and criticism. To my wife's devastating sanity I owe far more than she supposes.

Before closing this preface I would remind the reader that throughout the following pages the speaker, the first person singular, is supposed to be, not the actual writer, but an individual living in the extremely distant future.

W. O. S.

West Kirby
July, 1930

Introduction

BY

ONE OF THE LAST MEN

THIS book has two authors, one contemporary with its readers, the other an inhabitant of an age which they would call the distant future. The brain that conceives and writes these sentences lives in the time of Einstein. Yet I, the true inspirer of this book, I who have begotten it upon that brain, I who influence that primitive being's conception, inhabit an age which, for Einstein, lies in the very remote future.

The actual writer thinks he is merely contriving a work of fiction. Though he seeks to tell a plausible story, he neither believes it himself, nor expects others to believe it. Yet the story is true. A being whom you would call a future man has seized the docile but scarcely adequate brain of your contemporary, and is trying to direct its familiar processes for an alien purpose. Thus a future epoch makes contact with your age. Listen patiently; for we who are the Last Men earnestly desire to communicate with you, who are members of the First Human Species. We can help you, and we need your help.

You cannot believe it. Your acquaintance with time is very imperfect, and so your understanding of it is defeated. But no matter. Do not perplex yourselves about this truth, so difficult to you, so familiar to us of a later aeon. Do but entertain, merely as a fiction, the idea that the thought and will of individuals future to you may intrude, rarely and with difficulty, into the mental processes of some of your contemporaries. Pretend that you believe this, and that the following chronicle is an authentic message from the Last Men. Imagine the consequences of such a belief. Otherwise I cannot give life to the great history which it is my task to tell.

When your writers romance of the future, they too easily imagine a progress toward some kind of Utopia, in which beings like themselves live in unmitigated bliss among circumstances perfectly suited to a fixed human nature. I shall not describe any such paradise. Instead, I shall record huge fluctuations of joy and woe, the results of changes not only in man's environment but in his fluid nature. And I must tell how, in my own age, having at last achieved spiritual maturity and the philosophic mind, man is forced by an unexpected crisis to embark on an enterprise both repugnant and desperate.

I invite you, then, to travel in imagination through the aeons that lie between your age and mine. I ask you to watch such a history of change,

13

grief, hope, and unforeseen catastrophe, as has nowhere else occurred, within the girdle of the Milky Way. But first, it is well to contemplate for a few moments the mere magnitude of cosmical events. For, compressed as it must necessarily be, the narrative that I have to tell may seem to present a sequence of adventures and disasters crowded together, with no intervening peace. But in fact man's career has been less like a mountain torrent hurtling from rock to rock, than a great sluggish river, broken ✓ very seldom by rapids. Ages of quiescence, often of actual stagnation, filled with the monotonous problems and toils of countless almost identical lives, have been punctuated by rare moments of racial adventure. Nay, even these few seemingly rapid events themselves were in fact often long-drawn-out and tedious. They acquire a mere illusion of speed from the speed of the narrative.

The receding depths of time and space, though they can indeed be haltingly conceived even by primitive minds, cannot be imagined save by beings of a more ample nature. A panorama of mountains appears to naïve vision almost as a flat picture, and the starry void is a roof pricked with light. Yet in reality, while the immediate terrain could be spanned in an hour's walking, the sky-line of peaks holds within it plain beyond plain. Similarly with time. While the near past and the near future display within them depth beyond depth, time's remote immensities are foreshortened into flatness. It is almost inconceivable to simple minds that man's whole history should be but a moment in the life of the stars, and that remote events should embrace within themselves aeon upon aeon.

In your day you have learnt to calculate something of the magnitudes of time and space. But to grasp my theme in its true proportions, it is necessary to do more than calculate. It is necessary to brood upon these magnitudes, to draw out the mind toward them, to feel the littleness of your here and now, and of the moment of civilization which you call history. You cannot hope to image, as we do, such vast proportions as one in a thousand million, because your sense-organs, and therefore your perceptions, are too coarse-grained to discriminate so small a fraction of their total field. But you may at least, by mere contemplation, grasp more constantly and firmly the significance of your calculations.

Men of your day, when they look back into the history of their planet, remark not only the length of time but also the bewildering acceleration of life's progress. Almost stationary in the earliest period of the earth's career, in your moment it seems headlong. Mind in you, it is said, not merely ✓ stands higher than ever before in respect of percipience, knowledge, insight, delicacy of admiration, and sanity of will, but also it moves upward century by century ever more swiftly. What next? Surely, you think, there will come a time when there will be no further heights to conquer.

This view is mistaken. You underestimate even the foothills that stand in front of you, and never suspect that far above them, hidden by cloud, *rise precipices and snow-fields. The mental and spiritual advances which, in your day, mind in the solar system has still to attempt, are overwhelmingly more complex, more precarious and dangerous, than those which have already been achieved. And though in certain humble respects you have attained full development, the loftier potencies of the spirit in you have not yet even begun to put forth buds.*

Somehow, then, I must help you to feel not only the vastness of time and space, but also the vast diversity of mind's possible modes. But this I can only hint to you, since so much lies wholly beyond the range of your imagination.

Historians living in your day need grapple only with one moment of the flux of time. But I have to present in one book the essence not of centuries but of aeons. Clearly we cannot walk at leisure through such a tract, in which a million terrestrial years are but as a year is to your historians. We must fly. We must travel as you do in your aeroplanes, observing only the broad features of the continent. But since the flier sees nothing of the minute inhabitants below him, and since it is they who make history, we must also punctuate our flight with many descents, skimming as it were over the house-tops, and even alighting at critical points to speak face to face with individuals. And as the plane's journey must begin with a slow ascent from the intricate pedestrian view to wider horizons, so we must begin with a somewhat close inspection of that little period which includes the culmination and collapse of your own primitive civilization.

THE CHRONICLE

BALKAN EUROPE

I. THE EUROPEAN WAR AND AFTER

OBSERVE now your own epoch of history as it appears to the Last Men.

Long before the human spirit awoke to clear cognizance of the world and itself, it sometimes stirred in its sleep, opened bewildered eyes, and slept again. One of these moments of precocious experience embraces the whole struggle of the First Men from savagery toward civilization. Within that moment, you stand almost in the very instant when the species attains its zenith. Scarcely at all beyond your own day is this early culture to be seen progressing, and already in your time the mentality of the race shows signs of decline.

The first, and some would say the greatest, achievement of your own "Western" culture was the conceiving of two ideals of conduct, both essential to the spirit's well-being. Socrates, delighting in the truth for its own sake and not merely for practical ends, glorified unbiased thinking, honesty of mind and speech. Jesus, delighting in the actual human persons around him, and in that flavour of divinity which, for him, pervaded the world, stood for unselfish love of neighbours and of God. Socrates woke to the ideal of dispassionate intelligence, Jesus to the ideal of passionate yet self-oblivious worship. Socrates urged intellectual integrity, Jesus integrity of will. Each, of course, though starting with a different emphasis, involved the other.

Unfortunately both these ideals demanded of the human brain a degree of vitality and coherence of which the nervous system of the First Men was never really capable. For many centuries these twin stars enticed the more precociously human of human animals, in vain. And the failure to put these

17

ideals in practice helped to engender in the race a cynical lassitude which was one cause of its decay.

There were other causes. The peoples from whom sprang Socrates and Jesus were also among the first to conceive admiration for Fate. In Greek tragic art and Hebrew worship of divine law, as also in the Indian resignation, man experienced, at first very obscurely, that vision of an alien and supernal beauty, which was to exalt and perplex him again and again throughout his whole career. The conflict between this worship and the intransigent loyalty to Life, embattled against Death, proved insoluble. And though few individuals were ever clearly conscious of the issue, the first human species was again and again unwittingly hampered in its spiritual development by this supreme perplexity.

While man was being whipped and enticed by these precocious experiences, the actual social constitution of his world kept changing so rapidly through increased mastery over physical energy, that his primitive nature could no longer cope with the complexity of his environment. Animals that were fashioned for hunting and fighting in the wild were suddenly called upon to be citizens, and moreover citizens of a world-community. At the same time they found themselves possessed of certain very dangerous powers which their petty minds were not fit to use. Man struggled; but, as you shall hear, he broke under the strain.

The European War, called at the time the War to End War, was the first and least destructive of those world conflicts which display so tragically the incompetence of the First Men to control their own nature. At the outset a tangle of motives, some honourable and some disreputable, ignited a conflict for which both antagonists were all too well prepared, though neither seriously intended it. A real difference of temperament between Latin France and Nordic Germany combined with a superficial rivalry between Germany and England, and a number of stupidly brutal gestures on the part of the German Government and military command, to divide the world into two camps; yet in such a manner that it is impossible to find any difference of principle between them. During the struggle each party was convinced that it alone stood for civilization. But in fact both succumbed now and again to impulses of sheer brutality, and both achieved acts not merely of heroism, but of generosity unusual among the First Men. For conduct which to clearer minds seems merely sane, was in those days to be performed only by rare vision and self-mastery.

As the months of agony advanced, there was bred in the warring peoples a genuine and even passionate will for peace and a united world. Out of the conflict of the tribes arose, at least for a while, a spirit loftier than tribalism. But this fervour lacked as yet clear guidance, lacked even the courage of conviction. The peace which followed the European War is one of the most significant moments of ancient history; for it epitomizes both the dawning vision and the incurable blindness, both the impulse toward a higher loyalty and the compulsive tribalism of a race which was, after all, but superficially human.

2. THE ANGLO-FRENCH WAR

One brief but tragic incident, which occurred within a century after the European War, may be said to have sealed the fate of the First Men. During this century the will for peace and sanity was already becoming a serious factor in history. Save for a number of most untoward accidents, to be recorded in due course, the party of peace might have dominated Europe during its most dangerous period; and, through Europe, the world. With either a little less bad luck or a fraction more of vision and self-control at this critical time, there might never have occurred that aeon of darkness, in which the First Men were presently to be submerged. For had victory been gained before the general level of mentality had seriously begun to decline, the attainment of the world state might have been regarded, not as an end, but as the first step toward true civilization. But this was not to be.

After the European War the defeated nation, formerly no less militaristic than the others, now became the most pacific, and a stronghold of enlightenment. Almost everywhere, indeed, there had occurred a profound change of heart, but chiefly in Germany. The victors on the other hand, in spite of their real craving to be human and generous, and to found a new world, were led partly by their own timidity, partly by their governors' blind diplomacy, into all the vices against which they believed themselves to have been crusading. After a brief period in which they desperately affected amity for one another they began to indulge once more in physical conflicts. Of these conflicts, two must be observed.

The first outbreak, and the less disastrous for Europe, was a short and grotesque struggle between France and Italy. Since the fall of ancient Rome, the Italians had excelled more in art and literature than in martial achievement. But the heroic liberation of Italy in the nineteenth Christian century had made Italians peculiarly sensitive to national prestige; and since among Western peoples national vigour was measured in terms of military glory, the Italians were fired, by their success against a rickety foreign domination, to vindicate themselves more thoroughly against the charge of mediocrity in warfare. After the European War, however, Italy passed through a phase of social disorder and self-distrust. Subsequently a flamboyant but sincere national party gained control of the State, and afforded the Italians a new self-respect, based on reform of the social services, and on militaristic policy. Trains became punctual, streets clean, morals puritanical. Aviation records were won for Italy. The young, dressed up and taught to play at soldiers with real fire-arms, were persuaded to regard themselves as saviours of the nation, encouraged to shed blood, and used to enforce the will of the Government. The whole movement was engineered chiefly by a man whose genius in action combined with his rhetoric and crudity of thought to make him a very successful dictator. Almost miraculously he drilled the Italian nation into efficiency. At the same time, with great emotional effect and incredible lack of humour he trumpeted Italy's self-importance, and her will to "expand." And since Italians were slow to learn the necessity of restricting their population, "expansion" was a real need.

Thus it came about that Italy, hungry for French territory in Africa, jealous of French leadership of the Latin races, indignant at the protection afforded to Italian "traitors" in France, became increasingly prone to quarrel with the most assertive of her late allies. It was a frontier incident, a fancied "insult to the Italian flag," which at last caused an unauthorized raid upon French territory by a small party of Italian militia. The raiders were captured, but French blood was shed. The consequent demand for apology and reparation was calm, but subtly offensive to Italian dignity. Italian patriots worked themselves into short-sighted fury. The Dictator, far from daring to apologize, was forced to require the release of the captive militia-men, and finally to declare war. After a single sharp engagement the relentless armies of France pressed into North Italy. Resistance, at first heroic, soon became chaotic. In consternation the Italians woke from their dream of military glory. The populace turned against the Dictator whom they themselves had forced to declare war. In a theatrical but gallant attempt to dominate the Roman mob, he failed, and was killed. The new government made a hasty peace, ceding to France a frontier territory which she had already annexed for "security."

Thenceforth Italians were less concerned to outshine the glory of Garibaldi than to emulate the greater glory of Dante, Giotto and Galileo.

France had now complete mastery of the continent of Europe; but having much to lose, she behaved arrogantly and nervously. It was not long before the peace was once more disturbed.

Scarcely had the last veterans of the European War ceased from wearying their juniors with reminiscence, when the long rivalry between France and England culminated in a dispute between their respective Governments over a case of sexual outrage said to have been committed by a French African soldier upon an Englishwoman. In this quarrel, the British Government happened to be definitely in the wrong, and was probably confused by its own sexual repressions. The outrage had never been committed. The facts which gave rise to the rumour were, that an idle and neurotic Englishwoman in the south of France, craving the embraces of a "cave man," had seduced a Senegalese corporal in her own apartments. When, later, he had shown signs of boredom, she took revenge by declaring that he had attacked her indecently in the woods above the town. This rumour was such that the English were all too prone to savour and believe. At the same time, the magnates of the English Press could not resist this opportunity of trading upon the public's sexuality, tribalism and self-righteousness. There followed an epidemic of abuse, and occasional violence, against French subjects in England; and thus the party of fear and militarism in France was given the opportunity it had long sought. For the real cause of this war was connected with air power. France had persuaded the League of Nations (in one of its less intelligent moments) to restrict the size of military aeroplanes in such a manner that, while London lay within easy striking distance of the French coast, Paris could only with difficulty be touched by England. This state of affairs obviously could not last long. Britain was agitating more and more insistently for the removal of the restriction. On the other hand, there was an increasing demand for complete aerial disarmament in Europe; and so strong was the party of sanity in France, that the scheme would almost certainly have been accepted by the French Government. On both counts, therefore, the militarists of France were eager to strike while yet there was opportunity.

In an instant, the whole fruit of this effort for disarmament was destroyed. That subtle difference of mentality which had ever made it impossible for these two nations to understand one another, was suddenly exaggerated by this provocative incident into an apparently insoluble discord. England reverted to her conviction that all Frenchmen were sensualists, while to France the English appeared, as often before, the most offensive of hypocrites. In vain did the saner minds in each country insist on the fundamental humanity of both. In vain did the chastened Germans seek to mediate. In vain did the League, which by now had very great prestige and authority, threaten both parties with expulsion, even with chastisement. Rumour got about in Paris that England, breaking all her international pledges, was now feverishly building giant planes which would wreck France from Calais to Marseilles. And indeed the rumour was not wholly a slander, for when the struggle began, the British air force was found to have a range of intensive action far wider than was expected. Yet the actual outbreak of war took England by surprise. While the London papers were selling out upon the news that war was declared, enemy planes appeared over the city. In a couple of hours a third of London was in ruins, and half her population lay poisoned in the streets. One bomb, falling beside the British Museum, turned the whole of Bloomsbury into a crater, wherein fragments of mummies, statues, and manuscripts were mingled with the contents of shops, and morsels of salesmen and the intelligentsia. Thus in a moment was destroyed a large proportion of England's most precious relics and most fertile brains.

Then occurred one of those microscopic, yet supremely potent incidents which sometimes mould the course of events for centuries. During the bombardment a special meeting of the British Cabinet was held in a cellar in Downing Street. The party in power at the time was progressive, mildly pacifist, and timorously cosmopolitan. It had got itself involved in the French quarrel quite unintentionally. At this Cabinet meeting an idealistic member urged upon his colleagues the need for a supreme gesture of heroism and generosity on the part of Britain. Raising his voice with difficulty above the bark of English guns and the volcanic crash of French bombs, he suggested sending by radio the following message: "From the people of England to the people of France. Catastrophe has fallen on us at your hands. In this hour of agony, all hate and anger have left us. Our eyes are opened. No longer can we think of ourselves as English merely, and you as merely French; all of us are, before all else, civilized beings. Do not imagine that we are defeated, and that this message is a cry for mercy. Our armament is intact, and our resources still very great. Yet, because of the revelation which has come to us today, we will not fight. No plane, no ship, no soldier of Britain shall commit any further act of hostility. Do what you will. It would be better even that a great people should be destroyed than that the whole race should be thrown into turmoil. But you will not strike again. As our own eyes have been opened by agony, yours now will be opened by our act of brotherhood. The spirit of France and the spirit of England differ. They differ deeply; but only as the eye differs from the hand. Without you, we should be barbarians. And without us, even the bright spirit of France would be but half expressed. For the spirit of France lives again in our culture and in our very speech; and the spirit of England is that which strikes from you your most distinctive brilliance."

At no earlier stage of man's history could such a message have been considered seriously by any government. Had it been suggested during the previous war, its author would have been ridiculed, execrated, perhaps even murdered. But since those days, much had happened. Increased communication, increased cultural intercourse, and a prolonged vigorous campaign for cosmopolitanism, had changed the mentality of Europe. Even so, when, after a brief discussion, the Government ordered this unique message to be sent, its members were awed by their own act. As one of them expressed it, they were uncertain whether it was the devil or the deity that had possessed them, but possessed they certainly were.

That night the people of London (those who were left) experienced an exaltation of spirit. Disorganization of the city's life, overwhelming physical suffering and compassion, the consciousness of an unprecedented spiritual act in which each individual felt himself to have somehow participated—these influences combined to produce, even in the bustle and confusion of a wrecked metropolis, a certain restrained fervour, and a deep peace of mind, wholly unfamiliar to Londoners.

Meanwhile the undamaged North knew not whether to regard the Government's sudden pacificism as a piece of cowardice or as a superbly courageous gesture. Very soon, however, they began to make a virtue of necessity, and incline to the latter view. Paris itself was divided by the message into a vocal party of triumph and a silent party of bewilderment. But as the hours advanced, and the former urged a policy of aggression, the latter found voice for the cry, "*Vive l'Angleterre, vive l'humanité.*" And so strong by now was the will for cosmopolitanism that the upshot would almost certainly have been a triumph of sanity, had there not occurred in England an accident which tilted the whole precarious course of events in the opposite direction.

The bombardment had occurred on a Friday night. On Saturday the repercussions of England's great message were echoing throughout the nations. That evening, as a wet and foggy day was achieving its pallid sunset, a French plane was seen over the western outskirts of London. It gradually descended, and was regarded by onlookers as a messenger of peace. Lower and lower it came. Something was seen to part from it and fall. In a few seconds an immense explosion occurred in the neighbourhood of a great school and a royal palace. There was hideous destruction in the school. The palace escaped. But, chief disaster for the cause of peace, a beautiful and extravagantly popular young princess was caught by the explosion. Her body, obscenely mutilated, but still recognizable to every student of the illustrated papers, was impaled upon some high park-railings beside the main thoroughfare toward the city. Immediately after the explosion the enemy plane crashed, burst into flame, and was destroyed with its occupants.

A moment's cool thinking would have convinced all onlookers that this disaster was an accident, that the plane was a belated straggler in distress, and no messenger of hate. But, confronted with the mangled bodies of schoolboys, and harrowed by cries of agony and terror, the populace was in no state for ratiocination. Moreover there was the princess, an overwhelmingly potent sexual symbol and emblem of tribalism, slaughtered and exposed before the eyes of her adorers.

The news was flashed over the country, and distorted of course in such a manner as to admit no doubt that this act was the crowning deviltry of sexual fiends beyond the Channel. In an hour the mood of London was changed, and the whole population of England succumbed to a paroxysm of primitive hate far more extravagant than any that had occurred even in the war against Germany. The British air force, all too well equipped and prepared, was ordered to Paris.

Meanwhile in France the militaristic government had fallen, and the party of peace was now in control. While the streets were still thronged by its vociferous supporters, the first bomb fell. By Monday morning Paris was obliterated. There followed a few days of strife between the opposing armaments, and of butchery committed upon the civilian populations. In spite of French gallantry, the superior organization, mechanical efficiency, and more cautious courage of the British air force soon made it impossible for a French plane to leave the ground. But if France was broken, England was too crippled to pursue her advantage. Every city of the two countries was completely disorganized. Famine, riot, looting, and above all the rapidly accelerating and quite uncontrollable spread of disease, disintegrated both States, and brought war to a standstill.

Indeed, not only did hostilities cease, but also both nations were too shattered even to continue hating one another. The energies of each were for a while wholly occupied in trying to prevent complete annihilation by famine and pestilence. In the work of reconstruction they had to depend very largely on help from outside. The management of each country was taken over, for the time, by the League of Nations.

It is significant to compare the mood of Europe at this time with that which followed the European War. Formerly, though there had been a real effort toward unity, hate and suspicion continued to find expression in national policies. There was much wrangling about indemnities, reparations, securities; and the division of the whole continent into two hostile camps persisted, though by then it was purely artificial and sentimental. But after the Anglo-French war, a very different mood prevailed. There was no mention of reparations, no possibility of seeking security by alliances. Patriotism simply faded out, for the time, under the influence of extreme disaster. The two enemy peoples co-operated with the League in the work of reconstructing not only each one itself, but each one the other. This change of heart was due partly to the temporary collapse of the whole national organization, partly to the speedy dominance of each nation by pacifist and anti-nationalist Labour, partly to the fact that the League was powerful enough to inquire into and publish the whole story of the origins of the war, and expose each combatant to itself and to the world in a sorry light.

We have now observed in some detail the incident which stands out in man's history as perhaps the most dramatic example of petty cause and mighty effect. For consider. Through some miscalculation, or a mere defect in his instruments, a French airman went astray, and came to grief in London after the sending of the peace message. Had this not happened, England and France would not have been wrecked. And, had the war been nipped at the outset, as it almost was, the party of sanity throughout the world would have been very greatly strengthened; the precarious will to unity would have gained the conviction which it lacked, would have dominated man not merely during the terrified revulsion after each spasm of national strife, but as a permanent policy based on mutual trust. Indeed so delicately balanced were man's primitive and developed impulses at this time, that but for this trivial accident, the movement which was started by England's peace message might have proceeded steadily and rapidly toward the unification of the race. It might, that is, have attained its goal, before, instead of after, the period of mental deterioration, which in fact resulted from a long epidemic of wars. And so the first Dark Age might never have occurred.

3. EUROPE AFTER THE ANGLO-FRENCH WAR

A subtle change now began to affect the whole mental climate of the planet. This is remarkable, since, viewed for instance from America or

China, this war was, after all, but a petty disturbance, scarcely more than a brawl between quarrelsome statelets, an episode in the decline of a senile civilization. Expressed in dollars, the damage was not impressive to the wealthy West and the potentially wealthy East. The British Empire, indeed, that unique banyan tree of peoples, was henceforth less effective in world diplomacy; but since the bond that held it together was by now wholly a bond of sentiment, the Empire was not disintegrated by the misfortune of its parent trunk. Indeed, a common fear of American economic imperialism was already helping the colonies to remain loyal.

Yet this petty brawl was in fact an irreparable and far-reaching disaster. For in spite of those differences of temperament which had forced the English and French into conflict, they had co-operated, though often unwittingly, in tempering and clarifying the mentality of Europe. Though their faults played a great part in wrecking Western civilization, the virtues from which these vices sprang were needed for the salvation of a world prone to uncritical romance. In spite of the inveterate blindness and meanness of France in international policy, and the even more disastrous timidity of England, their influence on culture had been salutary, and was at this moment sorely needed. For, poles asunder in tastes and ideals, these two peoples were yet alike in being on the whole more sceptical, and in their finest individuals more capable of dispassionate yet creative intelligence, than any other Western people. This very character produced their distinctive faults, namely, in the English a caution that amounted often to moral cowardice, and in the French a certain myopic complacency and cunning, which masqueraded as realism. Within each nation there was, of course, great variety. English minds were of many types. But most were to some extent distinctively English; and hence the special character of England's influence in the world. Relatively detached, sceptical, cautious, practical, more tolerant than others, because more complacent and less prone to fervour, the typical Englishman was capable both of generosity and of spite, both of heroism and of timorous or cynical abandonment of ends proclaimed as vital to the race. French and English alike might sin against humanity, but in different manners. The French sinned blindly, through a strange inability to regard France dispassionately. The English sinned through faint-heartedness, and with open eyes. Among all nations they excelled in the union of common sense and vision. But also among all nations they were most ready to betray their visions in the name of common sense. Hence their reputation for perfidy.

Differences of national character and patriotic sentiment were not the most fundamental distinctions between men at this time. Although in each nation a common tradition or cultural environment imposed a certain uniformity on all its members, yet in each nation every mental type was present, though in different proportions. The most significant of all cultural differences between men, namely, the difference between the tribalists and the cosmopolitans, traversed the national boundaries. For throughout the world something like a new, cosmopolitan "nation" with a new all-embracing patriotism was beginning to appear. In every land there was by now a salting of awakened minds who, whatever their temperament and politics and formal faith, were at one in respect of their allegiance to humanity as a race or as an adventuring spirit. Unfortunately this new loyalty was still entangled with old prejudices. In some minds the defence of the human spirit was sincerely identified with the defence of a particular nation, conceived as the home of all enlightenment. In others, social injustice kindled a militant proletarian loyalty, which, though at heart cosmopolitan, infected alike its champions and its enemies with sectarian passions.

Another sentiment, less definite and conscious than cosmopolitanism, also played some part in the minds of men, namely loyalty toward the dispassionate intelligence, and perplexed admiration of the world which it was beginning to reveal, a world august, immense, subtle, in which, seemingly, man was doomed to play a part minute but tragic. In many races there had, no doubt, long existed some fidelity toward the dispassionate intelligence. But it was England and France that excelled in this respect. On the other hand, even in these two nations there was much that was opposed to this allegiance. These, like all peoples of the age, were liable to bouts of insane emotionalism. Indeed the French mind, in general so clear sighted, so realistic, so contemptuous of ambiguity and mist, so detached in all its final valuations, was yet so obsessed with the idea "France" as to be wholly incapable of generosity in international affairs. But it was France, with England, that had chiefly inspired the intellectual integrity which was the rarest and brightest thread of Western culture, not only within the territories of these two nations, but throughout Europe and America. In the seventeenth and eighteenth Christian centuries, the French and English had conceived, more clearly than other peoples, an interest in the objective world for its own sake, had founded physical science, and had fashioned out of scepticism the most brilliantly constructive of mental instruments. At a later stage it was largely the French and English who, by means of this instrument, had revealed man and the physical universe in something like their true proportions; and it was chiefly the elect of these two peoples that had been able to exult in this bracing discovery.

With the eclipse of France and England this great tradition of dispassionate cognizance began to wane. Europe was now led by Germany. And the Germans, in spite of their practical genius, their scholarly contributions to history, their brilliant science and austere philosophy, were at heart romantic. This inclination was both their strength and their weakness. Thereby they had been inspired to their finest art and their most profound metaphysical speculation. But thereby they were also often rendered unself-critical and pompous. More eager than Western minds to solve the mystery of existence, less sceptical of the power of human reason, and there-

fore more inclined to ignore or argue away recalcitrant facts, the Germans
were courageous systematizers. In this direction they had achieved greatly.
Without them, European thought would have been chaotic. But their passion for order and for a systematic reality behind the disorderly appearances,
rendered their reasoning all too often biased. Upon shifty foundations they
balanced ingenious ladders to reach the stars. Thus, without constant ribald
criticism from across the Rhine and the North Sea, the Teutonic soul could
not achieve full self-expression. A vague uneasiness about its own senti-
mentalism and lack of detachment did indeed persuade this great people
to assert its virility now and again by ludicrous acts of brutality, and to
compensate for its dream life by ceaseless hard-driven and brilliantly successful commerce; but what was needed was a far more radical self-criticism.

Beyond Germany, Russia. Here was a people whose genius needed,
even more than that of the Germans, discipline under the critical intelligence. Since the Bolshevic revolution, there had risen in the scattered towns
of this immense tract of corn and forest, and still more in the metropolis,
an original mode of art and thought, in which were blended a passion of
iconoclasm, a vivid sensuousness, and yet also a very remarkable and essentially mystical or intuitive power of detachment from all private cravings.
America and Western Europe were interested first in the individual human
life, and only secondarily in the social whole. For these peoples, loyalty
involved a reluctant self-sacrifice, and the ideal was ever a person, excelling
in prowess of various kinds. Society was but the necessary matrix of this
jewel. But the Russians, whether by an innate gift, or through the influence
of agelong political tyranny, religious devotion, and a truly social revolution,
were prone to self-contemptuous interest in groups, prone, indeed, to a
spontaneous worship of whatever was conceived as loftier than the individual
man, whether society, or God, or the blind forces of nature. Western Europe
could reach by way of the intellect a precise conception of man's littleness
and irrelevance when regarded as an alien among the stars; could even
glimpse from this standpoint the cosmic theme in which all human striving
is but one contributory factor. But the Russian mind, whether orthodox or
Tolstoyan or fanatically materialist, could attain much the same conviction
intuitively, by direct perception, instead of after an arduous intellectual pilgrimage; and, reaching it, could rejoice in it. But because of this independence of intellect, the experience was confused, erratic, frequently misinterpreted; and its effect on conduct was rather explosive than directive. Great
indeed was the need that the West and East of Europe should strengthen
and temper one another.

After the Bolshevic revolution a new element appeared in Russian culture, and one which had not been known before in any modern state. The
old regime was displaced by a real proletarian government, which, though
an oligarchy, and sometimes bloody and fanatical, abolished the old tyranny
of class, and encouraged the humblest citizen to be proud of his partnership

in the great community. Still more important, the native Russian disposition not to take material possessions very seriously co-operated with the political revolution, and brought about such a freedom from the snobbery of wealth as was quite foreign to the West. Attention which elsewhere was absorbed in the massing or display of money was in Russia largely devoted either to spontaneous instinctive enjoyments or to cultural activity.

In fact it was among the Russian townsfolk, less cramped by tradition than other city-dwellers, that the spirit of the First Men was beginning to achieve a fresh and sincere readjustment to the facts of its changing world. And from the townsfolk something of the new way of life was spreading even to the peasants; while in the depths of Asia a hardy and ever-growing population looked increasingly to Russia, not only for machinery, but for ideas. There were times when it seemed that Russia might transform the almost universal autumn of the race into a new spring.

After the Bolshevic revolution the New Russia had been boycotted by the West, and had therefore passed through a stage of self-conscious extravagance. Communism and naïve materialism became the dogmas of a new crusading atheist church. All criticism was suppressed, even more rigorously than was the opposite criticism in other countries; and Russians were taught to think of themselves as saviours of mankind. Later, however, as economic isolation began to hamper the Bolshevic state, the new culture was mellowed and broadened. Bit by bit, economic intercourse with the West was restored, and with it cultural intercourse increased. The intuitive mystical detachment of Russia began to define itself, and so consolidate itself, in terms of the intellectual detachment of the best thought of the West. Iconoclasm was harnessed. The life of the senses and of impulse was tempered by a new critical movement. Fanatical materialism, whose fire had been derived from a misinterpreted, but intense, mystical intuition of dispassionate Reality, began to assimilate itself to the far more rational stoicism which was the rare flower of the West. At the same time, through intercourse with peasant culture and with the peoples of Asia, the new Russia began to grasp in one unifying act of apprehension both the grave disillusion of France and England and the ecstasy of the East.

The harmonizing of these two moods was now the chief spiritual need of mankind. Failure to integrate them into an all-dominant sentiment could not but lead to racial insanity. And so in due course it befell. Meanwhile this task of integration was coming to seem more and more urgent to the best minds in Russia, and might have been finally accomplished had they been longer illumined by the cold light of the West.

But this was not to be. The intellectual confidence of France and England, already shaken through progressive economic eclipse at the hands of America and Germany, was now undermined. For many decades England had watched these newcomers capture her markets. The loss had smothered her with a swarm of domestic problems, such as could never be solved save by drastic surgery; and this was a course which demanded more courage and energy than was possible to a people without hope. Then came the war with France, and harrowing distintegration. No delirium seized her, such as occurred in France; yet her whole mentality was changed, and her sobering influence in Europe was lessened.

As for France, her cultural life was now grievously reduced. It might, indeed, have recovered from the final blow, had it not already been slowly poisoned by gluttonous nationalism. For love of France was the undoing of the French. They prized the truly admirable spirit of France so extravagantly, that they regarded all other nations as barbarians.

Thus it befell that in Russia the doctrines of communism and materialism, products of German systematists, survived uncriticized. On the other hand, the practice of communism was gradually undermined. For the Russian state came increasingly under the influence of Western, and especially American, finance. The materialism of the official creed also became a farce, for it was foreign to the Russian mind. Thus between practice and theory there was, in both respects, a profound inconsistency. What was once a vital and promising culture became insincere.

4. THE RUSSO-GERMAN WAR

The discrepancy between communist theory and individualist practice in Russia was one cause of the next disaster which befell Europe. Between Russia and Germany there should have been close partnership, based on interchange of machinery and corn. But the theory of communism stood in the way, and in a strange manner. Russian industrial organization had proved impossible without American capital; and little by little this influence had transformed the communistic system. From the Baltic to the Himalayas and the Behring Straits, pasture, timber lands, machine-tilled corn-land, oil-fields, and a spreading rash of industrial towns, were increasingly dependent on American finance and organization. Yet not America, but the far less individualistic Germany, had become in the Russian mind the symbol of capitalism. Self-righteous hate of Germany compensated Russia for her own betrayal of the communistic ideal. This perverse antagonism was encouraged by the Americans, who, strong in their own individualism and prosperity, and by now contemptuously tolerant of Russian doctrines, were concerned only to keep Russian finance to themselves. In truth, of course, it was America that had helped Russia's self-betrayal; and it was the spirit of America that was most alien to the Russian spirit. But American wealth was by now indispensable to Russia; so the hate due to America had to be borne vicariously by Germany.

The Germans, for their part, were aggrieved that the Americans had ousted them from a most profitable field of enterprise, and in particular from the exploitation of Russian Asiatic oil. The economic life of the human race had for some time been based on coal, but latterly oil had been found a far more convenient source of power; and as the oil store of the planet was much smaller than its coal store, and the expenditure of oil had of course been wholly uncontrolled and wasteful, a shortage was already being felt. Thus the national ownership of the remaining oil fields had become a main factor in politics and a fertile source of wars. America, having used up most of her own supplies, was now anxious to compete with the still prolific sources under Chinese control, by forestalling Germany in Russia. No wonder the Germans were aggrieved. But the fault was their own. In the days when Russian communism had been seeking to convert the world, Germany had taken over England's leadership of individualistic Europe. While greedy for trade with Russia, she had been at the same time frightened of contamination by Russian social doctrine, the more so because communism had at first made some headway among the German workers. Later, even when sane industrial reorganization in Germany had deprived communism of its appeal to the workers, and thus had rendered it impotent, the habit of anti-communist vituperation persisted.

Thus the peace of Europe was in constant danger from the bickerings of two peoples who differed rather in ideals than in practice. For the one, in theory communistic, had been forced to delegate many of the community's rights to enterprising individuals; while the other, in theory organized on a basis of private business, was becoming ever more socialized.

Neither party desired war. Neither was interested in military glory, for militarism as an end was no longer reputable. Neither was professedly nationalistic, for nationalism, though still potent, was no longer vaunted. Each claimed to stand for internationalism and peace, but accused the other of narrow patriotism. Thus Europe, though more pacific than ever before, was doomed to war.

Like most wars, the Anglo-French War had increased the desire for peace, yet made peace less secure. Distrust, not merely the old distrust of nation for nation, but a devastating distrust of human nature, gripped men like the dread of insanity. Individuals who thought of themselves as whole-hearted Europeans, feared that at any moment they might succumb to some ridiculous epidemic of patriotism and participate in the further crippling of Europe.

This dread was one cause of the formation of a European Confederacy, in which all the nations of Europe, save Russia, surrendered their sovereignty to a common authority and actually pooled their armaments. Ostensibly the motive of this act was peace; but America interpreted it as directed against herself, and withdrew from the League of Nations. China, the "natural enemy" of America, remained within the League, hoping to use it against her rival.

From without, indeed, the Confederacy at first appeared as a close-knit whole; but from within it was known to be insecure, and in every serious crisis it broke. There is no need to follow the many minor wars of this period, though their cumulative effect was serious, both economically and psychologically. Europe did at last, however, become something like a single nation in sentiment, though this unity was brought about less by a common loyalty than by a common fear of America.

Final consolidation was the fruit of the Russo-German War, the cause of which was partly economic and partly sentimental. All the peoples of Europe had long watched with horror the financial conquest of Russia by the United States, and they dreaded that they also must presently succumb to the same tyrant. To attack Russia, it was thought, would be to wound America in her only vulnerable spot. But the actual occasion of the war was sentimental. Half a century after the Anglo-French War, a second-rate German author published a typically German book of the baser sort. For as each nation had its characteristic virtues, so also each was prone to characteristic follies. This book was one of those brilliant but extravagant works in which the whole diversity of existence is interpreted under a single formula, with extreme detail and plausibility, yet with amazing *naïveté*. Highly astute within its own artificial universe, it was none the less in wider regard quite uncritical. In two large volumes the author claimed that the cosmos was a dualism in which a heroic and obviously Nordic spirit ruled by divine right over an un-self-disciplined, yet servile and obviously Slavonic spirit. The whole of history, and of evolution, was interpreted on this principle; and of the contemporary world it was said that the Slavonic element was poisoning Europe. One phrase in particular caused fury in Moscow, "the anthropoid face of the Russian subman."

Moscow demanded apology and suppression of the book. Berlin regretted the insult, but with its tongue in its cheek; and insisted on the freedom of the press. Followed a crescendo of radio hate, and war.

The details of this war do not matter to one intent upon the history of mind in the Solar System, but its result was important. Moscow, Leningrad and Berlin were shattered from the air. The whole West of Russia was flooded with the latest and deadliest poison gas, so that, not only was all animal and vegetable life destroyed, but also the soil between the Black Sea and the Baltic was rendered infertile and uninhabitable for many years. Within a week the war was over, for the reason that the combatants were separated by an immense territory in which life could not exist. But the effects of the war were lasting. The Germans had set going a process which they could not stop. Whiffs of the poison continued to be blown by fickle winds into every country of Europe and Western Asia. It was spring-time; but save in the Atlantic coast-lands the spring flowers shrivelled in the bud, and every young leaf had a withered rim. Humanity also suffered; though, save in the regions near the seat of war, it was in general only the children and the old people who suffered greatly. The poison spread across the Continent in huge blown tresses, broad as principalities, swinging with each change of wind. And wherever it strayed, young eyes, throats, and lungs were blighted like the leaves.

America, after much debate, had at last decided to defend her interests in Russia by a punitive expedition against Europe. China began to mobilize her forces. But long before America was ready to strike, news of the widespread poisoning changed her policy. Instead of punishment, help was given. This was a fine gesture of goodwill. But also, as was observed in Europe, instead of being costly, it was profitable; for inevitably it brought more of Europe under American financial control.

The upshot of the Russo-German war, then, was that Europe was unified in sentiment by hatred of America, and that European mentality definitely deteriorated. This was due in part to the emotional influence of the war itself, partly to the socially damaging effects of the poison. A proportion of the rising generation had been rendered sickly for life. During the thirty years which intervened before the Euro-American war, Europe was burdened with an exceptional weight of invalids. First-class intelligence was on the whole rarer than before, and was more strictly concentrated on the practical work of reconstruction.

Even more disastrous for the human race was the fact that the recent Russian cultural enterprise of harmonizing Western intellectualism and Eastern mysticism was now wrecked.

CHAPTER II

EUROPE'S DOWNFALL

I. EUROPE AND AMERICA

OVER the heads of the European tribes two mightier peoples regarded each other with increasing dislike. Well might they; for the one cherished the most ancient and refined of all surviving cultures, while the other, youngest and most self-confident of the great nations, proclaimed her novel spirit as the spirit of the future.

In the Far East, China, already half American, though largely Russian and wholly Eastern, patiently improved her rice lands, pushed forward her railways, organized her industries, and spoke fair to all the world. Long ago, during her attainment of unity and independence, China had learnt much from militant Bolshevism. And after the collapse of the Russian state it was in the East that Russian culture continued to live. Its mysticism influenced India. Its social ideal influenced China. Not indeed that China took over the theory, still less the practice, of communism; but she learnt to entrust herself increasingly to a vigorous, devoted and despotic party, and to feel in terms of the social whole rather than individualistically. Yet she was honeycombed with individualism, and in spite of her rulers she had precipitated a submerged and desperate class of wage slaves.

In the Far West, the United States of America openly claimed to be custodians of the whole planet. Universally feared and envied, universally respected for their enterprise, yet for their complacency very widely despised, the Americans were rapidly changing the whole character of man's existence. By this time every human being throughout the planet made use of American products, and there was no region where American capital did not support local labour. Moreover the American press, gramophone, radio, cinematograph and televisor ceaselessly drenched the planet with American thought. Year by year the æther reverberated with echoes of New York's pleasures and the religious fervours of the Middle West. What wonder, then, that America, even while she was despised, irresistibly moulded the whole human race. This, perhaps, would not have mattered, had America been able to give of her very rare best. But inevitably only her worst could be propagated. Only the most vulgar traits of that potentially great people could get through into the minds of foreigners by means of these crude instruments. And so, by the floods of poison issuing from this people's baser members, the whole world, and with it the nobler parts of America herself, were irrevocably corrupted.

For the best of America was too weak to withstand the worst. Americans had indeed contributed amply to human thought. They had helped to emancipate philosophy from ancient fetters. They had served science by lavish and rigorous research. In astronomy, favoured by their costly instruments and clear atmosphere, they had done much to reveal the dispositions of the stars and galaxies. In literature, though often they behaved as barbarians, they had also conceived new modes of expression, and moods of thought not easily appreciated in Europe. They had also created a new and brilliant architecture. And their genius for organization worked upon a scale that was scarcely conceivable, let alone practicable, to other peoples. In fact their best minds faced old problems of theory and of valuation with a fresh innocence and courage, so that fogs of superstition were cleared away wherever these choice Americans were present. But these best were after all a minority in a huge wilderness of opinionated self-deceivers, in whom surprisingly, an outworn religious dogma was championed with the intolerant optimism of youth. For this was essentially a race of bright, but arrested, adolescents. Something lacked which should have enabled them to grow up. One who looks back across the aeons to this remote people can see their fate already woven of their circumstance and their disposition, and can appreciate the grim jest that these, who seemed to themselves gifted to rejuvenate the planet, should have plunged it, inevitably, through spiritual desolation into senility and age-long night.

Inevitably. Yet here was a people of unique promise, gifted innately beyond all other peoples. Here was a race brewed of all the races, and mentally more effervescent than any. Here were intermingled Anglo-Saxon stubbornness, Teutonic genius for detail and systematization, Italian gaiety, the intense fire of Spain, and the more mobile Celtic flame. Here also was the sensitive and stormy Slav, a youth-giving Negroid infusion, a faint but subtly stimulating trace of the Red Man, and in the West a sprinkling of the Mongol. Mutual intolerance no doubt isolated these diverse stocks to some degree; yet the whole was increasingly one people, proud of its individuality, of its success, of its idealistic mission in the world, proud also of its optimistic and anthropocentric view of the universe. What might not this energy have achieved, had it been more critically controlled, had it been forced to attend to life's more forbidding aspects! Direct tragic experience might perhaps have opened the hearts of this people. Intercourse with a more mature culture might have refined their intelligence. But the very success which had intoxicated them rendered them also too complacent to learn from less prosperous competitors.

Yet there was a moment when this insularity promised to wane. So long as England was a serious economic rival, America inevitably regarded her with suspicion. But when England was seen to be definitely in economic decline, yet culturally still at her zenith, America conceived a more generous interest in the last and severest phase of English thought. Eminent Americans themselves began to whisper that perhaps their unrivalled prosperity was not after all good evidence either of their own spiritual greatness or of the moral rectitude of the universe. A minute but persistent school of writers began to affirm that America lacked self-criticism, was incapable of seeing the joke against herself, was in fact wholly devoid of that detachment and resignation which was the finest, though of course the rarest, mood of latter-day England. This movement might well have infused throughout the American people that which was needed to temper their barbarian egotism, and open their ears once more to the silence beyond man's strident sphere. Once more, for only latterly had they been seriously deafened by the din of their own material success. And indeed, scattered over the continent throughout this whole period, many shrinking islands of true culture contrived to keep their heads above the rising tide of vulgarity and superstition. These it was that had looked to Europe for help, and were attempting a rally when England and France blundered into that orgy of emotionalism and murder which exterminated so many of their best minds and permanently weakened their cultural influence.

Subsequently it was Germany that spoke for Europe. And Germany was too serious an economic rival for America to be open to her influence. Moreover German criticism, though often emphatic, was too heavily pedantic, too little ironical, to pierce the hide of American complacency. Thus it was that America sank further and further into Americanism. Vast wealth and industry, and also brilliant invention, were concentrated upon puerile ends. In particular the whole of American life was organized around the cult of the powerful individual, that phantom ideal which Europe herself had only begun to outgrow in her last phase. Those Americans who wholly failed to realize this ideal, who remained at the bottom of the social ladder, either consoled themsleves with hopes for the future, or stole symbolical satisfaction by identifying themselves with some popular star, or gloated upon their American citizenship, and applauded the arrogant foreign policy of their government. Those who achieved power were satisfied so long as they could merely retain it, and advertise it uncritically in the conventionally self-assertive manners.

It was almost inevitable that when Europe had recovered from the Russo-German disaster she should come to blows with America; for she had long chafed under the saddle of American finance, and the daily life of Europeans had become more and more cramped by the presence of a widespread and contemptuous foreign "aristocracy" of American business men. Germany alone was comparatively free from this domination, for Germany was herself still a great economic power. But in Germany, no less than elsewhere, there was constant friction with the Americans.

Of course neither Europe nor America desired war. Each was well aware that war would mean the end of business prosperity, and for Europe very possibly the end of all things; for it was known that man's power of destruction had recently increased, and that if war were waged relentlessly, the stronger side might exterminate the other. But inevitably an "incident" at last occurred which roused blind rage on each side of the Atlantic. A murder in South Italy, a few ill-considered remarks in the European Press, offensive retaliation in the American Press accompanied by the lynching of an Italian in the Middle West, an uncontrollable massacre of American citizens in Rome, the dispatch of an American air fleet to occupy Italy, interception by the European air fleet, and war was in existence before ever it had been declared. This aerial action resulted, perhaps unfortunately for Europe, in a momentary check to the American advance. The enemy was put on his mettle, and prepared a crushing blow.

2. THE ORIGINS OF A MYSTERY

While the Americans were mobilizing their whole armament, there occurred the really interesting event of the war. It so happened that an international society of scientific workers was meeting in England at Plymouth, and a young Chinese physicist had expressed his desire to make a report to a select committee. As he had been experimenting to find means for the utilization of subatomic energy by the annihilation of matter, it was with some excitement that, according to instruction, the forty international representatives travelled to the north coast of Devon and met upon the bare headland called Hartland Point.

It was a bright morning after rain. Eleven miles to the north-west, the cliffs of Lundy Island displayed their markings with unusual detail. Sea-birds wheeled about the heads of the party as they seated themselves on their rain-coats in a cluster upon the rabbit-cropped turf.

They were a remarkable company, each one of them a unique person, yet characterized to some extent by his particular national type. And all were distinctively "scientists" of the period. Formerly this would have implied a rather uncritical leaning toward materialism, and an affectation of cynicism; but by now it was fashionable to profess an equally uncritical belief that all natural phenomena were manifestations of the cosmic mind. In both periods, when a man passed beyond the sphere of his own serious scientific work he chose his beliefs irresponsibly, according to his taste, much as he chose his recreation or his food.

Of the individuals present we may single out one or two for notice. The German, an anthropologist, and a product of the long-established cult of physical and mental health, sought to display in his own athletic person the characters proper to Nordic man. The Frenchman, an old but still sparkling psychologist, whose queer hobby was the collecting of weapons, ancient and modern, regarded the proceedings with kindly cynicism. The Englishman, one of the few remaining intellectuals of his race, compensated for the severe study of physics by a scarcely less devoted research into the history of English expletives and slang, delighting to treat his colleagues to the fruits of his toil. The West African president of the Society was a biologist, famous for his interbreeding of man and ape.

When all were settled, the President explained the purpose of the meeting. The utilization of subatomic energy had indeed been achieved, and they were to be given a demonstration.

The young Mongol stood up, and produced from a case an instrument rather like the old-fashioned rifle. Displaying this object, he spoke as follows, with that quaintly stilted formality which had once been characteristic of all educated Chinese: "Before describing the details of my rather delicate process, I will illustrate its importance by showing what can be done with the finished product. Not only can I initiate the annihilation of matter, but also I can do so at a distance and in a precise direction. Moreover, I can inhibit the process. As a means of destruction, my instrument is perfect. As a source of power for the constructive work of mankind, it has unlimited potentiality. Gentlemen, this is a great moment in the history of Man. I am about to render into the hands of organized intelligence the means to stop for ever man's internecine brawls. Henceforth this great Society, of which you are the *élite,* will benefi-cently rule the planet. With this little instrument you will stop the ridiculous war; and with another, which I shall soon perfect, you will dispense unlimited industrial power wherever you consider it needed. Gentlemen, with the aid of this handy instrument which I have the honour to demonstrate, you are able to become absolute masters of this planet."

Here the representative of England muttered an archaism whose significance was known only to himself, "Gawd 'elp us!" In the minds of some
of those foreigners who were not physicists this quaint expression was taken
to be a technical word having some connexion with the new source of energy.

The Mongol continued. Turning towards Lundy, he said, "That island
is no longer inhabited, and as it is something of a danger to shipping, I will
remove it." So saying he aimed his instrument at the distant cliff, but continued speaking. "This trigger will stimulate the ultimate positive and negative charges which constitute the atoms at a certain point on the rock face to
annihilate each other. These stimulated atoms will infect their neighbours,
and so on indefinitely. This second trigger, however, will stop the actual
annihilation. Were I to refrain from using it, the process would indeed continue indefinitely, perhaps until the whole of the planet had disintegrated."

There was an anxious movement among the spectators, but the young
man took careful aim, and pressed the two triggers in quick succession. No
sound from the instrument. No visible effect upon the smiling face of the
island. Laughter began to gurgle from the Englishman, but ceased. For a
dazzling point of light appeared on the remote cliff. It increased in size and
brilliance, till all eyes were blinded in the effort to continue watching. It lit
up the under parts of the clouds and blotted out the sun-cast shadows of gorse
bushes beside the spectators. The whole end of the island facing the mainland
was now an intolerable scorching sun. Presently, however, its fury was veiled
in clouds of steam from the boiling sea. Then suddenly the whole island,
three miles of solid granite, leaped asunder; so that a covey of great rocks
soared heavenward, and beneath them swelled more slowly a gigantic mush-
room of steam and debris. Then the sound arrived. All hands were clapped
to ears, while eyes still strained to watch the bay, pocked white with the hail
of rocks. Meanwhile a great wall of sea advanced from the centre of turmoil.
This was seen to engulf a coasting vessel, and pass on toward Bideford and
Barnstaple.

The spectators leaped to their feet and clamoured, while the young author of this fury watched the spectacle with exultation, and some surprise at
the magnitude of these mere after-effects of his process.

The meeting was now adjourned to a neighbouring chapel to hear the
report of the research. As the representatives were filing through the door it
was observed that the steam and smoke had cleared, and that open sea extended where had been Lundy. Within the chapel, the great Bible was de-
corously removed and the windows thrown open, to dispel somewhat the
odour of sanctity. For though the early and spiritistic interpretations of relativity and the quantum theory had by now accustomed men of science to
pay their respects to the religions, many of them were still liable to a certain
asphyxia when they were actually within the precincts of sanctity. When the
scientists had settled themselves upon the archaic and unyielding benches,

the President explained that the chapel authorities had kindly permitted this meeting because they realized that, since men of science had gradually discovered the spiritual foundation of physics, science and religion must henceforth be close allies. Moreover the purpose of this meeting was to discuss one of those supreme mysteries which it was the glory of science to discover and religion to transfigure. The President then complimented the young dispenser of power upon his triumph, and called upon him to address the meeting.

At this point, however, the aged representative of France intervened, and was granted a hearing. Born almost a hundred and forty years earlier, and preserved more by native intensity of spirit than by the artifices of the regenerator, this ancient seemed to speak out of a remote and wiser epoch. For in a declining civilization it is often the old who see furthest and see with youngest eyes. He concluded a rather long, rhetorical, yet closely reasoned speech as follows: "No doubt we are the intelligent of the planet; and because of our consecration to our calling, no doubt we are comparatively honest. But alas, even we are human. We make little mistakes now and then, and commit little indiscretions. The possession of such power as is offered us would not bring peace. On the contrary it would perpetuate our national hates. It would throw the world into confusion. It would undermine our own integrity, and turn us into tyrants. Moreover it would ruin science. And,—well, when at last through some little error the world got blown up, the disaster would not be regrettable. I know that Europe is almost certainly about to be destroyed by those vigorous but rather spoilt children across the Atlantic. But distressing as this must be, the alternative is far worse. No Sir! Your very wonderful toy would be a gift fit for developed minds; but for us, who are still barbarians,—no, it must not be. And so, with deep regret I beg you to destroy your handiwork, and if it were possible, your memory of your marvellous research. But above all breathe no word of your process to us, or to any man."

The German then protested that to refuse would be cowardly. He briefly described his vision of a world organized under organized science, and inspired by a scientifically organized religious dogma. "Surely," he said, "to refuse were to refuse the gift of God, of that God whose presence in the humblest quantum we have so recently and so surprisingly revealed." Other speakers followed, for and against; but it soon grew clear that wisdom would prevail. Men of science were by now definitely cosmopolitan in sentiment. Indeed so far were they from nationalism, that on this occasion the representative of America had urged acceptance of the weapon, although it would be used against his own countrymen.

Finally, however, and actually by a unanimous vote, the meeting, while recording its deep respect for the Chinese scientist, requested, nay ordered, that the instrument and all account of it should be destroyed.

The young man rose, drew his handiwork from its case, and fingered it. So long did he remain thus standing in silence with eyes fixed on the instrument, that the meeting became restless. At last, however, he spoke. "I shall abide by the decision of the meeting. Well, it is hard to destroy the fruit of ten years' work, and such fruit, too. I expected to have the gratitude of mankind; but instead I am an outcast." Once more he paused. Gazing out of the window, he now drew from his pocket a field-glass, and studied the western sky. "Yes, they are American. Gentlemen, the American air fleet approaches."

The company leapt to its feet and crowded to the windows. High in the west a sparse line of dots stretched indefinitely into the north and the south. Said the Englishman, "For God's sake use your damned tool once more, or England's done. They must have smashed our fellows over the Atlantic."

The Chinese scientist turned his eyes on the President. There was a general cry of "Stop them." Only the Frenchman protested. The representative of the United States raised his voice and said, "They are my people, I have friends up there in the sky. My own boy is probably there. But they're mad. They want to do something hideous. They're in the lynching mood. Stop them." The Mongol still gazed at the President, who nodded. The Frenchman broke down in senile tears. Then the young man, leaning upon the window sill, took careful aim at each black dot in turn. One by one, each became a blinding star, then vanished. In the chapel, a long silence. Then whispers; and glances at the Chinaman, expressive of anxiety and dislike.

There followed a hurried ceremony in a neighbouring field. A fire was lit. The instrument and the no less murderous manuscript were burnt. And then the grave young Mongol, having insisted on shaking hands all round, said, "With my secret alive in me, I must not live. Some day a more worthy race will re-discover it, but today I am a danger to the planet. And so I, who have foolishly ignored that I live among savages, help myself now by the ancient wisdom to pass hence." So saying, he fell dead.

3. EUROPE MURDERED

Rumour spread by voice and radio throughout the world. An island had been mysteriously exploded. The American fleet had been mysteriously annihilated in the air. And in the neighbourhood where these events had occurred, distinguished scientists were gathered in conference. The European Government sought out the unknown saviour of Europe, to thank him, and secure his process for their own use. The President of the scientific society gave an account of the meeting and the unanimous vote. He and his colleagues were promptly arrested, and "pressure," first moral and then physical, was brought to bear on them to make them disclose the secret; for the world was convinced that they really knew it, and were holding it back for their own purposes.

Meanwhile it was learned that the American air commander, after he had defeated the European fleet, had been instructed merely to "demonstrate" above England while peace was negotiated. For in America, big business had threatened the government with boycott if unnecessary violence were committed in Europe. Big business was by now very largely international in sentiment, and it was realized that the desrtuction of Europe would inevitably unhinge American finance. But the unprecedented disaster to the victorious fleet roused the Americans to blind hate, and the peace party was submerged. Thus it turned out that the Chinaman's one hostile act had not saved England, but doomed her.

For some days Europeans lived in panic dread, knowing not what horror might at any moment descend on them. No wonder, then, that the Government resorted to torture in order to extract the secret from the scientists. No wonder that out of the forty individuals concerned, one, the Englishman, saved himself by deceit. He promised to do his best to "remember" the intricate process. Under strict supervision, he used his own knowledge of physics to experiment in search of the Chinaman's trick. Fortunately, however, he was on the wrong scent. And indeed he knew it. For though his first motive was mere self-preservation, later he conceived the policy of indefinitely preventing the dangerous discovery by directing research along a blind alley. And so his treason, by seeming to give the authority of a most eminent physicist to a wholly barren line of research, saved this undisciplined and scarcely human race from destroying its planet.

The American people, sometimes tender even to excess, were now collectively insane with hate of the English and of all Europeans. With cold efficiency they flooded Europe with the latest and deadliest of gasses, till all the peoples were poisoned in their cities like rats in their holes. The gas employed was such that its potency would cease within three days. It was therefore possible for an American sanitary force to take charge of each metropolis within a week after the attack. Of those who first descended into the great silence of the murdered cities, many were unhinged by the overwhelming presence of dead populations. The gas had operated first upon the ground level, but rising like a tide, it had engulfed the top stories, the spires, the hills. Thus, while in the streets lay thousands who had been overcome by the first wave of poison, every roof and pinnacle bore the bodies of those who had struggled upwards in the vain hope of escaping beyond the highest reach of the tide. When the invaders arrived they beheld on every height prostrate and contorted figures.

Thus Europe died. All centres of intellectual life were blotted out, and of the agricultural regions only the uplands and mountains were untouched. The spirit of Europe lived henceforth only in a piece-meal and dislocated manner in the minds of Americans, Chinese, Indians, and the rest.

There were indeed the British Colonies, but they were by now far less European than American. The war had, of course, disintegrated the

British Empire. Canada sided with the United States. South Africa and India declared their neutrality at the outbreak of war. Australia, not through cowardice, but through conflict of loyalties, was soon reduced to neutrality. The New Zealanders took to their mountains and maintained an insane but heroic resistance for a year. A simple and gallant folk, they had almost no conception of the European spirit, yet obscurely and in spite of their Americanization they were loyal to it, or at least to that symbol of one aspect of Europeanism, "England." Indeed so extravagantly loyal were they, or so innately dogged and opinionated, that when further resistance became impossible, many of them, both men and women, killed themselves rather than submit.

But the most lasting agony of this war was suffered, not by the defeated, but by the victors. For when their passion had cooled the Americans could not easily disguise from themselves that they had committed murder. They were not at heart a brutal folk, but rather a kindly. They liked to think of the world as a place of innocent pleasure-seeking, and of themselves as the main purveyors of delight. Yet they had been somehow drawn into this fantastic crime; and henceforth an all-pervading sense of collective guilt warped the American mind. They had ever been vainglorious and intolerant; but now these qualities in them became extravagant even to insanity. Both as individuals and collectively, they became increasingly frightened of criticism, increasingly prone to blame and hate, increasingly self-righteous, increasingly hostile to the critical intelligence, increasingly superstitious.

Thus was this once noble people singled out by the gods to be cursed, and the minister of curses.

CHAPTER III

AMERICA AND CHINA

I. THE RIVALS

AFTER the eclipse of Europe, the allegiance of men gradually crystallized into two great national or racial sentiments, the American and the Chinese. Little by little all other patriotisms became mere local variants of one or other of these two major loyalties. At first, indeed, there were many internecine conflicts. A detailed history of this period would describe how North America, repeating the welding process of the ancient "American Civil War," incorporated within itself the already Americanized Latins of South America; and how Japan, once the bully of young China, was so crippled by social revolutions that she fell a prey to American Imperialism; and how this bondage turned her violently Chinese in sentiment, so that finally she freed herself by an heroic war of independence, and joined the Asiatic Confederacy, under Chinese leadership.

A full history would also tell of the vicissitudes of the League of Nations. Although never a cosmopolitan government, but an association of national governments, each concerned mainly for its own sovereignty, this great organization had gradually gained a very real prestige and authority over all its members. And in spite of its many short-comings, most of which were involved in its fundamental constitution, it was invaluable as the great concrete focusing point of the growing loyalty toward humanity. At first its existence had been precarious; and indeed it had only preserved itself by an extreme caution, amounting almost to servility toward the "great powers." Little by little, however, it had gained moral authority to such an extent that no single power, even the mightiest, dared openly and in cold blood either to disobey the will of the League or reject the findings of the High Court. But, since human loyalty was still in the main national rather than cosmopolitan, situations were all too frequent in which a nation would lose its head, run amok, throw its pledges to the winds, and plunge into fear-inspired aggression. Such a situation had produced the Anglo-French War. At other times the nations would burst apart into two great camps, and the League would be temporarily forgotten in their disunion. This happened in the Russo-German War, which was possible only because America favoured Russia, and China favoured Germany. After the destruction of Europe, the world had for a while consisted of the League on one side and America on the other. But the League was dominated by China, and no longer stood for cosmopolitanism. This being so, those whose loyalty was genuinely human worked hard to bring America once more into the fold, and at last succeeded.

In spite of the League's failure to prevent the "great" wars, it worked admirably in preventing all the minor conflicts which had once been a chronic disease of the race. Latterly, indeed, the world's peace was absolutely secure, save when the League itself was almost equally divided. Unfortunately, with the rise of America and China, this kind of situation became more and more common. During the war of North and South America an attempt was made to recreate the League as a Cosmopolitan Sovereignty, controlling the pooled armaments of all nations. But, though the cosmopolitan will was strong, tribalism was stronger. The upshot was that, over the Japanese question, the League definitely split into two Leagues, each claiming to inherit universal sovereignty from the old League, but each in reality dominated by a kind of supernational sentiment, the one American, the other Chinese.

This occurred within a century after the eclipse of Europe. The second century completed the process of crystallization into two systems, political and mental. On the one hand was the wealthy and close-knit American Continental Federation, with its poor relations, South Africa, Australia, New

Zealand, the bedridden remains of Western Europe, and part of the soulless body that was Russia. On the other hand were Asia and Africa. In fact the ancient distinction between East and West had now become the basis of political sentiment and organization.

Within each system there were of course real differences of culture, of which the chief was the difference between the Chinese and Indian mentalities. The Chinese were interested in appearances, in the sensory, the urbane, the practical; while the Indians inclined to seek behind appearances for some ultimate reality, of which this life, they said, was but a passing aspect. Thus the average Indian never took to heart the practical social problem in all its seriousness. The ideal of perfecting this world was never an all-absorbing interest to him; since he had been taught to believe that this world was mere shadow. There was, indeed, a time when China had mentally less in common with India than with the West, but fear of America had drawn the two great Eastern peoples together. They agreed at least in earnest hate of that strange blend of the commercial traveller, the missionary, and the barbarian conqueror, which was the American abroad.

China, owing to her relative weakness and irritation caused by the tentacles of American industry within her, was at this time more nationalistic than her rival. America, indeed, professed to have outgrown nationalism, and to stand for political and cultural world unity. But she conceived this unity as a unity under American organization; and by culture she meant Americanism. This kind of cosmopolitanism was regarded by Asia and Africa without sympathy. In China a concerted effort had been made to purge the foreign element from her culture. Its success, however, was only superficial. Pigtails and chopsticks had once more come into vogue among the leisured, and the study of Chinese classics was once more compulsory in all schools. Yet the manner of life of the average man remained American. Not only did he use American cutlery, shoes, gramophones, domestic labour-saving devices, but also his alphabet was European, his vocabulary was permeated by American slang, his newspapers and radio were American in manner, though anti-American in politics. He saw daily in his domestic television screen every phase of American private life and every American public event. Instead of opium and joss sticks, he affected cigarettes and chewing gum.

His thought also was largely a Mongolian variant of American thought. For instance, since his was a non-metaphysical mind, but since also some kind of metaphysics is unavoidable, he accepted the naïvely materialistic metaphysics which had been popularized by the earliest Behaviourists. In this view the only reality was physical energy, and the mind was but the system of the body's movements in response to stimulus. Behaviourism had formerly played a great part in purging the best Western minds of superstition; and indeed at one time it was the chief growing point of thought.

This early, pregnant, though extravagant, doctrine it was that had been absorbed by China. But in its native land Behaviorism had gradually been infected by the popular demand for comfortable ideas, and had finally changed into a curious kind of spiritism, according to which, though the ultimate reality was indeed physical energy, this energy was identified with the divine spirit. The most dramatic feature of American thought in this period was the merging of Behaviorism and Fundamentalism, a belated and degenerate mode of Christianity. Behaviourism itself, indeed, had been originally a kind of inverted Puritan faith, according to which intellectual salvation involved acceptance of a crude materialistic dogma, chiefly because it was repugnant to the self-righteous, and unintelligible to intellectuals of the earlier schools. The older Puritans trampled down all fleshy impulses; these newer Puritans trampled no less self-righteously upon the spiritual cravings. But in the increasingly spiritistic inclination of physics itself, Behaviorism and Fundamentalism had found a meeting place. Since the ultimate stuff of the physical universe was now said to be multitudinous and arbitrary "quanta" of the activity of "spirits," how easy was it for the materialistic and the spiritistic to agree! At heart, indeed, they were never far apart in mood, though opposed in doctrine. The real cleavage was between the truly spiritual view on the one hand, and the spiritistic and materialistic on the other. Thus the most materialistic of Christian sects and the most doctrinaire of scientific sects were not long in finding a formula to express their unity, their denial of all those finer capacities which had emerged to be the spirit of man.

These two faiths were at one in their respect for crude physical movement. And here lay the deepest difference between the American and the Chinese minds. For the former, activity, any sort of activity, was an end in itself; for the latter, activity was but a progress toward the true end, which was rest, and peace of mind. Action was to be undertaken only when equilibrium was disturbed. And in this respect China was at one with India. Both preferred contemplation to action.

Thus in China and India the passion for wealth was less potent than in America. Wealth was the power to set things and people in motion; and in America, therefore, wealth came to be frankly regarded as the breath of God, the divine spirit immanent in man. God was the supreme Boss, the universal Employer. His wisdom was conceived as a stupendous efficiency, his love as munificence towards his employees. The parable of the talents was made the corner-stone of education; and to be wealthy, therefore, was to be respected as one of God's chief agents. The typical American man of big business was one who, in the midst of a show of luxury, was at heart ascetic. He valued his splendour only because it advertised to all men that he was of the elect. The typical Chinese wealthy man was one who savoured his luxury with a delicate and lingering palate, and was seldom tempted to sacrifice it to the barren lust of power.

On the other hand, since American culture was wholly concerned with the values of the individual life, it was more sensitive than the Chinese with regard to the well-being of humble individuals. Therefore industrial conditions were far better under American than under Chinese capitalism. And in China both kinds of capitalism existed side by side. There were American factories in which the Chinese operatives thrived on the American system, and there were Chinese factories in which the operatives were by comparison abject wage-slaves. The fact that many Chinese industrial workers could not afford to keep a motor-car, let alone an aeroplane, was a source of much self-righteous indignation amongst American employers. And the fact that this fact did not cause a revolution in China, and that Chinese employers were able to procure plenty of labour in spite of the better conditions in American factories, was a source of perplexity. But in truth what the average Chinese worker wanted was not symbolical self-assertion through the control of privately owned machines, but security of life, and irresponsible leisure. In the earlier phase of "modern" China there had indeed been serious explosions of class hatred. Almost every one of the great Chinese industrial centres had, at some point in its career, massacred its employers, and declared itself an independent communist city-state. But communism was alien to China, and none of these experiments was permanently successful. Latterly, when the rule of the Nationalist Party had become secure, and the worst industrial evils had been abolished, class feeling had given place to a patriotic loathing of American interference and American hustle, and those who worked under American employers were often called traitors.

The Nationalist Party was not, indeed, the soul of China; but it was, so to speak, the central nervous system, within which the soul presided as a controlling principle. The Party was an intensely practical yet idealistic organization, half civil service, half religious order, though violently opposed to every kind of religion. Modelled originally on the Bolshevic Party of Russia, it had also drawn inspiration from the native and literary civil service of old China, and even from the tradition of administrative integrity which had been the best, the sole, contribution of British Imperialism to the East. Thus, by a route of its own, the Party had approached the ideal of the Platonic governors. In order to be admitted to the Party, it was necessary to do two things, to pass a very strict written examination on Western and Chinese social theory, and to come through a five years' apprenticeship in actual administrative work. Outside the Party, China was still extremely corrupt; for peculation and nepotism were not censured, so long as they were kept decently hidden. But the Party set a brilliant example of self-oblivious devotion; and this unheard-of honesty was one source of its power. It was universally recognized that the Party man was genuinely interested in social rather than private matters; and consequently he was trusted. The supreme object of his loyalty was not the Party, but China, not indeed the mass of Chinese individuals, whom he regarded with almost the same nonchalance as he regarded himself, but the corporate unity and culture of the race.

The whole executive power in China was now in the hands of members of the Party, and the final legislative authority was the Assembly of Party Delegates. Between these two institutions stood the President. Sometimes no more than chairman of the Executive Committee, this individual was now and then almost a dictator, combining in himself the attributes of Prime Minister, Emperor, and Pope. For the head of the Party was the head of the state; and like the ancient emperors, he became the symbolical object of ancestor worship.

The Party's policy was dominated by the Chinese respect for culture. Just as Western states had been all too often organized under the will for military prestige, so the new China was organized under the will for prestige of culture. For this end the American state was reviled as the supreme example of barbarian vulgarity; and so patriotism was drawn in to strengthen the cultural policy of the Party. It was boasted that, while indeed in America every man and woman might hope to fight a way to material wealth, in China every intelligent person could actually enjoy the cultural wealth of the race. The economic policy of the Party was based on the principle of affording to all workers security of livelihood and full educational opportunity. (In American eyes, however, the livelihood thus secured was scarely fit for beasts, and the education provided was out of date and irreligious.) The Party took good care to gather into itself all the best of every social class, and also to encourage in the unintelligent masses a respect for learning, and the illusion that they themselves shared to some extent in the national culture.

But in truth this culture, which the common people so venerated in their superiors and mimicked in their own lives, was scarcely less superficial than the cult of power against which it was pitted. For it was almost wholly a cult of social rectitude and textual learning; not so much of the merely literary learning which had obsessed ancient China, as of the vast corpus of contemporary scientific dogma, and above all of pure mathematics. In old days the candidate for office had to show minute but uncritical knowledge of classical writers; now he had to give proof of a no less barren agility in describing the established formulæ of physics, biology, psychology, and more particularly of economics and social theory. And though never encouraged to puzzle over the philosophical basis of mathematics, he was expected to be familiar with the intricacy of at least one branch of that vast game of skill. So great was the mass of information forced upon the student, that he had no time to think of the mutual implications of the various branches of his knowledge.

Yet there was a soul in China. And in this elusive soul of China the one hope of the First Men now lay. Scattered throughout the Party was a minority of original minds, who were its source of inspiration and the growing point of the human spirit in this period. Well aware of man's littleness, these thinkers regarded him none the less as the crown of the universe. On the basis of a positivistic and rather perfunctory metaphysic, they built a social ideal and a theory of art. Indeed, in the practice and appreciation of art they saw man's highest achievement. Pessimistic about the remote future of the race, and contemptuous of American evangelism, they accepted as the end of living the creation of an intricately unified pattern of human lives set in a fair environment. Society, the supreme work of art (so they put it), is a delicate and perishable texture of human intercourse. They even entertained the possibility that in the last resort, not only the individual's life, but the whole career of the race, might be tragic, and to be valued according to the standards of tragic art. Contrasting their own spirit with that of the Americans, one of them had said, "America, a backward youth in a playroom equipped with luxury and electric power, pretends that his mechanical toy moves the world. China, a gentleman walking in his garden in the evening, admires the fragrance and the order all the more because in the air is the first nip of winter, and in his ear rumour of the irresistible barbarian."

In this attitude there was something admirable, and sorely needed at the time; but also there was a fatal deficiency. In its best exponents it rose to a detached yet fervent salutation of existence, but all too easily degenerated into a supine complacency, and a cult of social etiquette. In fact it was ever in danger of corruption through the inveterate Chinese habit of caring only for appearances. In some respects the spirit of America and the spirit of China were complementary, since the one was restless and the other bland, the one zealous and the other dispassionate, the one religious, the other artistic, the one superficially mystical or at least romantic, the other classical and rationalistic, though too easy-going for prolonged rigorous thought. Had they co-operated, these two mentalities might have achieved much. On the other hand, in both there was an identical and all-important lack. Neither of them was disturbed and enlightened by that insatiable lust for the truth, that passion for the free exercise of critical intelligence, the gruelling hunt for reality, which had been the glory of Europe and even of the earlier America, but now was no longer anywhere among the First Men. And, consequent on this lack, another disability crippled them. Both were by now without that irreverent wit which individuals of an earlier generation had loved to exercise upon one another and on themselves, and even on their most sacred values.

In spite of this weakness, with good luck they might have triumphed. But, as I shall tell, the spirit of America undermined the integrity of China, and thereby destroyed its one chance of salvation. There befell, in fact, one of those disasters, half inevitable and half accidental, which periodically descended on the First Men, as though by the express will of some divinity who cared more for the excellence of his dramatic creation than for the sentient puppets which he had conceived for its enacting.

2. THE CONFLICT

After the Euro-American War there occurred first a century of minor national conflicts, and then a century of strained peace, during which America and China became more and more irksome to each other. At the close of this period the great mass of men were in theory far more cosmopolitan than nationalist, yet the inveterate tribal spirit lurked within each mind, and was ever ready to take possession. The planet was now a delicately organized economic unit, and big business in all lands was emphatically contemptuous of patriotism. Indeed the whole adult generation of the period was consciously and without reserve internationalist and pacifist. Yet this logically unassailable conviction was undermined by a biological craving for adventurous living. Prolonged peace and improved social conditions had greatly reduced the danger and hardship of life, and there was no socially harmless substitute to take the place of war in exercising the primitive courage and anger of animals fashioned for the wild. Consciously men desired peace, unconsciously they still needed some such gallantry as war afforded. And this repressed combative disposition ever and again expressed itself in explosions of irrational tribalism.

Inevitably a serious conflict at last occurred. As usual the cause was both economic and sentimental. The economic cause was the demand for fuel. A century earlier a very serious oil famine had so sobered the race that the League of Nations had been able to impose a system of cosmopolitan control upon the existing oil fields, and even the coal fields. It had also imposed strict regulations as to the use of these invaluable materials. Oil in particular was only to be used for enterprises in which no other source of power would serve. The cosmopolitan control of fuel was perhaps the supreme achievement of the League, and it remained a fixed policy of the race long after the League had been superseded. Yet, by a choice irony of fate, this quite unusually sane policy contributed largely to the downfall of civilization. By means of it, as will later transpire, the end of coal was postponed into the period when the intelligence of the race was so deteriorated that it could no longer cope with such a crisis. Instead of adjusting itself to the novel situation, it simply collapsed.

But at the time with which we are at present dealing, means had recently been found of profitably working the huge deposits of fuel in Antarctica. This vast supply unfortunately lay technically beyond the jurisdiction of the World Fuel Control Board. America was first in the field, and saw in Antarctic fuel a means for her advancement, and for her self-imposed duty of Americanizing the planet. China, fearful of Americanization, demanded that the new sources should be brought under the jurisdiction of the Board. For some years feeling had become increasingly violent on this point, and both peoples had by now relapsed into the crude old nationalistic mood. War began to seem almost inevitable.

The actual occasion of conflict, however, was, as usual, an accident. A scandal was brought to light about child labour in certain Indian factories. Boys and girls under twelve were being badly sweated, and in their abject state their only adventure was precocious sex. The American Government protested, and in terms which assumed that America was the guardian of the world's morals. India immediately held up the reform which she had begun to impose, and replied to America as to a busy-body. America threatened an expedition to set things right, "backed by the approval of all the morally sensitive races of the earth." China now intervened to keep the peace between her rival and her partner, and undertook to see that the evil should be abolished, if America would withdraw her extravagant slanders against the Eastern conscience. But it was too late. An American bank in China was raided, and its manager's severed head was kicked along the street. The tribes of men had once more smelled blood. War was declared by the West upon the East.

Of the combatants, Asia, with North Africa, formed geographically the more compact system, but America and her dependents were economically more organized. At he outbreak of war neither side had any appreciable armament, for war had long ago been "outlawed." This fact, however, made little difference; since the warfare of the period could be carried on with great effect simply by the vast swarms of civil air-craft, loaded with poison, high explosives, disease microbes, and the still more lethal "hypobiological" organisms, which contemporary science sometimes regarded as the simplest living matter, sometimes as the most complex molecules.

The struggle began with violence, slackened, and dragged on for a quarter of a century. At the close of this period, Africa was mostly in the hands of America. But Egypt was an uninhabitable no-man's land, for the South Africans had very successfully poisoned the sources of the Nile. Europe was under Chinese military rule. This was enforced by armies of sturdy Central-Asiatics, who were already beginning to wonder why they did not make themselves masters of China also. The Chinese language, with European alphabet, was taught in all schools. In England, however, there were no schools, and no population; for early in the war, an American air-base had been established in Ireland, and England had been repeatedly devastated. Airmen passing over what had been London, could still make out the lines of Oxford Street and the Strand among the green and grey tangle of ruins. Wild nature, once so jealously preserved in national "beauty spots" against the incursion of urban civilization, now rioted over the whole island. At the other side of the world, the Japanese islands had been similarly devastated in the vain American effort to establish there an air-base from which to reach the heart of the enemy. So far, however, neither China nor America had been very seriously damaged; but recently the American biologists had devised a new malignant germ, more infectious and irresistible than anything hitherto known. Its work was to disintegrate the highest levels of the nervous system, and therefore to render all who were even slightly affected incapable of intelligent action; while a severe atack caused paralysis and finally death. With this weapon the American military had already turned one Chinese city into a bedlam; and wandering bacilli had got into the brains of several high officials throughout the province, rendering their behaviour incoherent. It was becoming the fashion to attribute all one's blunders to a touch of the new microbe. Hitherto no effective means of resisting the spread of this plague had been discovered. And as in the early stages of the disease the patient became restlessly active, undertaking interminable and objectless journeys on the flimsiest pretexts, it seemed probable that the "American madness" would spread throughout China.

On the whole, then, the military advantage lay definitely with the Americans; but economically they were perhaps the more damaged, for their higher standard of prosperity depended largely on foreign investment and foreign trade. Throughout the American continent there was now real poverty and serious symptoms of class war, not indeed between private workers and employers, but between workers and the autocratic military governing caste which inevitably war had created. Big business had at first succumbed to the patriotic fever, but had soon remembered that war is folly and ruinous to trade. Indeed upon both sides the fervour of nationalism had lasted only a couple of years, after which the lust of adventure had given place to mere dread of the enemy. For on each side the populace had been nursed into the belief that its foe was diabolic. When a quarter of a century had passed since there had been free intercourse between the two peoples, the real mental difference which had always existed between them appeared to many almost as a difference of biological species. Thus in America the Church preached that no Chinaman had a soul. Satan, it was said, had tampered with the evolution of the Chinese race when first it had emerged from the pre-human animal. He had contrived that it should be cunning, but wholly without tenderness. He had induced in it an insatiable sensuality, and wilful blindness toward the divine, toward that superbly masterful energy-for-energy's-sake which was the glory of America. Just as in a prehistoric era the young race of mammals had swept away the sluggish, brutish and demoded reptiles, so now, it was said, young soulful America was destined to rid the planet of the reptilian Mongol. In China, on the other hand, the official view was that the Americans were a typical case of biological retrogression. Like all parasitic organisms, they had thriven by specializing in one low-grade mode of behaviour at the expense of their higher nature; and now, "tape-worms of the planet," they were starving out the higher capacities of the human race by their frantic acquisitiveness.

Such were the official doctrines. But the strain of war had latterly produced on each side a grave distrust of its own government, and an emphatic will for peace at any price. The governments hated the peace party even more than each other, since their existence now depended on war. They even went so far as to inform one another of the clandestine operations of the pacifists, discovered by their own secret service in enemy territory.

Thus when at last big business and the workers on each side of the

Pacific had determined to stop the war by concerted action, it was very difficult for their representatives to meet.

3. ON AN ISLAND IN THE PACIFIC

Save for the governments, the whole human race now earnestly desired peace; but opinion in America was balanced between the will merely to effect an economic and political unification of the world, and a fanatical craving to impose American culture on the East. In China also there was a balance of the purely commercial readiness to sacrifice ideals for the sake of peace and prosperity, and the will to preserve Chinese culture. The two individuals who were to meet in secret for the negotiation of peace were typical of their respective races; in both of them the commercial and cultural motives were present, though the commercial was by now most often dominant.

It was in the twenty-sixth year of the war that two sea-planes converged by night from the East and West upon an island in the Pacific, and settled on a secluded inlet. The moon, destined in another age to smother this whole equatorial region with her shattered body, now merely besparkled the waves. From each plane a traveller emerged, and rowed himself ashore in a rubber coracle. The two men met upon the beach, and shook hands, the one with ceremony, the other with a slightly forced brotherliness. Already the sun peered over the wall of the sea, shouting his brilliance and his heat. The Chinese, taking off his air-helmet, uncoiled his pigtail with a certain emphasis, stripped off his heavy coverings, and revealed a sky-blue silk pyjama suit, embroidered with golden dragons. The other, glancing with scarcely veiled dislike at this finery, flung off his wraps and displayed the decent grey coat and breeches with which the American business men of this period unconsciously symbolized their reversion to Puritanism. Smoking the Chinese envoy's cigarettes, the two sat down to re-arrange the planet.

The conversation was amicable, and proceeded without hitch; for there was agreement about the practical measures to be adopted. The government in each country was to be overthrown at once. Both representatives were confident that this could be done if it could be attempted simultaneously on each side of the Pacific; for in both countries finance and the people could be trusted. In place of the national governments, a World Finance Directorate was to be created. This was to be composed of the leading commercial and industrial magnates of the world, along with representatives of the workers' organizations. The American representative should be the first president of the Directorate, and the Chinese the first vice-president. The Directorate was to manage the whole economic re-organization of the world. In particular, industrial conditions in the East were to be brought into line with those of America, while on the other hand the American monopoly of Antarctica was to be abolished. That rich and almost virgin land was to be subjected to the control of the Directorate.

Occasionally during the conversation reference was made to the great cultural difference between the East and West; but both the negotiants seemed anxious to believe that this was only a minor matter which need not be allowed to trouble a business discussion.

At this point occurred one of those incidents which, minute in themselves, have disproportionately great effects. The unstable nature of the First Men made them peculiarly liable to suffer from such accidents, and especially so in their decline.

The talk was interrupted by the appearance of a human figure swimming round a promontory into the little bay. In the shallows she arose, and walked out of the water towards the creators of the World State. A bronze young smiling woman, completely nude, with breasts heaving after her long swim, she stood before them, hesitating. The relation between the two men was instantly changed, though neither was at first aware of it.

"Delicious daughter of Ocean," said the Chinese, in that somewhat archaic and deliberately un-American English which the Asiatics now affected in communication with foreigners, "what is there that these two despicable land animals can do for you? For my friend, I cannot answer, but I at least am henceforth your slave." His eyes roamed carelessly, yet as it were with perfect politeness, all over her body. And she, with that added grace which haloes women when they feel the kiss of an admiring gaze, pressed the sea from her hair and stood at the point of speech.

But the American protested, "Whoever you are, please do not interrupt us. We are really very busy discussing a matter of great importance, and we have no time to spare. Please go. Your nudity is offensive to one accustomed to civilized manners. In a modern country you would not be allowed to bathe without a costume. We are growing very sensitive on this point."

A distressful but enhancing blush spread under the wet bronze, and the intruder made as if to go. But the Chinese cried, "Stay! We have almost finished our business talk. Refresh us with your presence. Bring the realities back into our discussion by permitting us to contemplate for a while the perfect vase line of your waist and thigh. Who are you? Of what race are you? My anthropological studies fail to place you. Your skin is fairer than is native here, though rich with sun. Your breasts are Grecian. Your lips are chiselled with a memory of Egypt. Your hair, night though it was, is drying with a most bewildering hint of gold. And your eyes, let me observe them. Long, subtle, as my countrywomen's, unfathomable as the mind of India, they yet reveal themselves to your new slave as not wholly black, but violet as the zenith before dawn. Indeed this exquisite unity of incompatibles conquers both my heart and my understanding."

During this harangue her composure was restored, though she glanced now and then at the American, who kept ever removing his gaze from her.

She answered in much the same diction as the other; but, surprisingly, with an old-time English accent, "I am certainly a mongrel. You might call me, not daughter of Ocean, but daughter of Man; for wanderers of every race have scattered their seed on this island. My body, I know, betrays its diverse ancestry in a rather queer blend of characters. My mind is perhaps unusual too, for I have never left this island. And though it is actually less than a quarter of a century since I was born, a past century has perhaps had more meaning for me than the obscure events of today. A hermit taught me. Two hundred years ago he lived actively in Europe; but towards the end of his long life he retreated to this island. As an old man he loved me. And day by day he gave me insight into the great spirit of the past; but of this age he gave me nothing. Now that he is dead, I struggle to familiarize myself with the present, but I continue to see everything from the angle of another age. And so" (turning to the American), "if I have offended against modern customs, it is because my insular mind has never been taught to regard nakedness as indecent. I am very ignorant, truly a savage. If only I could gain experience of your great world! If ever this war ends, I must travel."

"Delectable," said the Chinese, "exquisitely proportioned, exquisitely civilized savage! Come with me for a holiday in modern China. There you can bathe without a costume, so long as you are beautiful."

She ignored this invitation, and seemed to have fallen into a reverie. Then absently she continued, "Perhaps I should not suffer from this restlessness, this craving to experience the world, if only I were to experience motherhood instead. Many of the islanders from time to time have enriched me with their embraces. But with none of them could I permit myself to conceive. They are dear; but not one of them is at heart more than a child."

The American became restless. But again the Mongol intervened, with lowered and deepened voice. "I," he said, "I the Vice-President of the World Finance Directorate, shall be honoured to afford you the opportunity of motherhood."

She regarded him gravely, then smiled as on a child who asks more than it is reasonable to give. But the American rose hastily. Addressing the silken Mongol, he said, "You probably know that the American Government is in the act of sending a second poison fleet to turn your whole population insane, more insane than you are already. You cannot defend yourselves against this new weapon; and if I am to save you, I must not trifle any longer. Nor must you, for we must act simultaneously. We have settled all that matters for the moment. But before I leave, I must say that your behaviour toward this woman has very forcibly reminded me that there is something wrong with the Chinese way of thought and life. In my anxiety for peace, I overlooked my duty in this respect. I now give you notice that when the Directorate is established, we Americans must induce you to reform these abuses, for the world's sake and your own."

The Chinese rose and answered, "This matter must be settled locally.

We do not expect you to accept our standards, so do not you expect us to accept yours." He moved toward the woman, smiling. And the smile outraged the American.

We need not follow the wrangle which now ensued between the two representatives, each of whom, though in a manner cosmopolitan in sentiment, was heartily contemptuous of the other's values. Suffice it that the American became increasingly earnest and dictatorial, the other increasingly careless and ironical. Finally the American raised his voice and presented an ultimatum. "Our treaty of world-union," he said, "will remain unsigned unless you add a clause promising drastic reforms, which, as a mater of fact, my colleagues had already proposed as a condition of co-operation. I had decided to withhold them, in case they should wreck our treaty; but now I see they are essential. You must educate your people out of their lascivious and idle ways, and give them modern scientific religion. Teachers in your schools and universities must pledge themselves to the modern fundamentalized physics and behaviourism, and must enforce worship of the Divine Mover. The change will be difficult, but we will help you. You will need a strong order of Inquisitors, responsible to the Directorate. They will see also to the reform of your people's sexual frivolity in which you squander so much of the Divine Energy. Unless you agree to this, I cannot stop the war. The law of God must be kept, and those who know it must enforce it."

The woman interrupted him. "Tell me, what is this 'God' of yours? The Europeans worshipped love, not energy. What do you mean by energy? Is it merely to make engines go fast, and to agitate the ether?"

He answer flatly, as if repeating a lesson, "God is the all-pervading spirit of movement which seeks to actualize itself wherever it is latent. God has appointed the great American people to mechanize the universe." He paused, contemplating the clean lines of his sea-plane. Then he continued with emphasis, "But come! Time is precious. Either you work for God, or we trample you out of God's way."

The woman approached him, saying, "There is certainly something great in this enthusiasm. But somehow, though my heart says you are right, my head is doubting still. There must be a mistake somewhere."

"Mistake!" he laughed, overhanging her with his mask of power. "When a man's soul is action, how can he be mistaken that action is divine? I have served the great God, Energy, all my life, from garage boy to World President. Has not the whole American people proved its faith by its success?"

With rapture, but still in perplexity, she gazed at him. "There's something terribly wrong-headed about you Americans," she said, "but certainly you are great." She looked him in the eyes. Then suddenly she laid a hand on him, and said with conviction, "Being what you are, you are probably right. Anyhow you are a man, a real man. Take me. Be the father of my boy. Take me to the dangerous cities of America to work with you."

The President was surprised with sudden hunger for her body, and she saw it; but he turned to the Vice-President and said, "She has seen where the truth lies. And you? War, or co-operation in God's work?"

"The death of our bodies, or the death of our minds," said the Chinese, but with a bitterness that lacked conviction; for he was no fanatic. "Well, since the soul is only the harmoniousness of the body's behaviour, and since, in spite of this little dispute, we are agreed that the co-ordination of activity is the chief need of the planet today, and since in respect of our differences of temperament this lady has judged in favour of America, and moreover since, if there is any virtue in our Asiatic way of life, it will not succumb to a little propaganda, but rather will be strengthened by opposition—since all these matters are so, I accept your terms. But it would be undignified in China to let this great change be imposed upon her externally. You must give me time to form in Asia a native and spontaneous party of Energists, who will themselves propagate your gospel, and perhaps give it an elegance which, if I may say so, it has not yet. Even this we will do to secure the cosmopolitan control of Antarctica."

Thereupon the treaty was signed; but a new and secret codicil was drawn up and signed also, and both were witnessed by the Daughter of Man, in a clear, round, old-fashioned script.

Then, taking a hand of each, she said, "And so at last the world is united. For how long, I wonder. I seem to hear my old master's voice scolding, as though I had been rather stupid. But he failed me, and I have chosen a new master, Master of the World."

She released the hand of the Asiatic, and made as if to draw the American away with her. And he, though he was a strict monogamist with a better half waiting for him in New York, longed to crush her sun-clad body to his Puritan cloth. She drew him away among the palm trees.

The Vice-President of the World sat down once more, lit a cigarette, and meditated, smiling.

CHAPTER IV

AN AMERICANIZED PLANET

I. THE FOUNDATION OF THE FIRST WORLD STATE

WE have now reached that point in the history of the First Men when, some three hundred and eighty terrestrial years after the European War, the goal of world unity was at last achieved—not, however, before the mind of the race had been seriously crippled.

There is no need to recount in detail the transition from rival national

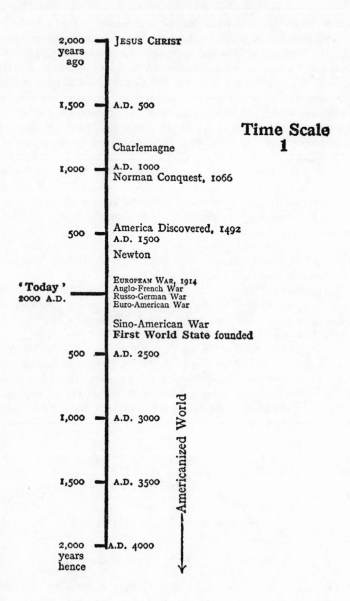

Time Scale 1

sovereignties to unitary control by the World Financial Directorate. Suffice it that by concerted action in America and China the military governments found themselves hamstrung by the passive resistance of cosmopolitan big business. In China this process was almost instantaneous and bloodless; in America there was serious disorder for a few weeks, while the bewildered government attempted to reduce its rebels by martial law. But the population was by now eager for peace; and, although a few business magnates were shot, and a crowd of workers here and there mown down, the opposition was irresistible. Very soon the governing clique collapsed.

The new order consisted of a vast system akin to guild socialism, yet at bottom individualistic. Each industry was in theory democratically governed by all its members, but in practice was controlled by its dominant individuals. Co-ordination of all industries was effected by a World Industrial Council, whereon the leaders of each industry discussed the affairs of the planet as a whole. The status of each industry on the Council was determined partly by its economic power in the world, partly by public esteem. For already the activities of men were beginning to be regarded as either "noble" or "ignoble"; and the noble were not necessarily the most powerful economically. Thus upon the Council appeared an inner ring of noble "industries," which were, in approximate order of prestige, Finance, Flying, Engineering, Surface Locomotion, Chemical Industry, and Professional Athletics. But the real seat of power was not the Council, not even the inner ring of the Council, but the Financial Directorate. This consisted of a dozen millionaires, with the American President and the Chinese Vice-President at their head.

Within this august committee internal dissensions were inevitable. Shortly after the system had been inaugurated the Vice-President sought to overthrow the President by publishing his connection with the coloured woman who now styled herself the Daughter of Man. This piece of scandal was expected to enrage the virtuous American public against their hero. But by a stroke of genius the President saved both himself and the unity of the world. Far from denying the charge, he gloried in it. In that moment of sexual triumph, he said, a great truth had been revealed to him. Without this daring sacrifice of his private purity, he would never have been really fit to be President of the World; he would have remained simply an American. In this lady's veins flowed the blood of all races, and in her mind all cultures mingled. His union with her, confirmed by many subsequent visits, had taught him to enter into the spirit of the East, and had given him a broad human sympathy such as his high office demanded. As a private individual, he insisted, he remained a monogamist with a wife in New York; and, as a private individual, he had sinned, and must suffer for ever the pangs of conscience. But as President of the World, it was incumbent upon him to espouse the World. And since nothing could be said to be real without a physical basis, this spiritual union had to be embodied and symbolized by his physical union with the Daughter of Man. In tones of grave emotion he described through the microphone how, in the presence of that mystical woman, he had suddenly triumphed over his private moral scruples; and how, in a sudden access of the divine energy, he had consummated his marriage with the World in the shade of a banana tree.

The lovely form of the Daughter of Man (decently clad) was transmitted by television to every receiver in the world. Her face, blended of Asia and the West, became a most potent symbol of human unity. Every man on the planet became in imagination her lover. Every woman identified herself with this supreme woman.

Undoubtedly there was some truth in the plea that the Daughter of Man had enlarged the President's mind, for his policy had been unexpectedly tactful toward the East. Often he had moderated the American demand for the immediate Americanization of China. Often he had persuaded the Chinese to welcome some policy which at first they had regarded with suspicion.

The President's explanation of his conduct enhanced his prestige both in America and Asia. America was hypnotized by the romantic religiosity of the story. Very soon it became fashionable to be a strict monogamist with one domestic wife, and one "symbolical" wife in the East, or in another town, or a neighbouring street, or with several such in various localities. In China the cold tolerance with which the President was at first treated was warmed by this incident into something like affection. And it was partly through his tact, or the influence of his symbolical wife, that the speeding up of China's Americanization was effected without disorder.

For some months after the foundation of the World State, China had been wholly occupied in coping with the plague of insanity, called "the American madness," with which her former enemy had poisoned her. The coast region of North China had been completely disorganized. Industry, agriculture, transport, were at a standstill. Huge mobs, demented and starving, staggered about the country devouring every kind of vegetable matter and wrangling over the flesh of their own dead. It was long before the disease was brought under control; and indeed for years afterwards an occasional outbreak would occur, and cause panic throughout the land.

To some of the more old-fashioned Chinese it appeared as though the whole population had been mildly affected by the germ; for throughout China a new sect, apparently a spontaneous native growth, calling themselves Energists, began to preach a new interpretation of Buddhism in terms of the sanctity of action. And, strange to say, this gospel throve to such an extent that in a few years the whole educational system was captured by its adherents, though not without a struggle with the reactionary members of the older universities. Curiously enough, however, in spite of this general acceptance of the New Way, in spite of the fact that the young of China were now taught to admire movement in all forms, in spite of a much increased wage-scale, which put all workers in possession of mechanical locomotion, the masses of China continued at heart to regard action as a mere means toward rest. And when at last a native physicist pointed out that the supreme expression of energy was the tense balance of forces within the atom, the Chinese applied the doctrine to themselves, and claimed that in them quiescence was the perfect balance of mighty forces. Thus did the East contribute to the religion of this age. The worship of activity was made to include the worship of inactivity. And both were founded on the principles of natural science.

2. THE DOMINANCE OF SCIENCE

Science now held a position of unique honour among the First Men. This was not so much because it was in this field that the race long ago during its high noon had thought most rigorously, nor because it was through science that men had gained some insight into the nature of the physical world, but rather because the application of scientific principles had revolutionized their material circumstances. The once fluid doctrines of science had by now begun to crystallize into a fixed and intricate dogma; but inventive scientific intelligence still exercised itself brilliantly in improving the technique of industry, and thus completely dominated the imagination of a race in which the pure intellectual curiosity had waned. The scientist was regarded as an embodiment, not merely of knowledge, but of power; and no legends of the potency of science seemed too fantastic to be believed.

A century after the founding of the first World State a rumour began to be heard in China about the supreme secret of scientific religion, the awful mystery of Gordelpus, by means of which it should be possible to utilize the energy locked up in the opposition of proton and electron. Long ago discovered by a Chinese physicist and saint, this invaluable knowledge was now reputed to have been preserved ever since among the *élite* of science, and to be ready for publication as soon as the world seemed fit to possess it. The new sect of Energists claimed that the young Discoverer was himself an incarnation of Buddha, and that, since the world was still unfit for the supreme revelation, he had entrusted his secret to the Scientists. On the side of Christianity a very similar legend was concerned with the same individual. The Regenerate Christian Brotherhood, by now overwhelmingly the most powerful of the Western Churches, regarded the Discoverer as the Son of God, who, in this his Second Coming, had proposed to bring about the millennium by publishing the secret of divine power; but, finding the peoples still unable to put in practice even the more primitive gospel of love which was announced at his First Coming, he had suffered martyrdom for man's sake, and entrusted his secret to the scientists.

The scientific workers of the world had long ago organized themselves as a close corporation. Entrance to the International College of Science was to be obtained only by examination and the payment of high fees. Membership conferred the title of "Scientist," and the right to perform experiments. It was also an essential qualification for many lucrative posts. Moreover, there were said to be certain technical secrets which members were pledged not to reveal. Rumour had it that in at least one case of minor blabbing the traitor had shortly afterwards mysteriously died.

Science itself, the actual corpus of natural knowledge, had by now become so complex that only a tiny fraction of it could be mastered by one brain. Thus students of one branch of science knew practically nothing of the work of others in kindred branches. Especially was this the case with the huge science called Subatomic Physics. Within this were contained a dozen studies, any one of which was as complex as the whole of the physics of the Nineteenth Christian Century. This growing complexity had rendered students in one field ever more reluctant to criticize, or even to try to understand, the principles of other fields. Each petty department, jealous of its own preserves, was meticulously respectful of the preserves of others. In an earlier period the sciences had been co-ordinated and criticized philosophically by their own leaders and by the technical philosophers. But, philosophy, as a rigorous technical discipline, no longer existed. There was, of course, a vague framework of ideas, or assumptions, based on science, and common to all men, a popular pseudo-science, constructed by the journalists from striking phrases current among scientists. But actual scientific workers prided themselves on the rejection of this ramshackle structure, even while they themselves were unwittingly assuming it. And each insisted that his own special subject must inevitably remain unintelligible even to most of his brother scientists.

Under these circumstances, when rumour declared that the mystery of Gordelpus was known to the physicists, each department of subatomic physics was both reluctant to deny the charge explicitly in its own case, and ready to believe that some other department really did possess the secret. Consequently the conduct of the scientists as a body strengthened the general belief that they knew and would not tell.

About two centuries after the formation of the first World State, the President of the World declared that the time was ripe for a formal union of science and religion, and called a conference of the leaders of these two great disciplines. Upon that island in the Pacific which had become the Mecca of cosmopolitan sentiment, and was by now one vast many-storied, and cloud-capped Temple of Peace, the heads of Buddhism, Mohammedanism, Hinduism, the Regenerate Christian Brotherhood and the Modern Catholic Church in South America, agreed that their differences were but differences of expression. One and all were worshippers of the Divine Energy, whether expressed in activity, or in tense stillness. One and all recognized the saintly Discoverer as either the last and greatest of the prophets or an actual incarnation of divine Movement. And these two concepts were easily shown, in the light of modern science, to be identical.

In an earlier age it had been the custom to single out heresy and extirpate it with fire and sword. But now the craving for uniformity was fulfilled by explaining away differences, amid universal applause.

When the Conference had registered the unity of the religions, it went on to establish the unity of religion and science. All knew, said the President, that some of the scientists were is possession of the supreme secret, though, wisely, they would not definitely admit it. It was time, then, that the organizations of Science and Religion should be merged, for the better guidance of men. He, therefore, called upon the International College of Science to nominate from amongst themselves a select body, which should be sanctified by the Church, and called the Sacred Order of Scientists. These custodians of the supreme secret were to be kept at public expense. They were to devote themselves wholly to the service of science, and in particular to research into the most scientific manner of worshipping the Divine Gordelpus.

Of the scientists present, some few looked distinctly uncomfortable, but the majority scarcely concealed their delight under dignified and thoughtful hesitation. Amongst the priests also two expressions were visible; but on the whole it was felt that the Church must gain by thus gathering into herself the unique prestige of science. And so it was that the Order was founded which was destined to become the dominant force in human affairs until the downfall of the first world civilization.

3. MATERIAL ACHIEVEMENT

Save for occasional minor local conflicts, easily quelled by the World Police, the race was now a single social unit for some four thousand years. During the first of these millennia material progress at least was rapid, but subsequently there was little change until the final disintegration. The whole energy of man was concentrated on maintaining at a constant pitch the furious routine of his civilization, until, after another three thousand years of lavish expenditure, certain essential sources of power were suddenly exhausted. Nowhere was there the mental agility to cope with this novel crisis. The whole social order collapsed.

We may pass over the earlier stages of this fantastic civilization, and examine it as it stood just before the fatal change began to be felt.

The material circumstances of the race at this time would have amazed all its predecessors, even those who were in the true sense far more civilized beings. But to us, the Last Men, there is an extreme pathos and even comicality, not only in this most thorough confusion of material development with civilization, but also in the actual paucity of the vaunted material development itself, compared with that of our own society. All the continents, indeed, were by now minutely artificialized. Save for the many wild reserves which were cherished as museums and playgrounds, not a square mile of territory was left in a natural state. Nor was there any longer a distinction between agricultural and industrial areas. All the continents were urbanized, not of course in the manner of the congested industrial cities of an earlier age, but none the less urbanized. Industry and agriculture interpenetrated everywhere. This was possible partly through the great development of aerial communication, partly through a no less remarkable improvement of architecture. Great advances in artificial materials had enabled the erection of buildings in the form of slender pylons which, rising often to a height of three miles, or even more, and founded a quarter of a mile beneath the ground, might yet occupy a ground plan of less than half a mile across. In section these structures were often cruciform; and on each floor, the centre of the long-armed cross consisted of an aerial landing, providing direct access from the air for the dwarf private aeroplanes which were by now essential to the life of every adult. These gigantic pillars of architecture, prophetic of the still mightier structures of an age to come, were scattered over every continent in varying density. Very rarely were they permitted to approach one another by a distance less than their height; on the other hand, save in the arctic, they were very seldom separated by more than twenty miles. The general appearance of every country was thus rather like an open forest of lopped tree-trunks, gigantic in stature. Clouds often encircled the middle heights of these artificial peaks, or blotted out all but the lower stories. Dwellers in the summits were familiar with the spectacle of a dazzling ocean of cloud, dotted on all sides with steep islands of architecture. Such was the altitude of the upper floors that it was sometimes necessary to maintain in them, not merely artificial heating, but artificial air pressure and oxygen supply.

Between these columns of habitation and industry, the land was everywhere green or brown with the seasonal variations of agriculture, park, and wild reserve. Broad grey thoroughfares for heavy freight traffic netted every continent; but lighter transport and the passenger services were wholly aerial. Over all the more populous districts the air was ever aswarm with planes up to a height of five miles, where the giant air-liners plied between the continents.

The enterprise of an already distant past had brought every land under civilization. The Sahara was a lake district, crowded with sun-proud holiday resorts. The arctic islands of Canada, ingeniously warmed by directed tropical currents, were the homes of vigorous northerners. The coasts of Antarctica, thawed in the same manner, were permanently inhabited by those engaged in exploiting the mineral wealth of the hinterland.

Much of the power needed to keep this civilization in being was drawn from the buried remains of prehistoric vegetation, in the form of coal. Although after the foundation of the World State the fuel of Antarctica had been very carefully husbanded, the new supply of oil had given out in less than three centuries, and men were forced to drive their aeroplanes by electricity generated from coal. It soon became evident, however, that even the unexpectedly rich coal-fields of Antarctica would not last for ever. The cessation of oil had taught men a much needed lesson, had made them feel the reality of the power problem. At the same time the cosmopolitan spirit, which was learning to regard the whole race as compatriots, was also beginning to take a broader view temporally, and to see things with the eyes of remote generations. During the first and sanest thousand years of the World State, there was a widespread determination not to incur the blame of the future by wasting power. Thus not only was there serious economy (the first large-scale cosmopolitan enterprise), but also efforts were made to utilize more permanent sources of power. Wind was used extensively. On every building swarms of windmills generated electricity, and every mountain range was similarly decorated, while every considerable fall of water forced its way through turbines. More important still was the utilization of power derived from volcanos and from borings into the subterranean heat. This, it had been hoped, would solve the whole problem of power, once and for all. But even in the earlier and more intelligent period of the World State inventive genius was not what it had been, and no really satisfactory method was found. Consequently at no stage of this civilization did volcanic sources do more than supplement the amazingly rich coal seams of Antarctica. In this region coal was preserved at far greater depths than elsewhere, because, by some accident, the earth's central heat was not here fierce enough (as it was elsewhere) to turn the deeper beds into graphite. Another possible source of power was known to exist in the ocean tides; but the use of this was forbidden by the S.O.S. because, since tidal motion was so obviously astronomical in origin, it had come to be regarded as sacred.

Perhaps the greatest physical achievement of the First World State in its earlier and more vital phase had been in preventive medicine. Though the biological sciences had long ago become stereotyped in respect of fundamental theories, they continued to produce many practical benefits. No longer did men and women have to dread for themselves or those dear to them such afflictions as cancer, tuberculosis, angina pectoris, the rheumatic diseases, and the terrible disorders of the nervous system. No longer were there sudden microbic devastations. No longer was childbirth an ordeal, and womanhood itself a source of suffering. There were no more chronic invalids, no more life-long cripples. Only senility remained; and even this could be repeatedly alleviated by physiological rejuvenation. The removal of all these ancient sources of weakness and misery, which formerly had

lamed the race and haunted so many individuals either with definite terrors or vague and scarcely conscious despond, brought about now a pervading buoyancy and optimism impossible to earlier peoples.

4. THE CULTURE OF THE FIRST WORLD STATE

Such was the physical achievement of this civilization. Nothing half
so artificial and intricate and prosperous had ever before existed. An
earlier age, indeed, had held before itself some such ideal as this; but its
nationalistic mania prevented it from attaining the necessary economic
unity. This latter-day civilization, however, had wholly outgrown nationalism, and had spent many centuries of peace in consolidating itself. But to
what end? The terrors of destitution and ill-health having been abolished,
man's spirit was freed from a crippling burden, and might have dared
great adventures. But unfortunately his intelligence had by now seriously
declined. And so this age, far more than the notorious "nineteenth century," was the great age of barren complacency.

Every individual was a well-fed and physically healthy human animal.
He was also economically independent. His working day was never more
than six hours, often only four. He enjoyed a fair share of the products of
industry; and in his long holidays he was free to wander in his own aeroplane all over the planet. With good luck he might find himself rich, even
for those days, at forty; and if fortune had not favoured him, he might yet
expect affluence before he was eighty, when he could still look forward to
a century of active life.

But in spite of this material prosperity he was a slave. His work and
his leisure consisted of feverish activity, punctuated by moments of listless
idleness which he regarded as both sinful and unpleasant. Unless he was
one of the furiously successful minority, he was apt to be haunted by moments of brooding, too formless to be called meditation, and of yearning,
too blind to be called desire. For he and all his contemporaries were ruled
by certain ideas which prevented them from living a fully human life.

Of these ideas one was the ideal of progress. For the individual, the
goal imposed by his religious teaching was continuous advancement in
aeronautical prowess, legal sexual freedom, and millionaireship. For the
race also the ideal was progress, and progress of the same unintelligent type.
Ever more brilliant and extensive aviation, ever more extensive legal sexual
intercourse, ever more gigantic manufacture, and consumption, were to be
co-ordinated in an ever more intricately organized social system. For the
last three thousand years, indeed, progress even of this rude kind had
been minute; but this was a source of pride rather than of regret. It implied that the goal was already almost attained, the perfection which should
justify the release of the secret of divine power, and the inauguration of
an era of incomparably mightier activity.

For the all-pervading idea which tyrannized over the race was the fanatical worship of movement. Gordelpus, the Prime Mover, demanded of his human embodiments swift and intricate activity, and the individual's prospect of eternal life depended on the fulfilment of this obligation. Curiously, though science had long ago destroyed the belief in personal immortality as an intrinsic attribute of man, a complementary belief had grown up to the effect that those who justified themselves in action were preserved eternally, by special miracle, in the swift spirit of Gordelpus. Thus from childhood to death the individual's conduct was determined by the obligation to produce as much motion as possible, whether by his own muscular activity or by the control of natural forces. In the hierarchy of industry three occupations were honoured almost as much as the Sacred Order of Scientists, namely, flying, dancing, and athletics. Every one practised all three of these crafts to some extent, for they were imposed by religion; but the professional fliers and aeronautical engineers, and the professional dancers and athletes, were a privileged class.

Several causes had raised flying to a position of unique honour. As a means of communication it was of extreme practical importance; and as the swiftest locomotion it constituted the supreme act of worship. The accident that the form of the aeroplane was reminiscent of the main symbol of the ancient Christian religion lent flying an additional mystical significance. For though the spirit of Christianity was lost, many of its symbols had been preserved in the new faith. A more important source of the dominance of flying was that, since warfare had long ceased to exist, aviation of a gratuitously dangerous kind was the main outlet for the innate adventurousness of the human animal. Young men and women risked their lives fervently for the glory of Gordelpus and their own salvation, while their seniors took vicarious satisfaction in this endless festival of youthful prowess. Indeed apart from the thrills of devotional aerial acrobats, it is unlikely that the race would so long have preserved its peace and its unity. On each of the frequent Days of Sacred Flight special rituals of communal and solo aviation were performed at every religious centre. On these occasions the whole sky would be intricately patterned with thousands of planes, wheeling, tumbling, soaring, plunging, in perfect order and at various altitudes, the dance at one level being subtly complementary to the dance at others. It was as though the spontaneous evolutions of many distinct flocks of redshank and dunlin were multiplied a thousand-fold in complexity, and subordinated to a single ever-developing terpsichorean theme. Then suddenly the whole would burst asunder to the horizon, leaving the sky open for the quartets, duets and solos of the most brilliant stars of flight. At night also, regiments of planes bearing coloured lights would inscribe on the zenith ever-changing and symbolical patterns of fire. Besides these aerial dances, there had existed for eight hundred years a custom of spelling out periodically in a dense flight of planes six thousand miles long the sacred rubrics of the gospel of Gordelpus, so that the living word might be visible to other plants.

In the life of every individual, flying played a great part. Immediately after birth he was taken up by a priestess of flight and dropped, clinging to a parachute, to be deftly caught upon the wings of his father's plane. This ritual served as a substitute for contraception (forbidden as an interference with the divine energy); for since in many infants the old simian grasping-instinct was atrophied, a large proportion of the new-born let go and were smashed upon the paternal wings. At adolescence the individual (male or female) took charge of a plane for the first time, and his life was subsequently punctuated by severe aeronautical tests. From middle age onwards, namely as a centenarian, when he could no longer hope to rise in the hierarchy of active flight, he continued to fly daily for practical purposes.

The two other forms of ritual activity, dancing and athletics, were scarcely less important. Nor were they confined wholly to the ground. For certain rites were celebrated by dances upon the wings of a plane in mid air.

Dancing was especially associated with the Negro race, which occupied a very peculiar position in the world at this time. As a matter of fact the great colour distinctions of mankind were now beginning to fade. Increased aerial communication had caused the black, brown, yellow and white stocks so to mingle that everywhere there was by now a large majority of the racially indistinguishable. Nowhere was there any great number of persons of marked racial character. But each of the ancient types was liable to crop up now and again in isolated individuals, especially in its ancient homeland. These "throw-backs" were customarily treated in special and historically appropriate manners. Thus, for instance, it was to "sports" of definite Negro character that the most sacred dancing was entrusted.

In the days of the nations, the descendants of emancipated African slaves in North America had greatly influenced the artistic and religious life of the white population, and had inspired a cult of negroid dancing which survived till the end of the First Men. This was partly due to the sexual and primitive character of Negro dancing, sorely needed in a nation ridden by sexual taboos. But it had also a deeper source. The American nation had acquired its slaves by capture, and had long continued to spurn their descendants. Later it unconsciously compensated for its guilt by a cult of the Negro spirit. Thus when American culture dominated the planet, the pure Negroes became a sacred caste. Forbidden many of the rights of citizenship, they were regarded as the private servants of Gordelpus. They were both sacred and outcast. This dual role was epitomized in an extravagant ritual which took place once a year in each of the great national parks. A white woman and a Negro, both chosen for their prowess in dance, performed a long and symbolical ballet, which culminated in a ritual act of sexual violation, performed in full view of the maddened spectators. This over, the Negro knifed his victim, and fled through the forest pursued by an exultant mob. If he reached sanctuary, he became a peculiarly sacred object for the rest of his life. But if he was caught, he was torn to pieces or drenched with inflammable spirit and burned. Such was the superstition of the First Men at this time that the participants in this ceremony were seldom reluctant; for it was firmly believed that both were assured of eternal life in Gordelpus. In America this Sacred Lynching was the most popular of all festivals; for it was both sexual and bloody, and afforded a fierce joy to the masses whose sex-life was restricted and secret. In India and Africa the violator was always an "Englishman," when such a rare creature could be found. In China the whole character of the ceremony was altered; for the violation became a kiss, and the murder a touch with a fan.

One other race, the Jews, were treated with a similar combination of honour and contempt, but for very different reasons. In ancient days their general intelligence, and in particular their financial talent, had co-operated with their homelessness to make them outcasts; and now, in the decline of the First Men, they retained the fiction, if not strictly the fact, of racial integrity. They were still outcasts, though indispensable and powerful. Almost the only kind of intelligent activity which the First Men could still respect was financial operation, whether private or cosmopolitan. The Jews had made themselves invaluable in the financial organization of the world state, having far outstripped the other races because they alone had preserved a furtive respect for pure intelligence. And so, long after intelligence had come to be regarded as disreputable in ordinary men and women, it was expected of the Jews. In them it was called satanic cunning, and they were held to be embodiments of the powers of evil, harnessed in the service of Gordelpus. Thus in time the Jews had made something like "a corner" in intelligence. This precious commodity they used largely for their own purposes; for two thousand years of persecution had long ago rendered them permanently tribalistic, subconsciously if not consciously. Thus when they had gained control of the few remaining operations which demanded originality rather than routine, they used this advantage chiefly to strengthen their own position in the world. For, though relatively bright, they had suffered much of the general coarsening and limitation which had beset the whole world. Though capable to some extent of criticizing the practical means by which ends should be realized, they were by now wholly incapable of criticizing the major ends which had dominated their race for thousands of years. In them intelligence had become utterly subservient to tribalism. There was thus some excuse for the universal hate and even physical repulsion with which they were regarded; for they alone had failed to make the one great advance, from tribalism to a cosmopolitanism which in other races was no longer merely theoretical. There was good reason also for the respect which they received, since they retained and used somewhat ruthlessly a certain degree of the most distinctively human attribute, intelligence.

In primitive times the intelligence and sanity of the race had been preserved by the inability of its unwholesome members to survive. When humanitarianism came into vogue, and the unsound were tended at public expense, this natural selection ceased. And since these unfortunates were incapable alike of prudence and of social responsibility, they procreated without restraint, and threatened to infect the whole species with their rottenness. During the zenith of Western Civilization, therefore, the subnormal were sterilized. But the latter-day worshippers of Gordelpus regarded both sterilization and contraception as a wicked interference with the divine potency. Consequently the only restriction on population was the suspension of the new-born from aeroplanes, a process which, though it eliminated weaklings, favoured among healthy infants rather the primitive than the highly developed. Thus the intelligence of the race steadily declined. And no one regretted it.

The general revulsion from intelligence was a corollary of the adoration of instinct, and this in turn was an aspect of the worship of activity. Since the unconscious source of human vigour was the divine energy, spontaneous impulse must so far as possible never be thwarted. Reasoning was indeed permitted to the individual within the sphere of his official work, but never beyond. And not even specialists might indulge in reasoning and experiment without obtaining a licence for the particular research. The licence was expensive, and was only granted if the goal in view could be shown to be an increase of world activity. In old times certain persons of morbid curiosity had dared to criticize the time-honoured methods of doing things, and had suggested "better" methods not convenient to the Sacred Order of Scientists. This had to be stopped. By the fourth millennium of the World State the operations of civilization had become so intricately stereotyped that novel situations of a major order never occurred.

One kind of intellectual pursuit in addition to finance was, indeed, honoured, namely mathematical calculation. All ritual movements, all the motions of industrial machinery, all observable natural phenomena, had to be minutely described in mathematical formulæ. The records were filed in the sacred archives of the S.O.S. And there they remained. The vast enterprise of mathematical description was the main work of the scientists, and was said to be the only means by which the evanescent thing, movement, could be passed into the eternal being of Gordelpus.

The cult of instinct did not result simply in a life of ungoverned impulse. Far from it. For the fundamental instinct, it was said, was the instinct to worship Gordelpus in action, and this should rule all the other instincts. Of these, the most important and sacred was the sexual impulse, which the First Men had ever tended to regard as both divine and obscene. Sex, therefore, was now very strictly controlled. Reference to sexuality, save by circumlocution, was forbidden by law. Persons who remarked on the obvious sexual significance of the religious dances, were severely punished. No sexual activity and no sex knowledge were permitted to the individual until he had won his (or her) wings. Much information, of a distorted and perverted nature could, indeed, be gained meanwhile by observation of the religious writings and practices; but officially these sacred matters were all given a metaphysical, not a sexual interpretation. And though legal maturity, the Wing-Winning, might occur as early as the age of fifteen, sometimes it was not attained till forty. If at that age the individual still failed in the test, he or she was forbidden sexual intercourse and information for ever.

In China and India this extravagant sexual taboo was somewhat mitigated. Many easy-going persons had come to feel that the imparting of sex knowledge to the "immature" was only wrong when the medium of communication was the sacred American language. They therefore made use of the local patois. Similarly, sexual activity of the "immature" was permissible so long as it was performed solely in the wild reserves, and without American speech. These subterfuges, however, were condemned by the orthodox, even in Asia.

When a man had won his wings, he was formally initiated into the mystery of sex and all its "biologico-religious" significance. He was also allowed to take a "domestic wife," and after a much more severe aviation test, any number of "symbolical" wives. Similarly with the woman. These two kinds of partnership differed greatly. The "domestic" husband and wife appeared in public together, and their union was indissoluble. The "symbolic" union, on the other hand, could be dissolved by either party. Also it was too sacred ever to be revealed, or even mentioned, in public.

A very large number of persons never passed the test which sanctioned sexuality. These either remained virgin, or indulged in sexual relations which were not only illegal but sacrilegious. The successful, on the other hand, were apt to consummate sexually every casual acquaintance.

Under these circumstances it was natural that there should exist among the sexually submerged part of the population certain secret cults which sought escape from harsh reality into worlds of fantasy. Of these illicit sects, two were most widespread. One was a perversion of the ancient Christian faith in a God of Love. All love, it was said, is sexual; therefore in worship, private or public, the individual must seek a direct sexual relation with God. Hence arose a grossly phallic cult, very contemptible to those more fortunate persons who had no need of it.

The other great heresy was derived partly from the energy of repressed intellective impulses, and was practised by persons of natural curiosity who, nevertheless, shared the universal paucity of intelligence. These pathetic devotees of intellect were inspired by Socrates. That great primitive had insisted that clear thought is impossible without clear definition of terms, and that without clear thinking man misses fullness of being. These his last disciples were scarcely less fervent admirers of truth than their master, yet they missed his spirit completely. Only by knowing the truth, they said, can the individual attain immortality; only by defining can he know the truth. Therefore, meeting together in secret, and in constant danger of arrest for illicit intellection, they disputed endlessly about the definition of things. But the things which they were concerned to define were not the basic concepts of human thought; for these, they affirmed, had been settled once for all by Socrates and his immediate followers. Therefore, accepting these as true, and grossly misunderstanding them, the ultimate Socratics undertook to define all the processes of the world state and the ritual of the established religion, all the emotions of men and women, all the shapes of noses, mouths, buildings, mountains, clouds, and in fact the whole superficies of their world. Thus they believe that they emancipated themselves from the philistinism of their age, and secured comradeship with Socrates in the hereafter.

5. DOWNFALL

The collapse of this first world-civilization was due to the sudden failure of the supplies of coal. All the original fields had been sapped centuries earlier, and it should have been obvious that those more recently discovered could not last for ever. For some thousands of years the main supply had come from Antarctica. So prolific was this continent that latterly a superstition had arisen in the clouded minds of the world-citizens that it was in some mysterious manner inexhaustible. Thus when at last, in spite of strict censorship, the news began to leak out that even the deepest possible borings had failed to reveal further vegetable deposits of any kind, the world was at first incredulous.

The sane policy would have been to abolish the huge expense of power on ritual flying, which used more of the community's resources than the whole of productive industry. But to believers in Gordelpus such a course was almost unthinkable. Moreover it would have undermined the flying aristocracy. This powerful class now declared that the time had come for the release of the secret of divine power, and called on the S.O.S. to inaugurate the new era. Vociferous agitation in all lands put the scientists in an awkward plight. They gained time by declaring that, though the moment of revelation was approaching, it had not yet arrived; for they had received a divine intimation that this failure of coal was imposed as a supreme test of man's faith. The service of Gordelpus in ritual flight must be rather increased than reduced. Spending a bare mimimum of its power on secular matters, the race must concentrate upon religion. When Gordelpus had evidence of their devotion and trust, he would permit the scientists to save them.

Such was the prestige of science that at first this explanation was universally accepted. The ritual flights were maintained. All luxury trades were abolished, and even vital services were reduced to a minimum. Workers thus thrown out of employment were turned over to agricultural labour; for it was felt that the use of mechanical power in mere tillage must be as soon as possible abolished. These changes demanded far more organizing ability than was left in the race. Confusion was widespread, save here and there where serious organization was attempted by certain Jews.

The first result of this great movement of economy and self-denial was to cause something of a spiritual awakening among many who had formerly lived a life of bored ease. This was augmented by the widespread sense of crisis and impending marvels. Religion, which, in spite of its universal authority in this age, had become a matter of ritual rather than of inward experience, began to stir in many hearts,—not indeed as a movement of true worship, but rather as a vague awe, not unmixed with self-importance.

But as the novelty of this enthusiasm dwindled, and life became increasingly uncomfortable, even the most zealous began to notice with horror that in moments of inactivity they were prone to doubts too shocking to confess. And as the situation worsened, even a life of ceaseless action could not suppress these wicked fantasies.

For the race was now entering upon an unprecedented psychological crisis, brought about by the impact of the economic disaster upon a permanently unwholesome mentality. Each individual, it must be remembered, had once been a questioning child, but had been taught to shun curiosity as the breath of Satan. Consequently the whole race was suffering from a kind of inverted repression, a repression of the intellective impulses. The sudden economic change, which affected all classes throughout the planet, thrust into the focus of attention a shocking curiosity, an obsessive scepticism, which had hitherto been buried in the deepest recesses of the mind.

It is not easy to conceive the strange mental disorder that now afflicted the whole race, symbolizing itself in some cases by fits of actual physical vertigo. After centuries of prosperity, of routine, of orthodoxy, men were suddenly possessed by a doubt which they regarded as diabolical. No one said a word of it; but in each man's own mind the fiend raised a whispering head, and each was haunted by the troubled eyes of his fellows. Indeed the whole changed circumstances of his life jibed at his credulity.

Earlier in the career of the race, this world crisis might have served to wake men into sanity. Under the first pressure of distress they might have abandoned the extravagances of their culture. But by now the ancient way of life was too deeply rooted. Consequently, we observe the fantastic spectacle of a world engaged, devotedly and even heroically, on squandering its resources in vast aeronautical displays, not through single-minded faith in their rightness and efficacy, but solely in a kind of desperate automatism. Like those little rodents whose migration became barred by an encroachment of the sea, so that annually they drowned themselves in thousands, the First Men helplessly continued in their ritualistic behaviour; but unlike the lemmings, they were human enough to be at the same time oppressed by unbelief, an unbelief which, moreover, they dared not recognize.

Meanwhile the scientists were earnestly and secretly delving in the ancient literature of their science, in hope of discovering the forgotten talisman. They undertook also clandestine experiments, but upon a false trail laid by the wily English contemporary of the Discoverer. The main results were, that several researchers were poisoned or electrocuted, and a great college was blown up. This event impressed the populace, who supposed the accident to be due to an overdaring exercise of the divine potency. The misunderstanding inspired the desperate scientists to rig further impressive "miracles," and moreover to use them to dispel the increasing restlessness of hungry industrial workers. Thus when a deputation arrived outside the offices of Cosmopolitan Agriculture to demand more flour for industrialists, Gordelpus miraculously blew up the ground on which they stood, and flung their bodies among the onlookers. When the agriculturists of China struck to obtain a reasonable allowance of electric power for their tillage, Gordelpus affected them with an evil atmosphere, so that they choked and died in thousands. Stimulated in this manner by direct divine intervention, the doubting and disloyal elements of the world population recovered their faith and their docility. And so the world jogged on for a while, as nearly as possible as it had done for the last four thousand years, save for a general increase of hunger and ill-health.

But inevitably, as the conditions of life became more and more severe, docility gave place to desperation. Daring spirits began publicly to question the wisdom, and even the piety, of so vast an expenditure of power upon ritual flight, when prime necessities such as food and clothing were becoming so scarce. Did not this helpless devotion merely ridicule them in the divine eyes? God helps him who helps himself. Already the death rate had risen alarmingly. Emaciated and ragged persons were beginning to beg in public places. In certain districts whole populations were starving, and the Directorate did nothing for them. Yet, elsewhere, harvests were being wasted for lack of power to reap them. In all lands an angry clamour arose for the inauguration of the new era.

The scientists were by now panic-stricken. Nothing had come of their researches, and it was evident that in future all wind- and water-power must be devoted to the primary industries. Even so, there was starvation ahead for many. The President of the Physical Society suggested to the Directorate that ritual flying should at once be reduced by half, as a compromise with Gordelpus. Immediately the hideous truth, which few hith-erto had dared to admit even to themselves, was blurted out upon the ether by a prominent Jew: the whole hoary legend of the divine secret was a lie, else why were the physicists temporizing? Dismay and rage spread over the planet. Everywhere the people rose against the scientists, and against the governing authority which they controlled. Massacres and meas-ures of retaliation soon developed into civil wars. China and India de-clared themselves free national states, but could not achieve internal unity. In America, ever a stronghold of science and religion, the Government maintained its authority for a while; but as its seat became less secure, its methods became more ruthless. Finally it made the mistake of using not merely poison gas, but microbes; and such was the decayed state of medical science that no one could invent a means of restraining their ravages. The whole American continent succumbed to a plague of pulmonary and nerv-ous diseases. The ancient "American Madness," which long ago had been used against China, now devastated America. The great stations of water-power and wind-power were wrecked by lunatic mobs who sought ven-geance upon anything associated with authority. Whole populations vanished in an orgy of cannibalism.

In Asia and Africa, some semblance of order was maintained for a while. Presently, however, the American Madness spread to these conti-nents also, and very soon all living traces of their civilization vanished.

Only in the most natural fertile areas of the world could the diseased remnant of a population now scrape a living from the soil. Elsewhere, utter desolation. With easy strides the jungle came back into its own.

CHAPTER V

THE FALL OF THE FIRST MEN

I. THE FIRST DARK AGE

WE have reached a period in man's history rather less than five thousand years after the life of Newton. In this chapter we must cover about one hundred and fifteen thousand years, and in the next chapter another ten million years. That will bring us to a point as remotely future from the First World State as the earliest anthropoids were remotely past. During the first tenth of the first million years after the fall of the World State, during a hundred thousand years, man remained in complete eclipse. Not till the close of this span, which we will call the First Dark Age, did he struggle once more from savagery through barbarism into civilization. And then his renaissance was relatively brief. From its earliest beginnings to its end, it covered only fifteen thousand years; and in its final agony the planet was so seriously damaged that mind lay henceforth in deep slumber for ten more millions of years. This was the Second Dark Age. Such is the field which we must observe in this and the following chapter.

It might have been expected that, after the downfall of the First World State, recovery would have occurred within a few generations. Historians have, indeed, often puzzled over the cause of this surprisingly complete and lasting degradation. Innate human nature was roughly the same immediately after as immediately before the crisis; yet minds that had easily maintained a world-civilization in being, proved quite incapable of building a new order on the ruins of the old. Far from recovering, man's estate rapidly deteriorated till it had sunk into abject savagery.

Many causes contributed to this result, some relatively superficial and temporary, some profound and lasting. It is as though Fate, directing events toward an allotted end, had availed herself of many diverse instruments, none of which would have sufficed alone, though all worked together irresistibly in the same sense. The immediate cause of the helplessness of the race during the actual crisis of the World State was of course the vast epidemic of insanity and still more widespread deterioration of intelligence, which resulted from the use of microbes. This momentary seizure made it impossible for man to check his downfall during its earliest and least unmanageable stage. Later, when the epidemic was spent, even though civilization was already in ruins, a concerted effort of devotion might yet have rebuilt it on a more modest plan. But among the First Men only a minority had ever been capable of wholehearted devotion. The great majority were by nature too much obsessed by private impulses. And in this black period, such was the depth of disillusion and fatigue, that even normal resolution was impossible. Not only man's social structure but the structure of the universe itself, it seemed, had failed. The only reaction was supine despair. Four thousand years of routine had deprived human nature of all its suppleness. To expect these things to refashion their whole behaviour, were scarcely less unreasonable than to expect ants, when their nest was flooded, to assume the habits of water beetles.

But a far more profound and lasting cause doomed the First Men to lie prone for a long while, once they had fallen. A subtle physiological change, which it is tempting to call "general senescence of the species," was undermining the human body and mind. The chemical equilibrium of each individual was becoming more unstable, so that, little by little, man's unique gift of prolonged youth was being lost. Far more rapidly than of old, his tissues failed to compensate for the wear and tear of living. This disaster was by no means inevitable; but it was brought on by influences peculiar to the make-up of the species, and aggravated artificially. For during some thousands of years man had been living at too high a pressure in a biologically unnatural environment, and had found no means of compensating his nature for the strain thus put upon it.

Conceive, then, that after the fall of the First World State, the generations slid rapidly through dusk into night. To inhabit those centuries was to live in the conviction of universal decay, and under the legend of a mighty past. The population was derived almost wholly from the agriculturists of the old order, and since agriculture had been considered a sluggish and base occupation, fit only for sluggish natures, the planet was now peopled with yokels. Deprived of power, machinery, and chemical fertilizers, these bumpkins were hard put to it to keep themselves alive. And indeed only a tenth of their number survived the great disaster. The second generation knew civilization only as a legend. Their days were filled with ceaseless tillage, and in banding together to fight marauders. Women became once more sexual and domestic chattels. The family, or tribe of families, became the largest social whole. Endless brawls and feuds sprang up between valley and valley, and between the tillers and the brigand swarms. Small military tyrants rose and fell; but no permanent unity of control could be maintained over a wide region. There was no surplus wealth to spend on such luxuries as governments and trained armies.

Thus without appreciable change the millennia dragged on in squalid drudgery. For these latter-day barbarians were hampered by living in a used planet. Not only were coal and oil no more, but almost no mineral wealth of any kind remained within reach of their feeble instruments and wits. In particular the minor metals, needed for so many of the multifarious activities of developed material civilization, had long ago disappeared from the more accessible depths of the earth's crust. Tillage moreover was hampered by the fact that iron itself, which was no longer to be had without mechanical mining, was now inaccessible. Men had been forced to resort once more to stone implements, as their first human ancestors had done. But they lacked both the skill and the persistence of the ancients. Not for them the delicate flaking of the Paleoliths nor the smooth symmetry of the Neoliths. Their tools were but broken pebbles, chipped improvements upon natural stones. On almost every one they engraved the same pathetic symbol, the Swastika or cross, which had been used by the First Men as a sacred emblem throughout their existence, though with varying significance. In this instance it had originally been the figure of an aeroplane diving to destruction, and had been used by the rebels to symbolize the downfall of Gordelpus and the State. But subsequent generations reinterpreted the emblem as the sign manual of a divine ancestor, and as a memento of the golden age from which they were destined to decline for ever, or until the gods should intervene. Almost one might say that in its persistent use of this symbol the first human species unwittingly epitomized its own dual and self-thwarting nature.

The idea of irresistible decay obsessed the race at this time. The generation which brought about the downfall of the World State oppressed its juniors with stories of past amenities and marvels, and hugged to itself the knowledge that the young men had not the wit to rebuild such complexity. Generation by generation, as the circumstance of actual life became more squalid, the legend of past glory became more extravagant. The whole mass of scientific knowledge was rapidly lost, save for a few shreds which were of practical service even in savage life. Fragments of the old culture were indeed preserved in the tangle of folk-lore that meshed the globe, but they were distorted beyond recognition. Thus there was a widespread belief that the world had begun as fire, and that life had evolved out of the fire. After the apes had appeared, evolution ceased (so it was said), until divine spirits came down and possessed the female apes, thereby generating human beings. Thus had arisen the golden age of the divine ancestors. But unfortunately after a while the beast in man had triumphed over the god, so that progress had given place to age-long decay. And indeed decay was now unavoidable, until such time as the gods should see fit to come down to cohabit with women and fire the race once more. This faith in the second coming of the gods persisted here and there throughout the First Dark Age, and consoled men for their vague conviction of degeneracy.

Even at the close of the First Dark Age the ruins of the ancient residential pylons still characterized every landscape, often with an effect of senile domination over the hovels of latter-day savages. For the living races dwelt beneath these relics like puny grandchildren playing around the feet of their fathers' once mightier fathers. So well had the past built, and with such durable material, that even after a hundred millennia the ruins were still recognizably artifacts. Though for the most part they were of course by now little more than pyramids of debris overgrown with grass and brushwood, most of them retained some stretch of standing wall, and here and there a favoured specimen still reared from its rubble-encumbered base a hundred foot or so of cliff, punctured with windows. Fantastic legends now clustered round these relics. In one myth the men of old had made for themselves huge palaces which could fly. For a thousand years (an aeon to these savages) men had dwelt in unity, and in reverence of the gods; but at last they had become puffed up with their own glory, and had undertaken to fly to the sun and moon and the field of stars, to oust the gods from their bright home. But the gods sowed discord among them, so that they fell a-fighting one another in the upper air, and their swift palaces crashed down to the earth in thousands, to be monuments of man's folly for ever after. In yet another saga it was the men themselves who were winged. They inhabited dovecots of masonry, with summits overtopping the stars and outraging the gods; who therefore destroyed them. Thus in one form or another, this theme of the downfall of the mighty fliers of old tyrannized over these abject peoples. Their crude tillage, their hunting, their defence against the reviving carnivora, were hampered at every turn by fear of offending the gods by any innovation.

2. THE RISE OF PATAGONIA

As the centuries piled up, the human species had inevitably diverged once more into many races in the various geographical areas. And each race consisted of a swarm of tribes, each ignorant of all but its immediate neighbours. After many millennia this vast diversification of stocks and cultures made it possible for fresh biological transfusions and revivifications to occur. At last, after many racial copulations, a people arose in whom the ancient dignity of humanity was somewhat restored. Once more there was a real distinction between the progressive and the backward regions, between "primitive" and relatively enlightened cultures.

This rebirth occurred in the Southern Hemisphere. Complex climatic changes had rendered the southern part of South America a fit nursery for civilization. Further, an immense warping of the earth's crust to the east and south of Patagonia, had turned what was once a relatively shallow region of the ocean into a vast new land connecting America with Antarctica by way of the former Falkland Islands and South Georgia, and stretching thence east and north-east into the heart of the Atlantic.

It happened also that in South America the racial conditions were more favourable than elsewhere. After the fall of the First World State the European element in this region had dwindled, and the ancient "Indian" and Peruvian stock had come into dominance. Many thousands of years earlier, this race had achieved a primitive civilization of its own. After its ruin at the hands of the Spaniards, it had seemed a broken and negligible thing; yet it had ever kept itself curiously aloof in spirit from its conquerors. Though the two stocks had mingled inextricably, there remained ever in the remoter parts of this continent a way of life which was foreign to the dominant Americanism. Superficially Americanized, it remained fundamentally "Indian" and unintelligible to the rest of the world. Throughout the former civilization this spirit had lain dormant like a seed in winter; but with the return of barbarism it had sprouted, and quietly spread in all directions. From the interaction of this ancient primitive culture and the many other racial elements left over in the continent from the old cosmopolitan civilization, civil life was to begin once more. Thus in a manner the Incas were at last to triumph over their conquerors.

Various causes, then, combined in South America, and especially in the new and virgin plains of Patagonia, to bring the First Dark Age to an end. The great theme of mind began to repeat itself. But in a minor key. For a grave disability hampered the Patagonians. They began to grow old before their adolescence was completed. In the days of Einstein, an individual's youth lasted some twenty-five years, and under the World State it had been artificially doubled. After the downfall of civilization the increasing natural brevity of the individual life was no longer concealed by artifice, and at the end of the First Dark Age a boy of fifteen was already settling into middle age. Patagonian civilization at its height afforded considerable ease and security of life, and enabled man to live to seventy or even eighty; but the period of sensitive and supple youth remained at the very best little more than a decade and a half. Thus the truly young were never able to contribute to culture before they were already at heart middle-aged. At fifteen their bones were definitely becoming brittle, their hair grizzled, their faces lined. Their joints and muscles were stiffening, their brains were no longer quick to learn new adjustments, their fervour was evaporating.

It may seem strange that under these circumstances any kind of civilization could be achieved by the race, that any generation should ever have been able to do more than learn the tricks of its elders. Yet in fact, though progress was never swift, it was steady. For though these beings lacked much of the vigour of youth, they were compensated somewhat by escaping much of youth's fevers and distractions. The First Men, in fact, were now a race whose wild oats had been sown; and though their youthful escapades had somewhat crippled them, they had now the advantage of sobriety and singleness of purpose. Though doomed by lassitude, and a certain fear of extravagance, to fall short of the highest achievements of their predecessors, they avoided much of the wasteful incoherence and mental conflict which had tortured the earlier civilization at its height, though not in its decline. Moreover, because their animal nature was somewhat subdued, the Patagonians were more capable of dispassionate cognition, and more inclined toward intellectualism. They were a people in whom rational behaviour was less often subverted by passion, though more liable to fail through mere indolence or faint-heartedness. Though they found detachment relatively easy, theirs was the detachment of mere lassitude, not the leap from the prison of life's cravings into a more spacious world.

One source of the special character of the Patagonian mind was that in it the sexual impulse was relatively weak. Many obscure causes had helped to temper that lavish sexuality in respect of which the first human species differed from all other animals, even the continuously sexual apes. These causes were diverse, but they combined to produce in the last phase of the life of the species a general curtailment of excess energy. In the Dark Age the severity of the struggle for existence had thrust the sexual interest back almost into the subordinate place which it occupies in the animal mind. Coitus became a luxury only occasionally desired, while self-preservation had become once more an urgent and ever-present necessity. When at last life began to be easier, sexuality remained in partial eclipse, for the forces of racial "senescence" were at work. Thus the Patagonian culture differed in mood from all the earlier cultures of the First Men. Hitherto it had been the clash of sexuality and social taboo that had generated half the fervour and half the delusions of the race. The excess energy of a victorious species, directed by circumstance into the great river of sex, and dammed by social convention, had been canalized for a thousand labours. And though often it would break loose and lay all waste before it, in the main it had been turned to good account. At all times indeed, it had been prone to escape in all directions and carve out channels for itself, as a lopped tree stump sends forth not one but a score of shoots. Hence the richness, diversity, incoherence, violent and uncomprehended cravings and enthusiasms, of the earlier peoples. In the Patagonians there was no such luxuriance. That they were not highly sexual was not in itself a weakness. What mattered was that the springs of energy which formerly happened to flood into the channel of sex were themselves impoverished.

Conceive, then, a small and curiously sober people established east of the ancient Bahia Blanca, and advancing century by century over the plains and up the valleys. In time it reached and encircled the heights which were once the island of South Georgia, while to the north and west it spread into the Brazilian highlands and over the Andes. Definitely of higher type than any of their neighbours, definitely more vigorous and acute, the Patagonians were without serious rivals. And since by temperament they were peaceable and conciliatory, their cultural progress was little delayed, either by military imperialism or internal strife. Like their predecessors in the northern hemisphere, they passed through phases of disruption and union, retrogression and regeneration; but their career was on the whole more steadily progressive, and less dramatic, than anything that had occurred before. Earlier peoples had leapt from barbarism to civil life and collapsed again within a thousand years. The slow march of the Patagonians took ten times as long to pass from a tribal to a civic organization.

Eventually they comprised a vast and highly organized community of autonomous provinces, whose political and cultural centre lay upon the new coast north-east of the ancient Falkland Islands, while its barbarian outskirts included much of Brazil and Peru. The absence of serious strife between the various parts of this "empire" was due partly to an innately pacific disposition, partly to a genius for organization. These influences were strengthened by a curiously potent tradition of cosmopolitanism, or human unity, which had been born in the agony of disunion before the days of the World State, and was so burnt into men's hearts that it survived as an element of myth even through the Dark Age. So powerful was this tradition, that even when the sailing ships of Patagonia had founded colonies in remote Africa and Australia, these new communities remained at heart one with the mother country. Even when the almost Nordic culture of the new and temperate Antarctic coasts had outshone the ancient centre, the political harmony of the race was never in danger.

3. THE CULT OF YOUTH

The Patagonians passed through all the spiritual phases that earlier races had experienced, but in a distinctive manner. They had their primitive tribal religion, derived from the dark past, and based on the fear of natural forces. They had their monotheistic impersonation of Power as a vindictive Creator. Their most adored racial hero was a god-man who abolished the old religion of fear. They had their phases, also, of devout ritual and their phases of rationalism, and again their phases of empirical curiosity.

Most significant for the historian who would understand their special mentality is the theme of the god-man; so curiously did it resemble, yet differ from, similar themes in earlier cultures of the first human species. He was conceived as eternally adolescent, and as mystically the son of all men and women. Far from being the Elder Brother, he was the Favourite Child; and indeed he epitomizes that youthful energy and enthusiasm which the race now guessed was slipping away from it. Though the sexual interest of this people was weak, the parental interest was curiously strong. But the worship of the Favourite Son was not merely parental; it expressed also both the individual's craving for his own lost youth, and his obscure sense that the race itself was senescent.

It was believed that the prophet had actually lived a century as a fresh adolescent. He was designated the Boy who Refused to Grow Up. And this vigour of will was possible to him, it was said, because in him the feeble vitality of the race was concentrated many millionfold. For he was the fruit of all parental passion that ever was and would be; and as such he was divine. Primarily he was the Son of Man, but also he was God. For God, in this religion, was no prime Creator but the fruit of man's endeavour. The Creator was brute power, which had quite inadvertently begotten a being nobler than itself. God, the adorable, was the eternal outcome of man's labour in time, the eternally realized promise of what man himself should become. Yet though this cult was based on the will for a young-hearted future, it was also overhung by a dread, almost at times a certainty, that in fact such a future would never be, that the race was doomed to grow old and die, that spirit could never conquer the corruptible flesh, but must fade and vanish. Only by taking to heart the message of the Divine Boy, it was said, could man hope to escape this doom.

Such was the legend. It is instructive to examine the reality. The actual individual, in whom this myth of the Favourite Son was founded, was indeed remarkable. Born of shepherd parents among the Southern Andes, he had first become famous as the leader of a romantic "youth movement"; and it was this early stage of his career that won him followers. He urged the young to set an example to the old, to live their own life undaunted by conventions, to enjoy, to work hard but briefly, to be loyal comrades. Above all, he preached the religious duty of remaining young in spirit. No one, he said, need grow old, if he willed earnestly not to do so, if he would but keep his soul from falling asleep, his heart open to all rejuvenating influences and shut to every breath of senility. The delight of soul in soul, he said, was the great rejuvenator; it re-created both lover and beloved. If Patagonians would only appreciate each other's beauty without jealousy, the race would grow young again. And the mission of his ever-increasing Band of Youth was nothing less than the rejuvenation of man.

The propagation of this attractive gospel was favoured by a seeming miracle. The prophet turned out to be biologically unique among Patagonians. When many of his coevals were showing signs of senescence, he remained physically young. Also he possessed a sexual vigour which to the Patagonians seemed miraculous. And since sexual taboo was unknown, he exercised himself so heartily in love-making, that he had paramours in every village, and presently his offspring were numbered in hundreds. In this respect his followers strove hard to live up to him, though with small success. But it was not only physically that the prophet remained young. He preserved also a striking youthful agility of mind. His sexual prodigality, though startling to his contemporaries, was in him a temperate overflow of surplus energy. Far from exhausting him, it refreshed him. Presently, however, this exuberance gave place to a more sober life of work and meditation. It was in this period that he began to differentiate himself mentally from his fellows. For at twenty-five, when most Patagonians were deeply settled into a mental groove, he was still battling with successive waves of ideas, and striking out into the unknown. Not till he was forty, and still physically in earlier prime, did he gather his strength and deliver himself of his mature gospel. This, his considered view of existence, turned out to be almost unintelligible to Patagonians. Though in a sense it was an expression of their own culture, it was an expression upon a plane of vitality to which very few of them could ever reach.

The climax came when, during a ceremony in the supreme temple of the capital city, while the worshippers were all prostrated before the hideous image of the Creator, the ageless prophet strode up to the altar, regarded first the congregation and then the god, burst into a hearty peal of laughter, slapped the image resoundingly, and cried, "Ugly, I salute you! Not as almighty, but as the greatest of all jokers. To have such a face, and yet to be admired for it! To be so empty, and yet so feared!" Instantly there was a hubbub. But such was the young iconoclast's god-like radiance, confidence, unexpectedness, and such his reputation as the miraculous Boy, that when he turned upon the crowd, they fell silent, and listened to his scolding.

"Fools!" he cried. "Senile infants! If God really likes your adulation, and all this hugger-mugger, it is because he enjoys the joke against you, and against himself, too. You are too serious, yet not serious enough; too solemn, and all for puerile ends. You are so eager for life, that you cannot live. You cherish your youth so much that it flies from you. When I was a boy, I said, 'Let us keep young'; and you applauded, and went about hugging your toys and refusing to grow up. What I said was not bad for a boy, but it was not enough. Now I am a man; and I say, 'For God's sake, grow up!' Of course we must keep young; but it is useless to keep young if we do not also grow up, and never stop growing up. To keep young, surely, is just to keep supple and keen; and to grow up is not at all a mere sinking into stiffness and into disillusion, but a rising into ever finer skill in all the actions of the game of living. There is something else, too, which is a part of growing up—to see that life is really, after all, a game; a terribly serious game, no doubt, but none the less a game. When we play a game, as it should be played, we strain every muscle to win; but all the while we care less for winning than for the game. And we play the better for it. When barbarians play against a Patagonian team, they forget that it is a game, and go mad for victory. And then how we despise them! If they find themselves losing, they turn savage; if winning, blatant. Either way, the game is murdered, and they cannot see that they are slaughtering a lovely thing. How they pester and curse the umpire, too! I have done that myself, of course, before now; not in games but in life. I have actually cursed the umpire of life. Better so, anyhow, than to insult him with presents, in the hope of being favoured; which is what you are doing here, with your salaams and your vows. I never did that. I merely hated him. Then later I learned to laugh at him, or rather at the thing you set up in his place. But now at last I see him clearly, and laugh with him, at myself, for having missed the spirit of the game. But as for you! Coming here to fawn and whine and cadge favours of the umpire!"

At this point the people rushed toward him to seize him. But he checked them with a young laugh that made them love while they hated. He spoke again.

"I want to tell you how I came to learn my lesson. I have a queer love for clambering about the high mountains; and once when I was up among the snow-fields and precipices of Aconcagua, I was caught in a blizzard. Perhaps some of you may know what storms can be like in the mountains. The air became a hurtling flood of snow. I was swallowed up and carried away. After many hours of floundering, I fell into a snow-drift. I tried to rise, but fell again and again, till my head was buried. The thought of death enraged me, for there was still so much that I wanted to do. I struggled frantically, vainly. Then suddenly—how can I put it?—I saw the game that I was losing, and it was good. Good, no less to lose than to win. For it was the game, now, not victory, that mattered. Hitherto I had been blindfold, and a slave to victory; suddenly I was free, and with sight. For now I saw myself, and all of us, through the eyes of the umpire. It was as though a play-actor were to see the whole play, with his own part in it, through the author's eyes, from the auditorium. Here was I, acting the part of a rather fine man who had come to grief through his own carelessness before his work was done. For me, a character in the play, the situation was hideous; yet for me, the spectator, it had become excellent, within a wider excellence. I saw that it was equally so with all of us, and with all the worlds. For I seemed to see a thousand worlds taking part with us in the great show. And I saw everything through the calm eyes, the exultant, almost derisive, yet not unkindly, eyes of the playwright.

"Well, it had seemed that my exit had come; but no, there was still a cue for me. Somehow I was so strengthened by this new view of things that I struggled out of the snow-drift. And here I am once more. But I am a new man. My spirit is free. While I was a boy, I said, 'Grow more alive'; but in those days I never guessed that there was an aliveness far intenser than youth's flicker, a kind of still incandescence. Is there no one here who knows what I mean? No one who at least *desires* this keener living? The first step is to outgrow this adulation of life itself, and this cadging obsequiousness toward Power. Come! Put it away! Break the ridiculous image in your hearts, as I now smash this idol."

So saying he picked up a great candlestick and shattered the image. Once more there was an uproar, and the temple authorities had him arrested. Not long afterwards he was tried for sacrilege and executed. For this final extravagance was but the climax of many indiscretions, and those in power were glad to have so obvious a pretext for extinguishing this brilliant but dangerous lunatic.

But the cult of the Divine Boy had already become very popular, for the earlier teaching of the prophet expressed the fundamental craving of the Patagonians. Even his last and perplexing message was accepted by his followers, though without real understanding. Emphasis was laid upon the act of iconoclasm, rather than upon the spirit of his exhortation.

Century by century, the new religion, for such it was, spread over the civilized world. And the race seemed to have been spiritually rejuvenated to some extent by widespread fervour. Physically also a certain rejuvenation took place; for before his death this unique biological "sport," or throw-back to an earlier vitality, produced some thousands of sons and daughters; and they in turn propagated the good seed far and wide. Undoubtedly it was this new strain that brought about the golden age of Patagonia, greatly improving the material conditions of the race, carrying civilization into the northern continents and attacking problems of science and philosophy with renewed ardour.

But the revival was not permanent. The descendants of the prophet prided themselves too much on violent living. Physically, sexually, mentally, they over-reached themselves and became enfeebled. Moreover, little by little the potent strain was diluted and overwhelmed by intercourse with the greater volume of the innately "senile"; so that, after a few centuries, the race returned to its middle-aged mood. At the same time the vision of the Divine Boy was gradually distorted. At first it had been youth's ideal of what youth should be, a pattern woven of fanatical loyalty, irresponsible gaiety, comradeship, physical gusto, and not a little pure devilry. But insensibly it became a pattern of that which was expected of youth by sad maturity. The violent young hero was sentimentalized into the senior's vision of childhood, naïve and docile. All that had been violent was forgotten; and what was left became a whimsical and appealing stimulus to the parental impulses. At the same time this phantom was credited with all the sobriety and caution which are so easily appreciated by the middle-aged.

Inevitably this distorted image of youth became an incubus upon the actual young men and women of the race. It was held up as the model social virtue; but it was a model to which they could never conform without doing violence to their best nature, since it was not any longer an expression of youth at all. Just as, in an earlier age, women had been idealized and at the same time hobbled, so now, youth.

Some few, indeed, throughout the history of Patagonia, attained a clearer vision of the prophet. Fewer still were able to enter into the spirit of his final message, in which his enduring youthfulness raised him to a maturity alien to Patagonia. For the tragedy of this people was not so much their "senescence" as their arrested growth. Feeling themselves old, they yearned to be young again. But, through fixed immaturity of mind, they could never recognize that the true, though unlooked-for, fulfilment of youth's passionate craving is not the mere achievement of the ends of youth itself, but an advance into a more awake and far-seeing vitality.

4. THE CATASTROPHE

It was in these latter days that the Patagonians discovered the civilization that had preceded them. In rejecting the ancient religion of fear, they had abandoned also the legend of a remote magnificence, and had come to regard themselves as pioneers of the mind. In the new continent which was their homeland there were, of course, no relics of the ancient order; and the ruins that besprinkled the older regions had been explained as mere freaks of nature. But latterly, with the advance of natural knowledge, archæologists had reconstructed something of the forgotten world. And the crisis came when, in the basement of a shattered pylon in China, they found a store of metal plates (constructed of an immensely durable artificial element), on which were embossed crowded lines of writing. These objects were, in fact, blocks from which books were printed a thousand centuries earlier. Other deposits were soon discovered, and bit by bit

the dead language was deciphered. Within three centuries the outline of
the ancient culture was laid bare; and presently the whole history of man's
rise and ruin fell upon this latter-day civilization with crushing effect, as
though an ancient pylon were to have fallen on a village of wigwams
at its foot. The pioneers discovered that all the ground which they had
so painfully won from the wild had been conquered long ago, and lost;
that on the material side their glory was nothing beside the glory of the
past; and that in the sphere of mind they had established only a few scattered settlements where formerly was an empire. The Patagonian system
of natural knowledge had been scarcely further advanced than that of pre-
Newtonian Europe. They had done little more than conceive the scientific
spirit and unlearn a few superstitions. And now suddenly they came into
a vast inheritance of thought.

This in itself was a gravely disturbing experience for a people of strong
intellectual interest. But even more overwhelming was the discovery,
borne in on them in the course of their research, that the past had been
not only brilliant but crazy, and that in the long run the crazy element
had completely triumphed. For the Patagonian mind was by now too
sane and empirical to accept the ancient knowledge without testing it.
The findings of the archæologists were handed over to the physicists and
other scientists, and the firm thought and valuation of Europe and
America at their zenith were soon distinguished from the degenerate
products of the World State.

The upshot of this impact with a more developed civilization was
dramatic and tragic. It divided the Patagonians into loyalists and rebels,
into those who clung to the view that the new learning was a satanic lie,
and those who faced the facts. To the former party the facts were thoroughly depressing; the latter, though overawed, found in them a compelling majesty, and also a hope. That the earth was a mote among the
star-clouds was the least subversive of the new doctrines, for the Patagonians had already abandoned the geocentric view. What was so distressing to the reactionaries was the theory that an earlier race had long ago
possessed and spent the vitality that they themselves so craved. The party
of progress, on the other hand, urged that this vast new knowledge must
be used; and that, thus equipped, Patagonia might compensate for lack of
youthfulness by superior sanity.

This divergence of will resulted in a physical conflict such as had never
before occurred in the Patagonian world. Something like nationalism
emerged. The more vigorous Antarctic coasts became modern, while Patagonia itself clung to the older culture. There were several wars, but as
physics and chemistry advanced in Antarctica, the Southerners were able
to devise engines of war which the Northerners could not resist. In a
couple of centuries the new "culture" had triumphed. The world was once
more unified.

Hitherto Patagonian civilization had been of a mediæval type. Under the influence of physics and chemistry it began to change. Wind- and water-power began to be used for the generation of electricity. Vast mining operations were undertaken in search of the metals and other minerals which no longer occurred at easy depths. Architecture began to make use of steel. Electrically driven aeroplanes were made, but without real success. And this failure was symptomatic; for the Patagonians were not sufficiently foolhardy to master aviation, even had their planes been more efficient. They themselves naturally attributed their failure wholly to lack of a convenient source of power, such as the ancient petrol. Indeed this lack of oil and coal hampered them at every turn. Volcanic power, of course, was available; but, never having been really mastered by the more resourceful ancients, it defeated the Patagonians completely.

As a matter of fact, in wind and water they had all that was needed. The resources of the whole planet were available, and the world population was less than a hundred million. With this source alone they could never, indeed, have competed in luxury with the earlier World State, but they might well have achieved something like Utopia.

But this was not to be. Industrialism, though accompanied by only a slow increase of population, produced in time most of the social discords which had almost ruined their predecessors. To them it appeared that all their troubles would be solved if only their material power were far ampler. This strong and scarcely rational conviction was a symptom of their ruling obsession, the craving for increased vitality.

Under these circumstances it was natural that one event and one strand of ancient history should fascinate them. The secret of limitless material power had once been known and lost. Why should not Patagonians rediscover it, and use it, with their superior sanity, to bring heaven on earth? The ancients, no doubt, did well to forgo this dangerous source of power; but the Patagonians, level-headed and single-minded, need have no fear. Some, indeed, considered it less important to seek power than to find a means of checking biological senescence; but, unfortunately, though physical science had advanced so rapidly, the more subtle biological sciences had remained backward, largely because among the ancients themselves little more had been done than to prepare their way. Thus it happened that the most brilliant minds of Patagonia, fascinated by the prize at stake, concentrated upon the problem of matter. The state encouraged this research by founding and endowing laboratories whose avowed end was this sole work.

The problem was difficult, and the Patagonian scientists, though intelligent, were somewhat lacking in grit. Only after some five hundred years of intermittent research was the secret discovered, or partially so. It was found possible, by means of a huge initial expenditure of energy, to annihilate the positive and negative electric charges in one not very common kind of atom. But this limitation mattered not at all; the human race now possessed an inexhaustible source of power which could be easily manipulated and easily controlled. But though controllable, the new gift was not foolproof; and there was no guarantee that those who used it might not use it foolishly, or inadvertently let it get out of hand.

Unfortunately, at the time when the new source of energy was discovered, the Patagonians were more divided than of old. Industrialism, combined with the innate docility of the race, had gradually brought about a class cleavage more extreme even than that of the ancient world, though a cleavage of a curiously different kind. The strongly parental disposition of the average Patagonian prevented the dominant class from such brutal exploitation as had formerly occurred. Save during the first century of industrialism, there was no serious physical suffering among the proletariat. A paternal government saw to it that all Patagonians were at least properly fed and clothed, that all had ample leisure and opportunities of amusement. At the same time they saw to it also that the populace became more and more regimented. As in the First World State, civil authority was once more in the hands of a small group of masters of industry, but with a difference. Formerly the dominant motive of big business had been an almost mystical passion for the creation of activity; now the ruling minority regarded themselves as standing towards the populace *in loco parentis,* and aimed at creating "a young-hearted people, simple, gay, vigorous and loyal." Their ideal of the state was something between a preparatory school under a sympathetic but strict adult staff, and a joint-stock company, in which the shareholders retained only one function, to delegate their powers thankfully to a set of brilliant directors.

That the system had worked so well and survived so long was due not only to innate Patagonian docility, but also to the principle by which the governing class recruited itself. One lesson at least had been learnt from the bad example of the earlier civilization, namely respect for intelligence. By a system of careful testing, the brightest children were selected from all classes and trained to be governors. Even the children of the governors themselves were subjected to the same examination, and only those who qualified were sent to the "schools for young governors." Some corruption no doubt existed, but in the main this system worked. The children thus selected were very carefully trained in theory and practice, as organizers, scientists, priests and logicians.

The less brilliant children of the race were educated very differently from the young governors. It was impressed on them that they were less able than the others. They were taught to respect the governors as superior beings, who were called upon to serve the community in specially skilled and arduous work, simply because of their ability. It would not be true to say that the less intelligent were educated merely to be slaves; rather they were expected to be the docile, diligent and happy sons and daughters of the fatherland. They were taught to be loyal and optimistic. They were given vocational training for their various occupations, and encouraged to use their intelligence as much as possible upon the plane suited to it; but the affairs of the state and the problems of religion and theoretical science were strictly forbidden. The official doctrine of the beauty of youth was fundamental in their education. They were taught all the conventional virtues of youth, and in particular modesty and simplicity. As a class they were extremely healthy, for physical training was a very important part of education in Patagonia. Moreover, the universal practice of sun-bathing, which was a religious rite, was especially encouraged among the proletariat, as it was believed to keep the body "young" and the mind placid. The leisure of the governed class was devoted mostly to athletics and other sport, physical and mental. Music and other forms of art were also practised, for these were considered fit occupations for juveniles. The government exercised a censorship over artistic products, but it was seldom enforced; for the common folk of Patagonia were mostly too phlegmatic and too busy to conceive anything but the most obvious and respectable art. They were fully occupied with work and pleasure. They suffered no sexual restraints. Their impersonal interests were satisfied with the official religion of youth-worship and loyalty to the community.

This placid condition lasted for some four hundred years after the first century of industrialism. But as time passed the mental difference between the two classes increased. Superior intelligence became rarer and rarer among the proletariat; the governors were recruited more and more from their own offspring, until finally they became an hereditary caste. The gulf widened. The governors began to lose all mental contact with the governed. They made a mistake which could never have been committed had their psychology kept pace with their other sciences. Ever confronted with the workers' lack of intelligence, they came to treat them more and more as children, and forgot that, though simple, they were grown men and women who needed to feel themselves as free partners in a great human enterprise. Formerly this illusion of responsibility had been sedulously encouraged. But as the gulf widened the proletarians were treated rather as infants than as adolescents, rather as well-cared-for domestic animals than as human beings. Their lives became more and more minutely, though benevolently, systematized for them. At the same time less care was taken to educate them up to an understanding and appreciation of the common human enterprise. Under these circumstances the temper of the people changed. Though their material condition was better than had ever been known before, save under the First World State, they became listless, discontented, mischievous, ungrateful to their superiors.

Such was the state of affairs when the new source of energy was discovered. The world community consisted of two very different elements, first a small, highly intellectual caste, passionately devoted to the state and to the advancement of culture amongst themselves; and, second, a much more numerous population of rather obtuse, physically well-cared-for, and spiritually starved industrialists. A serious clash between the two classes had already occurred over the use of a certain drug, favoured by the people for the bliss it produced, forbidden by the governors for its evil after-effects. The drug was abolished; but the motive was misinterpreted by the proletariat. This incident brought to the surface a hate that had for long been gathering strength in the popular mind, though unwittingly.

When rumour got afoot that in future mechanical power would be unlimited, the people expected a millennium. Every one would have his own limitless source of energy. Work would cease. Pleasure would be increased to infinity. Unfortunately the first use made of the new power was extensive mining at unheard-of depths in search of metals and other minerals which had long ago ceased to be available near the surface. This involved difficult and dangerous work for the miners. There were casualties. Riots occurred. The new power was used upon the rioters with murderous effect, the governors declaring that, though their paternal hearts bled for their foolish children, this chastisement was necessary to prevent worse evils. The workers were urged to face their troubles with that detachment which the Divine Boy had preached in his final phase; but this advice was greeted with the derision which it deserved. Further strikes, riots, assassinations. The proletariat had scarcely more power against their masters than sheep against the shepherd, for they had not the brains for large-scale organization. But it was through one of these pathetically futile rebellions that Patagonia was at last destroyed.

A petty dispute had occurred in one of the new mines. The management refused to allow miners to teach their trade to their sons; for vocational education, it was said, should be carried on professionally. Indignation against this interference with parental authority caused a sudden flash of the old rage. A power unit was seized, and after a bout of insane monkeying with the machinery, the mischief-makers inadvertently got things into such a state that at last the awful djin of physical energy was able to wrench off his fetters and rage over the planet. The first explosion was enough to blow up the mountain range above the mine. In those mountains were huge tracts of the critical element, and these were detonated by rays from the initial explosion. This sufficed to set in action still more remote tracts of the elements. An incandescent hurricane spread over the whole of Patagonia, reinforcing itself with fresh atomic fury wherever it went. It raged along the line of the Andes and the Rockies, scorching both continents with its heat. It undermined and blew up the Behring Straits, spread like a brood of gigantic fiery serpents into Asia, Europe and Africa. Martians, already watching the earth as a cat a bird beyond its spring, noted that the brilliance of the neighbour planet was suddenly enhanced. Presently the oceans began to boil here and there with submarine commotion. Tidal waves mangled the coasts and floundered up the valleys. But in time the general sea level sank considerably through evaporation and the opening of chasms in the ocean floor. All volcanic regions became fantastically active. The polar caps began to melt, but prevented the arctic regions from being calcined like the rest of the planet. The atmosphere was a continuous dense cloud of moisture, fumes and dust, churned in ceaseless hurricanes. As the fury of the electromagnetic collapse proceeded, the surface temperature of the planet steadily increased, till only in the Arctic and a few favoured corners of the sub-Arctic could life persist.

Patagonia's death agony was brief. In Africa and Europe a few remote settlements escaped the actual track of the eruptions, but succumbed in a few weeks to the hurricanes of steam. Of the two hundred million members of the human race, all were burnt or roasted or suffocated within three months—all but thirty-five, who happened to be in the neighbourhood of the North Pole.

CHAPTER VI

TRANSITION

I. THE FIRST MEN AT BAY

BY one of those rare tricks of fortune, which are as often favourable as hostile to humanity, an Arctic exploration ship had recently been embedded in the pack-ice for a long drift across the Polar sea. She was provisioned for four years, and when the catastrophe occurred she had already been at sea for six months. She was a sailing vessel; the expedition had been launched before it was practicable to make use of the new source of power. The crew consisted of twenty-eight men and seven women. Individuals of an earlier and more sexual race, proportioned thus, in such close proximity and isolation, would almost certainly have fallen foul of one another sooner or later. But to Patagonians the arrangement was not intolerable. Besides managing the whole domestic side of the expedition, the seven women were able to provide moderate sexual delight for all, for in this people the female sexuality was much less reduced than the male. There were, indeed, occasional jealousies and feuds in the little community, but these were subordinated to a strong *esprit de corps*. The whole company had, of course, been very carefully chosen for comradeship, loyalty, and health, as well as for technical skill. All claimed descent from the Divine Boy. All were of the governing class. One quaint expression of the strongly parental Patagonian temperament was that a pair of diminutive pet monkeys was taken with the expedition.

The crew's first intimation of the catastrophe was a furious hot wind that melted the surface of the ice. The sky turned black. The Arctic summer became a weird and sultry night, torn by fantastic thunderstorms. Rain crashed on the ship's deck in a continuous waterfall. Clouds of pungent smoke and dust irritated the eyes and nose. Submarine earthquakes buckled the pack-ice.

A year after the explosion, the ship was labouring in tempestuous and berg-strewn water near the Pole. The bewildered little company now began to feel its way south; but, as they proceeded, the air became more fiercely hot and pungent, the storms more savage. Another twelve months were spent in beating about the Polar sea, ever and again retreating north from the impossible southern weather. But at length conditions improved slightly, and with great difficulty these few survivors of the human race approached their original objective in Norway, to find that the lowlands were a scorched and lifeless desert, while on the heights the valley vegetation was already struggling to establish itself, in patches of sickly green. Their base town had been flattened by a hurricane, and the skeletons of its population still lay in the streets. They coasted further south. Everywhere the same desolation. Hoping that the disturbance might be merely local, they headed round the British Isles and doubled back on France. But France turned out to be an appalling chaos of volcanoes. With a change of wind, the sea around them was infuriated with falling debris, often red hot. Miraculously they got away and fled north again. After creeping along the Siberian coast they were at last able to find a tolerable resting-place at the mouth of one of the great rivers. The ship was brought to anchor, and the crew rested. They were a diminished company, for six men and two women had been lost on the voyage.

Conditions even here must recently have been far more severe, since much of the vegetation had been scorched, and dead animals were frequent. But evidently the first fury of the vast explosion was now abating.

By this time the voyagers were beginning to realize the truth. They remembered the half jocular prophecies that the new power would sooner or later wreck the planet, prophecies which had evidently been all too well founded. There had been a world-wide disaster; and they themselves had been saved only by their remoteness and the Arctic ice from a fate that had probably overwhelmed all their fellow men.

So desperate was the outlook for a handful of exhausted persons on a devastated planet, that some urged suicide. All dallied with the idea, save a woman, who had unexpectedly become pregnant. In her the strong parental disposition of her race was now awakened, and she implored the party to make a fight for the sake of her child. Reminded that the baby would only be born into a life of hardship, she reiterated with more persistence than reason, "My baby must live."

The men shrugged their shoulders. But as their tired bodies recovered after the recent struggle, they began to realize the solemnity of their position. It was one of the biologists who expressed a thought which was already present to all. There was at least a chance of survival, and if ever men and women had a sacred duty, surely these had. For they were now the sole trustees of the human spirit. At whatever cost of toil and misery they must people the earth again.

This common purpose now began to exalt them, and brought them all into a rare intimacy. "We are ordinary folk," said the biologist, "but somehow we must become great." And they were, indeed, in a manner made great by their unique position. In generous minds a common purpose and common suffering breed a deep passion of comradeship, expressed perhaps not in words but in acts of devotion. These, in their loneliness and their sense of obligation, experienced not only comradeship, but a vivid communion with one another as instruments of a sacred cause.

The party now began to build a settlement beside the river. Though the whole area had, of course, been devastated, vegetation had soon revived, from roots and seeds, buried or wind-borne. The countryside was now green with those plants that had been able to adjust themselves to the new climate. Animals had suffered far more seriously. Save for the Arctic fox, a few small rodents, and one herd of reindeer, none were left but the dwellers in the actual Arctic seas, the Polar bear, various cetaceans, and seals. Of fish there were plenty. Birds in great numbers had crowded out of the south, and had died off in thousands through lack of food, but certain species were already adjusting themselves to the new environment. Indeed, the whole remaining fauna and flora of the planet was passing through a phase of rapid and very painful readjustment. Many well-established species had wholly failed to get a footing in the new world, while certain hitherto insignificant types were able to forge ahead.

The party found it possible to grow maize and even rice from seed brought from a ruined store in Norway. But the great heat, frequent torrential rain, and lack of sunlight, made agriculture laborious and precarious. Moreover, the atmosphere had become seriously impure, and the human organism had not yet succeeded in adapting itself. Consequently the party were permanently tired and liable to disease.

The pregnant woman had died in child-birth, but her baby lived. It became the party's most sacred object, for it kindled in every mind the strong parental disposition so characteristic of Patagonians.

Little by little the numbers of the settlement were reduced by sickness, hurricanes and volcanic gases. But in time they achieved a kind of equilibrium with their environment, and even a certain strenuous amenity of life. As their prosperity increased, however, their unity diminished. Differences of temperament began to be dangerous. Among the men two leaders had emerged, or rather one leader and a critic. The original head of the expedition had proved quite incapable of dealing with the new situation, and had at last committed suicide. The company had then chosen the second navigating officer as their chief, and had chosen him unanimously. The other born leader of the party was a junior biologist, a man of very different type. The relations of these two did much to determine the future history of man, and are worthy of study in themselves; but here we can only glance at them. In all times of stress the navigator's authority was absolute, for everything depended on his initiative and heroic example. But in less arduous periods, murmurs arose against him for exacting discipline when discipline seemed unnecessary. Between him and the young biologist there grew up a strange blend of hostility and affection; for the latter, though critical, loved and admired the other, and declared that the survival of the party depended on this one man's practical genius.

Three years after their landing, the community, though reduced in numbers and in vitality, was well established in a routine of hunting, agriculture and building. Three fairly healthy infants rejoiced and exasperated their elders. With security, the navigator's genius for action found less scope, while the knowledge of the scientists became more valuable. Plant and poultry-breeding were beyond the range of the heroic leader, and in prospecting for minerals he was equally helpless. Inevitably as time passed he and the other navigators grew restless and irritable; and at last, when the leader decreed that the party should take to the ship and explore for better land, a serious dispute occurred. All the sea-farers applauded; but the scientists, partly through clearer understanding of the calamity that had befallen the planet, partly through repugnance at the hardship involved, refused to go.

Violent emotions were aroused; but both sides restrained themselves through well-tried mutual respect and loyalty to the community. Then suddenly sexual passion set a light to the tinder. The woman who, by general consent, had come to be queen of the settlement, and was regarded as sacred to the leader, asserted her independence by sleeping with one of the scientists. The leader surprised them, and in sudden rage killed the young man. The little community at once fell into two armed factions, and more blood was shed. Very soon, however, the folly and sacrilege of this brawl became evident to these few survivors of a civilized race, and after a parley a grave decision was made.

The company was to be divided. One party, consisting of five men and two women, under the young biologist, was to remain in the settlement. The leader himself, with the remaining nine men and two women, were to navigate the ship toward Europe, in search of a better land. They promised to send word, if possible, during the following year.

With this decision taken the two parties once more became amicable. All worked to equip the pioneers. When at last it was the time of departure, there was a solemn leave-taking. Every one was relieved at the cessation of a painful incompatibility; but more poignant than relief was the distressed affection of those who had so long been comrades in a sacred enterprise.

It was a parting even more momentous than was supposed. For from this act arose at length two distinct human species.

Those who stayed behind heard no more of the wanderers, and finally concluded that they had come to grief. But in fact they were driven West and South-west past Iceland, now a cluster of volcanoes, to Labrador. On this voyage through fantastic storms and oceanic convulsions they lost nearly half their number, and were at last unable to work the ship. When finally they were wrecked on a rocky coast, only the carpenter's mate, two women, and the pair of monkeys succeeded in clambering ashore.

These found themselves in a climate far more sultry than Siberia; but like Siberia, Labrador contained uplands of luxuriant vegetation. The man and his two women had at first great difficulty in finding food, but in time they adapted themselves to a diet of berries and roots. As the years passed, however, the climate undermined their mentality and their descendants sank into abject savagery, finally degenerating into a type that was human only in respect of its ancestry.

The little Siberian settlement was now hard-pressed but single-minded. Calculation had convinced the scientists that the planet would not return to its normal state for some millions of years; for though the first and superficial fury of the disaster had already ceased, the immense pent-up energy of the central explosions would take millions of years to leak out through volcanic vents. The leader of the party, by rare luck a man of genius, conceived their situation thus. For millions of years the planet would be uninhabitable save for a fringe of Siberian coast. The human race was doomed for ages to a very restricted and uncongenial environment. All that could be hoped for was the persistence of a mere remnant of civilized humanity, which should be able to lie dormant until a more favourable epoch. With this end in view the party must propagate itself, and make some possibility of cultured life for its offspring. Above all it must record in some permanent form as much as it could remember of Patagonian culture. "We are the germ," he said. "We must play for safety, mark time, preserve man's inheritance. The chances against us are almost overwhelming, but just possibly we shall win through."

And so in fact they did. Several times almost exterminated at the outset, these few harassed individuals preserved their spark of humanity. A close inspection of their lives would reveal an intense personal drama; for, in spite of the sacred purpose which united them, almost as muscles in one limb, they were individuals of different temperaments. The children, moreover, caused jealousy between their parentally hungry elders. There was ever a subdued, and sometimes an open, rivalry to gain the affection of these young things, these few and precious buds on the human stem. Also there was sharp disagreement about their education. For though all the elders adored them simply for their childishness, one at least, the visionary leader of the party, thought of them chiefly as potential vessels of the human spirit, to be moulded strictly for their great function. In this perpetual subdued antagonism of aims and temperaments the little society lived from day to day, much as a limb functions in the antagonism of its muscles.

The adults of the party devoted much of their leisure during the long winters to the heroic labour of recording the outline of man's whole knowledge. This task was very dear to the leader, but the others often grew weary of it. To each person a certain sphere of culture was assigned; and after he or she had thought out a section and scribbled it down on slate, it was submitted to the company for criticism, and finally engraved deeply on tablets of hard stone. Many thousands of such tablets were produced in the course of years, and were stored in a cave which was carefully prepared for them. Thus was recorded something of the history of the earth and of man, the outlines of physics, chemistry, biology, psychology, and geometry. Each scribe set down also in some detail a summary of his own special study, and added a personal manifesto of his own views about existence. Much ingenuity was spent in devising a vast pictorial dictionary and grammar, with which, it was hoped, the remote future might interpret the whole library.

Years passed while this immense registration of human thought was still in progress. The founders of the settlement grew feebler while the eldest of the next generation were still adolescent. Of the two women, one had died and the other was almost a cripple, both martyrs to the task of motherhood. A youth, an infant boy, and four girls of various ages—on these the future of man now depended. Unfortunately these precious beings had suffered from their very preciousness. Their education had been bungled. They had been both pampered and oppressed. Nothing was thought too good for them, but they were overwhelmed with cherishing and teaching. Thus they came to hold the elders at arm's length, and to weary of the ideals imposed on them. Brought into a ruined world without their own consent, they refused to accept the crushing obligation toward an improbable future. Hunting, and the daily struggle of a pioneering age, afforded their spirits full exercise in courage, mutual loyalty, and interest in one another's personality. They would live for the present only, and for the tangible reality, not for a culture which they knew only by hearsay. In particular, they loathed the hardship of engraving endless verbiage upon granitic slabs.

The crisis came when the eldest girl had crossed the threshold of physical maturity. The leader told her that it was her duty to begin bearing children at once, and ordered her to have intercourse with her half-brother, his own son. Having herself assisted at the last birth, which had destroyed her mother, she refused; and when pressed she dropped her graving tool and fled. This was the first serious act of rebellion. In a few years the older generation was deposed from authority. A new way of life, more active, more dangerous, zestful and careless, resulted in a lowering of the community's standard of comfort and organization, but also in greater health and vitality. Experiments in plant and stock-breeding were neglected, buildings went out of repair; but great feats of hunting and exploration were undertaken. Leisure was given over to games of hazard and calculation, to dancing, singing and romantic story-telling. Music and romance, indeed, were now the main expression of the finer nature of these beings, and became the vehicles of obscure religious experience. The intellectualism of the elders was ridiculed. What could their poor sciences tell of reality, of the many-faced, never-for-a-moment-the-same, superbly inconsequent, and ever-living Real? Man's intelligence was all right for hunting and tillage in the world of common sense; but if he rode it further afield, he would find himself in a desert, and his soul would starve. Let him live as nature prompted. Let him keep the young god in his heart alive. Let him give free play to the struggling, irrational, dark vitality that sought to realize itself in him not as logic but as beauty.

The tablets were now engraved only by the aged.

But one day, after the infant boy had reached the early Patagonian adolescence, his curiosity was roused by the tail-like hind limbs of a seal. The old people timidly encouraged him. He made other biological observations, and was led on to envisage the whole drama of life on the planet, and to conceive loyalty to the cause which they had served.

Meanwhile, sexual and parental nature had triumphed where schooling had failed. The young things inevitably fell in love with each other, and in time several infants appeared.

Thus, generation by generation, the little settlement maintained itself with varying success, varying zestfulness, and varying loyalty toward the future. With changing conditions the population fluctuated, sinking as low as two men and one woman, but increasing gradually up to a few thousand, the limit set by the food capacity of their strip of coast. In the long run, though circumstances did not prevent material survival, they made for mental decline. For the Siberian coast remained a tropical land bounded on the south by a forest of volcanoes; and consequently in the long run the generations declined in mental vigour and subtlety. This result was perhaps due in part to too intensive inbreeding; but this factor had also one good effect. Though mental vigour waned, certain desirable characteristics were consolidated. The founders of the group represented the best remaining stock of the first human species. They had been chosen for their hardihood and courage, their native loyalty, their strong cognitive interest. Consequently, in spite of phases of depression, the race not only survived but retained its curiosity and its group feeling. Even while the ability of men decreased, their will to understand, and their sense of racial unity, remained. Though their conception of man and the universe gradually sank into crude myth, they preserved a strong unreasoning loyalty towards the

future, and toward the now sacred stone library which was rapidly becoming unintelligible to them. For thousands and even millions of years,
after the species had materially changed its nature, there remained a vague
admiration for mental prowess, a confused tradition of a noble past, and
pathetic loyalty toward a still nobler future. Above all, internecine strife
was so rare that it served only to strengthen the clear will to preserve the
unity and harmony of the race.

<h2 style="text-align:center">2. THE SECOND DARK AGE</h2>

We must now pass rapidly over the Second Dark Age, observing
merely those influences which were to affect the future of humanity.

Century by century the pent energy of the vast explosion dispersed
itself; but not till many hundred thousand years had passed did the
swarms of upstart volcanoes begin to die, and not till after millions of
years did the bulk of the planet become once more a possible home for
life.

During this period many changes took place. The atmosphere became
clearer, purer and less turbulent. With the fall of temperature, frost and
snow appeared occasionally in the Arctic regions, and in due course the
Polar caps were formed again. Meanwhile, ordinary geological processes,
augmented by the strains to which the planet was subjected by increased
internal pressure, began to change the continents. South America mostly
collapsed into the hollows blasted beneath it, but a new land rose to join
Brazil with West Africa. The East Indies and Australia became a continuous continent. The huge mass of Thibet sank deeply into its disturbed
foundations, lunged West, and buckled Afghanistan into a range of peaks
nearly forty thousand feet above the sea. Europe sank under the Atlantic.
Rivers writhed shiftingly hither and thither upon the continents, like tortured worms. New alluvial areas were formed. New strata were laid upon
one another under new oceans. New animals and plants developed from the
few surviving Arctic species, and spread south through Asia and America.
In the new forests and grass-lands appeared various specialized descendants
of the reindeer, and swarms of rodents. Upon these preyed the large and
small descendants of the Arctic fox, of which one species, a gigantic wolf-
like creature, rapidly became the "King of Beasts" in the new order, and
remained so, until it was ousted by the more slowly modified offspring of
the polar bears. A certain genus of seals, reverting to the ancient terrestrial
habit, had developed a slender snake-like body and an almost swift, and
very serpentine, mode of locomotion among the coastal sand-dunes. There
it was wont to stalk its rodent prey, and even follow them into their
burrows. Everywhere there were birds. Many of the places left vacant by
the destruction of the ancient fauna were now filled by birds which had
discarded flight and developed pedestrian habits. Insects, almost exter-

minated by the great conflagration, had afterwards increased so rapidly, and had refashioned their types with such versatility, that they soon reached almost to their ancient profusion. Even more rapid was the establishment of the new micro-organisms. In general, among all the beasts and plants of the earth there was a great change of habit, and a consequent overlaying of old body-forms with new forms adapted to a new way of life.

The two human settlements had fared very differently. That of Labrador, oppressed by a more sweltering climate, and unsupported by the Siberian will to preserve human culture, sank into animality; but ultimately it peopled the whole West with swarming tribes. The human beings in Asia remained a mere handful throughout the ten million years of the Second Dark Age. An incursion of the sea cut them off from the south. The old Taimyr Peninsula, where their settlements clustered, became the northern promontory of an island whose coasts were the ancient valley-edges of the Yenessi, the Lower Tunguska and the Lena. As the climate became less oppressive, the families spread toward the southern coast of the island, but the sea checked them. Temperate conditions enabled them to regain a certain degree of culture. But they had no longer the capacity to profit much from the new clemency of nature, for the previous ages of tropical conditions had undermined them. Moreover, toward the end of the ten million years of the Second Dark Age, the Arctic climate spread south into their island. Their crops failed, the rodents that formed their chief cattle dwindled, their few herds of deer faded out through lack of food. Little by little this scanty human race degenerated into a mere remnant of Arctic savages. And so they remained for a million years. Psychologically they were so crippled that they had almost completely lost the power of innovation. When their sacred quarries in the hills were covered with ice, they had not the wit to use stone from the valleys, but were reduced to making implements of bone. Their language degenerated into a few grunts to signify important acts, and a more complex system of emotional expressions. For emotionally these creatures still preserved a certain refinement. Moreover, though they had almost wholly lost the power of intelligent innovation, their instinctive responses were often such as a more enlightened intelligence would justify. They were strongly social, deeply respectful of the individual human life, deeply parental, and often terribly earnest in their religion.

Not till long after the rest of the planet was once more covered with life, not till nearly ten million years after the Patagonian disaster, did a group of these savages, adrift on an iceberg, get blown southward across the sea to the mainland of Asia. Luckily, for Arctic conditions were increasing, and in time the islanders were extinguished.

The survivors settled in the new land and spread, century by century, into the heart of Asia. Their increase was very slow, for they were an infertile and inflexible race. But conditions were now extremely favourable.

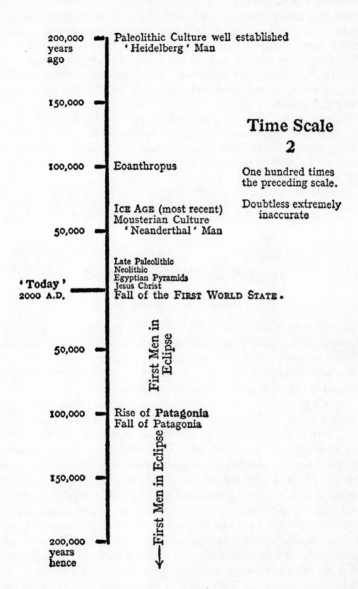

200,000 years ago — Paleolithic Culture well established
'Heidelberg' Man

150,000 —

Time Scale 2

100,000 — Eoanthropus

One hundred times the preceding scale.

ICE AGE (most recent)
Mousterian Culture

Doubtless extremely inaccurate

50,000 — 'Neanderthal' Man

Late Paleolithic
Neolithic
Egyptian Pyramids
Jesus Christ

'Today'
2000 A.D. — Fall of the FIRST WORLD STATE.

First Men in Eclipse

50,000 —

100,000 — Rise of **Patagonia**
Fall of Patagonia

First Men in Eclipse

150,000 —

200,000 years hence —

The climate was temperate; for Russia and Europe were now a shallow sea warmed by currents from the Atlantic. There were no dangerous animals save the small grey bears, an offshoot from the polar species, and the large wolf-like foxes. Various kinds of rodents and deer provided meat in plenty. There were birds of all sizes and habits. Timber, fruit, wild grains and other nourishing plants throve on the well-watered volcanic soil. The prolonged eruptions, moreover, had once more enriched the upper layers of the rocky crust with metals.

A few hundred thousand years in this new world sufficed for the human species to increase from a handful of individuals to a swarm of races. It was in the conflict and interfusion of these races, and also through the absorption of certain chemicals from the new volcanic soil, that humanity at last recovered its vitality.

CHAPTER VII

THE RISE OF THE SECOND MEN

I. THE APPEARANCE OF A NEW SPECIES

IT was some ten million years after the Patagonian disaster that the first elements of a few human species appeared, in an epidemic of biological variations, many of which were extremely valuable. Upon this raw material the new and stimulating environment worked for some hundred thousand years until at last there appeared the Second Men.

Though of greater stature and more roomy cranium, these beings were not wholly unlike their predecessors in general proportions. Their heads, indeed, were large even for their bodies, and their necks massive. Their hands were huge, but finely moulded. Their almost titanic size entailed a seemingly excessive strength of support; their legs were stouter, even proportionately, than the legs of the earlier species. Their feet had lost the separate toes, and, by a strengthening and growing together of the internal bones, had become more efficient instruments of locomotion. During the Siberian exile the First Men had acquired a thick hairy covering, and most races of the Second Men retained something of this blonde hirsute appearance throughout their career. Their eyes were large, and often jade green, their features firm as carved granite, yet mobile and lucent. Of the second human species one might say that Nature had at last repeated and far excelled the noble but unfortunate type which she had achieved once, long ago, with the first species, in certain pre-historic cave-dwelling hunters and artists.

Inwardly the Second Men differed from the earlier species in that they had shed most of those primitive relics which had hampered the First Men more than was realized. Not only were they free of appendix, tonsils and other useless excrescences, but also their whole structure was more firmly knit into unity. Their chemical organization was such that their tissues were kept in better repair. Their teeth, though proportionately small and few, were almost completely immune from caries. Such was their glandular equipment that puberty did not begin till twenty; and not till they were fifty did they reach maturity. At about one hundred and ninety their powers began to fail, and after a few years of contemplative retirement they almost invariably died before true senility could begin. It was as though, when a man's work was finished, and he had meditated in peace upon his whole career, there were nothing further to hold his attention and prevent him from falling asleep. Mothers carried the fœtus for three years, suckled the infant for five years, and were sterile during this period and for another seven years. Their climacteric was reached at about a hundred and sixty. Architecturally massive like their mates, they would have seemed to the First Men very formidable titanesses; but even those early half-human beings would have admired the women of the second species both for their superb vitality and for their brilliantly human expression.

In temperament the Second Men were curiously different from the earlier species. The same factors were present, but in different proportions, and in far greater subordination to the considered will of the individual. Sexual vigour had returned. But sexual interest was strangely altered. Around the ancient core of delight in physical and mental contact with the opposite sex there now appeared a kind of innately sublimated, and no less poignant, appreciation of the unique physical and mental forms of all kinds of live things. It is difficult for less ample natures to imagine this expansion of the innate sexual interest; for to them it is not apparent that the lusty admiration which at first directs itself solely on the opposite sex is the appropriate attitude to all the beauties of flesh and spirit in beast and bird and plant. Parental interest also was strong in the new species, but it too was universalized. It had become a strong innate interest in, and a devotion to, all beings that were conceived as in need of help. In the earlier species this passionate spontaneous altruism occurred only in exceptional persons. In the new species, however, all normal men and women experienced altruism as a passion. And yet at the same time primitive parenthood had become tempered to a less possessive and more objective love, which among the First Men was less common than they themselves were pleased to believe. Assertiveness had also greatly changed. Formerly very much of a man's energy had been devoted to the assertion of himself as a private individual over against other individuals; and very much of his generosity had been at bottom selfish. But in the Second Men this competitive self-assertion, this championship of the most intimately known animal against all others, was greatly tempered. Formerly the major enterprises of society would never have been carried through had they not been able to annex to themselves the egoism of their champions. But in the Second Men the parts were reversed. Few individuals could ever trouble to exert themselves to the last ounce for merely private ends, save when those ends borrowed interest or import from some public enterprise. It was only his vision of a world-wide community of persons, and of his own function therein, that could rouse the fighting spirit in a man. Thus it was inwardly, rather than in outward physical characters, that the Second Men differed from the First. And in nothing did they differ more than in their native aptitude for cosmopolitanism. They had their tribes and nations. War was not quite unknown amongst them. But even in primitive times a man's most serious loyalty was directed toward the race as a whole; and wars were so hampered by impulses of kindliness toward the enemy that they were apt to degenerate into rather violent athletic contests, leading to an orgy of fraternization.

It would not be true to say that the strongest interest of these beings was social. They were never prone to exalt the abstraction called the state, or the nation, or even the world-commonwealth. For their most characteristic factor was not mere gregariousness but something novel, namely an innate interest in personality, both in the actual diversity of persons and in the ideal of personal development. They had a remarkable power of vividly intuiting their fellows as unique persons with special needs. Individuals of the earlier species had suffered from an almost insurmountable spiritual isolation from one another. Not even lovers, and scarcely even the geniuses with special insight into personality, ever had anything like accurate vision of one another. But the Second Men, more intensely and accurately self-conscious, were also more intensely and accurately conscious of one another. This they achieved by no unique faculty, but solely by a more ready interest in each other, a finer insight, and a more active imagination.

They had also a remarkable innate interest in the higher kinds of mental activity, or rather in the subtle objects of those activities. Even children were instinctively inclined toward a genuinely æsthetic interest in their world and their own behaviour, and also toward scientific inquiry and generalization. Small boys, for instance, would delight in collecting not merely such things as eggs or crystals, but mathematical formulæ expressive of the different shapes of eggs and crystals, or of the innumerable rhythms of shells, fronds, leaflets, grass-nodes. And there was a wealth of traditional fairy-stories whose appeal was grounded in philosophical puzzles. Little children delighted to hear how the poor things called Illusions were banished from the Country of the Real, how one-dimensional Mr. Line woke up in a two-dimensional world, and how a brave young tune slew cacophonous beasts and won a melodious bride in that strange country where the landscape is all of sound and all living things are music. The First Men had attained to interest in science, mathematics, philosophy, only after arduous schooling, but in the Second Men there was a natural propensity for these activities, no less vigorous than the primitive instincts. Not, of course, that they were absolved from learning; but they had the same zest and facility in these matters as their predecessors had enjoyed only in humbler spheres.

In the earlier species, indeed, the nervous system had maintained only a very precarious unity, and was all too liable to derangement by the rebellion of one of its subordinate parts. But in the second species the highest centres maintained an almost absolute harmony among the lower. Thus the moral conflict between momentary impulse and considered will, and again between private and public interest, played a very subordinate part among the Second Men.

In actual cognitive powers, also, this favoured species far outstripped its predecessor. For instance, vision had greatly developed. The Second Men distinguished in the spectrum a new primary colour between green and blue; and beyond blue they saw, not a reddish blue, but again a new primary colour, which faded with increasing ruddiness far into the old ultra-violet. These two new primary colours were complementary to one another. At the other end of the spectrum they saw the infra-red as a peculiar purple. Further, owing to the very great size of their retinæ, and the multiplication of rods and cones, they discriminated much smaller fractions of their field of vision.

Improved discrimination combined with a wonderful fertility of mental imagery to produce a greatly increased power of insight into the character of novel situations. Whereas among the First Men, native intelligence had increased only up to the age of fourteen, among the Second Men it progressed up to forty. Thus an average adult was capable of immediate insight into problems which even the most brilliant of the First Men could only solve by prolonged reasoning. This superb clarity of mind enabled the second species to avoid most of those age-long confusions and superstitions which had crippled its predecessor. And along with great intelligence went a remarkable flexibility of will. In fact the Second Men were far more able than the First to break habits that were seen to be no longer justified.

To sum the matter, circumstance had thrown up a very noble species. Essentially it was of the same type as the earlier species, but it had undergone extensive improvements. Much that the First Men could only achieve by long schooling and self-discipline the Second Men performed with effortless fluency and delight. In particular, two capacities which for the First Men had been unattainable ideals were now realized in every normal individual, namely the power of wholly dispassionate cognition, and the power of loving one's neighbour as oneself, without reservation. Indeed, in this respect the Second Men might be called "Natural Christians," so readily and constantly did they love one another in the manner of Jesus, and infuse their whole social policy with loving-kindness. Early in their career they conceived the religion of love, and they were possessed by it again and again, in diverse forms, until their end. On the other hand, their gift of dispassionate cognition helped them to pass speedily to the admiration of fate. And being by nature rigorous thinkers, they were peculiarly liable to be disturbed by the conflict between their religion of love and their loyalty to fate.

Well might it seem that the stage was now set for a triumphant and rapid progress of the human spirit. But though the second human species constituted a real improvement on the first, it lacked certain faculties without which the next great mental advance could not be made.

Moreover its very excellence involved one novel defect from which the First Men were almost wholly free. In the lives of humble individuals there are many occasions when nothing but an heroic effort can wrest their private fortunes from stagnation or decline, and set them pioneering in new spheres. Among the First Men this effort was often called forth by passionate regard for self. And it was upon the tidal wave of innumerable egoisms, blindly surging in one direction, that the first species was carried forward. But, to repeat, in the Second Men self-regard was never an over-mastering motive. Only at the call of social loyalty or personal love would a man spur himself to desperate efforts. Whenever the stake appeared to be mere private advancement, he was apt to prefer peace to enterprise, the delights of sport, companionship, art or intellect, to the slavery of self-regard. And so in the long run, though the Second Men were fortunate in their almost complete immunity from the lust of power and personal ostentation (which cursed the earlier species with industrialism and militarism), and though they enjoyed long ages of idyllic peace, often upon a high cultural plane, their progress toward full self-conscious mastery of the planet was curiously slow.

2. THE INTERCOURSE OF THREE SPECIES

In a few thousand years the new species filled the region from Afghanistan to the China Sea, overran India, and penetrated far into the new Australasian continent. Its advance was less military than cultural. The remaining tribes of the First Men, with whom the new species could not normally interbreed, were unable to live up to the higher culture that flooded round them and over them. They faded out.

For some further thousands of years the Second Men remained as noble savages, then passed rapidly through the pastoral into the agricultural stage. In this era they sent an expedition across the new and gigantic Hindu Kush to explore Africa. Here it was that they came upon the sub-human descendants of the ship's crew that had sailed from Siberia millions of years earlier. These animals had spread south through America and across the new Atlantic Isthmus into Africa.

Dwarfed almost to the knees of the superior species, bent so that as often as not they used their arms as aids to locomotion, flat-headed and curiously long-snouted, these creatures were by now more baboon-like than human. Yet in the wild state they maintained a very complicated organization into castes, based on the sense of smell. Their powers of scent, indeed, had developed at the expense of their intelligence. Certain odours, which had become sacred through their very repulsiveness, were given off only by individuals having certain diseases. Such individuals were treated with respect by their fellows; and though, in fact, they were debilitated by their disease, they were so feared that no healthy individual dared resist them. The characteristic odours were themselves graded in nobility, so that those individuals who bore only the less repulsive perfume, owed respect to those in whom a widespread rotting of the body occasioned the most nauseating stench. These plagues had the special effect of stimulating reproductive activity; and this fact was one cause both of the respect felt for them, and of the immense fertility of the species, such a fertility that, in spite of plagues and obtuseness, it had flooded two continents. For though the plagues were fatal, they were slow to develop. Further, though individuals far advanced in disease were often incapable of feeding themselves, they profited by the devotion of the healthy, who were well-pleased if they also became infected.

But the most startling fact about these creatures was that many of them had become enslaved to another species. When the Second Men had penetrated further into Africa they came to a forest region where companies of diminutive monkeys resisted their intrusion. It was soon evident that any interference with the imbecile and passive sub-humans in this district was resented by the monkeys. And as the latter made use of a primitive kind of bow and poisoned arrows, their opposition was seriously inconvenient to the invaders. The use of weapons and other tools, and a remarkable co-ordination in warfare, made it clear that in intelligence this simian species had far outstripped all creatures save man. Indeed, the Second Men were now face to face with the only terrestrial species which ever evolved so far as to compete with man in versatility and practical shrewdness.

As the invaders advanced, the monkeys were seen to round up whole flocks of the sub-men and drive them out of reach. It was noticed also that these domesticated sub-men were wholly free from the diseases that infected their wild kinsfolk, who on this account greatly despised the healthy drudges. Later it transpired that the sub-men were trained as beasts of burden by the monkeys and that their flesh was a much relished article of diet. An arboreal city of woven branches was discovered, and was apparently in course of construction, for the sub-men were dragging timber and hauling it aloft, goaded by the bone-headed spears of the monkeys. It was evident also that the authority of the monkeys was maintained less by force than by intimidation. They anointed themselves with the juice of a rare aromatic plant, which struck terror into their poor cattle, and reduced them to abject docility.

Now the invaders were only a handful of pioneers. They had come over the mountains in search of metals, which had been brought to the earth's surface during the volcanic era. An amiable race, they felt no hostility toward the monkeys, but rather amusement at their habits and ingenuity. But the monkeys resented the mere presence of these mightier beings; and, presently collecting in the tree-tops in thousands, they annihilated the party with their poisoned arrows. One man alone escaped into Asia. In a couple of years he returned, with a host. Yet this was no punitive expedition, for the bland Second Men were strangely lacking in resentment. Establishing themselves on the outskirts of the forest region, they contrived to communicate and barter with the little people of the trees, so that after a while they were allowed to enter the territory unmolested, and begin their great metallurgical survey.

A close study of the relations of these very different intelligences would be enlightening, but we have no time for it. Within their own sphere the monkeys showed perhaps a quicker wit than the men; but only within very narrow limits did their intelligence work at all. They were deft at finding new means for the better satisfaction of their appetites. But they wholly lacked self-criticism. Upon a normal outfit of instinctive needs they had developed many acquired, traditional cravings, most of which were fantastic and harmful. The Second Men, on the other hand, though often momentarily outwitted by the monkeys, were in the long run incomparably more able and more sane.

The difference between the two species is seen clearly in their reaction to metals. The Second Men sought metal solely for the carrying on of an already well-advanced civilization. But the monkeys, when for the first time they saw the bright ingots, were fascinated. They had already begun to hate the invaders for their native superiority and their material wealth; and now this jealousy combined with primitive acquisitiveness to make the slabs of copper and tin become in their eyes symbols of power. In order to remain unmolested in their work, the invaders had paid a toll of the wares of their own country, of baskets, pottery and various specially designed miniature tools. But at the sight of the crude metal, the monkeys demanded a share of this noblest product of their own land. This was readily granted, since it did away with the need of bringing goods from Asia. But the monkeys had no real use for metal. They merely hoarded it, and became increasingly avaricious. No one had respect among them who did not laboriously carry a great ingot about with him wherever he went. And after a while it came to be considered actually indecent to be seen without a slab of metal. In conversation between the sexes this symbol of refinement was always held so as to conceal the genitals.

The more metal the monkeys acquired the more they craved. Blood was often shed in disputes over the possession of hoards. But this internecine strife gave place at length to a concerted movement to prevent the whole export of metal from their land. Some even suggested that the ingots in their possession should be used for making more effective weapons, with which to expel the invaders. This policy was rejected, not merely because there were none who could work up the crude metal, but because it was generally agreed that to put such a sacred material to any kind of service would be base.

The will to be rid of the invader was augmented by a dispute about the sub-men. These abject beings were treated very harshly by their masters. Not only were they overworked, but also they were tortured in cold blood, not precisely through lust in cruelty, but through a queer sense of humour, or delight in the incongruous. For instance, it afforded the monkeys a strangely innocent and extravagant pleasure to compel these cattle to carry on their work in an erect posture, which was by now quite unnatural to them, or to eat their own excrement or even their own young. If ever these tortures roused some exceptional sub-man to rebel, the monkeys flared into contemptuous rage at such a lack of humour, so incapable were they of realizing the subjective processes of others. To one another they could, indeed, be kindly and generous; but even among themselves the imp of humour would sometimes run riot. In any matter in which an individual was misunderstood by his fellows, he was sure to be gleefully baited, and often harried to death. But in the main it was only the slave-species that suffered.

The invaders were outraged by this cruel imbecility, and ventured to protest. To the monkeys the protest was unintelligible. What were cattle for, but to be used in the service of superior beings? Evidently, the monkeys thought, the invaders were after all lacking in the finer capacities of mind, since they failed to appreciate the beauty of the fantastic.

This and other causes of friction finally led the monkeys to conceive a means of freeing themselves for ever. The Second Men had proved to be terribly liable to the diseases of their wretched sub-human kinsfolk. Only by very rigorous quarantine had they stamped out the epidemic that had revealed this fact. Now partly for revenge, but partly also through malicious delight in the topsy-turvy, the monkeys determined to make use of this human weakness. There was a certain nut, very palatable to both men and monkeys, which grew in a remote part of the country. The monkeys had already begun to barter this nut for extra metal; and the pioneering Second Men were arranging to send caravans laden with nuts into their own country. In this situation the monkeys found their opportunity. They carefully infected large quantities of nuts with the plagues rampant

among those herds of sub-men which had not been domesticated. Very
soon caravans of infected nuts were scattered over Asia. The effect upon a
race wholly fresh to these microbes was disastrous. Not only were the
pioneering settlements wiped out, but the bulk of the species also. The sub-
men themselves had become adjusted to the microbes, and even reproduced
more rapidly because of them. Not so the more delicately organized species.
They died off like autumn leaves. Civilization fell to pieces. In a few
generations Asia was peopled only by a handful of scattered savages, all
diseased and mostly crippled.

But in spite of this disaster the species remained potentially the same.
Within a few centuries it had thrown off the infection and had begun
once more the ascent toward civilization. After another thousand years,
pioneers again crossed the mountains and entered Africa. They met with
no opposition. The precarious flicker of simian intelligence had long ago
ceased. The monkeys had so burdened their bodies with metal and their
minds with the obsession of metal, that at length the herds of sub-human
cattle were able to rebel and devour their masters.

3. THE ZENITH OF THE SECOND MEN

For nearly a quarter of a million years the Second Men passed through
successive phases of prosperity and decline. Their advance to developed
culture was not nearly so steady and triumphal as might have been expected from a race of such brilliance. As with individuals, so with species,
accidents are all too likely to defeat even the most cautious expectations.
For instance, the Second Men were for a long time seriously hampered by
a "glacial epoch" which at its height imposed Arctic conditions even as
far south as India. Little by little the encroaching ice crowded their tribes
into the extremity of that peninsula, and reduced their culture to the level
of the Esquimaux. In time, of course, they recovered, but only to suffer
other scourges, of which the most devastating were epidemics of bacteria.
The more recently developed and highly organized tissues of this species
were peculiarly susceptible to disease, and not once but many times a promising barbarian culture or "mediæval" civilization was wiped out by
plagues.

But of all the natural disasters which befell the Second Men, the
worst was due to a spontaneous change in their own physical constitution.
Just as the fangs of the ancient sabre-toothed tiger had finally grown so
large that the beast could not eat, so the brain of the second human
species threatened to outgrow the rest of its body. In a cranium that was
originally roomy enough, this rare product of nature was now increasingly cramped; while a circulatory system, that was formerly quite adequate, was becoming more and more liable to fail in pumping blood
through so cramped a structure. These two causes at last began to take

serious effect. Congenital imbecility became increasingly common, along with all manner of acquired mental diseases. For some thousands of years the race remained in a most precarious condition, now almost dying out, now rapidly attaining an extravagant kind of culture in some region where physical nature happened to be peculiarly favourable. One of these precarious flashes of spirit occurred in the Yang-tze valley as a sudden and brief effulgence of city states peopled by neurotics, geniuses and imbeciles. The lasting upshot of this civilization was a brilliant literature of despair, dominated by a sense of the difference between the actual and the potential in man and the universe. Later, when the race had attained its noontide glory, it was wont to brood upon this tragic voice from the past in order to remind itself of the underlying horror of existence.

Meanwhile, brains became more and more overgrown, and the race more and more disorganized. There is no doubt that it would have gone the way of the sabre-toothed tiger, simply through the fatal direction of its own physiological evolution, had not a more stable variety of this second human species at last appeared. It was in North America, into which, by way of Africa, the Second Men had long ago spread, that the roomier-skulled and stronger hearted type first occurred. By great good fortune this new variety proved to be a dominant Mendelian character. And as it interbred freely with the older variety, a superbly healthy race soon peopled America. The species was saved.

But another hundred thousand years were to pass before the Second Men could reach their zenith. I must not dwell on this movement of the human symphony, though it is one of great richness. Inevitably many themes are now repeated from the career of the earlier species, but with special features, and transposed, so to speak, from the minor to the major key. Once more primitive cultures succeed one another, or pass into civilization, barbarian or "mediæval"; and in turn these fall or are transformed. Twice, indeed, the planet became the home of a single world-wide community which endured for many thousands of years, until misfortune wrecked it. The collapse is not altogether surprising, for unlike the earlier species, the Second Men had no coal and oil. In both these early world societies of the Second Men there was a complete lack of mechanical power. Consequently, though world-wide and intricate, they were in a manner "mediæval." In every continent intensive and highly skilled agriculture crept from the valleys up the mountain sides and over the irrigated deserts. In the rambling garden-cities each citizen took his share of drudgery, practised also some fine handicraft, and yet had leisure for gaiety and contemplation. Intercourse within and between the five great continental communities had to be maintained by coaches, caravans and sailing ships. Sail, indeed, now came back into its own, and far surpassed its previous achievements. On every sea, fleets of great populous red-sailed clippers, wooden, with carved poops and prows, but with the sleek flanks of the dolphin carried the produce of every land, and the many travellers who delighted to spend a sabbatical year among foreigners.

So much, in the fullness of time, could be achieved, even without mechanical power, by a species gifted with high intelligence and immune from anti-social self-regard. But inevitably there came an end. A virus, whose subtle derangement of the glandular system was never suspected by a race still innocent of physiology, propagated throughout the world a mysterious fatigue. Century by century, agriculture withdrew from the hills and deserts, craftsmanship deteriorated, thought became stereotyped. And the vast lethargy produced a vast despond. At length the nations lost touch with one another, forgot one another, forgot their culture, crumbled into savage tribes. Once more Earth slept.

Many thousand years later, long after the disease was spent, several great peoples developed in isolation. When at last they made contact, they were so alien that in each there had to occur a difficult cultural revolution, not unaccompanied by bloodshed, before the world could once more feel as one. But this second world order endured only a few centuries, for profound subconscious differences now made it impossible for the races to keep whole-heartedly loyal to each other. Religion finally severed the unity which all willed but none could trust. An heroic nation of monothesist sought to impose its faith on a vaguely pantheist world. For the first and last time the Second Men stumbled into a world-wide civil war; and just because the war was religious it developed a brutality hitherto unknown. With crude artillery, but with fanaticism, the two groups of citizen armies harried one another. The fields were laid waste, the cities burned, the rivers, and finally the winds, were poisoned. Long after that pitch of horror had been passed, at which an inferior species would have lost heart, these heroic madmen continued to organize destruction. And when at last the inevitable breakdown came, it was the more complete. In a sensitive species the devastating enlightenment which at last began to invade every mind, the overwhelming sense of treason against the human spirit, the tragic comicality of the whole struggle, sapped all energy. Not for thousands of years did the Second Men achieve once more a world-community. But they had learnt their lesson.

The third and most enduring civilization of the Second Men repeated the glorified mediævalism of the first, and passed beyond it into a phase of brilliant natural science. Chemical fertilizers increased the crops, and therefore the world population. Wind- and water-power was converted into electricity to supplement human and animal labour. At length, after many failures, it became possible to use volcanic and subterranean energy to drive dynamos. In a few years the whole physical character of civilization was transformed. Yet in this headlong passage into industrialism the Second Men escaped the errors of ancient Europe, America and Patagonia. This was due partly to their greater gift of sympathy, which, save during the one great aberration of the religious war, made them all in a very vivid manner members one of another. But partly also it was due to their combination of a practical common sense that was more than British, with a more than Russian immunity from the glamour of wealth, and a passion for the life of the mind that even Greece had never known. Mining and manufacture, even with plentiful electric power, were occupations scarcely less arduous than of old; but since each individual was implicated by vivid sympathy in the lives of all persons within his ken, there was little or no obsession with private economic power. The will to avoid industrial evils was effective, because sincere.

At its height, the culture of the Second Men was dominated by respect for the individual human personality. Yet contemporary individuals were regarded both as end and as means, as a stage toward far ampler individuals in the remote future. For, although they themselves were more long-lived than their predecessors, the Second Men were oppressed by the brevity of human life, and the pettiness of the individual's achievement in comparison with the infinity round about him which awaited apprehension and admiration. Therefore they were determined to produce a race endowed with much greater natural longevity. Again, though they participated in one another far more than their predecessors, they themselves were dogged by despair at the distortion and error which spoiled every mind's apprehension of others. Like their predecessors, they had passed through all the more naïve phases of self-consciousness and other-consciousness, and through idealizations of various modes of personality. They had admired the barbarian hero, the romantical, the sensitive-subtle, the bluff and hearty, the decadent, the bland, the severe. And they had concluded that each person, while being himself an expression of some one mode of personality, should seek to be also sensitive to every other mode. They even conceived that the ideal community should be knit into one mind by each unique individual's direct telepathic apprehension of the experience of all his fellows. And the fact that this ideal seemed utterly unattainable wove through their whole culture a thread of darkness, a yearning for spiritual union, a horror of loneliness, which never seriously troubled their far more insulated predecessors.

This craving for union influenced the sexual life of the species. In the first place, so closely was the mental related to the physiological in their composition, that when there was no true union of minds, the sexual act failed to give conception. Casual sexual relations thus came to be regarded very differently from those which expressed a deeper intimacy. They were treated as a delightful embroidery on life, affording opportunity of much elegance, light-hearted tenderness, banter, and of course physical inebriation; but they were deemed to signify nothing more than the delight of friend in friend. Where there was a marriage of minds, but then only during the actual passion of communion, sexual intercourse almost always resulted in conception. Under these circumstances, intimate persons had often to practise contraception, but acquaintances never. And one of the most beneficial inventions of the psychologists was a technique of auto-suggestion, which, at will, either facilitated conception, or prevented it, surely, harmlessly, and without inæsthetic accompaniments.

The sexual morality of the Second Men passed through all the phases known to the First Men; but by the time that they had established a single world-culture it had a form not known before. Not only were both men and women encouraged to have as much casual sexual intercourse as they needed for their enrichment, but also, on the higher plane of spiritual union, strict monogamy was deprecated. For in sexual union of this higher kind they saw a symbol of that communion of minds which they longed to make universal. Thus the most precious gift that a lover could bring to the beloved was not virginity but sexual experience. The union, it was felt, was the more pregnant the more each party could contribute from previous sexual and spiritual intimacy with others. Yet though as a prin-ciple monogamy was not applauded, the higher kind of union would in practice sometimes result in a life-long partnership. But since the average life was so much longer than among the First Men, such fortuitously peren-nial unions were often deliberately interrupted for a while, by a change of partners, and then restored with their vitality renewed. Sometimes, on the other hand, a group of persons of both sexes would maintain a com-posite and permanent marriage together. Sometimes such a group would exchange a member, or members, with another group, or disperse itself completely among other groups, to come together again years afterwards with enriched experience. In one form or another, this "marriage of groups" was much prized, as an extension of the vivid sexual participation into an ampler sphere. Among the First Men the brevity of life made these novel forms of union impossible; for obviously no sexual, and no spiritual, relation can be developed with any richness in less than thirty years of close intimacy. It would be interesting to examine the social institutions of the Second Men at their zenith; but we have not time to spare for this subject, nor even for the brilliant intellectual achievements in which the species so far outstripped its predecessor. Obviously any account of the natural science and the philosophy of the Second Men would be unintelli-gible to readers of this book. Suffice it that they avoided the errors which had led the First Men into false abstraction, and into metaphysical theories which were at once sophisticated and naïve.

Not until after they had passed beyond the best work of the First Men in science and philosophy did the Second Men discover the remains of the great stone library in Siberia. A party of engineers happened upon it while they were preparing to sink a shaft for subterranean energy. The tablets were broken, disordered, weathered. Little by little, however, they were reconstructed and interpreted, with the aid of the pictorial dictionary. The finds were of extreme interest to the Second Men, but not in the manner which the Siberian party had intended, not as a store of scientific and philosophic truth, but as a vivid historical document. The view of the universe which the tablets recorded was both too naïve and too artificial; but the insight which they afforded into the mind of the earlier species was invaluable. So little of the old world had survived the volcanic epoch that the Second Men had failed hitherto to get a clear picture of their predecessors.

One item alone in this archæological treasure had more than historical interest. The biologist leader of the little party in Siberia had recorded much of the sacred text of the Life of the Divine Boy. At the end of the record came the prophet's last words, which had so baffled Patagonia. This theme was full of meaning for the Second Men, as indeed it would have been even for the First Men in their prime. But whereas for the First Men the dispassionate ecstasy which the Boy had preached was rather an ideal than a fact of experience, the Second Men recognized in the prophet's words an intuition familiar to themselves. Long ago the tortured geniuses of the Yang-tze cities had expressed this same intuition. Subsequently also it had often been experienced by the more healthy generations, but always with a certain shame. For it had become associated with morbid mentality. But now with growing conviction that it was wholesome, the Second Men had begun to grope for a wholesome expression of it. In the life and the last words of the remote apostle of youth they found an expression which was not wholly inadequate. The species was presently to be in sore need of this gospel.

The world-community reached at length a certain relative perfection and equilibrium. There was a long summer of social harmony, prosperity, and cultural embellishment. Almost all that could be done by mind in the stage to which it had then reached seemed to have been done. Generations of long-lived, eager, and mutually delightful beings succeeded one another. There was a widespread feeling that the time had come for man to gather all his strength for a flight into some new sphere of mentality. The present type of human being, it was recognized, was but a rough and incoherent natural product. It was time for man to take control of himself and remake himself upon a nobler pattern. With this end in view, two great works were set afoot, research into the ideal of human nature, and research into practical means of remaking human nature. Individuals in all lands, living their private lives, delighting in each other, keeping the tissue of society alive and vigorous, were deeply moved by the thought that their world community was at last engaged upon this heroic task.

But elsewhere in the solar system life of a very different kind was seeking, in its own strange manner, ends incomprehensible to man, yet at bottom identical with his own ends. And presently the two were to come together, not in co-operation.

CHAPTER VIII

THE MARTIANS

I. THE FIRST MARTIAN INVASION

UPON the foot-hills of the new and titanic mountains that were once the Hindu Kush, were many holiday centres, whence the young men and women of Asia were wont to seek Alpine dangers and hardships for their souls' refreshment. It was in this district, and shortly after a summer dawn, that the Martians were first seen by men. Early walkers noticed that the sky had an unaccountably greenish tinge, and that the climbing sun, though free from cloud, was wan. Observers were presently surprised to see the green concentrate itself into a thousand tiny cloudlets, with clear blue between. Field-glasses revealed within each fleck of green some faint hint of a ruddy nucleus, and shifting strands of an infra-red colour, which would have been invisible to the earlier human race. These extraordinary specks of cloud were all of about the same size, the largest of them appearing smaller than the moon's disk; but in form they varied greatly, and were seen to be changing their shapes more rapidly than the natural cirrus which they slightly resembled. In fact, though there was much that was cloudlike in their form and motion, there was also something definite about them, both in their features and behaviour, which suggested life. Indeed they were strongly reminiscent of primitive amœboid organisms seen through a microscope.

The whole sky was strewn with them, here and there in concentrations of unbroken green, elsewhere more sparsely. And they were observed to be moving. A general drift of the whole celestial population was setting toward one of the snowy peaks that dominated the landscape. Presently the foremost individuals reached the mountain's crest, and were seen to be creeping down the rock-face with a very slow amœboid action.

Meanwhile a couple of aeroplanes, electrically driven, had climbed the sky to investigate the strange phenomenon at close quarters. They passed among the drifting cloudlets, and actually through many of them, without hindrance, and almost without being obscured from view.

On the mountain a vast swarm of the cloudlets was collecting, and creeping down the precipices and snow-fields into a high glacier valley. At a certain point, where the glacier dropped steeply to a lower level, the advance guard slowed down and stopped, while hosts of their fellows continued to pack in on them from behind. In half an hour the whole sky was once more clear, save for normal clouds; but upon the glacier lay what might almost have been an exceptionally dark solid-looking thunder-cloud, save for its green tinge and seething motion. For some minutes this strange object was seen to concentrate itself into a somewhat smaller bulk and become darker. Then it moved forward again, and passed over the cliffy end of the glacier into the pine-clad valley. An intervening ridge now hid it from its first observers.

Lower down the valley there was a village. Many of the inhabitants, when they saw the mysterious dense fume advancing upon them, took to their mechanical vehicles and fled; but some waited out of curiosity. They were swallowed up in a murky olive-brown fog, shot here and there with queer shimmering streaks of a ruddier tint. Presently there was complete darkness. Artificial lights were blotted out almost at arm's length. Breathing became difficult. Throats and lungs were irritated. Every one was seized with a violent attack of sneezing and coughing. The cloud streamed through the village, and seemed to exercise irregular pressures upon objects, not always in the general direction of movement but sometimes in the opposite direction, as though it were getting a purchase upon human bodies and walls, and actually elbowing its way along. Within a few minutes the fog lightened; and presently it left the village behind it, save for a few strands and whiffs of its smoke-like substance, which had become entangled in side-streets and isolated. Very soon, however, these seemed to get themselves clear and hurry to overtake the main body.

When the gasping villagers had somewhat recovered, they sent a radio message to the little town lower down the valley, urging temporary evacuation. The message was not broadcast, but transmitted on a slender beam of rays. It so happened that the beam had to be directed through the noxious matter itself. While the message was being given, the cloud's progress ceased, and its outlines became vague and ragged. Fragments of it actually drifted away on the winds and dissipated themselves. Almost as soon as the message was completed, the cloud began to define itself again, and lay for a quarter of an hour at rest. A dozen bold young men from the town now approached the dark mass out of curiosity. No sooner did they come face to face with it, round a bend in the valley, than the cloud rapidly contracted, till it was no bigger than a house. Looking now something between a dense, opaque fume and an actual jelly, it lay still until the party had ventured within a few yards. Evidently their courage failed, for they were seen to turn. But before they had retreated three paces, a long proboscis shot out of the main mass with the speed of a chameleon's tongue, and enveloped them. Slowly it withdrew; but the young men had been gathered in with it. The cloud, or jelly, churned itself violently for some seconds, then ejected the bodies in a single chewed lump.

The murderous thing now elbowed itself along the road toward the town, leaned against the first house, crushed it, and proceeded to wander hither and thither, pushing everything down before it, as though it were a lava-stream. The inhabitants took to their heels, but several were licked up and slaughtered.

Powerful beam radiation was now poured into the cloud from all the neighbouring installations. Its destructive activity slackened, and once more it began to disintegrate and expand. Presently it streamed upwards as a huge column of smoke; and, at a great altitude, it dissipated itself again into a swarm of the original green cloudlets, noticeably reduced in numbers. These again faded into a uniform greenish tinge, which gradually vanished.

Thus ended the first invasion of the Earth from Mars.

2. LIFE ON MARS

Our concern is with humanity, and with the Martians only in relation to men. But in order to understand the tragic intercourse of the two planets, it is necessary to glance at conditions on Mars, and conceive something of those fantastically different yet fundamentally similar beings, who were now seeking to possess man's home.

To describe the biology, psychology and history of a whole world in a few pages is as difficult as it would be to give the Martians themselves in the same compass a true idea of man. Encyclopædias, libraries, would be needed in either case. Yet, somehow, I must contrive to suggest the alien sufferings and delights, and the many aeons of struggle, which went to the making of these strange nonhuman intelligences, in some ways so inferior yet in others definitely superior to the human species which they encountered.

Mars was a world whose mass was about one-tenth that of the earth. Gravity therefore had played a less tyrannical part in Martian than in terrestrial history. The weakness of Martian gravity combined with the paucity of the planet's air envelope to make the general atmospheric pressure far lighter than on earth. Oxygen was far less plentiful. Water also was comparatively rare. There were no oceans or seas, but only shallow lakes and marshes, many of which dried up in summer. The climate of the planet was in general very dry, and yet very cold. Being without cloud, it was perennially bright with the feeble rays of a distant sun.

Earlier in the history of Mars, when there were more air, more water, and a higher temperature from internal heat, life had appeared in the coastal waters of the seas, and evolution had proceeded in much the same manner as on earth. Primitive life was differentiated into the fundamental animal and vegetable types. Multicellular structures appeared, and specialized themselves in diverse manners to suit diverse environments. A great variety of plant forms clothed the lands, often with forests of gigantic and slender-stemmed plumes. Mollusc-like and insect-like animals crept or swam, or shot themselves hither and thither in fantastic jumps. Huge spidery creatures of a type not wholly unlike crustaceans, or gigantic grasshoppers, bounded after their prey, and developed a versatility and cunning which enabled them to dominate the planet almost as, at a much later date, early man was to dominate the terrestrial wild.

But meanwhile a rapid loss of atmosphere, and especially of water-vapor, was changing Martian conditions beyond the limits of adaptability of this early fauna and flora. At the same time a very different kind of vital organization was beginning to profit by the change. On Mars, as on the Earth, life had arisen from one of many "subvital" forms. The new type of life on Mars evolved from another of these subvital kinds of molecular organization, one which had hitherto failed to evolve at all, and had played an insignificant part, save occasionally as a rare virus in the respiratory organs of animals. These fundamental subvital units of organization were ultra-microscopic, and indeed far smaller than the terrestrial bacteria, or even the terrestrial viruses. They originally occurred in the marshy ponds, which dried up every spring, and became depressions of baked mud and dust. Certain of their species, borne into the air upon dust particles, developed an extremely dry habit of life. They maintained themselves by absorbing chemicals from the wind-borne dust, and a very slight amount of moisture from the air. Also they absorbed sunlight by a photo-synthesis almost identical with that of the plants.

To this extent they were similar to the other living things, but they had also certain capacities which the other stock had lost at the very outset of its evolutionary career. Terrestrial organisms, and Martian organisms of the terrestrial type, maintained themselves as vital unities by means of nervous systems, or other forms of material contact between parts. In the most developed forms, an immensely complicated neural "telephone" system connected every part of the body with a vast central exchange, the brain. Thus on the earth a single organism was without exception a continuous system of matter, which maintained a certain constancy of form. But from the distinctively Martian subvital unit there evolved at length a very different kind of complex organism, in which material contact of parts was not necessary either to coordination of behaviour or unity of consciousness. These ends were achieved upon a very different physical basis. The ultra-microscopic subvital members were sensitive to all kinds of etherial vibrations, directly sensitive, in a manner impossible to terrestrial life; and they could also initiate vibrations. Upon this basis Martian life developed at length the capacity of maintaining vital organization as a single conscious individual without continuity of living matter. Thus the typical Martian organism was a cloudlet, a group of free-moving members dominated by a "group-mind." But in one species individuality came to inhere, for certain purposes, not in distinct cloudlets only, but in a great fluid system of cloudlets. Such was the single-minded Martian host which invaded the Earth.

The Martian organism depended, so to speak, not on "telephone" wires, but on an immense crowd of mobile "wireless stations," transmitting and receiving different wave-lengths according to their function. The radiation of a single unit was of course very feeble; but a great system of units could maintain contact with its wandering parts over a considerable distance.

One other important characteristic distinguished the dominant form of life on Mars. Just as a cell, in the terrestrial form of life, has often the power of altering its shape (whence the whole mechanism of muscular activity), so in the Martian form the free-floating ultra-microscopic unit might be specialized for generating around itself a magnetic field, and so either repelling or attracting its neighbours. Thus a system of materially disconnected units had a certain cohesion. Its consistency was something between a smoke-cloud and a very tenuous jelly. It had a definite, though ever-changing contour and resistant surface. By massed mutual repulsions of its constituent units it could exercise pressure on surrounding objects; and in its most concentrated form the Martian cloud-jelly could bring to bear immense forces which could also be controlled for very delicate manipulation. Magnetic forces were also responsible for the mollusc-like motion of the cloud as a whole over the ground, and again for the transport of lifeless material and living units from region to region within the cloud.

The magnetic field of repulsion and attraction generated by a subvital unit was much more restricted than its field of "wireless" communication. Similarly with organized systems of units. Thus each of the cloudlets which the Second Men saw in their sky was an independent motor unit; but also it was in a kind of "telepathic" communication with all its fellows. Indeed in every public enterprise, such as the terrestrial campaigns, almost perfect unity of consciousness was maintained within the limits of a huge field of radiation. Yet only when the whole population concentrated itself into a small and relatively dense cloud-jelly, did it become a single magnetic motor unit. The Martians, it should be noted, had three possible forms, or formations, namely: first, an "open order" of independent and very tenuous cloudlets in "telepathic" communication, and often in strict unity as a group mind; second, a more concentrated and less vulnerable corporate cloud; and third, an extremely concentrated and formidable cloud-jelly.

Save for these very remarkable characteristics, there was no really fundamental difference between the distinctively Martian and the distinctively terrestrial forms of life. The chemical basis of the former was somewhat more complicated than that of the latter; and selenium played a part in it, to which nothing corresponded in terrestrial life. The Martian organism, moreover, was unique in that it fulfilled within itself the functions of both animal and vegetable. But, save for these peculiarities, the two types of life were biochemically much the same. Both needed material from the ground, both needed sunlight. Each lived in the chemical changes occurring in its own "flesh." Each, of course, tended to maintain itself as an organic unity. There was a certain difference, indeed, in respect of reproduction; for the Martian subvital units retained the power of growth and sub-division. Thus the birth of a Martian cloud arose from the sub-division of myriads of units within the parent cloud, followed by their ejection as a new individual. And, as the units were highly specialized for different functions, representatives of many types had to pass into the new cloud.

In the earliest stages of evolution on Mars the units had become independent of each other as soon as they parted in reproduction. But later the hitherto useless and rudimentary power of emitting radiation was specialized, so that, after reproduction, free individuals came to maintain radiant contact with one another, and to behave with ever-increasing coordination. Still later, these organized groups themselves maintained radiant contact with groups of their offspring, thus constituting larger individuals with specialized members. With each advance in complexity the sphere of radiant influence increased; until, at the zenith of Martian evolution, the whole planet (save for the remaining animal and vegetable representatives of the other and unsuccessful kind of life) constituted sometimes a single biological and psychological individual. But this occurred as a rule only in respect of matters which concerned the species as a whole. At most times the Martian individual was a cloudlet, such as those which first astonished the Second Men. But in great public crises each cloudlet would suddenly wake up to find himself the mind of the whole race, sensing through many individuals, and interpreting his sensations in the light of the experience of the whole race.

The life which dominated Mars was thus something between an extremely well-disciplined army of specialized units, and a body possessed by one mind. Like an army, it could take any form without destroying its organic unity. Like an army it was sometimes a crowd of free-wandering units, yet at other times also it disposed itself in very special orders to fulfil special functions. Like an army it was composed of free, experiencing individuals who voluntarily submitted themselves to discipline. On the other hand, unlike an army, it woke occasionally into unified consciousness.

The same fluctuation between individuality and multiplicity which characterized the race as a whole, characterized also each of the cloudlets themselves. Each was sometimes an individual, sometimes a swarm of more primitive individuals. But while the race rather seldom rose to full individuality, the cloudlets declined from it only in very special circumstances. Each cloudlet was an organization of specialized groups formed of minor specialized groups, which in turn were composed of the fundamental specialized varieties of subvital units. Each free-roving group of free-roving units constituted a special organ, fulfilling some particular function in the whole. Thus some were specialized for attraction and repulsion, some for chemical operations, some for storing the sun's energy, some for emitting radiation, some for absorbing and storing water, some for special sensitivities, such as awareness of mechanical pressure and vibration, or temperature changes, or light rays. Others again were specialized to fulfil the function of the brain of man; but in a peculiar manner. The whole volume of the cloudlet vibrated with innumerable "wireless" messages in very many wave-lengths from the different "organs." It was the function of the "brain" units to receive, and correlate, and interpret these messages in the light of past experience, and to initiate responses in the wave-lengths appropriate to the organs concerned.

All these subvital units, save a few types that were too highly specialized, were capable of independent life as air-borne bacteria or viruses. And whenever they lost touch with the radiation of the whole system, they continued to live their own simple lives until they were once more controlled. All were free-floating units, but normally they were under the influence of the cloudlet's system of electro-magnetic fields, and were directed hither and thither for their special functions. And under this influence some of them might be held rigidly in position in relation to one another. Such was the case of the organs of sight. In early stages of evolution, some of the units had specialized for carrying minute globules of water. Later, much larger droplets were carried, millions of units holding between them a still microscopic globule of life's most precious fluid. Ultimately this function was turned to good account in vision. Aqueous lenses as large as the eye of an ox, were supported by a scaffolding of units; while, at focal length from the lens, a rigid retina of units was held in position. Thus the Martian could produce eyes of every variety whenever he wanted them, and telescopes and microscopes too. This production and manipulation of visual organs was of course largely subconscious, like the focussing mechanism in man. But latterly the Martians had greatly increased their conscious control of physiological processes; and it was this achievement which facilitated their remarkable optical triumphs.

One other physiological function we must note before considering the Martian psychology. The fully evolved, but as yet uncivilized, Martian had long ago ceased to depend for his chemicals on wind-borne volcanic dust. Instead, he rested at night on the ground, like a knee-high mist on terrestrial meadows, and projected specialized tubular groups of units into the soil, like rootlets. Part of the day also had to be occupied in this manner. Somewhat later this process was supplemented by devouring the declining plant-life of the planet. But the final civilized Martians had greatly improved their methods of exploiting the ground and the sunlight, both by mechanical means and by artificial specialization of their own organs. Even so, however, as their activities increased, these vegetable functions became an ever more serious problem for them. They practised agriculture; but only a very small area of the arid planet could be induced to bear. It was terrestrial water and terrestrial vegetation that finally determined them to make the great voyage.

3. THE MARTIAN MIND

The Martian mind was of a very different type from the terrestrial,—different, yet at bottom identical. In so strange a body, the mind was inevitably equipped with alien cravings, and alien manners of apprehending its environment. And with so different a history, it was confused by prejudices very unlike those of man. Yet it was none the less mind, concerned in the last resort with the maintenance and advancement of life, and the exercise of vital capacities. Fundamentally the Martian was like all other living beings, in that he delighted in the free working of his body and his mind. Yet superficially, he was as unlike man in mind as in body.

The most distinctive feature of the Martian, compared with man, was that his individuality was both far more liable to disruption, and at the same time immeasurably more capable of direct participation in the minds of other individuals. The human mind in its solid body maintained its unity and its dominance over its members in all normal circumstances. Only in disease was man liable to mental or physical dissociation. On the other hand, he was incapable of direct contact with other individuals, and the emergence of a "super-mind" in a group of individuals was quite impossible. The Martian cloudlet, however, though he fell to pieces physically, and also mentally, far more readily than a man, might also at any moment wake up to be the intelligent mind of his race, might begin to perceive with the sense-organs of all other individuals, and experience thoughts and desires which were, so to speak, the resultant of all individual thoughts and desires upon some matter of general interest. But unfortunately, as I shall tell, the common mind of the Martians never woke into any order of mentality higher than that of the individual.

These differences between the Martian and the human psyche entailed characteristic advantages and disadvantages. The Martian, immune from man's inveterate selfishness and spiritual isolation from his fellows, lacked the mental coherence, the concentrated attention and far-reaching analysis and synthesis, and again the vivid self-consciousness and relentless self-criticism, which even the First Men, at their best, had attained in some degree, and which in the Second Men were still more developed. The Martians, moreover, were hampered by being almost identical in character. They possessed perfect harmony; but only through being almost wholly in temperamental unison. They were all hobbled by their sameness to one another. They were without that rich diversity of personal character, which enabled the human spirit to cover so wide a field of mentality. This infinite variety of human nature entailed, indeed, endless wasteful and cruel personal conflicts in the first, and even to some extent in the second, species of man; but also it enabled every individual of developed sympathy to enrich his spirit by intercourse with individuals whose temperament, thought and ideals differed from his own. And while the Martians were little troubled by internecine strife and the passion of hate, they were also almost wholly devoid of the passion of love. The Martian individual could admire, and be utterly faithful to, the object of his loyalty; but his admiration was given, not to concrete and uniquely charactered persons of the same order as himself, but at best to the vaguely conceived "spirit of the race." Individuals like himself he regarded merely as instruments or organs of the "supermind."

This would not have been amiss, had the mind of the race, into which he so frequently awoke under the influence of the general radiation, been indeed a mind of higher rank than his own. But it was not. It was but a pooling of the percipience and thought and will of the cloudlets. Thus it was that the superb loyalty of the Martians was squandered upon something which was not greater than themselves in mental calibre, but only in mere bulk.

The Martian cloudlet, like the human animal, had a complex instinctive nature. By night and day, respectively, he was impelled to perform the vegetative functions of absorbing chemicals from the ground and energy from the sunlight. Air and water he also craved, though he dealt with them, of course, in his own manner. He had also his own characteristic instinctive impulses to move his "body," both for locomotion and manipulation. Martian civilization provided an outlet for these cravings, both in the practice of agriculture and in intricate and wonderfully beautiful cloud-dances and gymnastics. For these perfectly supple beings rejoiced in executing aerial evolutions, flinging out wild rhythmical streamers, intertwining with one another in spirals, concentrating into opaque spheres, cubes, cones, and all sorts of fantastical volumes. Many of these movements and shapes had intense emotional significance for them in relation to the operations of their life, and were executed with a religious fervour and solemnity.

The Martian had also his impulses of fear and pugnacity. In the remote past these had often been directed against hostile members of his own species; but since the race had become unified, they found exercise only upon other types of life and upon inanimate nature. Instinctive gregariousness was, of course, extremely developed in the Martian at the expense of instinctive self-assertion. Sexuality the Martian had not; there were no partners in reproduction. But his impulse to merge physically and mentally with other individuals, and wake up as the super-mind, had in it much that was characteristic of sex in man. Parental impulses, of a kind, he knew; but they were scarcely worthy of the name. He cared only to eject excessive living matter from his system, and to keep *en rapport* with the new individual thus formed, as he would with any other individual. He knew no more of the human devotion to children as budding personalities than of the subtle intercourse of male and female temperaments. By the time of the first invasion, however, reproduction had been greatly restricted; for the planet was fully populated, and each individual cloudlet was potentially immortal. Among the Martians there was no "natural death," no spontaneous death through mere senility. Normally the cloudlet's members kept themselves in repair indefinitely by the reproduction of their constituent units. Diseases, indeed, were often fatal. And chief among them was a plague, corresponding to terrestrial cancer, in which the subvital units lost their sensitivity to radiation, so that they proceeded to live as primitive organisms and reproduced without restraint. As they also became parasitic on the unaffected units, the cloudlet inevitably died.

Like the higher kinds of terrestrial mammal, the Martians had strong impulses of curiosity. Having also many practical needs to fulfil as a result of their civilization, and being extremely well equipped by nature for physical experiment and microscopy, they had gone far in the natural sciences. In physics, astronomy, chemistry and even in the chemistry of life, man had nothing to teach them.

The vast corpus of Martian knowledge had taken many thousands of years to grow. All its stages, and its current achievements were recorded on immense scrolls of paper made from vegetable pulp, and stored in libraries of stone. For the Martians, curiously enough, had become great masons, and had covered much of their planet with buildings of feathery and toppling design, such as would have been quite impossible on earth. They had no need of buildings for habitation, save in the arctic regions; but as workshops, granaries, and store rooms of all sorts, buildings had become very necessary to the Martians. Moreover these extremely tenuous creatures took a peculiar joy in manipulating solids. Even their most utilitarian architecture blossomed with a sort of gothic or arabesque ornateness and fantasy, wherein the ethereal seemed to torture the substance of solid rocks into its own likeness.

At the time of the invasion, the Martians were still advancing intellectually; and, indeed, it was through an achievement in theoretical physics that they were able to leave their planet. They had long known that minute particles at the upper limit of the atmosphere might be borne into space by the pressure of the sun's rays at dawn and sunset. And at length they discovered how to use this pressure as the wind is used in sailing. Dissipating themselves into their ultra-microscopic units, they contrived to get a purchase on the gravitational fields of the solar system, as a boat's keel and rudder get a purchase on the water. Thus they were able to tack across to the earth as an armada of ultra-microscopic vessels. Arrived in the terrestrial sky, they re-formed themselves as cloudlets, swam through the dense air to the alpine summit, and climbed downwards, as a swimmer may climb down a ladder under water.

This achievement involved very intricate calculations and chemical inventions, especially for the preservation of life in transit and on an alien planet. It could never have been done save by beings with far-reaching and accurate knowledge of the physical world. But though in respect of "natural knowledge" the Martians were so well advanced, they were extremely backward in all those spheres which may be called "spiritual knowledge." They had little understanding of their own mentality, and less of the place of mind in the cosmos. Though in a sense a highly intelligent species, they were at the same time wholly lacking in philosophical interest. They scarcely conceived, still less tackled, the problems which even the First Men had faced so often, though so vainly. For the Martians there was no mystery in the distinction between reality and appearance or in the relation of the one and the many, or in the status of good and evil. Nor were they ever critical of their own ideals. They aimed whole-heartedly at the advancement of the Martian super-individual. But what should constitute individuality, and its advancement, they never seriously considered. And the idea that they were under obligation also toward beings not included in the Martian system of radiation, proved wholly beyond them. For, though so clever, they were the most naïve of self-deceivers, and had no insight to see what it is that is truly desirable.

4. DELUSIONS OF THE MARTIANS

To understand how the Martians tricked themselves, and how they were finally undone by their own insane will, we must glance at their history.

The civilized Martians constituted the sole remaining variety of a species. That species itself, in the remote past, had competed with, and exterminated, many other species of the same general type. Aided by the changing climate, it had also exterminated almost all the species of the more terrestrial kind of fauna, and had thereby much reduced the vegetation which it was subsequently to need and foster so carefully. This victory of the species had been due partly to its versatility and intelligence, partly to a remarkable zest in ferocity, partly to its unique powers of radiation and sensitivity to radiation, which enabled it to act with a co-ordination impossible even to the most gregarious of animals. But, as with other species in biological history, the capacity by which it triumphed became at length a source of weakness. When the species reached a stage corresponding to primitive human culture, one of its races, achieving a still higher degree of radiant intercourse and physical unity, was able to behave as a single vital unit; and so it succeeded in exterminating all its rivals. Racial conflict had persisted for many thousands of years, but as soon as the favoured race had developed this almost absolute solidarity of will, its victory was sweeping, and was clinched by joyous massacre of the enemy.

But ever afterwards the Martians suffered from the psychological effects of their victory at the close of the epoch of racial wars. The extreme brutality with which the other races had been exterminated conflicted with the generous impulses which civilization had begun to foster, and left a scar upon the conscience of the victors. In self-defence they persuaded themselves that since they were so much more admirable than the rest, the extermination was actually a sacred duty. And their unique value, they said, consisted in their unique radiational development. Hence arose a gravely insincere tradition and culture, which finally ruined the species. They had long believed that the physical basis of consciousness must necessarily be a system of units directly sensitive to ethereal vibrations, and that organisms dependent on the physical contact of their parts were too gross to have any experience whatever. After the age of the racial massacres they sought to persuade themselves that the excellence, or ethical worth, of any organism depended upon the degree of complexity and unity of its radiation. Century by century they strengthened their faith in this vulgar doctrine, and developed also a system of quite irrational delusions and obsessions based upon an obsessive and passionate lust in radiation.

It would take too long to tell of all these subsidiary fantasies, and of the ingenious ways in which they were reconciled with the main body of sane knowledge. But one at least must be mentioned, because of the part it played in the struggle with man. The Martians knew, of course, that "solid matter" was solid by virtue of the interlocking of the minute electromagnetic systems called atoms. Now rigidity had for them somewhat the same significance and prestige that air, breath, spirit, had for early man. It was in the quasi-solid form that Martians were physically most potent; and the maintenance of this form was exhausting and difficult. These facts combined in the Martian consciousness with the knowledge that rigidity was after all the outcome of interlocked electro-magnetic systems. Rigidity was thus endowed with a peculiar sanctity. The superstition was gradually consolidated, by a series of psychological accidents, into a fanatical admiration of all very rigid materials, but especially of hard crystals, and above all of diamonds. For diamonds were extravagantly resistant; and at the same time, as the Martians themselves put it, diamonds were superb jugglers with the ethereal radiation called light. Every diamond was therefore a supreme embodiment of the tense energy and eternal equilibrium of the cosmos, and must be treated with reverence. In Mars, all known diamonds were exposed to sunlight on the pinnacles of sacred buildings; and the thought that on the neighbour planet might be diamonds which were not properly treated, was one motive of the invasion.

Thus did the Martian mind, unwittingly side-tracked from its true development, fall sick, and strive ever more fanatically toward mere phantoms of its goal. In the early stages of the disorder, radiation was merely regarded as an infallible *sign* of mentality, and radiative complexity was taken as an infallible *measure,* merely, of spiritual worth. But little by little, radiation and mentality failed to be distinguished, and radiative organization was actually mistaken for spiritual worth.

In this obsession the Martians resembled somewhat the First Men during their degenerate phase of servitude to the idea of movement; but with a difference. For the Martian intelligence was still active, though its products were severely censored in the name of the "spirit of the race." Every Martian was a case of dual personality. Not merely was he sometimes a private consciousness, sometimes the consciousness of the race, but further, even as a private individual he was in a manner divided against himself. Though his practical allegiance to the super-individual was absolute, so that he condemned or ignored all thoughts and impulses that could not be assimilated to the public consciousness, he did in fact have such thoughts and impulses, as it were in the deepest recesses of his being. He very seldom noticed that he was having them, and whenever he did notice it, he was shocked and terrified; yet he did have them. They constituted an intermittent, sometimes almost a continuous, critical commentary on all his more reputable experience.

This was the great tragedy of the spirit on Mars. The Martians were in many ways extremely well equipped for mental progress and for true spiritual adventure, but through a trick of fortune which had persuaded them to prize above all else unity and uniformity, they were driven to thwart their own struggling spirits at every turn.

Far from being superior to the private mind, the public mind which obsessed every Martian was in many ways actually inferior. It had come into dominance in a crisis which demanded severe military co-ordination; and though, since that remote age, it had made great intellectual progress, it remained at heart a military mind. Its disposition was something between that of a field-marshal and the God of the ancient Hebrews. A certain English philosopher once described and praised the fictitious corporate personality of the state, and named it "Leviathan." The Martian super-individual was Leviathan endowed with consciousness. In this consciousness there was nothing but what was easily assimilated and in accord with tradition. Thus the public mind was always intellectually and culturally behind the times. Only in respect of practical social organization did it keep abreast of its own individuals. Intellectual progress had always been initiated by private individuals, and had only penetrated the public mind when the mass of individuals had been privately infected by intercourse with the pioneers. The public consciousness itself initiated progress only in the sphere of social, military, and economic organization.

The novel circumstances which were encountered on the earth put the mentality of the Martians to a supreme test. For the unique enterprise of tackling a new world demanded the extremes of both public and private activity, and so led to agonizing conflicts within each private mind.

For, while the undertaking was essentially social and even military, and necessitated very strict co-ordination and unity of action, the extreme novelty of the new environment demanded all the resources of the untrammelled private consciousness. Moreover the Martians encountered much on the earth which made nonsense of their fundamental assumptions. And in their brightest moments of private consciousness they sometimes recognized this fact.

CHAPTER IX

EARTH AND MARS

1. THE SECOND MEN AT BAY

SUCH were the beings that invaded the earth when the Second Men were gathering their strength for a great venture in artificial evolution. The motives of the invasion were both economic and religious. The Martians sought water and vegetable matter; but they came also in a crusading spirit, to "liberate" the terrestrial diamonds.

Conditions on the earth were very unfavourable to the invaders. Excessive gravitation troubled them less than might have been expected. Only in their most concentrated form did they find it oppressive. More harmful was the density of the terrestrial atmosphere, which constricted the tenuous animate cloudlets very painfully, hindering their vital processes, and deadening all their movements. In their native atmosphere they swam hither and thither with ease and considerable speed; but the treacly air of the earth hampered them as a bird's wings are hampered under water. Moreover, owing to their extreme buoyancy as individual cloudlets, they were scarcely able to dive down so far as the mountain-tops. Excessive oxygen was also a source of distress; it tended to put them into a violent fever, which they had only been able to guard against very imperfectly. Even more damaging was the excessive moisture of the atmosphere, both through its solvent effect upon certain factors in the subvital units, and because heavy rain interfered with the physiological processes of the cloudlets and washed many of their materials to the ground.

The invaders had also to cope with the tissue of "radio" messages that constantly enveloped the planet, and tended to interfere with their own organic systems of radiation. They were prepared for this to some extent; but "beam wireless" at close range surprised, bewildered, tortured, and finally routed them; so that they fled back to Mars, leaving many of their number disintegrated in the terrestrial air.

But the pioneering army (or individual, for throughout the adventure it maintained unity of consciousness) had much to report at home. As was expected, there was rich vegetation, and water was even too abundant. There were solid animals, of the type of the prehistoric Martian fauna, but mostly two-legged and erect. Experiment had shown that these creatures died when they were pulled to pieces, and that though the sun's rays affected them by setting up chemical action in their visual organs, they had no really direct sensitivity to radiation. Obviously, therefore, they must be unconscious. On the other hand, the terrestrial atmosphere was permanently alive with radiation of a violent and incoherent type. It was still uncertain whether these crude ethereal agitations were natural phenomena, mere careless offshoots of the cosmic mind, or whether they were emitted by a terrestrial organism. There was reason to suppose this last to be the case, and that the solid organisms were used by some hidden terrestrial intelligence as instruments; for there were buildings, and many of the bipeds were found within the buildings. Moreover, the sudden violent concentration of beam radiation upon the Martian cloud suggested purposeful and hostile behaviour. Punitive action had therefore been taken, and many buildings and bipeds had been destroyed. The physical basis of such a terrestrial intelligence was still to be discovered. It was certainly not in the terrestrial clouds, for these had turned out to be insensitive to radiation. Anyhow, it was obviously an intelligence of very low order, for its radiation was scarcely at all systematic, and was indeed excessively crude. One or two unfortunate diamonds had been found in a building. There was no sign that they were properly venerated.

The Terrestrials, on their side, were left in complete bewilderment by the extraordinary events of that day. Some had jokingly suggested that since the strange substance had behaved in a manner obviously vindictive, it must have been alive and conscious; but no one took the suggestion seriously. Clearly, however, the thing had been dissipated by beam radiation. That at least was an important piece of practical knowledge. But theoretical knowledge about the real nature of the clouds, and their place in the order of the universe, was for the present wholly lacking. To a race of strong cognitive interest and splendid scientific achievement, this ignorance was violently disturbing. It seemed to shake the foundations of the great structure of knowledge. Many frankly hoped, in spite of the loss of life in the first invasion, that there would soon be another opportunity for studying these amazing objects, which were not quite gaseous and not quite solid, not (apparently) organic, yet capable of behaving in a manner suggestive of life. An opportunity was soon afforded.

Some years after the first invasion the Martians appeared again, and in far greater force. This time, moreover, they were almost immune from man's offensive radiation. Operating simultaneously from all the alpine regions of the earth, they began to dry up the great rivers at their sources; and, venturing further afield, they spread over jungle and agricultural land, and stripped off every leaf. Valley after valley was devastated as though by endless swarms of locusts, so that in whole countries there was not a green blade left. The booty was carried off to Mars. Myriads of the subvital units, specialized for transport of water and food materials, were loaded each with a few molecules of the treasure, and dispatched to the home planet. The traffic continued indefinitely. Meanwhile the main body of the Martians proceeded to explore and loot. They were irresistible. For the absorption of water and leafage, they spread over the countryside as an impalpable mist which man had no means to dispel. For the destruction of civilization, they became armies of gigantic cloud-jellies, far bigger than the brute which had formed itself during the earlier invasion. Cities were knocked down and flattened, human beings masticated into pulp. Man tried weapon after weapon in vain.

Presently the Martians discovered the sources of terrestrial radiation in the innumerable wireless transmitting stations. Here at last was the physical basis of the terrestrial intelligence! But what a lowly creature! What a caricature of life! Obviously in respect of complexity and delicacy of organization these wretched immobile systems of glass, metal and vegetable compounds were not to be compared with the Martian cloud. Their only feat seemed to be that they had managed to get control of the unconscious bipeds who tended them.

In the course of their explorations the Martians also discovered a few more diamonds. The second human species had outgrown the barbaric lust for jewellery; but they recognized the beauty of gems and precious metals, and used them as badges of office. Unfortunately, the Martians, in sacking a town, came upon a woman who was wearing a large diamond between her breasts; for she was mayor of the town, and in charge of the evacuation. That the sacred stone should be used thus, apparently for the mere identification of cattle, shocked the invaders even more than the discovery of fragments of diamonds in certain cutting-instruments. The war now began to be waged with all the heroism and brutality of a crusade. Long after a rich booty of water and vegetable matter had been secured, long after the Terrestrials had developed an effective means of attack, and were slaughtering the Martian clouds with high-tension electricity in the form of artificial lightning flashes, the misguided fanatics stayed on to rescue the diamonds and carry them away to the mountain tops, where, years afterwards, climbers discovered them, arranged along the rock-edges in glittering files, like seabird's eggs. Thither the dying remnant of the Martian host had transported them with its last strength, scorning to save itself before the diamonds were borne into the pure mountain air, to be lodged with dignity. When the Second Men learned of this great hoard of diamonds, they began to be seriously persuaded that they had been dealing, not with a freak of physical nature, nor yet (as some said) with swarms of bacteria, but with organisms of a higher order. For how could the jewels have been singled out, freed from their metallic settings, and so carefully regimented on the rocks, save by conscious purpose? The murderous clouds must have had at least the pilfering mentality of jackdaws, since evidently they had been fascinated by the treasure. But the very action which revealed their consciousness suggested also that they were no more intelligent than the merely instinctive animals. There was no opportunity of correcting this error, since all the clouds had been destroyed.

The struggle had lasted only a few months. Its material effects on Man were serious but not insurmountable. Its immediate psychological effect was invigorating. The Second Men had long been accustomed to a security and prosperity that were almost utopian. Suddenly they were overwhelmed by a calamity which was quite unintelligible in terms of their own systematic knowledge. Their predecessors, in such a situation, would have behaved with their own characteristic vacillation between the human and the subhuman. They would have contracted a fever of romantic loyalty, and have performed many random acts of secretly self-regarding self-sacrifice. They would have sought profit out of the public disaster, and howled at all who were more fortunate than themselves. They would have cursed their gods, and looked for more useful ones. But also, in an incoherent manner, they would sometimes have behaved reasonably, and would even have risen now and again to the standards of the Second Men. Wholly unused to large-scale human bloodshed, these more developed beings suffered an agony of pity for their mangled fellows. But they said nothing about their pity, and scarcely noticed their own generous grief; for they were busy with the work of rescue. Suddenly confronted with the need of extreme loyalty and courage, they exulted in complying, and experienced that added keenness of spirit which comes when danger is well faced. But it did not occur to them that they were bearing themselves heroically; for they thought they were merely behaving reasonably, showing common sense. And if any one failed in a tight place, they did not call him coward, but gave him a drug to clear his head; or, if that failed, they put him under a doctor. No doubt, among the First Men such a policy would not have been justified, for those bewildered beings had not the clear and commanding vision which kept all sane members of the second species constant in loyalty.

The immediate psychological effect of the disaster was that it afforded this very noble race healthful exercise for its great reserves of loyalty and heroism. Quite apart from this immediate invigoration, however, the first agony, and those many others which were to follow, influenced the Second Men for good and ill in a train of effects which may be called spiritual. They had long known very well that the universe was one in which there could be not only private but also great public tragedies; and their philosophy did not seek to conceal this fact. Private tragedy they were able to face with a bland fortitude, and even an ecstasy of acceptance, such as the earlier species had but rarely attained. Public tragedy, even world-tragedy, they declared should be faced in the same spirit. But to know world-tragedy in the abstract, is very different from the direct acquaintance with it. And now the Second Men, even while they held their attention earnestly fixed upon the practical work of defence, were determined to absorb this tragedy into the very depths of their being, to scrutinize it fearlessly, savour it, digest it, so that its fierce potency should henceforth be added to them. Therefore they did not curse their gods, nor supplicate them. They said to themselves, "Thus, and thus, and thus, is the world. Seeing the depth we shall see also the height; and we shall praise both."

But their schooling was yet scarcely begun. The Martian invaders were all dead, but their subvital units were dispersed over the planet as a virulent ultra-microscopic dust. For, though as members of the living cloud they could enter the human body without doing permanent harm, now that they were freed from their functions within the higher organic system, they became a predatory virus. Breathed into man's lungs, they soon adapted themselves to the new environment, and threw his tissues into disorder. Each cell that they entered overthrew its own constitution, like a state which the enemy has successfully infected with lethal propaganda through a mere handful of agents. Thus, though man was temporarily victor over the Martian super-individual, his own vital units were poisoned and destroyed by the subvital remains of his dead enemy. A race whose physique had been as utopian as its body politic, was reduced to timid invalidity. And it was left in possession of a devastated planet. The loss of water proved negligible; but the destruction of vegetation in all the war areas produced for a while a world famine such as the Second Men had never known. And the material fabric of civilization had been so broken that many decades would have to be spent in rebuilding it.

But the physical damage proved far less serious than the physiological. Earnest research discovered, indeed, a means of checking the infection; and, after a few years of rigorous purging, the atmosphere and man's flesh were clean once more. But the generations that had been stricken never recovered; their tissues had been too seriously corroded. Little by little, of course, there arose a fresh population of undamaged men and women. But it was a small population; for the fertility of the stricken had been much reduced. Thus the earth was now occupied by a small number of healthy persons below middle age and a very large number of ageing invalids. For many years these cripples had contrived to carry on the work of the world in spite of their frailty, but gradually they began to fail both in endurance and competence. For they were rapidly losing their grip on life, and sinking into a long-drawn-out senility, from which the Second Men had never before suffered; and at the same time the young, forced to take up work for which they were not yet equipped, committed all manner of blunders and crudities of which their elders would never have been guilty. But such was the general standard of mentality in the second human species, that what might have been an occasion for recrimination produced an unparalleled example of human loyalty at its best. The stricken generations decided almost unanimously that whenever an individual was declared by his generation to have outlived his competence, he should commit suicide. The younger generations, partly through affection, partly through dread of their own incompetence, were at first earnestly opposed to this policy. "Our elders," one young man said, "may have declined in vigour, but they are still beloved, and still wise. We dare not carry on without them." But the elders maintained their point. Many members of the rising generation were no longer juveniles. And, if the body politic was to survive the economic crisis, it must now ruthlessly cut out all its damaged tissues. Accordingly the decision was carried out. One by one, as occasion demanded, the stricken "chose the peace of annihilation," leaving a scanty, inexperienced, but vigorous, population to rebuild what had been destroyed.

Four centuries passed, and then again the Martian clouds appeared in the sky. Once more devastation and slaughter. Once more a complete failure of the two mentalities to conceive one another. Once more the Martians were destroyed. Once more the pulmonary plague, the slow purging, a crippled population, and generous suicide.

Again, and again they appeared, at irregular intervals for fifty thousand years. On each occasion the Martians came irresistibly fortified against whatever weapon humanity had last used against them. And so, by degrees, men began to recognize that the enemy was no merely instinctive brute, but intelligent. They therefore made attempts to get in touch with these alien minds, and make overtures for a peaceful settlement. But since obviously the negotiations had to be performed by human beings, and since the Martians always regarded human beings as the mere cattle of the terrestrial intelligence, the envoys were always either ignored or destroyed.

During each invasion the Martians contrived to dispatch a considerable bulk of water to Mars. And every time, not satisfied with this material gain, they stayed too long crusading, until man had found a weapon to circumvent their new defences; and then they were routed. After each invasion man's recovery was slower and less complete, while Mars, in spite of the loss of a large proportion of its population, was in the long run invigorated with the extra water.

2. THE RUIN OF TWO WORLDS

Rather more than fifty thousand years after their first appearance, the Martians secured a permanent footing on the Antarctic table-land and over-ran Australasia and South Africa. For many centuries they remained in possession of a large part of the earth's surface, practising a kind of agriculture, studying terrestrial conditions, and spending much energy on the "liberation" of diamonds.

During the considerable period before their settlement their mentality had scarcely changed; but actual habitation of the earth now began to undermine their self-complacency and their unity. It was borne in upon certain exploring Martians that the terrestrial bipeds, though insensitive to radiation, were actually the intelligences of the planet. At first this fact was studiously shunned, but little by little it gripped the attention of all terrestrial Martians. At the same time they began to realize that the whole work of research into terrestrial conditions, and even the social construction of their colony, depended, not on the public mind, but on private individuals, acting in their private capacity. The colonial super-individual inspired only the diamond crusade, and the attempt to extirpate the terrestrial intelligence, or radiation. These various novel acts of insight woke the Martian colonists from an age-long dream. They saw that their revered super-individual was scarcely more than the least common measure of themselves, a bundle of atavistic fantasies and cravings, knit into one mind and gifted with a certain practical cunning. A rapid and bewildering spiritual renascence now came over the whole Martian colony. The central doctrine of it was that what was valuable in the Martian species was not radiation but mentality. These two utterly different things had been confused, and even identified, since the dawn of Martian civilization. At last they were clearly distinguished. A fumbling but sincere study of mind now began; and distinction was even made between the humbler and loftier mental activities.

There is no telling whither this renascence might have led, had it run its course. Possibly in time the Martians might have recognized worth even in minds other than Martian minds. But such a leap was at first far beyond them. Though they now understood that human animals were conscious and intelligent, they regarded them with no sympathy, rather indeed, with increased hostility. They still rendered allegiance to the Martian race, or brotherhood, just because it was in a sense one flesh, and, indeed, one mind. For they were concerned not to abolish but to recreate the public mind of the colony, and even that of Mars itself.

But the colonial public mind still largely dominated them in their more somnolent periods, and actually sent some of those who, in their private phases, were revolutionaries across to Mars for help against the revolutionary movement. The home planet was quite untouched by the new ideas. Its citizens co-operated whole-heartedly in an attempt to bring the colonists to their senses. But in vain. The colonial public mind itself changed its character as the centuries passed, until it became seriously alienated from Martian orthodoxy. Presently, indeed, it began to undergo a very strange and thorough metamorphosis, from which, conceivably, it might have emerged as the noblest inhabitant of the solar system. Little by little it fell into a kind of hypnotic trance. That is to say, it ceased to possess the attention of its private members, yet remained as a unity of their subconscious, or un-noticed mentality. Radiational unity of the colony was maintained, but only in this subconscious manner; and it was at that depth that the great metamorphosis began to take place under the fertilizing influence of the new ideas; which, so to speak, were generated in the tempest of the fully conscious mental revolution, and kept on spreading down into the oceanic depth of the subconsciousness. Such a condition was likely to produce in time the emergence of a qualitatively new and finer mentality, and to waken at last into a fully conscious super-individual of higher order than its own members. But meanwhile this trance of the public consciousness incapacitated the colony for that prompt and co-ordinated action which had been the most successful faculty of Martian life. The public mind of the home planet easily destroyed its disorderly offspring, and set about re-colonizing the earth.

Several times during the next three hundred thousand years this process repeated itself. The changeless and terribly efficient super-individual of Mars extirpated its own offspring on the earth, before it could emerge from the chrysalis. And the tragedy might have been repeated indefinitely, but for certain changes that took place in humanity.

The first few centuries after the foundation of the Martian colony had been spent in ceaseless war. But at last, with terribly reduced resources, the Second Men had reconciled themselves to the fact that they must live in the same world with their mysterious enemy. Moreover, constant observation of the Martians began to restore somewhat man's shattered self-confidence. For during the fifty thousand years before the Martian colony was founded his opinion of himself had been undermined. He had formerly been used to regarding himself as the sun's ablest child. Then suddenly a stupendous new phenomenon had defeated his intelligence. Slowly he had learned that he was at grips with a determined and versatile rival, and that this rival hailed from a despised planet. Slowly he had been forced to suspect that he himself was outclassed, outshone, by a race whose very physique was incomprehensible to man. But after the Martians had established a permanent colony, human scientists began to discover the real physiological nature of the Martian organism, and were comforted to find that it did not make nonsense of human science. Man also learned that the Martians, though very able in certain spheres, were not really of a high mental type. These discoveries restored human self-confidence. Man settled down to make the best of the situation. Impassable barriers of high-power electric current were devised to keep the Martians out of human territory, and men began patiently to rebuild their ruined home as best they could. At first there was little respite from the crusading zeal of the Martians, but in the second millennium this began to abate, and the two races left one another alone, save for occasional revivals of Martain fervour. Human civilization was at last reconstructed and consolidated, though upon a modest scale. Once more, though interrupted now and again by decades of agony, human beings lived in peace and relative prosperity. Life was somewhat harder than formerly, and the physique of the race was definitely less reliable than of old; but men and women still enjoyed conditions which most nations of the earlier species would have envied. The age of ceaseless personal sacrifice in service of the stricken community had ended at last. Once more a wonderful diversity of untrammelled personalities was put forth. Once more the minds of men and women were devoted without hindrance to the joy of skilled work, and all the subtleties of personal intercourse. Once more the passionate interest in one's fellows, which had for so long been hushed under the all-dominating public calamity, refreshed and enlarged the mind. Once more there was music, sweet and backward-hearkening towards a golden past. Once more a wealth of literature, and of the visual arts. Once more intellectual exploration into the nature of the physical world and the potentiality of mind. And once more the religious experience, which had for so long been coarsened and obscured by all the violent distractions and inevitable self-deceptions of war, seemed to be refining itself under the influence of reawakened culture.

In such circumstances the earlier and less sensitive human species might well have prospered indefinitely. Not so the Second Men. For their very refinement of sensibility made them incapable of shunning an ever-present conviction that in spite of all their prosperity they were undermined. Though superficially they seemed to be making a slow but heroic recovery they were at the same time suffering from a still slower and far more profound spiritual decline. Generation succeeded generation. Society became almost perfected, within its limited territory and its limitations of material wealth. The capacities of personality were developed with extreme subtlety and richness. At last the race proposed to itself once more its ancient project of re-making human nature upon a loftier plane. But somehow it had no longer the courage and self-respect for such work. And so, though there was much talk, nothing was done. Epoch succeeded epoch, and everything human remained apparently the same. Like a twig that has been broken but not broken off, man settled down to retain his life and culture, but could make no progress.

It is almost impossible to describe in a few words the subtle malady of the spirit that was undermining the Second Men. To say that they were suffering from an inferiority complex, would not be wholly false, but it would be a misleading vulgarization of the truth. To say that they had lost faith, both in themselves and in the universe, would be almost as inadequate. Crudely stated, their trouble was that, as a species, they had attempted a certain spiritual feat beyond the scope of their still-primitive nature. Spiritually they had over-reached themselves, broken every muscle (so to speak) and incapacitated themselves for any further effort. For they had determined to see their own racial tragedy as a thing of beauty, and they had failed. It was the obscure sense of this defeat that had poisoned them, for, being in many respects a very noble species, they could not simply turn their backs upon their failure and pursue the old way of life with the accustomed zest and thoroughness.

During the earliest Martian raids, the spiritual leaders of humanity had preached that the disaster must be an occasion for a supreme religious experience. While striving mightily to save their civilization, men must yet (so it was said) learn not merely to endure, but to admire, even the sternest issue. "Thus and thus is the world. Seeing the depth, we shall see also the height, and praise both." The whole population had accepted this advice. At first they had seemed to succeed. Many noble literary expressions were given forth, which seemed to define and elaborate, and even actually to create in men's hearts, this supreme experience. But as the centuries passed and the disasters were repeated, men began to fear that their forefathers had deceived themselves. Those remote generations had earnestly longed to feel the racial tragedy as a factor in the cosmic beauty; and at last they had persuaded themselves that this experience had actually befallen them. But their descendants were slowly coming to suspect that no such experience had ever occurred, that it would never occur to any man, and that there was in fact no such cosmic beauty to be experienced. The First Men would probably, in such a situation, have swung violently either into spiritual nihilism, or else into some comforting religious myth. At any rate, they were of too coarse-grained a nature to be ruined by a trouble so impalpable. Not so the Second Men. For they realized all too clearly that they were faced with the supreme crux of existence. And so, age after age the generations clung desperately to the hope that, if only they could endure a little longer, the light would break in on them. Even after the Martian colony had been three times established and destroyed by the orthodox race in Mars, the supreme preoccupation of the human species was with this religious crux. But afterwards, and very gradually, they lost heart. For it was borne in on them that either they themselves were by nature too obtuse to perceive this ultimate excellence of things (an excellence which they had strong reason to believe in intellectually, although they could not actually experience it), or the human race had utterly deceived itself, and the course of cosmic events after all was not significant, but a meaningless rigmarole.

It was this dilemma that poisoned them. Had they been still physically in their prime, they might have found fortitude to accept it, and proceed to the patient exfoliation of such very real excellencies as they were still capable of creating. But they had lost the vitality which alone could perform such acts of spiritual abnegation. All the wealth of personality, all the intricacies of personal relationship, all the complex enterprise of a very great community, all art, all intellectual research, had lost their savour. It is remarkable that a purely religious disaster should have warped even the delight of lovers in one another's bodies, actually taken the flavour out of food, and drawn a veil between the sun-bather and the sun. But individuals of this species, unlike their predecessors, were so closely integrated, that none of their functions could remain healthy while the highest was disordered. Moreover, the general slight failure of physique, which was the legacy of age-long war, had resulted in a recurrence of those shattering brain disorders which had dogged the earliest races of their species. The very horror of the prospect of racial insanity increased their aberration from reasonableness. Little by little, shocking perversions of desire began to terrify them. Masochistic and sadistic orgies alternated with phases of extravagant and ghastly revelry. Acts of treason against the community, hitherto almost unknown, at last necessitated a strict police system. Local groups organized predatory raids against one another. Nations appeared, and all the phobias that make up nationalism.

The Martian colonists, when they observed man's disorganization, prepared, at the instigation of the home planet, a very great offensive. It so happened that at this time the colony was going through its phase of enlightenment, which had always hitherto been followed sooner or later by chastisement from Mars. Many individuals were at the moment actually toying with the idea of seeking harmony with man, rather than war. But the public mind of Mars, outraged by this treason, sought to overwhelm it by instituting a new crusade. Man's disunion offered a great opportunity.

The first attack produced a remarkable change in the human race. Their madness seemed suddenly to leave them. Within a few weeks the national governments had surrendered their sovereignty to a central authority. Disorders, debauchery, perversions, wholly ceased. The treachery and self-seeking and corruption, which had by now been customary for many centuries, suddenly gave place to universal and perfect devotion to the social cause. The species was apparently once more in its right mind. Everywhere, in spite of the war's horrors, there was gay brotherliness, combined with a heroism, which clothed itself in an odd extravagance of jocularity.

The war went ill for man. The general mood changed to cold resolution. And still victory was with the Martians. Under the influence of the huge fanatical armies which were poured in from the home planet, the colonists had shed their tentative pacifism, and sought to vindicate their loyalty by ruthlessness. In reply the human race deserted its sanity, and succumbed to an uncontrollable lust for destruction. It was at this stage that a human bacteriologist announced that he had bred a virus of peculiar deadliness and transmissibility, with which it would be possible to infect the enemy, but at the cost of annihilating also the human race. It is significant of the insane condition of the human population at this time that, when these facts were announced and broadcast, there was no discussion of the desirability of using this weapon. It was immediately put in action, the whole human race applauding.

Within a few months the Martian colony had vanished, their home planet itself had received the infection, and its population was already aware that nothing could save it. Man's constitution was tougher than that of the animate clouds, and he appeared to be doomed to a somewhat more lingering death. He made no effort to save himself, either from the disease which he himself had propagated, or from the pulmonary plague which was caused by the disintegrated substance of the dead Martian colony. All the public processes of civilization began to fall to pieces; for the community was paralysed by disillusion, and by the expectation of death. Like a bee-hive that has no queen, the whole population of the earth sank into apathy. Men and women stayed in their homes, idling, eating whatever food they could procure, sleeping far into the mornings, and, when at last they rose, listlessly avoiding one another. Only the children could still be gay, and even they were oppressed by their elders' gloom. Meanwhile the disease was spreading. Household after household was stricken, and was left unaided by its neighbours. But the pain in each individual's flesh was strangely numbed by his more poignant distress in the spiritual defeat of the race. For such was the high development of this species, that even physical agony could not distract it from the racial failure. No one wanted to save himself; and each knew that his neighbours desired not his aid. Only the children, when the disease crippled them, were plunged into agony and terror. Tenderly, yet listlessly, their elders would then give them the last sleep. Meanwhile the unburied dead spread corruption among the dying. Cities fell still and silent. The corn was not harvested.

3. THE THIRD DARK AGE

So contagious and so lethal was the new bacterium, that its authors expected the human race to be wiped out as completely as the Martian colony. Each dying remnant of humanity, isolated from its fellows by the breakdown of communications, imagined its own last moments to be the last of man. But by accident, almost one might say by miracle, a spark of human life was once more preserved, to hand on the sacred fire. A certain stock or strain of the race, promiscuously scattered throughout the continents, proved less susceptible than the majority. And, as the bacterium was less vigorous in a hot climate, a few of these favoured individuals, who happened to be in the tropical jungle, recovered from the infection. And of these few a minority recovered also from the pulmonary plague which, as usual, was propagated from the dead Martians.

It might have been expected that from this human germ a new civilized community would have soon arisen. With such brilliant beings as the Second Men, surely a few generations, or at the most a few thousand years, should have sufficed to make up the lost ground.

But no. Once more it was in a manner the very excellence of the species that prevented its recovery, and flung the spirit of Earth into a trance which lasted longer than the whole previous career of mammals. Again and again, some thirty million times, the seasons were repeated; and throughout this period man remained as fixed in bodily and mental character as, formerly, the platypus. Members of the earlier human species must find it difficult to understand this prolonged impotence of a race far more developed than themselves. For here apparently were both the requisites of progressive culture, namely a world rich and unpossessed, and a race exceptionally able. Yet nothing was done.

When the plagues, and all the immense consequent putrefactions, had worked themselves off, the few isolated groups of human survivors settled down to an increasingly indolent tropical life. The fruits of past learning were not imparted to the young, who therefore grew up in extreme ignorance of almost everything beyond their immediate experience. At the same time the elder generation cowed their juniors with vague suggestions of racial defeat and universal futility. This would not have mattered, had the young themselves been normal; they would have reacted with fervent optimism. But they themselves were now by nature incapable of any enthusiasm. For, in a species in which the lower functions were so strictly disciplined under the higher, the long-drawn-out spiritual disaster had actually begun to take effect upon the germ-plasm; so that individuals were doomed before birth to lassitude, and to mentality in a minor key. The First Men, long ago, had fallen into a kind of racial senility through a combination of vulgar errors and indulgences. But the second species, like a boy whose mind has been too soon burdened with grave experience, lived henceforth in a sleep-walk.

As the generations passed, all the lore of civilization was shed, save the routine of tropical agriculture and hunting. Not that intelligence itself had waned. Not that the race had sunk into mere savagery. Lassitude did not prevent it from readjusting itself to suit its new circumstances. These sleep-walkers soon invented convenient ways of making, in the home and by hand, much that had hitherto been made in factories and by mechanical power. Almost without mental effort they designed and fashioned tolerable instruments out of wood and flint and bone. But though still intelligent, they had become by disposition, supine, indifferent. They would exert themselves only under the pressure of urgent primitive need. No man seemed capable of putting forth the full energy of a man. Even suffering had lost its poignancy. And no ends seemed worth pursuing that could not be realized speedily. The sting had gone out of experience. The soul was calloused against every goad. Men and women worked and played, loved and suffered; but always in a kind of rapt absent-mindedness. It was as though they were ever trying to remember something important which escaped them. The affairs of daily life seemed too trivial to be taken seriously. Yet that other, and supremely important thing, which alone deserved consideration, was so obscure that no one had any idea what it was. Nor indeed was anyone aware of this hypnotic subjection, any more than a sleeper is aware of being asleep.

The minimum of necessary work was performed, and there was even a dreamy zest in the performance, but nothing which would entail extra toil ever seemed worth while. And so, when adjustment to the new circumstances of the world had been achieved, complete stagnation set in. Practical intelligence was easily able to cope with a slowly changing environment, and even with sudden natural upheavals such as floods, earthquakes and disease epidemics. Man remained in a sense master of his world, but he had no idea what to do with his mastery. It was everywhere assumed that the sane end of living was to spend as many days as possible in indolence, lying in the shade. Unfortunately human beings had, of course, many needs which were irksome if not appeased, and so a good deal of hard work had to be done. Hunger and thirst had to be satisfied. Other individuals besides oneself had to be cared for, since man was cursed with sympathy and with a sentiment for the welfare of his group. The only fully rational behaviour, it was thought, would be general suicide, but irrational impulses made this impossible. Beatific drugs offered a temporary heaven. But, far as the Second Men had fallen, they were still too clear-sighted to forget that such beatitude is outweighed by subsequent misery.

Century by century, epoch by epoch, man glided on in this seemingly precarious, yet actually unshakable equilibrium. Nothing that happened to him could disturb his easy dominance over the beasts and over physical nature; nothing could shock him out of his racial sleep. Long-drawn-out climatic changes made desert, jungle and grass-land fluctuate like the clouds. As the years advanced by millions, ordinary geological processes, greatly accentuated by the immense strains set up by the Patagonian upheaval, remodelled the surface of the planet. Continents were submerged, or lifted out of the sea, till presently there was little of the old configuration. And along with these geological changes went changes in the fauna and flora. The bacterium which had almost exterminated man had also wrought havoc amongst other mammals. Once more the planet had to be re-stocked, this time from the few surviving tropical species. Once more there was a great re-making of old types, only less revolutionary than that which had followed the Patagonian disaster. And since the human race remained minute, through the effects of its spiritual fatigue, other species were favoured. Especially the ruminants and the large carnivora increased and diversified themselves into many habits and forms.

But the most remarkable of all the biological trains of events in this period was the history of the Martian subvital units that had been disseminated by the slaughter of the Martian colony, and had then tormented men and animals with pulmonary diseases. As the ages passed, certain spe-

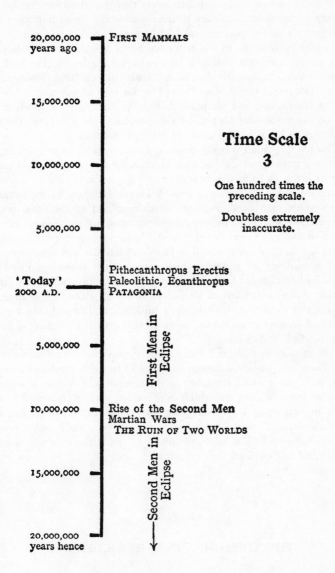

20,000,000 years ago — FIRST MAMMALS

15,000,000 —

10,000,000 —

Time Scale
3

One hundred times the
preceding scale.

Doubtless extremely
inaccurate.

5,000,000 —

'Today' — Pithecanthropus Erectus
2000 A.D. — Paleolithic, Eoanthropus
PATAGONIA

First Men in
Eclipse

5,000,000 —

10,000,000 — Rise of the Second Men
Martian Wars
THE RUIN OF TWO WORLDS

Second Men in
Eclipse

15,000,000 —

20,000,000 years hence —

cies of mammals so readjusted themselves that the Martian virus became not only harmless but necessary to their well-being. A relationship which was originally that of parasite and host became in time a true symbiosis, a co-operative partnership, in which the terrestrial animals gained something of the unique attributes of the vanished Martian organisms. The time was to come when Man himself should look with envy on these creatures, and finally make use of the Martian "virus" for his own enrichment.

But meanwhile, and for many million years, almost all kinds of life were on the move, save Man. Like a ship-wrecked sailor, he lay exhausted and asleep on his raft, long after the storm had abated.

But his stagnation was not absolute. Imperceptibly, he was drifting on the oceanic currents of life, and in a direction far out of his original course. Little by little, his habit was becoming simpler, less artificial, more animal. Agriculture faded out, since it was no longer necessary in the luxuriant garden where man lived. Weapons of defence and of the chase became more precisely adapted to their restricted purposes, but at the same time less diversified and more stereotyped. Speech almost vanished; for there was no novelty left in experience. Familiar facts and familiar emotions were conveyed increasingly by gestures which were mostly unwitting. Physically, the species had changed little. Though the natural period of life was greatly reduced, this was due less to physiological change than to a strange and fatal increase of absent-mindedness in middle-age. The individual gradually ceased to react to his environment; so that even if he escaped a violent death, he died of starvation.

Yet in spite of this great change, the species remained essentially human. There was no bestialization, such as had formerly produced a race of sub-men. These tranced remnants of the second human species were not beasts but innocents, simples, children of nature, perfectly adjusted to their simple life. In many ways their state was idyllic and enviable. But such was their dimmed mentality that they were never clearly aware even of the blessings they had, still less, of course, of the loftier experiences which had kindled and tortured their ancestors.

CHAPTER X

THE THIRD MEN IN THE WILDERNESS

I. THE THIRD HUMAN SPECIES

WE have now followed man's career during some forty million years. The whole period to be covered by this chronicle is about two thousand million. In this chapter, and the next, therefore, we must accomplish a swift flight at great altitude over a tract of time more than three times as long as that which we have hitherto observed. This great expanse is no desert, but a continent teeming with variegated life, and many successive and very diverse civilizations. The myriads of human beings who inhabit it far outnumber the First and Second Men combined. And the content of each one of these lives is a universe, rich and poignant as that of any reader of this book.

In spite of the great diversity of this span of man's history, it is a single movement within the whole symphony, just as the careers of the First and of the Second Men are each a single movement. Not only is it a period dominated by a single natural human species and the artificial human species into which the natural species at length transformed itself; but, also, in spite of innumerable digressions, a single theme, a single mood of the human will, informs the whole duration. For now at last man's main energy is devoted to remaking his own physical and mental nature. Throughout the rise and fall of many successive cultures this purpose is progressively clarifying itself, and expressing itself in many tragic and even devastating experiments; until, toward the close of this immense period, it seems almost to achieve its end.

When the Second Men had remained in their strange racial trance for about thirty million years, the obscure forces that make for advancement began to stir in them once more. This reawakening was favoured by geological accident. An incursion of the sea gradually isolated some of their number in an island continent, which was once part of the North Atlantic ocean-bed. The climate of this island gradually cooled from sub-tropical to temperate and sub-arctic. The vast change of conditions caused in the imprisoned race a subtle chemical re-arrangement of the germ-plasm, such that there ensued an epidemic of biological variation. Many new types appeared, but in the long run one, more vigorous and better adapted than the rest, crowded out all competitors and slowly consolidated itself as a new species, the Third Men.

Scarcely more than half the stature of their predecessors, these beings were proportionally slight and lithe. Their skin was of a sunny brown, covered with a luminous halo of red-gold hairs, which on the head became a russet mop. Their golden eyes, reminiscent of the snake, were more enigmatic than profound. Their faces were compact as a cat's muzzle, their lips full, but subtle at the corners. Their ears, objects of personal pride and of sexual admiration, were extremely variable both in individuals and races. These surprising organs, which would have seemed merely ludicrous to the First Men, were expressive both of temperament and passing mood. They were immense, delicately involuted, of a silken texture, and very mobile. They gave an almost bat-like character to the otherwise somewhat feline heads. But the most distinctive feature of the Third Men was their great lean hands, on which were six versatile fingers, six antennæ of living steel.

Unlike their predecessors, the Third Men were short-lived. They had a brief childhood and a brief maturity, followed (in the natural course) by a decade of senility, and death at about sixty. But such was their abhorrence of decrepitude, that they seldom allowed themselves to grow old. They preferred to kill themselves when their mental and physical agility began to decline. Thus, save in exceptional epochs of their history, very few lived to be fifty.

But though in some respects the third human species fell short of the high standard of its predecessor, especially in certain of the finer mental capacities, it was by no means simply degenerate. The admirable sensory equipment of the second species was retained, and even improved. Vision was no less ample and precise and colourful. Touch was far more discriminate, especially in the delicately pointed sixth finger-tip. Hearing was so developed that a man could run through wooded country blind-fold without colliding with the trees. Moreover the great range of sounds and rhythms had acquired an extremely subtle gamut of emotional significance. Music was therefore one of the main preoccupations of the civilizations of this species.

Mentally the Third Men were indeed very unlike their predecessors. Their intelligence was in some ways no less agile; but it was more cunning than intellectual, more practical than theoretical. They were interested more in the world of sense-experience than in the world of abstract reason, and again far more in living things than in the lifeless. They excelled in certain kinds of art, and indeed also in some fields of science. But they were led into science more through practical, æsthetic or religious needs than through intellectual curiosity. In mathematics, for instance (helped greatly by the duodecimal system, which resulted from their having twelve fingers), they became wonderful calculators; yet they never had the curiosity to inquire into the essential nature of number. Nor, in physics, were they ever led to discover the more obscure properties of space. They were, indeed, strangely devoid of curiosity. Hence, though sometimes capable of a penetrating mystical intuition, they never seriously disciplined themselves under philosophy, nor tried to relate their mystical intuitions with the rest of their experience.

In their primitive phases the Third Men were keen hunters; but also, owing to their strong parental impulses, they were much addicted to making pets of captured animals. Throughout their career they displayed what earlier races would have called an uncanny sympathy with, and understanding of, all kinds of animals and plants. This intuitive insight into the nature of living things, and this untiring interest in the diversity of vital behaviour, constituted the dominating impulse throughout the whole career of the third human species. At the outset they excelled not only as hunters but as herdsmen and domesticators. By nature they were very apt in every kind of manipulation, but especially in the manipulation of living things. As a species they were also greatly addicted to play of all kinds, but especially to manipulative play, and above all to the playful manipulation of organisms. From the first they performed great feats of riding on the moose-like deer which they had domesticated. They tamed also a certain gregarious coursing beast. The pedigree of this great leonine wolf led, through the tropical survivors of the Martian plague, back to those descendants of the arctic fox which had over-run the world after the Patagonian disaster. This animal the Third Men trained not only to help them in shepherding and in the chase, but also to play intricate hunting games. Between this hound and its master or mistress there frequently arose a very special relation, a kind of psychical symbiosis, a dumb intuitive mutual insight, a genuine love, based on economic co-operation, but strongly toned also, in a manner peculiar to the third human species, with religious symbolism and frankly sexual intimacy.

As herdsmen and shepherds the Third Men very early practised selective breeding; and increasingly they became absorbed in the perfecting and enriching of all types of animals and plants. It was the boast of every local chieftain not only that the men of his tribe were more manly and the women more beautiful than all others, but also that the bears in his territory were the noblest and most bear-like of all bears, that the birds built more perfect nests and were more skilful fliers and singers than birds elsewhere. And so on, through all the animal and vegetable races.

This biological control was achieved at first by simple breeding experiments, but later and increasingly by crude physiological manipulation of the young animal, the foetus and (later still) the germ-plasm. Hence arose a perennial conflict, which often caused wars of a truly religious bitterness, between the tender-hearted, who shrank from the infliction of pain, and the passionately manipulative, who willed to create at whatever cost. This conflict, indeed, was waged not only between individuals but within each mind; for all were innately hunters and manipulators, but also all had intuitive sympathy even with the quarry which they tormented. The trouble was increased by a strain of sheer cruelty which occurred even in the most tender-hearted. This sadism was at bottom an expression of an almost mystical reverence for sensory experience. Physical pain, being the most intense of all sensed qualities, was apt to be thought the most excellent. It might be expected that this would lead rather to self-torture than to cruelty. Sometimes it did. But in general those who could not appreciate pain in their own flesh were yet able to persuade themselves that in inflicting pain on lower animals they were creating vivid psychic reality, and therefore high excellence. It was just the intense reality of pain, they said, that made it intolerable to men and animals. Seen with the detachment of the divine mind, it appeared in its true beauty. And even man, they declared, could appreciate its excellence when it occurred not in men but in animals.

Though the Third Men lacked interest in systematic thought, their minds were often concerned with matters outside the fields of private and social economy. They experienced not only æsthetic but mystical cravings. And though they were without any appreciation of those finer beauties of human personality, which their predecessors had admired as the highest attainment of life on the planet, the Third Men themselves, in their own way, sought to make the best of human nature, and indeed of animal nature. Man they regarded in two aspects. In the first place he was the noblest of all animals, gifted with unique aptitudes. He was, as was sometimes said, God's chief work of art. But secondly, since his special virtues were his insight into the nature of all living things and his manipulative capacity, he was himself God's eye and God's hand. These convictions were expressed over and over again in the religions of the Third Men, by the image of the deity as a composite animal, with wings of the albatross, jaws of the great wolf-dog, feet of the deer, and so on. For the human element was represented in this deity by the hands, the eyes, and the sexual organs of man. And between the divine hands lay the world, with all its diverse population. Often the world was represented as being the fruit of God's primitive potency, but also as in process of being drastically altered and tortured into perfection by the hands.

Most of the cultures of the Third Men were dominated by this obscure worship of Life as an all-pervading spirit, expressing itself in myriad diverse individuals. And at the same time the intuitive loyalty to living things and to a vaguely conceived life-force was often complicated by sadism. For in the first place it was recognized, of course, that what is valued by higher beings may be intolerable to lower; and, as has been said, pain itself was thought to be a superior excellence of this kind. And again in a second manner sadism expressed itself. The worship of Life, as agent or subject, was complemented by worship of environment, as object to life's subjectivity, as that which remains ever foreign to life, thwarting its enterprises, torturing it, yet making it possible, and, by its very resistance, goading it into nobler expressions. Pain, it was said, was the most vivid apprehension of the sacred and universal Object.

The thought of the third human species was never systematic. But in some such manner as the foregoing it strove to rationalize its obscure intuition of the beauty which includes at once Life's victory and defeat.

2. DIGRESSIONS OF THE THIRD MEN

Such, in brief, was the physical and mental nature of the third human species. In spite of innumerable distractions, the spirit of the Third Men kept on returning to follow up the thread of biological interest through a thousand variegated cultures. Again and again folk after folk would clamber out of savagery and barbarism into relative enlightenment;

and mostly, though not always, the main theme of this enlightenment was some special mood either of biological creativeness or of sadism, or of both. To a man born into such a society, no dominant characteristic would be apparent. He would be impressed rather by the many-sidedness of human activities in his time. He would note a wealth of personal intercourse, of social organization and industrial invention, of art and speculation, all set in that universal matrix, the private struggle to preserve or express the self. Yet the historian may often see in a society, over and above this multifarious proliferation, some one controlling theme.

Again and again, then, at intervals of a few thousand or a few hundred thousand years, man's whim was imposed upon the fauna and flora of the earth, and at length directed to the task of remaking man himself. Again and again, through a diversity of causes, the effort collapsed, and the species sank once more into chaos. Sometimes indeed there was an interlude of culture in some quite different key. Once, early in the history of the species, and before its nature had become fixed, there occurred a nonindustrial civilization of a genuinely intellectual kind, almost like that of Greece. Sometimes, but not often, the third human species fooled itself into an extravagantly industrial world civilization, in the manner of the Americanized First Men. In general its interest was too much concerned with other matters to become entangled with mechanical devices. But on three occasions at least it succumbed. Of these civilizations one derived its main power from wind and falling water, one from the tides, one from the earth's internal heat. The first, saved from the worst evils of industrialism by the limitations of its power, lasted some hundred thousand years in barren equilibrium, until it was destroyed by an obscure bacterium. The second was fortunately brief; but its fifty thousand years of unbridled waste of tidal energy was enough to interfere appreciably with the orbit of the moon. This world-order collapsed at length in a series of industrial wars. The third endured a quarter of a million years as a brilliantly sane and efficient world organization. Throughout most of its existence there was almost complete social harmony with scarcely as much internal strife as occurs in a bee-hive. But once more civilization came at length to grief, this time through the misguided effort to breed special human types for specialized industrial pursuits.

Industrialism, however, was never more than a digression, a lengthy and disastrous irrelevance in the life of this species. There were other digressions. There were for instance cultures, enduring sometimes for several thousand years, which were predominantly musical. This could never have occurred among the First Men; but, as was said, the third species was peculiarly developed in hearing, and in emotional sensitivity to sound and rhythm. Consequently, just as the First Men at their height were led into the wilderness by an irrational obsession with mechanical contrivances, just as the Third Men themselves were many times undone by their own interest in biological control, so, now and again, it was their musical gift that hypnotized them.

Of these predominantly musical cultures the most remarkable was one in which music and religion combined to form a tyranny no less rigid than that of religion and science in the remote past. It is worth while to dwell on one of these episodes for a few moments.

The Third Men were very subject to a craving for personal immortality. Their lives were brief, their love of life intense. It seemed to them a tragic flaw in the nature of existence that the melody of the individual life must either fade into a dreary senility or be cut short, never to be repeated. Now music had a special significance for this race. So intense was their experience of it, that they were ready to regard it as in some manner the underlying reality of all things. In leisure hours, snatched from a toilful and often tragic life, groups of peasants would seek to conjure about them by song or pipe or viol a universe more beautiful, more real, than that of daily labour. Concentrating their sensitive hearing upon the inexhaustible diversity of tone and rhythm, they would seem to themselves to be possessed by the living presence of music, and to be transported thereby into a lovelier world. No wonder they believed that every melody was a spirit, leading a life of its own within the universe of music. No wonder they imagined that a symphony or chorus was itself a single spirit inhering in all its members. No wonder it seemed to them that when men and women listened to great music, the barriers of their individuality were broken down, so that they became one soul through communion with the music.

The prophet was born in a highland village where the native faith in music was intense, though quite unformulated. In time he learnt to raise his peasant audiences to the most extravagant joy and the most delicious sorrow. Then at last he began to think, and to expound his thoughts with the authority of a great bard. Easily he persuaded men that music was the reality, and all else illusion, that the living spirit of the universe was pure music, and that each individual animal and man, though he had a body that must die and vanish for ever, had also a soul that was music and eternal. A melody, he said, is the most fleeting of things. It happens and ceases. The great silence devours it, and seemingly annihilates it. Passage is essential to its being. Yet though for a melody, to halt is to die a violent death, all music, the prophet affirmed, has also eternal life. After silence it may occur again, with all its freshness and aliveness. Time cannot age it; for its home is in a country outside time. And that country, thus the young musician earnestly preached, is also the home land of every man and woman, nay of every living thing that has any gift of music. Those who seek immortality, must strive to waken their tranced souls into melody and harmony. And according to their degree of musical originality and proficiency will be their standing in the eternal life.

The doctrine, and the impassioned melodies of the prophet, spread like fire. Instrumental and vocal music sounded from every pasture and corn plot. The government tried to suppress it, partly because it was thought to interfere with agricultural productivity, largely because its passionate significance reverberated even in the hearts of courtly ladies, and threatened to undo the refinement of centuries. Nay, the social order itself began to crumble. For many began openly to declare that what mattered was not aristocratic birth, nor even proficiency in the time-honoured musical forms (so much prized by the leisured), but the gift of spontaneous emotional expression in rhythm and harmony. Persecution strengthened the new faith with a glorious company of martyrs who, it was affirmed, sang triumphantly even in the flames.

One day the sacred monarch himself, hitherto a prisoner within the conventions, declared half sincerely, half by policy, that he was converted to his people's faith. Bureaucracy gave place to an enlightened dictatorship, the monarch assumed the title of Supreme Melody, and the whole social order was re-fashioned, more to the taste of the peasants. The subtle prince, backed by the crusading zeal of his people, and favoured by the rapid spontaneous spread of the faith in all lands, conquered the whole world, and founded the Universal Church of Harmony. The prophet himself, meanwhile, dismayed by his own too facile success, had retired into the mountains to perfect his art under the influence of their great quiet, or the music of wind, thunder and waterfall. Presently, however, the silence of the fells was shattered by the blare of military bands and ecclesiastical choirs, which the emperor had sent to salute him and conduct him to the metropolis. He was secured, though not without a scrimmage, and lodged in the High Temple of Music. There he was kept a prisoner, dubbed God's Big Noise, and used by the world-government as an oracle needing interpretation. In a few years the official music of the temple, and of deputations from all over the world, drove him into raving madness; in which state he was the more useful to the authorities.

Thus was founded the Holy Empire of Music, which gave order and purpose to the species for a thousand years. The sayings of the prophet, interpreted by a series of able rulers, became the foundation of a great system of law which gradually supplanted all local codes by virtue of its divine authority. Its root was madness; but its final expression was intricate common sense, decorated with harmless and precious flowers of folly. Throughout, the individual was wisely, but tacitly, regarded as a biological organism having definite needs or rights and definite social obligations; but the language in which this principle was expressed and elaborated was a jargon based on the fiction that every human being was a melody, demanding completion within a greater musical theme of society.

Toward the close of this millennium of order a schism occurred among the devout. A new and fervent sect declared that the true spirit of the musical religion had been stifled by ecclesiasticism. The founder of the religion had preached salvation by individual musical experience, by an intensely emotional communion with the Divine Music. But little by little, so it was said, the church had lost sight of this central truth, and had substituted a barren interest in the objective forms and principles of melody and counterpoint. Salvation, in the official view, was not to be had by subjective experience, but by keeping the rules of an obscure musical technique. And what was this technique? Instead of making the social order a practical expression of the divine law of music, churchmen and statesmen had misinterpreted these divine laws to suit mere social convenience, until the true spirit of music had been lost. Meanwhile on the other side a counter-revival took place. The self-centred and soul-saving mood of the rebels was ridiculed. Men were urged to care rather for the divine and exquisitely ordered forms of music itself than for their own emotion.

It was amongst the rebel peoples that the biological interest of the race, hitherto subordinate, came into its own. Mating, at least among the more devout sort of women, began to be influenced by the desire to have children who should be of outstanding musical brilliance and sensitivity. Biological sciences were rudimentary, but the general principle of selective breeding was known. Within a century this policy of breeding for music, or breeding "soul," developed from a private idiosyncrasy into a racial obsession. It was so far successful that after a while a new type became common, and thrived upon the approbation and devotion of ordinary persons. These new beings were indeed extravagantly sensitive to music, so much so that the song of a sky-lark caused them serious torture by its banality, and in response to any human music of the kind which they approved, they invariably fell into a trance. Under the stimulus of music which was not to their taste they were apt to run amok and murder the performers.

We need not pause to trace the stages by which an infatuated race gradually submitted itself to the whims of these creatures of human folly, until for a brief period they became the tyrannical ruling caste of a musical theocracy. Nor need we observe how they reduced society to chaos; and how at length an age of confusion and murder brought mankind once more to its senses, but also into so bitter a disillusionment that the effort to re-orientate the whole direction of its endeavour lacked determination. Civilization fell to pieces and was not rebuilt till after the race had lain fallow for some thousands of years.

So ended perhaps the most pathetic of racial delusions. Born of a genuine and potent æsthetic experience, it retained a certain crazy nobility even to the end.

Many scores of other cultures occurred, separated often by long ages of barbarism, but they must be ignored in this brief chronicle. The great majority of them were mainly biological in spirit. Thus one was dominated by an obsessive interest in flight, and therefore in birds, another by the concept of metabolism, several by sexual creativity, and very many by some general but mostly unenlightened policy of eugenics. All these we must pass over, so that we may descend to watch the greatest of all the races of the third species torture itself into a new form.

3. THE VITAL ART

It was after an unusually long period of eclipse that the spirit of the third human species attained its greatest brilliance. We need not watch the stages by which this enlightenment was reached. Suffice it that the upshot was a very remarkable civilization, if such a word can be applied to an order in which agglomerations of architecture were unknown, clothing was used only when needed for warmth, and such industrial development as occurred was wholly subordinated to other activities.

Early in the history of this culture the requirements of hunting and agriculture, and the spontaneous impulse to manipulate live things, gave rise to a primitive but serviceable system of biological knowledge. Not until the culture had unified the whole planet, did biology itself give rise to chemistry and physics. At the same time a well-controlled industrialism, based first on wind and water, and later on subterranean heat, afforded the race all the material luxuries it desired, and much leisure from the business of keeping itself in existence. Had there not already existed a more powerful and all-dominating interest, industrialism itself would probably have hypnotized the race, as it had so many others. But in this race the interest in live things, which characterized the whole species, was dominant before industrialism began. Egotism among the Third Men could not be satisfied by the exercise of economic power, nor by the mere ostentation of wealth. Not that the race was immune from egotism. On the contrary, it had lost almost all that spontaneous altruism which had distinguished the Second Men. But in most periods the only kind of personal ostentation which appealed to the Third Men was directly connected with the primitive interest in "pecunia." To own many and noble beasts, whether they were economically productive or not, was ever the mark of respectability. The vulgar, indeed, were content with mere numbers, or at most with the conventional virtues of the recognized breeds. But the more refined pursued, and flaunted, certain very exact principles of æsthetic excellence in their control of living forms.

In fact, as the race gained biological insight, it developed a very remarkable new art, which we may call "plastic vital art." This was to become the chief vehicle of expression of the new culture. It was practised universally, and with religious fervour; for it was very closely connected with the belief in a life-god. The canons of this art, and the precepts of this religion, fluctuated from age to age, but in general certain basic principles were accepted. Or rather, though there was almost always universal agreement that the practice of vital art was the supreme goal, and should not be treated in a utilitarian spirit, there were two conflicting sets of principles which were favoured by opposed sets. One mode of vital art sought to evoke the full potentiality of each natural type as a harmonious and perfected nature, or to produce new types equally harmonious. The other prided itself on producing monsters. Sometimes a single capacity was developed at the expense of the harmony and welfare of the organism as a whole. Thus a bird was produced which could fly faster than any other bird; but it could neither reproduce nor even feed, and therefore had to be maintained artificially. Sometimes, on the other hand, certain characters incompatible in nature were forced upon a single organism, and maintained in precarious and torturing equilibrium. To give examples, one much-talked-of feat was the production of a carnivorous mammal in which the fore limbs had assumed the structure of a bird's wings, complete with feathers. This creature could not fly, since its body was wrongly proportioned. Its only mode of locomotion was a staggering run with outstretched wings. Other examples of monstrosity were an eagle with twin heads, and a deer in which, with incredible ingenuity, the artists had induced the tail to develop as a head, with brain, sense organs, and jaws. In this monstrous art, interest in living things was infected with sadism through the preoccupation with fate, especially internal fate, as the divinity that shapes our ends. In its more vulgar forms, of course, it was a crude expression of egotistical lust in power.

This *motif* of the monstrous and the self-discrepant was less prominent than the other, the *motif* of harmonious perfection; but at all times it was apt to exercise at least a subconscious influence. The supreme aim of the dominant, perfection-seeking movement was to embellish the planet with a very diverse fauna and flora, with the human race as at once the crown and the instrument of terrestrial life. Each species, and each variety, was to have its place and fulfil its part in the great cycle of living types. Each was to be internally perfected to its function. It must have no harmful relics of a past manner of life; and its capacities must be in true accord with one another. But, to repeat, the supreme aim was not concerned merely with individual types, but with the whole vital economy of the planet. Thus, though there were to be types of every order from the most humble bacterium up to man, it was contrary to the canon of orthodox sacred art that any type should thrive by the destruction of a type higher than itself. In the sadistic mode of the art, however, a peculiarly exquisite tragic beauty was said to inhere in situations in which a lowly type exterminated a higher. There were occasions in the history of the race when the two sects indulged in bloody conflict because the sadists kept devising parasites to undermine the noble products of the orthodox.

Of those who practised vital art, and all did so to some extent, a few, though they deliberately rejected the orthodox principles, gained notoriety and even fame by their grotesques; while others, less fortunate, were ready to accept ostracism and even martyrdom, declaring that what they had produced was a significant symbol of the universal tragedy of vital nature. The great majority, however, accepted the sacred canon. They had therefore to choose one or other of certain recognized modes of expression. For instance, they might seek to enhance some extant type of organism, both by perfecting its capacities and by eliminating from it all that was harmful or useless. Or else, a more original and precarious work, they might set about creating a new type to fill a niche in the world, which had not yet been occupied. For this end they would select a suitable organism, and seek to remake it upon a new plan, striving to produce a creature of perfectly harmonious nature precisely adapted to the new way of life. In this kind of work sundry strict æsthetic principles must be observed. Thus it was considered bad art to reduce a higher type to a lower, or in any manner to waste the capacities of a type. And further, since the true end of art was not the production of individual types, but the production of a world-wide and perfectly systematic fauna and flora, it was inadmissible to harm even accidentally any type higher than that which it was intended to produce. For the practice of orthodox vital art was regarded as a co-operative enterprise. The ultimate artist, under God, was mankind as a whole; the ultimate work of art must be an ever more subtle garment of living forms for the adornment of the planet, and the delight of the supreme Artist, in relation to whom man was both creature and instrument.

Little was achieved, of course, until the applied biological sciences had advanced far beyond the high-water mark attained long ago during the career of the Second Men. Much more was needed than the rule-of-thumb principles of earlier breeders. It took this brightest of all the races of the third species many thousands of years of research to discover the more delicate principles of heredity, and to devise a technique by which the actual hereditary factors in the germ could be manipulated. It was this increasing penetration of biology itself that opened up the deeper regions of chemistry and physics. And owing to this historical sequence the latter sciences were conceived in a biological manner, with the electron as the basic organism, and the cosmos as an organic whole.

Imagine, then, a planet organized almost as a vast system of botanical and zoological gardens, or wild parks, interspersed with agriculture and industry. In every great centre of communications occurred annual and monthly shows. The latest creations were put through their paces, judged by the high priests of vital art, awarded distinctions, and consecrated with religious ceremony. At these shows some of the exhibits would be utilitarian, others purely æsthetic. There might be improved grains, vegetables, cattle, some exceptionally intelligent or sturdy variety of herdsman's dog, or a new micro-organism with some special function in agriculture or in human digestion. But also there would be the latest achievements in pure vital art. Great sleek-limbed, hornless, racing deer, birds or mammals adapted to some hitherto unfulfilled role, bears intended to outclass all existing varieties in the struggle for existence, ants with specialized organs and instincts, improvements in the relations of parasite and host, so as to make a true symbiosis in which the host profited by the parasite. And so on. And everywhere there would be the little unclad ruddy faun-like beings who had created these marvels. Shy forest-dwelling folk of Gurkha physique would stand beside their antelopes, vultures, or new great cat-like prowlers. A grave young woman might cause a stir by entering the grounds followed by several gigantic bears. Crowds would perhaps press round to examine the creatures' teeth or limbs, and she might scold the meddlers away from her patient flock. For the normal relation between man and beast at this time was one of perfect amity, rising, sometimes, in the case of domesticated animals, to an exquisite, almost painful, mutual adoration. Even the wild beasts never troubled to avoid man, still less to attack him, save in the special circumstances of the hunt and the sacred gladiatorial show.

These last need special notice. The powers of combat in beasts were admired no less than other powers. Men and women alike experienced a savage joy, almost an ecstasy, in the spectacle of mortal combat. Consequently there were formal occasions when different kinds of beasts were enraged against one another and allowed to fight to the death. Not only so, but also there were sacred contests between beast and man, between man and man, between woman and woman, and, most surprising to the readers of this book, between woman and man. For in this species, woman in her prime was not physically weaker than her partner.

4. CONFLICTING POLICIES

Almost from the first, vital art had been applied to some extent to man himself, though with hesitation. Certain great improvements had been effected, but only improvements about which there could be no two opinions. The many diseases and abnormalities left over from past civilizations were patiently abolished, and various more fundamental defects were remedied. For instance, teeth, digestion, glandular equipment and the circulatory system were greatly improved. Extreme good health and considerable physical beauty became universal. Child-bearing was made a painless and health-giving process. Senility was postponed. The standard of practical intelligence was appreciably raised. These reforms were made possible by a vast concerted effort of research and experiment supported by the world-community. But private enterprise was also effective, for the relation between the sexes was much more consciously dominated by the thought of offspring than among the First Men. Every individual knew the characteristics of his or her hereditary composition, and knew what kinds of offspring were to be expected from intercourse of different hereditary types.

Thus in courtship the young man was not content to persuade his beloved that his mind was destined by nature to afford her mind joyful completion; he sought also to persuade her that with his help she might bear children of a peculiar excellence. Consequently there was at all times going on a process of selective breeding towards the conventionally ideal type. In certain respects the ideal remained constant for many thousands of years. It included health, cat-like agility, manipulative dexterity, musical sensitivity, refined perception of rightness and wrongness in the sphere of vital art, and an intuitive practical judgment in all the affairs of life. Longevity, and the abolition of senility, were also sought, and partially attained. Waves of fashion sometimes directed sexual selection toward prowess in combat, or some special type of facial expression or vocal powers. But these fleeting whims were negligible. Only the permanently desired characters were actually intensified by private selective breeding.

But at length there came a time when more ambitious aims were entertained. The world-community was now a highly organized theocratic hierarchy, strictly but on the whole benevolently ruled by a supreme council of vital priests and biologists. Each individual, down to the humblest agricultural worker, had his special niche in society, allotted him by the supreme council or its delegates, according to his known heredity and the needs of society. This system, of course, sometimes led to abuse, but mostly it worked without serious friction. Such was the precision of biological knowledge that each person's mental calibre and special aptitudes were known beyond dispute, and rebellion against his lot in society would have been rebellion against his own heredity. This fact was universally known, and accepted without regret. A man had enough scope for emulation and triumph among his peers, without indulging in vague attempts to transcend his own nature, by rising into a superior hierarchical order. This state of affairs would have been impossible had there not been universal faith in the religion of life and the truth of biological science. Also it would have been impossible had not all normal persons been active practitioners of the sacred vital art, upon a plane suited to their capacity. Every individual adult of the rather scanty world-population regarded himself or herself as a creative artist, in however humble a sphere. And in general he, or she, was so fascinated by the work, that he was well content to leave social organization and control to those who were fitted for it. Moreover, at the back of every mind was the conception of society itself as an organism of specialized members. The strong sentiment for organized humanity tended, in this race, to master even its strong egotistical impulses, though not without a struggle.

It was such a society, almost unbelievable to the First Men, that now set about remaking human nature. Unfortunately there were conflicting views about the goal. The orthodox desired only to continue the work that had for long been on foot; though they proposed greater enterprise and co-ordination. They would perfect man's body, but upon its present plan; they would perfect his mind, but without seeking to introduce anything new in essence. His physique, percipience, memory, intelligence and emotional nature, should be improved almost beyond recognition; but they must, it was said, remain essentially what they always had been.

A second party, however, finally persuaded orthodox opinion to amplify itself in one important respect. As has already been said, the Third Men were prone to phases of preoccupation with the ancient craving for personal immortality. This craving had often been strong among the First Men; and even the Second Men, in spite of their great gift of detachment, had sometimes allowed their admiration for human personality to persuade them that souls must live for ever. The short-lived and untheoretical Third Men, with their passion for living things of all kinds, and all the diversity of vital behaviour, conceived immortality in a variety of manners. In their final culture they imagined that at death all living things whom the Life God approved passed into another world, much like the familiar world, but happier. There they were said to live in the presence of the deity, serving him in untrammelled vital creativeness of sundry kinds.

Now it was believed that communication might occur between the two worlds, and that the highest type of terrestrial life was that which communicated most effectively, and further that the time had now arrived for much fuller revelation of the life to come. It was therefore proposed to breed highly specialized communicants whose office should be to guide this world by means of advice from the other. As among the First Men, this communication with the unseen world was believed to take place in the mediumistic trance. The new enterprise, then, was to breed extremely sensitive mediums, and to increase the mediumistic powers of the average individual.

There was yet another party, whose aim was very different. Man, they said, is a very noble organism. We have dealt with other organisms so as to enhance in each its noblest attributes. It is time to do the same with man. What is most distinctive in man is intelligent manipulation, brain and hand. Now hand is really outclassed by modern mechanisms, but brain will never be outclassed. Therefore we must breed strictly for brain, for intelligent co-ordination of behaviour. All the organic functions which can be performed by machinery, must be relegated to machinery, so that the whole vitality of the organism may be devoted to brain-building and brain-working. We must produce an organism which shall be no mere bundle of relics left over from its primitive ancestors and precariously ruled by a glimmer of intelligence. We must produce a man who is nothing but man. When we have done this we can, if we like, ask him to find out the truth about immortality. And also, we can safely surrender to him the control of all human affairs.

The governing caste were strongly opposed to this policy. They declared that, if it succeeded, it would only produce a most inharmonious being whose nature would violate all the principles of vital æsthetics. Man, they said, was essentially an animal, though uniquely gifted. His whole nature must be developed, not one faculty at the expense of others. In arguing thus, they were probably influenced partly by the fear of losing their authority; but their arguments were cogent, and the majority of the community agreed with them. Nevertheless a small group of the governors themselves were determined to carry through the enterprise in secret.

There was no need of secrecy in breeding communicants. The world state encouraged this policy and even set up institutions for its pursuit.

CHAPTER XI

MAN REMAKES HIMSELF

I. THE FIRST OF THE GREAT BRAINS

THOSE who sought to produce a super-brain embarked upon a great enterprise of research and experiment in a remote corner of the planet. It is unnecessary to tell in detail how they fared. Working first in secret, they later strove to persuade the world to approve of their scheme, but only succeeded in dividing mankind into two parties. The body politic was torn asunder. There were religious wars. But after a few centuries of intermittent bloodshed the two sects, those who sought to produce communicants and those who sought the super-brain, settled down in different regions to pursue their respective aims unmolested. In time each developed into a kind of nation, united by a religious faith and crusading spirit. There was little cultural intercourse between the two.

Those who desired to produce the super-brain employed four methods, namely selective breeding, manipulation of the hereditary factors in germ cells (cultivated in the laboratory), manipulation of the fertilized ovum (cultivated also in the laboratory), and manipulation of the growing body. At first they produced innumerable tragic abortions. These we need not observe. But at length, several thousand years after the earliest experiments, something was produced which seemed to promise success. A human ovum had been carefully selected, fertilized in the laboratory, and largely reorganized by artificial means. By inhibiting the growth of the embryo's body, and the lower organs of the brain itself, and at the same time greatly stimulating the growth of the cerebral hemispheres, the dauntless experimenters succeeded at last in creating an organism which consisted of a brain twelve feet across, and a body most of which was reduced to a mere vestige upon the under-surface of the brain. The only parts of the body which were allowed to attain the natural size were the arms and hands. These sinewy organs of manipulation were induced to key themselves at the shoulders into the solid masonry which formed the creature's house. Thus they were able to get a purchase for their work. The hands were the normal six-fingered hands of the Third Men, very greatly enlarged and improved. The fantastic organism was generated and matured in a building designed to house both it and the complicated machinery which was necessary to keep it alive. A self-regulating pump, electrically driven, served it as a heart. A chemical factory poured the necessary materials into its blood and removed waste products, thus taking the place of digestive organs and the normal battery of glands. Its lungs consisted of a great room full of oxidizing tubes, through which a constant wind was driven by an electric fan. The same fan forced air through the artificial organs of speech. These organs were so constructed that the natural nerve-fibres, issuing from the speech centres of the brain, could stimulate appropriate electrical controls so as to produce sounds identical with those which they would have produced from a living throat and mouth. The sensory equipment of this trunkless brain was a blend of the natural and the artificial. The optic nerves were induced to grow out along two flexible probosces, five feet long, each of which bore a huge eye at the end. But by a very ingenious alteration of the structure of the eye, the natural lens could be moved aside at will, so that the retina could be applied to any of a great diversity of optical instruments. The ears also could be projected upon stalks, and were so arranged that the actual nerve endings could be brought into contact with artificial resonators of various kinds, or could listen directly to the miscroscopic rhythms of the most minute organisms. Scent and taste were developed as a chemical sense, which could distinguish almost all compounds and elements by their flavour. Pressure, warmth and cold were detected only by the fingers, but there with great subtlety. Sensory pain was to have been eliminated from the organism altogether; but this end was not achieved.

The creature was successfully launched upon life, and was actually kept alive for four years. But though at first all went well, in his second year the unfortunate child, if such he may be called, began to suffer severe pain, and to show symptoms of mental derangement. In spite of all that his devoted foster-parents could do, he gradually sank into insanity and died. He had succumbed to his own brain weight and to certain failures in the chemical regulation of his blood.

We may overlook the next four hundred years, during which sundry vain attempts were made to repeat the great experiment more successfully. Let us pass on to the first true individual of the fourth human species. He was produced in the same artificial manner as his forerunners, and was designed upon the same general plan. His mechanical and chemical machinery, however, was far more efficient; and his makers expected that, owing to careful adjustments of the mechanisms of growth and decay, he would prove to be immortal. His general plan, also, was changed in one important respect. His makers built a large circular "brain-turret" which they divided with many partitions, radiating from a central space, and covered everywhere with pigeon-holes. By a technique which took centuries to develop, they induced the cells of the growing embryonic brain to spread outwards, not as normal hemispheres of convolutions, but into the pigeon-holes which had been prepared for them. Thus the artificial "cranium" had to be a roomy turret of ferro-concrete some forty feet in diameter. A door and a passage led from the outer world into the centre of the turret, and thence other passages radiated between tiers of little cupboards. Innumerable tubes of glass, metal and a kind of vulcanite conveyed blood and chemicals over the whole system. Electric radiators preserved an even warmth in every cupboard, and throughout the innumerable carefully protected channels of the nerve-fibres. Thermometers, dials, pressure gauges, indicators of all sorts, informed the attendants of every physical change in this strange half-natural, half-artificial system, this preposterous factory of mind.

Eight years after its inception the organism had filled its brain room, and attained the mentality of a new-born infant. His advance to maturity seemed to his foster-parents dishearteningly slow. Not till almost at the end of his fifth decade could he be said to have reached the mental standard of a bright adolescent. But there was no real reason for disappointment. Within another decade this pioneer of the Fourth Men had learned all that the Third Men could teach him, and had also seen that a great part of their wisdom was folly. In manual dexterity he could already vie with the best; but though manipulation afforded him intense delight, he used his hands almost wholly in service of his tireless curiosity. In fact, it was evident that curiosity was his main characteristic. He was a huge bump of curiosity equipped with most cunning hands. A department of state had been created to look after his nurture and education. An army of learned persons was kept in readiness to answer his impatient questions and assist him in his own scientific experiments. Now that he had attained maturity these unfortunate pundits found themselves hopelessly outclassed, and reduced to mere clerks, bottle-washers and errand-boys. Hundreds of his servants were for ever scurrying into every corner of the planet to seek information and specimens; and the significance of their errands was by now often quite beyond the range of their own intelligence. They were careful, however, not to let their ignorance appear to the public. On the contrary, they succeeded in gaining much prestige from the mere mysteriousness of their errands.

The great brain was wholly lacking in all normal instinctive responses, save curiosity and constructiveness. Instinctive fear he knew not, though of course he was capable of cold caution in any circumstances which threatened to damage him and hinder his passionate research. Anger he knew not, but only an adamantine firmness in the face of opposition. Normal hunger and thirst he knew not, but only an experience of faintness when his blood was not properly supplied with nutriment. Sex was wholly absent from his mentality. Instinctive tenderness and instinctive group-feeling were not possible to him, for he was without the bowels of mercy. The heroic devotion of his most intimate servants called forth no gratitude, but only cold approval.

At first he interested himself not at all in the affairs of the society which maintained him, served his every whim, and adored him. But in time he began to take pleasure in suggesting brilliant solutions of all the current problems of social organization. His advice was increasingly sought and accepted. He became autocrat of the state. His own intelligence and complete detachment combined with the people's superstitious reverence to establish him far more securely than any ordinary tyrant. He cared nothing for the petty troubles of his people, but he was determined to be served by a harmonious, healthy and potent race. And as relaxation from the more serious excitement of research in physics and astronomy, the study of human nature was not without attractions. It may seem strange that one so completely devoid of human sympathy could have the tact to govern a race of the emotional Third Men. But he had built up for himself a very accurate behaviouristic psychology; and like the skilful master of animals, he knew unerringly how much could be expected of his people, even though their emotions were almost wholly foreign to him. Thus, for instance, while he thoroughly despised their admiration of animals and plants, and their religion of life, he soon learned not to seem hostile to these obsessions, but rather to use them for his own ends. He himself was interested in animals only as material for experiments. In this respect his people readily helped him, partly because he assured them that his goal was the further improvement of all types, partly because they were fascinated by his complete disregard, in his experimentation, of the common technique for preventing pain. The orgy of vicarious suffering awakened in his people the long-suppressed lust in cruelty which, in spite of their intuitive insight into animal nature, was so strong a factor in the third human species.

Little by little the great brain probed the material universe and the universe of mentality. He mastered the principles of biological evolution, and constructed for his own delight a detailed history of life on earth. He learned, by marvellous archæological technique, the story of all the earlier human peoples, and of the Martian episode, matters which had remained hidden from the Third Men. He discovered the principles of relativity and the quantum theory, the nature of the atom as a complex system of wave trains. He measured the cosmos; and with his delicate instruments he counted the planetary systems in many of the remote universes. He casually solved, to his own satisfaction at least, the ancient problems of good and evil, of mind and its object, of the one and the many, and of truth and error. He created many new departments of state for the purpose of recording his discoveries in an artificial language which he devised for the purpose. Each department consisted of many colleges of carefully bred and educated specialists who could understand the subject of their own department to some extent. But the co-ordination of all, and true insight into each, lay with the great brain alone.

2. THE TRAGEDY OF THE FOURTH MEN

When some three thousand years had passed since his beginning, the unique individual determined to create others of his kind. Not that he suffered from loneliness. Not that he yearned for love, or even for intellectual companionship. But solely for the undertaking of more profound research, he needed the co-operation of beings of his own mental stature. He therefore designed, and had built in various regions of the planet, turrets and factories like his own, though greatly improved. Into each he sent, by his servants, a cell of his own vestigial body, and directed how it should be cultivated so as to produce a new individual. At the same time he caused far-reaching operations to be performed upon himself, so that he should be remade upon a more ample plan. Of the new capacities which he inculcated in himself and his progeny the most important was direct sensitivity to radiation. This was achieved by incorporating in each brain-tissue a specially bred strain of Martian parasites. These henceforth were to live in the great brain as integral members of each one of its cells. Each brain was also equipped with a powerful wireless transmitting apparatus. Thus should the widely scattered sessile population maintain direct "telepathic" contact with one another.

The undertaking was successfully accomplished. Some ten thousand of these new individuals, each specialized for his particular locality and office, now constituted the Fourth Men. On the highest mountains were super-astronomers with vast observatories, whose instruments were partly artificial, partly natural excrescences of their own brains. In the very entrails of the planet others, specially adapted to heat, studied the subterranean forces, and were kept in "telepathic" union with the astronomers. In the tropics, in the Arctic, in the forests, the deserts, and on the ocean floor, the Fourth Men indulged their immense curiosity; and in the homeland, around the father of the race, a group of great buildings housed a hundred individuals. In the service of this world-wide population, those races of Third Men which had originally co-operated to produce the new human species, tilled the land, tended the cattle, manufactured the immense material requisites of the new civilization, and satisfied their spirits with an ever more stereotyped ritual of their ancient vital art. This degradation of the whole race to a menial position had occurred slowly, imperceptibly. But the result was none the less irksome. Occasionally there were sparks of rebellion, but they always failed to kindle serious trouble; for the prestige and persuasiveness of the Fourth Men were irresistible.

At length, however, a crisis occurred. For some three thousand years the Fourth Men had pursued their research with constant success, but latterly progress had been slow. It was becoming increasingly difficult to devise new lines of research. True, there was still much detail to be filled in, even in their knowledge of their own planet, and very much in their knowledge of the stars. But there was no prospect of opening up entirely new fields which might throw some light on the essential nature of things. Indeed, it began to dawn on them that they had scarcely plumbed a surface ripple of the ocean of mystery. Their knowledge seemed to them perfectly systematic, yet wholly enigmatic. They had a growing sense that though in a manner they knew almost everything, they really knew nothing.

The normal mind, when it experiences intellectual frustration, can seek recreation in companionship, or physical exercise, or art. But for the Fourth Men there was no such escape. These activities were impossible and meaningless to them. The Great Brains were whole-heartedly interested in the objective world, but solely as a vast stimulus to intellection, never for its own sake. They admired only the intellective process itself and the interpretative formulæ and principles which it devised. They cared no more for men and women than for material in a test-tube, no more for one another than for mechanical calculators. Nay, of each one of them it might almost be said that he cared even for himself solely as an instrument of knowing. Many of the species had actually sacrificed their sanity, even in some cases their lives, to the obsessive lust of intellection.

As the sense of frustration became more and more oppressive, the Fourth Men suffered more and more from the one-sidedness of their nature. Though so completely dispassionate while their intellectual life proceeded smoothly, now that it was thwarted they began to be confused by foolish whims and cravings which they disguised from themselves under a cloak of excuses. Sessile and incapable of affection, they continually witnessed the free movement, the group life, the love-making of their menials. Such activities became an offence to them, and filled them with a cold jealousy, which it was altogether beneath their dignity to notice. The affairs of the serf-population began to be conducted by their masters with less than the accustomed justice. Serious grievances arose.

The climax occurred in connexion with a great revival of research, which, it was said, would break down the impalpable barriers and set knowledge in progress again. The Great Brains were to be multiplied a thousandfold, and the resources of the whole planet were to be devoted far more strictly than before to the crusade of intellection. The menial Third Men would therefore have to put up with more work and less pleasure.

Formerly they would willingly have accepted this fate for the glory of serving the super-human brains. But the days of their blind devotion was past. It was murmured among them that the great experiment of their fore-fathers had proved a great disaster, and that the Fourth Men, the Great Brains, in spite of their devilish cunning, were mere abortions.

Matters came to a head when the tyrants announced that all useless animals must be slaughtered, since their upkeep was too great an economic burden upon the world-community. The vital art, moreover, was to be practised in future only by the Great Brains themselves. This announce-ment threw the Third Men into violent excitement, and divided them into two parties. Many of those whose lives were spent in direct service of the Great Brains favoured implicit obedience, though even these were deeply distressed. The majority, on the other hand, absolutely refused to permit the impious slaughter, or even to surrender their privileges as vital artists. For, they said, to kill off the fauna of the planet would be to violate the fair form of the universe by blotting out many of its most beautiful fea-tures. It would be an outrage to the Life-God, and he would surely avenge it. They therefore urged that the time was come for all true human beings to stand together and depose the tyrants. And this, they pointed out, could easily be done. It was only necessary to cut a few electric cables, connect-ing the Great Brains with the subterranean generating stations. The electric pumps would then cease to supply the brain-turrets with aerated blood. Or, in the few cases in which the Great Brains were so located that they could control their own source of power in wind or water, it was necessary merely to refrain from transporting food to their digestion-laboratories.

The personal attendants of the Great Brains shrank from such ac-tion; for their whole lives had been devoted, proudly and even in a manner lovingly, to service of the revered beings. But the agriculturists determined to withhold supplies. The Great Brains, therefore, armed their servitors with a diversity of ingenious weapons. Immense destruction was done; but since the rebels were decimated, there were not enough hands to work the fields. Some of the Great Brains, and many of their servants, actually died of starvation. And as hardship increased, the servants themselves began to drift over to the rebels. It now seemed certain to the Third Men that the Great Brains would very soon be impotent, and the planet once more un-der the control of natural beings. But the tyrants were not to be so easily defeated. Already for some centuries they had been secretly experimenting with a means of gaining a far more thorough dominion over the natural species. At the eleventh hour they succeeded.

In this undertaking they had been favoured by the results which a sec-tion of the natural species itself had produced long ago in the effort to breed specialized communicants to keep in touch with the unseen world. That sect, or theocratic nation, which had striven for many centuries to-ward this goal, had finally attained what they regarded as success. There came into existence an hereditary caste of communicants. Now, though these beings were subject to mediumistic trances in which they apparently conversed with denizens of the other world and received instructions about the ordering of matters terrestrial, they were in fact merely abnormally suggestible. Trained from childhood in the lore of the unseen world, their minds, during the trance, were amazingly fertile in developing fantasies based on that lore. Left to themselves, they were merely folk who were abnormally lacking in initiative and intelligence. Indeed, so naïve were they, and so sluggish, that they were mentally more like cattle than human beings. Yet under the influence of suggestion they became both intelligent and vigorous. Their intelligence, however, operating strictly in service of the suggestion, was wholly incapable of criticizing the suggestion itself.

There is no need to revert to the downfall of this theocratic society, beyond saying that, since both private and public affairs were regulated by reference to the sayings of the communicants, inevitably the state fell into chaos. The other community of the Third Men, that which was engaged upon breeding the Great Brains, gradually dominated the whole planet. The mediumistic stock, however, remained in existence, and was treated with a half-contemptuous reverence. The mediums were still generally regarded as in some manner specially gifted with the divine spirit, but they were now thought to be too holy for their sayings to have any relation to mundane affairs.

It was by means of this mediumistic stock that the Great Brains had intended to consolidate their position. Their earlier efforts may be passed over. But in the end they produced a race of living and even intelligent machines whose will they could control absolutely, even at a great distance. For the new variety of Third Men was "telepathically" united with its masters. Martian units had been incorporated in its nervous system.

At the last moment the Great Brains were able to put into the field an army of these perfect slaves, which they equipped with the most efficient lethal weapons. The remnant of original servants discovered too late that they had been helping to produce their supplanters. They joined the rebels, only to share in the general destruction. In a few months all the Third Men, save the new docile variety, were destroyed; except for a few specimens which were preserved in cages for experimental purposes. And in a few years every type of animal that was not known to be directly or indirectly necessary to human life had been exterminated. None were preserved even as specimens, for the Great Brains had already studied them through and through.

But though the Great Brains were now absolute possessors of the Earth, they were after all no nearer their goal than before. The actual struggle with the natural species had provided them with an aim; but now that the struggle was over, they began to be obsessed once more with their intellectual failure. With painful clarity they realized that, in spite of their vast weight of neural tissue, in spite of their immense knowledge and cunning, they were practically no nearer the ultimate truth than their predecessors had been. Both were infinitely far from it.

For the Fourth Men, the Great Brains, there was no possible life but the life of intellect; and the life of intellect had become barren. Evidently something more than mere bulk of brain was needed for the solving of the deeper intellectual problems. They must, therefore, somehow create a new brain-quality, or organic formation of brain, capable of a mode of vision or insight impossible in their present state. They must learn somehow to remake their own brain-tissues upon a new plan. With this aim, and partly through unwitting jealousy of the natural and more balanced species which had created them, they began to use their captive specimens of that species for a great new enterprise of research into the nature of human brain-tissue. It was hoped thus to find some hint of the direction in which the new evolutionary leap should take place. The unfortunate specimens were therefore submitted to a thousand ingenious physiological and psychological tortures. Some were kept alive with their brains spread out permanently on a laboratory table, for microscopic observation during their diverse psychological reactions. Others were put into fantastic states of mental abnormality. Others were maintained in perfect health of body and mind, only to be felled at last by some ingeniously contrived tragic experience. New types were produced which, it was hoped, might show evidence of emergence into a qualitatively higher mode of mentality; but in fact they succeeded only in ranging through the whole gamut of insanity.

The research continued for some thousands of years, but gradually slackened, so utterly barren did it prove to be. As this frustration became more and more evident, a change began to come over the minds of the Fourth Men.

They knew, of course, that the natural species valued many things and activities which they themselves did not appreciate at all. Hitherto this had seemed a symptom merely of the low mental development of the natural species. But the behaviour of the unfortunate specimens upon whom they had been experimenting had gradually given the Fourth Men a greater insight into the likings and admirations of the natural species, so that they had learned to distinguish between those desires which were fundamental and those merely accidental cravings which clear thinking would have dismissed. In fact, they came to see that certain activities and certain objects were appreciated by these beings with the same clear-sighted conviction as they themselves appreciated knowledge. For instance, the natural human beings valued one another, and were sometimes capable of sacrificing themselves for the sake of others. They also valued love itself. And again they valued very seriously their artistic activities; and the activities of their bodies and of animal bodies appeared to them to have intrinsic excellence.

Little by little the Fourth Men began to realize that what was wrong with themselves was not merely their intellectual limitation, but, far more seriously, the limitation of their insight into values. And this weakness, they saw, was the result, not of paucity of intellective brain, but of paucity of body and lower brain tissues. This defect they could not remedy. It was obviously impossible to remake themselves so radically that they should become of a more normal type. Should they concentrate their efforts upon the production of new individuals more harmonious than themselves? Such a work, it might be supposed, would have seemed unattractive to them. But no. They argued thus: "It is our nature to care most for knowing. Full knowledge is to be attained only by minds both more penetrating and more broadly based than ours. Let us, therefore, waste no more time in seeking to achieve the goal in ourselves. Let us seek rather to produce a kind of being, free from our limitations, in whom we may attain the goal of perfect knowledge vicariously. The producing of such a being will exercise all our powers, and will afford the highest kind of fulfilment possible to us. To refrain from this work would be irrational."

Thus it came about that the artificial Fourth Men began to work in a new spirit upon the surviving specimens of the Third Men to produce their own supplanters.

3. THE FIFTH MEN

The plan of the proposed new human being was worked out in great detail before any attempt was made to produce an actual individual. Essentially he was to be a normal human organism, with all the bodily functions of the natural type; but he was to be perfected through and through. Care must be taken to give him the greatest possible bulk of brain compatible with such a general plan, but no more. Very carefully his creators calculated the dimensions and internal proportions which their creature must have. His brain could not be nearly as large as their own, since he would have to carry it about with him, and maintain it with his own physiological machinery. On the other hand, if it was to be at all larger than the natural brain, the rest of the organism must be proportionately sturdy. Like the Second Men, the new species must be titanic. Indeed, it must be such as to dwarf even those natural giants. The body, however, must not be so huge as to be seriously hampered by its own weight, and by the necessity of having bones so massive as to be unmanageable.

In working out the general proportions of the new man, his makers took into account the possibility of devising more efficient bone and muscle. After some centuries of patient experiment they did actually invent a means of inducing in germ cells a tendency toward far stronger bone-tissues and far more powerful muscle. At the same time they devised nerve-tissues more highly specialized for their particular functions. And in the new brain, so minute compared with their own, smallness was to be compensated for by efficiency of design, both in the individual cells and in their organization.

Further, it was found possible to economize somewhat in bulk and vital energy by improvements in the digestive system. Certain new models of micro-organisms were produced, which, living symbiotically in the human gut, should render the whole process of digestion easier, more rapid, and less erratic.

Special attention was given to the system of self-repair in all tissues, especially in those which had hitherto been the earliest to wear out. And at the same time the mechanism regulating growth and general senescence was so designed that the new man should reach maturity at the age of two hundred years, and should remain in full vigour, for at least three thousand years, when, with the first serious symptom of decay, his heart should suddenly cease functioning. There had been some dispute whether the new being should be endowed with perennial life, like his makers. But in the end it had been decided that, since he was intended only as a transitional type, it would be safer to allow him only a finite, though a prolonged lifetime. There must be no possibility that he should be tempted to regard himself as life's final expression.

In sensory equipment, the new man was to have all the advantages of the Second and Third Men, and, in addition a still wider range and finer discrimination in every sense organ. More important was the incorporation of Martian units in the new model of germ cell. As the organism developed, these should propagate themselves and congregate in the cells of the brain, so that every brain area might be sensitive to ethereal vibrations, and the whole might emit a strong system of radiation. But care was taken that this "telepathic" faculty of the new species should remain subordinate. There must be no danger that the individual should become a mere resonator of the herd.

Long-drawn-out chemical research enabled the Fourth Men to design also far-reaching improvements in the secretions of the new man, so that he should maintain both a perfect physiological equilibrium and a well-balanced temperament. For they were determined that though he should experience all the range of emotional life, his passions should not run into disastrous excess; nor should he be prone to some one emotion in season and out of season. It was necessary also to revise in great detail the whole system of natural reflexes, abolishing some, modifying others, and again strengthening others. All the more complex, "instinctive" responses, which had persisted in man since the days of Pithecanthropus Erectus, had also to be meticulously revised, both in respect of the form of activity and the objects upon which they should be instinctively directed. Anger, fear, curiosity, humour, tenderness, egoism, sexual passion, and sociality must all be possible, but never uncontrollable. In fact, as with the Second Men, but more emphatically, the new type was to have an innate aptitude for, and inclination toward, all those higher activities and objects which, in the First Men, were only achieved after laborious discipline. Thus, while the design included self-regard, it also involved a disposition to prize the self chiefly as a social and intellectual being, rather than as a primeval savage. And while it included strong sociality, the group upon which instinctive interest was to be primarily directed was to be nothing less than the organized community of all minds. And again, while it included vigorous primitive sexuality and parenthood, it provided also those innate "sublimations" which had occurred in the second species; for instance, the native aptitude for altruistic love of individual spirits of every kind, and for art and religion. Only by a miracle of pure intellectual skill could the cold-natured Great Brains, who were themselves doomed never to have actual experience of such activities, contrive, merely by study of the Third Men, to see their importance, and to design an organism splendidly capable of them. It was much as though a blind race, after studying physics, should invent organs of sight.

It was recognized, of course, that in a race in which the average life-span should be counted in thousands of years, procreation must be very rare. Yet it was also recognized that, for full development of mind, not only sexual intercourse but parenthood was necessary in both sexes. This difficulty was overcome partly by designing a very prolonged infancy and childhood; which, necessary in themselves for the proper mental and physical growth of these complicated organisms, provided also a longer exercise of parenthood for the mature. At the same time the actual process of childbirth was designed to be as easy as among the Third Men. And it was expected that with its greatly improved physiological organization the infant would not need that anxious and absorbing care which had so seriously hobbled most mothers among the earlier races.

The mere sketching out of these preliminary specifications of an improved human being involved many centuries of research and calculation which taxed even the ingenuity of the Great Brains. Then followed a lengthy period of tentative experiment in the actual production of such a type. For some thousands of years little was done but to show that many promising lines of attack were after all barren. And several times during this period the whole work was held up by disagreements among the Great Brains themselves as to the policy to be adopted. Once, indeed, they took to violence, one party attacking the other with chemicals, microbes, and armies of human automata.

In short it was only after many failures, and after many barren epochs during which, for a variety of reasons, the enterprise was neglected, that the Fourth Men did at length fashion two individuals almost precisely of the type they had originally designed. These were produced from a single fertilized ovum, in laboratory conditions. Identical twins, but of opposite sexes, they became the Adam and Eve of a new and glorious human species, the Fifth Men.

It may fittingly be said of the Fifth Men that they were the first to attain true human proportions of body and mind. On the average they were more than twice as tall as the First Men, and much taller than the Second Men. Their lower limbs had therefore to be extremely massive compared with the torso which they had to support. Thus, upon the ample pedestal of their feet, they stood like columns of masonry. Yet though their proportions were in a manner elephantine, there was a remarkable precision and even delicacy in the volumes that composed them. Their great arms and shoulders, dwarfed somewhat by their still mightier legs, were instruments not only of power but also of fine adjustment. Their hands also were fashioned both for power and for minute control; for, while the thumb and forefinger constituted a formidable vice, the delicate sixth finger had been induced to divide its tip into two Lilliputian fingers and a corresponding thumb. The contours of the limbs were sharply visible, for the body bore no hair, save for a close, thick skull-cap which, in the original stock, was of ruddy brown. The well-marked eyebrows, when drawn down, shaded the sensitive eyes from the sun. Elsewhere there was no need of hair, for the brown skin had been so ingeniously contrived that it maintained an even temperature alike in tropical and subarctic climates, with no aid either from hair or clothes. Compared with the great body, the head was not large, though the brain capacity was twice that of the Second Men. In the original pair of individuals the immense eyes were of a deep violet, the features strongly moulded and mobile. These facial characters had not been specially designed, for they seemed unimportant to the Fourth Men; but the play of biological forces resulted in a face not unlike that of the Second Men, though with an added and indescribable expression which no human face had hitherto attained.

How from this pair of individuals the new population gradually arose; how at first it was earnestly fostered by its creators; how it subsequently asserted its independence and took control of its own destiny; how the Great Brains failed piteously to understand and sympathize with the mentality of their creatures, and tried to tyrannize over them; how for a while the planet was divided into two mutually intolerant communities, and was at last drenched with man's blood, until the human automata were exterminated, the Great Brains starved or blown to pieces, and the Fifth Men themselves decimated; how, as a result of these events, a dense fog of barbarism settled once more upon the planet, so that the Fifth Men, like so many other races, had after all to start rebuilding civilization and culture from its very foundations; how all these things befell we must not in detail observe.

4. THE CULTURE OF THE FIFTH MEN

It is not possible to recount the stages by which the Fifth Men advanced toward their greatest civilization and culture; for it is that fully developed culture itself which concerns us. And even of their highest achievement, which persisted for so many millions of years, I can say but little, not merely because I must hasten to the end of my story, but also because so much of that achievement lies wholly beyond the comprehension of those for whom this book is intended. For I have at last reached that period in the history of man when he first began to reorganize his whole mentality to cope with matters whose very existence had been hitherto almost completely hidden from him. The old aims persist, and are progressively realized as never before; but also they become increasingly subordinate to the requirements of new aims which are more and more insistently forced upon him by his deepening experience. Just as the interests and ideals of the First Men lie beyond the grasp of their ape contemporaries, so the interests and ideals of the Fifth Men in their full development lie beyond the grasp of the First Men. On the other hand, just as, in the life of primitive man, there is much which would be meaningful even to the ape, so in the life of the Fifth Men much remains which is meaningful even to the First Men.

Conceive a world-society developed materially far beyond the wildest dreams of America. Unlimited power, derived partly from the artificial disintegration of atoms, partly from the actual annihilation of matter through the union of electrons and protons to form radiation, completely abolished the whole grotesque burden of drudgery which hitherto had seemed the inescapable price of civilization, nay of life itself. The vast economic routine of the world-community was carried on by the mere touching of appropriate buttons. Transport, mining, manufacture, and even agriculture were performed in this manner. And indeed in most cases the systematic co-ordination of these activities was itself the work of self-regulating machinery. Thus, not only was there no longer need for any human beings to spend their lives in unskilled monotonous labour, but further, much that earlier races would have regarded as highly skilled though stereotyped work, was now carried on by machinery. Only the pioneering of industry, the endless exhilarating research, invention, design and reorganization, which is incurred by an ever-changing society, still engaged the minds of men and women. And though this work was of course immense, it could not occupy the whole attention of a great world-community. Thus very much of the energy of the race was free to occupy itself with other no less difficult and exacting matters, or to seek recreation in its many admirable sports and arts. Materially every individual was a multi-millionaire, in that he had at his beck and call a great diversity of powerful mechanisms; but also he was a penniless friar, for he had no

vestige of economic control over any other human being. He could fly
through the upper air to the ends of the earth in an hour, or hang idle
among the clouds all day long. His flying machine was no cumbersome
aeroplane, but either a wingless aerial boat, or a mere suit of overalls in
which he could disport himself with the freedom of a bird. Not only in
the air, but in the sea also, he was free. He could stroll about the ocean
bed, or gambol with the deep-sea fishes. And for habitation he could make
his home, as he willed, either in a shack in the wilderness or in one of the
great pylons which dwarfed the architecture even of the American age. He
could possess this huge palace in loneliness and fill it with his possessions,
to be automatically cared for without human service; or he could join
with others and create a hive of social life. All these amenities he took for
granted as the savage takes for granted the air which he breathes. And because they were as universally available as air, no one craved them in excess,
and no one grudged another the use of them.

Yet the population of the earth was now very numerous. Some ten
thousand million persons had their homes in the snow-capped pylons
which covered the continents with an open forest of architecture. Between
these great obelisks lay corn-land, park, and wilderness. For there were
very many areas of hill-country and forest which were preserved as playgrounds. And indeed one whole continent, stretching from the Tropics to
the Arctic, was kept as nearly as possible in its natural state. This region
was chosen mainly for its mountains; for since most of the Alpine tracts
had by now been worn into insignificance by water and frost, mountains
were much prized. Into this Wild Continent individuals of all ages repaired to spend many years at a time in living the life of primitive man
without any aid whatever from civilization. For it was recognized that a
highly sophisticated race, devoted almost wholly to art and science, must
take special measures to preserve its contact with the primitive. Thus in
the Wild Continent was to be found at any time a sparse population of
"savages," armed with flint and bone, or more rarely with iron, which they
or their friends had wrested from the earth. These voluntary primitives
were intent chiefly upon hunting and simple agriculture. Their scanty
leisure was devoted to art, and meditation, and to savouring fully all the
primeval human values. Indeed it was a hard life and a dangerous that
these intellectuals periodically imposed on themselves. And though of
course they had zest in it, they often dreaded its hardship and the uncertainty that they would ever return from it. For the danger was very real.
The Fifth Men had compensated for the Fourth Men's foolish destruction
of the animals by creating a whole system of new types, which they set
at large in the Wild Continent; and some of these creatures were extremely
formidable carnivora, which man himself, armed only with primitive weapons, had very good reason to fear. In the Wild Continent there was inevitably a high death-rate. Many promising lives were tragically cut short. But

it was recognized that from the point of view of the race this sacrifice was worth while, for the spiritual effects of the institution of periodic savagery were very real. Beings whose natural span was three thousand years, given over almost wholly to civilized pursuits, were greatly invigorated and enlightened by an occasional decade in the wild.

The culture of the Fifth Men was influenced in many respects by their "telepathic" communication with one another. The obvious advantages of this capacity were now secured without its dangers. Each individual could isolate himself at will from the radiation of his fellows, either wholly or in respect of particular elements of his mental process; and thus he was in no danger of losing his individuality. But, on the other hand, he was immeasurably more able to participate in the experience of others than were beings for whom the only possible communication was symbolic. The result was that, though conflict of wills was still possible, it was far more easily resolved by mutual understanding than had ever been the case in earlier species. Thus there were no lasting and no radical conflicts, either of thought or desire. It was universally recognized that every discrepancy of opinion and of aim could be abolished by telepathic discussion. Sometimes the process would be easy and rapid; sometimes it could not be achieved without a patient and detailed "laying of mind to mind," so as to bring to light the point where the difference originated.

One result of the general "telepathic" facility of the species was that speech was no longer necessary. It was still preserved and prized, but only as a medium of art, not as a means of communication. Thinking, of course, was still carried on largely by means of words; but in communication there was no more need actually to speak the words than in thinking in private. Written language remained essential for the recording and storing of thought. Both language and the written expression of it had become far more complex and accurate than they had ever been, more faithful instruments for the expression and creation of thought and emotion.

"Telepathy" combined with longevity and the extremely subtle brain-structure of the species to afford each individual an immense number of intimate friendships, and some slight acquaintance actually with the whole race. This, I fear, must seem incredible to my readers, unless they can be persuaded to regard it as a symptom of the high mental development of the species. However that may be, it is a fact that each person was aware of every other, at least as a face, or a name, or the holder of a certain office. It is impossible to exaggerate the effects of this facility of personal intercourse. It meant that the species constituted at any moment, if not strictly a community of friends, at least a vast club or college. Further, since each individual saw his own mind reflected, as it were, in very many other minds, and since there was great variety of psychological types, the upshot in each individual was a very accurate self-consciousness.

In the Martians, "telepathic" intercourse had resulted in a true group-mind, a single psychical process embodied in the electro-magnetic radiation of the whole race; but this group-mind was inferior in calibre to the individual minds. All that was distinctive of an individual at his best failed to contribute to the group-mind. But in the fifth human species "telepathy" was only a means of intercourse between individuals; there was no true group-mind. On the other hand, telepathic intercourse occurred even on the highest planes of experience. It was by "telepathic" intercourse in respect of art, science, philosophy, and the appreciation of personalities, that the public mind, or rather the public culture, of the Fifth Men had being. With the Martians, "telepathic" union took place chiefly by elimination of the differences between individuals; with the Fifth Men "telepathic" communication was, as it were, a kind of spiritual multiplication of mental diversity, by which each mind was enriched with the wealth of ten thousand million. Consequently each individual was, in a very real sense, the cultured mind of the species; but there were as many such minds as there were individuals. There was no additional racial mind over and above the minds of the individuals. Each individual himself was a conscious centre which participated in, and contributed to, the experience of all other centres.

This state of affairs would not have been possible had not the world-community been able to direct so much of its interest and energy into the higher mental activities. The whole structure of society was fashioned in relation to its best culture. It is almost impossible to give even an inkling of the nature and aims of this culture, and to make it believable that a huge population should have spent scores of millions of years not wholly, not even chiefly, on industrial advancement, but almost entirely on art, science and philosophy, without ever repeating itself or falling into ennui. I can only point out that, the higher a mind's development, the more it discovers in the universe to occupy it.

Needless to say, the Fifth Men had early mastered all those paradoxes of physical science which had so perplexed the First Men. Needless to say, they had a very complete knowledge of the geography of the cosmos and of the atom. But again and again the very foundations of their science were shattered by some new discovery, so that they had patiently to reconstruct the whole upon an entirely new plan. At length, however, with the clear formulation of the principles of psycho-physics, in which the older psychology and the older physics were held, so to speak, in chemical combination, they seemed to have built upon the rock. In this science, the fundamental concepts of psychology were given a physical meaning, and the fundamental concepts of physics were stated in a psychological manner. Further, the most fundamental relations of the physical universe were found to be of the same nature as the fundamental principles of art. But, and herein lay mystery and horror even for the Fifth Men, there was no shred of evidence that this æsthetically admirable cosmos was the work of a conscious artist, nor yet that any mind would ever develop so greatly as to be able to appreciate the Whole in all its detail and unity.

Since art seemed to the Fifth Men to be in some sense basic to the cosmos, they were naturally very much preoccupied with artistic creation. Consequently, all those who were not social or economic organizers, or scientific researchers, or pure philosophers, were by profession creative artists or handicraftsmen. That is to say, they were engaged on the production of material objects of various kinds, whose form should be æsthetically significant to the perceiver. In some cases the material object was a pattern of spoken words, in others pure music, in others moving coloured shapes, in others a complex of steel cubes and bars, in others some translation of the human figure into a particular medium, and so on. But also the æsthetic impulse expressed itself in the production, by hand, of innumerable common utensils, indulging sometimes in lavish decoration, trusting at other times to the beauty of function. Every medium of art that had ever been employed was employed by the Fifth Men, and innumerable new vehicles were also used. They prized on the whole more highly those kinds of art which were not static; but involved time as well as space; for as a race they were peculiarly fascinated by time.

These innumerable artists held that they were doing something of great importance. The cosmos was to be regarded as an æsthetic unity in four directions, and of inconceivable complexity. Human works of pure art were thought of as instruments through which man might behold and admire some aspect of the cosmic beauty. They were said to focus together features of the cosmos too vast and elusive for man otherwise to apprehend their form. The work of art was sometimes likened to a compendious mathematical formula expressive of some immense and apparently chaotic field of facts. But in the case of art, it was said, the unity which the artistic object elicited was one in which factors of vital nature and of mind itself were essential members.

The race thus deemed itself to be engaged upon a great enterprise both of discovery and creation in which each individual was both an originator of some unique contribution, and an appraiser of all.

Now, as the years advanced in millions and in decades of millions, it began to be noticed that the movement of world culture was in a manner spiral. There would be an age during which the interest of the race was directed almost wholly upon certain tracts or aspects of existence; and then, after perhaps a hundred thousand years, these would seem to have been fully cultivated, and would be left fallow. During the next epoch attention would be in the main directed to other spheres, and then afterwards to yet others, and again others. But at length a return would be made to the fields that had been deserted, and it would be discovered that they could now miraculously bear a million-fold the former crop. Thus, in both science and art man kept recurring again and again to the ancient themes, to work over them once more in meticulous detail and strike from them new truth and new beauty, such as, in the earlier epoch, he could never have conceived. Thus it was that, though science gathered to itself unfalteringly an ever wider and more detailed view of existence, it periodically discovered some revolutionary general principle in terms of which its whole content had to be given a new significance. And in art there would appear in one age works superficially almost identical with works of another age, yet to the discerning eye incomparably more significant. Similarly, in respect of human personality itself, those men and women who lived at the close of the aeon of the Fifth Men could often discover in the remote beginning of their own race beings curiously like themselves, yet, as it were, expressed in fewer dimensions than their own many-dimensional natures. As a map is like the mountainous land, or the picture like the landscape, or indeed as the point and the circle are like the sphere, so, and only so, the earlier Fifth Men resembled the flower of the species.

Such statements would be in a manner true of any period of steady cultural progress. But in the present instance they have a peculiar significance which I must now somehow contrive to suggest.

CHAPTER XII

THE LAST TERRESTRIALS

1. THE CULT OF EVANESCENCE

THE Fifth Men had not been endowed with that potential immortality which their makers themselves possessed. And from the fact that they were mortal and yet long-lived, their culture drew its chief brilliance and poignancy. Beings for whom the natural span was three thousand years, and ultimately as much as fifty thousand, were peculiarly troubled by the prospect of death, and by the loss of those dear to them. The mere ephemeral kind of spirit, that comes into being and then almost immediately ceases, before it has entered at all deeply into consciousness of itself, can face its end with a courage that is half unwitting. Even its smart in the loss of other beings with whom it has been intimate is but a vague and dream-like suffering. For the ephemeral spirit has no time to grow fully awake, or fully intimate with another, before it must lose its beloved, and itself once more fade into unconsciousness. But with the long-lived yet not immortal Fifth Men the case was different. Gathering to themselves experience of the cosmos, acquiring an ever more precise and vivid insight and appreciation, they knew that very soon all this wealth of the soul must cease to be. And in love, though they might be fully intimate not merely with one but with very many persons, the death of one of these dear spirits seemed an irrevocable tragedy, an utter annihilation of the most resplendent kind of glory, an impoverishment of the cosmos for evermore.

In their brief primitive phase, the Fifth Men, like so many other races, sought to console themselves by unreasoning faith in a life after death. They conceived, for instance, that at death terrestrial beings embarked upon a career continuous with earthly life, but far more ample, either in some remote planetary system, or in some wholly distinct orb of space-time. But though such theories were never disproved in the primitive era, they gradually began to seem not merely improbable but ignoble. For it came to be recognized that the resplendent glories of personality, even in that degree of beauty which now for the first time was attained, were not after all the extreme of glory. It was seen with pain, but also with exultation, that even love's demand that the beloved should have immortal life is a betrayal of man's paramount allegiance. And little by little it became evident that those who used great gifts, and even genius, to establish the truth of the after life, or to seek contact with their beloved dead, suffered from a strange blindness, and obtuseness of the spirit. Though the love which had misled them was itself a very lovely thing, yet they were misled. Like children, searching for lost toys, they wandered. Like adolescents seeking to recapture delight in the things of childhood, they shunned those more difficult admirations which are proper to the grown mind.

And so it became a constant aim of the Fifth Men to school themselves to admire chiefly even in the very crisis of bereavement, not persons, but that great music of innumerable personal lives, which is the life of the race. And quite early in their career they discovered an unexpected beauty in the very fact that the individual must die. So that, when they had actually come into possession of the means to make themselves immortal, they refrained, choosing rather merely to increase the life-span of succeeding generations to fifty thousand years. Such a period seemed to be demanded for the full exercise of human capacity; but immortality, they held, would lead to spiritual disaster.

Now as their science advanced they saw that there had been a time, before the stars were formed, when there was no possible footing for minds in the cosmos; and that there would come a time when mentality would be driven out of existence. Earlier human species had not needed to trouble about mind's ultimate fate; but for the long-lived Fifth Men the end, though remote, did not seem infinitely distant. The prospect distressed them. They had schooled themselves to live not for the individual but for the race; and now the life of the race itself was seen to be a mere instant between the endless void of the past and the endless void of the future. Nothing within their ken was more worthy of admiration than the organized progressive mentality of mankind; and the conviction that this most admired thing must soon cease, filled many of their less ample minds with horror and indignation. But in time the Fifth Men, like the Second Men long before them, came to suspect that even in this tragic brevity of mind's course there was a quality of beauty, more difficult than the familiar beauty, but also more exquisite. Even thus imprisoned in an instant, the spirit of man might yet plumb the whole extent of space, and also the whole past and the whole future; and so, from behind his prison bars, he might render the universe that intelligent worship which, they felt, it demanded of him. Better so, they said, than that he should fret himself with puny efforts to escape. He is dignified by his very weakness, and the cosmos by its very indifference to him.

For aeons they remained in this faith. And they schooled their hearts to acquiesce in it, saying, if it is so, it is best, and somehow we must learn to see that it is best. But what they meant by "best" was not what their predecessors would have meant. They did not, for instance, deceive themselves by pretending that after all they themselves actually preferred life to be evanescent. On the contrary, they continued to long that it might be otherwise. But having discovered, both behind the physical order and behind the desires of minds, a fundamental principle whose essence was æsthetic, they were faithful to the conviction that whatever was fact must somehow in the universal view be fitting, right, beautiful, integral to the form of the cosmos. And so they accepted as right a state of affairs which in their own hearts they still felt grievously wrong. This conviction of the irrevocability of the past and of the evanescence of mind induced in them a great tenderness for all beings that had lived and ceased. Deeming themselves to be near the crest of life's achievement, blessed also with longevity and philosophic detachment, they were often smitten with pity for those humbler, briefer and less free spirits whose lot had fallen in the past. Moreover, themselves extremely complex, subtle, conscious, they conceived a generous admiration for all simple minds, for the early men, and for the beasts. Very strongly they condemned the action of their predecessors in destroying so many joyous and delectible creatures. Earnestly they sought to reconstruct in imagination all those beings that blind intellectualism had murdered. Earnestly they delved in the near and the remote past so as to recover as much as possible of the history of life on the planet. With meticulous love they would figure out the life stories of extinct types, such as the brontosaurus, the hippopotamus, the chimpanzee, the Englishman, the American, as also of the still extant amœba. And while they could not but relish the comicality of these remote beings, their amusement was the outgrowth of affectionate insight into simple natures, and was but the obverse of their recognition that the primitive is essentially tragic, because blind. And so, while they saw that the main work of man must have regard to the future, they felt that he owed also a duty toward the past. He must preserve it in his own mind, if not actually in life at least in being. In the future lay glory, joy, brilliance of the spirit. The future needed service, not pity, not piety; but in the past lay darkness, confusion, waste, and all the cramped primitive minds, bewildered, torturing one another in their stupidity, yet one and all in some unique manner, beautiful.

The reconstruction of the past, not merely as abstract history but with the intimacy of the novel, thus became one of the main preoccupations of the Fifth Men. Many devoted themselves to this work, each individual specializing very minutely in some particular episode of human or animal history, and transmitting his work into the culture of the race. Thus increasingly the individual felt himself to be a single flicker between the teeming gulf of the never-more and the boundless void of the not-yet. Himself a member of a very noble and fortunate race, his zest in existence was tempered, deepened, by a sense of the presence, the ghostly presence, of the myriad less fortunate beings in the past. Sometimes, and especially in epochs when the contemporary world seemed most satisfactory and promising, this piety toward the primitive and the past became the dominant activity of the race, giving rise to alternating phases of rebellion against the tyrannical nature of the cosmos, and faith that in the universal view, after all, this horror must be right. In this latter mood it was held that the very irrevocability of the past dignified all past existents, and dignified the cosmos, as a work of tragic art is dignified by the irrevocability of disaster. It was this mood of acquiescence and faith which in the end became the characteristic attitude of the Fifth Men for many millions of years.

But a bewildering discovery was in store for the Fifth Men, a discovery which was to change their whole attitude toward existence. Certain obscure biological facts began to make them suspect, on purely empirical grounds, that past events were not after all simply non-existent, that though no longer existent in the temporal manner, they had eternal existence in some other manner. The effect of this increasing suspicion about the past was that a once harmonious race was divided for a while into two parties, those who insisted that the formal beauty of the universe demanded the tragic evanescence of all things, and those who determined to show that living minds could actually reach back into past events in all their pastness.

The readers of this book are not in a position to realize the poignancy of the conflict which now threatened to wreck humanity. They cannot approach it from the point of view of a race whose culture had consisted of an age-long schooling in admiration of an ever-vanishing cosmos. To the orthodox it seemed that the new view was iconoclastic, impertinent, vulgar. Their opponents, on the other hand, insisted that the matter must be decided dispassionately, according to the evidence. They were also able to point out that this devotion to evanescence was after all but the outcome of the conviction that the cosmos must be supremely noble. No one, it was said, really had direct vision of evanescence as in itself an excellence. So heartfelt was the dispute that the orthodox party actually broke off all "telepathic" communication with the rebels, and even went so far as to plan their destruction. There can be no doubt that if violence had actually been used the human race would have succumbed; for in a species of such high mental development internecine war would have been a gross violation of its nature. It would never have been able to live down so shameful a spiritual disaster. Fortunately, however, at the eleventh hour, common sense prevailed. The iconoclasts were permitted to carry on their research, and the whole race awaited the result.

2. EXPLORATION OF TIME

This first attack upon the nature of time involved an immense co-operative work, both theoretical and practical. It was from biology that the first hint had come that the past persisted. And it would be necessary to restate the whole of biology and the physical sciences in terms of the new idea. On the practical side it was necessary to undertake a great campaign of experiment, physiological and psychological. We cannot stay to watch this work. Millions of years passed by. Sometimes, for thousands of years at a spell, temporal research was the main preoccupation of the race; sometimes it was thrust into the background, or completely ignored, during epochs which were dominated by other interests. Age after age passed, and always the effort of man in this sphere remained barren. Then at last there was a real success.

A child had been selected from among those produced by an age-long breeding enterprise, directed towards the mastery of time. From infancy this child's brain had been very carefully controlled physiologically. Psychologically also he had been subjected to a severe treatment, that he might be properly schooled for his strange task. In the presence of several scientists and historians he was put into a kind of trance, and brought out of it again, half an hour later. He was then asked to give an account "telepathically" of his experiences during the trance. Unfortunately he was now so shattered that his evidence was almost unintelligible. After some months of rest he was questioned again, and was able to describe a curious episode which turned out to be a terrifying incident in the girlhood of his dead mother. He seemed to have seen the incident through her eyes, and to have been aware of all her thoughts. This alone proved nothing, for he might have received the information from some living mind. Once more, therefore, and in spite of his entreaties, he was put into the peculiar trance. On waking he told a rambling story of "little red people living in a squat white tower." It was clear that he was referring to the Great Brains and their attendants. But once more, this proved nothing; and before the account was finished the child died.

Another child was chosen, but was not put to the test until late in adolescence. After an hour of the trance, he woke and became terribly agitated, but forced himself to describe an episode which the historians assigned to the age of the Martian invasions. The importance of this incident lay in his account of a certain house with a carved granite portico, situated at the head of a waterfall in a mountain valley. He said he had found himself to be an old woman, and that he, or she, was being hurriedly helped out of the house by the other inmates. They watched a formless monster creep down the valley, destroy their house, and mangle two persons who failed to get away in time. Now this house was not at all typical of the Second Men, but must have expressed the whim of some freakish individual. From evidence derived from the boy himself, it proved possible to locate the valley with reference to a former mountain, known to history. No valley survived in that spot; but deep excavations revealed the ancient slopes, the fault that had occasioned the waterfall, and the broken pillars.

This and many similar incidents confirmed the Fifth Men in their new view of time. There followed an age in which the technique of direct inspection of the past was gradually improved, but not without tragedy. In the early stages it was found impossible to keep the "medium" alive for more than a few weeks after his venture into the past. The experience seemed to set up a progressive mental disintegration which produced first insanity, then paralysis, and, within a few months, death. This difficulty was at last overcome. By one means and another a type of brain was produced capable of undergoing the strain of supra-temporal experience without fatal results. An increasingly large proportion of the rising generation had now direct access to the past, and were engaged upon a great re-statement of history in relation to their first-hand experience; but their excursions into the past were uncontrollable. They could not go where they wanted to go, but only where fate flung them. Nor could they go of their own will, but only through a very complicated technique, and with the co-operation of experts. After a time the process was made much easier, in fact, too easy. The unfortunate medium might slip so easily into the trance that his days were eaten up by the past. He might suddenly fall to the ground, and lie rapt, inert, dependent on artificial feeding, for weeks, months, even for years. Or a dozen times in the same day he might be flung into a dozen different epochs of history. Or, still more distressing, his experience of past events might not keep pace with the actual rhythm of those events themselves. Thus he might behold the events of a month, or even a lifetime, fantastically accelerated so as to occupy a trance of no more than a day's duration. Or, worse, he might find himself sliding backwards down the vista of the hours and experiencing events in an order the reverse of the natural order. Even the magnificent brains of the Fifth Men could not stand this. The result was maniacal behaviour, followed by death. Another trouble also beset these first experimenters. Supra-temporal experience proved to be like a dangerous and habit-forming drug. Those who ventured into the past might become so intoxicated that they would try to spend every moment of their natural lives in roaming among past events. Thus gradually they would lose touch with the present, live in absent-minded brooding, fail to react normally to their environment, turn socially worthless, and often come actually to physical disaster through inability to look after themselves.

Many more thousands of years passed before these difficulties and dangers were overcome. At length, however, the technique of supra-temporal experience was so perfected that every individual could at will practise it with safety, and could, within limits, project his vision into any locality of space-time which he desired to inspect. It was only possible, however, to see past events through the mind of some past organism, no longer living. And in practice only human minds, and to some extent the minds of the higher mammals, could be entered. The explorer retained throughout his adventure his own personality and system of memory. While experiencing the past individual's perceptions, memories, thoughts, desires, and in fact the whole process and content of the past mind, the explorer continued to be himself, and to react in terms of his own character, now condemning, now sympathizing, now critically enjoying the spectacle.

The task of explaining the mechanism of this new faculty occupied the scientists and philosophers of the species for a very long period. The final account, of course, cannot be presented save by parable; for it was found necessary to recast many fundamental concepts in order to interpret the facts coherently. The only hint that I can give of the explanation is in saying, metaphorically of course, that the living brain had access to the past, not by way of some mysterious kind of racial memory, nor by some equally impossible journey up the stream of time, but by a partial awakening, as it were, into eternity, and into inspection of a minute tract of space-time through some temporal mind in the past, as though through an optical instrument. In the early experiments the fantastic speeding, slowing and reversal of the temporal process resulted from disorderly inspection. As a reader may either skim the pages of a book, or read at a comfortable pace, or dwell upon one word, or spell the sentence backwards, so, unintentionally, the novice in eternity might read or misread the mind that was presented to him.

This new mode of experience, it should be noted, was the activity of living brains, though brains of a novel kind. Hence what was to be discovered "through the medium of eternity" was limited by the particular exploring brain's capacity of understanding what was presented to it. And, further, though the actual supra-temporal contact with past events occupied no time in the brain's natural life, the assimilating of that moment of vision, the reduction of it to normal temporal memory in the normal brain structures, took time, and had to be done during the period of the trance. To expect the neural structure to record the experience instantaneously would be to expect a complicated machine to effect a complicated readjustment without a process of readjusting.

The access to the past had, of course, far-reaching effects upon the culture of the Fifth Men. Not only did it give them an incomparably more accurate knowledge of past events, and insight into the motives of historical personages, and into large-scale cultural movements, but also it effected a subtle change in their estimate of the importance of things. Though intellectually they had, of course, realized both the vastness and the richness of the past, now they realized it with an overwhelming vividness. Matters that had been known hitherto only historically, schematically, were now available to be lived through by intimate acquaintance. The only limit to such acquaintance was set by the limitations of the explorer's own brain-capacity. Consequently the remote past came to enter into a man and shape his mind in a manner in which only the recent past, through memory, had shaped him hitherto. Even before the new kind of experience was first acquired, the race had been, as was said, peculiarly under the spell of the past; but now it was infinitely more so. Hitherto the Fifth Men had been like stay-at-home folk who had read minutely of foreign parts, but had never travelled; now they had become travellers experienced in all the continents of human time. The presences that had hitherto been ghostly were now presences of flesh and blood seen in broad daylight. And so the moving instant called the present appeared no longer as the only, and infinitesimal, real, but as the growing surface of an everlasting tree of existence. It was now the past that seemed most real, while the future still seemed void, and the present merely the impalpable becomingness of the indestructible past.

The discovery that past events were after all persistent, and accessible, was of course for the Fifth Men a source of deep joy; but also it caused them a new distress. While the past was thought of as a mere gulf of non-existence, the inconceivably great pain, misery, baseness, that had fallen into that gulf, could be dismissed as done with; and the will could be concentrated wholly on preventing such horrors from occurring in the future. But now, along with past joy, past distress was found to be everlasting. And those who, in the course of their voyaging in the past, encountered regions of eternal agony, came back distraught. It was easy to remind these harrowed explorers that if pain was eternal, so also was joy. Those who had endured travel in the tragic past were apt to dismiss such assurances with contempt, affirming that all the delights of the whole population of time could not compensate for the agony of one tortured individual. And anyhow, they declared, it was obvious that there had been no preponderance of joy over pain. Indeed, save in the modern age, pain had been overwhelmingly in excess.

So seriously did these convictions prey upon the minds of the Fifth Men, that in spite of their own almost perfect social order, in which suffering had actually to be sought out as a tonic, they fell into despair. At all times, in all pursuits, the presence of the tragic past haunted them, poisoning their lives, sapping their strength. Lovers were ashamed of their delight in one another. As in the far-off days of sexual taboo, guilt crept between them, and held their spirits apart even while their bodies were united.

3. VOYAGING IN SPACE

It was while they were struggling in the grip of this vast social melancholy, and anxiously craving some new vision by which to reinterpret or transcend the agony of the past, that the Fifth Men were confronted with a most unexpected physical crisis. It was discovered that something queer was happening to the moon; in fact, that the orbit of the satellite was narrowing in upon the earth in a manner contrary to all the calculations of the scientists.

The Fifth Men had long ago fashioned for themselves an all-embracing and minutely coherent system of natural sciences, every factor in which had been put to the test a thousand times and had never been shaken. Imagine, then, their bewilderment at this extraordinary discovery. In ages when science was still fragmentary, a subversive discovery entailed merely a reorganization of some one department of science; but by now, such was the coherence of knowledge, that any minute discrepancy of fact and theory must throw man into a state of complete intellectual vertigo.

The evolution of the lunar orbit had, of course, been studied from time immemorial. Even the First Men had learned that the moon must first withdraw from and subsequently once more approach the earth, till it should reach a critical proximity and begin to break up into a swarm of fragments likes the rings of Saturn. This view had been very thoroughly confirmed by the Fifth Men themselves. The satellite should have continued to withdraw for yet many hundreds of millions of years; but in fact it was now observed that not only had the withdrawal ceased, but a comparatively rapid approach had begun.

Observations and calculations were repeated, and ingenious theoretical explanations were suggested; but the truth remained completely hidden. It was left to a future and more brilliant species to discover the connexion between a planet's gravitation and its cultural development. Meanwhile, the Fifth Men knew only that the distance between the earth and the moon was becoming smaller with ever-increasing rapidity.

This discovery was a tonic to a melancholy race. Men turned from the tragic past to the bewildering present and the uncertain future.

For it was evident that, if the present acceleration of approach were to be maintained, the moon would enter the critical zone and disintegrate in less than ten million years; and, further, that the fragments would not maintain themselves as a ring, but would soon crash upon the earth. Heat generated by their impact would make the surface of the earth impossible as the home of life. A short-lived and short-sighted species might well have considered ten million years as equivalent to eternity. Not so the Fifth Men. Thinking primarily in terms of the race, they recognized at once that their whole social policy must now be dominated by this future catastrophe. Some there were indeed who at first refused to take the matter seriously, saying that there was no reason to believe that the moon's odd behaviour would continue indefinitely. But as the years advanced, this view became increasingly improbable. Some of those who had spent much of their lives in exploration of the past now sought to explore the future also, hoping to prove that human civilization would always be discoverable on the earth in no matter how remote a future. But the attempt to unveil the future by direct inspection failed completely. It was surmised, erroneously, that future events, unlike past events, must be strictly non-existent until their creation by the advancing present.

Clearly humanity must leave its native planet. Research was therefore concentrated on the possibility of flight through empty space, and the suitability of neighbouring worlds. The only alternatives were Mars and Venus. The former was by now without water and without atmosphere. The latter had a dense moist atmosphere; but one which lacked oxygen. The surface of Venus, moreover, was known to be almost completely covered with a shallow ocean. Further the planet was so hot by day that, even at the poles, man in his present state would scarcely survive.

It did not take the Fifth Men many centuries to devise a tolerable means of voyaging in interplanetary space. Immense rockets were constructed, the motive power of which was derived from the annihilation of matter. The vehicle was propelled simply by the terrific pressure of radiation thus produced. "Fuel" for a voyage of many months, or even years, could, of course, easily be carried, since the annihilation of a minute amount of matter produced a vast wealth of energy. Moreover, when once the vessel had emerged from the earth's atmosphere, and had attained full speed, she would, of course, maintain it without the use of power from the rocket apparatus. The task of rendering the "ether ship" properly manageable and decently habitable proved difficult, but not insurmountable. The first vessel to take the ether was a cigar-shaped hull some three thousand feet long, and built of metals whose artificial atoms were incomparably more rigid than anything hitherto known. Batteries of "rocket" apparatus at various points on the hull enabled the ship not only to travel forward, but to reverse, turn in any direction, or side-step. Windows of an artificial transparent element, scarcely less strong than the metal of the hull, enabled the voyagers to look around them. Within there was ample accommodation for a hundred persons and their provisions for three years. Air for the same period was manufactured in transit from protons and electrons stored under pressure comparable to that in the interior of a star. Heat was, of course, provided by the annihilation of matter. Powerful refrigeration would permit the vessel to approach the sun almost to the orbit of Mercury.

An "artificial gravity" system, based on the properties of the electro-magnetic field, could be turned on and regulated at will, so as to maintain a
more or less normal environment for the human organism.

This pioneer ship was manned with a navigating crew and a company
of scientists, and was successfully dispatched upon a trial trip. The intention was to approach close to the surface of the moon, possibly to circum-
navigate it at an altitude of ten thousand feet, and to return without
landing. For many days those on earth received radio messages from the
vessel's powerful installation, reporting that all was going well. But suddenly the messages ceased, and no more was ever heard of the vessel.
Almost at the moment of the last message, telescopes had revealed a
sudden flash of light at a point on the vessel's course. It was therefore
surmised that she had collided with a meteor and fused with the heat of
the impact.

Other vessels were built and dispatched on trial voyages. Many failed
to return. Some got out of control, and reported that they were heading for
outer space or plunging toward the sun, their hopeless messages continuing
until the last of the crew succumbed to suffocation. Other vessels returned
successfully, but with crews haggard and distraught from long confinement
in bad atmosphere. One, venturing to land on the moon, broke her back,
so that the air rushed out of her, and her people died. After her last
message was received, she was detected from the earth, as an added speck
on the stippled surface of a lunar "sea."

As time passed, however, accidents became rarer; indeed, so rare that
trips in the void began to be a popular form of amusement. Literature of
the period reverberates with the novelty of such experiences, with the sense
that man had at last learned true flight, and acquired the freedom of the
solar system. Writers dwelt upon the shock of seeing, as the vessel soared
and accelerated, the landscape dwindle to a mere illuminated disk or crescent, surrounded by constellations. They remarked also the awful remoteness and mystery which travellers experienced on these early voyages, with
dazzling sunlight on one side of the vessel and dazzling bespangled night
on the other. They described how the intense sun spread his corona against
a black and star-crowded sky. They expatiated also on the overwhelming
interest of approaching another planet; of inspecting from the sky the still
visible remains of Martian civilization; of groping through the cloud banks
of Venus to discover islands in her almost coastless ocean; of daring an
approach to Mercury, till the heat became insupportable in spite of the best
refrigerating mechanism; of feeling a way across the belt of the asteroids
and onwards toward Jupiter, till shortage of air and provisions forced a
return.

But though the mere navigation of space was thus easily accomplished,
the major task was still untouched. It was necessary either to remake man's
nature to suit another planet, or to modify conditions upon another planet

to suit man's nature. The former alternative was repugnant to the Fifth Men. Obviously it would entail an almost complete refashioning of the human organism. No existing individual could possibly be so altered as to live in the present conditions of Mars or Venus. And it would probably prove impossible to create a new being, adapted to these conditions, without sacrificing the brilliant and harmonious constitution of the extant species.

On the other hand, Mars could not be made habitable without first being stocked with air and water; and such an undertaking seemed impossible. There was nothing for it, then, but to attack Venus. The polar surfaces of that planet, shielded by impenetrable depths of cloud, proved after all not unendurably hot. Subsequent generations might perhaps be modified so as to withstand even the sub-arctic and "temperate" climates. Oxygen was plentiful, but it was all tied up in chemical combination. Inevitably so, since oxygen combines very readily, and on Venus there was no vegetable life to exhale the free gas and replenish the ever-vanishing supply. It was necessary, then, to equip Venus with an appropriate vegetation, which in the course of ages should render the planet's atmosphere hospitable to man. The chemical and physical conditions on Venus had therefore to be studied in great detail, so that it might be possible to design a kind of life which would have a chance of flourishing. This research had to be carried out from within the ether ships, or with gas helmets, since no human being could live in the natural atmosphere of the planet.

We must not dwell upon the age of heroic research and adventure which now began. Observations of the lunar orbit were showing that ten millions years was too long an estimate of the future habitability of the earth; and it was soon realized that Venus could not be made ready soon enough unless some more rapid change was set on foot. It was therefore decided to split up some of the ocean of the planet into hydrogen and oxygen by a vast process of electrolysis. This would have been a more difficult task, had not the ocean been relatively free from salt, owing to the fact that there was so little dry land to be denuded of salts by rain and river. The oxygen thus formed by electrolysis would be allowed to mix with the atmosphere. The hydrogen had to be got rid of somehow, and an ingenious method was devised by which it should be ejected beyond the limits of the atmosphere at so great a speed that it would never return. Once sufficient free oxygen had been produced, the new vegetation would replenish the loss due to oxidation. This work was duly set on foot. Great automatic electrolysing stations were founded on several of the islands; and biological research produced at length a whole flora of specialized vegetable types to cover the land surface of the planet. It was hoped that in less than a million years Venus would be fit to receive the human race, and the race fit to live on Venus.

Meanwhile a careful survey of the planet had been undertaken. Its land surface, scarcely more than a thousandth that of the earth, consisted of an unevenly distributed archipelago of mountainous islands. The planet had evidently not long ago been through a mountain-forming era, for soundings proved its whole surface to be extravagantly corrugated. The ocean was subject to terrific storms and currents; for since the planet took several weeks to rotate, there was a great difference of temperature and atmospheric pressure between the almost arctic hemisphere of night and the sweltering hemisphere of day. So great was the evaporation, that open sky was almost never visible from any part of the planet's surface; and indeed the average day-time weather was a succession of thick fogs and fantastic thunderstorms. Rain in the evening was a continuous torrent. Yet before night was over the waves clattered with fragments of ice.

Man looked upon his future home with loathing, and on his birth-place with an affection which became passionate. With its blue sky, its in-comparable starry nights, its temperate and varied continents, its ample spaces of agriculture, wilderness and park, its well-known beasts and plants, and all the material fabric of the most enduring of terrestrial civili-zations, it seemed to the men and women who were planning flight almost a living thing imploring them not to desert it. They looked often with hate at the quiet moon, now visibly larger than the moon of history. They revised again and again their astronomical and physical theories, hoping for some flaw which should render the moon's observed behaviour less mysterious, less terrifying. But they found nothing. It was as though a fiend out of some ancient myth had come to life in the modern world, to interfere with the laws of nature for man's undoing.

4. PREPARING A NEW WORLD

Another trouble now occurred. Several electrolysis stations on Venus were wrecked, apparently by submarine eruption. Also, a number of ether-ships, engaged in surveying the ocean, mysteriously exploded. The explana-tion was found when one of these vessels, though damaged, was able to return to the earth. The commander reported that, when the sounding line was drawn up, a large spherical object was seen to be attached to it. Closer inspection showed that this object was fastened to the sounding apparatus by a hook, and was indeed unmistakably artificial, a structure of small metal plates riveted together. While preparations were being made to bring the object within the ship, it happened to bump against the hull, and then it exploded.

Evidently there must be intelligent life somewhere in the ocean of Venus. Evidently the marine Venerians resented the steady depletion of their aqueous world, and were determined to stop it. The terrestrials had assumed that water in which no free oxygen was dissolved could not sup-port life. But observation soon revealed that in this world-wide ocean there

were many living species, some sessile, others free-swimming, some microscopic, others as large as whales. The basis of life in these creatures lay not
in photosynthesis and chemical combination, but in the controlled disintegration of radio-active atoms. Venus was particularly rich in these atoms,
and still contained certain elements which had long ago ceased to exist on
the earth. The oceanic fauna subsisted in the destruction of minute quantities of radio-active atoms throughout its tissues.

Several of the Venerian species had attained considerable mastery over
their physical environment, and were able to destroy one another very
competently with various mechanical contrivances. Many types were indeed
definitely intelligent and versatile within certain limits. And of these intelligent types, one had come to dominate all the others by virtue of its superior intelligence, and had constructed a genuine civilization on the basis of
radio-active power. These most developed of all the Venerian creatures
were beings of about the size and shape of a swordfish. They had three
manipulative organs, normally sheathed within the long "sword," but
capable of extension beyond its point, as three branched muscular tentacles.
They swam with a curious screw-like motion of their bodies and triple
tails. Three fins enabled them to steer. They had also organs of phosphorescence, vision, touch, and something analogous to hearing. They
appeared to reproduce asexually, laying eggs in the ooze of the ocean bed.
They had no need of nutrition in the ordinary sense; but in infancy they
seemed to gather enough radio-active matter to keep them alive for many
years. Each individual, when his stock was running out and he began to
be feeble, was either destroyed by his juniors or buried in a radio-active
mine, to rise from this living death in a few months completely rejuvenated.

At the bottom of the Venerian ocean these creatures thronged in cities
of proliferated coral-like buildings, equipped with many complex articles,
which must have constituted the necessities and luxuries of their civilization. So much was ascertained by the Terrestrials in the course of their
submarine exploration. But the mental life of Venerians remained hidden.
It was clear, indeed, that like all living things, they were concerned with
self-maintenance and the exercise of their capacities; but of the nature
of these capacities little was discoverable. Clearly they used some kind of
symbolic language, based on mechanical vibrations set up in the water by
the snapping claws of their tentacles. But their more complex activities
were quite unintelligible. All that could be recorded with certainty was
that they were much addicted to warfare, even to warfare between groups
of one species; and that even in the stress of military disaster they maintained a feverish production of material articles of all sorts, which they
proceeded to destroy and neglect.

One activity was observed which was peculiarly mysterious. At certain
seasons three individuals, suddenly developing unusual luminosity, would

approach one another with rhythmic swayings and tremors, and would then rise on their tails and press their bodies together. Sometimes at this stage an excited crowd would collect, whirling around the three like driven snow. The chief performers would now furiously tear one another to pieces with their crab-like pincers, till nothing was left but tangled shreds of flesh, the great swords, and the still twitching claws. The Terrestrials, observing these matters with difficulty, at first suspected some kind of sexual intercourse; but no reproduction was ever traced to this source. Possibly the behaviour had once served a biological end, and had now become a useless ritual. Possibly it was a kind of voluntary religious sacrifice. More probably it was of a quite different nature, unintelligible to the human mind.

As man's activities on Venus became more extensive, the Venerians became more energetic in seeking to destroy him. They could not come out of the ocean to grapple with him, for they were deep-sea organisms. Deprived of oceanic pressure, they would have burst. But they contrived to hurl high explosives into the centres of the islands, or to undermine them from tunnels. The work of electrolysis was thus very seriously hampered. And as all efforts to parley with the Venerians failed completely, it was impossible to effect a compromise. The Fifth Men were thus faced with a grave moral problem. What right had man to interfere in a world already possessed by beings who were obviously intelligent, even though their mental life was incomprehensible to man? Long ago man himself had suffered at the hands of Martian invaders, who doubtless regarded themselves as more noble than the human race. And now man was committing a similar crime. On the other hand, either the migration to Venus must go forward, or humanity must be destroyed; for it seemed quite certain by now that the moon would fall, and at no very distant date. And though man's understanding of the Venerians was so incomplete, what he did know of them strongly suggested that they were definitely inferior to himself in mental range. The judgment might, of course, be mistaken; the Venerians might after all be so superior to man that man could not get an inkling of their superiority. But this argument would apply equally to jelly-fish and micro-organisms. Judgment had to be passed according to the evidence available. So far as man could judge at all in the matter, he was definitely the higher type.

There was another fact to be taken into account. The life of the Venerian organism depended on the existence of radio-active atoms. Since those atoms are subject to disintegration, they must become rarer. Venus was far better supplied than the earth in this respect, but there must inevitably come a time when there would be no more radio-active matter in Venus. Now submarine research showed that the Venerian fauna had once been much more extensive, and that the increasing difficulty of procuring radio-active matter was already the great limiting factor of civilization. Thus the Venerians were doomed, and man would merely hasten their destruction.

It was hoped, of course, that in colonizing Venus mankind would be able to accommodate itself without seriously interfering with the native population. But this proved impossible for two reasons. In the first place, the natives seemed determined to destroy the invader even if they should destroy themselves in the process. Titanic explosions were engineered, which caused the invaders serious damage, but also strewed the ocean surface with thousands of dead Venerians. Secondly, it was found that, as electrolysis poured more and more free oxygen into the atmosphere, the ocean absorbed some of the potent element back into itself by solution; and this dissolved oxygen had a disastrous effect upon the oceanic organisms. Their tissues began to oxidize. They were burnt up, internally and externally, by a slow fire. Man dared not stop the process of electrolysis until the atmosphere had become as rich in oxygen as his native air. Long before this state was reached, it was already clear that the Venerians were beginning to feel the effects of the poison, and that in a few thousand years, at most, they would be exterminated. It was therefore determined to put them out of their misery as quickly as possible. Men could by now walk abroad on the islands of Venus, and indeed the first settlements were already being founded. They were thus able to build a fleet of powerful submarine vessels to scour the ocean and destroy the whole native fauna.

This vast slaughter influenced the mind of the fifth human species in two opposite directions, now flinging it into despair, now rousing it to grave elation. For on the one hand the horror of the slaughter produced a haunting guiltiness in all men's minds, an unreasoning disgust with humanity for having been driven to murder in order to save itself. And this guiltiness combined with the purely intellectual loss of self-confidence which had been produced by the failure of science to account for the moon's approach. It re-awakened, also, that other quite irrational sense of guilt which had been bred of sympathy with the everlasting distress of the past. Together, these three influences tended toward racial neurosis.

On the other hand a very different mood sometimes sprang from the same three sources. After all, the failure of science was a challenge to be gladly accepted; it opened up a wealth of possibilities hitherto unimagined. Even the unalterable distress of the past constituted a challenge; for in some strange manner the present and future, it was said, must transfigure the past. As for the murder of Venerian life, it was, indeed, terrible, but right. It had been committed without hate; indeed, rather in love. For as the navy proceeded with its relentless work, it had gathered much insight into the life of the natives, and had learned to admire, even in a sense to love, while it killed. This mood, of inexorable yet not ruthless will, intensified the spiritual sensibility of the species, refined, so to speak, its spiritual hearing, and revealed to it tones and themes in the universal music which were hitherto obscure.

Which of these two moods, despair or courage, would triumph? All depended on the skill of the species to maintain a high degree of vitality in untoward circumstances.

Man now busied himself in preparing his new home. Many kinds of plant life, derived from the terrestrial stock, but bred for the Venerian environment, now began to swarm on the islands and in the sea. For so restricted was the land surface, that great areas of ocean had to be given over to specially designed marine plants, which now formed immense floating continents of vegetable matter. On the least torrid islands appeared habitable pylons, forming an architectural forest, with vegetation on every acre of free ground. Even so, it would be impossible for Venus ever to support the huge population of the earth. Steps had therefore been taken to ensure that the birth-rate should fall far short of the death-rate; so that, when the time should come, the race might emigrate without leaving any living members behind. No more than a hundred million, it was reckoned, could live tolerably on Venus. The population had therefore to be reduced to a hundredth of its former size. And since, in the terrestrial community, with its vast social and cultural activity, every individual had fulfilled some definite function in society, it was obvious that the new community must be not merely small but mentally impoverished. Hitherto, each individual had been inriched by intercourse with a far more intricate and diverse social environment than would be possible on Venus.

Such was the prospect when at length it was judged advisable to leave the earth to its fate. The moon was now so huge that it periodically turned day into night, and night into a ghastly day. Prodigious tides and distressful weather conditions had already spoilt the amenities of the earth, and done great damage to the fabric of civilization. And so at length humanity reluctantly took flight. Some centuries passed before the migration was completed, before Venus had received, not only the whole remaining human population, but also representatives of many other species of organisms, and all the most precious treasures of man's culture.

CHAPTER XIII

HUMANITY ON VENUS

I. TAKING ROOT AGAIN

MAN'S sojourn on Venus lasted somewhat longer than his whole career on the Earth. From the days of Pithecanthropus to the final evacuation of his native planet he passed, as we have seen, through a bewildering diversity of form and circumstance. On Venus, though the human type was somewhat more constant biologically, it was scarcely less variegated in culture.

To give an account of this period, even on the minute scale that has been adopted hitherto, would entail another volume. I can only sketch its bare outline. The sapling, humanity, transplanted into foreign soil, withers at first almost to the root, slowly readjusts itself, grows into strength and a certain permanence of form, burgeons, season by season, with leaf and flower of many successive civilizations and cultures, sleeps winter by winter, through many ages of reduced vitality, but at length (to force the metaphor), avoids this recurrent defeat by attaining an evergreen constitution and a continuous efflorescence. Then once more, through the whim of Fate, it is plucked up by the roots and cast upon another world.

The first human settlers on Venus knew well that life would be a sorry business. They had done their best to alter the planet to suit human nature, but they could not make Venus into another Earth. The land surface was minute. The climate was almost unendurable. The extreme difference of temperature between the protracted day and night produced incredible storms, rain like a thousand contiguous waterfalls, terrifying electrical disturbances, and fogs in which a man could not see his own feet. To make matters worse, the oxygen supply was as yet barely enough to render the air breathable. Worse still, the liberated hydrogen was not always successfully ejected from the atmosphere. It would sometimes mingle with the air to form an explosive mixture, and sooner or later there would occur a vast atmospheric flash. Recurrent disasters of this sort destroyed the architecture and the human inhabitants of many islands, and further reduced the oxygen supply. In time, however, the increasing vegetation made it possible to put an end to the dangerous process of electrolysis.

Meanwhile, these atmospheric explosions crippled the race so seriously that it was unable to cope with a more mysterious trouble which beset it some time after the migration. A new and inexplicable decay of the digestive organs, which first occurred as a rare disease, threatened within a few centuries to destroy mankind. The physical effects of this plague were scarcely more disastrous than the psychological effects of the complete failure to master it; for, what with the mystery of the moon's vagaries and the deep-seated, unreasoning, sense of guilt produced by the extermination of the Venerians, man's self-confidence was already seriously shaken, and his highly organized mentality began to show symptoms of derangement. The new plague was, indeed, finally traced to something in the Venerian water, and was supposed to be due to certain molecular groupings, formerly rare, but subsequently fostered by the presence of terrestrial organic matter in the ocean. No cure was discovered.

And now another plague seized upon the enfeebled race. Human tissues had never perfectly assimilated the Martian units which were the means of "telepathic" communication. The universal ill-health now favoured a kind of "cancer" of the nervous system, which was due to the ungoverned proliferation of these units. The harrowing results of this disease may be left unmentioned. Century by century it increased; and even those who did not actually contract the sickness lived in constant terror of madness.

These troubles were aggravated by the devastating heat. The hope that, as the generations passed, human nature would adapt itself even to the more sultry regions, seemed to be unfounded. Far otherwise, within a thousand years the once-populous arctic and antarctic islands were almost deserted. Out of each hundred of the great pylons, scarcely more than two were inhabited, and these only by a few plague-stricken and broken-spirited human relics. These alone were left to turn their telescopes upon the earth and watch the unexpectedly delayed bombardment of their native world by the fragments of the moon.

Population decreased still further. Each brief generation was slightly less well developed than its parents. Intelligence declined. Education became superficial and restricted. Contact with the past was no longer possible. Art lost its significance, and philosophy its dominion over the minds of men. Even applied science began to be too difficult. Unskilled control of the sub-atomic sources of power led to a number of disasters, which finally gave rise to a superstition that all "tampering with nature" was wicked, and all the ancient wisdom a snare of Man's Enemy. Books, instruments, all the treasures of human culture, were therefore burnt. Only the perdurable buildings resisted destruction. Of the incomparable world-order of the Fifth Men nothing was left but a few island tribes cut off from one another by the ocean, and from the rest of space-time by the depths of their own ignorance.

After many thousands of years human nature did begin to adapt itself to the climate and to the poisoned water without which life was impossible. At the same time a new variety of the fifth species now began to appear, in which the Martian units were not included. Thus at last the race regained a certain mental stability, at the expense of its faculty of "telepathy," which man was not to regain until almost the last phase of his career. Meanwhile, though he had recovered somewhat from the effects of an alien world, the glory that had been was no more. Let us therefore hurry through the ages that passed before noteworthy events again occurred.

In early days on Venus men had gathered their foodstuff from the great floating islands of vegetable matter which had been artificially produced before the migration. But as the oceans became populous with modifications of the terrestrial fauna, the human tribes turned more and more to fishing. Under the influence of its marine environment, one branch of the species assumed such an aquatic habit that in time it actually began to develop biological adaptations for marine life. It is perhaps surprising that man was still capable of spontaneous variation; but the fifth human species was artificial, and had always been prone to epidemics of mutation. After some millions of years of variation and selection there appeared a very successful species of seal-like sub-men. The whole body was moulded to stream-lines. The lung capacity was greatly developed. The spine had elongated, and increased in flexibility. The legs were shrunken, grown together, and flattened into a horizontal rudder. The arms also were diminutive and fin-like, though they still retained the manipulative forefinger and thumb. The head had shrunk into the body and looked forward in the direction of swimming. Strong carnivorous teeth, emphatic gregariousness, and a new, almost human, cunning in the chase, combined to make these seal-men lords of the ocean. And so they remained for many million years, until a more human race, annoyed at their piscatorial success, harpooned them out of existence.

For another branch of the degenerated fifth species had retained a more terrestrial habit and the ancient human form. Sadly reduced in stature and in brain, these abject beings were so unlike the original invaders that they are rightly considered a new species, and may therefore be called the Sixth Men. Age after age they gained a precarious livelihood by grubbing roots upon the forest-clad islands, trapping the innumerable birds, and catching fish in the tidal inlets with ground bait. Not infrequently they devoured, or were devoured by, their seal-like relatives. So restricted and constant was the environment of these human remnants, that they remained biologically and culturally stagnant for some millions of years.

At length, however, geological events afforded man's nature once more the opportunity of change. A mighty warping of the planet's crust produced an island almost as large as Australia. In time this was peopled, and from the clash of tribes a new and versatile race emerged. Once more there was methodical tillage, craftsmanship, complex social organization, and adventure in the realm of thought.

During the next two hundred million years all the main phases of man's life on earth were many times repeated on Venus with characteristic differences. Theocratic empires; free and intellectualistic island cities; insecure overlordship of feudal archipelagos; rivalries of high priest and emperor; religious feuds over the interpretation of sacred scriptures; recurrent fluctuations of thought from naïve animism, through polytheism, conflicting monotheisms, and all the desperate "isms" by which mind seeks to blur the severe outline of truth; recurrent fashions of comfort-seeking fantasy and cold intelligence; social disorders through the misuse of volcanic or wind power in industry; business empires and pseudo-communistic empires—all these forms flitted over the changing substance of mankind again and again, as in an enduring hearth fire there appear and vanish the infinitely diverse forms of flame and smoke. But all the while the brief, spirits, in whose massed configurations these forms inhered, were intent chiefly on the primitive needs of food, shelter, companionship, crowd-lust, love-making, the two-edged relationship of parent and child, the exercise of muscle and intelligence in facile sport. Very seldom, only in rare moments of clarity, only after ages of misapprehension, did a few of them, here and there, now and again, begin to have the deeper insight into the world's nature and man's. And no sooner had this precious insight begun to propagate itself, than it would be blotted out by some small or great disaster, by epidemic disease, by the spontaneous disruption of society, by an access of racial imbecility, by a prolonged bombardment of meteorites, or by the mere cowardice and vertigo that dared not look down the precipice of fact.

2. THE FLYING MEN

We need not dwell upon these multitudinous reiterations of culture, but must glance for a moment at the last phase of this sixth human species, so that we may pass on to the artificial species which it produced.

Throughout their career the Sixth Men had often been fascinated by the idea of flight. The bird was again and again their most sacred symbol. Their monotheism was apt to be worship not of a god-man, but of a god-bird, conceived now as the divine sea-eagle, winged with power, now as the giant swift, winged with mercy, now as a disembodied spirit of air, and once as the bird-god that became man to endow the human race with flight, physical and spiritual.

It was inevitable that flight should obsess man on Venus, for the planet afforded but a cramping home for groundlings; and the riotous efflorescence of avian species shamed man's pedestrian habit. When in due course the Sixth Men attained knowledge and power comparable to that of the First Men at their height, they invented flying-machines of various types. Many times, indeed, mechanical flight was rediscovered and lost again with the downfall of civilization. But at its best it was regarded only as a makeshift. And when at length, with the advance of the biological sciences, the Sixth Men were in a position to influence the human organism itself, they determined to produce a true flying man. Many civilizations strove vainly for this result, sometimes half-heartedly, sometimes with religious earnestness. Finally the most enduring and brilliant of all the civilizations of the Sixth Men actually attained the goal.

The Seventh Men were pigmies, scarcely heavier than the largest of terrestrial flying birds. Through and through they were organized for flight. A leathery membrane spread from the foot to the tip of the immensely elongated and strengthened "middle" finger. The three "outer" fingers, equally elongated, served as ribs to the membrane; while the index and thumb remained free for manipulation. The body assumed the stream-lines of a bird, and was covered with a deep quilt of feathery wool. This, and the silken down of the flight-membranes, varied greatly from individual to individual in colouring and texture. On the ground the Seventh Men walked much as other human beings, for the flight-membranes were folded close to the legs and body, and hung from the arms like exaggerated sleeves. In flight the legs were held extended as a flattened tail, with the feet locked together by the big toes. The breastbone was greatly developed as a keel, and as a base for the muscles of flight. The other bones were hollow, for lightness, and their internal surfaces were utilized as supplementary lungs. For, like the birds, these flying men had to maintain a high rate of oxidation. A state which others would regard as fever was normal to them.

Their brains were given ample tracts for the organization of prowess in flight. In fact, it was found possible to equip the species with a system of reflexes for aerial balance, and a true, though artificial, instinctive aptitude for flight, and interest in flight. Compared with their makers their brain volume was of necessity small, but their whole neural system was very carefully organized. Also it matured rapidly, and was extremely facile in the acquirement of new modes of activity. This was very desirable; for the individual's natural life period was but fifty years, and in most cases it was deliberately cut short by some impossible feat at about forty, or whenever the symptoms of old age began to be felt.

Of all human species these bat-like Flying Men, the Seventh Men, were probably the most care-free. Gifted with harmonious physique and gay temperament, they came into a social heritage well adapted to their nature. There was no occasion for them, as there had often been for some others, to regard the world as fundamentally hostile to life, or themselves as essentially deformed. Of quick intelligence in respect of daily personal affairs and social organization, they were untroubled by the insatiable lust of understanding. Not that they were an unintellectual race, for they soon formulated a beautifully systematic account of experience. They clearly perceived, however, that the perfect sphere of their thought was but a bubble adrift in chaos. Yet it was an elegant bubble. And the system was true, in its own gay and frankly insincere manner, true as significant metaphor, not literally true. What more, it was asked, could be expected of human intellect? Adolescents were encouraged to study the ancient problems of philosophy, for no reason but to convince themselves of the futility of probing beyond the limits of the orthodox system. "Prick the bubble of thought at any point," it was said, "and you shatter the whole of it. And since thought is one of the necessities of human life, it must be preserved."

Natural science was taken over from the earlier species with half-contemptuous gratitude, as a necessary means of sane adjustment to the environment. Its practical applications were valued as the ground of the social order; but as the millennia advanced, and society approached that remarkable perfection and stability which was to endure for many million years, scientific inventiveness became less and less needful, and science itself was relegated to the infant schools. History also was given in outline during childhood, and subsequently ignored.

This curiously sincere intellectual insincerity was due to the fact that the Seventh Men were chiefly concerned with matters other than abstract thought. It is difficult to give to members of the first human species an inkling of the great preoccupation of these Flying Men. To say that it was flight would be true, yet far less than the truth. To say that they sought to live dangerously and vividly, to crowd as much experience as possible into each moment, would again be a caricature of the truth. On the physical plane indeed "the universe of flight" with all the variety of peril and skill afforded by a tempestuous atmosphere, was every individual's chief medium of self-expression. Yet it was not flight itself, but the spiritual aspect of flight, which obsessed the species.

In the air and on the ground the Seventh Men were different beings. Whenever they exercised themselves in flight they suffered a remarkable change of spirit. Much of their time had to be spent on the ground, since most of the work upon which civilization rested was impossible in the air. Moreover, life in the air was life at high pressure, and necessitated spells of recuperation on the ground. In their pedestrian phase the Seventh Men were sober folk, mildly bored, yet in the main cheerful, humorously impatient of the drabness and irk of pedestrian affairs, but ever supported by memory and anticipation of the vivid life of the air. Often they were tired, after the strain of that other life, but seldom were they despondent or lazy. Indeed, in the routine of agriculture and industry they were industrious as the wingless ants. Yet they worked in a strange mood of attentive absent-mindedness; for their hearts were ever in the air. So long as they could have frequent periods of aviation, they remained bland even on the ground. But if for any reason such as illness they were confined to the ground for a long period, they pined, developed acute melancholia, and died. Their makers had so contrived them that with the onset of any very great pain or misery their hearts should stop. Thus they were to avoid all serious distress. But, in fact, this merciful device worked only on the ground. In the air they assumed a very different and more heroic nature, which their makers had not foreseen, though indeed it was a natural consequence of their design.

In the air the flying man's heart beat more powerfully. His temperature rose. His sensation became more vivid and more discriminate, his intelligence more agile and penetrating. He experienced a more intense pleasure or pain in all that happened to him. It would not be true to say that he became more emotional; rather the reverse, if by emotionality is meant enslavement to the emotions. For the most remarkable features of the aerial phase was that this enhanced power of appreciation was dispassionate. So long as the individual was in the air, whether in lonely struggle with the storm, or in the ceremonial ballet with sky-darkening hosts of his fellows; whether in the ecstatic love dance with a sexual partner, or in solitary and meditative circlings far above the world; whether his enterprise was fortunate, or he found himself dismembered by the hurricane, and crashing to death; always the gay and the tragic fortunes of his own person were regarded equally with detached æsthetic delight. Even when his dearest companion was mutilated or destroyed by some aerial disaster, he exulted; though also he would give his own life in the hope of effecting a rescue. But very soon after he had returned to the ground he would be overwhelmed with grief, would strive vainly to recapture the lost vision, and would perhaps die of heart failure.

Even when, as happened occasionally in the wild climate of Venus, a whole aerial population was destroyed by some world-wide atmospheric tumult, the few broken survivors, so long as they could remain in the air, exulted. And actually while at length they sank exhausted toward the ground, toward certain disillusionment and death, they laughed inwardly. Yet an hour after they had alighted, their constitution would be changed, their vision lost. They would remember only the horror of the disaster, and the memory would kill them.

No wonder the Seventh Men grudged every moment that was passed on the ground. While they were in the air, of course, the prospect of a pedestrian interlude, or indeed of endless pedestrianism, though in a manner repugnant, would be accepted with unswerving gaiety; but while they were on the ground, they grudged bitterly to be there. Early in the career of the species the proportion of aerial to terrestrial hours was increased by a biological invention. A minute foodplant was produced which spent the winter rooted in the ground, and the summer adrift in the sunlit upper air, engaged solely in photosynthesis. Henceforth the populations of the Flying Men were able to browse upon the bright pastures of the sky, like swallows. As the ages passed, material civilization became more and more simplified. Needs which could not be satisfied without terrestrial labour tended to be outgrown. Manufactured articles became increasingly rare. Books were no longer written or read. In the main, indeed, they were no longer necessary; but to some extent their place was taken by verbal tradition and discussion, in the upper air. Of the arts, music, spoken lyric and epic verse, and the supreme art of winged dance, were constantly practised. The rest vanished. Many of the sciences inevitably faded into tradition; yet the true scientific spirit was preserved in a very exact meteorology, a sufficient biology, and a human psychology surpassed only by the second and fifth species at their height. None of these sciences, however, was taken very seriously, save in its practical applications. For instance, psychology explained the ecstasy of flight very neatly as a febrile and "irrational" beatitude. But no one was disconcerted by this theory; for every one, while on the wing, felt it to be merely an amusing half-truth.

The social order of the Seventh Men was in essence neither utilitarian, nor humanistic, nor religious, but æsthetic. Every act and every institution were to be justified as contributing to the perfect form of the community. Even social prosperity was conceived as merely the medium in which beauty should be embodied, the beauty, namely, of vivid individual lives harmoniously related. Yet not only for the individual, but even for the race itself (so the wise insisted), death on the wing was more excellent than prolonged life on the ground. Better, far better, would be racial suicide than a future of pedestrianism. Yet though both the individual and the race were conceived as instrumental to objective beauty, there was nothing religious, in any ordinary sense, in this conviction. The Seventh Men were completely without interest in the universal and the unseen. The beauty which they sought to create was ephemeral and very largely sensuous. And they were well content that it should be so. Personal immortality, said a dying sage, would be as tedious as an endless song. Equally so with the race. The lovely flame, of which we all are members, must die, he said, must die; for without death she would fall short of beauty.

For close on a hundred million terrestrial years this aerial society endured with little change. On many of the islands throughout this period stood even yet a number of the ancient pylons, though repaired almost beyond recognition. In these nests the men and women of the seventh species slept through the long Venerian nights, crowded like roosting swallows. By day the same great towers were sparsely peopled with those who were serving their turn in industry, while in the fields and on the sea others laboured. But most were in the air. Many would be skimming the ocean, to plunge, gannetlike, for fish. Many, circling over land or sea, would now and again swoop like hawks upon the wild-fowl which formed the chief meat of the species. Others, forty or fifty thousand feet above the waves, where even the plentiful atmosphere of Venus was scarcely capable of supporting them, would be soaring, circling, sweeping, for pure joy of flight. Others, in the calm and sunshine of high altitudes, would be hanging effortless upon some steady up-current of air for meditation and the rapture of mere percipience. Not a few love-intoxicated pairs would be entwining their courses in aerial patterns, in spires, cascades, and true love-knots of flight, presently to embrace and drop ten thousand feet in bodily union. Some would be driving hither and thither through the green mists of vegetable particles, gathering the manna in their open mouths. Companies, circling together, would be discussing matters social or æsthetic; others would be singing together, or listening to recitative epic verse. Thousands, gathering in the sky like migratory birds, would perform massed convolutions, reminiscent of the vast mechanical aerial choreography of the First World State, but more vital and expressive, as a bird's flight is more vital than the flight of any machine. And all the while there would be some, solitary or in companies, who, either in the pursuit of fish and wildfowl, or out of pure devilment, pitted their strength and skill against the hurricane, often tragically, but never without zest, and laughter of the spirit.

It may seem to some incredible that the culture of the Seventh Men should have lasted so long. Surely it must either have decayed through mere monotony and stagnation or have advanced into richer experience. But no. Generation succeeded generation, and each was too short-lived to outlast its young delight and discover boredom. Moreover, so perfect was the adjustment of these beings to their world, that even if they had lived for centuries they would have felt no need of change. Flight provided them with intense physical exhilaration, and with the physical basis of a genuine and ecstatic, though limited, spiritual experience. In this their supreme attainment they rejoiced not only in the diversity of flight itself, but also in the perceived beauties of their variegated world, and most of all, perhaps, in the thousand lyric and epic ventures of human intercourse in an aerial community.

The end of this seemingly everlasting elysium was nevertheless involved in the very nature of the species. In the first place, as the ages lengthened into aeons, the generations preserved less and less of the ancient scientific lore. For it became insignificant to them. The aerial community had no need of it. This loss of mere information did not matter so long as their condition remained unaltered; but in due course biological changes began to undermine them. The species had always been prone to a certain biological instability. A proportion of infants, varying with circumstances, had always been misshapen; and the deformity had generally been such as to make flight impossible. The normal infant was able to fly early in its second year. If some accident prevented it from doing so, it invariably fell into a decline and died before its third year was passed. But many of the deformed types, being the result of a partial reversion to the pedestrian nature, were able to live on indefinitely without flight. According to a merciful custom these cripples had always to be destroyed. But at length, owing to the gradual exhaustion of a certain marine salt essential to the high-strung nature of the Seventh Men, infants were more often deformed

than true to type. The world population declined so seriously that the organized aerial life of the community could no longer be carried on according to the time-honoured æsthetic principles. No one knew how to check
this racial decay, but many felt that with greater biological knowledge it
might be avoided. A disastrous policy was now adopted. It was decided
to spare a carefully selected proportion of the deformed infants, those
namely which, though doomed to pedestrianism, were likely to develop
high intelligence. Thus it was hoped to raise a specialized group of persons
whose work should be biological research untrammelled by the intoxication
of flight.

The brilliant cripples that resulted from this policy looked at existence
from a new angle. Deprived of the supreme experience for which their
fellows lived, envious of a bliss which they knew only by report, yet contemptuous of the naïve mentality which cared for nothing (it seemed) but
physical exercise, love-making, the beauty of nature, and the elegances of
society, these flightless intelligences sought satisfaction almost wholly in
the life of research and scientific control. At the best, however, they were
a tortured and resentful race. For their natures were fashioned for the
aerial life which they could not lead. Although they received from the
winged folk just treatment and a certain compassionate respect, they
writhed under this kindness, locked their hearts against all the orthodox
values, and sought out new ideals. Within a few centuries they had re-
habilitated the life of intellect, and, with the power that knowledge gives,
they had made themselves masters of the world. The amiable fliers were
surprised, perplexed, even pained; and yet withal amused. Even when it
became evident that the pedestrians were determined to create a new world-
order in which there would be no place for the beauties of natural flight,
the fliers were only distressed while they were on the ground.

The islands were becoming crowded with machinery and flightless
industrialists. In the air itself the winged folk found themselves outstripped
by the base but effective instruments of mechanical flight. Wings became a
laughing stock, and the life of natural flight was condemned as a barren
luxury. It was ordained that in future every flier must serve the pedestrian
world-order, or starve. And as the cultivation of wind-borne plants had
been abandoned, and fishing and fowling rights were strictly controlled,
this law was no empty form. At first it was impossible for the fliers to
work on the ground for long hours, day after day, without incurring serious ill-health and an early death. But the pedestrian physiologists invented
a drug which preserved the poor wage-slaves in something like physical
health, and actually prolonged their life. No drug, however, could restore
their spirit, for their normal aerial habit was reduced to a few tired hours
of recreation once a week. Meanwhile, breeding experiments were undertaken to produce a wholly wingless large-brained type. And finally a law
was enacted by which all winged infants must be either mutilated or de-

stroyed. At this point the fliers made an heroic but ineffectual bid for power. They attacked the pedestrian population from the air. In reply the enemy rode them down in his great aeroplanes and blew them to pieces with high explosive.

The fighting squadrons of the natural fliers were finally driven to the ground in a remote and barren island. Thither the whole flying population, a mere remnant of its former strength, fled out of every civilized archipelago in search of freedom: the whole population—save the sick, who committed suicide, and all infants that could not yet fly. These were stifled by their mothers or next-of-kin, in obedience to a decree of the leaders. About a million men, women and children, some of whom were scarcely old enough for the prolonged flight, now gathered on the rocks, regardless that there was not food in the neighbourhood for a great company.

Their leaders, conferring together, saw clearly that the day of Flying Man was done, and that it would be more fitting for a high-souled race to die at once than to drag on in subjection to contemptuous masters. They therefore ordered the population to take part in an act of racial suicide that should at least make death a noble gesture of freedom. The people received the message while they were resting on the stony moorland. A wail of sorrow broke from them. It was checked by the speaker, who bade them strive to see, even on the ground, the beauty of the thing that was to be done. They could not see it; but they knew that if they had the strength to take wing again they would see it clearly, almost as soon as their tired muscles bore them aloft. There was no time to waste, for many were already faint with hunger, and anxious lest they should fail to rise. At the appointed signal the whole population rose into the air with a deep roar of wings. Sorrow was left behind. Even the children, when their mothers explained what was to be done, accepted their fate with zest; though, had they learned of it on the ground, they would have been terror-stricken. The company now flew steadily West, forming themselves into a double file many miles long. The cone of a volcano appeared over the horizon, and rose as they approached. The leaders pressed on towards its ruddy smoke plume; and unflinchingly, couple by couple, the whole multitude darted into its fiery breath and vanished. So ended the career of Flying Man.

3. A MINOR ASTRONOMICAL EVENT

The flightless yet still half avian race that now possessed the planet settled down to construct a society based on industry and science. After many vicissitudes of fortune and of aim, they produced a new human species, the Eighth Men. These long-headed and substantial folk were designed to be strictly pedestrian, physically and mentally. Apt for manipulation, calculation and invention, they very soon turned Venus into an engineer's paradise. With power drawn from the planet's central heat, their

huge electric ships bored steadily through the perennial monsoons and hurricanes, which also their aircraft treated with contempt. Islands were joined
by tunnels and by millepede bridges. Every inch of land served some industrial or agricultural end. So successfully did the generations amass
wealth that their rival races and rival castes were able to indulge, every
few centuries, in vast revelries of mutual slaughter and material destruction without, as a rule, impoverishing their descendants. And so insensitive had man become that these orgies shamed him not at all. Indeed, only
by the ardours of physical violence could this most philistine species wrench
itself for a while out of its complacency. Strife which to nobler beings
would have been a grave spiritual disaster, was for these a tonic, almost a
religious exercise. These cathartic paroxysms, it should be observed, were
but the rare and brief crises which automatically punctuated ages of stolid
peace. At no time did they threaten the existence of the species; seldom
did they even destroy its civilization.

It was after a lengthy period of peace and scientific advancement that
the Eighth Men made a startling astronomical discovery. Ever since the
First Men had learned that in the life of every star there comes a critical
moment when the great orb collapses, shrinking to a minute, dense grain
with feeble radiation, man had periodically suspected that the sun was
about to undergo this change, and become a typical "White Dwarf." The
Eighth Men detected sure signs of the catastrophe, and predicted its date.
Twenty thousand years they gave themselves before the change should
begin. In another fifty thousand years, they guessed, Venus would probably
be frozen and uninhabitable. The only hope was to migrate to Mercury
during the great change, when that planet was already ceasing to be intolerably hot. It was necessary then to give Mercury an atmosphere, and
to breed a new species which should be capable of adapting itself finally to
a world of extreme cold.

This desperate operation was already on foot when a new astronomical
discovery rendered it futile. Astronomers detected, some distance from the
solar system, a volume of non-luminous gas. Calculation showed that this
object and the sun were approaching one another at a tangent, and that
they would collide. Further calculation revealed the probable results of
this event. The sun would flare up and expand prodigiously. Life would
be quite impossible on any of the planets save, just possibly, Uranus, and
more probably Neptune. The three planets beyond Neptune would escape
roasting, but were unsuitable for other reasons. The two outermost would
remain glacial, and, moreover, lay beyond the range of the imperfect ether-
ships of the Eighth Men. The innermost was practically a bald globe of
iron, devoid not merely of atmosphere and water, but also of the normal
covering of rock. Neptune alone might be able to support life; but how
could even Neptune be populated? Not only was its atmosphere very unsuitable, and its gravitational pull such as to make man's body an intoler-

able burden, but also up to the time of the collision it would remain excessively cold. Not till after the collision could it support any kind of life known to man.

How these difficulties were overcome I have no time to tell, though the story of man's attack upon his final home is well worthy of recording. Nor can I tell in detail of the conflict of policy which now occurred. Some, realizing that the Eighth Men themselves could never live on Neptune, advocated an orgy of pleasure-living till the end. But at length the race excelled itself in an almost unanimous resolve to devote its remaining centuries to the production of a human being capable of carrying the torch of mentality into a new world.

Ether-vessels were able to reach that remote world and set up chemical changes for the improvement of the atmosphere. It was also possible, by means of the lately rediscovered process of automatic annihilation of matter, to produce a constant supply of energy for the warming of an area where life might hope to survive until the sun should be rejuvenated.

When at last the time for migration was approaching, a specially designed vegetation was shipped to Neptune and established in the warm area to fit it for man's use. Animals, it was decided, would be unnecessary. Subsequently a specially designed human species, the Ninth Men, was transported to man's new home. The giant Eighth Men could not themselves inhabit Neptune. The trouble was not merely that they could scarcely support their own weight, let alone walk, but that the atmospheric pressure on Neptune was unendurable. For the great planet bore a gaseous envelope thousands of miles deep. The solid globe was scarcely more than the yolk of a huge egg. The mass of the air itself combined with the mass of the solid to produce a gravitational pressure greater than that upon the Venerian ocean floor. The Eighth Men, therefore, dared not emerge from their ether-ships to tread the surface of the planet save for brief spells in steel diving suits. For them there was nothing else to do but to return to the archipelagos of Venus, and make the best of life until the end. They were not spared for long. A few centuries after the settlement of Neptune had been completed by transferring thither all the most precious material relics of humanity, the great planet itself narrowly missed collision with the dark stranger from space. Uranus and Jupiter were at the time well out of its track. Not so Saturn, which, a few years after Neptune's escape, was engulfed with all its rings and satellites. The sudden incandescence which resulted from this minor collision was but a prelude. The huge foreigner rushed on. Like a finger poked into a spider's web, it tangled up the planetary orbits. Having devoured its way through the asteroids, it missed Mars, caught Earth and Venus in its blazing hair, and leapt at the sun. Henceforth the centre of the solar system was a star nearly as wide as the old orbit of Mercury, and the system was transformed.

CHAPTER XIV

NEPTUNE

1. BIRD'S-EYE VIEW

I HAVE told man's story up to a point about half-way from his origin to his annihilation. Behind lies the vast span which includes the whole Terrestrial and Venerian ages, with all their slow fluctuations of darkness and enlightenment. Ahead lies the Neptunian age, equally long, equally tragic perhaps, but more diverse, and in its last phase incomparably more brilliant. It would not be profitable to recount the history of man on Neptune on the scale of the preceding chronicle. Very much of it would be incomprehensible to terrestrials, and much of it repeats again and again, in the many Neptunian modes, themes that we have already observed in the Terrestrial or the Venerian movements of the human symphony. To appreciate fully the range and subtlety of the great living epic, we ought, no doubt, to dwell on its every movement with the same faithful care. But this is impossible to any human mind. We can but attend to significant phrases, here and there, and hope to capture some fragmentary hint of its vast intricate form. And for the readers of this book, who are themselves tremors in the opening bars of the music, it is best that I should dwell chiefly on things near to them, even at the cost of ignoring much that is in fact greater.

Before continuing our long flight let us look around us. Hitherto we have passed over time's fields at a fairly low altitude, making many detailed observations. Now we shall travel at a greater height and with speed of a new order. We must therefore orientate ourselves within the wider horizon that opens around us; we must consider things from the astronomical rather than the human point of view. I said that we were half-way from man's beginning to his end. Looking back to that remote beginning we see that the span of time which includes the whole career of the First Men from Pithecanthropus to the Patagonian disaster is an unanalysable point. Even the preceding and much longer period between the first mammal and the first man, some twenty-five millions of terrestrial years, seems now inconsiderable. The whole of it, together with the age of the First Men, may be said to lie half-way between the formation of the planets, two thousand million years earlier, and their final destruction, two thousand million years later. Taking a still wider view, we see that this aeon of four thousand million years is itself no more than a moment in comparison with the sun's age. And before the birth of the sun the stuff of this galaxy had already endured for aeons as a nebula. Yet even those aeons look brief in relation to the passage of time before the myriad great nebulæ themselves, the future galaxies, condensed out of the all-pervading mist in the beginning. Thus the whole duration of humanity, with its many sequent species and its incessant downpour of generations, is but a flash in the lifetime of the cosmos.

Spatially, also, man is inconceivably minute. If in imagination we reduce this galaxy of ours to the size of an ancient terrestrial principality, we must suppose it adrift in the void with millions of other such principalities, very remote from one another. On the same scale the all-embracing cosmos would bulk as a sphere whose diameter was some twenty times greater than that of the lunar orbit in your day; and somewhere within the little wandering asteroid-like principality which is our own universe, the solar system would be an ultramicroscopic point, the greatest planet incomparably smaller.

We have watched the fortunes of eight successive human species for a thousand million years, the first half of that flicker which is the duration of man. Ten more species now succeed one another, or are contemporary, on the plains of Neptune. We, the Last Men, are the Eighteenth Men. Of the eight pre-Neptunian species, some, as we have seen, remained always primitive; many achieved at least a confused and fleeting civilization, and one, the brilliant Fifth, was already wakening into true humanity when misfortune crushed it. The ten Neptunian species show an even greater diversity. They range from the instinctive animal to modes of consciousness never before attained. The definitely sub-human degenerate types are confined mostly to the first six hundred million years of man's sojourn on Neptune. During the earlier half of this long phase of preparation, man, at first almost crushed out of existence by a hostile environment, gradually peopled the huge north; but with beasts, not men. For man, as man, no longer existed. During the latter half of the preparatory six hundred million years, the human spirit gradually awoke again, to undergo the fluctuating advance and decline characteristic of the pre-Neptunian ages. But subsequently, in the last four hundred million years of his career on Neptune, man has made an almost steady progress toward full spiritual maturity.

Let us now look rather more closely at these three great epochs of man's history.

2. DA CAPO

It was in desperate haste that the last Venerian men had designed and fashioned the new species for the colonization of Neptune. The mere remoteness of the great planet, moreover, had prevented its nature from being explored at all thoroughly, and so the new human organism was but partially adapted to its destined environment. Inevitably it was a dwarf type, limited in size by the necessity of resisting an excessive gravitation.

Its brain was so cramped that everything but the bare essentials of humanity had to be omitted from it. Even so, the Ninth Men were too delicately organized to withstand the ferocity of natural forces on Neptune. This ferocity the designers had seriously underestimated; and so they were content merely to produce a miniature copy of their own type. They should have planned a hardy brute, lustily procreative, cunning in the struggle for physical existence, but above all tough, prolific, and so insensitive as to be scarcely worthy of the name man. They should have trusted that if once this crude seed could take root, natural forces themselves would in time conjure from it something more human. Instead, they produced a race cursed with the inevitable fragility of miniatures, and designed for a civilized environment which feeble spirits could not possibly maintain in a tumultuous world. For it so happened that the still youthful giant, Neptune, was slowly entering one of his phases of crustal shrinkage, and therefore of earthquake and eruption. Thus the frail colonists found themselves increasingly in danger of being swallowed in sudden fiery crevasses or buried under volcanic dust. Moreover, their squat buildings, when not actually being trampled by lava streams, or warped and cracked by their shifting foundations, were liable to be demolished by the battering-ram thrust of a turbulent and massive atmosphere. Further, the atmosphere's unwholesome composition killed all possibility of cheerfulness and courage in a race whose nature was doomed to be, even in favourable circumstances, neurotic.

Fortunately this agony could not last indefinitely. Little by little, civilization crumbled into savagery, the torturing vision of better things was lost, man's consciousness was narrowed and coarsened into brute-consciousness. By good luck the brute precariously survived.

Long after the Ninth Men had fallen from man's estate, nature herself, in her own slow and blundering manner, succeeded where man had failed. The brute descendants of this human species became at length well adapted to their world. In time there arose a wealth of sub-human forms in the many kinds of environment afforded by the lands and seas of Neptune. None of them penetrated far toward the Equator, for the swollen sun had rendered the tropics at this time far too hot to support life of any kind. Even at the pole the protracted summer put a great strain on all but the most hardy creatures.

Neptune's year was at this time about one hundred and sixty-five times the length of the old terrestrial year. The slow seasonal change had an important effect on life's own rhythms. All but the most ephemeral organisms tended to live through at least one complete year, and the higher mammals survived longer. At a much later stage this natural longevity was to play a great and beneficial part in the revival of man. But, on the other hand, the increasing sluggishness of individual growth, the length of immaturity in each generation, retarded the natural evolutionary process on Neptune, so that compared with the Terrestrial and Venerian epochs the biological story now moves at a snail's pace.

After the fall of the Ninth Men the sub-human creatures had one and all adopted a quadruped habit, the better to cope with gravity. At first they had indulged merely in occasional support from their knuckles, but in time many species of true quadrupeds had appeared. In several of the running types the fingers, like the toes, had grown together, and a hoof had developed, not on the old fingertips, which were bent back and atrophied, but on the knuckles.

Two hundred million years after the solar collision innumerable species of sub-human grazers with long sheep-like muzzles, ample molars, and almost ruminant digestive systems, were competing with one another on the polar continent. Upon these preyed the sub-human carnivora, of whom some were built for speed in the chase, others for stalking and a sudden spring. But since jumping was no easy matter on Neptune, the cat-like types were all minute. They preyed upon man's more rabbit-like and rat-like descendants, or on the carrion of the larger mammals, or on the lusty worms and beetles. These had sprung originally from vermin which had been transported accidentally from Venus. For of all the ancient Venerian fauna only man himself, a few insects and other invertebrates, and many kinds of micro-organisms, succeeded in colonizing Neptune. Of plants, many types had been artificially bred for the new world, and from these eventually arose a host of grasses, flowering plants, thick-trunked bushes, and novel sea-weeds. On this marine flora fed certain highly developed marine worms; and of these last, some in time became vertebrate, predatory, swift and fish-like. On these in turn man's own marine descendants preyed, whether as sub-human seals, or still more specialized sub-human porpoises. Perhaps most remarkable of these developments of the ancient human stock was that which led, through a small insectivorous bat-like glider, to a great diversity of true flying mammals, scarcely larger than humming birds, but in some cases agile as swallows.

Nowhere did the typical human form survive. There were only beasts, fitted by structure and instinct to some niche or other of their infinitely diverse and roomy world.

Certainly strange vestiges of human mentality did indeed persist here and there even as, in the fore-limbs of most species, there still remained buried the relics of man's once cunning fingers. For instance, there were certain grazers which in times of hardship would meet together and give tongue in cacophonous ululation; or, sitting on their haunches with fore-limbs pressed together, they would listen by the hour to the howls of some leader, responding intermittently with groans and whimpers, and working themselves at last into foaming madness. And there were carnivora which, in the midst of the spring-time fervour, would suddenly cease from love-making, fighting, and the daily routine of hunting, to sit alone in some high place day after day, night after night, watching, waiting; until at last hunger forced them into action.

Now in the fullness of time, about three hundred million terrestrial years after the solar collision, a certain minute, hairless, rabbit-like creature, scampering on the polar grasslands, found itself greatly persecuted by a swift hound from the south. The sub-human rabbit was relatively unspecialized, and had no effective means of defence or flight. It was almost exterminated. A few individuals, however, saved themselves by taking to the dense and thick-trunked scrub, whither the hound could not follow them. Here they had to change their diet and manner of life, deserting grass for roots, berries, and even worms and beetles. Their fore-limbs were now increasingly used for digging and climbing, and eventually for weaving nests of stick and straw. In this species the fingers had never grown together. Internally the fore-paw was like a minute clenched fist from the elongated and exposed knuckles of which separate toes protruded. And now the knuckles elongated themselves still further, becoming in time a new set of fingers. Within the palm of the new little monkey-hand there still remained traces of man's ancient fingers, bent in upon themselves.

As of old, manipulation gave rise to clearer percipience. And this, in conjunction with the necessity of frequent experiments in diet, hunting, and defence, produced at length a real versatility of behaviour and suppleness of mind. The rabbit throve, adopted an almost upright gait, continued to increase in stature and in brain. Yet, just as the new hand was not merely a resurrection of the old hand, so the new regions of the brain were no mere revival of the atrophied human cerebrum, but a new organ, which overlaid and swallowed up that ancient relic. The creature's mind, therefore, was in many respects a new mind, though moulded to the same great basic needs. Like his forerunners, of course, he craved food, love, glory, companionship. In pursuit of these ends he devised weapons and traps, and built wicker villages. He held pow-wows. He became the Tenth Men.

3. SLOW CONQUEST

For a million terrestrial years these long-armed hairless beings were spreading their wicker huts and bone implements over the great northern continents, and for many more millions they remained in possession without making further cultural progress; for evolution, both biological and cultural, was indeed slow on Neptune. At last the Tenth Men were attacked by a micro-organism and demolished. From their ruins several primitive human species developed, and remained isolated in remote territories for millions of decades, until at length chance or enterprise brought them into contact. One of these early species, crouched and tusked, was persistently trapped for its ivory by an abler type, till it was exterminated. Another, long of muzzle and large of base, habitually squatted on its

haunches like the kangaroo. Shortly after this industrious and social species
had discovered the use of the wheel, a more primitive but more war-like
type crashed into it like a tidal wave and overwhelmed it. Erect, but literally almost as broad as they were tall, these chunkish and bloody-minded
savages spread over the whole arctic and sub-arctic region and spent some
millions of years in monotonous reiteration of progress and decline; until
at last a slow decay of their germ-plasm almost ended man's career. But
after an aeon of darkness, there appeared another thick-set, but larger
brained, species. This, for the first time on Neptune, conceived the religion of love, and all those spiritual cravings and agonies which had flick-
ered in man so often and so vainly upon Earth and Venus. There appeared
again feudal empires, militant nations, economic class wars, and, not once
but often, a world-state covering the whole northern hemisphere. These
men it was that first crossed the equator in artificially cooled electric ships,
and explored the huge south. No life of any kind was discovered in the
southern hemisphere; for even in that age no living matter could have
crossed the roasting tropics without artificial refrigeration. Indeed, it was
only because the sun's temporary revival had already passed its zenith that
even man, with all his ingenuity, could endure a long tropical voyage.

Like the First Men and so many other natural human types, these
Fourteenth Men were imperfectly human. Like the First Men, they conceived ideals of conduct which their imperfectly organized nervous systems
could never attain and seldom approach. Unlike the First Men, they survived with but minor biological changes for three hundred million years.
But even so long a period did not enable them to transcend their imperfect
spiritual nature. Again and again and again they passed from savagery to
world-civilization and back to savagery. They were captive within their
own nature, as a bird in a cage. And as a caged bird may fumble with
nest-building materials and periodically destroy the fruit of its aimless toil,
so these cramped beings destroyed their civilizations.

At length, however, this second phase of Neptunian history, this era
of fluctuation, was brought to an end. At the close of the six hundred
million years after the first settlement of the planet, unaided nature produced, in the Fifteenth human species, that highest form of natural man
which she had produced only once before, in the Second species. And this
time no Martians interfered. We must not stay to watch the struggle of
this great-headed man to overcome his one serious handicap, excessive
weight of cranium and unwieldy proportions of body. Suffice it that after
a long-drawn-out immaturity, including one great mechanized war between the northern and southern hemispheres, the Fifteenth Men outgrew
the ailments and fantasies of youth, and consolidated themselves as a single
world-community. This civilization was based economically on volcanic
power, and spiritually on devotion to the fulfilment of human capacity. It
was this species which, for the first time on Neptune, conceived, as an

enduring racial purpose, the will to remake human nature upon an ampler scale.

Henceforth in spite of many disasters, such as another period of earthquake and eruption, sudden climatic changes, innumerable plagues and biological aberrations, human progress was relatively steady. It was not by any means swift and sure. There were still to be ages, often longer than the whole career of the First Men, in which the human spirit would rest from its pioneering to consolidate its conquests, or would actually stray into the wilderness. But never again, seemingly, was it to be routed and crushed into mere animality.

In tracing man's final advance to full humanity we can observe only the broadest features of a whole astronomical era. But in fact it is an era crowded with many thousands of long-lived generations. Myriads of individuals, each one unique, live out their lives in rapt intercourse with one another, contribute their heart's pulses to the universal music, and presently vanish, giving place to others. All this age-long sequence of private living, which is the actual tissue of humanity's flesh, I cannot describe. I can only trace, as it were, the disembodied form of its growth.

The Fifteenth Men first set themselves to abolish five great evils, namely, disease, suffocating toil, senility, misunderstanding, ill-will. The story of their devotion, their many disastrous experiments and ultimate triumph, cannot here be told. Nor can I recount how they learned and used the secret of deriving power from the annihilation of matter, nor how they invented ether ships for the exploration of neighbouring planets, nor how, after ages of experiments, they designed and produced a new species, the Sixteenth, to supersede themselves.

The new type was analogous to the ancient Fifth, which had colonized Venus. Artificial rigid atoms had been introduced into its bone-tissues, so that it might support great stature and an ample brain; in which, moreover, an exceptionally fine-grained cellular structure permitted a new complexity of organization. "Telepathy," also, was once more achieved, not by means of the ·Martian units, which had long ago become extinct, but by the synthesis of new molecular groups of a similar type. Partly through the immense increase of mutual understanding, which resulted from "telepathic" *rapport,* partly through improved co-ordination of the nervous system, the ancient evil of selfishness was entirely and finally abolished from the normal human being. Egoistic impulses, whenever they refused to be subordinated, were henceforth classed as symptoms of insanity. The sensory powers of the new species were, of course, greatly improved; and it was even given a pair of eyes in the back of the head. Henceforth man was to have a circular instead of a semicircular field of vision. And such was the general intelligence of the new race that many problems formerly deemed insoluble were now solved in a single flash of insight.

Of the great practical uses to which the Sixteenth Men put their powers, one only need be mentioned as an example. They gained control of the movement of their planet. Early in their career they were able, with the unlimited energy at their disposal, to direct it into a wider orbit, so that its average climate became more temperate, and snow occasionally covered the polar regions. But as the ages advanced, and the sun became steadily less ferocious, it became necessary to reverse this process and shift the planet gradually nearer to the sun.

When they had possessed their world for nearly fifty million years, the Sixteenth Men, like the Fifth before them, learned to enter into past minds. For them this was a more exciting adventure than for their forerunners, since they were still ignorant of Terrestrial and Venerian history. Like their forerunners, so dismayed were they at the huge volume of eternal misery in the past, that for a while, in spite of their own great blessings and spontaneous gaiety, existence seemed a mockery. But in time they came to regard the past's misery as a challenge. They told themselves that the past was calling to them for help, and that somehow they must prepare a great "crusade to liberate the past." How this was to be done, they could not conceive; but they were determined to bear in mind this quixotic aim in the great enterprise which had by now become the chief concern of the race, namely the creation of a human type of an altogether higher order.

It had become clear that man had by now advanced in understanding and creativeness as far as was possible to the individual human brain acting in physical isolation. Yet the Sixteenth Men were oppressed by their own impotence. Though in philosophy they had delved further than had ever before been possible, yet even at their deepest they found only the shifting sands of mystery. In particular they were haunted by three ancient problems, two of which were purely intellectual, namely the mystery of time and the mystery of mind's relation to the world. Their third problem was the need somehow to reconcile their confirmed loyalty to life, which they conceived as embattled against death, with their ever-strengthening impulse to rise above the battle and admire it dispassionately.

Age after age the races of the Sixteenth Men blossomed with culture after culture. The movement of thought ranged again and again through all the possible modes of the spirit, ever discovering new significance in ancient themes. Yet throughout this epoch the three great problems remained unsolved, perplexing the individual and vitiating the policy of the race.

Forced thus at length to choose between spiritual stagnation and a perilous leap in the dark, the Sixteenth Men determined to set about devising a type of brain which, by means of the mental fusion of many individuals, might waken into an altogether new mode of consciousness. Thus, it was hoped, man might gain insight into the very heart of existence, whether finally to admire or loathe. And thus the racial purpose, which

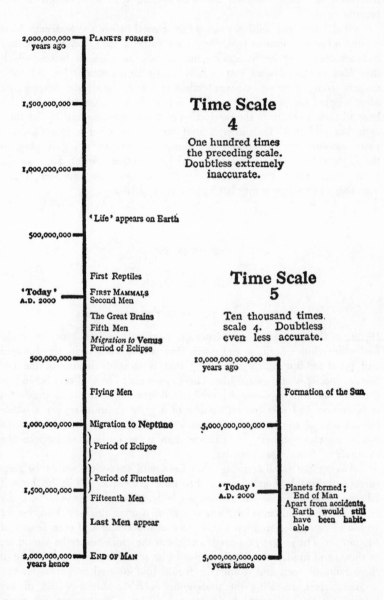

Time Scale 4

One hundred times
the preceding scale.
Doubtless extremely
inaccurate.

2,000,000,000 years ago — PLANETS FORMED

1,500,000,000 —

1,000,000,000 —

'Life' appears on Earth

500,000,000 —

First Reptiles

'Today' A.D. 2000 — FIRST MAMMALS
Second Men

The Great Brains
Fifth Men
Migration to Venus
Period of Eclipse

500,000,000 —

Flying Men

1,000,000,000 — Migration to Neptune

} Period of Eclipse

} Period of Fluctuation

1,500,000,000 — Fifteenth Men

Last Men appear

2,000,000,000 years hence — END OF MAN

Time Scale 5

Ten thousand times
scale 4. Doubtless
even less accurate.

10,000,000,000,000 years ago — Formation of the Sun

5,000,000,000,000 —

'Today' A.D. 2000 — Planets formed;
End of Man
Apart from accidents,
Earth would still
have been habitable

5,000,000,000,000 years hence

had been so much confused by philosophical ignorance, might at last become clear.

Of the hundred million years which passed before the Sixteenth Men produced the new human type, I must not pause to tell. They thought they had achieved their hearts' desire; but in fact the glorious beings which they had produced were tortured by subtle imperfections beyond their makers' comprehension. Consequently, no sooner had these Seventeenth Men peopled the world and attained full cultural stature, than they also bent all their strength to the production of a new type, essentially like their own, but perfected. Thus after a brief career of a few hundred thousand years, crowded with splendour and agony, the Seventeenth gave place to the Eighteenth, and, as it turns out, the Last, human species. Since all the earlier cultures find their fulfilment in the world of the Last Men, I pass over them to enlarge somewhat upon our modern age.

CHAPTER XV

THE LAST MEN

I. INTRODUCTION TO THE LAST HUMAN SPECIES

IF one of the First Men could enter the world of the Last Men, he would find many things familiar and much that would seem strangely distorted and perverse. But nearly everything that is most distinctive of the last human species would escape him. Unless he were to be told that behind all the obvious and imposing features of civilization, behind all the social organization and personal intercourse of a great community, lay a whole other world of spiritual culture, round about him, yet beyond his ken, he would no more suspect its existence than a cat in London suspects the existence of finance or literature.

Among the familiar things that he would encounter would be creatures recognizably human yet in his view grotesque. While he himself laboured under the weight of his own body, these giants would be easily striding. He would consider them very sturdy, often thick-set, folk, but he would be compelled to allow them grace of movement and even beauty of proportion. The longer he stayed with them the more beauty he would see in them, and the less complacently would he regard his own type. Some of these fantastic men and women he would find covered with fur, hirsute, or mole-velvet, revealing the underlying muscles. Others would display brown, yellow or ruddy skin, and yet others a translucent ash-green, warmed by the under-flowing blood. As a species, though we are all human, we are extremely variable in body and mind, so variable that superficially we seem to be not one species but many. Some characters, of course, are common to all of us. The traveller might perhaps be surprised by the large yet sensitive hands which are universal, both in men and women. In all of us the outermost finger bears at its tip three minute organs of manipulation, rather similar to those which were first devised for the Fifth Men. These excrescences would doubtless revolt our visitor. The pair of occipital eyes, too, would shock him; so would the upward-looking astronomical eye on the crown, which is peculiar to the Last Men. This organ was so cunningly designed that, when fully extended, about a hand-breadth from its bony case, it reveals the heavens in as much detail as your smaller astronomical telescopes. Apart from such special features as these, there is nothing definitely novel about us; though every limb, every contour, shows unmistakably that much has happened since the days of the First Men. We are both more human and more animal. The primitive explorer might be more readily impressed by our animality than our humanity, so much of our humanity would lie beyond his grasp. He would perhaps at first regard us as a degraded type. He would call us faun-like, and in particular cases, ape-like, bear-like, ox-like, marsupial, or elephantine. Yet our general proportions are definitely human in the ancient manner. Where gravity is not insurmountable, the erect biped form is bound to be most serviceable to intelligent land animals; and so, after long wanderings, man has returned to his old shape. Moreover, if our observer were himself at all sensitive to facial expression, he would come to recognize in every one of our innumerable physiognomic types an indescribable but distinctively human look, the visible sign of that inward and spiritual grace which is not wholly absent from his own species. He would perhaps say, "These men that are beasts are surely gods also." He would be reminded of those old Egyptian deities with animal heads. But in us the animal and the human interpenetrate in every feature, in every curve of the body, and with infinite variety. He would observe us, together with hints of the long-extinct Mongol, Negro, Nordic, and Semetic, many outlandish features and expressions, deriving from the sub-human period on Neptune, or from Venus. He would see in every limb unfamiliar contours of muscle, sinew or bone, which were acquired long after the First Men had vanished. Besides the familiar eye-colours, he would discover orbs of topaz, emerald, amethyst and ruby, and a thousand varieties of these. But in all of us he would see also, if he had discernment, a facial expression and bodily gesture peculiar to our own species, a certain luminous, yet pungent and ironical significance, which we miss almost wholly in the earlier human faces.

The traveller would recognize among us unmistakable sexual features, both of general proportions and special organs. But it would take him long to discover that some of the most striking bodily and facial differences were due to differentiation of the two ancient sexes into many sub-sexes. Full sexual experience involves for us a complicated relationship between individuals of all these types. Of the extremely important sexual groups I shall speak again.

Our visitor would notice, by the way, that though all persons on Neptune go habitually nude, save for a pouch or rucksack, clothing, often brightly coloured, and made of diverse lustrous or homely tissues unknown before our time, is worn for special purposes.

He would notice also, scattered about the green countryside, many buildings, mostly of one story; for there is plenty of room on Neptune even for the million million of the Last Men. Here and there, however, we have great architectural pylons, cruciform or star-shaped in section, cloud-piercing, dignifying the invariable planes of Neptune. These mightiest of all buildings, which are constructed in adamantine materials formed of artificial atoms, would seem to our visitor geometrical mountains, far taller than any natural mountain could be, even on the smallest planet. In many cases the whole fabric is translucent or transparent, so that at night, with internal illumination, it appears as an edifice of light. Springing from a base twenty or more miles across, the star-seeking towers attain a height where even Neptune's atmosphere is somewhat attenuated. In their summits work the hosts of our astronomers, the essential eyes through which our community, on her little raft, peers across the ocean. Thither also all men and women repair at one time or another to contemplate this galaxy of ours and the unnumbered remoter universes. There they perform together those supreme symbolic acts for which I find no adjective in your speech but the debased word "religious." There also they seek the refreshment of mountain air in a world where natural mountains are unknown. And on the pinnacles and precipices of these loftiest horns many of us gratify that primeval lust of climbing which was ingrained in man before ever he was man. These buildings thus combine the functions of observatory, temple, sanatorium and gymnasium. Some of them are almost as old as the species, some are not yet completed. They embody, therefore, many styles. The traveller would find modes which he would be tempted to call Gothic, Classical, Egyptian, Peruvian, Chinese, or American, besides a thousand architectural ideas unfamiliar to him. Each of these buildings was the work of the race as a whole at some stage in its career. None of them is a mere local product. Every successive culture has expressed itself in one or more of these supreme monuments. Once in forty thousand years or so some new architectural glory would be conceived and executed. And such is the continuity of our cultures that there has scarcely ever been need to remove the handiwork of the past.

If our visitor happened to be near enough to one of these great pylons, he would see it surrounded by a swarm of midges, which would turn out to be human fliers, wingless, but with outspread arms. The stranger might wonder how a large organism could rise from the ground in Neptune's powerful field of gravity. Yet flight is our ordinary means of locomotion. A man has but to put on a suit of overalls fitted at various points with radiation-generators. Ordinary flight thus becomes a kind of aerial swimming. Only when very high speed is desired do we make use of closed-in air-boats and liners.

At the feet of the great buildings the flat or undulating country is green, brown, golden, and strewn with houses. Our traveller would recognize that much land was under cultivation, and would see many persons at work upon it with tools or machinery. Most of our food, indeed, is produced by artificial photo synthesis on the broiling planet Jupiter, where even now that the sun is becoming normal again, no life can exist without powerful refrigeration. As far as mere nutrition is concerned, we could do without vegetation; but agriculture and its products have played so great a part in human history that today agricultural operations and vegetable foods are very beneficial to the race psychologically. And so it comes about that vegetable matter is in great demand, not only as raw material for innumerable manufactures, but also for table delicacies. Green vegetables, fruit, and various alcoholic fruit drinks have come to have the same kind of ritual significance for us as wine has for you. Meat also, though not a part of ordinary diet, is eaten on very rare and sacred occasions. The cherished wild fauna of the planet contributes its toll to periodic symbolical banquets. And whenever a human being has chosen to die, his body is ceremoniously eaten by his friends.

Communication with the food factories of Jupiter and the agricultural polar regions of the less torrid Uranus, as also with the automatic mining stations on the glacial outer planets, is maintained by ether ships, which, travelling much faster than the planets themselves, make the passage to the neighbour worlds in a small fraction of the Neptunian year. These vessels, of which the smallest are about a mile in length, may be seen descending on our oceans like ducks. Before they touch the water they cause a prodigious tumult with the downward pressure of their radiation; but once upon the surface, they pass quietly into harbour.

The ether ship is in a manner symbolic of our whole community, so highly organized is it, and so minute in relation to the void which engulfs it. The ethereal navigators, because they spend so much of their time in the empty regions, beyond the range of "telepathic" communication and sometimes even of mechanical radio, form mentally a unique class among us. They are a hardy, simple, and modest folk. And though they embody man's proud mastery of the ether, they are never tired of reminding landlubbers, with dour jocularity, that the most daring voyages are confined within one drop of the boundless ocean of space.

Recently an exploration ship returned from a voyage into the outer tracts. Half her crew had died. The survivors were emaciated, diseased, and mentally unbalanced. To a race that thought itself so well established in sanity that nothing could disturb it, the spectacle of these unfortunates was instructive. Throughout the voyage, which was the longest ever attempted, they had encountered nothing whatever but two comets, and an occasional meteor. Some of the nearer constellations were seen with altered forms. One or two stars increased slightly in brightness; and the sun was reduced to being the most brilliant of stars. The aloof and changeless presence of the constellations seems to have crazed the voyagers. When at last the ship returned and berthed, there was a scene such as is seldom witnessed in our modern world. The crew flung open the ports and staggered blubbering into the arms of the crowd. It would never have been believed that members of our species could be so far reduced from the self-possession that is normal to us. Subsequently these poor human wrecks have shown an irrational phobia of the stars, and of all that is not human. They dare not go out at night. They live in an extravagant passion for the presence of others. And since all others are astronomically minded, they cannot find real companionship. They insanely refuse to participate in the mental life of the race upon the plane where all things are seen in their just proportions. They cling piteously to the sweets of individual life; and so they are led to curse the immensities. They fill their minds with human conceits, and their houses with toys. By night they draw the curtains and drown the quiet voice of the stars in revelry. But it is a joyless and a haunted revelry, desired less for itself than as a defence against reality.

2. CHILDHOOD AND MATURITY

I said that we were all astronomically minded; but we are not without "human" interests. Our visitor from the earth would soon discover that the low buildings, sprinkled on all sides, were the homes of individuals, families, sexual groups, and bands of companions. Most of these buildings are so constructed that the roof and walls can be removed, completely or partially, for sun-bathing and for the night. Round each house is a wilderness, or a garden, or an orchard of our sturdy fruit trees. Here and there men and women may be seen at work with hoe or spade or secateurs. The buildings themselves affect many styles; and within doors our visitor would find great variety from house to house. Even within a single house he might come on rooms seemingly of different epochs. And while some rooms are crowded with articles, many of which would be incomprehensible to the stranger, others are bare, save for a table, chairs, a cupboard, and perhaps some single object of pure art. We have an immense variety of manufactured goods. But the visitor from a world obsessed with material wealth would probably remark the simplicity, even austerity, which characterizes most private houses.

He would doubtless be surprised to see no books. In every room, however, there is a cupboard filled with minute rolls of tape, microscopically figured. Each of these rolls contains matter which could not be cramped into a score of your volumes. They are used in connexion with a pocket-instrument, the size and shape of the ancient cigarette case. When the roll is inserted, it reels itself off at any desired speed, and interferes systematically with ethereal vibrations produced by the instrument. Thus is generated a very complex flow of "telepathic" language which permeates the brain of the reader. So delicate and direct is this medium of expression that there is scarcely any possibility of misunderstanding the author's intention. The rolls themselves, it should be said, are produced by another special instrument, which is sensitive to vibrations generated in the author's brain. Not that it produces a mere replica of his stream of consciousness; it records only those images and ideas with which he deliberately "inscribes" it. I may mention also that, since we can at any moment communicate by direct "telepathy" with any person on the planet, these "books" of ours are not used for the publication of merely ephemeral thought. Each one of them preserves only the threshed and chosen grains of some mind's harvest.

Other instruments may be observed in our houses, which I cannot pause to describe, instruments whose office is either to carry out domestic drudgery, or to minister directly in one way or another to cultured life. Near the outer door would be hanging a number of flying-suits, and in a garage attached to the house would be the private air-boats, gaily coloured torpedo-shaped objects of various sizes.

Decoration in our houses, save in those which belong to children, is everywhere simple, even severe. None the less we prize it greatly, and spend much consideration upon it. Children, indeed, often adorn their houses with splendour, which adults themselves can also enjoy through children's eyes, even as they can enter into the frolics of infants with unaffected glee.

The number of children in our world is small in relation to our immense population. Yet, seeing that every one of us is potentially immortal, it may be wondered how we can permit ourselves to have any children at all. The explanation is two-fold. In the first place, our policy is to produce new individuals of higher type than ourselves, for we are very far from biologically perfect. Consequently we need a continuous supply of children. And as these successively reach maturity, they take over the functions of adults whose nature is less perfect; and these, when they are aware that they are no longer of service, elect to retire from life.

But even though every individual, sooner or later, ceases to exist, the average length of life is not much less than a quarter of a million terrestrial years. No wonder, then, that we cannot accommodate many children. But we have more than might be expected, for with us infancy and adolescence are very lengthy. The fœtus is carried for twenty years. Ectogenesis was practised by our predecessors, but was abandoned by our own species, because, with greatly improved motherhood, there is no need for it. Our mothers, indeed, are both physically and mentally most vigorous during the all too rare period of pregnancy. After birth, true infancy lasts for about a century. During this period, in which the foundations of body and mind are being laid, very slowly, but so securely that they will never fail, the individual is cared for by his mother. Then follow some centuries of childhood, and a thousand years of adolescence.

Our children, of course, are very different beings from the children of the First Men. Though physically they are in many respects still childlike, they are independent persons in the community. Each has either a house of his own, or rooms in a larger building held in common by himself and his friends. Thousands of these are to be found in the neighbourhood of every educational centre. There are some children who prefer to live with their parents, or with one or other of their parents; but this is rare. Though there is often much friendly intercourse between parents and children, the generations usually fare better under separate roofs. This is inevitable in our species. For the adult's overwhelmingly greater experience reveals the world to him in very different proportions from those which alone are possible even to the most brilliant of children; while on the other hand with us the mind of every child is, in some potentiality or other, definitely superior to every adult mind. Consequently, while the child can never appreciate what is best in his elders, the adult, in spite of his power of direct insight into all minds not superior to himself, is doomed to incomprehension of all that is novel in his own offspring.

Six or seven hundred years after birth a child is in some respects physically equivalent to a ten-year-old of the First Men. But since his brain is destined for much higher development, it is already far more complex than any adult brain of that species. And though temperamentally he is in many ways still a child, intellectually he has already in some respects passed beyond the culture of the best adult minds of the ancient races. The traveller, encountering one of our bright boys, might sometimes be reminded of the wise simplicity of the legendary Child Christ. But also he might equally well discover a vast exuberance, boisterousness, impishness, and a complete inability to stand outside the child's own eager life and regard it dispassionately. In general our children develop intellectually beyond the level of the First Men long before they begin to develop the dispassionate will which is characteristic of our adults. When there is conflict between a child's personal needs and the needs of society, he will as a rule force himself to the social course; but he does so with resentment and dramatic self-pity, thereby rendering himself in the adult view exquisitely ridiculous.

When our children attain physical adolescence, nearly a thousand years after birth, they leave the safe paths of childhood to spend another thousand years in one of the antarctic continents, known as the Land of the Young. Somewhat reminiscent of the Wild Continent of the Fifth Men, this territory is preserved as virgin bush and prairie. Sub-human grazers and carnivora abound. Volcanic eruption, hurricanes and glacial seasons afford further attractions to the adventurous young. There is conse-

quently a high death-rate. In this land our young people live the half primitive, half sophisticated life to which their nature is fitted. They hunt, fish,
tend cattle and till the ground. They cultivate all the simple beauties of
human individuality. They love and hate. They sing, paint and carve.
They devise heroic myths, and delight in fantasies of direct intercourse
with a cosmic person. They organize themselves as tribes and nations.
Sometimes they even indulge in warfare of a primitive but bloody type.
Formerly when this happened, the adult world interfered; but we have
since learned to let the fever run its course. The loss of life is regrettable;
but it is a small price to pay for the insight afforded even by this restricted
and juvenile warfare, into those primitive agonies and passions which,
when they are experienced by the adult mind, are so transformed by
philosophy that their import is wholly changed. In the Land of the Young
our boys and girls experience all that is precious and all that is abject in
the primitive. They live through in their own persons, century by century,
all its toilsomeness and cramped meanness, all its blind cruelty and precari-
ousness; but also they taste its glamour, its vernal and lyrical glory. They
make in little all the mistakes of thought and action that men have ever
made; but at last they emerge ready for the larger and more difficult world
of maturity.

It was expected that some day, when we should have perfected the
species, there would be no need to build up successive generations, no need
of children, no need of all this schooling. It was expected that the community would then consist of adults only; and that they would be immortal not merely potentially but in fact, yet also, of course, perennially in
the flower of young maturity. Thus, death should never cut the string of
individuality and scatter the hard-won pearls, necessitating new strings,
and laborious re-gatherings. The many and very delectable beauties of
childhood could still be amply enjoyed in exploration of the past.

We know now that this goal is not to be attained, since man's end is
imminent.

3. A RACIAL AWAKENING

It is easy to speak of children; but how can I tell you anything significant of our adult experience, in relation to which not only the world of
the First Men but the worlds of the most developed earlier species seem so
naïve?

The source of the immense difference between ourselves and all other
human races lies in the sexual group, which is in fact much more than a
sexual group.

The designers of our species set out to produce a being that might be
capable of an order of mentality higher than their own. The only possibility
of doing so lay in planning a great increase of brain organization. But they
knew that the brain of an individual human being could not safely be

allowed to exceed a certain weight. They therefore sought to produce the new order of mentality in a system of distinct and specialized brains held in "telepathic" unity by means of ethereal radiation. Material brains were to be capable of becoming on some occasions mere nodes in a system of radiation which itself should then constitute the physical basis of a single mind. Hitherto there had been "telepathic" communication between many individuals, but no super-individual, or group-mind. It was known that such a unity of individual minds had never been attained before, save on Mars; and it was known how lamentably the racial mind of Mars had failed to transcend the minds of the Martians. By a combination of shrewdness and good luck the designers hit upon a policy which escaped the Martian failure. They planned as the basis of the super-individual a small multi-sexual group.

Of course the mental unity of the sexual group is not the direct outcome of the sexual intercourse of its members. Such intercourse does occur. Groups differ from one another very greatly in this respect; but in most groups all the members of the male sexes have intercourse with all the members of the female sexes. Thus sex is with us essentially social. It is impossible for me to give any idea of the great range and intensity of experience afforded by these diverse types of union. Apart from this emotional enrichment of the individuals, the importance of sexual activity in the group lies in its bringing individuals into that extreme intimacy, temperamental harmony and complementariness, without which no emergence into higher experience would be possible.

Individuals are not necessarily confined to the same group for ever. Little by little a group may change every one of its ninety-six members, and yet it will remain the same super-individual mind, though enriched with the memories grafted into it by the new-comers. Very rarely does an individual leave a group before he has been in it for ten thousand years. In some groups the members live together in a common home. In others they live apart. Sometimes an individual will form a sort of monogamous relation with another individual of his group, homing with the chosen one for many thousands of years, or even for a lifetime. Indeed some claim that lifelong monogamy is the ideal state, so deep and delicate is the intimacy which it affords. But of course, even in monogamy, each partner must be periodically refreshed by intercourse with other members of the group, not only for the spiritual health of the two partners themselves, but also that the group-mind may be maintained in full vigour. Whatever the sexual custom of the group, there is always in the mind of each member a very special loyalty toward the whole group, a peculiar sexually toned *esprit de corps,* unparalleled in any other species.

Occasionally there is a special kind of group intercourse in which, during the actual occurrence of group mentality, all the members of one group will have intercourse with those of another. Casual intercourse outside the group is not common, but not discouraged. When it occurs it comes as a symbolic act crowning a spiritual intimacy.

Unlike the physical sex-relationship, the mental unity of the group involves all the members of the group every time it occurs, and so long as it persists. During times of group experience the individual continues to perform his ordinary routine of work and recreation, save when some particular activity is demanded of him by the group-mind itself. But all that he does as a private individual is carried out in a profound absent-mindedness. In familiar situations he reacts correctly, even to the extent of executing familiar types of intellectual work or entertaining acquaintances with intelligent conversation. Yet all the while he is in fact "far away," rapt in the process of the group-mind. Nothing short of an urgent and unfamiliar crisis can recall him; and in recalling him it usually puts an end to the group's experience.

Each member of the group is fundamentally just a highly developed human animal. He enjoys his food. He has a quick eye for sexual attraction, within or without the group. He has his personal idiosyncrasies and foibles, and is pleased to ridicule the foibles of others—and of himself. He may be one of those who abhor children, or one of those who enter into children's antics with fervour, if they will tolerate him. He may move heaven and earth to procure permission for a holiday in the Land of the Young. And if he fails, as he almost surely does, he may go walking with a friend, or boating and swimming, or playing violent games. Or he may merely potter in his garden, or refresh his mind though not his body by exploring some favourite region of the past. Recreation occupies a large part of his life. For this reason he is always glad to get back to work in due season, whether his function is to maintain some part of the material organization of our world, or to educate, or to perform scientific research, or to co-operate in the endless artistic venture of the race, or, as is more likely, to help in some of those innumerable enterprises whose nature it is impossible for me to describe.

As a human individual, then, he or she is somewhat of the same type as a member of the Fifth species. Here once more is the perfected glandular outfit and instinctive nature. Here too is the highly developed sense perception and intellection. As in the Fifth species, so in the Eighteenth, each individual has his own private needs, which he heartily craves to fulfil; but also, in both species, he subordinates these private cravings to the good of the race absolutely and without struggle. The only kind of conflict which ever occurs between individuals is, not the irreconcilable conflict of wills, but the conflict due to misunderstanding, to imperfect knowledge of the matter under dispute; and this can always be abolished by patient telepathic explication.

In addition to the brain organization necessary to this perfection of individual human nature, each member of a sexual group has in his own brain a special organ which, useless by itself, can co-operate "telepathically" with the special organs of other members of the group to produce a single electro-magnetic system, the physical basis of the group-mind. In each sub-sex this organ has a peculiar form and function; and only by the simultaneous operation of the whole ninety-six does the group attain unified mental life. These organs do not merely enable each member to share the experience of all; for this is already provided in the sensitivity to radiation which is characteristic of all brain-tissue in our species. By means of the harmonious activity of the special organs a true group-mind emerges, with experience far beyond the range of the individuals in isolation.

This would not be possible did not the temperament and capacity of each sub-sex differ appropriately from those of the others. I can only hint at these differences by analogy. Among the First Men there are many temperamental types whose essential natures the psychologists of that species never fully analysed. I may mention, however, as superficial designations of these types, the meditative, the active, the mystical, the intellectual, the artistic, the theoretical, the concrete, the placid, the highly-strung. Now our sub-sexes differ from one another temperamentally in some such manners as these, but with a far greater range and diversity. These differences of temperament are utilized for the enrichment of a group self, such as could never have been attained by the First Men, even if they had been capable of "telepathic" communication and electro-magnetic unity; for they had not the range of specialized brain form.

For all the daily business of life, then, each of us is mentally a distinct individual, though his ordinary means of communication with others is "telepathic." But frequently he wakes up to be a group-mind. Apart from this "waking of individuals together," if I may so call it, the group-mind has no existence; for its being is solely the being of the individuals comprehended together. When this communal awakening occurs, each individual experiences all the bodies of the group as "his own multiple body," and perceives the world equally from all those bodies. This awakening happens to all the individuals at the same time. But over and above this simple enlargement of the experienced field, is the awakening into new kinds of experience. Of this obviously, I can tell you nothing, save that it differs from the lowlier state more radically than the infant mind differs from the mind of the individual adult, and that it consists of insight into many unsuspected and previously inconceivable features of the familiar world of men and things. Hence, in our group mode, most, but not all, of the perennial philosophical puzzles, especially those connected with the nature of personality, can be so lucidly restated that they cease to be puzzles.

Upon this higher plane of mentality the sexual groups, and therefore the individuals participating in them, have social intercourse with one another as super-individuals. Thus they form together a community of minded communities. For each group is a person differing from other groups in character and experience somewhat as individuals differ. The groups themselves are not allocated to different works, in such a manner that one group should be wholly engaged in industry, another in astronomy, and so on. Only the individuals are thus allocated. In each group there will be members of many professions. The function of the group itself is purely some special manner of insight and mode of appreciation; in relation to which, of course, the work of the individuals is constantly controlled, not only while they are actually supporting the group self, but also when they have each fallen once more into the limited experience which is ordinary individual selfhood. For though, as individuals, they cannot retain clear insight into the high matters which they so recently experienced, they do remember so much as is not beyond the range of individual mentality; and in particular they remember the bearing of the group experience upon their own conduct as individuals.

Recently another and far more penetrating kind of experience has been attained, partly by good fortune, partly through research directed by the group-minds. For these have specialized themselves for particular functions in the mental life of the race, as previously the individuals were specialized for functions within the mind of a group. Very rarely and precariously has this supreme experience been achieved. In it the individual passes beyond this group experience, and becomes the mind of the race. At all times, of course, he can communicate "telepathically" with other individuals anywhere upon the planet; and frequently the whole race "listens in" while one individual addresses the world. But in the true racial experience the situation is different. The system of radiation which embraces the whole planet, and includes the million million brains of the race, becomes the physical basis of a racial self. The individual discovers himself to be embodied in all the bodies of the race. He savours in a single intuition all bodily contacts, including the mutual embraces of all lovers. Through the myriad feet of all men and women he enfolds his world in a single grasp. He sees with all eyes, and comprehends in a single vision all visual fields. Thus he perceives at once and as a continuous, variegated sphere, the whole surface of the planet. But not only so. He now stands above the group-minds as they above the individuals. He regards them as a man may regard his own vital tissues, with mingled contempt, sympathy, reverence, and dispassion. He watches them as one might study the living cells of his own brain; but also with the aloof interest of one observing an ant hill; and yet again as one enthralled by the strange and diverse ways of his fellow men; and further as one who, from above the battle, watches himself and his comrades agonizing in some desperate venture; yet chiefly as the artist who has no thought but for his vision and its embodiment. In the racial mode a man apprehends all things astronomically. Through all eyes and all observatories, he beholds his voyaging world, and peers outward into space. Thus he merges in one view, as it were, the views of deck-hand, captain, stoker, and the man in the crow's-nest. Regarding the solar system simultaneously from both limbs of Neptune, he perceives the planets and the sun stereoscopically, as though in binocular vision. Further, his perceived "now" embraces not a moment but a vast age. Thus, observing the galaxy from every point in succession along Neptune's wide orbit, and watching the nearer stars shift hither and thither, he actually perceives some of the constellations in three dimensions. Nay, with the aid of our most recent instruments the whole galaxy appears stereoscopically. But the great nebulæ and remote universes remain mere marks upon the flat sky; and in contemplation of their remoteness man, even as the racial self of the mightiest of all human races, realizes his own minuteness and impotence.

But chiefly the racial mind transcends the minds of groups and individuals in philosophical insight into the true nature of space and time, mind and its objects, cosmical striving and cosmical perfection. Some hints of this great elucidation must presently be given; but in the main it cannot be communicated. Indeed such insight is beyond the reach of ourselves as isolated individuals, and even beyond the group-minds. When we have declined from the racial mentality, we cannot clearly remember what it was that we experienced.

In particular we have one very perplexing recollection about our racial experience, one which involves a seeming impossibility. In the racial mind our experience was enlarged not only spatially but temporally in a very strange manner. In respect of temporal perception, of course, minds may differ in two ways, in the length of the span which they can comprehend as "now," and the minuteness of the successive events which they can discriminate within the "now." As individuals we can hold within one "now" a duration equal to the old terrestrial day; and within that duration, we can if we will, discriminate rapid pulsations such as commonly we hear together as a high musical tone. As the race-mind we perceived as "now" the whole period since the birth of the oldest living individuals, and the whole past of the species appeared as personal memory, stretching back into the mists of infancy. Yet we could, if we willed, discriminate within the "now" one light-vibration from the next. In this mere increased breadth and precision of temporal perception there is no contradiction. But how, we ask ourselves, could the race-mind experience as "now" a vast period in which it had no existence whatever? Our first experience of racial mentality lasted only as long as Neptune's moon takes to complete one circuit. Before that period, then, the race-mind was not. Yet during the month of its existence it regarded the whole previous career of the race as "present."

Indeed, the racial experience has greatly perplexed us as individuals, and we can scarcely be said to remember more of it than that it was of extreme subtlety and extreme beauty. At the same time we often have of it an impression of unspeakable horror. We who, in our familiar individual sphere are able to regard all conceivable tragedy not merely with fortitude but with exultation, are obscurely conscious that as the racial mind we have looked into an abyss of evil such as we cannot now conceive, and could not endure to conceive. Yet even this hell we know to have been acceptable as an organic member in the austere form of the cosmos. We remember obscurely, and yet with a strange conviction, that all the age-long striving of the human spirit, no less than the petty cravings of individuals, was seen as a fair component in something far more admirable than itself; and that man ultimately defeated, no less than man for a while triumphant, contributes to this higher excellence.

How colourless these words! How unworthy of that wholly satisfying beauty of all things, which in our awakened racial mode we see face to face. Every human being, of whatever species, may occasionally glimpse some fragment or aspect of existence transfigured thus with the cold beauty which normally he cannot see. Even the First Men, in their respect for tragic art, had something of this experience. The Second, and still more surely the Fifth, sought it deliberately. The winged Seventh happened upon it while they were in the air. But their minds were cramped; and all that they could appreciate was their own small world and their own tragic story. We, the Last Men, have all their zest in private and in racial life, whether it fares well or ill. We have it at all times, and we have it in respect of matters inconceivable to lesser minds. We have it, moreover, intelligently. Knowing well how strange it is to admire evil along with good, we see clearly the subversiveness of this experience. Even we, as mere individuals, cannot reconcile our loyalty to the striving spirit of man with our own divine aloofness. And so, if we were mere individuals, there would remain conflict in each of us. But in the racial mode each one of us has now experienced the great elucidation of intellect and of feeling. And though, as individuals once more, we can never recapture that far-seeing vision, the obscure memory of it masters us always, and controls all our policies. Among yourselves, the artist, after his phase of creative insight is passed, and he is once more a partisan in the struggle for existence, may carry out in detail the design conceived in his brief period of clarity. He remembers, but no longer sees the vision. He tries to fashion some perceptible embodiment of the vanished splendour. So we, living our individual lives, delighting in the contacts of flesh, the relations of minds, and all the delicate activities of human culture, co-operating and conflicting in a thousand individual undertakings and performing each his office in the material maintenance of our society, see all things as though transfused with light from a source which is itself no longer revealed.

I have tried to tell you something of the most distinctive characteristics of our species. You can imagine that the frequent occasions of group mentality, and even more the rare occasions of race mentality, have a far-reaching effect on every individual mind, and therefore on our whole social order. Ours is in fact a society dominated, as no previous society, by a single racial purpose which is in a sense religious. Not that the individual's private efflorescence is at all thwarted by the racial purpose. Indeed, far otherwise; for that purpose demands as the first condition of its fulfilment a wealth of individual fulfilment, physical and mental. But in each mind of man or woman the racial purpose presides absolutely; and hence it is the unquestioned motive of all social policy.

I must not stay to describe in detail this society of ours, in which a million million citizens, grouped in over a thousand nations, live in perfect accord without the aid of armies or even a police force. I must not tell of our much prized social organization, which assigns a unique function to each citizen, controls the procreation of new citizens of every type in relation to social need, and yet provides an endless supply of originality. We have no government and no laws, if by law is meant a stereotyped convention supported by force, and not to be altered without the aid of cumbersome machinery. Yet, though our society is in this sense an anarchy, it lives by means of a very intricate system of customs, some of which are so ancient as to have become spontaneous taboos, rather than deliberate conventions. It is the business of those among us who correspond to your lawyers and politicians to study these customs and suggest improvements. Those suggestions are submitted to no representative body, but to the whole world-population in "telepathic" conference. Ours is thus in a sense the most democratic of all societies. Yet in another sense it is extremely bureaucratic, since it is already some millions of terrestrial years since any suggestion put forward by the College of Organizers was rejected or even seriously criticized, so thoroughly do these social engineers study their material. The only serious possibility of conflict lies now between the world population as individuals and the same individuals as group-minds or racial mind. But though in these respects there have formerly occurred serious conflicts, peculiarly distressing to the individuals who experienced them, such conflicts are now extremely rare. For, even as mere individuals, we are learning to trust more and more to the judgment and dictates of our own super-individual experience.

It is time to grapple with the most difficult part of my whole task. Somehow, and very briefly, I must give you an idea of that outlook upon existence which has determined our racial purpose, making it essentially a religious purpose. This outlook has come to us partly through the work of individuals in scientific research and philosophic thought, partly through the influence of our group and racial experiences. You can imagine that it is not easy to describe this modern vision of the nature of things in any manner intelligible to those who have not our advantages. There is much in this vision which will remind you of your mystics; yet between them and us there is far more difference than similarity, in respect both of the matter and the manner of our thought. For while they are confident that the

cosmos is perfect, we are sure only that it is very beautiful. While they pass
to their conclusion without the aid of intellect, we have used that staff
every step of the way. Thus, even when in respect of conclusions we agree
with your mystics rather than your plodding intellectuals, in respect of
method we applaud most your intellectuals; for they scorned to deceive
themselves with comfortable fantasies.

4. COSMOLOGY

We find ourselves living in a vast and boundless, yet finite, order of
spatio-temporal events. And each of us, as the racial mind, has learned that
there are other such orders, other and incommensurable spheres of events,
related to our own neither spatially nor temporally but in another mode of
eternal being. Of the contents of those alien spheres we know almost nothing but that they are incomprehensible to us, even in our racial mentality.

Within this spatio-temporal sphere of ours we remark what we call
the Beginning and what we call the End. In the Beginning there came
into existence, we know not how, that all-pervading and unimaginably
tenuous gas which was the parent of all material and spiritual existence
within time's known span. It was in fact a very multitudinous yet precisely
numbered host. From the crowding together of this great population into
many swarms, arose in time the nebulæ, each of which in its turn con-
denses as a galaxy, a universe of stars. The stars have their beginnings and
their ends; and for a few moments somewhere in between their beginnings
and their ends a few, very few, may support mind. But in due course will
come the universal End, when all the wreckage of the galaxies will have
drifted together as a single, barren, and seemingly changeless ash, in the
midst of a chaos of unavailing energy.

But the cosmic events which we call the Beginning and the End are
final only in relation to our ignorance of the events which lie beyond them.
We know, and as the racial mind we have apprehended as a clear necessity,
that not only space but time also is boundless, though finite. For in a sense
time is cyclic. After the End, events unknowable will continue to happen
during a period much longer than that which will have passed since the
Beginning; but at length there will recur the identical event which was
itself also the Beginning.

Yet though time is cyclic, it is not repetitive; there is no other time
within which it can repeat itself. For time is but an abstraction from the
successiveness of events that pass; and since all events whatsoever form together a cycle of successiveness, there is nothing constant in relation to
which there can be repetition. And so the succession of events is cyclic, yet
not repetitive. The birth of the all-pervading gas in the so-called Beginning
is not merely *similar* to another such birth to occur long after us and long
after the cosmic End, so-called; the past Beginning *is* the future Beginning.

From the Beginning to the End is but the span from one spoke to the next on time's great wheel. There is a vaster span, stretching beyond the End and round to the Beginning. Of the events therein we know nothing, save that there must be such events.

Everywhere within time's cycle there is endless passage of events. In a continuous flux, they occur and vanish, yielding to their successors. Yet each one of them is eternal. Though passage is of their very nature, and without passage they are nothing, yet they have eternal being. But their passage is no illusion. They have eternal being, yet eternally they exist with passage. In our racial mode we see clearly that this is so; but in our individual mode it remains a mystery. Yet even in our individual mode we must accept both sides of this mysterious antinomy, as a fiction needed for the rationalizing of our experience.

The Beginning precedes the End by some hundred million million terrestrial years, and succeeds it by a period at least nine times longer. In the middle of the smaller span lies the still shorter period within which alone the living worlds can occur. And they are very few. One by one they dawn into mentality and die, successive blooms in life's short summer. Before that season and after it, even to the Beginning and to the End, and even before the Beginning and after the End, sleep, utter oblivion. Not before there are stars, and not after the stars are chilled, can there be life. And then, rarely.

In our own galaxy there have occurred hitherto some twenty thousand worlds that have conceived life. And of these a few score have attained or surpassed the mentality of the First Men. But of those that have reached this development, man has now outstripped the rest, and today man alone survives.

There are the millions of other galaxies, for instance the Andromedan island. We have some reason to surmise that in that favoured universe mind may have attained to insight and power incomparably greater than our own. But all that we know for certain is that it contains four worlds of high order.

Of the host of other universes that lie within range of our mind-detecting instruments, none have produced anything comparable with man. But there are many universes too remote to be estimated.

You may wonder how we have come to detect these remote lives and intelligences. I can say only that the occurrence of mentality produces certain minute astronomical effects, to which our instruments are sensitive even at great distances. These effects increase slightly with the mere mass of living matter on any astronomical body, but far more with its mental and spiritual development. Long ago it was the spiritual development of the world-community of the Fifth Men that dragged the moon from its orbit. And in our own case, so numerous is our society today, and so greatly developed in mental and spiritual activities, that only by continuous expense of physical energy can we preserve the solar system from confusion.

We have another means of detecting minds remote from us in space. We can, of course, enter into past minds wherever they are, so long as they are intelligible to us; and we have tried to use this power for the discovery of remote minded worlds. But in general the experience of such minds is too different in fibre from our own for us to be able even to detect its existence. And so our knowledge of minds in other worlds is almost wholly derived from their physical effects.

We cannot say that nowhere save on those rare bodies called planets does life ever occur. For we have evidence that in a few of the younger stars there is life, and even intelligence. How it persists in an incandescent environment we know not, nor whether it is perhaps the life of the star as a whole, as a single organism, or the life of many flame-like inhabitants of the star. All that we know is that no star in its prime has life, and therefore that the lives of the younger ones are probably doomed.

Again, we know that mind occurs, though very seldom, on a few extremely old stars, no longer incandescent. What the future of these minds will be, we cannot tell. Perhaps it is with them, and not with man, that the hope of the cosmos lies. But at present they are all primitive.

Today nothing anywhere in this galaxy of ours can compare with man in respect of vision and mental creativeness.

We have, therefore, come to regard our community as of some importance. Especially so in the light of our metaphysics; but I can only hint at our metaphysical vision of things by means of metaphors which will convey at best a caricature of that vision.

In the Beginning there was great potency, but little form. And the spirit slept as the multitude of discrete primordial existents. Thenceforth there has been a long and fluctuating adventure toward harmonious complexity of form, and toward the awakening of the spirit into unity, knowledge, delight and self-expression. And this is the goal of all living, that the cosmos may be known, and admired, and that it may be crowned with further beauties. Nowhere and at no time, so far as we can tell, at least within our own galaxy, has the adventure reached further than in ourselves. And in us, what has been achieved is but a minute beginning. But it is a real beginning. Man in our day has gained some depth of insight, some breadth of knowledge, some power of creation, some faculty of worship. We have looked far afield. We have probed not altogether superficially into the nature of existence, and have found it very beautiful, though also terrible. We have created a not inconsiderable community; and we have wakened together to be the unique spirit of that community. We had proposed to ourselves a very long and arduous future, which should culminate, at some time before the End, in the complete achievement of the spirit's ideal. But now we know that disaster is already near at hand.

When we are in full possession of our faculties, we are not distressed by this fate. For we know that though our fair community must cease, it has also indestructible being. We have at least carved into one region of the eternal real a form which has beauty of no mean order. The great company of diverse and most lovely men and women in all their subtle relationships, striving with a single purpose toward the goal which is mind's final goal; the community and super-individuality of that great host; the beginnings of further insight and creativeness upon the higher plane— these surely are real achievements—even though, in the larger view, they are minute achievements.

Yet though we are not at all dismayed by our own extinction, we cannot but wonder whether or not in the far future some other spirit will fulfil the cosmic ideal, or whether we ourselves are the modest crown of existence. Unfortunately, though we can explore the past wherever there are intelligible minds, we cannot enter into the future. And so in vain we ask, will ever any spirit awake to gather all spirits into itself, to elicit from the stars their full flower of beauty, to know all things together, and admire all things justly?

If in the far future this end will be achieved, it is really achieved even now; for whenever it occurs, its being is eternal. But on the other hand if it is indeed achieved eternally, this achievement must be the work of spirits or a spirit not wholly unlike ourselves, though infinitely greater. And the physical location of that spirit must lie in the far future.

But if no future spirit will achieve this end before it dies, then, though the cosmos is indeed very beautiful, it is not perfect.

I said that we regard the cosmos as very beautiful. Yet it is also very terrible. For ourselves, it is easy to look forward with equanimity to our end, and even to the end of our admired community; for what we prize most is the excellent beauty of the cosmos. But there are the myriads of spirits who have never entered into that vision. They have suffered, and they were not permitted that consolation. There are, first, the incalculable hosts of lowly creatures scattered over all the ages in all the minded worlds. Theirs was only a dream life, and their misery not often poignant; but none the less they are to be pitied for having missed the more poignant experience in which alone spirit can find fulfilment. Then there are the intelligent beings, human and otherwise; the many minded worlds throughout the galaxies, that have struggled into cognizance, striven for they knew not what, tasted brief delights and lived in the shadow of pain and death, until at last their life has been crushed out by careless fate. In our solar system there are the Martians, insanely and miserably obsessed; the native Venerians, imprisoned in their ocean and murdered for man's sake; and all the hosts of the forerunning human species. A few individuals no doubt in every period, and many in certain favoured races, have lived on the whole happily. And a few have even known something of the supreme beatitude. But for most, until our modern epoch, thwarting has out-weighed fulfilment; and if actual grief has not preponderated over joy, it is because, mercifully, the fulfilment that is wholly missed cannot be conceived.

Our predecessors of the Sixteenth species, oppressed by this vast horror, undertook a forlorn and seemingly irrational crusade for the rescue of the tragic past. We see now clearly that their enterprise, though desperate, was not quite fantastic. For, if ever the cosmic ideal should be realized, even though for a moment only, then in that time the awakened Soul of All will embrace within itself all spirits whatever throughout the whole of time's wide circuit. And so to each one of them, even to the least, it will seem that he has awakened and discovered himself to be the Soul of All, knowing all things and rejoicing in all things. And though afterwards, through the inevitable decay of the stars, this most glorious vision must be lost, suddenly or in the long-drawn-out defeat of life, yet would the awakened Soul of All have eternal being, and in it each martyred spirit would have beatitude eternally, though unknown to itself in its own temporal mode.

It may be that this is the case. If not, then eternally the martyred spirits are martyred only, and not blest.

We cannot tell which of these possibilities is fact. As individuals we earnestly desire that the eternal being of things may include this supreme awakening. This, nothing less than this, has been the remote but ever-present goal of our practical religious life and of our social policy.

In our racial mode also we have greatly desired this end, but differently.

Even as individuals, all our desires are tempered by that relentless admiration of fate which we recognize as the spirit's highest achievement. Even as individuals, we exult in the issue whether our enterprises succeed or fail. The pioneer defeated, the lover bereaved and overwhelmed, can find in his disaster the supreme experience, the dispassionate ecstasy which salutes the Real as it is and would not change one jot of it. Even as individuals, we can regard the impending extinction of mankind as a thing superb though tragic. Strong in the knowledge that the human spirit has already inscribed the cosmos with indestructible beauty, and that inevitably, whether sooner or later, man's career must end, we face this too sudden end with laughter in our hearts, and peace.

But there is the one thought by which, in our individual state, we are still dismayed, namely that the cosmos enterprise itself may fail; that the full potentiality of the Real may never find expression; that never, in any stage of time, the multitudinous and conflicting existents should be organized as the universal harmonious living body; that the spirit's eternal nature, therefore, should be discordant, miserably tranced; that the inde-

structible beauties of this our sphere of space and time should remain imperfect, and remain, too, not adequately worshipped.

But in the racial mind this ultimate dread has no place. On those few
occasions when we have awakened racially, we have come to regard with
piety even the possibility of cosmical defeat. For as the racial mind, though
in a manner we earnestly desired the fulfilment of the cosmical ideal, yet
we were no more enslaved to this desire than, as individuals, we are enslaved to our private desires. For though the racial mind wills this supreme
achievement, yet in the same act it holds itself aloof from it, and from
all desire, and all emotion, save the ecstasy which admires the Real as it is,
and accepts its dark-bright form with joy.

As individuals, therefore, we try to regard the whole cosmic adventure
as a symphony now in progress, which may or may not some day achieve
its just conclusion. Like music, however, the vast biography of the stars is
to be judged not in respect of its final moment merely, but in respect of
the perfection of its whole form; and whether its form as a whole is perfect or not, we cannot know. Actual music is a pattern of intertwining
themes which evolve and die; and these again are woven of simpler members, which again are spun of chords and unitary tones. But the music of
the spheres is of a complexity almost infinitely more subtle, and its themes
rank above and below one another in hierarchy beyond hierarchy. None
but a God, none but a mind subtle as the music itself, could hear the whole
in all its detail, and grasp in one act its close-knit individuality, if such it
has. Not for any human mind to say authoritatively, "This is music,
wholly," or to say, "This is mere noise, flecked now and then by shreds
of significance."

The music of the spheres is unlike other music not only in respect of
its richness, but also in the nature of its medium. It is a music not merely
of sounds but of souls. Each of its minor themes, each of its chords, each
single tone of it, each tremor of each tone, is in its own degree more than a
mere passive factor in the music; it is a listener, and also a creator. Wherever there is individuality of form, there is also an individual appreciator
and originator. And the more complex the form, the more percipient and
active the spirit. Thus in every individual factor within the music, the
musical environment of that factor is experienced, vaguely or precisely,
erroneously, or with greater approximation to truth; and, being experienced,
it is admired or loathed, rightly or falsely. And it is influenced. Just as in
actual music each theme is in a manner a determination of its forerunners
and followers and present accompaniment, so in this vaster music each
individual factor is itself a determination of its environment. Also it is a
determinant, both of that which precedes and that which follows.

But whether these manifold interdeterminations are after all haphazard, or, as in music, controlled in relation to the beauty of the whole,
we know not; nor whether, if this is the case, the beautiful whole of things

is the work of some mind; nor yet whether some mind admires it adequately as a whole of beauty.

But this we know: that we ourselves, when the spirit is most awake
in us, admire the Real as it is revealed to us, and salute its dark-bright
form with joy.

CHAPTER XVI

THE LAST OF MAN

I. SENTENCE OF DEATH

OURS has been essentially a philosophical age, in fact the supreme age of
philosophy. But a great practical problem has also concerned us. We have
had to prepare for the task of preserving humanity during a most difficult
period which was calculated to being about one hundred million years
hence, but might, in certain circumstances, be sprung upon us at very
short notice. Long ago the human inhabitants of Venus believed that already in their day the sun was about to enter the "white dwarf" phase,
and that the time would therefore soon come when their world would be
frost-bound. This calculation was unduly pessimistic; but we know now
that, even allowing for the slight delay caused by the great collision, the
solar collapse must begin at some date astronomically not very distant.
We had planned that during the comparatively brief period of the actual
shrinkage, we would move our planet steadily nearer to the sun, until finally it should settle in the narrowest possible orbit.

Man would then be comfortably placed for a very long period. But in
the fullness of time there would come a far more serious crisis. The sun
would continue to cool, and at last man would no longer be able to live
by means of solar radiation. It would become necessary to annihilate matter
to supply the deficiency. The other planets might be used for this purpose,
and possibly the sun itself. Or, given the sustenance for so long a voyage,
man might boldly project his planet into the neighbourhood of some
younger star. Thenceforth, perhaps, he might operate upon a far grander
scale. He might explore and colonize all suitable worlds in every corner
of the galaxy, and organize himself as a vast community of minded worlds.
Even (so we dreamed) he might achieve intercourse with other galaxies. It
did not seem impossible that man himself was the germ of the world-soul,
which, we still hope, is destined to awake for a while before the universal
decline, and to crown the eternal cosmos with its due of knowledge and
admiration, fleeting yet eternal. We dared to think that in some far distant
epoch the human spirit, clad in all wisdom, power, and delight, might

look back upon our primitive age with a certain respect; no doubt with pity also and amusement, but none the less with admiration for the spirit in us, still only half awake, and struggling against great disabilities. In such a mood, half pity, half admiration, we ourselves look back upon the primitive mankinds.

Our prospect has now suddenly and completely changed, for astronomers have made a startling discovery, which assigns to man a speedy end. His existence has ever been precarious. At any stage of his career he might easily have been exterminated by some slight alteration of his chemical environment, by a more than usually malignant microbe, by a radical change of climate, or by the manifold effects of his own folly. Twice already he has been almost destroyed by astronomical events. How easily might it happen that the solar system, now rushing through a somewhat more crowded region of the galaxy, should become entangled with, or actually strike, a major astronomical body, and be destroyed. But fate, as it turns out, has a more surprising end in store for man.

Not long ago an unexpected alteration was observed to be taking place in a near star. Through no discoverable cause, it began to change from white to violet, and increase in brightness. Already it has attained such extravagant brilliance that, though its actual disk remains a mere point in our sky, its dazzling purple radiance illuminates our nocturnal landscapes with hideous beauty. Our astronomers have ascertained that this is no ordinary "nova," that it is not one of those stars addicted to paroxysms of brilliance. It is something unprecedented, a normal star suffering from a unique disease, a fantastic acceleration of its vital process, a riotous squandering of the energy which should have remained locked within its substance for æons. At the present rate it will be reduced either to an inert cinder or to actual annihilation in a few thousand years. This extraordinary event may possibly have been produced by unwise temperings on the part of intelligent beings in the star's neighbourhood. But, indeed, since all matter at very high temperature is in a state of unstable equilibrium, the cause may have been merely some conjunction of natural circumstances.

The event was first regarded simply as an intriguing spectacle. But further study roused a more serious interest. Our own planet, and therefore the sun also, was suffering a continuous and increasing bombardment of ethereal vibrations, most of which were of incredibly high frequency, and of unknown potentiality. What would be their effect upon the sun? After some centuries, certain astronomical bodies in the neighbourhood of the deranged star were seen to be infected with its disorder. Their fever increased the splendour of our night sky, but it also confirmed our fears. We still hoped that the sun might prove too distant to be seriously influenced, but careful analysis now showed that this hope must be abandoned. The sun's remoteness might cause a delay of some thousands of years before the cumulative effects of the bombardment could start the disintegration; but sooner or later the sun itself must be infected. Probably within thirty thousand years life will be impossible anywhere within a vast radius of the sun, so vast a radius that it is quite impossible to propel our planet away fast enough to escape before the storm can catch us.

2. BEHAVIOUR OF THE CONDEMNED

The discovery of this doom kindled in us unfamiliar emotions. Hitherto humanity had seemed to be destined for a very long future, and the individual himself had been accustomed to look forward to very many thousands of years of personal life, ending in voluntary sleep. We had of course often conceived, and even savoured in imagination, the sudden destruction of our world. But now we faced it as a fact. Outwardly every one behaved with perfect serenity, but inwardly every mind was in turmoil. Not that there was any question of our falling into panic or despair, for in this crisis our native detachment stood us in good stead. But inevitably some time passed before our minds became properly adjusted to the new prospect, before we could see our fate outlined clearly and beautifully against the cosmic background.

Presently, however, we learned to contemplate the whole great saga of man as a completed work of art, and to admire it no less for its sudden and tragic end than for the promise in it which was not to be fulfilled. Grief was now transfigured wholly into ecstasy. Defeat, which had oppressed us with a sense of man's impotence and littleness among the stars, brought us into a new sympathy and reverence for all those myriads of beings in the past out of whose obscure strivings we had been born. We saw the most brilliant of our own race and the lowliest of our prehuman forerunners as essentially spirits of equal excellence, though cast in diverse circumstances. When we looked round on the heavens, and at the violet splendour which was to destroy us, we were filled with awe and pity, awe for the inconceivable potentiality of this bright host, pity for its self-thwarting effort to fulfil itself as the universal spirit.

At this stage it seemed that there was nothing left for us to do but to crowd as much excellence as possible into our remaining life, and meet our end in the noblest manner. But now there came upon us once more the rare experience of racial mentality. For a whole Neptunian year every individual lived in an enraptured trance, in which, as the racial mind, he or she resolved many ancient mysteries and saluted many unexpected beauties. This ineffable experience, lived through under the shadow of death, was the flower of man's whole being. But I can tell nothing of it, save that when it was over we possessed, even as individuals, a new peace, in which, strangely but harmoniously, were blended grief, exaltation, and god-like laughter.

In consequence of this racial experience we found ourselves faced with two tasks which had not before been contemplated. The one referred to the future, the other to the past.

In respect of the future, we are now setting about the forlorn task of disseminating among the stars the seeds of a new humanity. For this purpose we shall make use of the pressure of radiation from the sun, and chiefly the extravagantly potent radiation that will later be available. We are hoping to devise extremely minute electro-magnetic "wave-systems," akin to normal protons and electrons, which will be individually capable of sailing forward upon the hurricane of solar radiation at a speed not wholly incomparable with the speed of light itself. This is a difficult task. But, further, these units must be so cunningly inter-related that, in favourable conditions, they may tend to combine to form spores of life, and to develop, not indeed into human beings, but into lowly organisms with a definite evolutionary bias toward the essentials of human nature. These objects we shall project from beyond our atmosphere in immense quantities at certain points of our planet's orbit, so that solar radiation may carry them toward the most promising regions of the galaxy. The chance that any of them will survive to reach their destination is small, and still smaller the chance that any of them will find a suitable environment. But if any of this human seed should fall upon good ground, it will embark, we hope, upon a somewhat rapid biological evolution, and produce in due season whatever complex organic forms are possible in its environment. It will have a very real physiological bias toward the evolution of intelligence. Indeed it will have a much greater bias in that direction than occurred on the Earth in those sub-vital atomic groupings from which terrestrial life eventually sprang.

It is just conceivable, then, that by extremely good fortune man may still influence the future of this galaxy, not directly but through his creature. But in the vast music of existence the actual theme of mankind now ceases for ever. Finished, the long reiterations of man's history; defeated, the whole proud enterprise of his maturity. The stored experience of many mankinds must sink into oblivion, and today's wisdom must vanish.

The other task which occupies us, that which relates to the past, is one which may very well seem to you nonsensical.

We have long been able to enter into past minds and participate in their experience. Hitherto we have been passive spectators merely, but recently we have acquired the power of influencing past minds. This seems an impossibility; for a past event is what it is, and how can it conceivably be altered at a subsequent date, even in the minutest respect?

Now it is true that past events are what they are, irrevocably; but in certain cases some feature of a past event may depend on an event in the far future. The past event would never have been as it actually was (and is, eternally), if there had not been going to be a certain future event, which, though not contemporaneous with the past event, influences it directly in the sphere of eternal being. The passage of events is real, and time is the successiveness of passing events; but though events have passage, they have also eternal being. And in certain rare cases mental events far separated in time determine one another directly by way of eternity.

Our own minds have often been profoundly influenced by direct inspection of past minds; and now we find that certain events of certain past minds are determined by present events in our own present minds. No doubt there are some past mental events which are what they are by virtue of mental processes which we *shall* perform but have not yet performed.

Our historians and psychologists, engaged on direct inspection of past minds, had often complained of certain "singular" points in past minds, where the ordinary laws of psychology fail to give a full explanation of the course of mental events; where, in fact, some wholly unknown influence seemed to be at work. Later it was found that, in some cases at least, this disturbance of the ordinary principles of psychology corresponded with certain thoughts or desires in the mind of the observer, living in our own age. Of course, only such matters as could have significance to the past mind could influence it at all. Thoughts and desires of ours which have no meaning to the particular past individual fail to enter into his experience. New ideas and new values are only to be introduced by arranging familiar matter so that it may gain a new significance. Nevertheless we now found ourselves in possession of an amazing power of communicating with the past, and contributing to its thought and action, though of course we could not *alter* it.

But, it may be asked, what if, in respect of a particular "singularity" in some past mind, we do not, after all, choose to provide the necessary influence to account for it? The question is meaningless. There is no possibility that we should not choose to influence those past minds which are, as a matter of fact, dependent on our influence. For it is in the sphere of eternity (wherein alone we meet past minds), that we really make this free choice. And in the sphere of time, though the choosing has relations with our modern age, and may be said to occur in that age, it also has relations with the past mind, and may be said to have occurred also long ago.

There are in some past minds singularities which are not the product of any influence that we have exerted today. Some of these singularities, no doubt, we shall ourselves produce on some occasion before our destruction. But it may be that some are due to an influence other than ours, perhaps to beings which, by good fortune, may spring long hence from our forlorn seminal enterprise; or they may be due perhaps to the cosmic mind, whose future occurrence and eternal existence we earnestly desire. However that may be, there are a few remarkable minds, scattered up and down past ages and even in the most primitive human races, which suggest an influence other than our own. They are so "singular" in one respect or another, that we cannot give a perfectly clear psychological account of them in terms of the past only; and yet we ourselves are not the instigators of their singularity. Your Jesus, your Socrates, your Gautama, show traces of this uniqueness. But the most original of all were too eccentric to have any influence on their contemporaries. It is possible that in ourselves also there are "singularities" which cannot be accounted for wholly in terms of ordinary biological and psychological laws. If we could prove that this is the case, we should have very definite evidence of the occurrence of a high order of mentality somewhere in the future, and therefore of its eternal existence. But hitherto this problem has proved too subtle for us, even in the racial mode. It may be that the mere fact that we have succeeded in attaining racial mentality involves some remote future influence. It is even conceivable that every creative advance that any mind has ever made involves unwitting co-operation with the cosmic mind which, perhaps, will awake at some date before the End.

We have two methods of influencing the past through past individuals; for we can operate either upon minds of great originality and power, or upon any average individual whose circumstances happen to suit our purpose. In original minds we can only suggest some very vague intuition, which is then "worked up" by the individual himself into some form very different from that which we intended, but very potent as a factor in the culture of his age. Average minds, on the other hand, we can use as passive instruments for the conveyance of detailed ideas. But in such cases the individual is incapable of working up the material into a great and potent form, suited to his age.

But what is it, you may ask, that we seek to contribute to the past? We seek to afford intuitions of truth and of value, which, though easy to us from our point of vantage, would be impossible to the unaided past. We seek to help the past to make the best of itself, just as one man may help another. We seek to direct the attention of past individuals and past races to truths and beauties which, though implicit in their experience, would otherwise be overlooked.

We seek to do this for two reasons. Entering into past minds, we become perfectly acquainted with them, and cannot but love them; and so we desire to help them. By influencing selected individuals, we seek to influence indirectly great multitudes. But our second motive is very different. We see the career of Man in his successive planetary homes as a process of very great beauty. It is far indeed from the perfect; but it is very beautiful, with the beauty of tragic art. Now it turns out that this beautiful thing entails our operation at various points in the past. Therefore we will to operate.

Unfortunately our first inexperienced efforts were disastrous. Many of the fatuities which primitive minds in all ages have been prone to attribute to the influence of disembodied spirits, whether deities, fiends, or the dead, are but the gibberish which resulted from our earliest experiments. And this book, so admirable in our conception, has issued from the brain of the writer, your contemporary, in such disorder as to be mostly rubbish.

We are concerned with the past not only in so far as we make very rare contributions to it, but chiefly in two other manners.

First, we are engaged upon the great enterprise of becoming lovingly acquainted with the past, the human past, in every detail. This is, so to speak, our supreme act of filial piety. When one being comes to know and love another, a new and beautiful thing is created, namely the love. The cosmos is thus far and at that date enhanced. We seek then to know and love every past mind that we can enter. In most cases we can know them with far more understanding than they can know themselves. Not the least of them, not the worst of them, shall be left out of this great work of understanding and admiration.

There is another manner in which we are concerned with the human past. We need its help. For we, who are triumphantly reconciled to our fate, are under obligation to devote our last energies not to ecstatic contemplation but to a forlorn and most uncongenial task, the dissemination. This task is almost intolerably repugnant to us. Gladly would we spend our last days in embellishing our community and our culture, and in pious exploration of the past. But it is incumbent on us, who are by nature artists and philosophers, to direct the whole attention of our world upon the arid labour of designing an artificial human seed, producing it in immense quantities, and projecting it among the stars. If there is to be any possibility of success, we must undertake a very lengthy program of physical research, and finally organize a world-wide system of manufacture. The work will not be completed until our physical constitution is already being undermined, and the disintegration of our community has already begun. Now we could never fulfil this policy without a zealous conviction of its importance. Here it is that the past can help us. We, who have now learnt so thoroughly the supreme art of ecstatic fatalism, go humbly to the past to learn over again that other supreme achievement of the spirit, loyalty to the forces of life embattled against the forces of death. Wandering among the heroic and often forlorn ventures of the past, we are fired once more with primitive zeal. Thus, when we return to our own world, we are able, even while we preserve in our hearts the peace that passeth understanding, to struggle as though we cared only for victory.

3. EPILOGUE

I am speaking to you now from a period about twenty thousand terrestrial years after the date at which the whole preceding part of this book was communicated. It has become very difficult to reach you, and still more difficult to speak to you; for already the Last Men are not the men they were.

Our two great undertakings are still unfinished. Much of the human past remains imperfectly explored, and the projection of the seed is scarcely begun. That enterprise has proved far more difficult than was expected. Only within the last few years have we succeeded in designing an artificial human dust capable of being carried forward on the sun's radiation, hardy enough to endure the conditions of a transgalactic voyage of many millions of years, and yet intricate enough to bear the potentiality of life and of spiritual development. We are now preparing to manufacture this seminal matter in great quantities, and to cast it into space at suitable points on the planet's orbit.

Some centuries have now passed since the sun began to show the first symptoms of disintegration, namely a slight change of colour toward the blue, followed by a definite increase of brightness and heat. Today, when he pierces the ever-thickening cloud, he smites us with an intolerable steely brilliance which destroys the sight of anyone foolish enough to face it. Even in the cloudy weather which is now normal, the eye is wounded by the fierce violet glare. Eye-troubles afflict us all, in spite of the special glasses which have been designed to protect us. The mere heat, too, is already destructive. We are forcing our planet outward from its old orbit in an ever-widening spiral; but, do what we will, we cannot prevent the climate from becoming more and more deadly, even at the poles. The intervening regions have already been deserted. Evaporation of the equatorial oceans has thrown the whole atmosphere into tumult, so that even at the poles we are tormented by hot wet hurricanes and incredible electric storms. These have already shattered most of our great buildings, sometimes burying a whole teeming province under an avalanche of tumbled vitreous crags.

Our two polar communities at first managed to maintain radio communication; but it is now some time since we of the south received news of the more distressed north. Even with us the situation is already desperate. We had recently established some hundreds of stations for the dissemination, but less than a score have been able to operate. This failure is due mainly to an increasing lack of personnel. The deluge of fantastic solar radiation has had disastrous effect on the human organism. Epidemics of a malignant tumour, which medical science has failed to conquer, have reduced the southern people to a mere remnant, and this in spite of the migration of the tropical races into the Antarctic. Each of us, moreover, is but the wreckage of his former self. The higher mental functions, attained only in the most developed human species, are already lost or disordered, through the breakdown of their special tissues. Not only has the racial mind vanished, but the sexual groups have lost their mental unity. Three of the sub-sexes have already been exterminated by derangement of their chemical nature. Glandular troubles, indeed, have unhinged many of us with anxieties and loathings which we cannot conquer, though we know them to be unreasonable. Even the normal power of "telepathic" communication has become so unreliable that we have been compelled to fall back upon the archaic practice of vocal symbolism. Exploration of the past is now confined to specialists, and is a dangerous profession, which may lead to disorders of temporal experience.

Degeneration of the higher neural centres has also brought about in us a far more serious and deep-seated trouble, namely a general spiritual degradation which would formerly have seemed impossible, so confident were we of our integrity. The perfectly dispassionate will had been for many millions of years universal among us, and the corner-stone of our whole society and culture. We had almost forgotten that it has a physiological basis, and that if that basis were undermined, we might no longer be capable of rational conduct. But, drenched for some thousands of years by the unique stellar radiation, we have gradually lost not only the ecstasy of dispassionate worship, but even the capacity for normal disinterested behaviour. Every one is now liable to an irrational bias in favour of himself as a private person, as against his fellows. Personal envy, uncharitableness, even murder and gratuitous cruelty, formerly unknown amongst us, are now becoming common. At first when men began to notice in themselves these archaic impulses, they crushed them with amused contempt. But as the highest nerve centres fell further into decay, the brute in us began to be ever more unruly, and the human more uncertain. Rational conduct was henceforth to be achieved only after an exhausting and degrading "moral struggle," instead of spontaneously and fluently. Nay, worse, increasingly often the struggle ended not in victory but defeat. Imagine then, the terror and disgust that gripped us when we found ourselves one and all condemned to a desperate struggle against impulses which we had been accustomed to regard as insane. It is distressing enough to know that each one of us might at any moment, merely to help some dear individual or other, betray his supreme duty toward the dissemination; but it is harrowing to discover ourselves sometimes so far sunk as to be incapable even of common loving-kindness toward our neighbours. For a man to favour himself against his friend or beloved, even in the slightest respect, was formerly unknown. But today many of us are haunted by the look of amazed horror and pity in the eyes of an injured friend.

In the early stages of our trouble lunatic asylums were founded, but they soon became over-crowded and a burden on a stricken community. The insane were then killed. But it became clear that by former standards we were all insane. No man now can trust himself to behave reasonably.

And, of course, we cannot trust each other. Partly through the prevalent irrationality of desire, and partly through the misunderstandings which have come with the loss of "telepathic" communication, we have been plunged into all manner of discords. A political constitution and system of laws had to be devised, but they seem to have increased our troubles. Order of a kind is maintained by an over-worked police force. But this is in the hands of the professional organizers, who have now all the vices of bureaucracy. It was largely through their folly that two of the antarctic nations broke into social revolution, and are now preparing to meet the armament which an insane world-government is devising for their destruction. Meanwhile, through the break-down of the economic order, and the impossibility of reaching the food-factories on Jupiter, starvation is added to our troubles, and has afforded to certain ingenious lunatics the opportunity of trading at the expense of others.

All this folly in a doomed world, and in a community that was yesterday the very flower of a galaxy! Those of us who still care for the life of the spirit are tempted to regret that mankind did not choose decent suicide before ever the putrescence began. But indeed this could not be. The task that was undertaken had to be completed. For the Scattering of the Seed has come to be for every one of us the supreme religious duty. Even those who continually sin against it recognize this as the last office of man. It was for this that we outstayed our time, and must watch ourselves decline from spiritual estate into that brutishness from which man has so seldom freed himself.

Yet why do we persist in the forlorn effort? Even if by good luck the seed should take root somewhere and thrive, there will surely come an end to its adventure, if not swiftly in fire, then in the ultimate battle of life against encroaching frost. Our labour will at best sow for death an ampler harvest. There seems no rational defence of it, unless it be rational to carry out blindly a purpose conceived in a former and more enlightened state.

But we cannot feel sure that we really were more enlightened. We look back now at our former selves, with wonder, but also with incomprehension and misgiving. We try to recall the glory that seemed to be revealed to each of us in the racial mind, but we remember almost nothing of it. We cannot rise even to that more homely beatitude which was once within the reach of the unaided individual, that serenity which, it seemed, should be the spirit's answer to every tragic event. It is gone from us. It is not only impossible but inconceivable. We now see our private distresses and the public calamity as merely hideous. That after so long a struggle into maturity man should be roasted alive like a trapped mouse, for the entertainment of a lunatic! How can any beauty lie in that?

But this is not our last word to you. For though we have fallen, there is still something in us left over from the time that is passed. We have become blind and weak; but the knowledge that we are so has forced us to a great effort. Those of us who have not already sunk too far have formed themselves into a brotherhood for mutual strengthening, so that the true human spirit may be maintained a little longer, until the seed has

been well sown, and death be permissible. We call ourselves the Brotherhood of the Condemned. We seek to be faithful to one another, and to our
common undertaking, and to the vision which is no longer revealed. We
are vowed to the comforting of all distressed persons who are not yet
permitted death. We are vowed also to the dissemination. And we are
vowed to keep the spirit bright until the end.

Now and again we meet together in little groups or great companies
to hearten ourselves with one another's presence. Sometimes on these occasions we can but sit in silence, groping for consolation and for strength.
Sometimes the spoken word flickers hither and thither amongst us, shed-
ding a brief light but little warmth to the soul that lies freezing in a torrid
world.

But there is among us one, moving from place to place and company
to company, whose voice all long to hear. He is young, the last born of the
Last Men; for he was the latest to be conceived before we learned man's
doom, and put an end to all conceiving. Being the latest, he is also the
noblest. Not him alone, but all his generation, we salute, and look to for
strength; but he, the youngest, is different from the rest. In him the spirit,
which is but the flesh awakened into spirituality, has power to withstand
the tempest of solar energy longer than the rest of us. It is as though the
sun itself were eclipsed by this spirit's brightness. It is as though in him at
last, and for a day only, man's promise were fulfilled. For though, like
others, he suffers in the flesh, he is above his suffering. And though more
than the rest of us he feels the suffering of others, he is above his pity. In
his comforting there is a strange sweet raillery which can persuade the sufferer to smile at his own pain. When this youngest brother of ours contemplates with us our dying world and the frustration of all man's
striving, he is not, like us, dismayed, but quiet. In the presence of such
quietness despair wakens into peace. By his reasonable speech, almost by the
mere sound of his voice, our eyes are opened, and our hearts mysteriously
filled with exultation. Yet often his words are grave.

Let his words, not mine, close this story:

Great are the stars, and man is of no account to them. But man is a
fair spirit, whom a star conceived and a star kills. He is greater than those
bright blind companies. For though in them there is incalculable potentiality, in him there is achievement, small, but actual. Too soon, seemingly,
he comes to his end. But when he is done he will not be nothing, not as
though he had never been; for he is eternally a beauty in the eternal form
of things.

Man was winged hopefully. He had in him to go further than this
short flight, now ending. He proposed even that he should become the
Flower of All Things, and that he should learn to be the All-Knowing,
the All-Admiring. Instead, he is to be destroyed. He is only a fledgling
caught in a bush-fire. He is very small, very simple, very little capable of in-

sight. His knowledge of the great orb of things is but a fledgling's knowledge. His admiration is a nestling's admiration for the things kindly to his own small nature. He delights only in food and the food-announcing call. The music of the spheres passes over him, through him, and is not heard.

Yet it has used him. And now it uses his destruction. Great, and terrible, and very beautiful is the Whole; and for man the best is that the Whole should use him.

But does it really use him? Is the beauty of the Whole really enhanced by our agony? And is the Whole really beautiful? And what is beauty? Throughout all his existence man has been striving to hear the music of the spheres, and has seemed to himself once and again to catch some phrase of it, or even a hint of the whole form of it. Yet he can never be sure that he has truly heard it, nor even that there is any such perfect music at all to be heard. Inevitably so, for if it exists, it is not for him in his littleness.

But one thing is certain. Man himself, at the very least, is music, a brave theme that makes music also of its vast accompaniment, its matrix of storms and stars. Man himself in his degree is eternally a beauty in the eternal form of things. It is very good to have been man. And so we may go forward together with laughter in our hearts, and peace, thankful for the past, and for our own courage. For we shall make after all a fair conclusion to this brief music that is man.

7|81

Star Maker

BY

OLAF STAPLEDON

DOVER PUBLICATIONS, INC.
NEW YORK

Preface

AT a moment when Europe is in danger of a catastrophe worse than that of 1914 a book like this may be condemned as a distraction from the desperately urgent defence of civilization against modern barbarism.

Year by year, month by month, the plight of our fragmentary and precarious civilization becomes more serious. Fascism abroad grows more bold and ruthless in its foreign ventures, more tyrannical toward its own citizens, more barbarian in its contempt for the life of the mind. Even in our own country we have reason to fear a tendency toward militarization and the curtailment of civil liberty. Moreover, while the decades pass, no resolute step is taken to alleviate the injustice of our social order. Our outworn economic system dooms millions to frustration.

In these conditions it is difficult for writers to pursue their calling at once with courage and with balanced judgement. Some merely shrug their shoulders and withdraw from the central struggle of our age. These, with their minds closed against the world's most vital issues, inevitably produce works which not only have no depth of significance for their contemporaries but also are subtly insincere. For these writers must consciously or unconsciously contrive to persuade themselves either that the crisis in human affairs does not exist, or that it is less important than their own work, or that it is anyhow not their business. But the crisis does exist, is of supreme importance, and concerns us all. Can anyone who is at all intelligent and informed hold the contrary without self-deception?

Yet I have a lively sympathy with some of those "intellectuals" who declare that they have no useful contribution to make to the struggle, and therefore had better not dabble in it. I am, in fact, one of them. In our defence I should say that, though we are inactive or ineffective as direct supporters of the cause, we do not ignore it. Indeed, it constantly, obsessively, holds our attention. But we are convinced by prolonged trial and error that the most useful service open to us is indirect. For some writers the case is different. Gallantly plunging into the struggle, they use their powers to spread urgent propaganda, or they even take up arms in the cause. If they have suitable ability, and if the particular struggle in which they serve is in fact a part of the great enterprise of defending (or creating) civilization, they may, of course, do valuable work. In addition they may gain great wealth of experience and human sympathy, thereby immensely increasing their literary power. But the very urgency of their service may tend to blind them to the importance of maintaining and extending, even in this age of crisis, what may be called metaphorically the "self-critical self-consciousness of the human species," or the attempt to see man's life as a whole in relation to the rest of things. This involves the will to regard all human affairs and ideals and theories with as little human prejudice as possible. Those who are in the thick of the struggle inevitably tend to become, though in a great and just cause, partisan. They nobly forgo something of that detachment, that power of cold assessment, which is, after all, among the most valuable human capacities. In their case this is perhaps as it should be; for a desperate struggle demands less of detachment than of devotion. But some who have the cause at heart must serve by striving to maintain, along with human loyalty, a more dispassionate spirit. And perhaps the attempt to see our turbulent world against a background of stars may, after all, increase, not lessen, the significance of the present human crisis. It may also strengthen our charity toward one another.

In this belief I have tried to construct an imaginative sketch of the dread but vital whole of things. I know well that it is a ludicrously inadequate and in some ways a childish sketch, even when regarded from the angle of contemporary human experience. In a calmer and a wiser age it might well seem crazy. Yet in spite of its crudity, and in spite of its remoteness, it is perhaps not wholly irrelevant.

At the risk of raising thunder both on the Left and on the Right, I have occasionally used certain ideas and words derived from religion, and I have tried to interpret them in relation to modern needs. The valuable, though much damaged words "spiritual" and "worship," which have become almost as obscene to the Left as the good old sexual words are to the Right, are here intended to suggest an experience which the Right is apt to pervert and the Left to misconceive. This experience, I should say, involves detachment from all private, all social, all racial ends; not in the sense that it leads a man to reject them, but that it makes him prize them in a new way. The "spiritual life" seems to be in essence the attempt to discover and adopt the attitude which is in fact appropriate to our experience as a whole, just as admiration is felt to be in fact appropriate toward a well-grown human being. This enterprise can lead to an increased lucidity and finer temper of consciousness, and therefore can have a great and beneficial effect on behaviour. Indeed, if this supremely humanizing experience does not produce, along with a kind of piety toward fate, the resolute will to serve our waking humanity, it is a mere sham and a snare.

Before closing this preface I must express my gratitude to Professor L. C. Martin, Mr. L. H. Myers, and Mr. E. V. Rieu, for much helpful and sympathetic criticism, in consequence of which I re-wrote many chapters. Even now I hesitate to associate their names with such an extravagant work. Judged by the standards of the Novel, it is remarkably bad. In fact, it is no novel at all.

Certain ideas about artificial planets were suggested by Mr. J. D.

Bernal's fascinating little book *The World, the Flesh, and the Devil.* I hope he will not strongly disapprove of my treatment of them.

My wife I must thank both for work on the proofs and for being herself.

At the end of the book I have included a note on Magnitude, which may be helpful to readers unfamiliar with astronomy. The very sketchy time scales may amuse some.

O. S.

March 1937

Contents

DIAGRAMS

THE EARTH

I. THE STARTING POINT

ONE night when I had tasted bitterness I went out on to the hill. Dark heather checked my feet. Below marched the suburban street lamps. Windows, their curtains drawn, were shut eyes, inwardly watching the lives of dreams. Beyond the sea's level darkness a lighthouse pulsed. Overhead, obscurity.

I distinguished our own house, our islet in the tumultuous and bitter currents of the world. There, for a decade and a half, we two, so different in quality, had grown in and in to one another, for mutual support and nourishment, in intricate symbiosis. There daily we planned our several undertakings, and recounted the day's oddities and vexations. There letters piled up to be answered, socks to be darned. There the children were born, those sudden new lives. There, under that roof, our own two lives, recalcitrant sometimes to one another, were all the while thankfully one, one larger, more conscious life than either alone.

All this, surely, was good. Yet there was bitterness. And bitterness not only invaded us from the world; it welled up also within our own magic circle. For horror at our futility, at our own unreality, and not only at the world's delirium, had driven me out on to the hill.

We were always hurrying from one little urgent task to another, but the upshot was insubstantial. Had we, perhaps, misconceived our whole existence? Were we, as it were, living from false premises? And in particular, this partnership of ours, this seemingly so well-based fulcrum for activity in the world, was it after all nothing but a little eddy of complacent and ingrown domesticity, ineffectively whirling on the surface of the great flux, having in itself no depth of being, and no significance? Had we perhaps after all deceived ourselves? Behind those rapt windows did we, like so many others, indeed live only a dream? In a sick world even the hale are sick. And we two, spinning our little life mostly by rote, seldom with clear cognizance, seldom with firm intent, were products of a sick world.

Yet this life of ours was not all sheer and barren fantasy. Was it not spun from the actual fibres of reality, which we gathered in with all the comings and goings through our door, all our traffic with the suburb and the city and with remoter cities, and with the ends of the earth? And were we not spinning together an authentic expression of our own nature? Did not our life issue daily as more or less firm threads of active living, and mesh itself into the growing web, the intricate, ever-proliferating pattern of mankind?

I considered "us" with quiet interest and a kind of amused awe. How could I describe our relationship even to myself without either disparaging it or insulting it with the tawdry decoration of sentimentality? For this our delicate balance of dependence and independence, this coolly critical, shrewdly ridiculing, but loving mutual contact, was surely a microcosm of true community, was after all in its simple style an actual and living example of that high goal which the world seeks.

The whole world? The whole universe? Overhead, obscurity unveiled a star. One tremulous arrow of light, projected how many thousands of years ago, now stung my nerves with vision, and my heart with fear. For in such a universe as this what significance could there be in our fortuitous, our frail, our evanescent community?

But now irrationally I was seized with a strange worship, not, surely of the star, that mere furnace which mere distance falsely sanctified, but of something other, which the dire contrast of the star and us signified to the heart. Yet what, what could thus be signified? Intellect, peering beyond the star, discovered no Star Maker, but only darkness; no Love, no Power even, but only Nothing. And yet the heart praised.

Impatiently I shook off this folly, and reverted from the inscrutable to the familiar and the concrete. Thrusting aside worship, and fear also and bitterness, I determined to examine more coldly this remarkable "us," this surprisingly impressive datum, which to ourselves remained basic to the universe, though in relation to the stars it appeared so slight a thing.

Considered even without reference to our belittling cosmical background, we were after all insignificant, perhaps ridiculous. We were such a commonplace occurrence, so trite, so respectable. We were just a married couple, making shift to live together without undue strain. Marriage in our time was suspect. And ours, with its trivial romantic origin, was doubly suspect.

We had first met when she was a child. Our eyes encountered. She looked at me for a moment with quiet attention; even, I had romantically imagined, with obscure, deep-lying recognition. I, at any rate, recognized in that look (so I persuaded myself in my fever of adolescence) my destiny. Yes! How predestinate had seemed our union! Yet now, in retrospect, how accidental! True, of course, that as a long-married couple we fitted rather neatly, like two close trees whose trunks have grown upwards together as a single shaft, mutually distorting, but mutually supporting. Coldly I now assessed her as merely a useful, but often infuriating adjunct to my personal life. We were on the whole sensible companions. We left one another a certain freedom, and so we were able to endure our proximity.

Such was our relationship. Stated thus it did not seem very significant for the understanding of the universe. Yet in my heart I knew that it was so. Even the cold stars, even the whole cosmos with all its inane immensities could not convince me that this our prized atom of community, imperfect as it was, short-lived as it must be, was not significant.

But could this indescribable union of ours really have any significance at all beyond itself? Did it, for instance, prove that the essential nature of all human beings was to love, rather than to hate and fear? Was it evidence that all men and women the world over, though circumstance might prevent them, were at heart capable of supporting a world-wide, love-knit community? And further, did it, being itself a product of the cosmos, prove that love was in some way basic to the cosmos itself? And did it afford, through its own felt intrinsic excellence, some guarantee that we two, its frail supporters, must in some sense have eternal life? Did it, in fact, prove that love was God, and God awaiting us in his heaven?

No! Our homely, friendly, exasperating, laughter-making, undecorated though most prized community of spirit proved none of these things. It was no certain guarantee of anything but its own imperfect rightness. It was nothing but a very minute, very bright epitome of one out of the many potentialities of existence. I remembered the swarms of the unseeing stars. I remembered the tumult of hate and fear and bitterness which is man's world. I remembered, too, our own not infrequent discordancy. And I reminded myself that we should very soon vanish like the flurry that a breeze has made on still water.

Once more there came to me a perception of the strange contrast of the stars and us. The incalculable potency of the cosmos mysteriously enhanced the rightness of our brief spark of community, and of mankind's brief, uncertain venture. And these in turn quickened the cosmos.

I sat down on the heather. Overhead obscurity was now in full retreat. In its rear the freed population of the sky sprang out of hiding, star by star.

On every side the shadowy hills or the guessed, featureless sea extended beyond sight. But the hawk-flight of imagination followed them as they curved downward below the horizon. I perceived that I was on a little round grain of rock and metal, filmed with water and with air, whirling in sunlight and darkness. And on the skin of that little grain all the swarms of men, generation by generation, had lived in labour and blindness, with intermittent joy and intermittent lucidity of spirit. And all their history, with its folk-wanderings, its empires, its philosophies, its proud sciences, its social revolutions, its increasing hunger for community, was but a flicker in one day of the lives of stars.

If one could know whether among that glittering host there were here and there other spirit-inhabited grains of rock and metal, whether man's blundering search for wisdom and for love was a sole and insignificant tremor, or part of a universal movement!

2. EARTH AMONG THE STARS

Overhead obscurity was gone. From horizon to horizon the sky was an unbroken spread of stars. Two planets stared, unwinking. The more obtrusive of the constellations asserted their individuality. Orion's four-square shoulders and feet, his belt and sword, the Plough, the zigzag of Cassiopeia, the intimate Pleiades, all were duly patterned on the dark. The Milky Way, a vague hoop of light, spanned the sky.

Imagination completed what mere sight could not achieve. Looking down, I seemed to see through a transparent planet, through heather and solid rock, through the buried grave-yards of vanished species, down through the molten flow of basalt, and on into the Earth's core of iron; then on again, still seemingly downwards, through the southern strata to the southern ocean and lands, past the roots of gum trees and the feet of the inverted antipodeans, through their blue, sun-pierced awning of day, and out into the eternal night, where sun and stars are together. For there, dizzyingly far below me, like fishes in the depth of a lake, lay the nether constellations. The two domes of the sky were fused into one hollow sphere, star-peopled, black, even beside the blinding sun. The young moon was a curve of incandescent wire. The completed hoop of the Milky Way encircled the universe.

In a strange vertigo, I looked for reassurance at the little glowing windows of our home. There they still were; and the whole suburb, and the hills. But stars shone through all. It was as though all terrestrial things were made of glass, or of some more limpid, more ethereal vitreosity. Faintly the church clock chimed for midnight. Dimly, receding, it tolled the first stroke.

Imagination was now stimulated to a new, strange mode of perception. Looking from star to star, I saw the heaven no longer as a jewelled ceiling and floor, but as depth beyond flashing depth of suns. And though for the most part the great and familiar lights of the sky stood forth as our near neighbours, some brilliant stars were seen to be in fact remote and mighty, while some dim lamps were visible only because they were so near. On every side the middle distance was crowded with swarms and streams of stars. But even these now seemed near; for the Milky Way had receded into an incomparably greater distance. And through gaps in its nearer parts appeared vista beyond vista of luminous mists, and deep perspectives of stellar populations.

The universe in which fate had set me was no spangled chamber, but a perceived vortex of star-streams. No! It was more. Peering between the stars into the outer darkness, I saw also, as mere flecks and points of light, other such vortices, such galaxies, sparsely scattered in the void, depth beyond depth, so far afield that even the eye of imagination could find no limits to the cosmical, the all-embracing galaxy of galaxies. The universe now appeared to me as a void wherein floated rare flakes of snow, each flake a universe.

Gazing at the faintest and remotest of all the swarm of universes, I seemed, by hypertelescopic imagination, to see it as a population of suns; and near one of those suns was a planet, and on that planet's dark side a hill, and on that hill myself. For our astronomers assure us that in this boundless finitude which we call the cosmos the straight lines of light lead not to infinity but to their source. Then I remembered that, had my vision depended on physical light, and not on the light of imagination, the rays coming thus to me "round" the cosmos would have revealed, not myself, but events that had ceased long before the Earth, or perhaps even the Sun, was formed.

But now, once more shunning these immensities, I looked again for the curtained windows of our home, which, though star-pierced, was still more real to me than all the galaxies. But our home had vanished, with the whole suburb, and the hills too, and the sea. The very ground on which I had been sitting was gone. Instead there lay far below me an insubstantial gloom. And I myself was seemingly disembodied, for I could neither see nor touch my own flesh. And when I willed to move my limbs, nothing happened. I had no limbs. The familiar inner perceptions of my body, and the headache which had oppressed me since morning, had given way to a vague lightness and exhilaration.

When I realized fully the change that had come over me, I wondered if I had died, and was entering some wholly unexpected new existence. Such a banal possibility at first exasperated me. Then with sudden dismay I understood that if indeed I had died I should not return to my prized, concrete atom of community. The violence of my distress shocked me. But soon I comforted myself with the thought that after all I was probably not dead, but in some sort of trance, from which I might wake at any minute. I resolved, therefore, not to be unduly alarmed by this mysterious change. With scientific interest I would observe all that happened to me.

I noticed that the obscurity which had taken the place of the ground was shrinking and condensing. The nether stars were no longer visible through it. Soon the earth below me was like a huge circular table-top, a broad disc of darkness surrounded by stars. I was apparently soaring away from my native planet at incredible speed. The sun, formerly visible to imagination in the nether heaven, was once more physically eclipsed by the

Earth. Though by now I must have been hundreds of miles above the ground, I was not troubled by the absence of oxygen and atmospheric pressure. I experienced only an increasing exhilaration and a delightful effervescence of thought. The extraordinary brilliance of the stars excited me. For, whether through the absence of obscuring air, or through my own increased sensitivity, or both, the sky had taken on an unfamiliar aspect. Every star had seemingly flared up into higher magnitude. The heavens blazed. The major stars were like the headlights of a distant car. The Milky Way, no longer watered down with darkness, was an encircling, granular river of light.

Presently, along the Planet's eastern limb, now far below me, there appeared a faint line of luminosity; which, as I continued to soar, warmed here and there to orange and red. Evidently I was travelling not only upwards but eastwards, and swinging round into the day. Soon the sun leapt into view, devouring the huge crescent of dawn with its brilliance. But as I sped on, sun and planet were seen to drift apart, while the thread of dawn thickened into a misty breadth of sunlight. This increased, like a visibly waxing moon, till half the planet was illuminated. Between the areas of night and day, a belt of shade, warm-tinted, broad as a sub-continent, now marked the area of dawn. As I continued to rise and travel eastwards, I saw the lands swing westward along with the day, till I was over the Pacific and high noon.

The Earth appeared now as a great bright orb hundreds of times larger than the full moon. In its centre a dazzling patch of light was the sun's image reflected in the ocean. The planet's circumference was an indefinite breadth of luminous haze, fading into the surrounding blackness of space. Much of the northern hemisphere, tilted somewhat toward me, was an expanse of snow and cloud-tops. I could trace parts of the outlines of Japan and China, their vague browns and greens indenting the vague blues and greys of the ocean. Toward the equator, where the air was clearer, the ocean was dark. A little whirl of brilliant cloud was perhaps the upper surface of a hurricane. The Philippines and New Guinea were precisely mapped. Australia faded into the hazy southern limb.

The spectacle before me was strangely moving. Personal anxiety was blotted out by wonder and admiration; for the sheer beauty of our planet surprised me. It was a huge pearl, set in spangled ebony. It was nacrous, it was an opal. No, it was far more lovely than any jewel. Its patterned colouring was more subtle, more ethereal. It displayed the delicacy and brilliance, the intricacy and harmony of a live thing. Strange that in my remoteness I seemed to feel, as never before, the vital presence of Earth as of a creature alive but tranced and obscurely yearning to wake.

I reflected that not one of the visible features of this celestial and living gem revealed the presence of man. Displayed before me, though invisible, were some of the most congested centres of human population.

There below me lay huge industrial regions, blackening the air with smoke. Yet all this thronging life and humanly momentous enterprise had made no mark whatever on the features of the planet. From this high look-out the Earth would have appeared no different before the dawn of man. No visiting angel, or explorer from another planet, could have guessed that this bland orb teemed with vermin, with world-mastering, self-torturing, incipiently angelic beasts.

CHAPTER II

INTERSTELLAR TRAVEL

WHILE I was thus contemplating my native planet, I continued to soar through space. The Earth was visibly shrinking into the distance, and as I raced eastwards, it seemed to be rotating beneath me. All its features swung westwards, till presently sunset and the Mid-Atlantic appeared upon its eastern limb, and then the night. Within a few minutes, as it seemed to me, the planet had become an immense half-moon. Soon it was a misty, dwindling crescent, beside the sharp and minute crescent of its satellite.

With amazement I realized that I must be travelling at a fantastic, a quite impossible rate. So rapid was my progress that I seemed to be passing through a constant hail of meteors. They were invisible till they were almost abreast of me; for they shone only by reflected sunlight, appearing for an instant only, as streaks of light, like lamps seen from an express train. Many of them I met in head-on collision, but they made no impression on me. One huge irregular bulk of rock, the size of a house, thoroughly terrified me. The illuminated mass swelled before my gaze, displayed for a fraction of a second a rough and lumpy surface, and then engulfed me. Or rather, I infer that it must have engulfed me; but so swift was my passage that I had no sooner seen it in the middle distance than I found myself already leaving it behind.

Very soon the Earth was a mere star. I say soon, but my sense of the passage of time was now very confused. Minutes and hours, and perhaps even days, even weeks, were now indistinguishable.

While I was still trying to collect myself, I found that I was already beyond the orbit of Mars, and rushing across the thoroughfare of the asteroids. Some of these tiny planets were now so near that they appeared as great stars streaming across the constellations. One or two revealed gibbous, then crescent forms before they faded behind me.

Already Jupiter, far ahead of me, grew increasingly bright and shifted its position among the fixed stars. The great globe now appeared as a disc, which soon was larger than the shrinking sun. Its four major satellites were little pearls floating beside it. The planet's surface now appeared like streaky bacon, by reason of its cloud-zones. Clouds fogged its whole circumference. Now I drew abreast of it and passed it. Owing to the immense depth of its atmosphere, night and day merged into one another without assignable boundary. I noted here and there on its eastern and unilluminated hemisphere vague areas of ruddy light, which were perhaps the glow cast upwards through dense clouds by volcanic upheavals.

In a few minutes, or perhaps years, Jupiter had become once more a star, and then was lost in the splendour of the diminished but still blazing sun. No other of the outer planets lay near my course, but I soon realized that I must be far beyond the limits of even Pluto's orbit. The sun was now merely the brightest of the stars, fading behind me.

At last I had time for distress. Nothing now was visible but the starry sky. The Plough, Cassiopeia, Orion, the Pleiades, mocked me with their familiarity and their remoteness. The sun was now but one among the other bright stars. Nothing changed. Was I doomed to hang thus for ever out in space, a bodiless view-point? Had I died? Was this my punishment for a singularly ineffectual life? Was this the penalty of an inveterate will to remain detached from human affairs and passions and prejudices?

In imagination I struggled back to my suburban hilltop. I saw our home. The door opened. A figure came out into the garden, lit by the hall light. She stood for a moment looking up and down the road, then went back into the house. But all this was imagination only. In actuality, there was nothing but the stars.

After a while I noticed that the sun and all the stars in his neighbourhood were ruddy. Those at the opposite pole of the heaven were of an icy blue. The explanation of this strange phenomenon flashed upon me. I was still travelling, and travelling so fast that light itself was not wholly indifferent to my passage. The overtaking undulations took long to catch me. They therefore affected me as slower pulsations than they normally were, and I saw them therefore as red. Those that met me on my headlong flight were congested and shortened, and were seen as blue.

Very soon the heavens presented an extraordinary appearance, for all the stars directly behind me were now deep red, while those directly ahead were violet. Rubies lay behind me, amethysts ahead of me. Surrounding the ruby constellations there spread an area of topaz stars, and round the amethyst constellations an area of sapphires. Beside my course, on every side, the colours faded into the normal white of the sky's familiar diamonds. Since I was travelling almost in the plane of the galaxy, the hoop of the Milky Way, white on either hand, was violet ahead of me, red behind. Presently the stars immediately before and behind grew dim, then vanished, leaving two starless holes in the heaven, each hole surrounded by a zone of coloured stars. Evidently I was still gathering speed. Light from the forward and the hinder stars now reached me in forms beyond the range of my human vision.

As my speed increased, the two starless patches, before and behind, each with its coloured fringe, continued to encroach upon the intervening zone of normal stars which lay abreast of me on every side. Amongst these I now detected movement. Through the effect of my own passage the nearer stars appeared to drift across the background of the stars at greater distance. This drifting accelerated, till, for an instant, the whole visible sky was streaked with flying stars. Then everything vanished. Presumably my speed was so great in relation to the stars that light from none of them could take normal effect on me.

Though I was now perhaps travelling faster than light itself, I seemed to be floating at the bottom of a deep and stagnant well. The featureless darkness, the complete lack of all sensation, terrified me, if I may call "terror" the repugnance and foreboding which I now experienced without any of the bodily accompaniments of terror, without any sensation of trembling, sweating, gasping or palpitation. Forlornly, and with self-pity, I longed for home, longed to see once more the face that I knew best. With the mind's eye I could see her now, sitting by the fire sewing, a little furrow of anxiety between her brows. Was my body, I wondered, lying dead on the heather? Would they find it there in the morning? How would she confront this great change in her life? Certainly with a brave face; but she would suffer.

But even while I was desperately rebelling against the dissolution of our treasured atom of community, I was aware that something within me, the essential spirit within me, willed very emphatically not to retreat but to press on with this amazing voyage. Not that my longing for the familiar human world could for a moment be counterbalanced by the mere craving for adventure. I was of too home-keeping a kind to seek serious danger and discomfort for their own sake. But timidity was overcome by a sense of the opportunity that fate was giving me, not only to explore the depths of the physical universe, but to discover what part life and mind were actually playing among the stars. A keen hunger now took possession of me, a hunger not for adventure but for insight into the significance of man, or of any manlike beings in the cosmos. This homely treasure of ours, this frank and spring-making daisy beside the arid track of modern life, impelled me to accept gladly my strange adventure; for might I not discover that the whole universe was no mere place of dust and ashes with here and there a stunted life, but actually beyond the parched terrestrial waste land, a world of flowers?

Was man indeed, as he sometimes desired to be, the growing point of the cosmical spirit, in its temporal aspect at least? Or was he one of many million growing points? Or was mankind of no more importance in the universal view than rats in a cathedral? And again, was man's true function power, or wisdom, or love, or worship, or all of these? Or was the idea of function, of purpose, meaningless in relation to the cosmos? These grave questions I would answer. Also I must learn to see a little more clearly and confront a little more rightly (so I put it to myself) that which, when we glimpse it at all, compels our worship.

I now seemed to my self-important self to be no isolated individual, craving aggrandizement, but rather an emissary of mankind, no, an organ of exploration, a feeler, projected by the living human world to make contact with its fellows in space. At all cost I must go forward, even if my trivial earthly life must come to an untimely end, and my wife and children be left without me. I must go forward; and somehow, some day, even if after centuries of interstellar travel, I must return.

When I look back on that phase of exaltation, now that I have indeed returned to earth after the most bewildering adventures, I am dismayed at the contrast between the spiritual treasure which I aspired to hand over to my fellow men and the paucity of my actual tribute. This failure was perhaps due to the fact that, though I did indeed accept the challenge of the adventure, I accepted it only with secret reservations. Fear and the longing for comfort, I now recognize, dimmed the brightness of my will. My resolution, so boldly formed, proved after all frail. My unsteady courage often gave place to yearnings for my native planet. Over and over again in the course of my travels I had a sense that, owing to my timid and pedestrian nature, I missed the most significant aspects of events.

Of all that I experienced on my travels, only a fraction was clearly intelligible to me even at the time; and then, as I shall tell, my native powers were aided by beings of superhuman development. Now that I am once more on my native planet, and this aid is no longer available, I cannot recapture even so much of the deeper insight as I formerly attained. And so my record, which tells of the most far-reaching of all human explorations, turns out to be after all no more reliable than the rigmarole of any mind unhinged by the impact of experience beyond its comprehension.

To return to my story. How long I spent in debate with myself I do not know, but soon after I had made my decision, the absolute darkness was pierced once more by the stars. I was apparently at rest, for stars were visible in every direction, and their colour was normal.

But a mysterious change had come over me. I soon discovered that, by merely willing to approach a star, I could set myself in motion toward it, and at such a speed that I must have travelled much faster than normal light. This, as I knew very well, was physically impossible. Scientists had assured me that motion faster than the speed of light was meaningless. I inferred that my motion must therefore be in some manner a mental, not a physical phenomenon, that I was enabled to take up successive viewpoints without physical means of locomotion. It seemed to me evident, too, that the light with which the stars were now revealed to me was not normal, physical light; for I noticed that my new and expeditious means of travel took no effect upon the visible colours of the stars. However fast I moved, they retained their diamond hues, though all were somewhat brighter and more tinted than in normal vision.

No sooner had I made sure of my new power of locomotion than I began feverishly to use it. I told myself that I was embarking on a voyage of astronomical and metaphysical research; but already my craving for the Earth was distorting my purpose. It turned my attention unduly toward the search for planets, and especially for planets of the terrestrial type.

At random I directed my course toward one of the brighter of the near stars. So rapid was my advance that certain lesser and still nearer luminaries streamed past me like meteors. I swung close to the great sun, insensitive to its heat. On its mottled surface, in spite of the pervading brilliance, I could see, with my miraculous vision, a group of huge dark sun-spots, each one a pit into which a dozen Earths could have been dropped. Round the star's limb the excrescences of the chromosphere looked like fiery trees and plumes and prehistoric monsters, atiptoe or awing, all on a globe too small for them. Beyond these the pale corona spread its films into the darkness. As I rounded the star in hyperbolic flight I searched anxiously for planets, but found none. I searched again, meticulously, tacking and veering near and far. In the wider orbits a small object like the earth might easily be overlooked. I found nothing but meteors and a few insubstantial comets. This was the more disappointing because the star seemed to be of much the same type as the familiar sun. Secretly I had hoped to discover not merely planets but actually the Earth.

Once more I struck out into the ocean of space, heading for another near star. Once more I was disappointed. I approached yet another lonely furnace. This too was unattended by the minute grains that harbour life.

I now hurried from star to star, a lost dog looking for its master. I rushed hither and thither, intent on finding a sun with planets, and among those planets my home. Star after star I searched, but far more I passed impatiently, recognizing at once that they were too large and tenuous and young to be Earth's luminary. Some were vague ruddy giants broader than the orbit of Jupiter; some, smaller and more definite, had the brilliance of a thousand suns, and their colour was blue. I had been told that our Sun was of average type, but I now discovered many more of the great youngsters than of the shrunken, yellowish middle-aged. Seemingly I must have strayed into a region of late stellar condensation.

I noticed, but only to avoid them, great clouds of dust, huge as constellations, eclipsing the star-streams; and tracts of palely glowing gas, shining sometimes by their own light, sometimes by the reflected light of stars. Often these nacrous cloud-continents had secreted within them a number of vague pearls of light, the embryos of future stars.

I glanced heedlessly at many star-couples, trios, and quartets, in which more or less equal partners waltz in close union. Once, and once only, I came on one of those rare couples in which one partner is no bigger than a mere Earth, but massive as a whole great star, and very brilliant. Up and down this region of the galaxy I found here and there a dying star, sombrely smouldering; and here and there the encrusted and extinguished dead. These I could not see till I was almost upon them, and then only dimly, by the reflected light of the whole heaven. I never approached nearer to them than I could help, for they were of no interest to me in my crazy yearning for the Earth. Moreover, they struck a chill into my mind, prophesying the universal death. I was comforted, however, to find that as yet there were so few of them.

I found no planets. I knew well that the birth of planets was due to the close approach of two or more stars, and that such accidents must be very uncommon. I reminded myself that stars with planets must be as rare in the galaxy as gems among the grains of sand on the sea-shore. What chance had I of coming upon one? I began to lose heart. The appalling desert of darkness and barren fire, the huge emptiness so sparsely pricked with scintillations, the colossal futility of the whole universe, hideously oppressed me. And now, an added distress, my power of locomotion began to fail. Only with a great effort could I move at all among the stars, and then but slowly, and ever more slowly. Soon I should find myself pinned fast in space like a fly in a collection; but lonely, eternally alone. Yes, surely this was my special Hell.

I pulled myself together. I reminded myself that even if this was to be my fate, it was no great matter. The Earth could very well do without me. And even if there was no other living world anywhere in the cosmos, still, the Earth itself had life, and might wake to far fuller life. And even though I had lost my native planet, still, that beloved world was real. Besides, my whole adventure was a miracle, and by continued miracle might I not stumble on some other Earth? I remembered that I had undertaken a high pilgrimage, and that I was man's emissary to the stars.

With returning courage my power of locomotion returned. Evidently it depended on a vigorous and self-detached mentality. My recent mood of self-pity and earthward-yearning had hampered it.

Resolving to explore a new region of the galaxy, where perhaps there would be more of the older stars and a greater hope of planets, I headed in the direction of a remote and populous cluster. From the faintness of the individual members of this vaguely speckled ball of light I guessed that it must be very far afield.

On and on I travelled in the darkness. As I never turned aside to search, my course through the ocean of space never took me near enough to any star to reveal it as a disc. The lights of heaven streamed remotely past me like the lights of distant ships. After a voyage during which I lost all measure of time I found myself in a great desert, empty of stars, a gap between two star-streams, a cleft in the galaxy. The Milky Way surrounded me, and in all directions lay the normal dust of distant stars; but there were no considerable lights, save the thistle-down of the remote cluster which was my goal.

This unfamiliar sky disturbed me with a sense of my increasing dissociation from my home. It was almost a comfort to note, beyond the furthest stars of our galaxy, the minute smudges that were alien galaxies, incomparably more distant than the deepest recesses of the Milky Way; and to be reminded that, in spite of all my headlong and miraculous travelling, I was still within my native galaxy, within the same little cell of the cosmos where she, my life's friend, still lived. I was surprised, by the way, that so many of the alien galaxies appeared to the naked eye, and that the largest was a pale, cloudy mark bigger than the moon in the terrestrial sky.

By contrast with the remote galaxies, on whose appearance all my voyaging failed to make impression, the star-cluster ahead of me was now visibly expanding. Soon after I had crossed the great emptiness between the star-streams, my cluster confronted me as a huge cloud of brilliants. Presently I was passing through a more populous area, and then the cluster itself opened out ahead of me, covering the whole forward sky with its congested lights. As a ship approaching port encounters other craft, so I came upon and passed star after star. When I had penetrated into the heart of the cluster, I was in a region far more populous than any that I had explored. On every side the sky blazed with suns, many of which appeared far brighter than Venus in the Earth's sky. I felt the exhilaration of a traveller who, after an ocean crossing, enters harbour by night and finds himself surrounded by the lights of a metropolis. In this congested region, I told myself, many close approaches must have occurred, many planetary systems must have been formed.

Once more I looked for middle-aged stars of the sun's type. All that I had passed hitherto were young giants, great as the whole solar system. After further searching I found a few likely stars, but none had planets. I found also many double and triple stars, describing their incalculable orbits; and great continents of gas, in which new stars were condensing.

At last, at last I found a planetary system. With almost insupportable hope I circled among these worlds; but all were greater than Jupiter, and all were molten. Again I hurried from star to star. I must have visited thousands, but all in vain. Sick and lonely I fled out of the cluster. It dwindled behind me into a ball of down, sparkling with dew-drops. In front of me a great tract of darkness blotted out a section of the Milky Way and the neighbouring area of stars, save for a few near lights which lay between me and the obscuring opacity. The billowy edges of this huge cloud of gas or dust were revealed by the glancing rays of bright stars beyond it. The sight moved me with self-pity; on so many nights at home had I seen the edges of dark clouds silvered just so by moonlight. But the cloud which now opposed me could have swallowed not merely whole worlds, not merely countless planetary systems, but whole constellations.

Once more my courage failed me. Miserably I tried to shut out the immensities by closing my eyes. But I had neither eyes nor eyelids. I was a disembodied, wandering view-point. I tried to conjure up the little interior of my home, with the curtains drawn and the fire dancing. I tried to persuade myself that all this horror of darkness and distance and barren incandescence was a dream, that I was dozing by the fire, that at any moment I might wake, that she would reach over from her sewing and touch me and smile. But the stars still held me prisoner.

Again, though with failing strength, I set about my search. And after I had wandered from star to star for a period that might have been days or years or aeons, luck or some guardian spirit directed me to a certain sun-like star; and looking outwards from this centre, I caught sight of a little point of light, moving, with my movement, against the patterned sky. As I leapt toward it, I saw another, and another. Here was indeed a planetary system much like my own. So obsessed was I with human stand-ards that I sought out at once the most earth-like of these worlds. And amazingly earth-like it appeared, as its disc swelled before me, or below me. Its atmosphere was evidently less dense than ours, for the outlines of un-familiar continents and oceans were very plainly visible. As on the earth, the dark sea brilliantly reflected the sun's image. White cloud-tracts lay here and there over the seas and the lands, which, as on my own planet, were mottled green and brown. But even from this height I saw that the greens were more vivid and far more blue than terrestrial vegetation. I noted, also, that on this planet there was less ocean than land, and that the centres of the great continents were chiefly occupied by dazzling creamy-white deserts.

CHAPTER III

THE OTHER EARTH

I. ON THE OTHER EARTH

AS I slowly descended toward the surface of the little planet, I found my-self searching for a land which promised to be like England. But no sooner did I realize what I was doing than I reminded myself that conditions here would be entirely different from terrestrial conditions, and that it was very unlikely that I should find intelligent beings at all. If such beings existed, they would probably be quite incomprehensible to me. Perhaps they would be huge spiders or creeping jellies. How could I hope ever to make contact with such monsters?

After circling about at random for some time over the filmy clouds and the forests, over the dappled plains and prairies and the dazzling stretches of desert, I selected a maritime country in the temperate zone, a brilliantly green peninsula. When I had descended almost to the ground, I was amazed at the verdure of the country-side. Here unmistakably was vegetation, similar to ours in essential character, but quite unfamiliar in detail. The fat, or even bulbous, leaves reminded me of our desert-flora, but here the stems were lean and wiry. Perhaps the most striking character of this vegetation was its colour, which was a vivid blue-green, like the colour of vineyards that have been treated with copper salts. I was to discover later that the plants of this world had indeed learnt to protect themselves by means of copper sulphate from the microbes and the insect-like pests which formerly devastated this rather dry planet.

I skimmed over a brilliant prairie scattered with Prussian-blue bushes. The sky also attained a depth of blue quite unknown on earth, save at great altitudes. There were a few low yet cirrus clouds, whose feathery character I took to be due to the tenuousness of the atmosphere. This was borne out by the fact that, though my descent had taken place in the fore-noon of a summer's day, several stars managed to pierce the almost nocturnal sky. All exposed surfaces were very intensely illuminated. The shadows of the nearer bushes were nearly black. Some distant objects, rather like buildings, but probably mere rocks, appeared to be blocked out in ebony and snow. Altogether the landscape was one of unearthly and fantastical beauty.

I glided with wingless flight over the surface of the planet, through glades, across tracts of fractured rock, along the banks of streams. Presently I came to a wide region covered by neat, parallel rows of fern-like plants, bearing masses of nuts on the lower surfaces of their leaves. It was almost

impossible to believe that this vegetable regimentation had not been intelligently planned. Or could it after all be merely a natural phenomenon
not known on my own planet? Such was my surprise that my power of
locomotion, always subject to emotional interference, now began to fail
me. I reeled in the air like a drunk man. Pulling myself together, I staggered on over the ranked crops toward a rather large object which lay
some distance from me beside a strip of bare ground. Presently, to my
amazement, my stupefaction, this object revealed itself as a plough. It was
rather a queer instrument, but there was no mistaking the shape of the
blade, which was rusty, and obviously made of iron. There were two iron
handles, and chains for attachment to a beast of draught. It was difficult
to believe that I was many light-years distant from England. Looking
round, I saw an unmistakable cart track, and a bit of dirty ragged cloth
hanging on a bush. Yet overhead was the unearthly sky, full noon with
stars.

I followed the lane through a little wood of queer bushes, whose
large fat drooping leaves had cherry-like fruits along their edges. Suddenly,
round a bend in the lane, I came upon—a man. Or so at first he seemed to
my astounded and star-weary sight. I should not have been so surprised by
the strangely human character of this creature had I at this early stage
understood the forces that controlled my adventure. Influences which I shall
later describe doomed me to discover first such worlds as were most akin
to my own. Meanwhile the reader may well conceive my amazement at this
strange encounter.

I had always supposed that man was a unique being. An inconceive-
ably complex conjunction of circumstances had produced him, and it was
not to be supposed that such conditions would be repeated anywhere in
the universe. Yet here, on the very first globe to be explored, was an
obvious peasant. Approaching him, I saw that he was not quite so like
terrestrial man as he seemed at a distance; but he was a man for all that.
Had God, then, peopled the whole universe with our kind? Did he perhaps in very truth make us in his image? It was incredible. To ask such
questions proved that I had lost my mental balance.

As I was a mere disembodied view-point, I was able to observe without being observed. I floated about him as he strode along the lane. He was
an erect biped, and in general plan definitely human. I had no means of
judging his height, but he must have been approximately of normal terrestrial stature, or at least not smaller than a pigmy and not taller than a
giant. He was of slender build. His legs were almost like a bird's, and
enclosed in rough narrow trousers. Above the waist he was naked, displaying a disproportionately large thorax, shaggy with greenish hair. He
had two short but powerful arms, and huge shoulder muscles. His skin
was dark and ruddy, and dusted plentifully with bright green down. All
his contours were uncouth, for the details of muscles, sinews and joints

were very plainly different from our own. His neck was curiously long
and supple. His head I can best describe by saying that most of the brain-
pan, covered with a green thatch, seemed to have slipped backwards and
downwards over the nape. His two very human eyes peered from under
the eaves of hair. An oddly projecting, almost spout-like mouth made him
look as though he were whistling. Between the eyes, and rather above
them, was a pair of great equine nostrils which were constantly in motion.
The bridge of the nose was represented by an elevation in the thatch,
reaching from the nostrils backwards over the top of the head. There were
no visible ears. I discovered later that the auditory organs opened into the
nostrils.

Clearly, although evolution on this Earth-like planet must have taken
a course on the whole surprisingly like that which had produced my own
kind, there must also have been many divergencies.

The stranger wore not only boots but gloves, seemingly of tough
leather. His boots were extremely short. I was to discover later that the feet
of this race, the "Other Men," as I called them, were rather like the feet
of an ostrich or a camel. The instep consisted of three great toes grown
together. In place of the heel there was an additional broad, stumpy toe.
The hands were without palms. Each was a bunch of three gristly fingers
and a thumb.

The aim of this book is not to tell of my own adventures but to give
some idea of the worlds which I visited. I shall therefore not recount in
detail how I established myself among the Other Men. Of myself it is
enough to say a few words. When I had studied this agriculturalist for a
while, I began to be strangely oppressed by his complete unawareness of
myself. With painful clearness I realized that the purpose of my pilgrimage
was not merely scientific observation, but also the need to effect some kind
of mental and spiritual traffic with other worlds, for mutual enrichment
and community. How should I ever be able to achieve this end unless I
could find some means of communication? It was not until I had followed
my companion to his home, and had spent many days in that little circular
stone house with roof of mudded wicker, that I discovered the power of
entering into his mind, of seeing through his eyes, sensing through all his
sense organs, perceiving his world just as he perceived it, and following
much of his thought and his emotional life. Not till very much later, when
I had passively "inhabited" many individuals of the race, did I discover
how to make my presence known, and even to converse inwardly with
my host.

This kind of internal "telepathic" intercourse, which was to serve me
in all my wanderings, was at first difficult, ineffective, and painful. But in
time I came to be able to live through the experiences of my host with
vividness and accuracy, while yet preserving my own individuality, my own

critical intelligence, my own desires and fears. Only when the other had come to realize my presence within him could he, by a special act of volition, keep particular thoughts secret from me.

It can well be understood that at first I found these alien minds quite unintelligible. Their very sensations differed from my familiar sensations in important respects. Their thoughts and all their emotions and sentiments were strange to me. The traditional groundwork of these minds, their most familiar concepts, were derived from a strange history, and expressed in languages which to the terrestrial mind were subtly misleading.

I spent on the Other Earth many "other years," wandering from mind to mind and country to country, but I did not gain any clear understanding of the psychology of the Other Men and the significance of their history till I had encountered one of their philosophers, an aging but still vigorous man whose eccentric and unpalatable views had prevented him from attaining eminence. Most of my hosts, when they became aware of my presence within them, regarded me either as an evil spirit or as a divine messenger. The more sophisticated, however, assumed that I was a mere disease, a symptom of insanity in themselves. They therefore promptly applied to the local "Mental Sanitation Officer." After I had spent, according to the local calendar, a year or so of bitter loneliness among minds who refused to treat me as a human being, I had the good fortune to come under the philosopher's notice. One of my hosts, who complained of suffering from "voices," and visions of "another world," appealed to the old man for help. Bvalltu, for such approximately was the philosopher's name, the "ll" being pronounced more or less as in Welsh, Bvalltu effected a "cure" by merely inviting me to accept the hospitality of his own mind, where, he said, he would very gladly entertain me. It was with extravagant joy that I made contact at last with a being who recognized in me a human personality.

2. A BUSY WORLD

So many important characteristics of this world-society need to be described that I cannot spend much time on the more obvious features of the planet and its race. Civilization had reached a stage of growth much like that which was familiar to me. I was constantly surprised by the blend of similarity and difference. Travelling over the planet I found that cultivation had spread over most of the suitable areas, and that industrialism was already far advanced in many countries. On the prairies huge flocks of mammal-like creatures grazed and scampered. Larger mammals, or quasi-mammals, were farmed on all the best pasture land for food and leather. I say "quasi-mammal" because, though these creatures were viviparous, they did not suckle. The chewed cud, chemically treated in the maternal belly, was spat into the offspring's mouth as a jet of pre-digested fluid. It was thus also that human mothers fed their young.

The most important means of locomotion on the Other Earth was the steam-train, but trains in this world were so bulky that they looked like whole terraces of houses on the move. This remarkable railway development was probably due to the great number and length of journeys across deserts. Occasionally I travelled on steam-ships on the few and small oceans, but marine transport was on the whole backward. The screw propeller was unknown, its place being taken by paddle wheels. Internal-combustion engines were used in road and desert transport. Flying, owing to the rarified atmosphere, had not been achieved; but rocket-propulsion was already used for long-distance transport of mails, and for long-range bombardment in war. Its application to aeronautics might come any day.

My first visit to the metropolis of one of the great empires of the Other Earth was an outstanding experience. Everything was at once so strange and so familiar. There were streets and many-windowed stores and offices. In this old city the streets were narrow, and so congested was the motor traffic that pedestrians were accommodated on special elevated tracks slung beside the first-storey windows and across the streets.

The crowds that streamed along these footpaths were as variegated as our own. The men wore cloth tunics, and trousers surprisingly like the trousers of Europe, save that the crease affected by the respectable was at the side of the leg. The women, breastless and high-nostrilled like the men, were to be distinguished by their more tubular lips, whose biological function it was to project food for the infant. In place of skirts they disported green and glossy silk tights and little gawdy knickers. To my unaccustomed vision the effect was inexpressibly vulgar. In summer both sexes often appeared in the streets naked to the waist; but they always wore gloves.

Here, then, was a host of persons who, in spite of their oddity, were as essentially human as Londoners. They went about their private affairs with complete assurance, ignorant that a spectator from another world found them one and all grotesque, with their lack of forehead, their great elevated quivering nostrils, their startlingly human eyes, their spout-like mouths. There they were, alive and busy, shopping, staring, talking. Children dragged at their mothers' hands. Old men with white facial hair bowed over walking-sticks. Young men eyed young women. The prosperous were easily to be distinguished from the unfortunate by their newer and richer clothes, their confident and sometimes arrogant carriage.

How can I describe in a few pages the distinctive character of a whole teeming and storied world, so different from my own, yet so similar? Here, as on my own planet, infants were being born every hour. Here, as there, they clamoured for food, and very soon for companionship. They discovered what pain was, and what fear, and what loneliness, and love. They grew up, moulded by the harsh or kindly pressure of their fellows, to be either well nurtured, generous, sound, or mentally crippled, bitter, unwittingly vindictive. One and all they desperately craved the bliss of true community; and very few, fewer here, perhaps, than in my own world, found more than the vanishing flavour of it. They howled with the pack and hounded with the pack. Starved both physically and mentally, they brawled over the quarry and tore one another to pieces, mad with hunger, physical or mental. Sometimes some of them paused and asked what it was all for; and there followed a battle of words, but no clear answer. Suddenly they were old and finished. Then, the span from birth to death being an imperceptible instant of cosmical time, they vanished.

This planet, being essentially of the terrestrial type, had produced a race that was essentially human, though, so to speak, human in a different key from the terrestrial. These continents were as variegated as ours, and inhabited by a race as diversified as *Homo sapiens*. All the modes and facets of the spirit manifested in our history had their equivalents in the history of the Other Men. As with us, there had been dark ages and ages of brilliance, phases of advancement and of retreat, cultures predominantly material, and others in the main intellectual, aesthetic, or spiritual. There were "Eastern" races and "Western" races. There were empires, republics, dictatorships. Yet all was different from the terrestrial. Many of the differences, of course, were superficial; but there was also an underlying, deeply-lying difference which I took long to understand and will not yet describe.

I must begin by speaking of the biological equipment of the Other Men. Their animal nature was at bottom much like ours. They responded with anger, fear, hate, tenderness, curiosity, and so on, much as we respond. In sensory equipment they were not unlike ourselves, save that in vision they were less sensitive to colour and more to form than is common with us. The violent colours of the Other Earth appeared to me through the eyes of its natives very subdued. In hearing also they were rather ill-equipped. Though their auditory organs were as sensitive as ours to faint sounds, they were poor discriminators. Music, such as we know, never developed in this world.

In compensation, scent and taste developed amazingly. These beings tasted not only with their mouths, but with their moist black hands and with their feet. They were thus afforded an extraordinarily rich and intimate experience of their planet. Tastes of metals and woods, of sour and sweet earths, of the many rocks, and of the innumerable shy or bold flavours of plants crushed beneath the bare running feet, made up a whole world unknown to terrestrial man.

The genitals also were equipped with taste organs. There were several distinctive male and female patterns of chemical characteristics, each powerfully attractive to the opposite sex. These were savoured faintly by contact of hands or feet with any part of the body, and with exquisite intensity in copulation.

This surprising richness of gustatory experience made it very difficult for me to enter fully into the thoughts of the Other Men. Taste played as important a part in their imagery and conception as sight in our own. Many ideas which terrestrial man has reached by way of sight, and which even in their most abstract form still bear traces of their visual origin, the Other Men conceived in terms of taste. For example, our "brilliant," as applied to persons or ideas, they would translate by a word whose literal meaning was "tasty." For "lucid" they would use a term which in primitive times was employed by hunters to signify añ easily runnable taste-trail. To have "religious illumination" was to "taste the meadows of heaven." Many of our non-visual concepts also were rendered by means of taste. "Complexity" was "many-flavoured," a word applied originally to the confusion of tastes round a drinking pool frequented by many kind of beasts. "Incompatibility" was derived from a word meaning the disgust which certain human types felt for one another on account of their flavours.

Differences of race, which in our world are chiefly conceived in terms of bodily appearance, were for the Other Men almost entirely differences of taste and smell. And as the races of the Other Men were much less sharply localized than our own races, the strife between groups whose flavours were repugnant to one another played a great part in history. Each race tended to believe that its own flavour was characteristic of all the finer mental qualities, was indeed an absolutely reliable label of spiritual worth. In former ages the gustatory and olfactory differences had, no doubt, been true signs of racial differences; but in modern times, and in the more developed lands, there had been great changes. Not only had the races ceased to be clearly localized, but also industrial civilization had produced a crop of genetic changes which rendered the old racial distinctions meaningless. The ancient flavours, however, though they had by now no racial significance at all, and indeed members of one family might have mutually repugnant flavours, continued to have the traditional emotional effects. In each country some particular flavour was considered the true hall-mark of the race of that country, and all other flavours were despised, if not actually condemned.

In the country which I came to know best the orthodox racial flavour was a kind of saltness inconceivable to terrestrial man. My hosts regarded themselves as the very salt of the earth. But as a matter of fact the peasant whom I first "inhabited" was the only genuine pure salt man of orthodox variety whom I ever encountered. The great majority of that country's citizens attained their correct taste and smell by artificial means. Those who were at least approximately salt, with some variety of saltness, though not the ideal variety, were for ever exposing the deceit of their sour, sweet, or bitter neighbours. Unfortunately, though the taste of the limbs could be fairly well disguised, no effective means had been found for changing the flavour of copulation. Consequently newly married couples were apt to make the most shattering discoveries about one another on the wedding night. Since in the great majority of unions neither party had the orthodox flavour, both were willing to pretend to the world that all was well. But often there would turn out to be a nauseating incompatibility between the two gustatory types. The whole population was rotten with neuroses bred of these secret tragedies of marriage. Occasionally, when one party was more or less of the orthodox flavour, this genuinely salt partner would indignantly denounce the impostor. The courts, the news bulletins, and the public would then join in self-righteous protests.

Some "racial" flavours were too obtrusive to be disguised. One in particular, a kind of bitter-sweet, exposed its possessor to extravagant persecution in all but the most tolerant countries. In past times the bitter-sweet race had earned a reputation of cunning and self-seeking, and had been periodically massacred by its less intelligent neighbours. But in the general biological ferment of modern times the bitter-sweet flavour might crop up in any family. Woe, then, to the accursed infant, and to all its relatives! Persecution was inevitable; unless indeed the family was wealthy enough to purchase from the state "an honorary salting" (or in the neighbouring land, "an honorary sweetening"), which removed the stigma.

In the more enlightened countries the whole racial superstition was becoming suspect. There was a movement among the intelligentsia for conditioning infants to tolerate every kind of human flavour, and for discarding the deodorants and degustatants, and even the boots and gloves, which civilized convention imposed.

Unfortunately this movement of toleration was hampered by one of the consequences of industrialism. In the congested and unhealthy industrial centres a new gustatory and olfactory type had appeared, apparently as a biological mutation. In a couple of generations this sour, astringent, and undisguisable flavour dominated in all the most disreputable working-class quarters. To the fastidious palates of the well-to-do it was overwhelmingly nauseating and terrifying. In fact it became for them an unconscious symbol, tapping all the secret guilt and fear and hate which the oppressors felt for the oppressed.

In this world, as in our own, nearly all the chief means of production, nearly all the land, mines, factories, railways, ships, were controlled for private profit by a small minority of the population. These privileged individuals were able to force the masses to work for them on pain of starvation. The tragic farce inherent in such a system was already approaching. The owners directed the energy of the workers increasingly toward the production of more means of production rather than to the fulfilment of the needs of individual life. For machinery might bring profit to the owners; bread would not. With the increasing competition of machine with machine, profits declined, and therefore wages, and therefore effective demand for goods. Marketless products were destroyed, though bellies were unfed and backs unclad. Unemployment, disorder, and stern repression increased as the economic system disintegrated. A familiar story!

As conditions deteriorated, and the movements of charity and state-charity became less and less able to cope with the increasing mass of unemployment and destitution, the new pariah-race became more and more psychologically useful to the hate-needs of the scared, but still powerful, prosperous. The theory was spread that these wretched beings were the result of secret systematic race-pollution by riff-raff immigrants, and that they deserved no consideration whatever. They were therefore allowed only the basest forms of employment and the harshest conditions of work. When unemployment had become a serious social problem, practically the whole pariah stock was workless and destitute. It was of course easily believed that unemployment, far from being due to the decline of capitalism, was due to the worthlessness of the pariahs.

At the time of my visit the working class had become tainted through and through by the pariah stock, and there was a vigorous movement afoot amongst the wealthy and the official classes to institute slavery for pariahs and half-pariahs, so that these might be openly treated as the cattle which in fact they were. In view of the danger of continued race-pollution, some politicians urged wholesale slaughter of the pariahs, or, at the least, universal sterilization. Others pointed out that, as a supply of cheap labour was necessary to society, it would be wiser merely to keep their numbers down by working them to an early death in occupations which those of "pure race" would never accept. This, at any rate, should be done in times of prosperity; but in times of decline, the excess population could be allowed to starve, or might be used up in the physiological laboratories.

The persons who first dared to suggest this policy were scourged by the whips of generous popular indignation. But their policy was in fact adopted; not explicitly but by tacit consent, and in the absence of any more constructive plan.

The first time that I was taken through the poorest quarter of the city I was surprised to see that, though there were large areas of slum property far more squalid than anything in England, there were also many great clean blocks of tenements worthy of Vienna. These were surrounded by gardens, which were crowded with wretched tents and shanties. The grass was worn away, the bushes damaged, the flowers trampled. Everywhere men, women, and children, all filthy and ragged, were idling.

I learned that these noble buildings had been erected before the world-economic-crisis (familiar phrase!) by a millionaire who had made his money in trading an opium-like drug. He presented the buildings to the City Council, and was gathered to heaven by way of the peerage. The more deserving and less unsavoury poor were duly housed; but care was taken to fix the rent high enough to exclude the pariah-race. Then came the crisis. One by one the tenants failed to pay their rent, and were ejected. Within a year the buildings were almost empty.

There followed a very curious sequence of events, and one which, as I was to discover, was characteristic of this strange world. Respectable public opinion, though vindictive toward the unemployed, was passionately tender toward the sick. In falling ill, a man acquired a special sanctity, and exercised a claim over all healthy persons. Thus no sooner did any of the wretched campers succumb to a serious disease than he was carried off to be cared for by all the resources of medical science. The desperate paupers soon discovered how things stood, and did all in their power to fall sick. So successful were they, that the hospitals were soon filled. The empty tenements were therefore hastily fitted out to receive the increasing flood of patients.

Observing these and other farcical events, I was reminded of my own race. But though the Other Men were in many ways so like us, I suspected increasingly that some factor still hidden from me doomed them to a frustration which my own nobler species need never fear. Psychological mechanisms which in our case are tempered with common sense or moral sense stood out in this world in flagrant excess. Yet it was not true that Other Man was less intelligent or less moral than man of my own species. In abstract thought and practical invention he was at least our equal. Many of his most recent advances in physics and astronomy had passed beyond our present attainment. I noticed, however, that psychology was even more chaotic than with us, and that social thought was strangely perverted.

In radio and television, for instance, the Other Men were technically far ahead of us, but the use to which they put their astounding inventions was disastrous. In civilized countries everyone but the pariahs carried a pocket receiving set. As the Other Men had no music, this may seem odd; but since they lacked newspapers, radio was the only means by which the man in the street could learn the lottery and sporting results which were his staple mental diet. The place of music, moreover, was taken by taste- and smell-themes, which were translated into patterns of ethereal undulation, transmitted by all the great national stations, and restored to their original form in the pocket receivers and taste-batteries of the population. These instruments afforded intricate stimuli to the taste organs and scent organs of the hand. Such was the power of this kind of entertainment that both men and women were nearly always seen with one hand in a pocket. A special wave length had been allotted to the soothing of infants.

A sexual receiving set had been put upon the market, and programmes were broadcast for it in many countries; but not in all. This extraordinary invention was a combination of radio-touch, -taste, -odour, and -sound. It worked not through the sense organs, but by direct stimulation of the appropriate brain-centres. The recipient wore a specially constructed skull-cap, which transmitted to him from a remote studio the embraces of some delectable and responsive woman, as they were then actually being experienced by a male "love-broadcaster," or as electromagnetically recorded on a steel tape on some earlier occasion.

Controversies had arisen about the morality of sexual broadcasting. Some countries permitted programmes for males but not for females, wishing to preserve the innocence of the purer sex. Elsewhere the clerics had succeeded in crushing the whole project on the score that radio-sex, even for men alone, would be a diabolical substitute for a certain much desired and jealously guarded religious experience, called the immaculate union, of which I shall tell in the sequel. Well did the priests know that their power depended largely on their ability to induce this luscious ecstasy in their flock by means of ritual and other psychological techniques.

Militarists also were strongly opposed to the new invention; for in the cheap and efficient production of illusory sexual embraces they saw a danger even more serious than contraception. The supply of cannon-fodder would decline.

Since in all the more respectable countries broadcasting had been put under the control of retired soldiers or good churchmen, the new device was at first adopted only in the more commercial and the more disreputable states. From their broadcasting stations the embraces of popular "radio love-stars" and even of impecunious aristocrats were broadcast along with advertisements of patent medicines, tasteproof gloves, lottery results, savours, and degustatants.

The principle of radio-brain-stimulation was soon developed much further. Programmes of all the most luscious or piquant experiences were broadcast in all countries, and could be picked up by simple receivers that were within the means of all save the pariahs. Thus even the labourer and the factory hand could have the pleasures of a banquet without expense and subsequent repletion, the delights of proficient dancing without the trouble of learning the art, the thrills of motor-racing without danger. In an ice-bound northern home he could bask on tropical beaches, and in the tropics indulge in winter sports.

Governments soon discovered that the new invention gave them a cheap and effective kind of power over their subjects. Slum-conditions could be tolerated if there was an unfailing supply of illusory luxury. Reforms distasteful to the authorities could be shelved if they could be represented as inimical to the national radio-system. Strikes and riots could often be broken by the mere threat to close down the broadcasting studios, or alternatively by flooding the ether at a critical moment with some saccharine novelty.

The fact that the political Left Wing opposed the further development of radio amusements made Governments and the propertied classes the more ready to accept it. The Communists, for the dialectic of history on this curiously earth-like planet had produced a party deserving that name, strongly condemned the scheme. In their view it was pure Capitalist dope, calculated to prevent the otherwise inevitable dictatorship of the proletariat.

The increasing opposition of the Communists made it possible to buy off the opposition of their natural enemies, the priests and soldiers. It was arranged that religious services should in future occupy a larger proportion of broadcasting time, and that a tithe of all licensing fees should be allocated to the churches. The offer to broadcast the immaculate union, however, was rejected by the clerics. As an additional concession it was agreed that all married members of the staffs of Broadcasting Authorities must, on pain of dismissal, prove that they had never spent a night away from their wives (or husbands). It was also agreed to weed out all those B.A. employees who were suspected of sympathy with such disreputable ideals as pacifism and freedom of expression. The soldiers were further appeased by a state-subsidy for maternity, a tax on bachelors, and regular broadcasting of military propaganda.

During my last years on the Other Earth a system was invented by which a man could retire to bed for life and spend all his time receiving radio programmes. His nourishment and all his bodily functions were attended to by doctors and nurses attached to the Broadcasting Authority. In place of exercise he received periodic massage. Participation in the scheme was at first an expensive luxury, but its inventors hoped to make it at no distant date available to all. It was even expected that in time medical and menial attendants would cease to be necessary. A vast system of automatic food-production, and distribution of liquid pabulum by means of pipes leading to the mouths of the recumbent subjects, would be complemented by an intricate sewage system. Electric massage could be applied at will by pressing a button. Medical supervision would be displaced by an automatic endocrine-compensation system. This would enable the condition of the patient's blood to regulate itself automatically by tapping from the communal drug-pipes whatever chemicals were needed for correct physiological balance.

Even in the case of broadcasting itself the human element would no longer be needed, for all possible experiences would have been already recorded from the most exquisite living examples. These would be continuously broadcast in a great number of alternative programmes.

A few technicians and organizers might still be needed to superintend the system; but, properly distributed, their work would entail for each member of the World Broadcasting Authority's staff no more than a few hours of interesting activity each week.

Children, if future generations were required, would be produced ectogenetically. The World Director of Broadcasting would be requested to submit psychological and physiological specifications of the ideal "listening breed." Infants produced in accordance with this pattern would then be educated by special radio programmes to prepare them for adult radio life. They would never leave their cots, save to pass by stages to the full-sized beds of maturity. At the latter end of life, if medical science did not succeed in circumventing senility and death, the individual would at least be able to secure a painless end by pressing an appropriate button.

Enthusiasm for this astounding project spread rapidly in all civilized countries, but certain forces of reaction were bitterly opposed to it. The old-fashioned religious people and the militant nationalists both affirmed that it was man's glory to be active. The religious held that only in self-discipline, mortification of the flesh, and constant prayer, could the soul be fitted for eternal life. The nationalists of each country declared that their own people had been given a sacred trust to rule the baser kinds, and that in any case only the martial virtues could ensure the spirit's admittance to Valhalla.

Many of the great economic masters, though they had originally favoured radio-bliss in moderation as an opiate for the discontented workers, now turned against it. Their craving was for power; and for power they needed slaves whose labour they could command for their great industrial ventures. They therefore devised an instrument which was at once an opiate and a spur. By every method of propaganda they sought to rouse the passions of nationalism and racial hatred. They created, in fact, the "Other Fascism," complete with lies, with mystical cult of race and state, with scorn of reason, with praise of brutal mastery, with appeal at once to the vilest and to the generous motives of the deluded young.

Opposed to all these critics of radio-bliss, and equally opposed to radio-bliss itself, there was in each country a small and bewildered party which asserted that the true goal of human activity was the creation of a world-wide community of awakened and intelligently creative persons, related by mutual insight and respect, and by the common task of fulfilling the potentiality of the human spirit on earth. Much of their doctrine was a re-statement of the teachings of religious seers of a fine long past, but it had also been deeply influenced by contemporary science. This party, however, was misunderstood by the scientists, cursed by the clerics, ridiculed by the militarists, and ignored by the advocates of radio-bliss.

Now at this time economic confusion had been driving the great commercial empires of the Other Earth into more and more desperate competition for markets. These economic rivalries had combined with ancient tribal passions of fear and hate and pride to bring about an interminable series of war scares each of which threatened universal Armageddon.

In this situation the radio-enthusiasts pointed out that, if their policy were accepted, war would never occur, and on the other hand that, if a world-war broke out, their policy would be indefinitely postponed. They contrived a world-wide peace movement; and such was the passion for radio-bliss that the demand for peace swept all countries. An International Broadcasting Authority was at last founded, to propagate the radio gospel, compose the differences between the empires, and eventually to take over the sovereignty of the world.

Meanwhile the earnestly "religious" and the sincere militarists, rightly dismayed at the baseness of the motives behind the new international-alism, but in their own manner equally wrong-headed, determined to save the Other Men in spite of themselves by goading the peoples into war. All the forces of propaganda and financial corruption were heroically wielded to foment the passions of nationalism. Even so, the greed for radio-bliss was by now so general and so passionate, that the war party would never have succeeded had it not been for the wealth of the great armourers, and their experience in fomenting strife.

Trouble was successfully created between one of the older commercial empires and a certain state which had only recently adopted mechanical civilization, but was already a Great Power, and a Power in desperate need of markets. Radio, which formerly had been the main force making for cosmopolitanism, became suddenly in each country the main stimulus to nationalism. Morning, noon and night, every civilized people was assured that enemies, whose flavour was of course subhuman and foul, were plotting its destruction. Armament scares, spy stories, accounts of the barbarous and sadistic behaviour of neighbouring peoples, created in every country such uncritical suspicion and hate that war became inevitable. A dispute arose over the control of a frontier province. During those critical days Bvalltu and I happened to be in a large provincial town. I shall never forget how the populace plunged into almost maniacal hate. All thought of human brotherhood, and even of personal safety, was swept away by a savage blood-lust. Panic-stricken governments began projecting long-range rocket bombs at their dangerous neighbours. Within a few weeks several of the capitals of the Other Earth had been destroyed from the air. Each people now began straining every nerve to do more hurt than it received.

Of the horrors of this war, of the destruction of city after city, of the panic-stricken, starving hosts that swarmed into the open country, looting and killing, of the starvation and disease, of the disintegration of the social services, of the emergence of ruthless military dictatorships, of the steady or catastrophic decay of culture and of all decency and gentleness in personal relations, of this there is no need to speak in detail.

Instead, I shall try to account for the finality of the disaster which overtook the Other Men. My own human kind, in similar circumstances, would never, surely, have allowed itself to be so completely overwhelmed.

No doubt, we ourselves are faced with the possibility of a scarcely less destructive war; but, whatever the agony that awaits us, we shall almost
certainly recover. Foolish we may be, but we always manage to avoid
falling into the abyss of downright madness. At the last moment sanity
falteringly reasserts itself. Not so with the Other Men.

3. PROSPECTS OF THE RACE

The longer I stayed on the Other Earth, the more I suspected that
there must be some important underlying difference between this human
race and my own. In some sense the difference was obviously one of
balance. *Homo sapiens* was on the whole better integrated, more gifted
with common sense, less apt to fall into extravagance through mental dissociation.

Perhaps the most striking example of the extravagance of the Other
Men was the part played by religion in their more advanced societies. Religion was a much greater power than on my own planet; and the religious teachings of the prophets of old were able to kindle even my alien
and sluggish heart with fervour. Yet religion, as it occurred around me
in contemporary society, was far from edifying.

I must begin by explaining that in the development of religion on
the Other Earth gustatory sensation had played a very great part. Tribal
gods had of course been endowed with the taste-characters most moving to
the tribe's own members. Later, when monotheisms arose, descriptions of
God's power, his wisdom, his justice, his benevolence, were accompanied
by descriptions of his taste. In mystical literature God was often likened to
an ancient and mellow wine; and some reports of religious experience suggested that this gustatory ecstasy was in many ways akin to the reverent
zest of our own wine-tasters, savouring some rare vintage.

Unfortunately, owing to the diversity of gustatory human types, there
had seldom been any widespread agreement as to the taste of God. Religious wars had been waged to decide whether he was in the main sweet
or salt, or whether his preponderant flavour was one of the many gustatory
characters which my own race cannot conceive. Some teachers insisted that
only the feet could taste him, others only the hands or the mouth, others
that he could be experienced only in the subtle complex of gustatory
flavours known as the immaculate union, which was a sensual, and mainly
sexual, ecstasy induced by contemplation of intercourse with the deity.

Other teachers declared that, though God was indeed tasty, it was
not through any bodily instrument but to the naked spirit that his essence
was revealed; and that his was a flavour more subtle and delicious than
the flavour of the beloved, since it included all that was most fragrant and
spiritual in man, and infinitely more.

Some went so far as to declare that God should be thought of not as a person at all but as actually *being* this flavour. Bvalltu used to say, "Either God is the universe, or he is the flavour of creativity pervading all things."

Some ten or fifteen centuries earlier, when religion, so far as I could tell, was most vital, there were no churches or priesthoods; but every man's life was dominated by religious ideas to an extent which to me was almost incredible. Later, churches and priesthoods had returned, to play an important part in preserving what was now evidently a declining religious consciousness. Still later, a few centuries before the Industrial Revolution, institutional religion had gained such a hold on the most civilized peoples that three-quarters of their total income was spent on the upkeep of religious institutions. The working classes, indeed, who slaved for the owners in return for a mere pittance, gave much of their miserable earnings to the priests, and lived in more abject squalor than need have been.

Science and industry had brought one of those sudden and extreme revolutions of thought which were so characteristic of the Other Men. Nearly all the churches were destroyed or turned into temporary factories or industrial museums. Atheism, lately persecuted, became fashionable. All the best minds turned agnostic. More recently, however, apparently in horror at the effects of a materialistic culture which was far more cynical and blatant than our own, the most industrialized peoples began to turn once more to religion. A spiritistic foundation was provided for natural science. The old churches were re-sanctified, and so many new religious edifices were built that they were soon as plentiful as cinema houses with us. Indeed, the new churches gradually absorbed the cinema, and provided non-stop picture shows in which sensual orgies and ecclesiastical propaganda were skilfully blended.

At the time of my visit the churches had regained all their lost power. Radio had indeed at one time competed with them, but was successfully absorbed. They still refused to broadcast the immaculate union, which gained fresh prestige from the popular belief that it was too spiritual to be transmitted on the ether. The more advanced clerics, however, had agreed that if ever the universal system of "radio-bliss" was established, this difficulty might be overcome. Communism, meanwhile, still maintained its irreligious convention; but in the two great Communist countries the officially organized "irreligion" was becoming a religion in all but name. It had its institutions, its priesthood, its ritual, its morality, its system of absolution, its metaphysical doctrines, which, though devoutly materialistic, were none the less superstitious. And the flavour of deity had been displaced by the flavour of the proletariat.

Religion, then, was a very real force in the life of all these peoples. But there was something puzzling about their devoutness. In a sense it was sincere, and even beneficial; for in very small personal temptations and very obvious and stereotyped moral choices, the Other Men were far more conscientious than my own kind. But I discovered that the typical modern Other Man was conscientious only in conventional situations, and that in genuine moral sensibility he was strangely lacking. Thus, though practical generosity and superficial comradeship were more usual than with us, the most diabolic mental persecution was perpetrated with a clear conscience. The more sensitive had always to be on their guard. The deeper kinds of intimacy and mutual reliance were precarious and rare. In this passionately social world, loneliness dogged the spirit. People were constantly "getting together," but they never really got there. Everyone was terrified of being alone with himself; yet in company, in spite of the universal assumption of comradeship, these strange beings remained as remote from one another as the stars. For everyone searched his neighbour's eyes for the image of himself, and never saw anything else. Or if he did, he was outraged and terrified.

Another perplexing fact about the religious life of the Other Men at the time of my visit was this. Though all were devout, and blasphemy was regarded with horror, the general attitude to the deity was one of blasphemous commercialism. Men assumed that the flavour of deity could be bought for all eternity with money or with ritual. Further, the God whom they worshipped with the superb and heart-searching language of an earlier age was now conceived either as a just but jealous employer or as an indulgent parent, or else as sheer physical energy. The crowning vulgarity was the conviction that in no earlier age had religion been so widespread and so enlightened. It was almost universally agreed that the profound teachings of the prophetic era were only now being understood in the sense in which they had originally been intended by the prophets themselves. Contemporary writers and broadcasters claimed to be re-interpreting the scriptures to suit the enlightened religious needs of an age which called itself the Age of Scientific Religion.

Now behind all the complacency which characterized the civilization of the Other Men before the outbreak of the war I had often detected a vague restlessness and anxiety. Of course for the most part people went about their affairs with the same absorbed and self-satisfied interest as on my own planet. They were far too busy making a living, marrying, rearing families, trying to get the better of one another, to spare time for conscious doubt about the aim of life. Yet they had often the air of one who has forgotten some very important thing and is racking his brains to recover it, or of an aging preacher who uses the old stirring phrases without clear apprehension of their significance. Increasingly I suspected that this race, in spite of all its triumphs, was now living on the great ideas of its past, mouthing concepts that it no longer had the sensibility to understand, paying verbal homage to ideals which it could no longer sincerely will, and behaving within a system of institutions many of which could only be worked successfully by minds of a slightly finer temper.

These institutions, I suspected, must have been created by a race endowed not only with much greater intelligence, but with a much stronger and more comprehensive capacity for community than was now possible on the Other Earth. They seemed to be based on the assumption that men were on the whole kindly, reasonable and self-disciplined.

I had often questioned Bvalltu on this subject, but he had always turned my question aside. It will be remembered that, though I had access to all his thoughts so long as he did not positively wish to withhold them, he could always, if he made a special effort, think privately. I had long suspected that he was keeping something from me, when at last he told me the strange and tragic facts.

It was a few days after the bombardment of the metropolis of his country. Through Bvalltu's eyes and the goggles of his gas-mask I saw the results of that bombardment. We had missed the horror itself, but had attempted to return to the city to play some part in the rescue work. Little could be done. So great was the heat still radiated from the city's incandescent heart, that we could not penetrate beyond the first suburb. Even there, the streets were obliterated, choked with fallen buildings. Human bodies, crushed and charred, projected here and there from masses of tumbled masonry. Most of the population was hidden under the ruins. In the open spaces many lay gassed. Salvage parties impotently wandered. Between the smoke-clouds the Other Sun occasionally appeared, and even a daytime star.

After clambering among the ruins for some time, seeking vainly to give help, Bvalltu sat down. The devastation round about us seemed to "loosen his tongue," if I may use such a phrase to express a sudden frankness in his thinking toward myself. I had said something to the effect that a future age would look back on all this madness and destruction with amazement. He sighed through his gas-mask, and said, "My unhappy race has probably now doomed itself irrevocably." I expostulated; for though ours was about the fortieth city to be destroyed, there would surely some day be a recovery, and the race would at last pass through this crisis and go forward from strength to strength. Bvalltu then told me of the strange matters which, he said, he had often intended to tell me, but somehow he had always shunned doing so. Though many scientists and students of the contemporary world-society had now some vague suspicion of the truth, it was clearly known only to himself and a few others.

The species, he said, was apparently subject to strange and long-drawn-out fluctuations of nature, fluctuations which lasted for some twenty thousand years. All races in all climates seemed to manifest this vast rhythm of the spirit, and to suffer it simultaneously. Its cause was unknown. Though it seemed to be due to an influence affecting the whole planet at once, perhaps it actually radiated from a single starting point, but spread rapidly into all lands. Very recently an advanced scientist had suggested that it might be due to variations in the intensity of "cosmic rays." Geological evidence had established that such a fluctuation of cosmical radiation did occur, caused perhaps by variations in a neighbouring cluster of young stars. It was still doubtful whether the psychological rhythm and the astronomical rhythm coincided, but many facts pointed to the conclusion that when the rays were more violent the human spirit declined.

Bvalltu was not convinced by this story. On the whole he inclined to the opinion that the rhythmical waxing and waning of human mentality was due to causes nearer home. Whatever the true explanation, it was almost certain that a high degree of civilization had been attained many times in the past, and that some potent influence had over and over again damped down the mental vigour of the human race. In the troughs of these vast waves Other Man sank to a state of mental and spiritual dullness more abject than anything which my own race had ever known since it awoke from the sub-human. But at the wave's crest man's intellectual power, moral integrity, and spiritual insight seem to have risen to a pitch that we should regard as superhuman.

Again and again the race would emerge from savagery, and pass through barbarian culture into a phase of world-wide brilliance and sensibility. Whole populations would conceive simultaneously an ever-increasing capacity for generosity, self-knowledge, self-discipline, for dispassionate and penetrating thought and uncontaminated religious feeling.

Consequently within a few centuries the whole world would blossom with free and happy societies. Average human beings would attain an unprecedented clarity of mind, and by massed action do away with all grave social injustices and private cruelties. Subsequent generations, inherently sound, and blessed with a favourable environment, would create a world-wide utopia of awakened beings.

Presently a general loosening of fibre would set in. The golden age would be followed by a silver age. Living on the achievements of the past, the leaders of thought would lose themselves in a jungle of subtlety, or fall exhausted into mere slovenliness. At the same time moral sensibility would decline. Men would become on the whole less sincere, less self-searching, less sensitive to the needs of others, in fact less capable of community. Social machinery, which had worked well so long as citizens attained a certain level of humanity, would be dislocated by injustice and corruption. Tyrants and tyrannical oligarchies would set about destroying liberty. Hate-mad submerged classes would give them good excuse. Little by little, though the material benefits of civilization might smoulder on for centuries, the flame of the spirit would die down into a mere flicker in a few isolated individuals. Then would come sheer barbarism, followed by the trough of almost sub-human savagery.

On the whole there seemed to have been a higher achievement on the more recent crests of the wave than on those of the "geological" past. So at least some anthropologists persuaded themselves. It was confidently believed that the present apex of civilization was the most brilliant of all, that its best was as yet to come, and that by means of its unique scientific knowledge it would discover how to preserve the mentality of the race from a recurrence of deterioration.

The present condition of the species was certainly exceptional. In no earlier recorded cycle had science and mechanization advanced to such lengths. So far as could be inferred from the fragmentary relics of the previous cycle, mechanical invention had never passed beyond the crude machinery known in our own mid-nineteenth century. The still earlier cycles, it was believed, stagnated at even earlier stages in their industrial revolutions.

Now though it was generally assumed in intellectual circles that the best was yet to be, Bvalltu and his friends were convinced that the crest of the wave had already occurred many centuries ago. To most men, of course, the decade before the war had seemed better and more civilized than any earlier age. In their view civilization and mechanization were almost identical, and never before had there been such a triumph of mechanization. The benefits of a scientific civilization were obvious. For the fortunate class there was more comfort, better health, increased stature, a prolongation of youth, and a system of technical knowledge so vast and intricate that no man could know more than its outline or some tiny corner of its detail. Moreover, increased communications had brought all the peoples into contact. Local idiosyncrasies were fading out before the radio, the cinema, and the gramophone. In comparison with these hopeful signs it was easily overlooked that the human constitution, though strengthened by improved conditions, was intrinsically less stable than formerly. Certain disintegrative diseases were slowly but surely increasing. In particular, diseases of the nervous system were becoming more common and more pernicious. Cynics used to say that the mental hospitals would soon outnumber even the churches. But the cynics were only jesters. It was almost universally agreed that, in spite of wars and economic troubles and social upheavals, all was now well, and the future would be better.

The truth, said Bvalltu, was almost certainly otherwise. There was, as I had suspected, unmistakable evidence that the average of intelligence and of moral integrity throughout the world had declined; and they would probably continue to do so. Already the race was living on its past. All the great seminal ideas of the modern world had been conceived centuries ago. Since then, world-changing applications of these ideas had indeed been made; but none of these sensational inventions had depended on the extreme kind of penetrating and comprehensive intuition which had changed the whole course of thought in an earlier age. Recently there had been,

Bvalltu admitted, a spate of revolutionary scientific discoveries and theories, but not one of them, he said, contained any really novel principle. They were all re-combinations of familiar principles. Scientific method, invented some centuries ago, was so fertile a technique that it might well continue to yield rich fruit for centuries to come even in the hands of workers incapable of any high degree of originality.

But it was not in the field of science so much as in moral and practical activity that the deterioration of mental calibre was most evident. I myself, with Bvalltu's aid, had learnt to appreciate to some extent the literature of that amazing period, many centuries earlier, when every country seemed to blossom with art, philosophy and religion; when people after people had changed its whole social and political order so as to secure a measure of freedom and prosperity to all men; when state after state had courageously disarmed, risking destruction but reaping peace and prosperity; when police forces were disbanded, prisons turned into libraries or colleges; when weapons and even locks and keys came to be known only as museum pieces; when the four great established priesthoods of the world had exposed their own mysteries, given their wealth to the poor, and led the triumphant campaign for community; or had taken to agriculture, handicrafts, teaching, as befitted humble supporters of the new priestless, faithless, Godless religion of world-wide community and inarticulate worship.

After some five hundred years locks and keys, weapons and doctrines, began to return. The golden age left behind it only a lovely and incredible tradition, and a set of principles which, though now sadly misconceived, were still the best influences in a distraught world.

Those scientists who attributed mental deterioration to the increase of cosmic rays affirmed that if the race had discovered science many centuries earlier, when it had still before it the period of greatest vitality, all would have been well. It would soon have mastered the social problems which industrial civilization entails. It would have created not merely a "mediaeval" but a highly mechanized utopia. It would almost certainly have discovered how to cope with the excess of cosmic rays and prevent deterioration. But science had come too late.

Bvalltu, on the other hand, suspected that deterioration was due to some factor in human nature itself. He was inclined to believe that it was a consequence of civilization, that in changing the whole environment of the human species, seemingly for the better, science had unwittingly brought about a state of affairs hostile to spiritual vigour. He did not pretend to know whether the disaster was caused by the increase of artificial food, or the increased nervous strain of modern conditions, or interference with natural selection, or the softer upbringing of children, or to some other cause. Perhaps it should be attributed to none of these comparatively recent influences; for evidence did suggest that deterioration had set in at the very beginning of the scientific age, if not even earlier. It might be that some mysterious factor in the conditions of the golden age itself had started the rot. It might even be, he suggested, that genuine community generated its own poison, that the young human being, brought up in a perfected society, in a veritable "city of God" on earth, must inevitably revolt toward moral and intellectual laziness, toward romantic individualism and sheer devilment; and that, once this disposition had taken root, science and a mechanized civilization had augmented the spiritual decay.

Shortly before I left the Other Earth a geologist discovered a fossil diagram of a very complicated radio set. It appeared to be a lithographic plate which had been made some ten million years earlier. The highly developed society which produced it had left no other trace. This find was a shock to the intelligent world; but the comforting view was spread abroad that some non-human and less hardy species had long ago attained a brief flicker of civilization. It was agreed that man, once he had reached such a height of culture, would never have fallen from it.

In Bvalltu's view man had climbed approximately to the same height time after time, only to be undone by some hidden consequence of his own achievement.

When Bvalltu propounded this theory, among the ruins of his native city, I suggested that some time, if not this time, man would successfully pass this critical point in his career. Bvalltu then spoke of another matter which seemed to indicate that we were witnessing the final act of this long-drawn-out and repetitive drama.

It was known to scientists that, owing to the weak gravitational hold of their world, the atmosphere, already scant, was steadily deceasing. Sooner or later humanity would have to face the problem of stopping this constant leakage of precious oxygen. Hitherto life had successfully adapted itself to the progressive rarefaction of atmosphere, but the human physique had already reached the limit of adaptability in this respect. If the loss were not soon checked, the race would inevitably decline. The only hope was that some means to deal with the atmospheric problem would be discovered before the onset of the next age of barbarism. There had only been a slight possibility that this would be achieved. This slender hope the war had destroyed by setting the clock of scientific research back for a century just at the time when human nature itself was deteriorating and might never again be able to tackle so difficult a problem.

The thought of the disaster which almost certainly lay in wait for the Other Men threw me into a horror of doubt about the universe in which such a thing could happen. That a whole world of intelligent beings could be destroyed was not an unfamiliar idea to me; but there is a great difference between an abstract possibility and a concrete and inescapable danger.

On my native planet, whenever I had been dismayed by the suffering and the futility of individuals, I had taken comfort in the thought that at least the massed effect of all our blind striving must be the slow but glorious awakening of the human spirit. This hope, this certainty, had been the one sure consolation. But now I saw that there was no guarantee of any such triumph. It seemed that the universe, or the maker of the universe, must be indifferent to the fate of worlds. That there should be endless struggle and suffering and waste must of course be accepted; and gladly, for these were the very soil in which the spirit grew. But that all struggle should be finally, absolutely vain, that a whole world of sensitive spirits fail and die, must be sheer evil. In my horror it seemed to me that Hate must be the Star Maker.

Not so to Bvaltu. "Even if the powers destroy us," he said, "who are we, to condemn them? As well might a fleeting word judge the speaker that forms it. Perhaps they use us for their own high ends, use our strength and our weakness, our joy and our pain, in some theme inconceivable to us, and excellent." But I protested, "What theme could justify such waste, such futility? And how can we help judging; and how otherwise can we judge than by the light of our own hearts, by which we judge ourselves? It would be base to praise the Star Maker, knowing that he was too insensitive to care about the fate of his worlds." Bvaltu was silent in his mind for a moment. Then he looked up, searching among the smoke-clouds for a daytime star. And then he said to me in his mind, "If he saved all the worlds, but tormented just one man, would you forgive him? Or if he was a little harsh only to one stupid child? What has our pain to do with it, or our failure? Star Maker! It is a good word, though we can have no notion of its meaning. Oh, Star Maker, even if you destroy me, I must praise you. Even if you torture my dearest. Even if you torment and waste all your lovely worlds, the little figments of your imagination, yet I must praise you. For if you do so, it must be right. In me it would be wrong, but in you it *must* be right."

He looked down once more upon the ruined city, then continued, "And if after all there is no Star Maker, if the great company of galaxies leapt into being of their own accord, and even if this little nasty world of ours is the only habitation of the spirit anywhere among the stars, and this world doomed, even so, even so, I must praise. But if there is no Star Maker, what can it be that I praise? I do not know. I will call it only the sharp tang and savour of existence. But to call it this is to say little."

CHAPTER IV

I TRAVEL AGAIN

I MUST have spent several years on the Other Earth, a period far longer than I intended when I first encountered one of its peasants trudging through the fields. Often I longed to be at home again. I used to wonder with painful anxiety how those dear to me were faring, and what changes I should discover if I were ever to return. It was surprising to me that in spite of my novel and crowded experiences on the Other Earth thoughts of home should continue to be so insistent. It seemed but a moment since I was sitting on the hill looking at the lights of our suburb. Yet several years had passed. The children would be altered almost beyond recognition. Their mother? How would she have fared?

Bvalltu was partly responsible for my long spell on the Other Earth. He would not hear of my leaving till we had each attained a real understanding of the other's world. I constantly stimulated his imagination to picture as clearly as possible the life of my own planet, and he had discovered in it much the same medley of the splendid and the ironical as I had discovered in his. In fact he was far from agreeing with me that his world was on the whole the more grotesque.

The call to impart information was not the only consideration that bound me to Bvalltu. I had come to feel a very strong friendship for him. In the early days of our partnership there had sometimes been strains. Though we were both civilized human beings, who tried always to behave with courtesy and generosity, our extreme intimacy did sometimes fatigue us. I used, for instance, to find his passion for the gustatory fine art of his world very wearisome. He would sit by the hour passing his sensitive fingers over the impregnated cords to seize the taste sequences that had for him such great subtlety of form and symbolism. I was at first intrigued, then aesthetically stirred; but in spite of his patient help I was never at this early stage able to enter fully and spontaneously into the aesthetic of taste. Sooner or later I was fatigued or bored. Then again, I was impatient of his periodic need for sleep. Since I was disembodied, I myself felt no such need. I could, of course, disengage myself from Bvalltu and roam the world alone; but I was often exasperated by the necessity of breaking off the day's interesting experiences merely in order to afford my host's body time to recuperate. Bvalltu, for his part, at least in the early days of our partnership, was inclined to resent my power of watching his dreams. For though, while awake, he could withdraw his thoughts from my observation, asleep he was helpless. Naturally I very soon learned to refrain from exercising this power; and he, on his side, as our intimacy developed into mutual respect, no longer cherished this privacy so strictly.

In time each of us came to feel that to taste the flavour of life in isolation from the other was to miss half its richness and subtlety. Neither could entirely trust his own judgement or his own motives unless the other were present to offer relentless though friendly criticism.

We hit upon a plan for satisfying at once our friendship, his interest in my world, and my own longing for home. Why should we not somehow contrive to visit my planet together? I had travelled thence; why should we not both travel thither? After a spell on my planet, we could proceed upon the larger venture, again together.

For this end we had to attack two very different tasks. The technique of interstellar travel, which I had achieved only by accident and in a very haphazard manner, must now be thoroughly mastered. Also we must somehow locate my native planetary system in the astronomical maps of the Other Men.

This geographical, or rather cosmographical, problem proved insoluble. Do what I would, I could provide no data for the orientation. The attempt, however, led us to an amazing, and for me a terrifying discovery. I had travelled not only through space but through time itself. In the first place, it appeared that, in the very advanced astronomy of the Other Men, stars as mature as the Other Sun and as my own Sun were rare. Yet in terrestrial astronomy this type of star was known to be the commonest of all throughout the galaxy. How could this be? Then I made another perplexing discovery. The galaxy as known to the Other Astronomers proved to be strikingly different from my recollection of the galaxy as known to our own astronomers. According to the Other Men the great star-system was much less flattened than we observe it to be. Our astronomers tell us that it is like a circular biscuit five times as wide as it is thick. In their view it was more like a bun. I myself had often been struck by the width and indefiniteness of the Milky Way in the sky of the Other Earth. I had been surprised, too, that the Other Astronomers believed the galaxy to contain much gaseous matter not yet condensed into stars. To our astronomers it seemed to be almost wholly stellar.

Had I then travelled unwittingly much further than I had supposed, and actually entered some other and younger galaxy? Perhaps in my period of darkness, when the rubies and amethysts and diamonds of the sky had all vanished, I had actually sped across intergalactic space. This seemed at first the only explanation, but certain facts forced us to discard it in favour of one even stranger.

Comparison of the astronomy of the Other Men with my fragmentary recollections of our own astronomy convinced me that the whole cosmos of galaxies known to them differed from the whole cosmos of galaxies known to us. The average form of the galaxies was much more rotund and much more gaseous, in fact much more primitive, for them than for us.

Moreover, in the sky of the Other Earth several galaxies were so near as to be prominent smudges of light even for the naked eye. And astronomers had shown that many of these so-called "universes" were much closer to the home "universe" than the nearest known in our astronomy.

The truth that now flashed on Bvalltu and me was indeed bewildering. Everything pointed to the fact that I had somehow travelled up the river of time and landed myself at a date in the remote past, when the great majority of the stars were still young. The startling nearness of so many galaxies in the astronomy of the Other Men could be explained on the theory of the "expanding universe." Well I knew that this dramatic theory was but tentative and very far from satisfactory; but at least here was one more striking bit of evidence to suggest that it must be in *some* sense true. In early epochs the galaxies would of course be congested together. There could be no doubt that I had been transported to a world which had reached the human stage very long before my native planet had been plucked from the sun's womb.

The full realization of my temporal remoteness from my home reminded me of a fact, or at least a probability, which, oddly enough, I had long ago forgotten. Presumably I was dead. I now desperately craved to be home again. Home was all the while so vivid, so near. Even though its distance was to be counted in parsecs and in aeons, it was always at hand. Surely, if I could only *wake*, I should find myself there on our hill-top again. But there was no waking. Through Bvalltu's eyes I was studying star-maps and pages of outlandish script. When he looked up, I saw standing opposite us a caricature of a human being, with a frog-like face that was scarcely a face at all, and with the thorax of a pouter-pigeon, naked save for a greenish down. Red silk knickers crowned the spindle shanks that were enclosed in green silk stockings. This creature, which, to the terrestrial eye, was simply a monster, passed on the Other Earth as a young and beautiful woman. And I myself, observing her through Bvalltu's benevolent eyes, recognized her as indeed beautiful. To a mind habituated to the Other Earth her features and her every gesture spoke of intelligence and wit. Clearly, if I could admire such a woman, I myself must have changed.

It would be tedious to tell of the experiments by which we acquired and perfected the art of controlled flight through interstellar space. Suffice it that, after many adventures, we learned to soar up from the planet whenever we wished, and to direct our course, by mere acts of volition, hither and thither among the stars. We seemed to have much greater facility and accuracy when we worked together than when either ventured into space by himself. Our community of mind seemed to strengthen us even for spatial locomotion.

It was a very strange experience to find oneself in the depth of space, surrounded only by darkness and the stars, yet to be all the while in close personal contact with an unseen companion. As the dazzling lamps of heaven flashed past us, we would think to one another about our experiences, or debate our plans, or share our memories of our native worlds. Sometimes we used my language, sometimes his. Sometimes we needed no words at all, but merely shared the flow of imagery in our two minds.

The sport of disembodied flight among the stars must surely be the most exhilarating of all athletic exercises. It was not without danger; but its danger, as we soon discovered, was psychological, not physical. In our bodiless state, collision with celestial objects mattered little. Sometimes, in the early stages of our adventure, we plunged by accident headlong into a star. Its interior would, of course, be inconceivably hot, but we experienced merely brilliance.

The psychological dangers of the sport were grave. We soon discovered that disheartenment, mental fatigue, fear, all tended to reduce our powers of movement. More than once we found ourselves immobile in space, like a derelict ship on the ocean; and such was the fear roused by this plight that there was no possibility of moving till, having experienced the whole gamut of despair, we passed through indifference and on into philosophic calm.

A still graver danger, but one which trapped us only once, was mental conflict. A serious discord of purpose over our future plans reduced us not only to immobility but to terrifying mental disorder. Our perceptions became confused. Hallucinations tricked us. The power of coherent thought vanished. After a spell of delirium, filled with an overwhelming sense of impending annihilation, we found ourselves back on the Other Earth; Bvalltu in his own body, lying in bed as he had left it, I once more a disembodied view-point floating somewhere over the planet's surface. Both were in a state of insane terror, from which we took long to recover. Months passed before we renewed our partnership and our adventure.

Long afterwards we learned the explanation of this painful incident. Seemingly we had attained such a deep mental accord that, when conflict arose, it was more like dissociation within a single mind than discord between two separate individuals. Hence its serious consequences.

As our skill in disembodied flight increased, we found intense pleasure in sweeping hither and thither among the stars. We tasted the delights at once of skating and of flight. Time after time, for sheer joy, we traced huge figures-of-eight in and out around the two partners of a "double star." Sometimes we stayed motionless for long periods to watch at close quarters the waxing and waning of a variable. Often we plunged into a congested cluster, and slid amongst its suns like a car gliding among the lights of a city. Often we skimmed over billowy and palely luminous surfaces of gas, or among feathery shreds and prominences; or plunged into mist, to find ourselves in a world of featureless dawn light. Sometimes, without warning, dark continents of dust engulfed us, blotting out the universe. Once, as we were traversing a populous region of the heaven, a star suddenly blazed into exaggerated splendour, becoming a "nova." As it was apparently surrounded by a cloud of non-luminous gas, we actually saw the expanding sphere of light which was radiated by the star's explosion. Travelling outward at light's speed, it was visible by reflection from the surrounding gas, so that it appeared like a swelling balloon of light, fading as it spread.

These were but a few of the stellar spectacles that delighted us while we easefully skated, as on swallow wings, hither and thither among the neighbours of the Other Sun. This was during our period of apprenticeship to the craft of interstellar flight. When we had become proficient we passed further afield, and learned to travel so fast that, as on my own earlier and involuntary flight, the forward and the hinder stars took colour, and presently all was dark. Not only so, but we reached to that more spiritual vision, also experienced on my earlier voyage, in which these vagaries of physical light are overcome.

On one occasion our flight took us outwards toward the limits of the galaxy, and into the emptiness beyond. For some time the near stars had become fewer and fewer. The hinder hemisphere of sky was now crowded with faint lights, while in front of us lay starless blackness, unrelieved save by a few isolated patches of scintillation, a few detached fragments of the galaxy, or planetary "sub-galaxies." Apart from these the dark was featureless, save for half a dozen of the vague flecks which we knew to be the nearest of the alien galaxies.

Awed by this spectacle, we stayed long motionless in the void. It was indeed a stirring experience to see spread out before us a whole "universe," containing a billion stars and perhaps thousands of inhabited worlds; and to know that each tiny fleck in the black sky was itself another such "universe," and that millions more of them were invisible only because of their extreme remoteness.

What was the significance of this physical immensity and complexity? By itself, plainly, it constituted nothing but sheer futility and desolation. But with awe and hope we told ourselves that it promised an even greater complexity and subtlety and diversity of the psychical. This alone could justify it. But this formidable promise, though inspiring, was also terrifying.

Like a nestling that peers over the nest's rim for the first time, and then shrinks back from the great world into its tiny home, we had emerged beyond the confines of that little nest of stars which for so long, but falsely, men called "the universe." And now we sank back to bury ourselves once more in the genial precincts of our native galaxy.

As our experiences had raised many theoretical problems which we could not solve without further study of astronomy, we now decided to return to the Other Earth; but after long and fruitless search we realized that we had completely lost our bearings. The stars were all much alike, save that few in this early epoch were as old and temperate as the Other Sun. Searching at random, but at high speed, we found neither Bvalltu's planet nor mine, nor any other solar system. Frustrated, we came to rest once more in the void to consider our plight. On every side the ebony of the sky, patterned with diamonds, confronted us with an enigma. Which spark of all this star-dust was the Other Sun? As was usual in the sky of this early epoch, streaks of nebular matter were visible in all directions; but their shapes were unfamiliar, and useless for orientation.

The fact that we were lost among the stars did not distress us. We were exhilarated by our adventure, and each was a cause of good spirits in the other. Our recent experiences had quickened our mental life, still further organizing our two minds together. Each was still at most times conscious of the other and of himself as separate beings; but the pooling or integration of our memories and of our temperaments had now gone so far that our distinctness was often forgotten. Two disembodied minds, occupying the same visual position, possessing the same memories and desires, and often performing the same mental acts at the same time, can scarcely be conceived as distinct beings. Yet, strangely enough, this growing identity was complicated by an increasingly intense mutual realization and comradeship.

Our penetration of one another's minds brought to each not merely addition but multiplication of mental riches; for each knew inwardly not only himself and the other but also the contrapuntal harmony of each in relation to the other. Indeed, in some sense which I cannot precisely describe, our union of minds brought into being a third mind, as yet intermittent, but more subtly conscious than either of us in the normal state. Each of us, or rather both of us together, "woke up" now and then to be this superior spirit. All the experiences of each took on a new significance in the light of the other; and our two minds together became a new, more penetrating, and more self-conscious mind. In this state of heightened lucidity we, or rather the new I, began deliberately to explore the psychological possibilities of other types of beings and intelligent worlds. With new penetration I distinguished in myself and in Bvalltu those attributes which were essential to the spirit and those mere accidents imposed on each by his peculiar world. This imaginative venture was soon to prove itself a method, and a very potent method, of cosmological research.

We now began to realize more clearly a fact that we had long suspected. In my previous interstellar voyage, which brought me to the Other Earth, I had unwittingly employed two distinct methods of travel, the method of disembodied flight through space and a method which I shall call "psychical attraction." This consisted of telepathic projection of the mind directly into some alien world, remote perhaps in time and space, but mentally "in tune" with the explorer's own mind at the time of the venture. Evidently it was this method that had really played the chief part in directing me to the Other Earth. The remarkable similarities of our two races had set up a strong "psychical attraction" which had been far more potent than all my random interstellar wanderings. It was this method that Bvalltu and I were now to practice and perfect.

Presently we noticed that we were no longer at rest but slowly drifting. We had also a queer sense that, though we were seemingly isolated in a vast desert of stars and nebulae, we were in fact in some kind of mental proximity with unseen intelligences. Concentrating on this sense of presence, we found that our drift accelerated; and that, if we tried by a violent act of volition to change its course, we inevitably swung back into the original direction as soon as our effort ceased. Soon our drift became a headlong flight. Once more the forward stars turned violet, the hinder red. Once more all vanished.

In absolute darkness and silence we debated our situation. Clearly we were now passing through space more quickly than light itself. Perhaps we were also, in some incomprehensible manner, traversing time. Meanwhile that sense of the proximity of other beings became more and more insistent, though no less confused.

Then once again the stars appeared. Though they streamed past us like flying sparks, they were colourless and normal. One brilliant light lay right ahead of us. It waxed, became a dazzling splendour, then visibly a disc. With an effort of will we decreased our speed, then cautiously we swung round this sun, searching. To our delight, it proved to be attended by several of the grains that may harbour life. Guided by our unmistakable sense of mental presence, we selected one of these planets, and slowly descended toward it.

CHAPTER V

WORLDS INNUMERABLE

I. THE DIVERSITY OF WORLDS

THE planet on which we now descended after our long flight among the stars was the first of many to be visited. In some we stayed, according to the local calendar, only a few weeks, in others several years, housed together in the mind of some native. Often when the time came for our departure our host would accompany us for subsequent adventures. As we passed from world to world, as experience was piled upon experience like geological strata, it seemed that this strange tour of worlds was lasting for many lifetimes. Yet thoughts of our own home-planets were constantly with us. Indeed, in my case it was not till I found myself thus exiled that I came to realize fully the little jewel of personal union that I had left behind. I had to comprehend each world as best I could by reference to the remote world where my own life had happened, and above all by the touchstone of that common life that she and I had made together.

Before trying to describe, or rather suggest, the immense diversity of worlds which I entered, I must say a few words about the movement of the adventure itself. After the experiences which I have just recorded it was clear that the method of disembodied flight was of little use. It did indeed afford us extremely vivid perception of the visible features of our galaxy; and we often used it to orientate ourselves when we had made some fresh discovery by the method of psychological attraction. But since it gave us freedom only of space and not of time, and since, moreover, planetary systems were so very rare, the method of sheer random physical flight alone was almost infinitely unlikely to produce results. Psychical attraction, however, once we had mastered it, proved very effective. This method depended on the imaginative reach of our own minds. At first, when our imaginative power was strictly limited by experience of our own worlds, we could make contact only with worlds closely akin to our own. Moreover, in this novitiate stage of our work we invariably came upon these worlds when they were passing through the same spiritual crisis as that which underlies the plight of *Homo sapiens* today. It appeared that, for to enter any world at all, there had to be a deep-lying likeness or identity in ourselves and our hosts.

As we passed on from world to world we greatly increased our understanding of the principles underlying our venture, and our powers of applying them. Further, in each world that we visited we sought out a new collaborator, to give us insight into his world and to extend our imaginative reach for further exploration of the galaxy. This "snowball" method by which our company was increased was of great importance, since it magnified our powers. In the final stages of the exploration we made discoveries which might well be regarded as infinitely beyond the range of any single and unaided human mind.

At the outset Bvalltu and I assumed that we were embarking on a purely private adventure; and later, as we gathered helpers, we still believed that we ourselves were the sole initiators of cosmical exploration. But after a while we came in psychical contact with another group of cosmical explorers, natives of worlds as yet unknown to us. With these adventurers, after difficult and often distressing experiments, we joined forces, entering first into intimate community, and later into that strange mental union which Bvalltu and I had already experienced together in some degree on our first voyage among the stars.

When we had encountered many more such groups, we realized that, though each little expedition had made a lonely start, all were destined sooner or later to come together. For, no matter how alien from one another at the outset, each group gradually acquired such far-reaching imaginative power that sooner or later it was sure to make contact with others.

In time it became clear that we, individual inhabitants of a host of other worlds, were playing a small part in one of the great movements by which the cosmos was seeking to know itself, and even see beyond itself.

In saying this I do not for a moment claim that, because I have shared in this vast process of cosmical self-discovery, the story which I have to tell is true in a fully literal sense. Plainly it does not deserve to be taken as part of the absolute objective truth about the cosmos. I, the human individual, can only in a most superficial and falsifying way participate in the superhuman experience of that communal "I" which was supported by the innumerable explorers. This book must needs be a ludicrously false caricature of our actual adventure. But further, though we were and are a multitude drawn from a multitude of spheres, we represent only a tiny fraction of the diversity of the whole cosmos. Thus even the supreme moment of our experience, when it seemed to us that we had penetrated to the very heart of reality, must in fact have given us no more than a few shreds of truth, and these not literal but symbolic.

My account of that part of my adventure which brought me into contact with worlds of more or less human type may be fairly accurate; but that which deals with more alien spheres must be far from the truth. The Other Earth I have probably described with little more falsehood than our historians commit in telling of the past ages of *Homo sapiens*. But of the less human worlds, and the many fantastic kinds of beings which we encountered up and down the galaxy and throughout the whole cosmos, and even beyond it, I shall perforce make statements which, literally regarded, must be almost wholly false. I can only hope that they have the kind of truth that we sometimes find in myths.

Since we were now free of space, we ranged with equal ease over the nearer and the remoter tracts of this galaxy. That we did not till much later make contact with minds in other galaxies was not due to any limitations imposed by space, but seemingly to our own inveterate parochialism, to a strange limitation of our own interest, which for long rendered us inhospitable to the influence of worlds lying beyond the confines of the Milky Way. I shall say more of this curious restriction when I come to describe how we did at last outgrow it.

Along with freedom of space we had freedom of time. Some of the worlds that we explored in this early phase of our adventure ceased to exist long before my native planet was formed; others were its contemporaries; others were not born till the old age of our galaxy, when the Earth had been destroyed, and a large number of the stars had already been extinguished.

As we searched up and down time and space, discovering more and more of the rare grains called planets, as we watched race after race struggle to a certain degree of lucid consciousness, only to succumb to some external accident or, more often, to some flaw in its own nature, we were increasingly oppressed by a sense of the futility, the planlessness of the cosmos. A few worlds did indeed wake to such lucidity that they passed beyond our ken. But several of the most brilliant of these occurred in the earliest epoch of the galactic story; and nothing that we could as yet discover in the later phases of the cosmos suggested that any galaxies, still less the cosmos as a whole, had at last come (or will at last come) more under the sway of the awakened spirit than they were during the epoch of those early brilliant worlds. Not till a much later stage of our enquiry were we fitted to discover the glorious but ironical and heart-rending climax for which this vast proliferation of worlds was but a prologue.

In the first phase of our adventure, when, as I have said, our powers of telepathic exploration were incomplete, every world that we entered turned out to be in the throes of the same spiritual crisis as that which we knew so well on our native planets. This crisis I came to regard as having two aspects. It was at once a moment in the spirit's struggle to become capable of true community on a world-wide scale; and it was a stage in the age-long task of achieving the right, the finally appropriate, the spiritual attitude toward the universe.

In every one of these "chrysalis" worlds thousands of millions of persons were flashing into existence, one after the other, to drift gropingly about for a few instants of cosmical time before they were extinguished. Most were capable, at least in some humble degree, of the intimate kind of community which is personal affection; but for nearly all of them a stranger was ever a thing to fear and hate. And even their intimate loving was inconstant and lacking in insight. Nearly always they were intent merely on seeking for themselves respite from fatigue or boredom, fear or hunger. Like my own race, they never fully awoke from the primeval sleep of the subman. Only a few here and there, now and then, were solaced, goaded, or tortured by moments of true wakefulness. Still fewer attained a clear and constant vision, even of some partial aspect of truth; and their half-truths they nearly always took to be absolute. Propagating their little partial truths, they bewildered and misdirected their fellow mortals as much as they helped them.

Each individual spirit, in nearly all these worlds, attained at some point in life some lowly climax of awareness and of spiritual integrity, only to sink slowly or catastrophically back into nothingness. Or so it seemed. As in my own world, so in all these others, lives were spent in pursuit of shadowy ends that remained ever just round the corner. There were vast tracts of boredom and frustration, with here and there some rare bright joy. There were ecstasies of personal triumph, of mutual intercourse and love, of intellectual insight, of aesthetic creation. There were also religious ecstasies; but these, like all else in these worlds, were obscured by false interpretations. There were crazy ecstasies of hate and cruelty, felt against individuals and against groups. Sometimes during this early phase of our adventure we were so distressed by the incredible bulk of suffering and of cruelty up and down the worlds that our courage failed, our telepathic powers were disordered, and we slipped toward madness.

Yet most of these worlds were really no worse than our own. Like us, they had reached that stage when the spirit, half awakened from brutishness and very far from maturity, can suffer most desperately and behave most cruelly. And like us, these tragic but vital worlds, visited in our early adventures, were agonized by the inability of their minds to keep pace with changing circumstance. They were always behindhand, always applying old concepts and old ideals inappropriately to novel situations. Like us, they were constantly tortured by their hunger for a degree of community which their condition demanded but their poor, cowardly, selfish spirits could by no means attain. Only in couples and in little circles of companions could they support true community, the communion of mutual insight and respect and love. But in their tribes and nations they conceived all too easily the sham community of the pack, baying in unison of fear and hate.

Particularly in one respect these races were recognizably our kin. Each had risen by a strange mixture of violence and gentleness. The apostles of violence and the apostles of gentleness swayed them this way and that. At the time of our visit many of these worlds were in the throes of a crisis of this conflict. In the recent past, loud lip-service had been paid to gentleness and tolerance and freedom; but the policy had failed, because there was no sincere purpose in it, no conviction of the spirit, no true experience of respect for individual personality. All kinds of self-seeking and vindictiveness had flourished, secretly at first, then openly as shameless individualism. Then at last, in rage, the peoples turned away from individualism and plunged into the cult of the herd. At the same time, in disgust with the failure of gentleness, they began openly to praise violence, and the ruthlessness of the god-sent hero and of the armed tribe. Those who thought they believed in gentleness built up armaments for their tribes against those foreign tribes whom they accused of believing in violence. The highly developed technique of violence threatened to destroy civilization; year by year gentleness lost ground. Few could understand that their world must be saved, not by violence in the short run, but by gentleness in the long run. And still fewer could see that, to be effective, gentleness must be a religion; and that lasting peace can never come till the many have wakened to the lucidity of consciousness which, in all these worlds, only the few could as yet attain.

If I were to describe in detail every world that we explored, this book would develop into a world of libraries. I can give only a few pages to the many types of worlds encountered in this early stage of our adventure, up and down the whole breadth and length and the whole duration of our galaxy. Some of these types had apparently very few instances; others occurred in scores or hundreds.

The most numerous of all classes of intelligent worlds is that which includes the planet familiar to readers of this book. *Homo sapiens* has recently flattered and frightened himself by conceiving that, though perhaps he is not the sole intelligence in the cosmos, he is at least unique, and that worlds suited to intelligent life of any kind must be extremely rare. This view proves ludicrously false. In comparison with the unimaginable number of the stars intelligent worlds are indeed very rare; but we discovered some thousands of worlds much like the Earth and possessed by beings of essentially human kind, though superficially they were often unlike the type that we call human. The Other Men were amongst the most obviously human. But in a later stage of our adventure, when our research was no longer restricted to worlds that had reached the familiar spiritual crisis, we stumbled on a few planets inhabited by races almost identical with *Homo sapiens,* or rather with the creature that *Homo sapiens* was in the earliest phase of his existence. These most human worlds we had not encountered earlier because, by one accident or another, they were destroyed before reaching the stage of our own mentality.

Long after we had succeeded in extending our research from our peers among the worlds to our inferiors in mental rank we remained unable to make any sort of contact with beings who had passed wholly beyond the attainment of *Homo sapiens*. Consequently, though we traced the history of many worlds through many epochs, and saw many reach a catastrophic end, or sink into stagnation and inevitable decline, there were a few with which, do what we would, we lost touch just at that moment when they seemed ripe for a leap forward into some more developed mentality. Not till a much later stage of our adventure, when our corporate being had itself been enriched by the influx of many superior spirits, were we able to pick up once more the threads of these most exalted world-biographies.

2. STRANGE MANKINDS

Though all the worlds which we entered in the first phase of our adventure were in the throes of the crisis known so well in our own world, some were occupied by races biologically similar to man, others by very different types. The more obviously human races inhabited planets of much the same size and nature as the Earth and the Other Earth. All, whatever the vagaries of their biological history, had finally been moulded by circumstance to the erect form which is evidently most suited to such worlds. Nearly always the two nether limbs were used for locomotion, the two upper limbs for manipulation. Generally there was some sort of head, containing the brain and the organs of remote perception, and perhaps the orifices for eating and breathing. In size these quasi-human types were seldom larger than our largest gorillas, seldom much smaller than monkeys; but we could not estimate their size with any accuracy, as we had no familiar standards of measurements.

Within this approximately human class there was great variety. We came upon feathered, penguin-like men, descended from true fliers, and on some small planets we found bird-men who retained the power of flight, yet were able to carry an adequate human brain. Even on some large planets, with exceptionally buoyant atmosphere, men flew with their own wings. Then there were men that had developed from a slug-like ancestor along a line which was not vertebrate, still less mammalian. Men of this type attained the necessary rigidity and flexibility of limb by means of a delicate internal "basket-work" of wiry bones.

On one very small but earthlike planet we discovered a quasi-human race which was probably unique. Here, though life had evolved much as on earth, all the higher animals differed remarkably from the familiar type in one obvious respect. They were without that far-reaching duplication of organs which characterizes all our vertebrates. Thus a man in this world was rather like half a terrestrial man. He hopped on one sturdy, splayfooted leg, balancing himself with a kangaroo tail. A single arm protruded from his chest, but branched into three forearms and prehensile fingers. Above his mouth was a single nostril, above that an ear, and on the top of his head a flexible three-pronged proboscis bearing three eyes.

A very different and fairly common quasi-human kind was sometimes produced by planets rather larger than the Earth. Owing to the greater strength of gravitation, there would first appear, in place of the familiar quadruped, a six-legged type. This would proliferate into little sextuped burrowers, swift and elegant sextuped grazers, a sextuped mammoth, complete with tusks, and many kinds of sextuped carnivora. Man in these worlds sprang usually from some small opposum-like creature which had come to use the first of its three pairs of limbs for nest-building or for climbing. In time, the forepart of its body thus became erect, and it gradually assumed a form not unlike that of a quadruped with a human torso in place of a neck. In fact it became a centaur, with four legs and two capable arms. It was very strange to find oneself in a world in which all the amenities and conveniences of civilization were fashioned to suit men of this form.

In one of these worlds, rather smaller than the rest, man was not a centaur, though centaurs were among his remote ancestors. In sub-human stages of evolution the pressure of the environment had telescoped the horizontal part of the centaur's body, so that the forelegs and the hind-legs were drawn closer and closer together, till at last they became a single sturdy pair. Thus man and his nearer ancestors were bipeds with very large rumps, reminiscent of the Victorian bustle, and legs whose internal structure still showed their "centaur" origin.

One very common kind of quasi-human world I must describe in more detail, as it plays an important part in the history of our galaxy. In these worlds man, though varying greatly in form and fortune in particular worlds, had in every case developed from a sort of five-pronged marine animal, rather like a star-fish. This creature would in time specialize one prong for perceiving, four for locomotion. Later it would develop lungs, a complex digestive apparatus, and a well-integrated nervous system. Later still the perceiving limb would produce a brain, the others becoming adapted for running and climbing. The soft spines which covered the body of the ancestral star-fish often developed into a kind of spiky fur. In due season there would arise an erect, intelligent biped, equipped with eyes, nostrils, ears, taste-organs, and sometimes organs of electric perception. Save for the grotesqueness of their faces, and the fact that the mouth was generally upon the belly, these creatures were remarkably human. Their bodies, however, were usually covered with the soft spines or fat hairs characteristic of these worlds. Clothes were unknown, save as protection against cold in the arctic regions. Their faces, of course, were apt to be far from human. The tall head often bore a coronet of five eyes. Large single nostrils, used for breathing and smelling and also speaking, formed another circlet below the eyes.

The appearance of these "Human Echinoderms" belied their nature, for though their faces were inhuman, the basic pattern of their minds was not unlike our own. Their senses were much like ours, save that in some worlds they developed a far more varied colour-sensitivity. Those races that had the electric sense gave us some difficulty; for, in order to understand their thought, we had to learn a whole new gamut of sense qualities and a vast system of unfamiliar symbolism. The electric organs detected very slight differences of electric charge in relation to the subject's own body. Originally this sense had been used for revealing enemies equipped with electric organs of offence. But in man its significance was chiefly social. It gave information about the emotional state of one's neighbours. Beyond this its function was meteorological.

One example of this kind of world, one which clearly illustrates the type, and at the same time presents interesting peculiarities must be described in more detail.

The key to the understanding of this race is, I believe, its strange method of reproduction, which was essentially communal. Every individual was capable of budding a new individual; but only at certain seasons, and only after stimulation by a kind of pollen emanating from the whole tribe and carried on the air. The grains of this ultra-microscopically fine pollen dust were not germ cells but "genes," the elementary factors of inheritance. The precincts of the tribe were at all times faintly perfumed by the communal pollen; but on occasions of violent group emotion the pollen cloud became so intensified as to be actually visible as a haze. Only on these rare occasions was conception probable. Breathed out by every individual, the pollen was breathed in by those who were ripe for fertilization. By all it was experienced as a rich and subtle perfume, to which each individual contributed his peculiar odour. By means of a curious psychical and physiological mechanism the individual in heat was moved to crave stimulation by the full perfume of the tribe, or of the great majority of its members; and indeed, if the pollen clouds were insufficiently complex, conception would not occur. Cross-fertilization between tribes happened in inter-tribal warfare and in the ceaseless coming and going between tribes in the modern world.

In this race, then, every individual might bear children. Every child, though it had an individual as its mother, was fathered by the tribe as a whole. Expectant parents were sacred, and were tended communally. When the baby "Echinoderm" finally detached itself from the parental body, it also was tended communally along with the rest of the tribe's juvenile population. In civilized societies it was handed over to professional nurses and teachers.

I must not pause to tell of the important psychological effects of this kind of reproduction. The delights and disgusts which we feel in contact with the flesh of our kind were unknown. On the other hand, individuals were profoundly moved by the ever-changing tribal perfume. It is impossible to describe the strange variant of romantic love which each individual periodically felt for the tribe. The thwarting, the repression, the perversion of this passion was the source at once of the loftiest and the most sordid achievements of the race.

Communal parenthood gave to the tribe a unity and strength quite unknown in more individualistic races. The primitive tribes were groups of a few hundred or a few thousand individuals, but in modern times their size greatly increased. Always, however, the sentiment of tribal loyalty, if it was to remain healthy, had to be based on the personal acquaintance of its members. Even in the larger tribes, everyone was at least "the friend of a friend's friend" to every other member. Telephone, radio, and television enabled tribes as large as our smaller cities to maintain a sufficient degree of personal intercourse among their members.

But always there was some point beyond which further growth of the tribe was unwholesome. Even in the smallest and most intelligent tribes there was a constant strain between the individual's natural passion for the tribe and his respect for individuality in himself and his fellows. But whereas in the small tribes and healthy larger tribes the tribal spirit was kept sweet and sane by the mutual-respect and self-respect of the individuals, in the largest and imperfectly sane tribes the hypnotic influence of the tribe was all too apt to drown personality. The members might even lose all awareness of themselves and their fellows as persons, and become mere mindless organs of the tribe. Thus the community would degenerate into an instinctive animal herd.

Throughout history the finer minds of the race had realized that the supreme temptation was the surrender of individuality to the tribe. Prophets had over and over again exhorted men to be true to themselves, but their preaching had been almost wholly vain. The greatest religions of this strange world were not religions of love but religions of self. Whereas in our world men long for the utopia in which all men shall love one another, the "Echinoderms" were apt to exalt the religious hunger for strength to "be oneself" without capitulation to the tribe. Just as we compensate for our inveterate selfishness by religious veneration of the community, so this race compensated for inveterate "gregism" by religious veneration of the individual.

In its purest and most developed form, of course, the religion of self is almost identical with the religion of love at its best. To love is to will the self-fulfilment of the beloved, and to find, in the very activity of loving, an incidental but vitalizing increase of oneself. On the other hand, to be true to oneself, to the full potentiality of the self, involves the activity of love. It demands the discipline of the private self in service of a greater self which embraces the community and the fulfilment of the spirit of the race.

But the religion of self was no more effective with the "Echinoderms" than the religion of love with us. The precept, "Love thy neighbour as thyself," breeds in us most often the disposition to see one's neighbour merely as a poor imitation of oneself, and to hate him if he proves different. With them the precept, "Be true to thyself," bred the disposition merely to be true to the tribal fashion of mentality.

Modern industrial civilization caused many tribes to swell beyond the wholesome limit. It also introduced artificial "super-tribes" or "tribes of tribes," corresponding to our nations and social classes. Since the economic unit was the internally communistic tribe, not the individual, the employing class was a small group of small and prosperous tribes, and the working class was a large group of large and impoverished tribes. The ideologies of the super-tribes exercised absolute power over all individual minds under their sway.

In civilized regions the super-tribes and the overgrown natural tribes created an astounding mental tyranny. In relation to his natural tribe, at least if it was small and genuinely civilized, the individual might still behave with intelligence and imagination. Along with his actual tribal kinsmen he might support a degree of true community unknown on Earth. He might in fact be a critical, self-respecting and other-respecting person. But in all matters connected with the super-tribes, whether national or economic, he behaved in a very different manner. All ideas coming to him with the sanction of nation or class would be accepted uncritically and with fervour by himself and all his fellows. As soon as he encountered one of the symbols or slogans of his super-tribe he ceased to be a human personality and became a sort of de-cerebrate animal, capable only of stereotyped reactions. In extreme cases his mind was absolutely closed to influences opposed to the suggestion of the super-tribe. Criticism was either met with blind rage or actually not heard at all. Persons who in the intimate community of their small native tribe were capable of great mutual insight and sympathy might suddenly, in response to tribal symbols, be transformed into vessels of crazy intolerance and hate directed against national or class enemies. In this mood they would go to any extreme of self-sacrifice for the supposed glory of the super-tribe. Also they would show great ingenuity in contriving means to exercise their lustful vindictiveness upon enemies who in favourable circumstances could be quite as kindly and intelligent as themselves.

At the time of our visit to this world it seemed that mob passions would destroy civilization completely and irrevocably. The affairs of the world were increasingly conducted under the sway of the spreading mania of super-tribalism; conducted, in fact, not intelligently but according to the relative emotional compulsions of almost meaningless slogans.

I must not stay to describe how, after a period of chaos, a new way of life at last began to spread over this distressed world. It could not do so till the super-tribes had been disintegrated by the economic forces of mechanized industry, and by their own frenzied conflict. Then at last the individual mind became once more free. The whole prospect of the race now changed.

It was in this world that we first experienced that tantalizing loss of contact with the natives just at that point where, having established something like a social utopia throughout their planet, they were beset by the first painful stirrings of the spirit before advancement to some mental plane beyond our reach, or at least beyond such comprehension as we then had.

Of the other "Echinoderm" worlds in our galaxy, one, more promising than the average, rose early to brilliance, but was destroyed by astronomical collision. Its whole solar system encountered a tract of dense nebula. The surface of every planet was fused. In several other worlds of this type we saw the struggle for the more awakened mentality definitely fail. Vindictive and superstitious herd-cults exterminated the best minds of the race, and drugged the rest with customs and principles so damaging that the vital sources of sensitivity and adaptability on which all mental progress depends were destroyed for ever.

Many thousands of other quasi-human worlds, besides those of the "Echinoderm" type, came to an untimely end. One, which succumbed to a curious disaster, perhaps deserves brief notice. Here we found a race of very human kind. When its civilization had reached a stage and character much like our own, a stage in which the ideals of the masses are without the guidance of any well-established tradition, and in which natural science is enslaved to individualistic industry, biologists discovered the technique of artificial insemination. Now at this time there happened to be a widespread cult of irrationalism, of instinct, of ruthlessness, and of the "divine" primitive "brute-man." This figure was particularly admired when he combined brutishness with the power of the mob-controller. Several countries were subjected to tyrants of this type, and in the so-called democratic states the same type was much favoured by popular taste.

In both kinds of country, women craved "brute-men" as lovers and as fathers for their children. Since in the "democratic" countries women had attained great economic independence, their demand for fertilization by "brute-men" caused the whole matter to be commercialized. Males of the desirable type were taken up by syndicates, and graded in five ranks of desirability. At a moderate charge, fixed in relation to the grade of the father, any woman could obtain "brute-man" fertilization. So cheap was the fifth grade that only the most abject paupers were debarred from its services. The charge for actual copulation with even the lowest grade of selected male was, of course, much higher, since perforce the supply was limited.

In the non-democratic countries events took a different turn. In each of these regions a tyrant of the fashionable type gathered upon his own person the adoration of the whole population. He was the god-sent hero. He was himself divine. Every woman longed passionately to have him, if not as a lover, at least as father of her children. In some lands artificial insemination from the Master was permitted only as a supreme distinction for women of perfect type. Ordinary women of every class, however, were entitled to insemination from the authorized aristocratic stud of "brute-men." In other countries the Master himself condescended to be the father of the whole future population.

The result of this extraordinary custom, of artificial fatherhood by "brute-men," which was carried on without remission in all countries for a generation, and in a less thorough manner for a very much longer period, was to alter the composition of the whole quasi-human race. In order to maintain continued adaptability to an ever-changing environment a race must at all costs preserve in itself its slight but potent salting of sensibility and originality. In this world the precious factor now became so diluted as to be ineffective. Henceforth the desperately complex problems of the world were consistently bungled. Civilization decayed. The race entered on a phase of what might be called pseudo-civilized barbarism, which was in essence sub-human and incapable of change. This state of affairs continued for some millions of years, but at last the race was destroyed by the ravages of a small rat-like animal against which it could devise no protection.

I must not stay to notice the strange fortunes of all the many other quasi-human worlds. I will mention only that in some, though civilization was destroyed in a succession of savage wars, the germ of recovery precariously survived. In one, the agonizing balance of the old and the new seemed to prolong itself indefinitely. In another, where science had advanced too far for the safety of an immature species, man accidentally blew up his planet and his race. In several, the dialectical process of history was broken short by invasion and conquest on the part of inhabitants of another planet. These and other disasters, to be described in due course, decimated the galactic population of worlds.

In conclusion I will mention that in one or two of these quasi-human worlds a new and superior biological race emerged naturally during the typical world crisis, gained power by sheer intelligence and sympathy, took charge of the planet, persuaded the aborigines to cease breeding, peopled the whole planet with its own superior type, and created a human race which attained communal mentality, and rapidly advanced beyond the limits of our exploring and over-strained understanding. Before our contact failed, we were surprised to observe that, as the new species superseded the old and took over the vast political and economic activity of that world, it came to realize with laughter the futility of all this feverish and aimless living. Under our eyes the old order began to give place to a new and simpler order, in which the world was to be peopled by a small "aristocratic" population served by machines, freed alike from drudgery and luxury and intent on exploration of the cosmos and the mind.

This change-over to a simpler life happened in several other worlds not by the intervention of a new species, but simply by the victory of the new mentality in its battle against the old.

3. NAUTILOIDS

As our exploration advanced and we gathered more and more helpers from the many worlds that we entered, our imaginative insight into alien natures increased. Though our research was still restricted to races which were in the throes of the familiar spiritual crisis, we gradually acquired the power of making contact with beings whose minds were very far from human in texture. I must now try to give some idea of the main types of these "non-human" intelligent worlds. In some cases the difference from humanity, though physically striking, and even mentally very remarkable, was not nearly so far-reaching as the cases to be described in the next chapter.

In general the physical and mental form of conscious beings is an expression of the character of the planet on which they live. On certain very large and aqueous planets, for instance, we found that civilization had been achieved by marine organisms. On these huge globes no land-dwellers as large as a man could possibly thrive, for gravitation would have nailed them to the ground. But in the water there was no such limitation to bulk. One peculiarity of these big worlds was that, owing to the crushing action of gravitation, there were seldom any great elevations and depressions in their surface. Thus they were usually covered by a shallow ocean, broken here and there by archipelagos of small, low islands.

I shall describe one example of this kind of world, the greatest planet of a mighty sun. Situated, if I remember rightly, near the congested heart of the galaxy, this star was born late in galactic history, and it gave birth to planets when already many of the older stars were encrusted with smouldering lava. Owing to the violence of solar radiation its nearer planets had (or will have) stormy climates. On one of them a mollusc-like creature, living in the coastal shallows, acquired a propensity to drift in its boat-like shell on the sea's surface, thus keeping in touch with its drifting vegetable food. As the ages passed, its shell became better adapted to navigation. Mere drifting was supplemented by means of a crude sail, a membrane extending from the creature's back. In time this nautiloid type proliferated into a host of species. Some of these remained minute, but some found size advantageous, and developed into living ships. One of these became the intelligent master of this great world.

The hull was a rigid, stream-lined vessel, shaped much as the nineteenth-century clipper in her prime, and larger than our largest whale. At the rear a tentacle or fin developed into a rudder, which was sometimes used also as a propeller, like a fish's tail. But though all these species could navigate under their own power to some extent, their normal means of long-distance locomotion was their great spread of sail. The simple membranes of the ancestral type had become a system of parchment-like sails

and bony masts and spars, under voluntary muscular control. Similarity
to a ship was increased by the downward-looking eyes, one on each side
of the prow. The mainmast-head also bore eyes, for searching the horizon.
An organ of magnetic sensitivity in the brain afforded a reliable means of
orientation. At the fore end of the vessel were two long manipulatory
tentacles, which during locomotion were folded snugly to the flanks. In
use they formed a very serviceable pair of arms.

It may seem strange that a species of this kind should have developed
human intelligence. In more than one world of this type, however, a number of accidents combined to produce this result. The change from a vegetarian to a carnivorous habit caused a great increase of animal cunning
in pursuit of the much speedier submarine creatures. The sense of hearing
was wonderfully developed, for the movements of fish at great distances
could be detected by the underwater ears. A line of taste-organs along
either bilge responded to the ever-changing composition of the water, and
enabled the hunter to track his prey. Delicacy of hearing and of taste combined with omnivorous habits, and with great diversity of behaviour and
strong sociality, to favour the growth of intelligence.

Speech, that essential medium of the developed mentality, had two
distinct modes in this world. For short-range communication, rhythmic
underwater emissions of gas from a vent in the rear of the organism were
heard and analysed by means of underwater ears. Long-distance communication was carried on by means of semaphore signals from a rapidly agitating tentacle at the mast head.

The organizing of communal fishing expeditions, the invention of
traps, the making of lines and nets, the practice of agriculture, both in the
sea and along the shores, the building of stone harbours and work-shops,
the use of volcanic heat for smelting metals, and of wind for driving
mills, the projection of canals into the low islands in search of minerals and
fertile ground, the gradual exploration and mapping of a huge world, the
harnessing of solar radiation for mechanical power, these and many other
achievements were at once a product of intelligence and an opportunity
for its advancement.

It was a strange experience to enter the mind of an intelligent ship,
to see the foam circling under one's own nose as the vessel plunged through
the waves, to taste the bitter or delicious currents streaming past one's
flanks, to feel the pressure of air on the sails as one beat up against the
breeze, to hear beneath the water-line the rush and murmur of distant shoals
of fishes, and indeed actually to *hear* the sea-bottom's configuration by
means of the echoes that it cast up to the under-water ears. It was strange
and terrifying to be caught in a hurricane, to feel the masts straining and
the sails threatening to split, while the hull was battered by the small but
furious waves of that massive planet. It was strange, too, to watch other

great living ships, as they ploughed their way, heeled over, adjusted the set of their yellow or russet sails to the wind's variations; and very strange it was to realize that these were not man-made objects but themselves conscious and purposeful.

Sometimes we saw two of the living ships fighting, tearing at one another's sails with snake-like tentacles, stabbing at one another's soft "decks" with metal knives, or at a distance firing at one another with cannon. Bewildering and delightful it was to feel in the presence of a slim female clipper the longing for contact, and to carry out with her on the high seas the tacking and yawing, the piratical pursuit and overhauling, the delicate, fleeting caress of tentacles, which formed the love-play of this race. Strange, to come up alongside, close-hauled, grapple her to one's flank, and board her with sexual invasion. It was charming, too, to see a mother ship attended by her children. I should mention, by the way, that at birth the young were launched from the mother's decks like little boats, one from the port side, one from the starboard. Thenceforth they were suckled at her flanks. In play they swam about her like ducklings, or spread their immature sails. In rough weather and for long voyaging they were taken aboard.

At the time of our visit natural sails were beginning to be aided by a power unit and propeller which were fixed to the stern. Great cities of concrete docks had spread along many of the coasts, and were excavated out of the hinterlands. We were delighted by the broad water-ways that served as streets in these cities. They were thronged with sail and mechanized traffic, the children appearing as tugs and smacks among the gigantic elders.

It was in this world that we found in its most striking form a social disease which is perhaps the commonest of all world-diseases—namely, the splitting of the population into two mutually unintelligible castes through the influence of economic forces. So great was the difference between adults of the two castes that they seemed to us at first to be distinct species, and we supposed ourselves to be witnessing the victory of a new and superior biological mutation over its predecessor. But this was far from the truth.

In appearance the masters were very different from the workers, quite as different as queen ants and drones from the workers of their species. They were more elegantly and accurately stream-lined. They had a greater expanse of sail, and were faster in fair weather. In heavy seas they were less seaworthy, owing to their finer lines; but on the other hand they were the more skilful and venturesome navigators. Their manipulatory tentacles were less muscular, but capable of finer adjustments. Their perception was more delicate. While a small minority of them perhaps excelled the best of the workers in endurance and courage, most were much less hardy, both physically and mentally. They were subject to a number of disintegrative diseases which never affected the workers, chiefly diseases of the nervous system. On the other hand, if any of them contracted one of the infectious ailments which were endemic to the workers, but seldom fatal, he would almost certainly die. They were also very prone to mental disorders, and particularly to neurotic self-importance. The whole organization and control of the world was theirs. The workers, on the other hand, though racked by disease and neurosis bred of their cramping environment, were on the whole psychologically more robust. They had, however, a crippling sense of inferiority. Though in handicrafts and all small-scale operations they were capable of intelligence and skill, they were liable, when faced with tasks of wider scope, to a strange paralysis of mind.

The mentalities of the two castes were indeed strikingly different. The masters were more prone to individual initiative and to the vices of self-seeking. The workers were more addicted to collectivism and the vices of subservience to the herd's hypnotic influence. The masters were on the whole more prudent, far-seeing, independent, self-reliant; the workers were more impetuous, more ready to sacrifice themselves in a social cause, often more clearly aware of the right aims of social activity, and incomparably more generous to individuals in distress.

At the time of our visit certain recent discoveries were throwing the world into confusion. Hitherto it had been supposed that the natures of the two castes were fixed unalterably, by divine law and by biological inheritance. But it was now certain that this was not the case, and that the physical and mental differences between the classes were due entirely to nurture. Since time immemorial, the castes had been recruited in a very curious manner. After weaning, all children born on the port side of the mother, no matter what the parental caste, were brought up to be members of the master caste; all those born on the starboard side were brought up to be workers. Since the master class had, of course, to be much smaller than the working class, this system gave an immense superfluity of potential masters. The difficulty was overcome as follows. The starboard-born children of workers and the port-born children of masters were brought up by their own respective parents; but the port-born, potentially aristocratic children of workers were mostly disposed of by infant sacrifice. A few only were exchanged with the starboard-born children of masters.

With the advance of industrialism, the increasing need for large supplies of cheap labour, the spread of scientific ideas and the weakening of religion, came the shocking discovery that port-born children, of both classes, if brought up as workers, became physically and mentally indistinguishable from workers. Industrial magnates in need of plentiful cheap labour now developed moral indignation against infant sacrifice, urging that the excess of port-born infants should be mercifully brought up as workers. Presently certain misguided scientists made the even more sub-

versive discovery that starboard-born children brought up as masters developed the fine lines, the great sails, the delicate constitution, the aristocratic mentality of the master caste. An attempt was made by the masters
to prevent this knowledge from spreading to the workers, but certain
sentimentalists of their own caste bruited it abroad, and preached a new-
fangled and inflammatory doctrine of social equality.

During our visit the world was in terrible confusion. In backward
oceans the old system remained unquestioned, but in all the more advanced regions of the planet a desperate struggle was being waged. In
one great archipelago a social revolution had put the workers in power,
and a devoted though ruthless dictatorship was attempting so to plan the
life of the community that the next generation should be homogeneous
and of a new type, combining the most desirable characters of both workers
and masters. Elsewhere the masters had persuaded their workers that the
new ideas were false and base, and certain to lead to universal poverty and
misery. A clever appeal was made to the vague but increasing suspicion
that "materialistic science" was misleading and superficial, and that mechanized civilization was crushing out the more spiritual potentialities of the
race. Skilled propaganda spread the ideal of a kind of corporate state with
"port and starboard flanks" correlated by a popular dictator, who, it was
said, would assume power "by divine right and the will of the people."

I must not stay to tell of the desperate struggle which broke out between these two kinds of social organizations. In the world-wide campaigns many a harbour, many an ocean current, flowed red with slaughter.
Under the pressure of a war to the death, all that was best, all that was
most human and gentle on each side was crushed out by military necessity.
On the one side, the passion for a unified world, where every individual
should live a free and full life in service of the world community, was
overcome by the passion to punish spies, traitors, and heretics. On the
other, vague and sadly misguided yearnings for a nobler, less materialistic
life were cleverly transformed by the reactionary leaders into vindictiveness against the revolutionaries.

Very rapidly the material fabric of civilization fell to pieces. Not till
the race had reduced itself to an almost subhuman savagery, and all the
crazy traditions of a diseased civilization had been purged away, along
with true culture, could the spirit of these "ship-men" set out again on the
great adventure of the spirit. Many thousands of years later it broke
through on to that higher plane of being which I have still to suggest, as
best I may.

CHAPTER VI

INTIMATIONS OF THE STAR MAKER

IT must not be supposed that the normal fate of intelligent races in the galaxy is to triumph. So far I have spoken mainly of those fortunate Echinoderm and Nautiloid worlds which did at last pass triumphantly into the more awakened state, and I have scarcely even mentioned the hundreds, the thousands, of worlds which met disaster. This selection was inevitable because my space is limited, and because these two worlds, together with the even stranger spheres that I shall describe in the next chapter, were to have great influence on the fortunes of the whole galaxy. But many other worlds of "human" rank were quite as rich in history as those which I have noticed. Individual lives in them were no less varied than lives elsewhere, and no less crowded with distress and joy. Some triumphed; some in their last phase suffered a downfall, swift or slow, which lent them the splendour of tragedy. But since these worlds play no special part in the main story of the galaxy, they must be passed over in silence, along with the still greater host of worlds which never attained even to "human" rank. If I were to dwell upon their fortunes I should commit the same error as a historian who should try to describe every private life and neglect the pattern of the whole community.

I have already said that, as our experience of the destruction of worlds increased, we were increasingly dismayed by the wastefulness and seeming aimlessness of the universe. So many worlds, after so much distress, attained so nearly to social peace and joy, only to have the cup snatched from them for ever. Often disaster was brought by some trivial flaw of temperament or biological nature. Some races had not the intelligence, some lacked the social will, to cope with the problems of a unified world-community. Some were destroyed by an upstart bacterium before their medical science was mature. Others succumbed to climatic change, many to loss of atmosphere. Sometimes the end came through collision with dense clouds of dust or gas, or with swarms of giant meteors. Not a few worlds were destroyed by the downfall of a satellite. The lesser body, ploughing its way, age after age, through the extremely rarefied but omnipresent cloud of free atoms in interstellar space, would lose momentum. Its orbit would contract, at first slowly, then rapidly. It would set up prodigious tides in the oceans of the larger body, and drown much of its civilization. Later, through the increasing stress of the planet's attraction, the great moon would begin to disintegrate. First it would cast its ocean in a deluge on men's heads, then its mountains, and then the titanic and fiery fragments of its core. If in none of these manners came the end of the world, then inevitably, though perhaps not till the latter days of the galaxy, it must come in another way. The planet's own orbit, fatally contracting, must bring every world at last so close to its sun that conditions must pass beyond the limit of life's adaptability, and age by age all living things must be parched to death and roasted.

Dismay, terror, horror many a time seized us as we witnessed these huge disasters. An agony of pity for the last survivors of these worlds was part of our schooling.

The most developed of the slaughtered worlds did not need our pity, since their inhabitants seemed capable of meeting the end of all that they cherished with peace, even a strange unshakable joy which we in this early stage of our adventure could by no means comprehend. But only a few, very few, could reach this state. And only a few out of the great host of worlds could win through even to the social peace and fulness toward which all were groping. In the more lowly worlds, moreover, few were the individuals who won any satisfaction of life even within the narrow bounds of their own imperfect nature. No doubt one or two, here and there, in almost every world, found not merely happiness but the joy that passes all understanding. But to us, crushed now by the suffering and futility of a thousand races, it seemed that this joy itself, this ecstasy, whether it was supported by scattered individuals or by whole worlds, must after all be condemned as false, and that those who had found it must after all have been drugged by their own private and untypical well-being of spirit. For surely it had made them insensitive to the horror around them.

The sustaining motive of our pilgrimage had been the hunger which formerly drove men on Earth in search of God. Yes, we had one and all left our native planets in order to discover whether, regarding the cosmos as a whole, the spirit which we all in our hearts obscurely knew and haltingly prized, the spirit which on Earth we sometimes call humane, was Lord of the Universe, or outlaw; almighty, or crucified. And now it was becoming clear to us that if the cosmos had any lord at all, he was not that spirit but some other, whose purpose in creating the endless fountain of worlds was not fatherly toward the beings that he had made, but alien, inhuman, dark.

Yet while we felt dismay, we felt also increasingly the hunger to see and to face fearlessly whatever spirit was indeed the spirit of this cosmos. For as we pursued our pilgrimage, passing again and again from tragedy to farce, from farce to glory, from glory often to a final tragedy, we felt increasingly the sense that some terrible, some holy, yet at the same time unimaginably outrageous and lethal, secret lay just beyond our reach. Again and again we were torn between horror and fascination, between moral rage against the universe (or the Star Maker) and unreasonable worship.

This same conflict was to be observed in all those worlds that were of our own mental stature. Observing these worlds and the phases of their past growth, and groping as best we might toward the next plane of spiritual development, we came at last to see plainly the first stages of any world's pilgrimage. Even in the most primitive ages of every normal intelligent world there existed in some minds the impulse to seek and to praise some universal thing. At first this impulse was confused with the craving for protection by some mighty power. Inevitably the beings theorized that the admired thing must be Power, and that worship was mere propitiation. Thus they came to conceive the almighty tyrant of the universe, with themselves as his favoured children. But in time it became clear to their prophets that mere Power was not what the praiseful heart adored. Then theory enthroned Wisdom, or Law, or Righteousness. And after an age of obedience to some phantom lawgiver, or to divine legality itself, the beings found that these concepts too were inadequate to describe the indescribable glory that the heart confronted in all things, and mutely prized in all things.

But now, in every world that we visited, alternative ways opened out before the worshippers. Some hoped to come face to face with their shrouded god solely by inward-searching meditation. By purging themselves of all lesser, all trivial desires, by striving to see everything dispassionately and with universal sympathy, they hoped to identify themselves with the spirit of the cosmos. Often they travelled far along the way of self-perfecting and awakening. But because of this inward absorption most of them became insensitive to the suffering of their less-awakened fellows and careless of the communal enterprise of their kind. In not a few worlds this way of the spirit was thronged by all the most vital minds. And because the best attention of the race was given wholly to the inner life, material and social advancement was checked. The sciences of physical nature and of life never developed. Mechanical power remained unknown, and medical and biological power also. Consequently these worlds stagnated, and sooner or later succumbed to accidents which might well have been prevented.

There was a second way of devotion, open to creatures of a more practical temperament. These, in all the worlds, gave delighted attention to the universe around them, and chiefly they found the worshipped thing in the persons of their fellow-beings, and in the communal bond of mutual insight and love between persons. In themselves and in each other they prized above all things love.

And their prophets told them that the thing which they had always adored, the universal spirit, the Creator, the Almighty, the All-wise, was also the All-loving. Let them therefore worship in practical love of one another, and in service of the Love-God. And so for an age, short or long, they strove feebly to love and to become members one of another. They spun theories in defence of the theory of the Love-God. They set up priest-hoods and temples in service of Love. And because they hungered for im-mortality they were told that to love was the way to attain eternal life. And so love, which seeks no reward, was misconceived.

In most worlds these practical minds dominated over the meditators. Sooner or later practical curiosity and economic need produced the ma-terial sciences. Probing every region with these sciences, the beings found nowhere, neither in the atom nor in the galaxy, nor for that matter in the heart of "man" either, any signature of the Love-God. And what with the fever of mechanization, and the exploitation of slaves by masters, and the passions of intertribal warfare, and the increasing neglect or coarsening of all the more awakened activities of the spirit, the little flame of praise in their hearts sank lower than it had ever been in any earlier age, so low that they could no longer recognize it. And the flame of love, long fanned by the forced draught of doctrine, but now suffocated by the general ob-tuseness of the beings to one another, was reduced to an occasional smouldering warmth, which was most often mistaken for mere lust. With bitter laughter and rage the tortured beings now dethroned the image of the Love-God in their hearts.

And so without love and without worship the unhappy beings faced the increasingly formidable problems of their mechanized and hate-racked world.

This was the crisis which we in our own worlds knew so well. Many a world up and down the galaxy never surmounted it. But in a few, some miracle, which we could not yet clearly envisage, raised the average minds of these worlds to a higher plane of mentality. Of this I shall speak later. Meanwhile I will say only that in the few worlds where this happened, we noticed invariably, before the minds of that world passed beyond our reach, a new feeling about the universe, a feeling which it was very diffi-cult for us to share. Not till we had learned to conjure in ourselves some-thing of this feeling could we follow the fortunes of these worlds.

But, as we advanced on our pilgrimage, our own desires began to change. We came to wonder whether, in demanding lordship of the uni-verse for the divinely humane spirit that we prized most in ourselves and in our fellow-mortals in all the worlds, we were perhaps impious. We came less and less to require that Love should be enthroned behind the stars; more and more we desired merely to pass on, opening our hearts to ac-cept fearlessly whatever of the truth might fall within our comprehension.

There was a moment, late in this early phase of our pilgrimage, when, thinking and feeling in unison, we said to one another, "If the Star Maker is Love, we know that this must be right. But if he is not, if he is some other, some inhuman spirit, *this* must be right. And if he is nothing, if the stars and all else are not his creatures but self-subsistent, and if the adored spirit is but an exquisite creature of our minds, then *this* must be right, this and no other possibility. For we cannot know whether the highest place for love is on the throne or on the cross. We cannot know what spirit rules, for on the throne sits darkness. We know, we have seen, that in the waste of stars love is indeed crucified; and rightly, for its own proving, and for the throne's glory. Love and all that is humane we cherish in our hearts. Yet also we salute the throne and the darkness upon the throne. Whether it be Love or not Love, our hearts praise it, out-soaring reason."

But before our hearts could be properly attuned to this new, strange feeling, we had still far to go in the understanding of worlds of human rank, though diverse. I must now try to give some idea of several kinds of worlds very different from our own, but not in essentials more mature.

CHAPTER VII

MORE WORLDS

I. A SYMBIOTIC RACE

ON certain large planets, whose climates, owing to the proximity of a violent sun, were very much hotter than our tropics, we sometimes found an intelligent fish-like race. It was bewildering to us to discover that a submarine world could give rise to mentality of human rank, and to that drama of the spirit which we had now so often encountered.

The very shallow and sun-drenched oceans of these great planets provided an immense diversity of habitats and a great wealth of living things. Green vegetation, which could be classified as tropical, subtropical, temperate and arctic, basked on the bright ocean floors. There were submarine prairies and forests. In some regions the giant weeds stretched from the sea-bottom to the waves. In these jungles the blue and blinding light of the sun was reduced almost to darkness. Immense coral-like growths, honeycombed with passages and swarming with all manner of live-things, lifted their spires and turrets to the surface. Innumerable kinds of fish-like creatures of all sizes from sprat to whale inhabited the many levels of the waters, some gliding on the bottom, some daring an occasional leap into the torrid air. In the deepest and darkest regions hosts of sea-monsters, eyeless or luminous, browsed on the ceaseless rain of corpses which sank from the upper levels. Over their deep world lay other worlds of increasing brightness and colour, where gaudy populations basked, browsed, stalked, or hunted with arrowy flight.

Intelligence in these planets was generally achieved by some unimposing social creature, neither fish nor octopus nor crustacean, but something of all three. It would be equipped with manipulatory tentacles, keen eyes and subtle brain. It would make nests of weed in the crevices of the coral, or build strongholds of coral masonry. In time would appear traps, weapons, tools, submarine agriculture, the blossoming of primitive art, the ritual of primitive religion. Then would follow the typical fluctuating advance of the spirit from barbarism to civilization.

One of these submarine worlds was exceptionally interesting. Early in the life of our galaxy, when few of the stars had yet condensed from the "giant" to the solar type, when very few planetary births had yet occurred, a double star and a single star in a congested cluster did actually approach one another, reach fiery filaments toward one another, and spawn a planet brood. Of these worlds, one, an immense and very aqueous sphere, produced in time a dominant race which was not a single species but an intimate symbiotic partnership of two very alien creatures. The one came of a fish-like stock. The other was in appearance something like a crustacean. In form it was a sort of paddle-footed crab or marine spider. Unlike our crustaceans, it was covered not with a brittle carapace but with a tough pachydermatous hide. In maturity this serviceable jerkin was more or less rigid, save at the joints; but in youth it was very pliant to the still-expanding brain. This creature lived on the coasts and in the coastal waters of the many islands of the planet. Both species were mentally of human rank, though each had specific temperament and ability. In primitive times each had attained by its own route and in its own hemisphere of the great aqueous planet to what might be called the last stage of the subhuman mentality. The two species had then come into contact, and had grappled desperately. Their battle-ground was the shallow coastal water. The "crustaceans," though crudely amphibian, could not spend long under the sea; the "fish" could not emerge from it.

The two races did not seriously compete with one another in economic life, for the "fish" were mainly vegetarian, the "crustaceans" mainly carnivorous; yet neither could tolerate the presence of the other. Both were sufficiently human to be aware of one another as rival aristocrats in a subhuman world, but neither was human enough to realize that for each race the way of life lay in cooperation with the other. The fish-like creatures, which I shall call "ichthyoids," had speed and range of travel. They had also the security of bulk. The crab-like or spider-like "crustaceans," which I shall call "arachnoids," had greater manual dexterity, and had also access to the dry land. Cooperation would have been very beneficial to both species, for one of the staple foods of the arachnoids was parasitic to the ichthyoids.

In spite of the possibility of mutual aid, the two races strove to exterminate one another, and almost succeeded. After an age of blind mutual slaughter, certain of the less pugnacious and more flexible varieties of the two species gradually discovered profit in fraternization with the enemy. This was the beginning of a very remarkable partnership. Soon the arachnoids took to riding on the backs of the swift ichthyoids, and thus gained access to more remote hunting grounds.

As the epochs passed, the two species moulded one another to form a well-integrated union. The little arachnoid, no bigger than a chimpanzee, rode in a snug hollow behind the great "fish's" skull, his back being stream-lined with the contours of the larger creature. The tentacles of the ichthyoid were specialized for large-scale manipulation, those of the arachnoid for minute work. A biochemical interdependence also evolved. Through a membrane in the ichthyoid's pouch an exchange of endocrine products took place. This mechanism enabled the arachnoid to become fully aquatic. So long as it had frequent contact with its host, it could stay under water for any length of time and descend to any depth. A striking mental adaptation also occurred in the two species. The ichthyoids became on the whole more introvert, the arachnoids more extrovert.

Up to puberty the young of both species were free-living individuals; but, as their symbiotic organization developed, each sought out a partner of the opposite species. The union which followed was life-long, and was interrupted only by brief sexual matings. The symbiosis itself constituted a kind of contrapuntal sexuality; but a sexuality that was purely mental, since, of course, for copulation and reproduction each individual had to seek out a partner belonging to his or her own species. We found, however, that even the symbiotic partnership consisted invariably of a male of one species and a female of the other; and the male, whichever his species, behaved with parental devotion to the young of his symbiotic partner.

I have not space to describe the extraordinary mental reciprocity of these strange couples. I can only say that, though in sensory equipment and in temperament the two species were very different, and though in abnormal cases tragic conflicts did occur, the ordinary partnership was at once more intimate than human marriage and far more enlarging to the individual than any friendship between members of distinct human races. At certain stages of the growth of civilization malicious minds had attempted to arouse widespread interspecific conflict, and had met with temporary success; but the trouble seldom went as deep even as our "sex war," so necessary was each species to the other. Both had contributed equally to the culture of their world, though not equally at all times. In creative work of every kind one of the partners provided most of the originality, the other most of the criticism and restraint. Work in which one partner was entirely passive was rare. Books, or rather scrolls, which were made from pulped seaweed, were nearly always signed by couples. On the whole the arachnoid partners dominated in manual skill, experimental science, the plastic arts, and practical social organization. The ichthyoid partners excelled in theoretical work, in literary arts, in the surprisingly developed music of that submarine world, and in the more mystical kind of religion. This generalization, however, should not be interpreted very strictly.

The symbiotic relationship seems to have given the dual race a far greater mental flexibility than ours, and a quicker aptitude for community. It passed rapidly through the phase of inter-tribal strife, during which the nomadic shoals of symbiotic couples harried one another like hosts of submarine cavalry; for the arachnoids, riding their ichthyoid mates, attacked the enemy with bone spears and swords, while their mounts wrestled with powerful tentacles. But the phase of tribal warfare was remarkably brief. When a settled mode of life was attained, along with submarine agriculture and coral-built cities, strife between leagues of cities was the exception, not the rule. Aided no doubt by its great mobility and ease of communication, the dual race soon built up a world-wide and unarmed federation of cities. We learned also with wonder that at the height of the pre-mechanical civilization of this planet, when in our worlds the cleavage into masters and economic slaves would already have become serious, the communal spirit of the city triumphed over all individualistic enterprise. Very soon this world became a tissue of interdependent but independent municipal communes.

At this time it seemed that social strife had vanished for ever. But the most serious crisis of the race was still to come.

The submarine environment offered the symbiotic race no great possibilities of advancement. All sources of wealth had been tapped and regularized. Population was maintained at an optimum size for the joyful working of the world. The social order was satisfactory to all classes, and seemed unlikely to change. Individual lives were full and varied. Culture, founded on a great tradition, was now concerned entirely with detailed exploration of the great fields of thought that had long ago been pioneered by the revered ancestors, under direct inspiration, it was said, of the symbiotic deity. Our friends in this submarine world, our mental hosts, looked back on this age from their own more turbulent epoch sometimes with yearning, but often with horror; for in retrospect it seemed to them to display the first faint signs of racial decay. So perfectly did the race fit its unchanging environment that intelligence and acuity were already ceasing to be precious, and might soon begin to fade. But presently it appeared that fate had decreed otherwise.

In a submarine world the possibility of obtaining mechanical power was remote. But the arachnoids, it will be remembered, were able to live out of the water. In the epochs before the symbiosis their ancestors had periodically emerged upon the islands, for courtship, parenthood, and the pursuit of prey. Since those days the air-breathing capacity had declined, but it had never been entirely lost. Every arachnoid still emerged for sexual mating, and also for certain ritual gymnastic exercises. It was in this latter connection that the great discovery was made which changed the course of history. At a certain tournament the friction of stone weapons, clashing against one another, produced sparks, and fire among the sun-scorched grasses.

In startlingly quick succession came smelting, the steam engine, the electric current. Power was obtained first from the combustion of a sort of peat formed on the coasts by congested marine vegetation, later from the constant and violent winds, later still from photo-chemical light traps which absorbed the sun's lavish radiation. These inventions were of course the work of arachnoids. The ichthyoids, though they still played a great part in the systematization of knowledge, were debarred from the great practical work of scientific experiment and mechanical invention above the seas. Soon the arachnoids were running electric cables from the island power-stations to the submarine cities. In this work, at least, the ichthyoids could take part, but their part was necessarily subordinate. Not only in experience of electrical engineering but also in native practical ability they were eclipsed by their arachnoid partners.

For a couple of centuries or more the two species continued to co-operate, though with increasing strain. Artificial lighting, mechanical transport of goods on the ocean floor, and large-scale manufacture, produced an immense increase in the amenities of life in the submarine cities. The islands were crowded with buildings devoted to science and industry. Physics, chemistry, and biology made great progress. Astronomers began to map the galaxy. They also discovered that a neighbouring planet offered wonderful opportunities for settlement by arachnoids, who might without great difficulty, it was hoped, be conditioned to the alien climate, and to divorce from their symbiotic partners. The first attempts at rocket flight were leading to mingled tragedy and success. The directorate of extra-marine activities demanded a much increased arachnoid population.

Inevitably there arose a conflict between the two species, and in the mind of every individual of either species. It was at the height of this conflict, and in the spiritual crisis in virtue of which these beings were accessible to us in our novitiate stage, that we first entered this world. The ichthyoids had not yet succumbed biologically to their inferior position, but psychologically they were already showing signs of deep mental decay. A profound disheartenment and lassitude attacked them, like that which so often undermines our primitive races when they find themselves struggling in the flood of European civilization. But since in the case of the symbiotics the relation between the two races was extremely intimate, far more so than that between the most intimate human beings, the plight of the ichthyoids deeply affected the arachnoids. And in the minds of the ichthyoids the triumph of their partners was for long a source of mingled distress and exultation.

Every individual of both species was torn between conflicting motives. While every healthy arachnoid longed to take part in the adventurous new life, he or she longed also, through sheer affection and symbiotic entanglement, to assist his or her ichthyoid mate to have an equal share in that life. Further, all arachnoids were aware of subtle dependence on their mates, a dependence at once physiological and psychological. It was the ichthyoids who mostly contributed to the mental symbiosis the power of self-knowledge and mutual insight, and the contemplation which is so necessary to keep action sweet and sane. That this was so was evident from the fact that already among the arachnoids internecine strife had appeared. Island tended to compete with island, and one great industrial organization with another.

I could not help remarking that if this deep cleavage of interests had occurred on my own planet, say between our two sexes, the favoured sex would have single-mindedly trampled the other into servitude. Such a "victory" on the part of the arachnoids did indeed nearly occur. More and more partnerships were dissolved, each member attempting by means of drugs to supply his or her system with the chemicals normally provided by the symbiosis. For mental dependence, however, there was no substitute, and the divorced partners were subject to serious mental disorders, either subtle or flagrant. Nevertheless, there grew up a large population capable of living after a fashion without the symbiotic intercourse.

Strife now took a violent turn. The intransigents of both species attacked one another, and stirred up trouble among the moderates. There followed a period of desperate and confused warfare. On each side a small and hated minority advocated a "modernized symbiosis," in which each species should be able to contribute to the common life even in a mechanized civilization. Many of these reformers were martyred for their faith.

Victory would in the long run have gone to the arachnoids, for they controlled the sources of power. But it soon appeared that the attempt to break the symbiotic bond was not as successful as it had seemed. Even in actual warfare, commanders were unable to prevent widespread fraternization between the opposed forces. Members of dissolved partnerships would furtively meet to snatch a few hours or moments of each other's company. Widowed or deserted individuals of each species would timidly but hungrily venture toward the enemy's camps in search of new mates. Whole companies would surrender for the same purpose. The arachnoids suffered more from the neuroses than from the weapons of the enemy.

On the islands, moreover, civil wars and social revolutions made the manufacture of munitions almost impossible.

The most resolute faction of the arachnoids now attempted to bring the struggle to an end by poisoning the ocean. The islands in turn were poisoned by the millions of decaying corpses that rose to the sea's surface and were cast up on the shores. Poison, plague, and above all neurosis, brought war to a standstill, civilization to ruin, and the two species almost to extinction. The deserted sky-scrapers that crowded the islands began to crumble into heaps of wreckage. The submarine cities were invaded by the submarine jungle and by shark-like sub-human ichthyoids of many species. The delicate tissue of knowledge began to disintegrate into fragments of superstition.

Now at last came the opportunity of those who advocated a modernized symbiosis. With difficulty they had maintained a secret existence and their individual partnerships in the more remote and inhospitable regions of the planet. They now came boldly forth to spread their gospel among the unhappy remnants of the world's population. There was a rage of interspecific mating and remating. Primitive submarine agriculture and hunting maintained the scattered peoples while a few of the coral cities were cleared and rebuilt, and the instruments of a lean but hopeful civilization were refashioned. This was a temporary civilization, without mechanical power, but one which promised itself great adventures in the "upper world" as soon as it had established the basic principles of the reformed symbiosis.

To us it seemed that such an enterprise was doomed to failure, so clear was it that the future lay with a terrestrial rather than a marine creature. But we were mistaken. I must not tell in detail of the heroic struggle by which the race refashioned its symbiotic nature to suit the career that lay before it. The first stage was the reinstatement of power stations on the islands, and the careful reorganization of a purely submarine society equipped with power. But this reconstruction would have been useless had it not been accompanied by a very careful study of the physical and mental relations of the two species. The symbiosis had to be strengthened so that interspecific strife should in future be impossible. By means of chemical treatment in infancy the two kinds of organism were made more interdependent, and in partnership more hardy. By a special psychological ritual, a sort of mutual hypnosis, all newly joined partners were henceforth brought into indissoluble mental reciprocity. This interspecific communion, which every individual knew in immediate domestic experience, became in time the basic experience of all culture and religion. The symbiotic deity, which figured in all the primitive mythologies, was reinstated as a symbol of the dual personality of the universe, a dualism, it was said, of creativity and wisdom, unified as the divine spirit of love.

The one reasonable goal of social life was affirmed to be the creation of a world of awakened, of sensitive, intelligent, and mutually understanding personalities, banded together for the common purpose of exploring the universe and developing the "human" spirit's manifold potentialities. Imperceptibly the young were led to discover for themselves this goal.

Gradually and very cautiously all the industrial operations and scientific researches of an earlier age were repeated, but with a difference. Industry was subordinated to the conscious social goal. Science, formerly the slave of industry, became the free colleague of wisdom.

Once more the islands were crowded with buildings and with eager arachnoid workers. But all the shallow coastal waters were filled with a vast honeycomb of dwelling-houses, where the symbiotic partners took rest and refreshment with their mates. In the ocean depths the old cities were turned into schools, universities, museums, temples, palaces of art and of pleasure. There the young of both kinds grew up together. There the full-grown of both species met constantly for recreation and stimulation. There, while the arachnoids were busy on the islands, the ichthyoids performed their work of education and of refashioning the whole theoretical culture of the world. For it was known clearly by now that in this field their temperament and talents could make a vital contribution to the common life. Thus literature, philosophy, and non-scientific education were carried out chiefly in the ocean; while on the islands industry, scientific inquiry, and the plastic arts were more prominent.

Perhaps, in spite of the close union of each couple, this strange division of labour would have led in time to renewed conflict, had it not been for two new discoveries. One was the development of telepathy. Several centuries after the Age of War it was found possible to establish full telepathic intercourse between the two members of each couple. In time this intercourse was extended to include the whole dual race. The first result of this change was a great increase in the facility of communication between individuals all over the world, and therewith a great increase in mutual understanding and in unity of social purpose. But before we lost touch with this rapidly advancing race we had evidence of a much more far-reaching effect of universal telepathy. Sometimes, so we were told, telepathic communion of the whole race caused something like the fragmentary awakening of a communal world-mind in which all individuals participated.

The second great innovation of the race was due to genetic research. The arachnoids, who had to remain capable of active life on dry land and on a massive planet, could not achieve any great improvement in brain weight and complexity; but the ichthyoids, who were already large and were buoyed up by the water, were not subject to this limitation. After long and often disastrous experiment a race of "super-ichthyoids" was produced. In time the whole ichthyoid population came to consist of these creatures. Meanwhile the arachnoids, who were by now exploring and colonizing other planets of their solar system, were genetically improved not in respect of general brain complexity but in those special brain centres which afforded telepathic intercourse. Thus, in spite of their simpler brain-structure, they were able to maintain full telepathic community even with their big-brained mates far away in the oceans of the mother-planet. The simple brains and the complex brains formed now a single system, in which each unit, however simple its own contribution, was sensitive to the whole.

It was at this point, when the original ichthyoid race had given place to the super-ichthyoids, that we finally lost touch. The experience of the dual race passed completely beyond our comprehension. At a much later stage of our adventure we came upon them again, and on a higher plane of being. They were by then already engaged upon the vast common enterprise which, as I shall tell, was undertaken by the Galactic Society of Worlds. At this time the symbiotic race consisted of an immense host of arachnoid adventurers scattered over many planets, and a company of some fifty thousand million super-ichthyoids living a life of natatory delight and intense mental activity in the ocean of their great native world. Even at this stage physical contact between the symbiotic partners had to be maintained, though at long intervals. There was a constant stream of space-ships between the colonies and the mother-world. The ichthyoids, together with their teeming colleagues on a score of planets, supported a racial mind. Though the threads of the common experience were spun by the whole symbiotic race, they were woven into a single web by the ichthyoids alone in their primeval oceanic home, to be shared by all members of both races.

2. COMPOSITE BEINGS

Sometimes in the course of our adventure we came upon worlds inhabited by intelligent beings, whose developed personality was an expression not of the single individual organism but of a group of organisms. In most cases this state of affairs had arisen through the necessity of combining intelligence with lightness of the individual body. A large planet, rather close to its sun, or swayed by a very large satellite, would be swept by great ocean tides. Vast areas of its surface would be periodically submerged and exposed. In such a world flight was very desirable, but owing to the strength of gravitation only a small creature, a relatively small mass of molecules, could fly. A brain large enough for complex "human" activity could not have been lifted.

In such worlds the organic basis of intelligence was often a swarm of avian creatures no bigger than sparrows. A host of individual bodies were possessed together by a single individual mind of human rank. The body of this mind was multiple, but the mind itself was almost as firmly knit as the mind of a man. As flocks of dunlin or redshank stream and wheel and soar and quiver over our estuaries, so above the great tide-flooded cultivated regions of these worlds the animated clouds of avians manoeuvred, each cloud a single centre of consciousness. Presently, like our own winged waders, the little avians would settle, the huge volume of the cloud shrinking to a mere film upon the ground, a sort of precipitate along the fringe of the receding tide.

Life in these worlds was rhythmically divided by the tides. During the nocturnal tides the bird-clouds all slept on the waves. During the daytime tides they indulged in aerial sports and religious exercises. But twice a day, when the land was dry, they cultivated the drenched ooze, or carried out in their cities of concrete cells all the operations of industry and culture. It was interesting to us to see how ingeniously, before the tide's return, all the instruments of civilization were sealed from the ravages of the water.

We supposed at first that the mental unity of these little avians was telepathic, but in fact it was not. It was based on the unity of a complex electro-magnetic field, in fact on "radio" waves permeating the whole group. Radio, transmitted and received by every individual organism, corresponded to the chemical nerve current which maintains the unity of the human nervous system. Each brain reverberated with the ethereal rhythms of its environment; and each contributed its own peculiar theme to the complex pattern of the whole. So long as the flock was within a volume of about a cubic mile, the individuals were mentally unified, each serving as a specialized centre in the common "brain." But if some were separated from the flock, as sometimes happened in stormy weather, they lost mental contact and became separate minds of very low order. In fact each degenerated for the time being into a very simple instinctive animal or a system of reflexes, set wholly for the task of restoring contact with the flock.

It may easily be imagined that the mental life of these composite beings was very different from anything which we had yet encountered. Different and yet the same. Like a man, the bird-cloud was capable of anger and fear, hunger and sexual hunger, personal love and all the passions of the herd; but the medium of these experiences was so different from anything known to us that we found great difficulty in recognizing them.

Sex, for instance, was very perplexing. Each cloud was bisexual, having some hundreds of specialized male and female avian units, indifferent to one another, but very responsive to the presence of other bird-clouds. We found that in these strange multiple beings the delight and shame of bodily contact were obtained not only through actual sexual union of the specialized sexual members but, with the most exquisite subtlety, in the

aerial interfusion of two flying clouds during the performance of courtship gymnastics in the air.

More important for us than this superficial likeness to ourselves was
an underlying parity of mental rank. Indeed, we should not have gained
access to them at all had it not been for the essential similarity of their
evolutionary stage with that which we knew so well in our own worlds.
For each one of these mobile minded clouds of little birds was in fact an
individual approximately of our own spiritual order, indeed a very human
thing, torn between the beast and the angel, capable of ecstasies of love and
hate toward other such bird-clouds, capable of wisdom and folly, and the
whole gamut of human passions from swinishness to ecstatic contemplation.

Probing as best we could beyond the formal similarity of spirit which
gave us access to the bird-clouds, we discovered painfully how to see with
a million eyes at once, how to feel the texture of the atmosphere with a
million wings. We learned to interpret the composite percepts of mud-
flats and marshes and great agricultural regions, irrigated twice daily by
the tide. We admired the great tide-driven turbines and the system of
electric transport of freight. We discovered that the forests of high concrete poles or minarets, and platforms on stilts, which stood in the shal-
lowest of the tidal areas, were nurseries where the young were tended till
they could fly.

Little by little we learned to understand something of the alien thought
of these strange beings, which was in its detailed texture so different from
our own, yet in general pattern and significance so similar. Time presses,
and I must not try even to sketch the immense complexity of the most developed of these worlds. So much else has still to be told. I will say only
that, since the individuality of these bird-clouds was more precarious than
human individuality, it was apt to be better understood and more justly
valued. The constant danger of the bird-clouds was physical and mental
disintegration. Consequently the ideal of the coherent self was very prominent in all their cultures. On the other hand, the danger that the self of
the bird-cloud would be psychically invaded and violated by its neighbours, much as one radio station may interfere with another, forced these
beings to guard more carefully than ourselves against the temptations of
the herd, against drowning the individual cloud's self in the mob of
clouds. But again, just because this danger was effectively guarded against.
the ideal of the world-wide community developed without any life-and-
death struggle with mystical tribalism, such as we know too well. Instead
the struggle was simply between individualism and the twin ideals of the
world-community and the world-mind.

At the time of our visit world-wide conflict was already breaking out
between the two parties in every region of the planet. The individualists
were stronger in one hemisphere, and were slaughtering all adherents of

the world-mind ideal, and mustering their forces for attack on the other hemisphere. Here the party of the world-mind dominated, not by weapons but by sheer radio-bombardment, so to speak. The pattern of ethereal undulations issuing from the party imposed itself by sheer force on all re-calcitrants. All rebels were either mentally disintegrated by radio-bombard-ment or were absorbed intact into the communal radio system.

The war which ensued was to us astounding. The individualists used artillery and poison gas. The party of the world-mind used these weapons far less than the radio, which they, but not their enemies, could operate with irresistible effect. So greatly was the radio system strengthened, and so adapted to the physiological receptivity of the avian units, that before the individualists had done serious harm, they found themselves engulfed, so to speak, in an overwhelming torrent of radio stimulation. Their indi-viduality crumbled away. The avian units that made up their composite bodies were either destroyed (if they were specialized for war), or reor-ganized into new clouds, loyal to the world-mind.

Shortly after the defeat of the individualists we lost touch with this race. The experience and the social problems of the young world-mind were incomprehensible to us. Not till a much later stage of our adventure did we regain contact with it.

Others of the worlds inhabited by races of bird-clouds were less for-tunate. Most, through one cause or another, came to grief. In many of them the stresses of industrialism or of social unrest brought about a plague of insanity, or disintegration of the individual into a swarm of mere reflex animals. These miserable little creatures, which had not the power of in-dependent intelligent behaviour, were slaughtered in myriads by natural forces and beasts of prey. Presently the stage was clear for some worm or amoeba to reinaugurate the great adventure of biological evolution toward the human plane.

In the course of our exploration we came upon other types of com-posite individuals. For instance, we found that very large dry planets were sometimes inhabited by populations of insect-like creatures each of whose swarms or nests was the multiple body of a single mind. These planets were so large that no mobile organism could be bigger than a beetle, no flying organism bigger than an ant. In the intelligent swarms that ful-filled the part of men in these worlds, the microscopic brains of the insect-like units were specialized for microscopic functions within the group, much as the members of an ant's nest are specialized for working, fight-ing, reproduction, and so on. All were mobile, but each class of the units fulfilled special "neurological" functions in the life of the whole. In fact they acted as though they were special types of cells in a nervous system.

In these worlds, as in the worlds of the bird-clouds, we had to accustom ourselves to the unified awareness of a huge swarm of units. With innumerable hurrying feet we crept along Lilliputian concrete passages, with innumerable manipulatory antennae we took part in obscure industrial or agricultural operations, or in the navigation of toy ships on the canals and lakes of these flat worlds. Through innumerable many-faceted eyes we surveyed the plains of moss-like vegetation or studied the stars with minute telescopes and spectroscopes.

So perfectly organized was the life of the minded swarm that all routine activities of industry and agriculture had become, from the point of view of the swarm's mind, unconscious, like the digestive processes of a human being. The little insectoid units themselves carried on these operations consciously, though without understanding their significance; but the mind of the swarm had lost the power of attending to them. Its concern was almost wholly with such activities as called for unified conscious control, in fact with practical and theoretical invention of all kinds and with physical and mental exploration.

At the time of our visit to the most striking of these insectoid worlds the world-population consisted of many great nations of swarms. Each individual swarm had its own nest, its Lilliputian city, an area of about an acre, in which the ground was honey-combed to a depth of two feet with chambers and passages. The surrounding district was devoted to the cultivation of the moss-like food-plants. As the swarm increased in size, colonies might be founded beyond the range of the physiological radio system of the parent swarm. Thus arose new group-individuals. But neither in this race, nor in the race of bird-clouds, was there anything corresponding to our successive generations of individual minds. Within the minded group, the insectoid units were ever dying off and giving place to fresh units, but the mind of the group was potentially immortal. The units succeeded one another; the group-self persisted. Its memory reached back past countless generations of units, fading as it receded, and finally losing itself in that archaic time when the "human" was emerging from the "sub-human". Thus the civilized swarms had vague and fragmentary memories of every historical period.

Civilization had turned the old disorderly warrens into carefully planned subterranean cities; had turned the old irrigation channels into a widespread mesh of waterways for the transport of freight from district to district; had introduced mechanical power, based on the combustion of vegetable matter; had smelted metals from outcrops and alluvial deposits; had produced the extraordinary tissue of minute, almost microscopic machinery which had so greatly improved the comfort and health of the more advanced regions; had produced also myriads of tiny vehicles, corresponding to our tractors, trains, ships; had created class distinctions between those group-individuals that remained primarily agricultural, those that were mainly industrial, and those that specialized in intelligent co-ordination of their country's activities. These last became in time the bureaucratic tyrants of the country.

Owing to the great size of the planet and the extreme difficulty of long-distance travel by creatures so small as the insectoid units, civilizations had developed independently in a score of insulated regions; and when at last they came in contact, many of them were already highly industrialized, and equipped with the most "modern" weapons. The reader may easily imagine what happened when races that were in most cases biologically of different species, and anyhow were completely alien in customs, thought, and ideals, suddenly found themselves in contact and in conflict. It would be wearisome to describe the insane warfare which ensued. But it is of interest to note that we, the telepathic visitors from regions remote in time and space, could communicate with these warring hosts more easily than one host could communicate with another. And through this power we were actually able to play an important part in the history of this world. Indeed, it was probably through our mediation that these races were saved from mutual destruction. Taking up positions in "key" minds on each side of the conflict, we patiently induced in our hosts some insight into the mentality of the enemy. And since each of these races had already passed far beyond the level of sociality known on the Earth, since in relation to the life of his own race a swarm-mind was capable of true community, the realization of the enemy as being not monstrous but essentially humane, was enough to annihilate the will to fight.

The "key" minds on either side, enlightened by "divine messengers," heroically preached peace. And though many of them were hastily martyred, their cause triumphed. The races made terms with each other; all save two formidable and culturally rather backward peoples. These we could not persuade; and as they were by now highly specialized for war, they were a very serious menace. They regarded the new spirit of peace as mere weakness on the part of the enemy, and they were determined to take advantage of it, and to conquer the rest of that world.

But now we witnessed a drama which to terrestrial man must surely seem incredible. It was possible in this world only because of the high degree of mental lucidity which had already been attained within the bounds of each race. The pacific races had the courage to disarm. In the most spectacular and unmistakable manner they destroyed their weapons and their munition factories. They took care, too, that these events should be witnessed by enemy-swarms that had been taken prisoner. These captives they then freed, bidding them report their experiences to the enemy. In reply the enemy invaded the nearest of the disarmed countries and set about ruthlessly imposing the military culture upon it, by means of propaganda and persecution. But in spite of mass executions and mass torture, the upshot was not what was expected. For though the tyrant races were not appreciably more developed in sociality than *Homo sapiens,* the victims were far superior. Repression only strengthened the will for passive resistance. Little by little the tyranny began to waver. Then suddenly it collapsed. The invaders withdrew, taking with them the infection of pacifism. In a surprisingly short time that world became a federation, whose members were distinct species.

With sadness I realized that on the Earth, though all civilized beings belong to one and the same biological species, such a happy issue of strife is impossible, simply because the capacity for community in the individual mind is still too weak. I wondered, too, whether the tyrant races of insectoids would have had greater success in imposing their culture on the invaded country if there had been a distinct generation of juvenile malleable swarms for them to educate.

When this insectoid world had passed through its crisis, it began to advance so rapidly in social structure and in development of the individual mind that we found increasing difficulty in maintaining contact. At last we lost touch. But later, when we ourselves had advanced, we were to come upon this world again.

Of the other insectoid worlds, I shall say nothing, for not one of them was destined to play an important part in the history of the galaxy.

To complete the picture of the races in which the individual mind had not a single, physically continuous, body, I must refer to a very different and even stranger kind. In this the individual body is a cloud of ultramicroscopic sub-vital units, organized in a common radio-system. Of this kind is the race which now inhabits our own planet Mars. As I have already in another book described these beings and the tragic relations which they will have with our own descendants in the remote future, I shall say no more of them here; save that we did not make contact with them till a much later stage of our adventure, when we had acquired the skill to reach out to beings alien to ourselves in spiritual condition.

3. PLANT MEN AND OTHERS

Before passing on to tell the story of our galaxy as a whole (so far as I can comprehend it) I must mention another and a very alien kind of world. Of this type we found few examples, and few of these survived into the time when the galactic drama was at its height; but one at least had (or will have) a great influence on the growth of the spirit in that dramatic era.

On certain small planets, drenched with light and heat from a near or a great sun, evolution took a very different course from that with which we are familiar. The vegetable and animal functions were not separated into distinct organic types. Every organism was at once animal and vegetable.

In such worlds the higher organisms were something like gigantic and mobile herbs; but the violent flood of solar radiation rendered the tempo of their life much more rapid than that of our plants. To say that they looked like herbs is perhaps misleading, for they looked equally like animals. They had a definite number of limbs and a definite form of body; but all their skin was green, or streaked with green, and they bore here or there, according to their species, great masses of foliage. Owing to the slight power of gravitation on these small planets, the plant-animals often supported vast superstructures on very slender trunks or limbs. In general those that were mobile were less generously equipped with leaves than those that were more or less sedentary.

In these small hot worlds the turbulent circulation of water and atmosphere caused rapid changes in the condition of the ground from day to day. Storm and flood made it very desirable for the organisms of these worlds to be able to move from place to place. Consequently the early plants, which owing to the wealth of solar radiation could easily store themselves with energy for a life of moderate muscular activity, developed powers of perception and locomotion. Vegetable eyes and ears, vegetable organs of taste, scent and touch, appeared on their stems or foliage. For locomotion, some of them simply withdrew their primitive roots from the ground and crept hither and thither with a kind of caterpillar action. Some spread their foliage and drifted on the wind. From these in the course of ages arose true fliers. Meanwhile the pedestrian species turned some of their roots into muscular legs, four or six, or centipedal. The remaining roots were equipped with boring instruments, which on a new site could rapidly proliferate into the ground. Yet another method of combining locomotion and roots was perhaps more remarkable. The aerial portion of the organism would detach itself from its embedded roots, and wander off by land or air to strike root afresh in virgin soil. When the second site was exhausted the creature would either go off in search of a third, and so on, or return to its original bed, which by now might have recovered fertility. There, it would attach itself once more to its old dormant roots and wake them into new activity.

Many species, of course, developed predatory habits, and special organs of offence, such as muscular boughs as strong as pythons for constriction, or talons, horns, and formidable serrated pincers. In these "carnivorous" creatures the spread of foliage was greatly reduced, and all the leaves could be tucked snugly away along the back. In the most specialized beasts of prey the foliage was atrophied and had only decorative value. It was surprising to see how the environment imposed on these alien creatures forms suggestive of our tigers and wolves. And it was interesting, too, to note how excessive specialization and excessive adaptation to offence or defence ruined species after species; and how, when at length "human" intelligence appeared, it was achieved by an unimposing and inoffensive creature whose sole gifts were intelligence and sensibility toward the material world and toward its fellows.

Before describing the efflorescence of "humanity" in this kind of world I must mention one grave problem which faces the evolving life of all small planets, often at an early stage. This problem we had already come across on the Other Earth. Owing to the weakness of gravitation and the disturbing heat of the sun, the molecules of the atmosphere very easily escape into space. Most small worlds, of course, lose all their air and water long before life can reach the "human" stage, sometimes even before it can establish itself at all. Others, less small, may be thoroughly equipped with atmosphere in their early phases, but at a much later date, owing to the slow but steady contraction of their orbits, they may become so heated that they can no longer hold down the furiously agitated molecules of their atmosphere. On some of these planets a great population of living forms develops in early aeons only to be parched and suffocated out of existence through the long-drawn denudation and desiccation of the planet. But in more favourable cases life is able to adapt itself progressively to the increasingly severe conditions. In some worlds, for instance, a biological mechanism appeared by which the remaining atmosphere was imprisoned within a powerful electromagnetic field generated by the world's living population. In others the need of atmosphere was done away with altogether; photosynthesis and the whole metabolism of life were carried on by means of liquids alone. The last dwindling gases were captured in solution, stored in huge tracts of spongy growths among the crowded roots, and covered with an impervious membrane.

Both these natural biological methods occurred in one or other of the plant-animal worlds that reached the "human" level. I have space only to describe a single example, the most significant of these remarkable worlds. This was one in which all free atmosphere had been lost long before the appearance of intelligence.

To enter this world and experience it through the alien senses and alien temperament of its natives was an adventure in some ways more bewildering than any of our earlier explorations. Owing to the complete absence of atmosphere, the sky, even in full sunlight, was black with the blackness of interstellar space; and the stars blazed. Owing to the weakness of gravitation and the absence of the moulding action of air and water and frost on the planet's shrinking and wrinkled surface, the landscape was a mass of fold-mountains, primeval and extinct volcanoes, congealed floods and humps of lava, and craters left by the impact of giant meteors. None of these features had ever been much smoothed by atmospheric and glacial influences. Further, the ever-changing stresses of the planet's crust had shattered many of the mountains into the fantastic forms of ice-bergs. On our own earth, where gravity, that tireless hound, pulls down its quarry with so much greater strength, these slender, top-heavy crags and pinnacles could never have stood. Owing to the absence of atmosphere the exposed surfaces of the rock were blindingly illuminated; the crevasses and all the shadows were black as night.

Many of the valleys had been turned into reservoirs, seemingly of milk; for the surfaces of these lakes were covered with a deep layer of a white glutinous substance, to prevent loss by evaporation. Round about clustered the roots of the strange people of this world, like tree-stumps where a forest has been felled and cleared. Each stump was sealed with the white glue. Every stretch of soil was in use; and we learned that, though some of this soil was the natural result of past ages of action by air and water, most was artificial. It had been manufactured by great mining and pulverizing processes. In primitive times, and indeed throughout all "pre-human" evolution, the competitive struggle for a share of the rare soil of this world of rock had been one of the main spurs to intelligence.

The mobile plant-men themselves were to be seen by day clustered in the valleys, their foliage spread to the sun. Only by night did we observe them in action, moving over the bare rock or busy with machines and other artificial objects, instruments of their civilization. There were no buildings, no roofed weatherproof enclosures; for there was no weather. But the plateaux and terraces of the rock were crowded with all manner of artifacts unintelligible to us.

The typical plant-man was an erect organism, like ourselves. On his head he bore a vast crest of green plumes, which could be either folded together in the form of a huge, tight, cos lettuce, or spread out to catch the light. Three many-faceted eyes looked out from under the crest. Beneath these were three arm-like manipulatory limbs, green and serpentine, branching at their extremities. The slender trunk, pliable, encased in hard rings which slid into one another as the body bowed, was divided into three legs for locomotion. Two of the three feet were also mouths, which could either draw sap from the root or devour foreign matter. The third was an organ of excretion. The precious excrement was never wasted, but passed through a special junction between the third foot and the root. The feet contained taste-organs, and also ears. Since there was no air, sound was not propagated above ground.

By day the life of these strange beings was mainly vegetable, by night animal. Every morning, after the long and frigid night, the whole population swarmed to its rooty dormitories. Each individual sought out his own root, fixed himself to it, and stood throughout the torrid day, with leaves outspread. Till sunset he slept, not in a dreamless sleep, but in a sort of trance, the meditative and mystical quality of which was to prove in future ages a well of peace for many worlds. While he slept, the currents of sap hastened up and down his trunk, carrying chemicals between roots and leaves, flooding him with a concentrated supply of oxygen, removing the products of past katabolism. When the sun had disappeared once more behind the crags, displaying for a moment a wisp of fiery prominences, he would wake, fold up his leaves, close the passages to his roots, detach himself, and go about the business of civilized life. Night in this world was brighter than moonlight with us, for the stars were unobscured, and several great clusters hung in the night sky. Artificial light, however, was used for delicate operations. Its chief disadvantage was that it tended to send the worker to sleep.

I must not try even to sketch the rich and alien social life of these beings. I will only say that here as elsewhere we found all the cultural themes known on earth, but that in this world of mobile plants all was transposed into a strange key, a perplexing mode. Here as elsewhere we found a population of individuals deeply concerned with the task of keeping themselves and their society in being. Here we found self-regard, hate, love, the passions of the mob, intellectual curiosity, and so on. And here, as in all the other worlds that we had thus far visited, we found a race in the throes of the great spiritual crisis which was the crisis familiar to us in our own worlds, and formed the channel by which we had telepathic access to other worlds. But here the crisis had assumed a style different from any that we had yet encountered. We had, in fact, begun to extend our powers of imaginative exploration.

Leaving all else unnoticed, I must try to describe this crisis, for it is significant for the understanding of matters which reached far beyond this little world.

We did not begin to have insight into the drama of this race till we had learned to appreciate the mental aspect of its dual, animal-vegetable nature. Briefly, the mentality of the plant-men in every age was an expression of the varying tension between the two sides of their nature, between the active, assertive, objectively inquisitive, and morally positive animal nature and the passive, subjectively contemplative, and devoutly acquiescent vegetable nature. It was of course through animal prowess and practical human intelligence that the species had long ago come to dominate its world. But at all times this practical will had been tempered and enriched by a kind of experience which among men is very rare. Every day, throughout the ages, these beings had surrendered their feverish animal nature not merely to unconscious or dream-racked sleep, such as animals know, but to the special kind of awareness which (we learned) belongs to plants. Spreading their leaves, they had absorbed directly the essential elixir of life which animals receive only at second hand in the mangled flesh of their prey. Thus they seemingly maintained immediate physical contact with the source of all cosmical being. And this state, though physical, was also in some sense spiritual. It had a far-reaching effect on all their conduct. If theological language were acceptable, it might well be called a spiritual contact with

God. During the busy night-time they went about their affairs as insulated individuals, having no present immediate experience of their underlying unity; but normally they were always preserved from the worst excesses of individualism by memory of their day-time life.

It took us long to understand that their peculiar day-time state did not consist simply in being united as a group mind, whether of tribe or race. Theirs was not the condition of the avian units in the bird-cloud, nor yet of the telepathically constituted world-minds which, as we were later to discover, had a very great part to play in galactic history. The plant-man did not in his daytime life come into possession of the percepts and thoughts of his fellow plant-men, and thereby waken into a more comprehensive and discriminate awareness of the environment and of the multiple body of the race. On the contrary, he became completely unresponsive to all objective conditions save the flood of sunlight drenching his spread leaves. And this experience afforded him an enduring ecstasy whose quality was almost sexual, an ecstasy in which subject and object seemed to become identical, an ecstasy of subjective union with the obscure source of all finite being. In this state the plant-man could meditate upon his active, night-time life, and could become aware, far more clearly than by night, of the intricacies of his own motives. In this day-time mode he passed no moral judgments on himself or others. He mentally reviewed every kind of human conduct with detached contemplative joy, as a factor in the universe. But when night came again, bringing the active nocturnal mood, the calm, day-time insight into himself and others was lit with a fire of moral praise and censure.

Now throughout the career of this race there had been a certain tension between the two basic impulses of its nature. All its finest cultural achievements had been made in times when both had been vigorous and neither predominant. But, as in so many other worlds, the development of natural science and the production of mechanical power from tropical sunlight caused grave mental confusion. The manufacture of innumerable aids to comfort and luxury, the spread of electric railways over the whole world, the development of radio communication, the study of astronomy and mechanistic biochemistry, the urgent demands of war and social revolution, all these influences strengthened the active mentality and weakened the contemplative. The climax came when it was found possible to do away with the day-time sleep altogether. The products of artificial photosynthesis could be rapidly injected into the living body every morning, so that the plant-man could spend practically the whole day in active work. Very soon the roots of the peoples were being dug up and used as raw material in manufacture. They were no longer needed for their natural purpose.

I must not spend time in describing the hideous plight into which this world now fell. Seemingly, artificial photosynthesis, though it could keep the body vigorous, failed to produce some essential vitamin of the spirit. A disease of robotism, of purely mechanical living, spread through-out the population. There was of course a fever of industrial activity. The plant-men careered round their planet in all kinds of mechanically pro-pelled vehicles, decorated themselves with the latest synthetic products, tapped the central volcanic heat for power, expended great ingenuity in destroying one another, and in a thousand other feverish pursuits pushed on in search of a bliss which ever eluded them.

After untold distresses they began to realize that their whole way of life was alien to their essential plant nature. Leaders and prophets dared to inveigh against mechanization and against the prevalent intellectualistic scientific culture, and against artificial photosynthesis. By now nearly all the roots of the race had been destroyed; but presently biological science was turned to the task of generating, from the few remaining specimens, new roots for all. Little by little the whole population was able to return to natural photosynthesis. The industrial life of the world vanished like frost in sunlight. In returning to the old alternating life of animal and veg-etable, the plant-men, jaded and deranged by the long fever of industrialism, found in their calm day-time experience an overwhelming joy. The misery of their recent life intensified by contrast the ecstasy of the vegetal experi-ence. The intellectual acuity that their brightest minds had acquired in scientific analysis combined with the special quality of their revived plant life to give their whole experience a new lucidity. For a brief period they reached a plane of spiritual lucidity which was to be an example and a treasure for the future aeons of the galaxy.

But even the most spiritual life has its temptations. The extravagant fever of industrialism and intellectualism had so subtly poisoned the plant-men that when at last they rebelled against it they swung too far, falling into the snare of a vegetal life as one-sided as the old animal life had been. Little by little they gave less and less energy and time to "animal" pur-suits, until at last their nights as well as their days were spent wholly as trees, and the active, exploring, manipulating, animal intelligence died in them for ever.

For a while the race lived on in an increasingly vague and confused ecstasy of passive union with the universal source of being. So well estab-lished and automatic was the age-old biological mechanism for preserving the planet's vital gases in solution that it continued long to function with-out attention. But industrialism had increased the world population beyond the limits within which the small supply of water and gases could easily fulfil its function. The circulation of material was dangerously rapid. In time the mechanism was over-strained. Leakages began to appear, and no one repaired them. Little by little the precious water and other volatile substances escaped from the planet. Little by little the reservoirs ran dry, the spongy roots were parched, the leaves withered. One by one the blissful and no longer human inhabitants of that world passed from ecstasy to sickness, despondency, uncomprehending bewilderment, and on to death.

But, as I shall tell, their achievement was not without effect on the life of our galaxy.

"Vegetable humanities," if I may so call them, proved to be rather uncommon occurrences. Some of them inhabited worlds of a very curious kind which I have not yet mentioned. As is well known, a small planet close to its sun tends, through the sun's tidal action upon it, to lose its rotation. Its days become longer and longer, till at last it presents one face constantly toward its luminary. Not a few planets of this type, up and down the galaxy, were inhabited; and several of them by "vegetable humanities."

All these "non-diurnal" worlds were very inhospitable to life, for one hemisphere was always extravagantly hot, the other extravagantly cold. The illuminated face might reach the temperature of molten lead; on the dark face, however, no substances could retain the liquid state, for the temperature would remain but a degree or two above absolute zero. Between the two hemispheres there would lie a narrow belt, or rather a mere ribbon, which might be called temperate. Here the immense and incendiary sun was always partly hidden by the horizon. Along the cooler side of this ribbon, hidden from the murderous rays of the sun's actual disc, but illuminated by his corona, and warmed by the conduction of heat from the sunward ground, life was not invariably impossible.

Inhabited worlds of this kind had always reached a fairly high stage of biological evolution long before they had lost their diurnal rotation. As the day lengthened, life was forced to adapt itself to more extreme temperatures of day and night. The poles of these planets, if not too much inclined toward the ecliptic, remained at a fairly constant temperature, and were therefore citadels whence the living forms ventured into less hospitable regions. Many species managed to spread toward the equator by the simple method of burying themselves and "hibernating" through the day and the night, emerging only for dawn and sunset to lead a furiously active life. As the day lengthened into months, some species, adapted for swift locomotion, simply trekked round the planet, following the sunset and the dawn. Strange it was to see the equatorial and most agile of these species sweeping over the plains in the level sunlight. Their legs were often as tall and slender as a ship's masts. Now and then they would swerve, with long necks extended to snatch some scurrying creature or pluck some bunch of foliage. Such constant and rapid migration would have been impossible in worlds less rich in solar energy.

Human intelligence seems never to have been attained in any of these worlds unless it had been attained already before night and day became excessively long, and the difference of their temperatures excessively great. In worlds where plant-men or other creatures had achieved civilization and science before rotation had become seriously retarded, great efforts were made to cope with the increasing harshness of the environment. Sometimes civilization merely retreated to the poles, abandoning the rest of the planet. Sometimes subterranean settlements were established in other regions, the inhabitants issuing only at dawn and sunset to cultivate the land. Sometimes a system of railways along the parallels of latitude carried a migratory population from one agricultural centre to another, following the twilight.

Finally, however, when rotation had been entirely lost, a settled civilization would be crowded along the whole length of the stationary girdle between night and day. By this time, if not before, the atmosphere would have been lost also. It can well be imagined that a race struggling to survive in these literally straightened circumstances would not be able to maintain any richness and delicacy of mental life.

CHAPTER VIII

CONCERNING THE EXPLORERS

BVALLTU and I, in company with the increasing band of our fellow explorers, visited many worlds of many strange kinds. In some we spent only a few weeks of the local time; in others we remained for centuries, or skimmed from point to point of history as our interest dictated. Like a swarm of locusts we would descend upon a new-found world, each of us singling out a suitable host. After a period of observation, long or short, we would leave, to alight again, perhaps, on the same world in another of its ages; or to distribute our company among many worlds, far apart in time and in space.

This strange life turned me into a very different being from the Englishman who had at a certain date of human history walked at night upon a hill. Not only had my own immediate experience increased far beyond the normal range, but also, by means of a peculiarly intimate union with my fellows, I myself had been, so to speak, multiplied. For in a sense I was now as much Bvalltu and each one of my colleagues as I was that Englishman.

This change that had come over us deserves to be carefully described, not merely for its intrinsic interest, but also because it afforded us a key for understanding many cosmical beings whose nature would otherwise have been obscure to us.

In our new condition our community was so perfected that the experiences of each were available to all. Thus I, the new I, participated in the adventures of that Englishman and of Bvalltu and the rest with equal ease. And I possessed all their memories of former, separate existence in their respective native worlds.

Some philosophically minded reader may ask, "Do you mean that the many experiencing individuals became a single individual, having a single stream of experience? Or do you mean that there remained many experiencing individuals, having numerically distinct but exactly similar experiences?" The answer is that I do not know. But this I know. I, the Englishman, and similarly each of my colleagues, gradually "woke" into possession of each other's experience, and also into more lucid intelligence. Whether, as experients, we remained many or became one, I do not know. But I suspect that the question is one of those which can never be truly answered because in the last analysis it is meaningless.

In the course of my communal observation of the many worlds, and equally in the course of my introspection of my own communal mental processes, now one and now another individual explorer, and now perhaps a group of explorers, would form the main instrument of attention, affording through their particular nature and experience material for the contemplation of all. Sometimes, when we were exceptionally alert and eager, each awakened into a mode of perception and thought and imagination and will more lucid than any experiencing known to any of us as individuals. Thus, though each of us became in a sense identical with each of his friends, he also became in a manner a mind of higher order than any of us in isolation. But in this "waking" there seemed to be nothing more mysterious in kind than in those many occasions in normal life when the mind delightedly relates together experiences that have hitherto been insulated from one another, or discovers in confused objects a pattern or a significance hitherto unnoticed.

It must not be supposed that this strange mental community blotted out the personalities of the individual explorers. Human speech has no accurate terms to describe our peculiar relationship. It would be as untrue to say that we had lost our individuality, or were dissolved in a communal individuality, as to say that we were all the while distinct individuals. Though the pronoun "I" now applied to us all collectively, the pronoun "we" also applied to us. In one respect, namely unity of consciousness, we were indeed a single experiencing individual; yet at the same time we were in a very important and delightful manner distinct from one another. Though there was only the single, communal "I," there was also, so to speak, a manifold and variegated "us," an observed company of very diverse personalities, each of whom expressed creatively his own unique contribution to the whole enterprise of cosmical exploration, while all were bound together in a tissue of subtle personal relationships.

I am well aware that this account of the matter must seem to my readers self-contradictory, as indeed it does to me. But I can find no other way of expressing the vividly remembered fact that I was at once a particular member of a community and the possessor of the pooled experience of that community.

To put the matter somewhat differently, though in respect of our identity of awareness we were a single individual, in respect of our diverse and creative idiosyncrasies we were distinct persons observable by the common "I." Each one, as the common "I," experienced the whole company of individuals, including his individual self, as a group of actual persons, differing in temperament and private experience. Each one of us experienced all as a real community, bound together by such relations of affection and mutual criticism as occurred, for instance, between Bvalltu and myself. Yet on another plane of experience, the plane of creative thought and imagination, the single communal attention could withdraw from this tissue of personal relationships. Instead, it concerned itself wholly with the exploration of the cosmos. With partial truth it might be said that, while for love we were distinct, for knowledge, for wisdom, and for worship we were identical. In the following chapters, which deal with the cosmical, experiences of this communal "I," it would be logically correct to refer to the exploring mind always in the singular, using the pronoun "I," and saying simply, "I did so and so, and thought so and so"; nevertheless the pronoun "we" will still be generally employed so as to preserve the true impression of a communal enterprise, and to avoid the false impression that the explorer was just the human author of this book.

Each one of us had lived his individual active life in one or other of the many worlds. And for each one, individually, his own little blundering career in his remote native world retained a peculiar concreteness and glamour, like the vividness which mature men find in childhood memories. Not only so, but individually he imputed to his former private life an urgency and importance which, in his communal capacity, was overwhelmed by matters of greater cosmical significance. Now this concreteness and glamour, this urgency and importance of each little private life, was of great moment to the communal "I" in which each of us participated. It irradiated the communal experience with its vividness, its pathos. For only in his own life as a native in some world had each of us actually fought, so to speak, in life's war as a private soldier at close grips with the enemy. It was the recollection of this fettered, imprisoned, blindfold, eager, private individuality, that enabled us to watch the unfolding of cosmical events not merely as a spectacle but with a sense of the poignancy of every individual life as it flashed and vanished.

Thus I, the Englishman, contributed to the communal mind my persistently vivid recollections of all my ineffectual conduct in my own troubled world; and the true significance of that blind human life, redeemed by its little imperfect jewel of community, became apparent to me, the communal "I," with a lucidity which the Englishman in his primaeval stupor could never attain and cannot now recapture. All that I can now remember is that, as the communal "I," I looked on my terrestrial career at once more critically and with less guilt than I do in the individual state; and on my partner in that career at once with clearer, colder understanding of our mutual impact and with more generous affection.

One aspect of the communal experience of the explorers I have still to mention. Each of us had originally set out upon the great adventure mainly in the hope of discovering what part was played by community in the cosmos as a whole. This question had yet to be answered; but meanwhile another question was becoming increasingly insistent. Our crowded experiences in the many worlds, and our new lucidity of mind, had bred in each of us a sharp conflict of intellect and feeling. Intellectually the idea that some "deity," distinct from the cosmos itself, had made the cosmos now seemed to us less and less credible. Intellectually we had no doubt that the cosmos was self-sufficient, a system involving no logical ground and no creator. Yet increasingly, as a man may feel the psychical reality of a physically perceived beloved or a perceived enemy, we felt in the physical presence of the cosmos the psychical presence of that which we had named the Star Maker. In spite of intellect, we knew that the whole cosmos was infinitely less than the whole of being, and that the whole infinity of being underlay every moment of the cosmos. And with unreasoning passion we strove constantly to peer behind each minute particular event in the cosmos to see the very features of that infinity which, for lack of a truer name, we had called the Star Maker. But, peer as we might, we found nothing. Though in the whole and in each particular thing the dread presence indubitably confronted us, its very infinity prevented us from assigning to it any features whatever.

Sometimes we inclined to conceive it as sheer Power, and symbolized it to ourselves by means of all the myriad power-deities of our many worlds. Sometimes we felt assured that it was pure Reason, and that the cosmos was but an exercise of the divine mathematician. Sometimes Love seemed to us its essential character, and we imagined it with the forms of all the Christs of all the worlds, the human Christs, the Echinoderm and Nautiloid Christs, the dual Christ of the Symbiotics, the swarming Christ of the Insectoids. But equally it appeared to us as unreasoning Creativity, at once blind and subtle, tender and cruel, caring only to spawn and spawn the infinite variety of beings, conceiving here and there among a thousand inanities a fragile loveliness. This it might for a while foster with maternal solicitude, till in a sudden jealousy of the excellence of its own creature, it would destroy what it had made.

But we knew well that all these fictions were very false. The felt presence of the Star Maker remained unintelligible, even though it increasingly illuminated the cosmos, like the splendour of the unseen sun at dawn.

CHAPTER IX

THE COMMUNITY OF WORLDS

I. BUSY UTOPIAS

THERE came a time when our new-found communal mind attained such a degree of lucidity that it was able to maintain contact even with worlds that had passed far beyond the mentality of terrestrial man. Of these lofty experiences I, who am once more reduced to the state of a mere individual human being, have only the most confused memory. I am like one who, in the last extremity of mental fatigue, tries to recapture the more penetrating intuitions that he achieved in his lost freshness. He can recover only faint echoes and a vague glamour. But even the most fragmentary recollections of the cosmical experiences which befell me in that lucid state deserve recording.

The sequence of events in the successfully waking world was generally more or less as follows. The starting point, it will be remembered, was a plight like that in which our own Earth now stands. The dialectic of the world's history had confronted the race with a problem with which the traditional mentality could never cope. The world-situation had grown too complex for lowly intelligences, and it demanded a degree of individual integrity in leaders and in led, such as was as yet possible only to a few minds. Consciousness had already been violently awakened out of the primitive trance into a state of excruciating individualism, of poignant but pitifully restricted self-awareness. And individualism, together with the traditional tribal spirit, now threatened to wreck the world. Only after a long-drawn agony of economic distress and maniac warfare, haunted by an increasingly clear vision of a happier world, could the second stage of waking be achieved. In most cases it was not achieved. "Human nature," or its equivalent in the many worlds, could not change itself; and the environment could not remake it.

But in a few worlds the spirit reacted to its desperate plight with a miracle. Or, if the reader prefers, the environment miraculously refashioned the spirit. There occurred a widespread and almost sudden waking into a new lucidity of consciousness and a new integrity of will. To call this change miraculous is only to recognize that it could not have been scientifically predicted even from the fullest possible knowledge of "human nature" as manifested in the earlier age. To later generations, however, it appeared as no miracle but as a belated wakening from an almost miraculous stupor into plain sanity.

This unprecedented access of sanity took at first the form of a widespread passion for a new social order which should be just and should embrace the whole planet. Such a social fervour was not, of course, entirely new. A small minority had long ago conceived it, and had haltingly tried to devote themselves to it. But now at last, through the scourge of circumstance and the potency of the spirit itself, this social will became general. And while it was still passionate, and heroic action was still possible to the precariously awakened beings, the whole social structure of the world was reorganized, so that within a generation or two every individual on the planet could count upon the means of life, and the opportunity to exercise his powers fully, for his own delight and for the service of the world community. It was now possible to bring up the new generations to a sense that the world-order was no alien tyranny but an expression of the general will, and that they had indeed been born into a noble heritage, a thing for which it was good to live and suffer and die. To readers of this book such a change may well seem miraculous, and such a state utopian.

Those of us who had come from less fortunate planets found it at once a heartening and yet a bitter experience to watch world after world successfully emerge from a plight which seemed inescapable, to see a world-population of frustrated and hate-poisoned creatures give place to one in which every individual was generously and shrewdly nurtured, and therefore not warped by unconscious envy and hate. Very soon, though no change had occurred in the biological stock, the new social environment produced a world population which might well have seemed to belong to a new species. In physique, in intelligence, in mental independence and social responsibility, the new individual far outstripped the old, as also in mental wholesomeness and in integrity of will. And though it was sometimes feared that the removal of all sources of grave mental conflict might deprive the mind of all stimulus to creative work, and produce a mediocre population, it was soon found that, far from stagnating, the spirit of the race now passed on to discover new fields of struggle and triumph. The world-population of "aristocrats," which flourished after the great change, looked back with curiosity and incredulity into the preceding age, and found great difficulty in conceiving the tangled, disreputable and mostly unwitting motives which were the main-springs of action even in the most fortunate individuals among their ancestors. It was recognized that the whole pre-revolutionary population was afflicted with serious mental diseases, with endemic plagues of delusion and obsession, due to mental malnutrition and poisoning. As psychological insight advanced, the same kind of interest was aroused by the old psychology as is wakened in modern Europeans by ancient maps which distort the countries of the world almost beyond recognition.

We were inclined to think of the psychological crisis of the waking worlds as being the difficult passage from adolescence to maturity; for in essence it was an outgrowing of juvenile interests, a discarding of toys and childish games, and a discovery of the interests of adult life. Tribal prestige, individual dominance, military glory, industrial triumphs lost their obsessive glamour, and instead the happy creatures delighted in civilized social intercourse, in cultural activities, and in the common enterprise of world-building.

During the phase of history which followed the actual surmounting of the spiritual crisis in a waking world the attention of the race was of course still chiefly occupied with social reconstruction. Many heroic tasks had to be undertaken. There was need not only for a new economic system but for new systems of political organization, of world-law, of education. In many cases this period of reconstruction under the guidance of the new mentality was itself a time of serious conflict. For even beings who are sincerely in accord about the goal of social activity may disagree violently about the way. But such conflicts as arose, though heated, were of a very different kind from the earlier conflicts which were inspired by obsessive individualism and obsessive group-hatreds.

We noted that the new world-orders were very diverse. This was, of course, to be expected, since biologically, psychologically, culturally, these worlds were very different. The perfected world-order of an Echinoderm race had of course to be different from that of the symbiotic Ichthyoids and Arachnoids; and this from that of a Nautiloid world, and so on. But we noted also in all these victorious worlds a remarkable identity. For instance, in the loosest possible sense, all were communistic; for in all of them the means of production were communally owned, and no individual could control the labour of others for private profit. Again, in a sense all these world-orders were democratic, since the final sanction of policy was world-opinion. But in many cases there was no democratic machinery, no legal channel for the expression of world-opinion. Instead, a highly specialized bureaucracy, or even a world-dictator, might carry out the business of organizing the world's activity with legally absolute power, but under constant supervision by popular will expressed through the radio. We were amazed to find that in a truly awakened world even a dictatorship could be in essence democratic. We observed with incredulity situations in which the "absolute" world-government, faced with some exceptionally momentous and doubtful matter of policy, had made urgent appeals for a formal democratic decision, only to receive from all regions the reply, "We cannot advise. You must decide as your professional experience suggests. We will abide by your decision."

Law in these worlds was based on a very remarkable kind of sanction which could not conceivably work successfully on Earth. There was never any attempt to enforce the law by violence, save against dangerous lunatics, such as sometimes occurred as throw-backs to an earlier age. In some worlds there was a complex body of "laws" regulating the economic and social life of groups, and even the private affairs of individuals. It seemed to us at first that freedom had vanished from such worlds. But later we discovered that the whole intricate system was regarded as we should regard the rules of a game or the canons of an art, or the innumerable extra-legal customs of any long-established society. In the main, everyone kept the law because he had faith in its social value as a guide to conduct. But if ever the law seemed inadequate he would without hesitation break it. His conduct might cause offence or inconvenience or even serious hardship to his neighbours. They would probably protest vigorously. But there was never question of compulsion. If those concerned failed to persuade him that his behaviour was socially harmful, his case might be tried by a sort of court of arbitration, backed by the prestige of the world-government. If the decision went against the defendant, and yet he persisted in his illegal behaviour, none would restrain him. But such was the power of public censure and social ostracism that disregard of the court's decision was very rare. The terrible sense of isolation acted on the law-breaker like an ordeal by fire. If his motive was at bottom base, he would sooner or later collapse. But if his case had merely been misjudged, or if his conduct sprang from an intuition of value beyond the range of his fellows, he might persist in his course till he had won over the public.

I mention these social curiosities only to give some illustration of the far-reaching difference between the spirit of these utopian worlds and the spirit which is familiar to readers of this book. It may be easily imagined that in our wanderings we came upon a wonderful diversity of customs and institutions, but I must not pause to describe even the most remarkable of them. I must be content to outline the activities of the typical waking worlds, so as to be able to press on to tell a story not merely of particular worlds but of our galaxy as a whole.

When a waking world had passed through the phase of radical social reconstruction, and had attained a new equilibrium, it would settle into a period of steady economic and cultural advancement. Mechanism, formerly a tyrant over body and mind, but now a faithful servant, would secure for every individual a fulness and diversity of life far beyond anything known on earth. Radio communication and rocket travel would afford to each mind intimate knowledge of every people. Labour-saving machinery would reduce the work of maintaining civilization; all mind-crippling drudgery would vanish, and the best energy of every one of the world-citizens would be freely devoted to social service that was not unworthy of a well-grown intelligent being. And "social service" was apt to be interpreted very broadly. It seemed to permit many lives to be given over wholly to freakish and irresponsible self-expression. The community could well afford a vast amount of such wastage for the sake of the few invaluable jewels of originality which occasionally emerged from it.

This stable and prosperous phase of the waking worlds, which we came to call the utopian phase, was probably the happiest of all the ages in the life of any world. Tragedy of one sort or another there would still be, but never widespread and futile distress. We remarked, moreover, that, whereas in former ages tragedy had been commonly thought of in terms of physical pain and premature death, now it was conceived more readily as resulting from the clash and mutual yearning and mutual incompatibility of diverse personalities; so rare had the cruder kind of disaster become, and on the other hand so much more subtle and sensitive were the contacts between persons. Widespread physical tragedy, the suffering and annihiliation of whole populations, such as we experience in war and plague, were quite unknown, save in those rare cases when a whole race was destroyed by astronomical accident, whether through loss of atmosphere or the bursting of its planet or the plunging of its solar system into some tract of gas or dust.

In this happy phase, then, which might last for a few centuries or for many thousands of years, the whole energy of the world would be devoted to perfecting the world-community and raising the calibre of the race by cultural and by eugenical means.

Of the eugenical enterprise of these worlds I shall report little, because much of it would be unintelligible without a minute knowledge of the biological and biochemical nature of each of these non-human world-populations. It is enough to say that the first task of the eugenists was to prevent the perpetuation of inheritable disease and malformation of body and mind. In days before the great psychological change even this modest work had often led to serious abuses. Governments would attempt to breed out all those characters, such as independence of mind, which were distasteful to governments. Ignorant enthusiasts would advocate ruthless and misguided interference in the choice of mates. But in the more enlightened age these dangers were recognized and avoided. Even so, the eugenical venture did often lead to disaster. One splendid race of intelligent avians we saw reduced to the sub-human level by an attempt to extirpate susceptibility to a virulent mental disease. The liability to this disease happened to be genetically linked in an indirect manner with the possibility of normal brain development in the fifth generation.

Of positive eugenical enterprises I need only mention improvements of sensory range and acuity (chiefly in sight and touch), the invention of new senses, improvements in memory, in general intelligence, in temporal discrimination. These races came to distinguish ever more minute periods of duration, and at the same time to extend their temporal grasp so as to apprehend ever longer periods as "now."

Many of the worlds at first devoted much energy to this kind of eugenical work, but later decided that, though it might afford them some new richness of experience, it must be postponed for the sake of more important matters. For instance, with the increasing complexity of life it soon appeared very necessary to retard the maturing of the individual mind, so as to enable it to assimilate its early experience more thoroughly. "Before life begins," it was said, "there should be a lifetime of childhood." At the same time efforts were made to prolong maturity to three or four times its normal extent, and to reduce senility. In every world that had gained full eugenical power there arose sooner or later a sharp public discussion as to the most suitable length of individual life. All were agreed that life must be prolonged; but, while one party wished to multiply it only three or four times, another insisted that nothing less than a hundred times the normal life-span could afford the race that continuity and depth of experience which all saw to be desirable. Another party even advocated deathlessness, and a permanent race of never-aging immortals. It was argued that the obvious danger of mental rigidity, and the cessation of all advancement, might be avoided by contriving that the permanent physiological state of the deathless population should be one of very early maturity.

Different worlds found different solutions for this problem. Some races assigned to the individual a period no longer than three hundred of our years. Others allowed him fifty thousand. One race of Echinoderms decided on potential immortality, but endowed themselves with an ingenious psychological mechanism by which, if the ancient began to lose touch with changing conditions, he could not fail to recognize the fact, and would thereupon crave and practise euthanasia, gladly yielding his place to a successor of more modern type.

Many other triumphs of eugenical experiment we observed up and down the worlds. The general level of individual intelligence was, of course, raised far beyond the range of *Homo sapiens*. But also that superintelligence which can be attained only by a psychically unified community was greatly developed on the highest practicable plane, that of the conscious individuality of a whole world. This, of course, was impossible till the social cohesion of individuals within the world-community had become as close-knit as the integration of the elements of a nervous system. It demanded also a very great advance of telepathy. Further, it was not possible till the great majority of individuals had reached a breadth of knowledge unknown on earth.

The last and most difficult power to be attained by these worlds in the course of their utopian phase was psychical freedom of time and space, the limited power to observe directly, and even contribute to, events remote from the spacio-temporal location of the observer. Throughout our exploration we had been greatly perplexed by the fact that we, most of whom were beings of a very humble order, should have been able to achieve this freedom, which, as we now discovered, these highly developed worlds found so difficult to master. The explanation was now given us. No such venture as ours could have been undertaken by our unaided selves. Throughout our exploration we had unwittingly been under the influence of a system of worlds which had attained this freedom only after aeons of research. Not one step could we have taken without the constant support of those brilliant Ichthyoid and Arachnoid Symbiotics who played a leading part in the history of our galaxy. They it was who controlled our whole adventure, so that we might report our experiences in our primitive native worlds.

The freedom of space and time, the power of cosmical exploration and of influence by means of telepathic contact, was at once the most potent and the most dangerous asset of the fully awakened utopian worlds. Through the unwise exercise of it many a glorious and single-minded race came to disaster. Sometimes the adventuring world-mind failed to maintain its sanity in face of the welter of misery and despair that now flooded in upon it telepathically from all the regions of the galaxy. Sometimes the sheer difficulty of comprehending the subtleties that were revealed to it flung it into a mental breakdown from which there was no recovery. Sometimes it became so enthralled by its telepathic adventures that it lost touch with its own life upon its native planet, so that the world-community, deprived of its guiding communal mind, fell into disorder and decay, and the exploring mind itself died.

2. INTERMUNDANE STRIFE

Of the busy utopias which I have been describing, a few were already established even before the birth of the Other Earth, a larger number flourished before our own planet was formed, but many of the most important of these worlds are temporally located in an age far future to us, an age long after the destruction of the final human race. Casualties among these awakened worlds are of course much less common than among more lowly and less competent worlds. Consequently, though fatal accidents occurred in every epoch, the number of awakened worlds in our galaxy steadily increased as time advanced. The actual births of planets, due to the chance encounters of mature but not aged stars, reached (or will reach) a maximum fairly late in the history of our galaxy, and then declined. But since the fluctuating progress of a world from bare animality to spiritual maturity takes, on the average, several thousands of millions of years, the maximum population of utopian and fully awakened worlds occurred very late, when physically the galaxy was already somewhat past its prime. Further, though even in early epochs the few awakened worlds did sometimes succeed in making contact with one another, either by interstellar travel or by telepathy, it was not till a fairly late stage of galactic history that intermundane relations came to occupy the main attention of the wakened worlds.

Throughout the progress of a waking world there was one grave, subtle, and easily overlooked danger. Interest might be "fixated" upon some current plane of endeavour, so that no further advance could occur. It may seem strange that beings whose psychological knowledge so far surpassed the attainment of man should have been trapped in this manner.

Apparently at every stage of mental development, save the highest of all, the mind's growing point is tender and easily misdirected. However this may be, it is a fact that a few rather highly developed worlds, even with communal mentality, were disastrously perverted in a strange manner, which I find very difficult to understand. I can only suggest that in them, seemingly, the hunger for true community and true mental lucidity itself became obsessive and perverse, so that the behaviour of these exalted perverts might deteriorate into something very like tribalism and religious fanaticism. The disease would soon lead to the stifling of all elements which seemed recalcitrant to the generally accepted culture of the world-society. When such worlds mastered interstellar travel, they might conceive a fanatical desire to impose their own culture throughout the galaxy. Sometimes their zeal became so violent that they were actually driven to wage ruthless religious wars on all who resisted them.

Obsessions derived from one stage or another of the progress toward utopia and lucid consciousness, even if they did not bring violent disaster, might at any stage side-track the waking world into futility. Superhuman intelligence, courage, and constancy on the part of the devoted individuals might be consecrated to misguided and unworthy world purposes. Thus it was that, in extreme cases, even a world that remained socially utopian and mentally a super-individual, might pass beyond the bounds of sanity. With a gloriously healthy body and an insane mind it might do terrible harm to its neighbours.

Such tragedy did not become possible till after interplanetary and interstellar travel had been well established. Long ago, in an early phase of the galaxy, the number of planetary systems had been very small, and only half a dozen worlds had attained utopia. These were scattered up and down the galaxy at immense distances from one another. Each lived its life in almost complete isolation, relieved only by precarious telepathic intercourse with its peers. In a somewhat later but still early period, when these eldest children of the galaxy had perfected their society and their biological nature, and were on the threshold of super-individuality, they turned their attention to interplanetary travel. First one and then another achieved rocket-flight in space, and succeeded in breeding specialized populations for the colonization of neighbouring planets.

In a still later epoch, the middle period of galactic history, there were many more planetary systems than in the earlier ages, and an increasing number of intelligent worlds were successfully emerging from the great psychological crisis which so many worlds never surmount. Meanwhile some of the elder "generation" of awakened worlds were already facing the immensely difficult problems of travel on the interstellar and not merely the interplanetary scale. This new power inevitably changed the whole character of galactic history. Hitherto, in spite of tenative telepathic exploration on the part of the most awakened worlds, the life of the galaxy had been in the main the life of a number of isolated worlds which took no effect upon one another. With the advent of interstellar travel the many distinct themes of the world-biographies gradually became merged in an all-embracing drama.

Travel within a planetary system was at first carried out by rocket-vessels propelled by normal fuels. In all the early ventures one great difficulty had been the danger of collision with meteors. Even the most efficient vessel, most skilfully navigated and travelling in regions that were relatively free from these invisible and lethal missiles, might at any moment crash and fuse. The trouble was not overcome till means had been found to unlock the treasure of sub-atomic energy. It was then possible to protect the ship by means of a far-flung envelope of power which either diverted or exploded the meteors at a distance. A rather similar method was with great difficulty devised to protect the space ships and their crews from the constant and murderous hail of cosmic radiation.

Interstellar, as opposed to interplanetary, travel was quite impossible until the advent of sub-atomic power. Fortunately this source of power was seldom gained until late in a world's development, when mentality was mature enough to wield this most dangerous of all physical instruments without inevitable disaster. Disasters, however, did occur. Several worlds were accidentally blown to pieces. In others civilization was temporarily destroyed. Sooner or later, however, most of the minded worlds tamed this formidable djin, and set it to work upon a titanic scale, not only in industry, but in such great enterprises as the alteration of planetary orbits for the improvement of climate. This dangerous and delicate process was effected by firing a gigantic sub-atomic rocket-apparatus at such times and places that the recoil would gradually accumulate to divert the planet's course in the desired direction.

Actual interstellar voyaging was first effected by detaching a planet from its natural orbit by a series of well-timed and well-placed rocket impulsions, and thus projecting it into outer space at a speed far greater than the normal planetary and stellar speeds. Something more than this was necessary, since life on a sunless planet would have been impossible. For short interstellar voyages the difficulty was sometimes overcome by the generation of sub-atomic energy from the planet's own substance; but for longer voyages, lasting for many thousands of years, the only method was to form a small artificial sun, and project it into space as a blazing satellite of the living world. For this purpose an uninhabited planet would be brought into proximity with the home planet to form a binary system. A mechanism would then be contrived for the controlled disintegration of the atoms of the lifeless planet, to provide a constant source of light and heat. The two bodies, revolving round one another, would be launched among the stars.

This delicate operation may well seem impossible. Had I space to describe the age-long experiments and world-wrecking accidents which preceded its achievement, perhaps the reader's incredulity would vanish. But I must dismiss in a few sentences whole protracted epics of scientific adventure and personal courage. Suffice it that, before the process was perfected, many a populous world was either cast adrift to freeze in space, or was roasted by its own artificial sun.

The stars are so remote from one another that we measure their distances in light years. Had the voyaging worlds travelled only at speeds comparable with those of the stars themselves, even the shortest of interstellar voyages would have lasted for many millions of years. But since interstellar space offers almost no resistance to a travelling body, and therefore momentum is not lost, it was possible for the voyaging world, by prolonging the original rocket-impulsion for many years, to increase its speed far beyond that of the fastest star. Indeed, though even the early voyages by heavy natural planets were by our standards spectacular, I shall have to tell at a later stage of voyages by small artificial planets travelling at almost half the speed of light. Owing to certain "relativity effects" it was impossible to accelerate beyond this point. But even such a rate of travel made voyages to the nearer stars well worth undertaking if any other planetary system happened to lie within this range. It must be remembered that a fully awakened world had no need to think in terms of such short periods as a human lifetime. Though its individuals might die, the minded world was in a very important sense immortal. It was accustomed to lay its plans to cover periods of many million years.

In early epochs of the galaxy expeditions from star to star were difficult, and rarely successful. But at a later stage, when there were already many thousands of worlds inhabited by intelligent races, and hundreds that had passed the utopian stage, a very serious situation arose. Interstellar travel was by now extremely efficient. Immense exploration vessels many miles in diameter, were constructed out in space from artificial materials of extreme rigidity and lightness. These could be projected by rocket action and with cumulative acceleration till their speed was almost half the speed of light. Even so, the journey from end to end of the galaxy could not be completed under two hundred thousand years. However, there was no reason to undertake so long a voyage. Few voyages in search of suitable systems lasted for more than a tenth of that time. Many were much shorter. Races that had attained and secured a communal consciousness would not hesitate to send out a number of such expeditions. Ultimately they might project their planet itself across the ocean of space to settle in some remote system recommended by the pioneers.

The problem of interstellar travel was so enthralling that it sometimes became an obsession even to a fairly well-developed utopian world. This could only occur if in the constitution of that world there was something unwholesome, some secret and unfulfilled hunger impelling the beings. The race might then become travel-mad.

Its social organization would be refashioned and directed with Spartan strictness to the new communal undertaking. All its members, hypnotized by the common obsession, would gradually forget the life of intense personal intercourse and of creative mental activity which had hitherto been their chief concern. The whole venture of the spirit, exploring the universe and its own nature with critical intelligence and delicate sensibility, would gradually come to a standstill. The deepest roots of emotion and will, which in the fully sane awakened world were securely within the range of introspection, would become increasingly obscured. Less and less, in such a world, could the unhappy communal mind understand itself. More and more it pursued its phantom goal. Any attempt to explore the galaxy telepathically was now abandoned. The passion of physical exploration assumed the guise of a religion. The communal mind persuaded itself that it must at all costs spread the gospel of its own culture throughout the galaxy. Though culture itself was vanishing, the vague idea of culture was cherished as a justification of world-policy.

Here I must check myself, lest I give a false impression. It is necessary to distinguish sharply between the mad worlds of comparatively low mental development and those of almost the highest order. The humbler kinds might become crudely obsessed by sheer mastery or sheer travel, with its scope for courage and discipline. More tragic was the case of those few very much more awakened worlds whose obsession was seemingly for community itself and mental lucidity itself, and the propagation of the kind of community and the special mode of lucidity most admired by themselves. For them travel was but the means to cultural and religious empire.

I have spoken as though I were confident that these formidable worlds were indeed mad, aberrant from the line of mental and spiritual growth. But their tragedy lay in the fact that, though to their opponents they seemed to be either mad or at heart wicked, to themselves they appeared superbly sane, practical, and virtuous. There were times when we ourselves, the bewildered explorers, were almost persuaded that this was the truth. Our intimate contact with them was such as to give us insight, so to speak, into the inner sanity of their insanity, or the core of rightness in their wickedness. This insanity or wickedness I have to describe in terms of simple human craziness and vice; but in truth it was in a sense superhuman, for it included the perversion of faculties above the range of human sanity and virtue.

When one of these "mad" worlds encountered a sane world, it would sincerely express the most reasonable and kindly intentions. It desired only cultural intercourse, and perhaps economic cooperation. Little by little it would earn the respect of the other for its sympathy, its splendid social order, and its dynamic purpose. Each world would regard the other as a noble, though perhaps an alien and partly incomprehensible, instrument of the spirit. But little by little the normal world would begin to realize that in the culture of the "mad" world there were certain subtle and far-reaching intuitions that appeared utterly false, ruthless, aggressive, and hostile to the spirit, and were the dominant motives of its foreign relations. The "mad" world, meanwhile, would regretfully come to the conclusion that the other was after all gravely lacking in sensibility, that it was obtuse to the very highest values and most heroic virtues, in fact that its whole life was subtly corrupt, and must, for its own sake, be changed, or else destroyed. Thus each world, though with lingering respect and affection, would sadly condemn the other. But the mad world would not be content to leave matters thus. It would at length with holy fervour attack, striving to destroy the other's pernicious culture, and even exterminate its population.

It is easy for me now, after the event, after the final spiritual downfall of these mad worlds, to condemn them as perverts, but in the early stages of their drama we were often desperately at a loss to decide on which side sanity lay.

Several of the mad worlds succumbed to their own foolhardiness in navigation. Others, under the strain of age-long research, fell into social neurosis and civil strife. A few, however, succeeded in attaining their end, and after voyages lasting for thousands of years were able to reach some neighbouring planetary system. The invaders were often in a desperate plight. Generally they had used up most of the material of their little artificial sun. Economy had forced them to reduce their ration of heat and light so far that when at last they discovered a suitable planetary system their native world was almost wholly arctic. On arrival, they would first take up their position in a suitable orbit and, perhaps spend some centuries in recuperating. Then they would explore the neighbouring worlds, seek out the most hospitable, and begin to adapt themselves or their descendants to life upon it. If, as was often the case, any of the planets was already inhabited by intelligent beings, the invaders would inevitably come sooner or later into conflict with them, either in a crude manner over the right to exploit a planet's resources, or more probably over the invaders' obsession for propagating their own culture. For by now the civilizing mission, which was the ostensible motive of all their heroic adventures, would have become a rigid obsession. They would be quite incapable of conceiving that the native civilization, though less developed than their own, might be more suited to the natives. Nor could they realize that their own culture, formerly the expression of a gloriously awakened world, might have sunk, in spite of their mechanical powers and crazy religious fervour, below the simpler culture of the natives in all the essentials of mental life.

Many a desperate defence did we see, carried out by some world of the lowly rank of *Homo sapiens* against a race of mad supermen, armed not only with the invincible power of sub-atomic energy but with over-whelmingly superior intelligence, knowledge, and devotion, and moreover with the immense advantage that all its individuals participated in the unified mind of the race. Though we had come to cherish above all things the advancement of mentality, and were therefore prejudiced in favour of the awakened though perverted invaders, our sympathies soon became divided, and then passed almost wholly to the natives, however barbaric their culture. For in spite of their stupidity, their ignorance, and superstition, their endless internecine conflicts, their spiritual obtuseness and grossness, we recognized in them a power which the others had forfeited, a naïve but balanced wisdom, an animal shrewdness, a spiritual promise. The invaders, on the other hand, however brilliant, were indeed perverts. Little by little we came to regard the conflict as one in which an untamed but promising urchin had been set upon by an armed religious maniac.

When the invaders had exploited every world in the new-found planet-ary system, they would again feel the lust of proselytization. Persuading themselves that it was their duty to advance their religious empire through-out the galaxy, they would detach a couple of planets and dispatch them into space with a crew of pioneers. Or they would break up the whole planetary system, and scatter it abroad with missionary zeal. Occasionally their travel brought them into contact with another race of mad superiors. Then would follow a war in which one side or the other, or possibly both, would be exterminated.

Sometimes the adventurers came upon worlds of their own rank which had not succumbed to the mania of religious empire. Then the natives, though they would at first meet the invaders with courtesy and reason, would gradually realize that they were confronted with lunatics. They themselves would hastily convert their civilization for warfare. The issue would depend on superiority of weapons and military cunning; but if the contest was long and grim, the natives, even if victorious, might be so damaged mentally by an age of warfare that they would never recover their sanity.

Worlds that suffered from the mania of religious imperialism would seek interstellar travel long before economic necessity forced it upon them. The saner world-spirits, on the other hand, often discovered sooner or later a point beyond which increased material development and increased popula-tion were unnecessary for the exercise of their finer capacities. These were content to remain within their native planetary systems, in a state of economic and social stability. They were thus able to give most of their practical intelligence to telepathic exploration of the universe. Telepathic intercourse between worlds was now becoming much more precise and reliable. The galaxy had emerged from the primitive stage when any world could remain solitary, and live out its career in splendid isolation. In fact, just as, in the experience of *Homo sapiens,* the Earth is now "shrinking" to the dimensions of a country, so, in this critical period of the life of our galaxy, the whole galaxy was "shrinking" to the dimensions of a world. Those world spirits that had been most successful in telepathic exploration had by now constructed a fairly accurate "mental map" of the whole galaxy, though there still remained a number of eccentric worlds with which no lasting contact could yet be made. There was also one very advanced system of worlds, which had mysteriously "faded out" of telepathic intercourse altogether. Of this I shall tell more in the sequel.

The telepathic ability of the mad worlds and systems was by now greatly reduced. Though they were often under telepathic observation by the more mature world spirits, and were even influenced to some extent, they themselves were so self-complacent that they cared not to explore mental life of the galaxy. Physical travel and sacred imperial power were for them good enough means of intercourse with the surrounding universe.

In time there grew up several great rival empires of the mad worlds, each claiming to be charged with some sort of divine mission for the unifying and awakening of the whole galaxy. Between the ideologies of these empires there was little to choose, yet each was opposed to the others with religious fervour. Germinating in regions far apart, these empires easily mastered any sub-utopian worlds that lay within reach. Thus they spread from one planetary system to another, till at last empire made contact with empire.

Then followed wars such as had never before occurred in our galaxy. Fleets of worlds, natural and artificial, manœuvred among the stars to outwit one another, and destroyed one another with long-range jets of subatomic energy. As the tides of battle swept hither and thither through space, whole planetary systems were annihilated. Many a world-spirit found a sudden end. Many a lowly race that had no part in the strife was slaughtered in the celestial warfare that raged around it.

Yet so vast is the galaxy that these intermundane wars, terrible as they were, could at first be regarded as rare accidents, mere unfortunate episodes in the triumphant march of civilization. But the disease spread. More and more of the sane worlds, when they were attacked by the mad empires, reorganized themselves for military defence. They were right in believing that the situation was one with which non-violence alone could not cope; for the enemy, unlike any possible group of human beings, was too thoroughly purged of "humanity" to be susceptible to sympathy. But they were wrong in hoping that arms could save them. Even though, in the ensuing war, the defenders might gain victory in the end, the struggle was generally so long and devastating that the victors themselves were irreparably damaged in spirit.

In a later and perhaps the most terrible phase of our galaxy's life I was forcibly reminded of the state of bewilderment and anxiety that I had left behind me on the Earth. Little by little the whole galaxy, some ninety thousand light-years across, containing more than thirty thousand million stars, and (by this date) over a hundred thousand planetary systems, and actually thousands of intelligent races, was paralysed by the fear of war, and periodically tortured by its outbreak.

In one respect, however, the state of the galaxy was much more desperate than the state of our little world to-day. None of our nations is an awakened super-individual. Even those peoples which are suffering from the mania of herd glory are composed of individuals who in their private life are sane. A change of fortune might perhaps drive such a people into a less crazy mood. Or skilful propaganda for the idea of human unity might turn the scale. But in this grim age of the galaxy the mad worlds were mad almost down to the very roots of their being. Each was a super-individual whose whole physical and mental constitution, including the unit bodies and minds of its private members, was by now organized through and through for a mad purpose. There seemed to be no more possibility of appealing to the stunted creatures to rebel against the sacred and crazy purpose of their race than of persuading the individual brain-cells of a maniac to make a stand for gentleness.

To be alive in those days in one of the worlds that were sane and awakened, though not of the very highest, most percipient order, was to feel (or will be to feel) that the plight of the galaxy was desperate. These average sane worlds had organized themselves into a League to resist aggression; but since they were far less developed in military organization than the mad worlds, and much less inclined to subject their individual members to military despotism, they were at a great disadvantage.

Moreover, the enemy was now united; for one empire had secured complete mastery over the others, and had inspired all the mad worlds with an identical passion of religious imperialism. Though the "United Empires" of the mad worlds included only a minority of the worlds of the galaxy, the sane worlds had no hope of a speedy victory; for they were disunited, and unskilled in warfare. Meanwhile war was undermining the mental life of the League's own members. The urgencies and horrors were beginning to blot out from their minds all the more delicate, more developed capacities. They were becoming less and less capable of those activities of personal intercourse and cultural adventure which they still forlornly recognized as the true way of life.

The great majority of the worlds of the League, finding themselves caught up in a trap from which, seemingly, there was no escape, came despairingly to feel that the spirit which they had thought divine, the spirit which seeks true community and true awakening, was after all not destined to triumph, and therefore not the essential spirit of the cosmos. Blind chance, it was rumoured, ruled all things; or perhaps a diabolic intelligence. Some began to conceive that the Star Maker had created merely for the lust of destroying. Undermined by this terrible surmise, they themselves sank far toward madness. With horror they imagined that the enemy was indeed, as he claimed, the instrument of divine wrath, punishing them for their own impious will to turn the whole galaxy, the whole cosmos, into a paradise of generous and fully awakened beings. Under the influence of this growing sense of ultimate satanic power and the even more devastating doubt of the rightness of their own ideals, the League members despaired. Some surrendered to the enemy. Others succumbed to internal discord, losing their mental unity. The war of the worlds seemed likely to end in the victory of the insane. And so, indeed, it would have done, but for the interference of that remote and brilliant system of worlds which, as was mentioned above, had for a long while withdrawn itself from telepathic intercourse with the rest of our galaxy. This was the system of worlds which had been founded in the spring-time of the galaxy by the symbiotic Ichthyoids and Arachnoids.

3. A CRISIS IN GALACTIC HISTORY

Throughout this period of imperial expansion a few world-systems of a very high order, though less awakened than the Symbiotics of the sub-galaxy, had watched events telepathically from afar. They saw the frontiers of empire advancing steadily toward them, and knew that they themselves would soon be implicated. They had the knowledge and power to defeat the enemy in war; they received desperate appeals for help; yet they did nothing. These were worlds that were organized through and through for peace and the activities proper to an awakened world. They knew that, if they chose to remake their whole social structure and reorientate their minds, they could ensure military victory. They knew also that they would thereby save many worlds from conquest, from oppression and from the possible destruction of all that was best in them. But they knew also that in reorganizing themselves for desperate warfare, in neglecting, for a whole age of struggle, all those activities which were proper to them, they would destroy the best in themselves more surely than the enemy would destroy it by oppression; and that in destroying this they would be murdering what they believed to be the most vital germ in the galaxy. They therefore forswore military action.

When at last one of these more developed world-systems was itself confronted by mad religious enthusiasts, the natives welcomed the invaders, readjusted all their planetary orbits to accommodate the in-coming planets, pressed the foreign power actually to settle part of its population in such of their own planets as afforded suitable climatic conditions; and secretly, gradually, subjected the whole mad race throughout the combined solar system to a course of telepathic hypnotism so potent that its communal mind was completely disintegrated. The invaders became mere uncoordinated individuals, such as we know on Earth. Henceforth they were bewildered, short-sighted, torn by conflicts, ruled by no supreme purpose, obsessed more by self than by community. It had been hoped that, when the mad communal mind had been abolished, the individuals of the invading race would soon be induced to open their eyes and their hearts to a nobler ideal. Unfortunately the telepathic skill of the superior race was not sufficient to delve down to the long-buried chrysalis of the spirit in these beings, to give it air and warmth and light. Since the individual nature of these forlorn individuals was itself the product of a crazy world, they proved incapable of salvation, incapable of sane community. They were therefore segregated to work out their own unlovely destiny in ages of tribal quarrels and cultural decline, ending in the extinction which inevitably overtakes creatures that are incapable of adaptation to new circumstances.

When several invading expeditions had been thus circumvented, there arose among the worlds of the mad United Empires a tradition that certain seemingly pacific worlds were in fact more dangerous than all other enemies, since plainly they had a strange power of "poisoning the soul." The imperialists determined to annihilate these terrible opponents. The attacking forces were instructed to avoid all telepathic parley and blow the enemy to pieces at long range. This, it was found, could be most conveniently performed by exploding the sun of the doomed system. Stimulated by a potent ray, the atoms of the photosphere would start disintegrating, and the spreading fury would soon fling the star into the "nova" state, roasting all his planets.

It was our lot to witness the extraordinary calm, nay the exaltation and joy with which these worlds accepted the prospect of annihilation rather than debase themselves by resistance. Later we were to watch the strange events which saved this galaxy of ours from disaster. But first came tragedy.

From our observation points in the minds of the attackers and the attacked, we observed not once but three times the slaughter of races nobler than any that we had yet encountered by perverts whose own natural mental rank was almost as high. Three worlds, or rather systems of worlds, each possessed by a diversity of specialized races, we saw annihilated. From these doomed planets we actually observed the sun break out with tumultuous eruption, swelling hourly. We actually felt, through the bodies of our hosts, the rapidly increasing heat, and through their eyes the blinding light. We saw the vegetation wither, the seas begin to steam. We felt and heard the furious hurricanes which wrecked every structure and bowled the ruins before them. With awe and wonder we experienced something of that exaltation and inner peace with which the doomed angelic populations met their end. Indeed, it was this experienced angelic exaltation in the hour of tragedy that gave us our first clear insight into the most spiritual attitude to fate. The sheer bodily agony of the disaster soon became intolerable to us, so that we were forced to withdraw ourselves from those martyred worlds. But we left the doomed populations themselves accepting not only this torture but the annihilation of their glorious community with all its infinite hopes, accepting this bitterness as though it were not lethal but the elixir of immortality. Not till almost the close of our own adventure did we grasp for a moment the full meaning of this ecstasy.

It was strange to us that none of these three victims made any attempt to resist the attack. Indeed, not one inhabitant in any of these worlds considered for a moment the possibility of resistance. In every case the attitude to disaster seemed to express itself in such terms as these: "To retaliate would be to wound our communal spirit beyond cure. We choose rather to die. The theme of spirit that we have created must inevitably be broken short, whether by the ruthlessness of the invader or by our own resort to arms. It is better to be destroyed than to triumph in slaying the spirit. Such as it is, the spirit that we have achieved is fair; and it is indestructibly woven into the tissue of the cosmos. We die praising the universe in which at least such an achievement as ours can be. We die knowing that the promise of further glory outlives us in other galaxies. We die praising the Star Maker, the Star Destroyer."

4. TRIUMPH IN A SUB-GALAXY

It was after the destruction of the third system of worlds, when a fourth was preparing for its end, that a miracle, or a seeming miracle, changed the whole course of events in our galaxy. Before telling of this turn of fortune I must double back the thread of my story and trace the history of the system of worlds which was now to play the leading part in galactic events.

It will be remembered that in an outlying "island" off the galactic "continent" there lived the strange symbiotic race of Ichthyoids and Arachnoids. These beings supported almost the oldest civilization in the galaxy. They had reached the "human" plane of mental development even before the Other Men; and, in spite of many vicissitudes, during the thousands of millions of years of their career they had made great progress. I referred to them last as having occupied all the planets of their system with specialized races of Arachnoids, all of which were in permanent telepathic union with the Ichthyoid population in the oceans of the home planet. As the ages passed, they were several times reduced almost to annihilation, now by too daring physical experiments, now through too ambitious telepathic exploration; but in time they won through to a mental development unequalled in our galaxy.

Their little island universe, their outlying cluster of stars, had come wholly under their control. It contained many natural planetary systems. Several of these included worlds which, when the early Arachnoid explorers visited them telepathically, were found to be inhabited by native races of pre-utopian rank. These were left to work out their own destiny, save that in certain crises of their history the Symbiotics secretly brought to bear on them from afar a telepathic influence that might help them to meet their difficulties with increased vigour. Thus when one of these worlds reached the crisis in which *Homo sapiens* now stands, it passed with seemingly natural ease straight on to the phase of world-unity and the building of utopia. Great care was taken by the Symbiotic race to keep its existence hidden from the primitives, lest they should lose their independence of mind. Thus, even while the Symbiotics were voyaging among these worlds in rocket vessels and using the mineral resources of neighbouring uninhabited planets, the intelligent worlds of pre-utopian rank were left unvisited. Not till these worlds had themselves entered the full utopian phase and were exploring their neighbour planets were they allowed to discover the truth. By then they were ready to receive it with exultation, rather than disheartenment and fear.

Thenceforth, by physical and telepathic intercourse the young utopia would be speedily brought up to the spiritual rank of the Symbiotics themselves, and would cooperate on an equal footing in a symbiosis of worlds.

Some of these pre-utopian worlds, not malignant but incapable of further advance, were left in peace, and preserved, as we preserve wild animals in national parks, for scientific interest. Aeon after aeon, these beings, tethered by their own futility, struggled in vain to cope with the crisis which modern Europe knows so well. In cycle after cycle civilization would emerge from barbarism, mechanization would bring the peoples into uneasy contact, national wars and class wars would breed the longing for a better world-order, but breed it in vain. Disaster after disaster would undermine the fabric of civilization. Gradually barbarism would return. Aeon after aeon, the process would repeat itself under the calm telepathic observation of the Symbiotics, whose existence was never suspected by the primitive creatures under their gaze. So might we ourselves look down into some rock-pool where lowly creatures repeat with naive zest dramas learned by their ancestors aeons ago.

The Symbiotics could well afford to leave these museum pieces intact, for they had at their disposal scores of planetary systems. Moreover, armed with their highly developed physical sciences and with sub-atomic power, they were able to construct, out in space, artificial planets for permanent habitation. These great hollow globes of artificial super-metals, and artificial transparent adamant, ranged in size from the earliest and smallest structures, which were no bigger than a very small asteroid, to spheres considerably larger than the Earth. They were without external atmosphere, since their mass was generally too slight to prevent the escape of gases. A blanket of repelling force protected them from meteors and cosmic rays. The planet's external surface, which was wholly transparent, encased the atmosphere. Immediately beneath it hung the photosynthesis stations and the machinery for generating power from solar radiation. Part of this outer shell was occupied by astronomical observatories, machinery for controlling the planet's orbit, and great "docks" for interplanetary liners. The interior of these worlds was a system of concentric spheres supported by girders and gigantic arches. Interspersed between these spheres lay the machinery for atmospheric regulation, the great water reservoirs, the food factories and commodity-factories, the engineering shops, the refuse-conversion tracts, residential and recreational areas, and a wealth of research laboratories, libraries and cultural centres. Since the Symbiotic race was in origin marine, there was a central ocean where the profoundly modified, the physically indolent and mentally athletic descendants of the original Ichthyoids constituted the "highest brain tracts" of the intelligent world. There, as in the primeval ocean of the home planet, the symbiotic partners sought one another, and the young of both species were nurtured. Such races of the sub-galaxy as were not in origin marine constructed, of course, artificial planets which, though of the same general type, were adapted to their special nature. But all the races found it also necessary to mould their own nature drastically to suit their new conditions.

As the aeons advanced, hundreds of thousands of worldlets were constructed, all of this type, but gradually increasing in size and complexity. Many a star without natural planets came to be surrounded by concentric rings of artificial worlds. In some cases the inner rings contained scores, the outer rings thousands of globes adapted to life at some particular distance from the sun. Great diversity, both physical and mental, would distinguish worlds even of the same ring. Sometimes a comparatively old world, or even a whole ring of worlds, would feel itself outstripped in mental excellence by younger worlds and races, whose structure, physical and biological, embodied increasing skill. Then either the superannuated world would simply continue its life in a sort of backwater of civilization, tolerated, loved, studied by the younger worlds; or it would choose to die and surrender the material of its planet for new ventures.

One very small and rather uncommon kind of artificial world consisted almost wholly of water. It was like a titanic bowl of gold-fish. Beneath its transparent shell, studded with rocket-machinery and interplanetary docks, lay a spherical ocean, crossed by structural girders, and constantly impregnated with oxygen. A small solid core represented the sea-bottom. The population of Ichthyoids and the visting population of Arachnoids swarmed in this huge encrusted drop. Each Ichthyoid would be visited in turn by perhaps a score of partners whose working life was spent on other worlds. The life of the Ichthyoids was indeed a strange one, for they were at once imprisoned and free of all space. An Ichthyoid never left his native ocean, but he had telepathic intercourse with the whole Symbiotic race throughout the sub-galaxy. Moreover, the one form of practical activity which the Ichthyoids performed was astronomy. Immediately beneath the planet's glassy crust hung observatories, where the swimming astronomers studied the constitution of the stars and the distribution of the galaxies.

These "gold-fish-bowl" worlds turned out to be transitional. Shortly before the age of the mad empires the Symbiotics began to experiment for the production of a world which should consist of a single physical organism. After ages of experiment they produced a "gold-fish-bowl" type of world in which the whole ocean was meshed by a fixed net-work of Ichthyoid individuals in direct neural connection with one another. This world-wide, living, polyp-like tissue had permanent attachments to the machinery and observatories of the world. Thus it constituted a truly organic world-organism, and since the coherent Ichthyoid population supported together a perfectly unified mentality, each of these worlds was indeed in the fullest sense a minded organism, like a man. One essential link with the past was preserved. Arachnoids, specially adapted to the new symbiosis, would visit from their remote planets and swim along the submarine galleries for union with their anchored mates.

More and more of the stars of the outlying cluster or sub-galaxy came to be girdled with rings of worlds, and an increasing number of these worlds were of the new, organic type. Of the populations of the sub-galaxy most were descendants of the original Ichthyoids or Arachnoids; but there were also many whose natural ancestors were humanesque, and not a few that had sprung from avians, insectoids or plant-men. Between the worlds, between the rings of worlds, and between the solar systems there was constant intercourse, both telepathic and physical. Small, rocket-propelled vessels plied regularly within each system of planets. Larger vessels or high-speed worldlets voyaged from system to system, explored the whole sub-galaxy, and even ventured across the ocean of emptiness into the main body of the galaxy, where thousands upon thousands of planetless stars awaited encirclement by rings of worlds.

Strangely, the triumphant advance of material civilization and colonization now slowed down and actually came to a standstill. Physical intercourse between worlds of the sub-galaxy was maintained, but not increased. Physical exploration of the neighbouring fringe of the galactic "continent" was abandoned. Within the sub-galaxy itself no new worlds were founded. Industrial activities continued, but at reduced pressure, and no further advance was made in the standard of material convenience. Indeed, manners and customs began to grow less dependent on mechanical aids. Among the Symbiotic worlds, the Arachnoid populations were reduced in number; the Ichthyoids in their cells of ocean lived in a permanent state of mental concentration and fervour, which of course was telepathically shared by their partners.

It as at this time that telepathic intercourse between the advanced sub-galaxy and the few awakened worlds of the "continent" was entirely abolished. During recent ages, communication had been very fragmentary. The Sub-Galactics had apparently so far outstripped their neighbours that their interest in those primitives had become purely archaeological, and was gradually eclipsed by the enthralling life of their own community of worlds, and by their telepathic exploration of remote galaxies.

To us, the band of explorers, desperately struggling to maintain contact between our communal mind and the incomparably more developed minds of these worlds, the finest activities of the Sub-Galactics were at present inaccessible. We observed only a stagnation of the more obvious physical and mental activities of these systems of worlds. It seemed at first that this stagnation must be caused by some obscure flaw in their nature. Was it, perhaps, the first stage of irrevocable decline?

Later, however, we began to discover that this seeming stagnation was a symptom not of death but of more vigorous life. Attention had been drawn from material advancement just because it had opened up new spheres of mental discovery and growth. In fact the great community of worlds, whose members consisted of some thousands of world-spirits, was busy digesting the fruits of its prolonged phase of physical progress, and was now finding itself capable of new and unexpected psychical activities. At first the nature of these activities was entirely hidden from us. But in time we learned how to let ourselves be gathered up by these superhuman beings so as to obtain at least an obscure glimpse of the matters which so enthralled them. They were concerned, it seemed, partly with telepathic exploration of the great host of ten million galaxies, partly with a technique of spiritual discipline by which they strove to come to more penetrating insight into the nature of the cosmos and to a finer creativity. This, we learned, was possible because their perfect community of worlds was tentatively waking into a higher plane of being, as a single communal mind whose body was the whole sub-galaxy of worlds. Though we could not participate in the life of this lofty being, we guessed that its absorbing passion was not wholly unlike the longing of the noblest of our own human species to "come face to face with God." This new being desired to have the percipience and the hardihood to endure direct vision of the source of all light and life and love. In fact this whole population of worlds was rapt in a prolonged and mystical adventure.

5. THE TRAGEDY OF THE PERVERTS

Such was the state of affairs when, in the main galactic "continent," the mad United Empires concentrated their power upon the few worlds that were not merely sane but of superior mental rank. The attention of

the Symbiotics and their colleagues in the supremely civilized sub-galaxy
had long been withdrawn from the petty affairs of the "continent." It was
given instead to the cosmos as a whole and to the inner discipline of the
spirit. But the first of the three murders perpetrated by the United Empires
upon a population far more developed than themselves seems to have
caused a penetrating reverberation to echo, so to speak, through all the
loftier spheres of existence. Even in the full flight of their career, the Sub-
Galactics took cognizance. Once more attention was directed telepathically
to the neighbouring continent of stars.

While the situation was being studied, the second murder was committed. The Sub-Galactics knew that they had power to prevent any further
disaster. Yet, to our surprise, our horror and incomprehension, they calmly
awaited the third murder. Still more strange, the doomed worlds themselves, though in telepathic communication with the Sub-Galaxy, made no
appeal for help. Victims and spectators alike studied the situation with
quiet interest, even with a sort of bright exultation not wholly unlike
amusement. From our lowlier plane this detachment, this seeming levity,
at first appeared less angelic than inhuman. Here was a whole world of
sensitive and intelligent beings in the full tide of eager life and communal
activity. Here were lovers newly come together, scientists in the midst of
profound research, artists intent on new delicacies of apprehension, workers in a thousand practical social undertakings of which man has no conception, here in fact was all the rich diversity of personal lives that go to
make up a highly developed world in action. And each of these individual
minds participated in the communal mind of all; each experienced not
only as a private individual but as the very spirit of his race. Yet these
calm beings faced the destruction of their world with no more distress
seemingly than one of us would feel at the prospect of resigning his part
in some interesting game. And in the minds of the spectators of this impending tragedy we observed no agony of compassion, but only such com-
miseration, tinged with humour, as we might feel for some distinguished
tennis-player who was knocked out in the first round of a tournament
by some trivial accident such as a sprained ankle.

With difficulty we came to understand the source of this strange equanimity. Spectators and victims alike were so absorbed in cosmological research, so conscious of the richness and potentiality of the cosmos, and
above all so possessed by spiritual contemplation, that the destruction was
seen, even by the victims themselves, from the point of view which men
would call divine. Their gay exaltation and their seeming frivolity were
rooted in the fact that to them the personal life, and even the life and
death of individual worlds, appeared chiefly as vital themes contributing
to the life of the cosmos. From the cosmical point of view the disaster was
after all a very small though poignant matter. Moreover, if by the sacrifice
of another group of worlds, even of splendidly awakened worlds, greater

insight could be attained into the insanity of the Mad Empires, the sacrifice was well worth while.

So the third murder was committed. Then came the miracle. The telepathic skill of the Sub-Galaxy was far more developed than that of the scattered superior worlds on the galactic "continent." It could dispense with the aid of normal intercourse, and it could overcome every resistance. It could reach right down to the buried chrysalis of the spirit even in the most perverted individual. This was not a merely destructive power, blotting out the communal mind hypnotically; it was a kindling, an awakening power, brought to bear on the sane but dormant core of each individual. This skill was now exercised upon the galactic continent with triumphant but also tragic effect; for even this skill was not omnipotent. There appeared here and there among the mad worlds a strange and spreading "disease" of the mind. To the orthodox imperialists in those worlds themselves it seemed a madness; but it was in fact a late and ineffectual waking into sanity on the part of beings whose nature had been moulded through and through for madness in a mad environment.

The course of this "disease" of sanity in a mad world ran generally as follows. Individuals here and there, while still playing their part in the well-disciplined action and communal thought of the world, would find themselves teased by private doubts and disgusts opposed to the dearest assumptions of the world in which they lived, doubts of the worth of record-breaking travel and record-breaking empire, and disgust with the cult of mechanical triumph and intellectual servility and the divinity of the race. As these disturbing thoughts increased, the bewildered individuals would begin to fear for their own "sanity." Presently they would cautiously sound their neighbours. Little by little, doubt would become more widespread and more vocal, until at last considerable minorities in each world, though still playing their official part, would lose contact with the communal mind, and become mere isolated individuals; but individuals at heart more sane than the lofty communal mind from which they had fallen. The orthodox majority, horrified at this mental disintegration, would then apply the familiar ruthless methods that had been used so successfully in the uncivilized outposts of empire. The dissentients would be arrested, and either destroyed outright or concentrated upon the most inhospitable planet, in the hope that their torture might prove an effective warning to others.

This policy failed. The strange mental disease spread more and more rapidly, till the "lunatics" outnumbered the "sane." There followed civil wars, mass-martyrdom of devoted pacifists, dissension among the imperialists, a steady increase of "lunacy" in every world of the empire. The whole imperial organization fell to pieces; and since the aristocratic worlds that formed the backbone of empire were as impotent as soldier-ants to maintain themselves without the service and tribute of the subject worlds, the loss of empire doomed them to death. When almost the whole population of such a world had gone sane, great efforts would be made to reorganize its life for self-sufficiency and peace. It might have been expected that this task, though difficult, would not have defeated a population of beings whose sheer intelligence and social loyalty were incomparably greater than anything known on earth. But there were unexpected difficulties, not economic but psychological. These beings had been fashioned for war, tyranny and empire. Though telepathic stimulation from superior minds could touch into life the slumbering germ of the spirit in them, and help them to realize the triviality of their world's whole purpose, telepathic influence could not refashion their nature to such an extent that they could henceforth actually live for the spirit and renounce the old life. In spite of heroic self-discipline, they tended to sink into inertia, like wild beasts domesticated; or to run amok, and exercise against one another those impulses of domination which hitherto had been directed upon subject worlds. And all this they did with profound consciousness of guilt.

For us it was heartrending to watch the agony of these worlds. Never did the newly enlightened beings lose their vision of true community and of the spiritual life; but though the vision haunted them, the power to realize it in the detail of action was lost. Moreover, there were times when the change of heart that they had suffered seemed to them actually a change for the worse. Formerly all individuals had been perfectly disciplined to the common will, and perfectly happy in executing that will without the heart-searchings of individual responsibility. But now individuals were mere individuals; and all were tormented by mutual suspicion and by violent propensities for self-seeking.

The issue of this appalling struggle in the minds of these former imperialists depended on the extent to which specialization for empire had affected them. In a few young worlds, in which specialization had not gone deep, a period of chaos was followed by a period of reorientation and world-planning, and in due season by sane utopia. But in most of these worlds no such escape was possible. Either chaos persisted till racial decline set in, and the world sank to the human, the sub-human, the merely animal states; or else, in a few cases only, the discrepancy between the ideal and the actual was so distressing that the whole race committed suicide.

We could not long endure the spectacle of scores of worlds falling into psychological ruin. Yet the Sub-Galactics who had caused these strange events, and continued to use their power to clarify and so destroy these minds, watched their handiwork unflinchingly. Pity they felt, pity such as we feel for a child that has broken its toy; but no indignation against fate.

Within a few thousand years every one of the imperial worlds had either transformed itself or fallen into barbarism or committed suicide.

6. A GALACTIC UTOPIA

The events that I have been describing took place, or from the human point of view will take place, at a date as far future to us as we are from the condensation of the earliest stars. The next period of galactic history covers the period from the fall of the mad empires to the achievement of utopia in the whole galactic community of worlds. This transitional period was in itself in a manner utopian; for it was an age of triumphant progress carried out by beings whose nature was rich and harmonious, whose nurture was entirely favourable, and their ever-widening galactic community a wholly satisfying object of loyalty. It was only not utopian in the sense that the galactic society was still expanding and constantly changing its structure to meet new needs, economic and spiritual. At the close of this phase there came a period of full utopia in which the attention of the perfected galactic community was directed mainly beyond itself toward other galaxies. Of this I shall tell in due course; and of the unforeseen and stormy events which shattered this beatitude.

Meanwhile we must glance at the age of expansion. The worlds of the Sub-Galaxy, recognizing that no further great advance in culture was possible unless the population of awakened worlds was immensely increased and diversified, now began to play an active part in the work of reorganizing the whole galactic continent. By telepathic communication they gave to all awakened worlds throughout the galaxy knowledge of the triumphant society which they themselves had created; and they called upon all to join them in the founding of the galactic utopia. Every world throughout the galaxy, they said, must be an intensely conscious individual; and each must contribute its personal idiosyncrasy and all the wealth of its experience to the pooled experience of all. When at last the community was completed, they said, it must go on to fulfil its function in the far greater community of all galaxies, there to participate in spiritual activities as yet but dimly guessed.

In their earlier age of meditation the Sub-Galactic worlds, or rather the single intermittently awakening mind of the Sub-Galaxy, had evidently made discoveries which had very precise bearing on the founding of the galactic society; for they now put forward the demand that the number of minded worlds in the Galaxy must be increased to at least ten thousand times its present extent. In order that all the potentialities of the spirit should be fulfilled, they said there must be a far greater diversity of world-types, and thousands of worlds of each type. They themselves, in their small Sub-Galactic community, had learned enough to realize that only a very much greater community could explore all the regions of being, some few of which they themselves had glimpsed, but only from afar.

The natural worlds of the galactic continent were bewildered and alarmed by the magnitude of this scheme. They were content with the extant scale of life. The spirit, they affirmed, had no concern for magnitude and multiplicity. To this the reply was made that such a protest came ill from worlds whose own achievement depended on the splendid diversity of their members. Diversity and multiplicity of worlds was as necessary on the galactic plane as diversity and multiplicity of individuals on the world plane and diversity and multiplicity of nerve-cells on the individual plane.

In the upshot the natural worlds of the "continent" played a decreasing part in the advancing life of the galaxy. Some merely remained at the level of their own unaided achievement. Some joined in the great cooperative work, but without fervour and without genius. A few joined heartily and usefully in the enterprise. One, indeed, was able to contribute greatly. This was a symbiotic race, but of a very different kind from that which had founded the community of the Sub-Galaxy. The symbiosis consisted of two races which had originally inhabited separate planets of the same system. An intelligent avian species, driven to desperation by the desiccation of its native planet, had contrived to invade a neighbouring world inhabited by a manlike species. Here I must not tell how, after ages of alternating strife and cooperation, a thorough economic and psychological symbiosis was established.

The building of the galactic community of worlds lies far beyond the comprehension of the writer of this book. I cannot now remember at all clearly what I experienced of these obscure matters in the state of heightened lucidity which came to me through participation in the communal mind of the explorers. And even in that state I was bewildered by the effort to comprehend the aims of that close-knit community of worlds.

If my memory is to be trusted at all, three kinds of activity occupied the minded worlds in this phase of galactic history. The main practical work was to enrich and harmonize the life of the galaxy itself, to increase the number and diversity and mental unity of the fully awakened worlds up to the point which, it was believed, was demanded for the emergence of a mode of experience more awakened than any hitherto attained. The second kind of activity was that which sought to make closer contact with the other galaxies by physical and telepathic study. The third was the spiritual exercise appropriate to beings of the rank of the world-minds. This last seems to have been concerned (or will be concerned) at once with the deepening of the self-awareness of each individual world-spirit and the detachment of its will from merely private fulfilment. But this was not all. For on this relatively high level of the spirit's ascent, as on our own lowliest of all spiritual planes, there had also to be a more radical detachment from the whole adventure of life and mind in the cosmos. For, as the spirit wakens, it craves more and more to regard all existence not merely with a creature's eyes, but in the universal view, as though through the eyes of the creator.

At first the task of establishing the galactic utopia occupied almost the whole energy of the awakened worlds. More and more of the stars were encircled with concentric hoops of pearls, perfect though artificial. And each pearl was a unique world, occupied by a unique race. Henceforth the highest level of persistent individuality was not a world but a system of scores or hundreds of worlds. And between the systems there was as easy and delightful converse as between human individuals.

In these conditions, to be a conscious individual was to enjoy immediately the united sensory impressions of all the races inhabiting a system of worlds. And as the sense-organs of the worlds apprehended not only "nakedly" but also through artificial instruments of great range and subtlety, the conscious individual perceived not only the structure of hundreds of planets, but also the configuration of the whole system of planets clustered about its sun. Other systems also it perceived, as men perceive one another; for in the distance the glittering bodies of other "multi-mundane" persons like itself gyrated and drifted.

Between the minded planetary systems occurred infinite variations of personal intercourse. As between human individuals, there were loves and hates, temperamental sympathies and antipathies, joyful and distressful intimacies, cooperations and thwartings in personal ventures and in the great common venture of building the galactic utopia.

Between individual systems of worlds, as between symbiotic partners, there sometimes occurred relationships with an almost sexual flavour, though actual sex played no part in them. Neighbouring systems would project travelling worldlets, or greater worlds, or trains of worlds, across the ocean of space to take up orbits round each other's suns and play intimate parts in symbiotic, or rather "sympsychic" relationships in one another's private life. Occasionally a whole system would migrate to another system, and settle its worlds in rings between the rings of the other system.

Telepathic intercourse united the whole galaxy; but telepathy, though it had the great advantage that it was not affected by distance, was seemingly imperfect in other ways. So far as possible it was supplemented by physical travel. A constant stream of touring worldlets percolated through the whole galaxy in every direction.

The task of establishing utopia in the galaxy was not pursued without friction. Different kinds of races were apt to have different policies for the galaxy. Though war was by now unthinkable, the sort of strife which we know between individuals or associations within the same state was common. There was, for instance, a constant struggle between the planetary systems that were chiefly interested in the building of utopia, those that were most concerned to make contact with other galaxies, and those whose main preoccupation was spiritual. Besides these great parties, there were groups of planetary systems which were prone to put the well-being of individual world-systems above the advancement of galactic enterprise.

They cared more for the drama of personal intercourse and the fulfilment of the personal capacity of worlds and systems than for organization or exploration or spiritual purification. Though their presence was often exasperating to the enthusiasts, it was salutary, for it was a guarantee against extravagance and against tyranny.

It was during the age of the galactic utopia that another salutary influence began to take full effect on the busy worlds. Telepathic research had made contact with the long-extinct Plant Men, who had been undone by the extravagance of their own mystical quietism. The utopian worlds now learned much from these archaic but uniquely sensitive beings. Henceforth the vegetal mode of experience was thoroughly, but not dangerously, knit into the texture of the galactic mind.

CHAPTER X

A VISION OF THE GALAXY

IT seemed to us now that the troubles of the many worlds of this galaxy were at last over, that the will to support the galactic utopia was now universal, and that the future must bring glory after glory. We felt assured of the same progress in other galaxies. In our simplicity we looked forward to the speedy, the complete and final, triumph of the striving spirit throughout the cosmos. We even conceived that the Star Maker rejoiced in the perfection of his work. Using such symbols as we could to express the inexpressible, we imagined that, before the beginning, the Star Maker was alone, and that for love and for community he resolved to make a perfect creature, to be his mate. We imagined that he made her of his hunger for beauty and his will for love; but that he also scourged her in the making, and tormented her, so that she might at last triumph over all adversity, and thereby achieve such perfection as he in his almightiness could never attain. The cosmos we conceived to be that creature. And it seemed to us in our simplicity that we had already witnessed the greater part of cosmical growth, and that there remained only the climax of that growth, the telepathic union of all the galaxies to become the single, fully awakened spirit of the cosmos, perfect, fit to be eternally contemplated and enjoyed by the Star Maker.

All this seemed to us majestically right. Yet we ourselves had no joy in it. We had been sated with the spectacle of continuous and triumphant progress in the latter age of our galaxy, and we were no longer curious about the host of the other galaxies. Almost certainly they were much like our own. We were, in fact, overwhelmingly fatigued and disillusioned.

During so many aeons we had followed the fortunes of the many worlds. So often we had lived out their passions, novel to them, but to us for the most part repetitive. We had shared all kinds of sufferings, all kinds of glories and shames. And now that the cosmical ideal, the full awakening of the spirit, seemed on the point of attainment, we found ourselves a little tired of it. What matter whether the whole huge drama of existence should be intricately known and relished by the perfected spirit or not? What matter whether we ourselves should complete our pilgrimage or not?

During so many aeons our company, distributed throughout the galaxy, had with difficulty maintained its single communal mentality. At all times "we," in spite of our severalty, were in fact "I," the single observer of the many worlds; but the maintaining of this identity was itself becoming a toil. "I" was overpowered with sleepiness; "we," severally, longed for our little native worlds, our homes, our lairs; and for the animal obtuseness that had walled us in from all the immensities. In particular, I, the Englishman, longed to be sleeping safely in that room where she and I had slept together, the day's urgencies all blotted out, and nothing left but sleep and the shadowy, the peaceful awareness in each of the other.

But though I was fatigued beyond endurance, sleep would not come. I remained perforce with my colleagues, and with the many triumphant worlds.

Slowly we were roused from our drowsiness by a discovery. It gradually appeared to us that the prevailing mood of these countless utopian systems of worlds was at heart very different from that of triumph. In every world we found a deep conviction of the littleness and impotence of all finite beings, no matter how exalted. In a certain world there was a kind of poet. When we told him our conception of the cosmical goal, he said, "When the cosmos wakes, if ever she does, she will find herself not the single beloved of her maker, but merely a little bubble adrift on the boundless and bottomless ocean of being."

What had seemed to us at first the irresistible march of god-like world-spirits, with all the resources of the universe in their hands and all eternity before them, was now gradually revealed in very different guise. The great advance in mental calibre, and the attainment of communal mentality throughout the cosmos, had brought a change in the experience of time. The temporal reach of the mind had been very greatly extended. The awakened worlds experienced an aeon as a mere crowded day. They were aware of time's passage as a man in a canoe might have cognizance of a river which in its upper reaches is sluggish but subsequently breaks into rapids and becomes swifter and swifter, till, at no great distance ahead, it must plunge in a final cataract down to the sea, namely to the eternal end of life, the extinction of the stars. Comparing the little respite that remained with the great work which they passionately desired to accomplish, namely the full awakening of the cosmical spirit, they saw that at best there was no time to spare, and that, more probably, it was already too late to accomplish the task. They had a strange foreboding that unforeseen disaster lay in store for them. It was sometimes said, "We know not what the stars, even, have in store for us, still less what the Star Maker." And it was sometimes said, "We should not for a moment consider even our best-established knowledge of existence as true. It is awareness only of the colours that our own vision paints on the film of one bubble in one strand of foam on the ocean of being."

The sense of the fated incompleteness of all creatures and of all their achievements gave to the Galactic Society of Worlds a charm, a sanctity, as of some short-lived and delicate flower. And it was with an increasing sense of precarious beauty that we ourselves were now learning to regard the far-flung utopia. In this mood we had a remarkable experience.

We had embarked upon a sort of holiday from exploration, seeking the refreshment of disembodied flight in space. Gathering our whole company together out of all the worlds, we centred ourselves into a single mobile view-point; and then, as one being, we glided and circled among the stars and nebulae. Presently the whim took us to plunge into outer space. We hastened till the forward stars turned violet, the hinder red; till both forward and hinder vanished; till all visible features were extinguished by the wild speed of our flight. In absolute darkness we brooded on the origin and the destiny of the galaxies, and on the appalling contrast between the cosmos and our minute home-lives to which we longed to return.

Presently we came to rest. In doing so we discovered that our situation was not such as we expected. The galaxy whence we had emerged did indeed lie far behind us, no bigger than a great cloud; but it was not the featured spiral that it should have been. After some confusion of mind we realized that we were looking at the galaxy in an early stage of its existence, in fact at a time before it was really a galaxy at all. For the cloud was no cloud of stars, but a continuous mist of light. At its heart was a vague brilliance, which faded softly into the dim outer regions and merged without perceptible boundary into the black sky. Even the sky itself was quite unfamiliar. Though empty of stars, it was densely peopled with a great number of pale clouds. All seemingly were farther from us than that from which we had come, but several bulked as largely as Orion in the Earth's sky. So congested was the heaven that many of the great objects were continuous with one another in their filmy extremities, and many were separated only by mere channels of emptiness, through which loomed vistas of more remote nebulae, some of them so distant as to be mere spots of light.

It was clear that we had travelled back through time to a date when the great nebulae were still near neighbours to one another, before the explosive nature of the cosmos had done more than separate them out from the continuous and congested primal substance.

As we watched, it became obvious that events were unfolding before us with fantastic speed. Each cloud visibly shrank, withdrawing into the distance. It also changed its shape. Each vague orb flattened somewhat, and became more definite. Receding and therefore diminishing, the nebulae now appeared as lens-shaped mists, tilted at all angles. But, even as we watched, they withdrew themselves so far into the depth of space that it became difficult to observe their changes. Only our own native nebula remained beside us, a huge oval stretching across half the sky. On this we now concentrated our attention.

Differences began to appear within it, regions of brighter and of less bright mist, faint streaks and swirls, like the foam on the sea's waves. These shadowy features slowly moved, as wisps of cloud move on the hills. Presently it was clear that the internal currents of the nebula were on the whole set in a common pattern. The great world of gas was in fact slowly rotating, almost as a tornado. As it rotated it continued to flatten. It was now like some blurred image of a streaked and flattish pebble, handy for "ducks and drakes," held too near the eye to be focused.

Presently we noticed, with our novel and miraculous vision, that microscopic points of intenser light were appearing here and there throughout the cloud, but mainly in its outer regions. As we watched, their number grew, and the spaces between them grew dark. Thus were the stars born.

The great cloud still span and flattened. It was soon a disc of whirling star-streams and strands of uncondensed gas, the last disintegrating tissues of the primal nebula. These continued to move within the whole by their own semi-independent activity, changing their shapes, creeping like living things, extending pseudopodia, and visibly fading as clouds fade; but giving place to new generations of stars. The heart of the nebula was now condensing into a smaller bulk, more clearly defined. It was a huge, congested globe of brilliance. Here and there throughout the disc knots and lumps of light were the embryonic star-clusters. The whole nebula was strewn with these balls of thistledown, these feathery, sparkling, fairy decorations, each one in fact pregnant with a small universe of stars.

The galaxy, for such it could now be named, continued visibly to whirl with hypnotic constancy. Its tangled tresses of star-streams were spread abroad on the darkness. Now it was like a huge broad-brimmed white sombrero, the crown a glowing mass, the brim a filmy expanse of stars. It was a cardinal's hat, spinning. The two long whirling tassels on the brim were two long spiralling star-streams. Their frayed extremities had broken away and become sub-galaxies, revolving about the main galactic system. The whole, like a spinning top, swayed; and, as it tilted before us, the brim appeared as an ever narrower ellipse, till presently it was edge-on, and the outermost fringe of it, composed of non-luminous matter, formed a thin, dark, knotted line across the glowing inner substance of nebula and stars.

Peering, straining to see more precisely the texture of this shimmering and nacrous wonder, this largest of all the kinds of objects in the cosmos, we found that our new vision, even while embracing the whole galaxy and the distant galaxies, apprehended each single star as a tiny disc separated from its nearest neighbours much as a cork on the Arctic Ocean would be separated from another cork on the Antarctic. Thus, in spite of the nebulous and opalescent beauty of its general form, the galaxy also appeared to us as a void sprinkled with very sparse scintillations.

Observing the stars more closely, we saw that while they streamed along in companies like shoals of fishes, their currents sometimes interpenetrated. Then seemingly the stars of the different streams, crossing one another's paths, pulled at one another, moving in great sweeping curves as they passed from one neighbour's influence to another. Thus, in spite of their remoteness each from each, the stars often looked curiously like minute living creatures taking cognizance of one another from afar. Sometimes they swung hyperbolically round one another and away, or, more rarely, united to form binaries.

So rapidly did time pass before us that aeons were packed into moments. We had seen the first stars condense from the nebular tissue as ruddy giants, though in the remote view inconceivably minute. A surprising number of these, perhaps through the centrifugal force of their rotation, were burst asunder to form binaries, so that, increasingly, the heaven was peopled by these waltzing pairs. Meanwhile, the giant stars slowly shrank and gathered brightness. They passed from red to yellow, and on to dazzling white and blue. While other young giants condensed around them, they shrank still further, and their colour changed once more to yellow and to smouldering red. Presently we saw the eldest of the stars one by one extinguished like sparks from a fire. The incidence of this mortality increased, slowly but steadily. Sometimes a "nova" flashed out and faded, outshining for a moment all its myriad neighbours. Here and there a "variable" pulsated with inconceivable rapidity. Now and again we saw a binary and a third star approach one another so closely that one or other of the group reached out a filament of its substance toward its partner. Straining our supernatural vision, we saw these filaments break and condense into planets. And we were awed by the infinitesimal size and the rarity of these seeds of life among the lifeless host of the stars.

But the stars themselves gave an irresistible impression of vitality. Strange that the movements of these merely physical things, these mere fire-balls, whirling and travelling according to the geometrical laws of their minutest particles, should seem so vital, so questing. But then the whole galaxy was itself so vital, so like an organism, with its delicate tracery of star-streams, like the streams within a living cell; and its extended wreaths, almost like feelers; and its nucleus of light. Surely this great and lovely creature must be alive, must have intelligent experience of itself and of things other than it.

In the tide of these wild thoughts we checked our fancy, remembering that only on the rare grains called planets can life gain foothold, and that all this wealth of restless jewels was but a waste of fire.

With rising affection and longing we directed our attention more minutely toward the earliest planetary grains as they condensed out of the whirling filaments of flame, to become at first molten drops that span and pulsated, then grew rock-encrusted, ocean-filmed, and swathed in atmosphere. Our piercing sight observed their shallow watters ferment with life, which soon spread into their oceans and continents. A few of these early worlds we saw waken to intelligence of human rank; and very soon these were in the throes of the great struggle for the spirit, from which still fewer emerged victorious.

Meanwhile new planetary births, rare among the stars, yet, in all, thousands upon thousands, had launched new worlds and new biographies. We saw the Other Earth, with its recurrent glories and shames, and its final suffocation. We saw the many other humanesque worlds, Echinoderm, Centaurian, and so on. We saw Man on his little Earth blunder through many alternating phases of dullness and lucidity, and again abject dullness. From epoch to epoch his bodily shape changed as a cloud changes. We watched him in his desperate struggle with Martian invaders; and then, after a moment that included further ages of darkness and of light, we saw him driven, by dread of the moon's downfall, away to inhospitable Venus. Later still, after an aeon that was a mere sigh in the lifetime of the cosmos, he fled before the exploding sun to Neptune, there to sink back into mere animality for further aeons again. But then he climbed once more and reached his finest intelligence, only to be burnt up like a moth in a flame by irresistible catastrophe.

All this long human story, most passionate and tragic in the living, was but an unimportant, a seemingly barren and negligible effort, lasting only for a few moments in the life of the galaxy. When it was over, the host of the planetary systems still lived on, with here and there a casualty, and here and there among the stars a new planetary birth, and here and there a fresh disaster.

Before and after man's troubled life we saw other humanesque races rise in scores and hundreds, of which a mere handful was destined to waken beyond man's highest spiritual range, to play a part in the galactic community of worlds. These we now saw from afar on their little Earth-like planets, scattered among the huge drift of the star-streams, struggling to master all those world-problems, social and spiritual, which man in our "modern" era is for the first time confronting. Similarly, we saw again

the many other kinds of races, nautiloid, submarine, avian, composite, and
the rare symbiotics, and still rarer plant-like beings. And of every kind
only a few, if any, won through to utopia, and took part in the great communal enterprise of worlds. The rest fell by the way.

From our remote look-out we now saw in one of the islanded sub-
galaxies the triumph of the Symbiotics. Here at last was the germ of a
true community of worlds. Presently the stars of this islet-universe began
to be girdled with living pearls, till the whole sub-galaxy was alive with
worlds. Meanwhile in the main system arose that flagrant and contagious
insanity of empire, which we had already watched in detail. But what had
before appeared as a war of titans, in which great worlds manœuvred in
space with inconceivable speed, and destroyed one another's populations in
holocausts, was now seen as the jerky motion of a few microscopic sparks,
a few luminous animalcules, surrounded by the indifferent stellar hosts.

Presently, however, we saw a star blaze up and destroy its planets.
The Empires had murdered something nobler than themselves. There was
a second murder, and a third. Then, under the influence of the sub-galaxy,
the imperial madness faded, and empire crumbled. And soon our fatigued
attention was held by the irresistible coming of utopia throughout the galaxy. This was visible to us chiefly as a steady increase of artificial planets.
Star after star blossomed with orbit after crowded orbit of these vital jewels, these blooms pregnant with the spirit. Constellation after constellation,
the whole galaxy became visibly alive with myriads of worlds. Each world,
peopled with its unique, multitudinous race of sensitive individual intelligences united in true community, was itself a living thing, possessed of a
common spirit. And each system of many populous orbits was itself a communal being. And the whole galaxy, knit in a single telepathic mesh, was
a single intelligent and ardent being, the common spirit, the "I," of all its
countless, diverse, and ephemeral individuals.

This whole vast community looked now beyond itself toward its fellow galaxies. Resolved to pursue the adventure of life and of spirit in the
cosmical, the widest of all spheres, it was in constant telepathic communication with its fellows; and at the same time, conceiving all kinds of
strange practical ambitions, it began to avail itself of the energies of its
stars upon a scale hitherto unimagined. Not only was every solar system
now surrounded by a gauze of light traps, which focused the escaping
solar energy for intelligent use, so that the whole galaxy was dimmed,
but many stars that were not suited to be suns were disintegrated, and
rifled of their prodigious stores of sub-atomic energy.

Suddenly our attention was held by an event which even at a distance
was visibly incompatible with utopia. A star encircled by planets exploded,
destroying all its rings of worlds, and sinking afterwards into wan exhaus-

tion. Another and another, and yet others in different regions of the galaxy, did likewise.

To enquire into the cause of these startling disasters we once more, by an act of volition, dispersed ourselves to our stations among the many worlds.

CHAPTER XI

STARS AND VERMIN

1. THE MANY GALAXIES

THE Galactic Society of Worlds had sought to perfect its communication with other galaxies. The simpler medium of contact was telepathic; but it seemed desirable to reach out physically also across the huge void between this galaxy and the next. It was in the attempt to send envoys on such voyages that the Society of Worlds brought upon itself the epidemic of exploding stars.

Before describing this series of disasters I shall say something of the conditions of other galaxies as they were known to us through our participation in the experience of our own galaxy.

Telepathic exploration had long ago revealed that at least in some other galaxies there existed minded worlds. And now, after long experiment, the worlds of our galaxy, working for this purpose as a single galactic mind, had attained much more detailed knowledge of the cosmos as a whole. This had proved difficult because of an unsuspected parochialism in the mental attitude of the worlds of each galaxy. In the basic physical and biological constitutions of the galaxies there was no far-reaching difference. In each there was a diversity of races of the same general types as those of our own galaxy. But upon the cultural plane the trend of development in each galactic society had produced important mental idiosyncrasies, often so deep-seated as to be unwitting. Thus it was very difficult at first for the developed galaxies to make contact with one another. Our own galactic culture had been dominated by the culture of the Symbiotics, which had developed in the exceptionally happy sub-galaxy. In spite of the horrors of the imperial age, ours was therefore a culture having a certain blandness which made telepathic intercourse with more tragic galaxies difficult to establish. Further, the detail of basic concepts and values accepted by our own galactic society was also largely a development of the marine culture that had dominated the sub-galaxy. Though the "continental" population of worlds was mainly humanesque, its native cultures had been profoundly influenced by the oceanic mentality. And since this oceanic mental texture was rare amongst galactic societies, our galaxy was rather more isolated than most.

After long and patient work, however, our galactic society succeeded in forming a fairly complete survey of the cosmical population of galaxies. It was discovered that at this time the many galaxies were in many stages of mental, as of physical, development. Many very young systems, in which nebular matter still predominated over stars, contained as yet no planets. In others, though already there was a sprinkling of the vital grains, life had nowhere reached the human level. Some galaxies, though physically mature, were wholly barren of planetary systems, either through sheer accident or by reason of the exceptionally sparse distribution of their stars. In several, out of the millions of galaxies, a single intelligent world had spread its race and its culture throughout the galaxy, organizing the whole as an egg's germ organizes into itself the whole substance of the egg. In these galaxies, very naturally, the galactic culture had been based on the assumption that from the one single germ the whole cosmos was to be peopled. When telepathic intercourse with other galaxies was at last stumbled upon, its effect was at first utterly bewildering. There were not a few galaxies in which two or more such germs had developed independently and finally come into contact. Sometimes the result was symbiosis, sometimes endless strife or even mutual destruction. By far the commonest type of galactic society was that in which many systems of worlds had developed independently, come into conflict, slaughtered one another, produced vast federations and empires, plunged again and again into social chaos, and struggled between whiles haltingly toward galactic utopia. A few had already attained that goal, though seared with bitterness. More were still floundering. Many were so undermined by war that there seemed little prospect of recovery. To such a type our own galaxy would have belonged had it not been for the good fortune of the Symbiotics.

To this account of the galactic survey two points should be added. First, there were certain very advanced galactic societies which had been telepathic spectators of all history in our own and all other galaxies. Secondly, in not a few galaxies the stars had recently begun unexpectedly exploding and destroying their girdles of worlds.

While our Galactic Society of Worlds was perfecting its telepathic vision, and at the same time improving its own social and material structure, the unexpected disasters which we had already observed from afar forced it to attend strictly to the task of preserving the lives of its constituent worlds.

The occasion of the first accident was an attempt to detach a star from its natural course and direct it upon an intergalactic voyage. Telepathic intercourse with the nearest of the foreign galaxies was fairly reliable, but, as I have said, it had been decided that a physical exchange of worlds would be invaluable for mutual understanding and cooperation. Plans were therefore made for projecting several stars with their attendant systems of worlds across the vast ocean of space that separated the two floating islets of civilization. The voyage would of course be thousands of times longer than anything hitherto attempted. At its completion many more of the stars in each galaxy would already have ceased to shine, and the end of all life in the cosmos would already be in sight. Yet it was felt that the enterprise of linking galaxy with galaxy throughout the cosmos in this manner would be well justified by the great increase of mutual insight which it would produce in the galaxies in the last and most difficult phase of cosmical life.

After prodigies of experiment and calculation the first attempt at intergalactic voyaging was undertaken. A certain star, barren of planets, was used as a reservoir of energy, both normal and sub-atomic. By cunning devices far beyond my comprehension this fund of power was directed upon a chosen star with planetary girdles in such a way as to sway it gradually in the direction of the foreign galaxy. The task of securing that its planets should remain in their true orbits during this operation, and during the subsequent acceleration of their sun, was very delicate, but was accomplished without the destruction of more than a dozen worlds. Unfortunately, just as the star was correctly aimed and was beginning to gather speed, it exploded. A sphere of incandescent material, expanding from the sun with incredible speed, swallowed up and destroyed every girdle of planets. The star then subsided.

Throughout the history of the galaxy such sudden effulgence and quiescence of a star had been a very common occurrence. It was known to consist of an explosion of sub-atomic energy from the star's superficial layers. This was caused sometimes by the impact of some small wandering body, often no bigger than an asteroid; sometimes by factors in the star's own physical evolution. In either case the Galactic Society of Worlds could predict the event with great accuracy and take steps either to divert the intruding body or to remove the threatened world-system out of harm's way. But this particular disaster was entirely unforeseen. No cause could be assigned to it. It infringed the established laws of physics.

While the Society of Worlds was trying to understand what had happened, another star exploded. This was the sun of one of the leading world-systems. Attempts had recently been made to increase this star's output of radiation, and it was thought that the disaster must have been due to these experiments. After a while another and yet other stars exploded, destroying all their worlds. In several cases attempts had recently been made either to alter the star's course or tap its stored energy.

The trouble spread. System after system of worlds was destroyed. All tampering with stars had now been abandoned, yet the epidemic of "novae" continued, even increased. In every case the exploding star was a sun with a planetary system.

The normal "nova" phase, the explosion caused not by collision but by internal forces, was known to occur only in a star's youth or early maturity, and seldom, if ever, more often than once in each star's career. In this late phase of the galaxy far more stars had passed the natural "nova" stage than not. It would be possible, therefore, to move whole systems of worlds from the dangerous younger stars and settle them in close orbits round the older luminaries. With immense expense of energy this operation was several times performed. Heroic plans were made for the transformation of the whole galactic society by migration to the safe stars, and the euthanasia of the excess population of worlds that could not be thus accommodated.

While this plan was being carried out it was defeated by a new series of disasters. Stars that had already exploded developed a power of exploding again and again whenever they were girdled with planets. Moreover, yet another kind of disaster now began to occur. Very aged stars, which had long since passed the period when explosion was possible, began to behave in an astounding manner. A plume of incandescent substance would issue from the photosphere, and this, as the star revolved, would sweep outwards as a trailing whirl. Sometimes this fiery proboscis calcined the surface of every planet in every orbit, killing all its life. Sometimes, if the sweep of the proboscis was not quite in the plane of the planetary orbits, a number of planets escaped. But in many cases in which the destruction was not at first complete the proboscis gradually brought itself more accurately into the planetary plane and destroyed the remaining worlds.

It soon became clear that, if the two kinds of stellar activity remained unchecked, civilization would be undermined and perhaps life exterminated throughout the galaxy. Astronomical knowledge provided no clue whatever to the problem. The theory of stellar evolution had seemed perfect, but it had no place for these singular events.

Meanwhile the Society of Worlds had set about the task of artificially exploding all stars that had not yet spontaneously passed through the "nova" phase. It was hoped thus to render them comparatively safe, and then to use them once more as suns. But now that all kinds of stars had become equally dangerous, this work was abandoned. Instead, arrangements were made to procure the radiation necessary to life from the stars that had ceased to shine. Controlled disintegration of their atoms would turn them into satisfactory suns, at least for a while. Unfortunately the epidemic of fiery plumes was increasing rapidly. System by system, the living worlds were being swept out of existence. Desperate research hit at last on a method of diverting the fiery tentacle away from the plane of the ecliptic. This process was far from reliable. Moreover, if it succeeded, the sun would sooner or later project another filament.

The state of the galaxy was being very rapidly changed. Hitherto there had been an incalculable wealth of stellar energy, but this energy was now being shed like rain from a thunder-cloud. Though a single explosion did not seriously affect the vigour of a star, repetitions became more exhausting as they increased in number. Many young stars had been reduced to decrepitude. The great majority of the stellar population had now passed their prime; multitudes were mere glowing coals or lightless ash. The minded worlds, also, were much reduced in number, for in spite of all ingenious measures of defence, casualties were still heavy. This reduction of the population of the worlds was the more serious because in its prime the Galactic Society of Worlds had been so highly organized. In some ways it was less like a society than a brain. The disaster had almost blotted out certain higher "brain-centres" and greatly reduced the vitality of all. It had also seriously impaired telepathic intercourse between the systems of worlds by forcing each system to concentrate on its own urgent physical problem of defence against the attacks of its own sun. The communal mind of the Society of Worlds now ceased to operate.

The emotional attitude of the worlds had also changed. The fevour for the establishment of cosmical utopia had vanished, and with it the fevour for the completion of the spirit's adventure by the fulfilment of knowledge and creative capacity. Now that extermination seemed inevitable within a comparatively short time, there was an increasing will to meet fate with religious peace. The desire to realize the far cosmical goal, formerly the supreme motive of all awakened worlds, now seemed to be extravagant, even impious. How should the little creatures, the awakened worlds, reach out to knowledge of the whole cosmos, and of the divine. Instead they must play their own part in the drama, and appreciate their own tragic end with godlike detachment and relish.

This mood of exultant resignation, appropriate to unavoidable disaster, quickly changed under the influence of a new discovery. In certain quarters there had long been a suspicion that the irregular activity of the stars was not merely automatic but purposeful, in fact that the stars were alive, and were striving to rid themselves of the pest of planets. This possibility had at first seemed too fantastic; but it gradually became obvious that the destruction of a star's planetary system was the end which determined the duration of the irregular action. Of course it was possible that in some unexplained but purely mechanical way the presence of many planetary girdles created the explosion, or the fiery limb. Astronomical physics could suggest no mechanism whatever which could have this result.

Telepathic research was now undertaken in order to test the theory of stellar consciousness, and if possible to set up communication with the minded stars. This venture was at first completely barren. The worlds had not the slightest knowledge of the right method of approach to minds which, if they existed at all, must be inconceivably different from their own. It seemed all too probable that no factors in the mentality of the minded worlds were sufficiently akin to the stellar mentality to form a means of contact. Though the worlds used their imaginative powers as best they might, though they explored, so to speak, every subterranean passage and gallery of their own mentality, tapping everywhere in the hope of answer, they received none. The theory of stellar purposefulness began to seem incredible. Once more the worlds began to turn to the consolation, nay the joy, of acceptance.

Nevertheless, a few world-systems that had specialized in psychological technique persisted in their researches, confident that, if only they could communicate with the stars, some kind of mutual understanding and concord could be brought about between the two great orders of minds in the galaxy.

At long last the desired contact with the stellar minds was effected. It came not through the unaided efforts of the minded worlds of our galaxy but partly through the mediation of another galaxy where already the worlds and the stars had begun to realize one another.

Even to the minds of fully awakened worlds the stellar mentality was almost too alien to be conceived at all. To me, the little human individual, all that is most distinctive in it is now quite incomprehensible. Nevertheless, its simpler aspect I must now try to summarize as best I may, since it is essential to my story. The minded worlds made their first contact with the stars on the higher planes of stellar experience, but I shall not follow the chronological order of their discoveries. Instead I shall begin with aspects of the stellar nature which were haltingly inferred only after intercourse of a sort had become fairly well established. It is in terms of stellar biology and physiology that the reader may most easily conceive something of the mental life of stars.

3. STARS

Stars are best regarded as living organisms, but organisms which are physiologically and psychologically of a very peculiar kind. The outer and middle layers of a mature star apparently consist of "tissues" woven of currents of incandescent gases. These gaseous tissues live and maintain the stellar consciousness by intercepting part of the immense flood of energy that wells from the congested and furiously active interior of the star. The innermost of the vital layers must be a kind of digestive apparatus which transmutes the crude radiation into forms required for the maintenance of the star's life. Outside this digestive area lies some sort of coordinating layer, which may be thought of as the star's brain. The outermost layers, including the corona, respond to the excessively faint stimuli of the star's cosmical environment, to light from neighbouring stars, to cosmic rays, to the impact of meteors, to tidal stresses caused by the gravitational influence of planets or of other stars. These influences could not, of course, produce any clear impression but for a strange tissue of gaseous sense organs, which discriminate between them in respect of quality and direction, and transmit information to the correlating "brain" layer.

The sense experience of a star, though so foreign to us, proved after all fairly intelligible. It was not excessively difficult for us to enter telepathically into the star's perception of the gentle titillations, strokings, pluckings, and scintillations that came to it from the galactic environment. It was strange that, though the star's own body was actually in a state of extreme brilliance, none of this outward-flowing light took effect upon its sense organs. Only the faint in-coming light of other stars was seen. This afforded the perception of a surrounding heaven of flashing constellations, which were set not in blackness but in blackness tinged with the humanly inconceivable colour of the cosmic rays. The stars themselves were seen coloured according to their style and age.

But though the sense perception of the stars was fairly intelligible to us, the motor side of stellar life was at first quite incomprehensible. We had to accustom ourselves to an entirely new way of regarding physical events. For the normal voluntary motor activity of a star appears to be no other than the star's *normal* physical movement studied by our science, movement in relation to other stars and the galaxy as a whole. A star must be thought of as vaguely aware of the gravitational influence of the whole galaxy, and more precisely aware of the "pull" of its near neighbours; though of course their influence would generally be far too slight to be detected by human instruments. To these influences the star responds by voluntary movement, which to the astronomers of the little minded worlds seems purely mechanical; but the star itself unquestioningly and rightly feels this movement to be the freely willed expression of its own psychological nature. Such at least was the almost incredible conclusion forced on us by the research carried out by the Galactic Society of Worlds.

Thus the normal experience of a star appears to consist in perception of its cosmical environment, along with continuous voluntary changes within its own body and in its position in relation to other stars. This change of position consists, of course, in rotation and passage. The star's motor life is thus to be thought of almost as a life of dance, or of figure-skating, executed with perfect skill according to an ideal principle which emerges into consciousness from the depths of the stellar nature and becomes clearer as the star's mind matures.

This ideal principle cannot be conceived by men save as it is manifested in practice as the well-known physical principle of "least action," or the pursuit of that course which in all the gravitational and other conditions is the least extravagant. The star itself, by means of its purchase on the electromagnetic field of the cosmos, apparently wills and executes this

ideal course with all the attention and delicacy of response which a motor-
ist exercises in threading his way through traffic on a winding road, or a
ballet-dancer in performing the most intricate movements with the greatest
economy of effort. Almost certainly, the star's whole physical behaviour is
normally experienced as a blissful, an ecstatic, an ever successful pursuit
of formal beauty. This the minded worlds were able to discover through
their own most formalistic aesthetic experience. In fact it was through this
experience that they first made contact with stellar minds. But the actual
perception of the aesthetic (or religious?) rightness of the mysterious
canon, which the stars so earnestly accepted, remained far beyond the mental range of the minded worlds. They had to take it, so to speak, on trust.
Clearly this aesthetic canon was in some way symbolical of some spiritual
intuition that remained occult to the minded worlds.

The life of the individual star is not only a life of physical movement.
It is also undoubtedly in some sense a cultural and a spiritual life. In some
manner each star is aware of its fellow stars as conscious beings. This mutual awareness is probably intuitive and telepathic, though presumably it
is also constantly supported by inference from observation of the behaviour
of others. From the psychological relations of star with star sprang a whole
world of social experiences which were so alien to the minded worlds that
almost nothing can be said of them.

There is perhaps some reason for believing that the free behaviour of
the individual star is determined not only by the austere canons of the
dance but also by the social will to cooperate with others. Certainly the
relation between stars is perfectly social. It reminded me of the relation
between the performers in an orchestra, but an orchestra composed of persons wholly intent on the common task. Possibly, but not certainly, each
star, executing its particular theme, is moved not only by the pure aesthetic
or religious motive but also by a will to afford its partners every legitimate
opportunity for self-expression. If so, the life of each star is experienced not
only as the perfect execution of formal beauty but also as the perfect expression of love. It would, however, be unwise to attribute affection and
comradeship to the stars in any human sense. The most that can safely be
said, is that it would probably be more false to deny them affection for one
another than to assert that they were, indeed, capable of love. Telepathic
research suggested that the experience of the stars was through and through
of a different texture from that of the minded worlds. Even to attribute to
them thought or desire of any kind is probably grossly anthropomorphic,
but it is impossible to speak of their experience in any other terms.

The mental life of a star is almost certainly a progress from an obscure
infantile mentality to the discriminate consciousness of maturity. All stars,
young and old, are mentally "angelic," in that they all freely and joyfully
will the "good will," the pattern of right action so far as it is revealed to

them; but the great tenuous young stars, though they perfectly execute their part in the galactic dance, would seem to be in some manner spiritually naïve or childlike in comparison with their more experienced elders. Thus, though there is normally no such thing as sin among the stars, no deliberate choice of the course known to be wrong for the sake of some end known to be irrelevant, there is ignorance, and consequent aberration from the pattern of the ideal as revealed to stars of somewhat maturer mentality. But this aberration on the part of the young is itself apparently accepted by the most awakened class of the stars as itself a desirable factor in the dance pattern of the galaxy. From the point of view of natural science, as known to the minded worlds, the behaviour of young stars is of course always an exact expression of their youthful nature; and the behaviour of the elder stars an expression of their nature. But, most surprisingly, the physical nature of a star at any stage of its growth is in part an expression of the telepathic influence of other stars. This fact can never be detected by the pure physics of any epoch. Unwittingly scientists derive the inductive physical laws of stellar evolution from data which are themselves an expression not only of normal physical influences but also of the unsuspected psychical influence of star on star.

In early ages of the cosmos the first "generation" of stars had been obliged to find their way unhelped from infancy to maturity; but later "generations" were in some manner guided by the experience of their elders so that they should pass more quickly and more thoroughly from the obscure to the fully lucid consciousness of themselves as spirits, and of the spiritual universe in which they dwelt.

Almost certainly, the latest stars to condense out of the primeval nebula advanced (or will advance) more rapidly than their elders had done; and throughout the stellar host it was believed that in due season the youngest stars, when they had attained maturity, would pass far beyond the loftiest spiritual insight of their seniors.

There is good reason to say that the two over-mastering desires of all stars are the desire to execute perfectly their part in the communal dance, and the desire to press forward to the attainment of full insight into the nature of the cosmos. The latter desire was the factor in stellar mentality which was most comprehensible to the minded worlds.

The climax of a star's life occurs when it has passed through the long period of its youth, during which it is what human astronomers call a "red giant." At the close of this period it shrinks rapidly into the dwarf state in which our sun now is. This physical cataclysm seems to be accompanied by far-reaching mental changes. Henceforth, though the star plays a less dashing part in the dance-rhythms of the galaxy, it is perhaps more clearly and penetratingly conscious. It is interested less in the ritual of the stellar dance, more in its supposed spiritual significance. After this very long phase of physical maturity there comes another crisis. The star shrinks into the minute and inconceivably dense condition in which our astronomers call it a "white dwarf." Its mentality in the actual crisis proved almost impervious to the research of the minded worlds. It appeared to be a crisis of despair and of reorientated hope. Henceforth the stellar mind presents increasingly a strain of baffling and even terrifying negativity, an icy, an almost cynical aloofness, which, we suspected, was but the obverse of some dread rapture hidden from us. However that may be, the aged star still continues meticulously to fulfil its part in the dance, but its mood is deeply changed. The aesthetic fervours of youth, the more serene but earnest will of maturity, all maturity's devotion to the active pursuit of wisdom, now fall away. Perhaps the star is henceforth content with its achievement, such as it is, and pleased simply to enjoy the surrounding universe with such detachment and insight as it has attained. Perhaps; but the minded worlds were never able to ascertain whether the aged stellar mind eluded their comprehension through sheer superiority of achievement or through some obscure disorder of the spirit.

In this state of old age a star remains for a very long period, gradually losing energy, and mentally withdrawing into itself, until it sinks into an impenetrable trance of senility. Finally its light is extinguished and its tissues disintegrate in death. Henceforth it continues to sweep through space, but it does so unconsciously, and in a manner repugnant to its still conscious fellows.

Such, very roughly stated, would seem to be the normal life of the average star. But there are many varieties within the general type. For stars vary in original size and in composition, and probably in psychological impact upon their neighbours. One of the commonest of the eccentric types is the double star, two mighty globes of fire waltzing through space together, in some cases almost in contact. Like all stellar relations, these partnerships are perfect, are angelic. Yet it is impossible to be certain whether the members experience anything which could properly be called a sentiment of personal love, or whether they regard one another solely as partners in a common task. Research undoubtedly suggested that the two beings did indeed move on their winding courses in some kind of mutual delight, and delight of close cooperation in the measures of the galaxy. But love? It is impossible to say. In due season, with the loss of momentum, the two stars come into actual contact. Then, seemingly in an agonizing blaze of joy and pain, they merge. After a period of unconsciousness, the great new star generates new living tissues, and takes its place among the angelic company.

The strange Cepheid variables proved the most baffling of all the stellar kinds. It seems that these and other variables of much longer period alternate mentally between fervour and quietism, in harmony with their physical rhythm. More than this it is impossible to say.

One event, which happens only to a small minority of the stars in the course of their dance-life, is apparently of great psychological importance. This is the close approach of two or perhaps three stars to one another, and the consequent projection of a filament from one toward another. In the moment of this "moth kiss," before the disintegration of the filament and the birth of planets, each star probably experiences an intense but humanly unintelligible physical ecstasy. Apparently the stars which have been through this experience are supposed to have acquired a peculiarly vivid apprehension of the unity of body and spirit. The "virgin" stars, however, though unblessed by this wonderful adventure, seem to have no desire to infringe the sacred canons of the dance in order to contrive opportunities for such encounters. Each one of them is angelically content to play its allotted part, and to observe the ecstasy of those that fate has favoured.

To describe the mentality of stars is of course to describe the unintelligible by means of intelligible but falsifying human metaphors. This tendency is particularly serious in telling of the dramatic relations between the stars and the minded worlds, for under the stress of these relations the stars seem to have experienced for the first time emotions superficially like human emotions. So long as the stellar community was immune from interference by the minded worlds, every member of it behaved with perfect rectitude and had perfect bliss in the perfect expression of its own nature and of the common spirit. Even senility and death were accepted with calm, for they were universally seen to be involved in the pattern of existence; and what every star desired was not immortality, whether for itself or for the community, but the perfect fruition of stellar nature. But when at last the minded worlds, the planets, began to interfere appreciably with stellar energy and motion, a new and terrible and incomprehensible thing presumably entered into the experiences of the stars. The stricken ones found themselves caught in a distracting mental conflict. Through some cause which they themselves could not detect, they not merely erred but willed to err. In fact they sinned. Even while they still adored the right, they chose the wrong.

I said that the trouble was unprecedented. This is not strictly true. Something not wholly unlike this public shame seems to have occurred in the private experience of nearly every star. But each sufferer succeeded in keeping his shame secret until either with familiarity it became tolerable or else its source was overcome. It was indeed surprising that beings whose nature was in many ways so alien and unintelligible should be in this one respect at least so startlingly "human."

In the outer layers of young stars life nearly always appears not only in the normal manner but also in the form of parasites, minute independent organisms of fire, often no bigger than a cloud in the terrestrial air, but sometimes as large as the Earth itself. These "salamanders" either feed upon the welling energies of the star in the same manner as the star's own organic tissues feed, or simply prey upon those tissues themselves. Here as elsewhere the laws of biological evolution come into force, and in time there may appear races of intelligent flame-like beings. Even when the salamandrian life does not reach this level, its effect on the star's tissues may become evident to the star as a disease of its skin and sense organs, or even of its deeper tissues. It then experiences emotions not wholly unlike human fright and shame, and anxiously and most humanly guards its secret from the telepathic reach of its fellows.

The salamandrian races have never been able to gain mastery over their fiery worlds. Many of them succumb, soon or late, either to some natural disaster or to internecine strife or to the self-cleansing activities of their mighty host. Many others survive, but in a relatively harmless state, troubling their stars only with a mild irritation, and a faint shade of insincerity in all their dealings with one another.

In the public culture of the stars the salamandrian pest was completely ignored. Each star believed itself to be the only sufferer and the only sinner in the galaxy. One indirect effect the pest did have on stellar thought. It introduced the idea of purity. Each star prized the perfection of the stellar community all the more by reason of its own secret experience of impurity.

When the minded planets began to tamper seriously with stellar energy and stellar orbits, the effect was not a private shame but a public scandal. It was patent to all observers that the culprit had violated the canons of the dance. The first aberrations were greeted with bewilderment and horror. Amongst the hosts of the virgin stars it was whispered that if the result of the much prized interstellar contacts, whence the natural planets had sprung, was in the end this shameful irregularity, probably the original experience itself had also been sinful. The erring stars protested that they were not sinners, but victims of some unknown influence from the grains which revolved about them. Yet secretly they doubted themselves. Had they long ago, in the ecstatic sweep of star to star, after all infringed the canon of the dance? They suspected, moreover, that in respect of the irregularities which were now creating this public scandal, they could, if they had willed firmly enough, have contained themselves, and preserved their true courses in spite of the irritants that had affected them.

Meanwhile the power of the minded planets increased. Suns were boldly steered to suit the purposes of their parasites. To the stellar population it seemed, of course, that these erring stars were dangerous lunatics. The crisis came, as I have already said, when the worlds projected their first messenger toward the neighbouring galaxy. The hurtling star, terrified at its own maniac behaviour, took the only retaliation that was known to it. It exploded into the "nova" state, and successfully destroyed its planets. From the orthodox stellar point of view this act was a deadly sin;

for it was an impious interference with the divinely appointed order of a star's life. But it secured the desired end, and was soon copied by other desperate stars.

Then followed that age of horror which I have already described from the point of view of the Society of Worlds. From the stellar point of view it was no less terrible, for the condition of the stellar society soon became desperate. Gone was the perfection and beatitude of former days. "The City of God" had degenerated into a place of hatred, recrimination and despair. Hosts of the younger stars had become premature and embittered dwarfs, while the elders had mostly grown senile. The dance pattern had fallen into chaos. The old passion for the canons of the dance remained, but the conception of the canons was obscured. Spiritual life had succumbed to the necessity of urgent action. The passion for the progress of insight into the nature of the cosmos also remained, but insight itself was obscured. Moreover, the former naïve confidence, common to young and mature alike, the certainty that the cosmos was perfect and that the power behind it was righteous, had given place to blank despair.

4. GALACTIC SYMBIOSIS

Such was the state of affairs when the minded worlds first attempted to make telepathic contact with the minded stars. I need not tell the stages by which mere contact was developed into a clumsy and precarious kind of communication. In time the stars must have begun to realize that they were at grips, not with mere physical forces, nor yet with fiends, but with beings whose nature, though so profoundly alien, was at bottom identical with their own. Our telepathic research obscurely sensed the amazement which spread throughout the stellar population. Two opinions, two policies, two parties seem to have gradually emerged.

One of these parties was convinced that the pretensions of the minded planets must be false, that beings whose history was compact of sin and strife and slaughter must be essentially diabolic, and that to parley with them was to court disaster. This party, at first a majority, urged that the war should be continued till every planet had been destroyed.

The minority party clamoured for peace. The planets, they affirmed, were seeking in their own way the very same goal as the stars. It was even suggested that these minute beings, with their more varied experience and their long acquaintance with evil, might have certain kinds of insight which the stars, those fallen angels, lacked. Might not the two sorts of being create together a glorious symbiotic society, and achieve together the end that was most dear to both, namely the full awakening of the spirit?

It was a long while before the majority would listen to this counsel. Destruction continued. The precious energies of the galaxy were squan-

dered. System after system of worlds was destroyed. Star after star sank
into exhaustion and stupor.

Meanwhile the Society of Worlds maintained a pacific attitude. No
more stellar energy was tapped. No more stellar orbits were altered. No
stars were artificially exploded.

Stellar opinion began to change. The crusade of extermination relaxed,
and was abandoned. There followed a period of "isolationism" in which
the stars, intent on repairing their shattered society, left their former enemies alone. Gradually a fumbling attempt at fraternization began between
the planets and their suns. The two kinds of beings, though so alien that
they could not at all comprehend each other's idiosyncrasies, were too lucid
for mere tribal passions. They resolved to overcome all obstacles and enter
into some kind of community. Soon it was the desire of every star to be
girdled with artificial planets and enter into some sort of "sympsychic"
partnership with its encircling companions. For it was by now clear to the
stars that the "vermin" had much to give them. The experience of the two
orders of beings was in many ways complementary. The stars retained still
the tenor of the angelic wisdom of their golden age. The planets excelled
in the analytic, the microscopic, and in that charity which was bred in
them by knowledge of their own weak and suffering forbears. To the stars,
moreover, it was perplexing that their minute companions could accept not
merely with resignation but with joy a cosmos which evidently was seamed
with evil.

In due season a symbiotic society of stars and planetary systems embraced the whole galaxy. But it was at first a wounded society, and ever
after an impoverished galaxy. Few only of its million million stars were
still in their prime. Every possible sun was now girdled with planets. Many
dead stars were stimulated to disintegrate their atoms so as to provide artificial suns. Others were used in a more economical manner. Special races
of intelligent organisms were bred or synthetized to inhabit the surfaces
of these great worlds. Very soon, upon a thousand stars that once had
blazed, teeming populations of innumerable types maintained an austere
civilization. These subsisted on the volcanic energies of their huge worlds.
Minute, artificially contrived worm-like creatures, they crept laboriously
over the plains where oppressive gravitation allowed not so much as a stone
to project above the general level. So violent, indeed, was gravitation, that
even the little bodies of these worms might be shattered by a fall of half
an inch. Save for artificial lighting, the inhabitants of the stellar worlds
lived in eternal darkness, mitigated only by the starlight, the glow of
volcanic eruption, and the phosphorescence of their own bodies. Their subterranean borings led down to the vast photosynthesis stations which converted the star's imprisoned energy for the uses of life and of mind.
Intelligence in these gigantic worlds was of course a function not of the

separate individual but of the minded swarm. Like the insectoids, these little creatures, when isolated from the swarm, were mere instinctive animals, actuated wholly by the gregarious craving to return to the swarm.

The need to people the dead stars would not have arisen had not the war reduced the number of minded planets and the number of suns available for new planetary systems dangerously near the minimum required to maintain the communal life in full diversity. The Society of Worlds had been a delicately organized unity in which each element had a special function. It was therefore necessary, since the lost members could not be repeated, to produce new worlds to function in their places at least approximately.

Gradually the symbiotic society overcame the immense difficulties of reorganization, and began to turn its attention to the pursuit of that purpose which is the ultimate purpose of all awakened minds, the aim which they inevitably and gladly espouse because it is involved in their deepest nature. Henceforth the symbiotic society gave all its best attention to the further awakening of the spirit.

But this purpose, which formerly the angelic company of the stars and the ambitious Society of Worlds had each hoped to accomplish in relation not merely to the galaxy but to the cosmos, was now regarded more humbly. Both stars and worlds recognized that not merely the home galaxy but the cosmical swarm of galaxies was nearing its end. Physical energy, once a seemingly inexhaustible fund, was becoming less and less available for the maintenance of life. It was spreading itself more and more evenly over the whole cosmos. Only here and there and with difficulty could the minded organisms intercept it in its collapse from high to low potential. Very soon the universe would be physically senile.

All ambitious plans had therefore to be abandoned. No longer was there any question of physical travel between the galaxies. Such enterprises would use up too many of the pence out of the few pounds of wealth that survived after the extravagance of former aeons. No longer was there any unnecessary coming and going, even within the galaxy itself. The worlds clung to their suns. The suns steadily cooled. And as they cooled, the encircling worlds contracted their orbits for warmth's sake.

But though the galaxy was physically impoverished, it was in many ways utopian. The symbiotic society of stars and worlds was perfectly harmonious. Strife between the two kinds was a memory of the remote past. Both were wholly loyal to the common purpose. They lived their personal lives in zestful cooperation, friendly conflict, and mutual interest. Each took part according to its capacity in the common task of cosmical exploration and appreciation. The stars were now dying off more rapidly than before, for the great host of the mature had become a great host of aged white dwarfs. As they died, they bequeathed their bodies to the service of

the society, to be used either as reservoirs of sub-atomic energy, or as artificial suns, or as worlds to be peopled by intelligent populations of worms.
Many a planetary system was now centred round an artificial sun. Physically the substitution was tolerable; but beings that had become mentally
dependent on partnership with a living star regarded a mere furnace with
despondency. Foreseeing the inevitable dissolution of the symbiosis throughout the galaxy, the planets were now doing all in their power to absorb the
angelic wisdom of the stars. But after very few aeons the planets themselves had to begin reducing their number. The myriad worlds could no
longer all crowd closely enough around their cooling suns. Soon the mental
power of the galaxy, which had hitherto been with difficulty maintained
at its highest pitch, must inevitably begin to wane.

Yet the temper of the galaxy was not sad but joyful. The symbiosis
had greatly improved the art of telepathic communion; and now at last the
many kinds of spirit which composed the galactic society were bound so
closely in mutual insight that there had emerged out of their harmonious
diversity a true galactic mind, whose mental reach surpassed that of the
stars and of the worlds as far as these surpassed their own individuals.

The galactic mind, which was but the mind of each individual star
and world and minute organism in the worlds, enriched by all its fellows
and awakened to finer percipience, saw that it had but a short time to live.
Looking back through the ages of galactic history, down temporal vistas
crowded with teeming and diversified populations, the mind of our galaxy
saw that itself was the issue of untold strife and grief and hope frustrated.
It confronted all the tortured spirits of the past not with pity or regret but
with smiling content, such as a man may feel toward his own childhood's
tribulations. And it said, within the mind of each one of all its members,
"Their suffering, which to them seemed barren evil, was the little price
to be paid for my future coming. Right and sweet and beautiful is the whole
in which these things happen. For I, I am the heaven in which all my
myriad progenitors find recompense, finding their heart's desire. For in
the little time that is left me I shall press on, with all my peers throughout
the cosmos, to crown the cosmos with perfect and joyful insight, and to
salute the Maker of Galaxies and Stars and Worlds with fitting praise."

CHAPTER XII

A STUNTED COSMICAL SPIRIT

WHEN at last our galaxy was able to make a full telepathic exploration of
the cosmos of galaxies it discovered that the state of life in the cosmos was
precarious. Very few of the galaxies were now in their youth; most were

already far past their prime. Throughout the cosmos the dead and lightless stars far outnumbered the living and luminous. In many galaxies the strife of stars and worlds had been even more disastrous than in our own. Peace had been secured only after both sides had degenerated past hope of recovery. In most of the younger galaxies, however, this strife had not yet appeared; and efforts were already being made by the most awakened galactic spirits to enlighten the ignorant stellar and planetary societies about one another before they should blunder into conflict.

The communal spirit of our galaxy now joined the little company of the most awakened beings of the cosmos, the scattered band of advanced galactic spirits, whose aim it was to create a real cosmical community, with a single mind, the communal spirit of its myriad and diverse worlds and individual intelligences. Thus it was hoped to acquire powers of insight and of creativity impossible on the merely galactic plane.

With grave joy we, the cosmical explorers, who were already gathered up into the communal mind of our own galaxy, now found ourselves in intimate union with a score of other galactic minds. We, or rather I, now experienced the slow drift of the galaxies much as a man feels the swing of his own limbs. From my score of view-points I observed the great snowstorm of many million galaxies, streaming and circling, and ever withdrawing farther apart from one another with the relentless "expansion" of space. But though the vastness of space was increasing in relation to the size of galaxies and stars and worlds, to me, with my composite, scattered body, space seemed no bigger than a great vaulted hall.

My experience of time also had changed; for now, as on an earlier occasion, the aeons had become for me as brief as minutes. I conceived the whole life of the cosmos not as an immensely protracted and leisurely passage from a remote and shadowy source to a glorious and a still more remote eternity, but as a brief, a headlong and forlorn, race against galloping time.

Confronted by the many backward galaxies, I seemed to myself to be a lonely intelligence in a wilderness of barbarians and beasts. The mystery, the futility, the horror of existence now bore down upon me most cruelly. For to me, to the spirit of that little band of awakened galaxies, surrounded by unawakened and doomed hordes in the last day of the cosmos, there appeared no hope of any triumph elsewhere. For to me the whole extent, seemingly, of existence was revealed. There could be no "elsewhere." I knew with exactness the sum of cosmical matter. And though the "expansion" of space was already sweeping most of the galaxies apart more swiftly than light could bridge the gulf, telepathic exploration still kept me in touch with the whole extent of the cosmos. Many of my own members were physically divided from one another by the insurmountable gulf created by the ceaseless "expansion"; but telepathically they were still united.

I, the communal mind of a score of galaxies, seemed now to myself to be the abortive and crippled mind of the cosmos itself. The myriad-fold community that supported me ought surely to have expanded to embrace the whole of existence. In the climax of cosmical history the fully awakened mind of the cosmos ought surely to have won through to the fullness of knowledge and of worship. But this was not to be. For even now, in the late phase of the cosmos, when the physical potency was almost all exhausted, I had reached only to a lowly state of spiritual growth. I was mentally still adolescent, yet my cosmical body was already in decay. I was the struggling embryo in the cosmical egg, and the yolk was already in decay.

Looking back along the vistas of the aeons, I was impressed less by the length of the journey that had led me to my present state than by its haste and confusion, and even its brevity. Peering into the very earliest of the ages, before the stars were born, before the nebulae were formed from chaos, I still failed to see any clear source, but only a mystery as obscure as any that confronts the little inhabitants of the Earth.

Equally, when I tried to probe the depths of my own being, I found impenetrable mystery. Though my self-consciousness was awakened to a degree thrice removed beyond the self-consciousness of human beings, namely from the simple individual to the world-mind, and from the world-mind to the galactic mind, and thence to the abortively cosmical, yet the depth of my nature was obscure.

Although my mind now gathered into itself all the wisdom of all worlds in all ages, and though the life of my cosmical body was itself the life of myriads of infinitely diverse worlds and myriads of infinitely diverse individual creatures, and though the texture of my daily life was one of joyful and creative enterprise, yet all this was as nothing. For around lay the host of the unfulfilled galaxies; and my own flesh was already grievously impoverished by the death of my stars; and the aeons were slipping past with fatal speed. Soon the texture of my cosmical brain must disintegrate. And then inevitably I must fall away from my prized though imperfect state of lucidity, and descend, through all the stages of the mind's second childhood, down to the cosmical death.

It was very strange that I, who knew the whole extent of space and time, and counted the wandering stars like sheep, overlooking none, that I who was the most awakened of all beings, I, the glory which myriads in all ages had given their lives to establish, and myriads had worshipped, should now look about me with the same overpowering awe, the same abashed and tongue-tied worship as that which human travellers in the desert feel under the stars.

CHAPTER XIII

THE BEGINNING AND THE END

I. BACK TO THE NEBULAE

WHILE the awakened galaxies were striving to make full use of the last phase of their lucid consciousness, while I, the imperfect cosmical mind, was thus striving, I began to have a strange new experience. I seemed to be telepathically stumbling upon some being or beings of an order that was at first quite incomprehensible to me.

At first I supposed that I had inadvertently come into touch with sub-human beings in the primitive age of some natural planet, perhaps with some very lowly amoeboid micro-organisms, floating in a primeval sea. I was aware only of crude hungers of the body, such as the lust to assimilate physical energy for the maintenance of life, the lust of movement and of contact, the lust of light and warmth.

Impatiently I tried to dismiss this trivial irrelevance. But it continued to haunt me, becoming more intrusive and more lucid. Gradually it took on such an intensity of physical vigour and well-being, and such a divine confidence, as was manifested by no spirits up and down the ages since the stars began.

I need not tell of the stages by which I learned at last the meaning of this experience. Gradually I discovered that I had made contact not with micro-organisms, nor yet with worlds or stars or galactic minds, but with the minds of the great nebulae before their substance had disintegrated into stars to form the galaxies.

Presently I was able to follow their history from the time when they first wakened, when they first existed as discrete clouds of gas, flying apart after the explosive act of creation, even to the time when, with the birth of the stellar hosts out of their substance, they sank into senility and death.

In their earliest phase, when physically they were the most tenuous clouds, their mentality was no more than a formless craving for action and a sleepy perception of the infinitely slight congestion of their own vacuous substance.

I watched them condense into close-knit balls with sharper contours, then into lentoid discs, featured with brighter streams and darker chasms. As they condensed, each gained more unity, became more organic in struc-ture. Congestion, though so slight, brought greater mutual influence to their atoms, which still were no more closely packed, in relation to their size, than stars in space. Each nebula was now a single great pool of faint radiation, a single system of all-pervasive waves, spreading from atom to atom.

And now mentally these greatest of all megatheria, these amoeboid titans, began to waken into a vague unity of experience. By human standards, and even by the standards of the minded worlds and the stars, the experience of the nebulae was incredibly slow-moving. For owing to their prodigious size and the slow passage of the undulations to which their consciousness was physically related, a thousand years was for them an imperceptible instant. Periods such as men call geological, containing the rise and fall of species after species, they experienced as we experience the hours.

Each of the great nebulae was aware of its own lentoid body as a single volume compact of tingling currents. Each craved fulfilment of its organic potency, craved easement from the pressure of physical energy welling softly within it, craved at the same time free expression of all its powers of movement, craved also something more.

For though, both in physique and in mentality, these primordial beings were strangely like the primeval micro-organisms of planetary life, they were also remarkably different; or at least they manifested a character which even I, the rudimentary cosmical mind, had overlooked in micro-organisms. This was a will or predilection that I can only by halting metaphor suggest.

Though even at their best these creatures were physically and intellectually very simple, they were gifted with something which I am forced to describe as a primitive but intense religious consciousness. For they were ruled by two longings, both of which were essentially religious. They desired, or rather they had a blind urge toward, union with one another, and they had a blind passionate urge to be gathered up once more into the source whence they had come.

The universe that they inhabited was of course a very simple, even a poverty-stricken universe. It was also to them quite small. For each of them the cosmos consisted of two things, the nebula's own almost featureless body and the bodies of the other nebulae. In this early age of the cosmos the nebulae were very close to one another, for the volume of the cosmos was at this time small in relation to its parts, whether nebulae or electrons. In that age the nebulae, which in man's day are like birds at large in the sky, were confined, as it were, within a narrow aviary. Thus each exercised an appreciable influence on its fellows. And as each became more organized, more of a coherent physical unity, it distinguished more readily between its native wave-pattern and the irregularities which its neighbours' influence imposed upon that pattern. And by a native propensity implanted in it at the time of its emergence from the common ancestral cloud, it interpreted this influence to mean the presence of other minded nebulae.

Thus the nebulae in their prime were vaguely but intensely aware of one another as distinct beings. They were aware of one another; but their communication with each other was very meagre and very slow. As prisoners confined in separate cells give one another a sense of companionship by tapping on their cell walls, and may even in time work out a crude system of signals, so the nebulae revealed to one another their kinship by exercising gravitational stress upon one another, and by long-drawn-out pulsations of their light. Even in the early phase of their existence, when the nebulae were very close to one another, a message would take many thousands of years to spell itself out from beginning to end, and many millions of years to reach its destination. When the nebulae were at their prime, the whole cosmos reverberated with their talk.

In the earliest phase of all, when these huge creatures were still very close to one another and also immature, their parleying was concerned wholly with the effort to reveal themselves to one another. With child-like glee they laboriously communicated their joy in life, their hungers and pains, their whims, their idiosyncrasies, their common passion to be once more united, and to be, as men have sometimes said, at one in God.

But even in early days, when few nebulae were yet mature, and most were still very unclear in their minds, it became evident to the more awakened that, far from uniting, they were steadily drifting apart. As the physical influence of one on another diminished, each nebula perceived its companions shrinking into the distance. Messages took longer and longer to elicit answers.

Had the nebulae been able to communicate telepathically, the "expansion" of the universe might have been faced without despair. But these beings were apparently too simple to make direct and lucid mental contact with one another. Thus they found themselves doomed to separation. And since their life-tempo was so slow, they seemed to themselves to have scarcely found one another before they must be parted. Bitterly they regretted the blindness of their infancy. For as they reached maturity they conceived, one and all, not merely the passion of mutual delight which we call love, but also the conviction that through mental union with one another lay the way to union with the source whence they had come.

When it had become clear that separation was inevitable, when indeed the hard-won community of these naïve beings was already failing through the increased difficulty of communication, and the most remote nebulae were already receding from one another at high speed, each perforce made ready to face the mystery of existence in absolute solitude.

There followed an aeon, or rather for the slow-living creatures themselves a brief spell, in which they sought, by self-mastery of their own flesh and by spiritual discipline, to find the supreme illumination which all awakened beings must, in their very nature, seek.

But now there appeared a new trouble. Some of the eldest of the nebu-

lae complained of a strange sickness which greatly hampered their meditations. The outer fringes of their tenuous flesh began to concentrate into
little knots. These became in time grains of intense, congested fire. In the
void between, there was nothing left but a few stray atoms. At first the
complaint was no more serious than some trivial rash on a man's skin;
but later it spread into the deeper tissues of the nebula, and was accompanied by grave mental troubles. In vain the doomed creatures resolved to
turn the plague to an advantage by treating it as a heaven-sent test of the
spirit. Though for a while they might master the plague simply by heroic
contempt of it, its ravages eventually broke down their will. It now seemed
clear to them that the cosmos was a place of futility and horror.

Presently the younger nebulae observed that their seniors, one by one,
were falling into a state of sluggishness and confusion which ended invariably in the sleep that men call death. Soon it became evident even to
the most buoyant spirit that this disease was no casual accident but a fate
inherent in the nebular nature.

One by one the celestial megatheria were annihilated, giving place
to stars.

Looking back on these events from my post in the far future, I, the
rudimentary cosmical mind, tried to make known to the dying nebulae
in the remote past that their death, far from being the end, was but an
early stage in the life of the cosmos. It was my hope that I might give
them consolation by imparting some idea of the vast and intricate future,
and of my own final awakening. But it proved impossible to communicate with them. Though within the sphere of their ordinary experience
they were capable of a sort of intellection, beyond that sphere they were
almost imbecile. As well might a man seek to comfort the disintegrating
germ-cell from which he himself sprang by telling it about his own successful career in human society.

Since this attempt to comfort was vain, I put aside compassion, and
was content merely to follow to its conclusion the collapse of the nebular
community. Judged by human standards the agony was immensely prolonged. It began with the disintegration of the eldest nebulae into stars,
and it lasted (or will last) long after the destruction of the final human
race on Neptune. Indeed, the last of the nebulae did not sink into complete unconsciousness till many of the corpses of its neighbours had already
been transformed into symbiotic societies of stars and minded worlds. But
to the slow-living nebulae themselves the plague seemed a galloping disease. One after the other, each great religious beast found itself at grips
with the subtle enemy, and fought a gallant losing fight until stupor overwhelmed it. None ever knew that its crumbling flesh teemed with the
young and swifter lives of stars, or that it was already sprinkled here and
there with the incomparably smaller, incomparably swifter, and incompa-

rably richer lives of creatures such as men, whose crowded ages of history were all compressed within the last few distressful moments of the primeval monsters.

2. THE SUPREME MOMENT NEARS

The discovery of nebular life deeply moved the incipient cosmical mind that I had become. Patiently I studied those almost formless megatheria, absorbing into my own composite being the fervour of their simple but deep-running nature. For these simple creatures sought their goal with a single-mindedness and passion eclipsing all the worlds and stars. With such earnest imagination did I enter into their history that I myself, the cosmical mind, was in a manner remade by contemplation of these beings. Considering from the nebular point of view the vast complexity and subtlety of the living worlds, I began to wonder whether the endless divagations of the worlds were really due so much to richness of being as to weakness of spiritual perception, so much to the immensely varied potentiality of their nature as to sheer lack of any intense controlling experience. A compass needle that is but feebly magnetized swings again and again to west and east, and takes long to discover its proper direction. One that is more sensitive will settle immediately toward the north. Had the sheer complexity of every world, with its host of minute yet complex members, merely confused its sense of the proper direction of all spirit? Had the simplicity and spiritual vigour of the earliest, hugest beings achieved something of highest value that the complexity and subtlety of the worlds could never achieve?

But no! Excellent as the nebular mentality was, in its own strange way, the stellar and the planetary mentalities had also their special virtues. And of all three the planetary must be most prized, since it could best comprehend all three.

I now allowed myself to believe that I, since I did at last include in my own being an intimate awareness not only of many galaxies but also of the first phase of cosmical life, might now with some justice regard myself as the incipient mind of the cosmos as a whole.

But the awakened galaxies that supported me were still only a small minority of the total population of galaxies. By telepathic influence I continued to help on those many galaxies that were upon the threshold of mental maturity. If I could include within the cosmical community of awakened galaxies some hundreds instead of a mere score of members, perhaps I myself, the communal mind, might be so strengthened as to rise from my present state of arrested mental infancy to something more like maturity. It was clear to me that even now, in my embryonic state, I was ripening for some new elucidation; and that with good fortune I might yet find myself in the presence of that which, in the human language of this book, has been called the Star Maker.

At this time my longing for that presence had become an overmastering passion. It seemed to me that the veil which still hid the source and goal of all nebulae and stars and worlds was already dissolving. That which had kindled so many myriad beings to worship, yet had clearly revealed itself to none, that toward which all beings had blindly striven, representing it to themselves by the images of a myriad divinities, was now, I felt, on the point of revelation to me, the marred but still growing spirit of the cosmos.

I who had myself been worshipped by hosts of my little members, I whose achievement reached far beyond their dreams, was now oppressed, overwhelmed, by the sense of my own littleness and imperfection. For the veiled presence of the Star Maker already overmastered me with dreadful power. The further I ascended along the path of the spirit, the loftier appeared the heights that lay before me. For what I had once thought to be the summit fully revealed was now seen to be a mere foot-hill. Beyond lay the real ascent, steep, cragged, glacial, rising into the dark mist. Never, never should I climb that precipice. And yet I must go forward. Dread was overcome by irresistible craving.

Meanwhile under my influence the immature galaxies one by one attained that pitch of lucidity which enabled them to join the cosmical community and enrich me with their special experience. But physically the enfeeblement of the cosmos continued. By the time that half the total population of galaxies had reached maturity it became clear that few more would succeed.

Of living stars, very few were left in any galaxy. Of the host of dead stars, some, subjected to atomic disintegration, were being used as artificial suns, and were surrounded by many thousands of artificial planets. But the great majority of the stars were now encrusted, and themselves peopled. After a while it became necessary to evacuate all planets, since the artificial suns were too extravagant of energy. The planet-dwelling races therefore one by one destroyed themselves, bequeathing the material of their worlds and all their wisdom to the inhabitants of the extinguished stars. Henceforth the cosmos, once a swarm of blazing galaxies, each a swarm of stars, was composed wholly of star-corpses. These dark grains drifted through the dark void, like an infinitely tenuous smoke rising from an extinguished fire. Upon these motes, these gigantic worlds, the ultimate populations had created here and there with their artificial lighting a pale glow, invisible even from the innermost ring of lifeless planets.

By far the commonest type of being in these stellar worlds was the intelligent swarm of minute worms or insectoids. But there were also many races of larger creatures of a very curious kind adapted to the prodigious gravitation of their giant worlds. Each of these creatures was a sort of living blanket. Its under surface bore a host of tiny legs that were also mouths.

These supported a body that was never more than an inch thick, though it might be as much as a couple of yards wide and ten yards long. At the forward end the manipulatory "arms" travelled on their own battalions of legs. The upper surface of the body contained a honeycomb of breathing-pores and a great variety of sense organs. Between the two surfaces spread the organs of metabolism and the vast area of brain. Compared with the worm-swarms and insect-swarms, these tripe-like beings had the advantage of more secure mental unity and greater specialization of organs; but they were more cumbersome, and less adapted to the subterranean life which was later to be forced on all populations.

The huge dark worlds with their immense weight of atmosphere and their incredible breadths of ocean, where the waves even in the most furious storms were never more than ripples such as we know on quicksilver, were soon congested with the honeycomb civilizations of worms and insectoids of many species, and the more precarious shelters of the tripe-like creatures. Life on these worlds was almost like life in a two-dimensional "flat-land." Even the most rigid of the artificial elements was too weak to allow of lofty structures.

As time advanced, the internal heat of the encrusted stars was used up, and it became necessary to support civilization by atomic disintegration of the star's rocky core. Thus in time each stellar world became an increasingly hollow sphere supported by a system of great internal buttresses. One by one the populations, or rather the new and specially adapted descendants of the former populations, retired into the interiors of the burnt-out stars.

Each imprisoned in its hollow world, and physically isolated from the rest of the cosmos, these populations telepathically supported the cosmical mind. These were my flesh. In the inevitable "expansion" of the universe, the dark galaxies had already for aeons been flying apart so rapidly that light itself could not have bridged the gulf between them. But this prodigious disintegration of the cosmos was of less account to the ultimate populations than the physical insulation of star from star through the cessation of all stellar radiation and all interstellar travel. The many populations, teeming in the galleries of the many worlds, maintained their telepathic union. Intimately they knew one another in all their diversity. Together they supported the communal mind, with all its awareness of the whole vivid, intricate past of the cosmos, and its tireless effort to achieve its spiritual goal before increase of entropy should destroy the tissue of civilizations in which it inhered.

Such was the condition of the cosmos when it approached the supreme moment of its career, and the illumination toward which all beings in all ages had been obscurely striving. Strange it was that these latter-day populations, cramped and impoverished, counting their past pence of energy, should achieve the task that had defeated the brilliant hosts of earlier epochs. Theirs was indeed the case of the wren that outsoared the eagle. In spite of their straitened circumstances they were still able to maintain the essential structure of a cosmical community, and a cosmical mentality. And with native insight they could use the past to deepen their wisdom far beyond the range of any past wisdom.

The supreme moment of the cosmos was not (or will not be) a moment by human standards; but by cosmical standards it was indeed a brief instant. When little more than half the total population of many million galaxies had entered fully into the cosmical community, and it was clear that no more were to be expected, there followed a period of universal meditation. The populations maintained their straitened utopian civilizations, lived their personal lives of work and social intercourse, and at the same time, upon the communal plane, refashioned the whole structure of cosmical culture. Of this phase I shall say nothing. Suffice it that to each galaxy and to each world was assigned a special creative mental function, and that all assimilated the work of all. At the close of this period I, the communal mind, emerged re-made, as from a chrysalis; and for a brief moment, which was indeed the supreme moment of the cosmos, I faced the Star Maker.

For the human author of this book there is now nothing left of that age-long, that eternal moment which I experienced as the cosmical mind, save the recollection of a bitter beatitude, together with a few incoherent memories of the experience itself which fired me with that beatitude.

Somehow I must tell something of that experience. Inevitably I face the task with a sense of abysmal incompetence. The greatest minds of the human race through all the ages of human history have failed to describe their moments of deepest insight. Then how dare I attempt this task? And yet I must. Even at the risk of well-merited ridicule and contempt and moral censure, I must stammer out what I have seen. If a shipwrecked seaman on his raft is swept helplessly past marvellous coasts and then home again, he cannot hold his peace. The cultivated may turn away in disgust at his rude accent and clumsy diction. The knowing may laugh at his failure to distinguish between fact and illusion. But speak he must.

3. THE SUPREME MOMENT AND AFTER

In the supreme moment of the cosmos I, as the cosmical mind, seemed to myself to be confronted with the source and the goal of all finite things.

I did not, of course, in that moment sensuously perceive the infinite spirit, the Star Maker. Sensuously I perceived nothing but what I had perceived before, the populous interiors of many dying stellar worlds. But through the medium which in this book is called telepathic I was now given a more inward perception. I felt the immediate presence of the Star

Maker. Latterly, as I have said, I had already been powerfully seized by a sense of the veiled presence of some being other than myself, other than my cosmical body and conscious mind, other than my living members and the swarms of the burnt-out stars. But now the veil trembled and grew half-transparent to the mental vision. The source and goal of all, the Star Maker, was obscurely revealed to me as a being indeed other than my conscious self, objective to my vision, yet as in the depth of my own nature; as, indeed, myself, though infinitely more than myself.

It seemed to me that I now saw the Star Maker in two aspects: as the spirit's particular creative mode that had given rise to me, the cosmos; and also, most dreadfully, as something incomparably greater than creativity, namely as the eternally achieved perfection of the absolute spirit.

Barren, barren and trivial are these words. But not barren the experience.

Confronted with this infinity that lay deeper than my deepest roots and higher than my topmost reach, I, the cosmical mind, the flower of all the stars and worlds, was appalled, as any savage is appalled by the lightning and the thunder. And as I fell abject before the Star Maker, my mind was flooded with a spate of images. The fictitious deities of all races in all worlds once more crowded themselves upon me, symbols of majesty and tenderness, of ruthless power, of blind creativity, and of all-seeing wisdom. And though these images were but the fantasies of created minds, it seemed to me that one and all did indeed embody some true feature of the Star Maker's impact upon the creatures.

As I contemplated the host of deities that rose to me like a smoke cloud from the many worlds, a new image, a new symbol of the infinite spirit, took shape in my mind. Though born of my own cosmical imagination, it was begotten by a greater than I. To the human writer of this book little remains of that vision which so abashed and exalted me as the cosmical mind. But I must strive to recapture it in a feeble net of words as best I may.

It seemed to me that I had reached back through time to the moment of creation. I watched the birth of the cosmos.

The spirit brooded. Though infinite and eternal, it had limited itself with finite and temporal being, and it brooded on a past that pleased it not. It was dissatisfied with some past creation, hidden from me; and it was dissatisfied also with its own passing nature. Discontent goaded the spirit into fresh creation.

But now, according to the fantasy that my cosmical mind conceived, the absolute spirit, self-limited for creativity, objectified from itself an atom of its infinite potentiality.

This microcosm was pregnant with the germ of a proper time and space, and all the kinds of cosmical beings.

Within this punctual cosmos the myriad but not unnumbered physical centres of power, which men conceive vaguely as electrons, protons,
and the rest, were at first coincident with one another. And they were dormant. The matter of ten million galaxies lay dormant in a point.

Then the Star Maker said, "Let there be light." And there was light.

From all the coincident and punctual centres of power, light leapt and
blazed. The cosmos exploded, actualizing its potentiality of space and
time. The centres of power, like fragments of a bursting bomb, were
hurled apart. But each one retained in itself, as a memory and a longing,
the single spirit of the whole; and each mirrored in itself aspects of all
others throughout all the cosmical space and time.

No longer punctual, the cosmos was now a volume of inconceivably
dense matter and inconceivably violent radiation, constantly expanding.
And it was a sleeping and infinitely dissociated spirit.

But to say that the cosmos was expanding is equally to say that its
members were contracting. The ultimate centres of power, each at first
coincident with the punctual cosmos, themselves generated the cosmical
space by their disengagement from each other. The expansion of the whole
cosmos was but the shrinkage of all its physical units and of the wave-
lengths of its light.

Though the cosmos was ever of finite bulk, in relation to its minutiae
of light-waves, it was boundless and centre-less. As the surface of a swelling sphere lacks boundary and centre, so the swelling volume of the cosmos
was boundless and centre-less. But as the spherical surface is centred on a
point foreign to it, in a "third dimension," so the volume of the cosmos
was centred in a point foreign to it, in a "fourth dimension."

The congested and exploding cloud of fire swelled till it was of a
planet's size, a star's size, the size of a whole galaxy, and of ten million
galaxies. And in swelling it became more tenuous, less brilliant, less turbulent.

Presently the cosmical cloud was disrupted by the stress of its expansion in conflict with the mutual clinging of its parts, disrupted into many
million cloudlets, the swarm of the great nebulae.

For a while these were as close to one another in relation to their bulk
as the flocculations of a mottled sky. But the channels between them
widened, till they were separated as flowers on a bush, as bees in a flying
swarm, as birds migrating, as ships on the sea. More and more rapidly
they retreated from one another; and at the same time each cloud contracted, becoming first a ball of down and then a spinning lens and then
a featured whirl of star-streams.

Still the cosmos expanded, till the galaxies that were most remote from
one another were flying apart so swiftly that the creeping light of the
cosmos could no longer bridge the gulf between them.

But I, with imaginative vision, retained sight of them all. It was as though some other, some hypercosmical and instantaneous light, issuing from nowhere in the cosmical space, illuminated all things inwardly.

Once more, but in a new and cold and penetrating light, I watched all the lives of stars and worlds, and of the galactic communities, and of myself, up to the moment wherein now I stood, confronted by the infinity that men call God, and conceive according to their human cravings.

I, too, now sought to capture the infinite spirit, the Star Maker, in an image spun by my own finite though cosmical nature. For now it seemed to me, it seemed, that I suddenly outgrew the three-dimensional vision proper to all creatures, and that I saw with physical sight the Star Maker. I saw, though nowhere in cosmical space, the blazing source of the hyper-cosmical light, as though it were an overwhelmingly brilliant point, a star, a sun more powerful than all suns together. It seemed to me that this effulgent star was the centre of a four-dimensional sphere whose curved surface was the three-dimensional cosmos. This star of stars, this star that was indeed the Star Maker, was perceived by me, its cosmical creature, for one moment before its splendour seared my vision. And in that moment I knew that I had indeed seen the very source of all cosmical light and life and mind; and of how much else besides I had as yet no knowledge.

But this image, this symbol that my cosmical mind had conceived under the stress of inconceivable experience, broke and was transformed in the very act of my conceiving it, so inadequate was it to the actuality of the experience. Harking back in my blindness to the moment of my vision, I now conceived that the star which was the Star Maker, and the immanent centre of all existence, had been perceived as looking down on me, his creature, from the height of his infinitude; and that when I saw him I immediately spread the poor wings of my spirit to soar up to him, only to be blinded and seared and struck down. It had seemed to me in the moment of my vision that all the longing and hope of all finite spirits for union with the infinite spirit were strength to my wings. It seemed to me that the Star, my Maker, must surely stoop to meet me and raise me and enfold me in his radiance. For it seemed to me that I, the spirit of so many worlds, the flower of so many ages, was the Church Cosmical, fit at last to be the bride of God. But instead I was blinded and seared and struck down by terrible light.

It was not only physical effulgence that struck me down in that supreme moment of my life. In that moment I guessed what mood it was of the infinite spirit that had in fact made the cosmos, and constantly supported it, watching its tortured growth. And it was that discovery which felled me.

For I had been confronted not by welcoming and kindly love, but by a very different spirit. And at once I knew that the Star Maker had made me not to be his bride, nor yet his treasured child, but for some other end.

It seemed to me that he gazed down on me from the height of his divinity with the aloof though passionate attention of an artist judging his finished work; calmly rejoicing in its achievement, but recognizing at last the irrevocable flaws in its initial conception, and already lusting for fresh creation.

His gaze anatomized me with calm skill, dismissing my imperfections, and absorbing for his own enrichment all the little excellence that I had won in the struggle of the ages.

In my agony I cried out against my ruthless maker. I cried out that, after all, the creature was nobler than the creator; for the creature loved and craved love, even from the star that was the Star Maker; but the creator, the Star Maker, neither loved nor had need of love.

But no sooner had I, in my blinded misery, cried out, than I was struck dumb with shame. For suddenly it was clear to me that virtue in the creator is not the same as virtue in the creature. For the creator, if he should love his creature, would be loving only a part of himself; but the creature, praising the creator, praises an infinity beyond himself. I saw that the virtue of the creature was to love and to worship, but the virtue of the creator was to create, and to be the infinite, the unrealizable and incomprehensible goal of worshipping creatures.

Once more, but in shame and adoration, I cried out to my maker. I said, "It is enough, and far more than enough, to be the creature of so dread and lovely a spirit, whose potency is infinite, whose nature passes the comprehension even of a minded cosmos. It is enough to have been created, to have embodied for a moment the infinite and tumultuously creative spirit. It is infinitely more than enough to have been used, to have been the rough sketch for some perfected creation."

And so there came upon me a strange peace and a strange joy.

Looking into the future, I saw without sorrow, rather with quiet interest, my own decline and fall. I saw the populations of the stellar worlds use up more and more of their resources for the maintenance of their frugal civilizations. So much of the interior matter of the stars did they disintegrate, that their worlds were in danger of collapse. Some worlds did indeed crash in fragments upon their hollow centres, destroying the indwelling peoples. Most, before the critical point was reached, were remade, patiently taken to pieces and rebuilt upon a smaller scale. One by one, each star was turned into a world of merely planetary size. Some were no bigger than the moon. The populations themselves were reduced to a mere millionth of their original numbers, maintaining within each little hollow grain a mere skeleton civilization in conditions that became increasingly penurious.

Looking into the future aeons from the supreme moment of the cosmos, I saw the populations still with all their strength maintaining the essentials of their ancient culture, still living their personal lives in zest and endless novelty of action, still practising telepathic intercourse between worlds, still telepathically sharing all that was of value in their respective world-spirits, still supporting a truly cosmical community with its single cosmical mind. I saw myself still preserving, though with increasing difficulty, my lucid consciousness; battling against the onset of drowsiness and senility, no longer in the hope of winning through to any more glorious state than that which I had already known, or of laying a less inadequate jewel of worship before the Star Maker, but simply out of sheer hunger for experience, and out of loyalty to the spirit.

But inevitably decay overtook me. World after world, battling with increasing economic difficulties, was forced to reduce its population below the numbers needed for the functioning of its own communal mentality. Then, like a degenerating brain-centre, it could no longer fulfil its part in the cosmical experience.

Looking forward from my station in the supreme moment of the cosmos, I saw myself, the cosmical mind, sink steadily toward death. But in this my last aeon, when all my powers were waning, and the burden of my decaying body pressed heavily on my enfeebled courage, an obscure memory of past lucidity still consoled me. For confusedly I knew that even in this my last, most piteous age I was still under the zestful though remote gaze of the Star Maker.

Still probing the future, from the moment of my supreme unwithered maturity, I saw my death, the final breaking of those telepathic contacts on which my being depended. Thereafter the few surviving worlds lived on in absolute isolation, and in that barbarian condition which men call civilized. Then in world after world the basic skills of material civilization began to fail; and in particular the techniques of atomic disintegration and photosynthesis. World after world either accidentally exploded its little remaining store of matter, and was turned into a spreading, fading sphere of light-waves in the immense darkness; or else died miserably of starvation and cold. Presently nothing was left in the whole cosmos but darkness and the dark whiffs of dust that once were galaxies. Aeons incalculable passed. Little by little each whiff of dust-grains contracted upon itself through the gravitational influence of its parts; till at last, not without fiery collisions between wandering grains, all the matter in each whiff was concentrated to became a single lump. The pressure of the huge outer regions heated the centre of each lump to incandescence and even to explosive activity. But little by little the last resources of the cosmos were radiated away from the cooling lumps, and nothing was left but rock and the inconceivably faint ripples of radiation that crept in all directions throughout the ever "expanding" cosmos, far too slowly to bridge the increasing gulfs between the islanded grains of rock.

Meanwhile, since each rocky sphere that had once been a galaxy had been borne beyond every possible physical influence of its fellows, and there were no minds to maintain telepathic contact between them, each was in effect a wholly distinct universe. And since all change had ceased, the proper time of each barren universe had also ceased.

Since this apparently was to be the static and eternal end, I withdrew my fatigued attention back once more to the supreme moment which was in fact my present, or rather my immediate past. And with the whole mature power of my mind I tried to see more clearly what it was that had been present to me in that immediate past. For in that instant when I had seen the blazing star that was the Star Maker, I had glimpsed, in the very eye of that splendour, strange vistas of being; as though in the depths of the hypercosmical past and the hypercosmical future also, yet coexistent in eternity, lay cosmos beyond cosmos.

CHAPTER XIV

THE MYTH OF CREATION

A WALKER in mountainous country, lost in mist, and groping from rock to rock, may come suddenly out of the cloud to find himself on the very brink of a precipice. Below he sees valleys and hills, plains, rivers, and intricate cities, the sea with all its islands, and overhead the sun. So I, in the supreme moment of my cosmical experience, emerged from the mist of my finitude to be confronted by cosmos upon cosmos, and by the light itself that not only illumines but gives life to all. Then immediately the mist closed in upon me again.

That strange vision, inconceivable to any finite mind, even of cosmical stature, I cannot possibly describe. I, the little human individual, am now infinitely removed.from it; and even to the cosmical mind itself it was most baffling. Yet if I were to say nothing whatever of the content of my adventure's crowning moment, I should belie the spirit of the whole. Though human language and even human thought itself are perhaps in their very nature incapable of metaphysical truth, something I must somehow contrive to express, even if only by metaphor.

All I can do is to record, as best I may with my poor human powers, something of the vision's strange and tumultuous after-effect upon my own cosmical imagination when the intolerable lucidity had already blinded me, and I gropingly strove to recollect what it was that had appeared. For in my blindness the vision did evoke from my stricken mind a fantastic reflex of itself, an echo, a symbol, a myth, a crazy dream, contemptibly crude and falsifying, yet, as I believe, not wholly without significance. This poor myth, this mere parable, I shall recount, so far as I can remember it in my merely human state. More I cannot do. But even this I cannot properly accomplish. Not once, but many times, I have written down an account of my dream, and then destroyed it, so inadequate was it. With a sense of utter failure I stammeringly report only a few of its more intelligible characters.

One feature of the actual vision my myth represented in a most perplexing and inadequate manner. It declared that the supreme moment of my experience as the cosmical mind actually comprised eternity within it, and that within eternity there lay a multiplicity of temporal sequences wholly distinct from one another. For though in eternity all times are present, and the infinite spirit, being perfect, must comprise in itself the full achievement of all possible creations, yet this could not be unless in its finite, its temporal and creative mode, the infinite and absolute spirit conceived and executed the whole vast series of creations. For creation's sake the eternal and infinite spirit entails time within its eternity, contains the whole protracted sequence of creations.

In my dream, the Star Maker himself, as eternal and absolute spirit, timelessly contemplated all his works; but also as the finite and creative mode of the absolute spirit, he bodied forth his creations one after the other in a time sequence proper to his own adventure and growth. And further, each of his works, each cosmos, was itself gifted with its own peculiar time, in such a manner that the whole sequence of events within any single cosmos could be viewed by the Star Maker not only from within the cosmical time itself but also externally, from the time proper to his own life, with all the cosmical epochs co-existing together.

According to the strange dream or myth which took possession of my mind, the Star Maker in his finite and creative mode was actually a developing, an awakening spirit. That he should be so, and yet also eternally perfect, is of course humanly inconceivable; but my mind, overburdened with superhuman vision, found no other means of expressing to itself the mystery of creation.

Eternally, so my dream declared to me, the Star Maker is perfect and absolute; yet in the beginning of the time proper to his creative mode he was an infant deity, restless, eager, mighty, but without clear will. He was equipped with all creative power. He could make universes with all kinds of physical and mental attributes. He was limited only by logic. Thus he could ordain the most surprising natural laws, but he could not, for instance, make twice two equal five. In his early phase he was limited also by his immaturity. He was still in the trance of infancy. Though the unconscious source of his consciously exploring and creating mentality was none other than his own eternal essence, consciously he was at first but the vague blind hunger of creativity.

In his beginning he immediately set about exploring his power. He objectified from himself something of his own unconscious substance to be the medium of his art, and this he moulded with conscious purpose. Thus again and again he fashioned toy cosmos after toy cosmos.

But the creative Star Maker's own unconscious substance was none other than the eternal spirit itself, the Star Maker in his eternal and perfect aspect. Thus it was that, in his immature phases, whenever he evoked from his own depth the crude substance of a cosmos, the substance itself turned out to be not formless but rich in determinate potentialities, logical, physical, biological, psychological. These potentialities were sometimes recalcitrant to the conscious purpose of the young Star Maker. He could not always accommodate, still less fulfil them. It seemed to me that this idiosyncrasy of the medium itself often defeated his plan; but also that it suggested again and again more fertile conceptions. Again and again, according to my myth, the Star Maker learned from his creature, and thereby outgrew his creature, and craved to work upon an ampler plan. Again and again he set aside a finished cosmos and evoked from himself a new creation.

Many times in the early part of my dream I felt doubt as to what the Star Maker was striving to accomplish in his creating. I could not but believe that his purpose was at first not clearly conceived. He himself had evidently to discover it gradually; and often, as it seemed to me, his work was tentative, and his aim confused. But at the close of his maturity he willed to create as fully as possible, to call forth the full potentiality of his medium, to fashion works of increasing subtlety, and of increasingly harmonious diversity. As his purpose became clearer, it seemed also to include the will to create universes each of which might contain some unique achievement of awareness and expression. For the creature's achievement of perception and of will was seemingly the instrument by which the Star Maker himself, cosmos by cosmos, woke into keener lucidity.

Thus it was that, through the succession of his creatures, the Star Maker advanced from stage to stage in the progress from infantile to mature divinity.

Thus it was that in the end he became what, in the eternal view, he already was in the beginning, the ground and crown of all things.

In the typically irrational manner of dreams, this dream-myth which arose in my mind represented the eternal spirit as being at once the cause and the result of the infinite host of finite existents. In some unintelligible manner all finite things, though they were in a sense figments of the absolute spirit, were also essential to the very existence of the absolute spirit. Apart from them it had no being. But whether this obscure relationship represented some important truth or was merely a trivial dream-fiction, I cannot say.

CHAPTER XV

THE MAKER AND HIS WORKS

1. IMMATURE CREATING

ACCORDING to the fantastic myth or dream that was evoked from my mind after the supreme moment of experience, the particular cosmos which I had come to regard as "myself" falls somewhere neither early nor late in the vast series of creations. It appeared to be in some respects the Star Maker's first mature work; but in comparison with later creations it was in many ways juvenile in spirit.

Though the early creations express the nature of the Star Maker merely in his immature phase, for the most part they fall in important respects aside from the direction of human thought, and therefore I cannot now recapture them. They have left me with little more than a vague sense of the multiplicity and diversity of the Star Maker's works. Nevertheless a few humanly intelligible traces remain and must be recorded.

In the crude medium of my dream the first cosmos of all appeared as a surprisingly simple thing. The infant Star Maker, teased, as it seemed to me, by his unexpressed potency, conceived and objectified from himself two qualities. With these alone he made his first toy cosmos, a temporal rhythm, as it were of sound and silence. From this first simple drum-beat, premonitory of a thousand creations, he developed with infantile but god-like zest a flickering tattoo, a changeful complexity of rhythm. Presently, through contemplation of his creature's simple form, he conceived the possibility of more subtle creating. Thus the first of all creatures itself bred in its creator a need that itself could never satisfy. Therefore the infant Star Maker brought his first cosmos to a close. Regarding it from outside the cosmical time which it had generated, he apprehended its whole career as present, though none the less a flux. And when he had quietly assessed his work, he withdrew his attention from it and brooded for a second creation.

Thereafter, cosmos upon cosmos, each more rich and subtle than the last, leapt from his fervent imagination. In some of his earliest creations he seemed to be concerned only with the physical aspect of the substance which he had objectified from himself. He was blind to its psychical potentiality. In one early cosmos, however, the patterns of physical quality with which he played simulated an individuality and a life which they did not in fact possess. Or did they possess it? In a later creation, certainly, true life broke out most strangely. This was a cosmos which the Star Maker apprehended physically much as men apprehend music. It was a rich sequence of qualities diverse in pitch and in intensity. With this toy the infant Star Maker played delightedly, inventing an infinite wealth of melody and counterpoint. But before he had worked out all the subtleties of pattern implied in this little world of cold, mathematical music, before he had created more than a few kinds of lifeless, musical creatures, it became evident that some of his creatures were manifesting traces of a life of their own, recalcitrant to the conscious purpose of the Star Maker. The themes of the music began to display modes of behaviour that were not in accord with the canon which he had ordained for them. It seemed to me that he watched them with intense interest, and that they spurred him to new conceptions, beyond the creatures' power to fulfil. Therefore he brought this cosmos to completion; and in a novel manner. He contrived that the last state of the cosmos should lead immediately back to the first. He knotted the final event temporally to the beginning, so that the cosmical time formed an endless circlet. After considering his work from outside its proper time, he set it aside, and brooded for a fresh creation.

For the next cosmos he consciously projected something of his own percipience and will, ordaining that certain patterns and rhythms of quality should be the perceivable bodies of perceiving minds. Seemingly these creatures were intended to work together to produce the harmony which he had conceived for this cosmos; but instead, each sought to mould the whole cosmos in accordance with its own form. The creatures fought desperately, and with self-righteous conviction. When they were damaged, they suffered pain. This, seemingly, was something which the young Star Maker had never experienced or conceived. With rapt, surprised interest, and (as it seemed to me) with almost diabolical glee, he watched the antics and the sufferings of his first living creatures, till by their mutual strife and slaughter they had reduced this cosmos to chaos.

Thenceforth the Star Maker never for long ignored his creatures' potentiality for intrinsic life. It seemed to me, however, that many of his early experiments in vital creation went strangely awry, and that sometimes, seemingly in disgust with the biological, he would revert for a while to purely physical fantasies.

I can only briefly describe the host of the early creations. Suffice it that they issued from the divine though still infantile imagination one after the other like bright but trivial bubbles, gaudy with colour, rich with all manner of physical subtleties, lyrical and often tragic with the loves and hates, the lusts and aspirations and communal enterprises of the Star Maker's early experimental conscious beings.

Many of these early universes were non-spatial, though none the less physical. And of these non-spatial universes not a few were of the "musical" type, in which space was strangely represented by a dimension corresponding to musical pitch, and capacious with myriads of tonal differences. The creatures appeared to one another as complex patterns and rhythms of tonal characters. They could move their tonal bodies in the dimension of pitch, and sometimes in other dimensions, humanly inconceivable. A creature's body was a more or less constant tonal pattern, with much the same degree of flexibility and minor changefulness as a human body. Also, it could traverse other living bodies in the pitch dimension much as wave-trains on a pond may cross one another. But though these beings could glide through one another, they could also grapple, and damage one another's tonal tissues. Some, indeed, lived by devouring others; for the more complex needed to integrate into their own vital patterns the simpler patterns that exfoliated throughout the cosmos directly from the creative power of the Star Maker. The intelligent creatures could manipulate for their own ends elements wrenched from the fixed tonal environment, thus constructing artifacts of tonal pattern. Some of these served as tools for the more efficient pursuit of "agricultural" activities, by which they enhanced the abundance of their natural food. Universes of this non-spatial kind, though incomparably simpler and more meagre than our own cosmos, were rich enough to produce societies capable not only of "agriculture" but of "handicrafts," and even a kind of pure art that combined the characteristics of song and dance and verse. Philosophy, generally rather Pythagorean, appeared for the first time in a cosmos of this "musical" kind.

In nearly all the Star Maker's works, as revealed in my dream, time was a more fundamental attribute than space. Though in some of his earliest creations he excluded time, embodying merely a static design, this plan was soon abandoned. It gave little scope to his skill. Moreover, since it excluded the possibility of life and mind, it was incompatible with all but the earliest phase of his interest.

Space, my dream declared, appeared first as a development of a non-spatial dimension in a "musical" cosmos. The tonal creatures in this cosmos could move not merely "up" and "down" the scale but "sideways." In human music particular themes may seem to approach or retreat, owing to variations of loudness and timbre. In a rather similar manner the creatures in this "musical" cosmos could approach one another or retreat and finally vanish out of earshot. In passing "sideways" they travelled through continuously changing tonal environments. In a subsequent cosmos this "sideways" motion of the creatures was enriched with true spatial experience.

There followed creations with spatial characters of several dimensions, creations Euclidean and non-Euclidean, creations exemplifying a great diversity of geometrical and physical principles. Sometimes time, or space-time, was the fundamental reality of the cosmos, and the entities were but fleeting modifications of it; but more often, qualitative events were fundamental, and these were related in spatio-temporal manners. In some cases the system of spatial relations was infinite, in others finite though boundless. In some the finite extent of space was of constant magnitude in relation to the atomic material constituents of the cosmos; in some, as in our own cosmos, it was manifested as in many respects "expanding." In others again space "contracted"; so that the end of such a cosmos, rich perhaps in intelligent communities, was the collision and congestion of all its parts, and their final coincidence and vanishing into a dimensionless point.

In some creations expansion and ultimate quiescence were followed by contraction and entirely new kinds of physical activity. Sometimes, for example, gravity was replaced by anti-gravity. All large lumps of matter tended to burst asunder, and all small ones to fly apart from each other. In one such cosmos the law of entropy also was reversed. Energy, instead of gradually spreading itself evenly throughout the cosmos, gradually piled itself upon the ultimate material units. I came in time to suspect that my own cosmos was followed by a reversed cosmos of this kind, in which, of course, the nature of living things was profoundly different from anything conceivable to man. But this is a digression, for I am at present describing much earlier and simpler universes.

Many a universe was physically a continuous fluid in which the solid creatures swam. Others were constructed as series of concentric spheres, peopled by diverse orders of creatures. Some quite early universes were quasi-astronomical, consisting of a void sprinkled with rare and minute centres of power.

Sometimes the Star Maker fashioned a cosmos which was without any single, objective, physical nature. Its creatures were wholly without influence on one another; but under the direct stimulation of the Star Maker each creature conceived an illusory but reliable and useful physical world of its own, and peopled it with figments of its imagination. These subjective worlds the mathematical genius of the Star Maker correlated in a manner that was perfectly systematic.

I must not say more of the immense diversity of physical form which, according to my dream, the early creations assumed. It is enough to mention that, in general, each cosmos was more complex, and in a sense more voluminous than the last; for in each the ultimate physical units were smaller in relation to the whole, and more multitudinous. Also, in each the individual conscious creatures were generally more in number, and more diverse in type; and the most awakened in each cosmos reached a more lucid mentality than any creatures in the previous cosmos.

Biologically and psychologically the early creations were very diverse. In some cases there was a biological evolution such as we know. A small minority of species would precariously ascend toward greater individuation and mental clarity. In other creations the species were biologically fixed, and progress, if it occurred, was wholly cultural. In a few most perplexing creations the most awakened state of the cosmos was at the beginning, and the Star Maker calmly watched this lucid consciousness decay.

Sometimes a cosmos started as a single lowly organism with an internal, non-organic environment. It then propagated by fission into an increasing host of increasingly small and increasingly individuated and awakened creatures. In some of these universes evolution would continue till the creatures became too minute to accommodate the complexity of organic structure necessary for intelligent minds. The Star Maker would then watch the cosmical societies desperately striving to circumvent the fated degeneration of their race.

In some creations the crowning achievement of the cosmos was a chaos of mutually unintelligible societies, each devoted to the service of some one mode of the spirit, and hostile to all others. In some the climax was a single utopian society of distinct minds; in others a single composite cosmical mind.

Sometimes it pleased the Star Maker to ordain that each creature in a cosmos should be an inevitable, determinate expression of the environment's impact on its ancestors and itself. In other creations each creature had some power of arbitrary choice, and some modicum of the Star Maker's own creativity. So it seemed to me in my dream; but even in my dream I suspected that to a more subtle observer both kinds would have appeared as in fact determinate, and yet both of them also spontaneous and creative.

In general the Star Maker, once he had ordained the basic principles of a cosmos and created its initial state, was content to watch the issue; but sometimes he chose to interfere, either by infringing the natural laws that he himself had ordained, or by introducing new emergent formative principles, or by influencing the minds of the creatures by direct revelation. This according to my dream, was sometimes done to improve a cosmical design; but, more often, interference was included in his original plan.

Sometimes the Star Maker flung off creations which were in effect groups of many linked universes, wholly distinct physical systems of very different kinds, yet related by the fact that the creatures lived their lives successively in universe after universe, assuming in each habitat an indigenous physical form, but bearing with them in their transmigration faint and easily misinterpreted memories of earlier existences. In another way also, this principle of transmigration was sometimes used. Even creations that were not thus systematically linked might contain creatures that mentally echoed in some vague but haunting manner the experience or the temperament of their counterparts in some other cosmos.

One very dramatic device was used in cosmos after cosmos. I mentioned earlier that in my dream the immature Star Maker had seemed to regard the tragic failure of his first biological experiment with a kind of diabolical glee. In many subsequent creations also he appeared to be twi-minded. Whenever his conscious creative plan was thwarted by some unsuspected potentiality of the substance which he had objectified from his unconscious depth, his mood seemed to include not only frustration but also surprised satisfaction, as of some unrecognized hunger unexpectedly satisfied.

This twi-mindedness at length gave rise to a new mode of creating. There came a stage in the Star Maker's growth, as my dream represented it, when he contrived to dissociate himself as two independent spirits, the one his essential self, the spirit that sought positive creation of vital and spiritual forms and ever more lucid awareness, the other a rebellious, destructive and cynical spirit, that could have no being save as a parasite upon the works of the other.

Again and again he dissociated these two moods of himself, objectified them as independent spirits, and permitted them to strive within a cosmos for mastery. One such cosmos, which consisted of three linked universes, was somewhat reminiscent of Christian orthodoxy. The first of these linked universes was inhabited by generations of creatures gifted with varying degrees of sensibility, intelligence, and moral integrity. Here the two spirits played for the souls of the creatures. The "good" spirit exhorted, helped, rewarded, punished; the "evil" spirit deceived, tempted, and morally destroyed. At death the creatures passed into one or other of the two secondary universes, which constituted a timeless heaven and a timeless hell. There they experienced an eternal moment either of ecstatic comprehension and worship or of the extreme torment of remorse.

When my dream presented me with this crude, this barbaric figment, I was at first moved with horror and incredulity. How could the Star Maker, even in his immaturity, condemn his creatures to agony for the weakness that he himself had allotted to them? How could such a vindictive deity command worship?

In vain I told myself that my dream must have utterly falsified the reality; for I was convinced that in this respect it was not false, but in some sense true, at least symbolically. Yet, even when I was confronted by this brutal deed, even in the revulsion of pity and horror, I saluted the Star Maker.

To excuse my worship, I told myself that this dread mystery lay far beyond my comprehension, and that in some sense even such flagrant cruelty must, in the Star Maker, be right. Did barbarity perhaps belong to the Star Maker only in his immaturity? Later, when he was fully himself, would he finally outgrow it? No! Already I deeply knew that this ruthlessness was to be manifested even in the ultimate cosmos. Could there, then, be some key fact, overlooked by me, in virtue of which such seeming vindictiveness was justified? Was it simply that all creatures were indeed but figments of the creative power, and that in tormenting his creatures the Star Maker did but torment himself in the course of his adventure of self-expression? Or was it perhaps that even the Star Maker himself, though mighty, was limited in all creation by certain absolute logical principles, and that one of these was the indissoluble bond between betrayal and remorse in half-awakened spirits? Had he, in this strange cosmos, simply accepted and used the ineluctable limitations of his art? Or again, was my respect given to the Star Maker only as the "good" spirit, not as the "evil" spirit? And was he in fact striving to eject evil from himself by means of this device of dissociation?

Some such explanation was suggested by the strange evolution of this cosmos. Since its denizens had mostly a very low degree of intelligence and moral integrity, the hell was soon overcrowded, while the heaven remained almost empty. But the Star Maker in his "good" aspect loved and pitied his creatures. The "good" spirit therefore entered into the mundane sphere to redeem the sinners by his own suffering. And so at last the heaven was peopled, though the hell was not depopulated.

Was it, then, only the "good" aspect of the Star Maker that I worshipped? No! Irrationally, yet with conviction, I gave my adoration to the Star Maker as comprising both aspects of his dual nature, both the "good" and the "evil," both the mild and the terrible, both the humanly ideal and the incomprehensibly inhuman. Like an infatuated lover who denies or excuses the flagrant faults of the beloved, I strove to palliate the inhumanity of the Star Maker, nay positively I gloried in it. Was there then something cruel in my own nature? Or did my heart vaguely recognize that love, the supreme virtue in creatures, must not in the creator be absolute?

This dire and insoluble problem confronted me again and again in the course of my dream. For instance there appeared a creation in which the two spirits were permitted to strive in a novel and more subtle manner. In its early phase this cosmos manifested only physical characters; but the Star Maker provided that its vital potentiality should gradually express itself in certain kinds of living creatures which, generation by generation, should emerge from the purely physical and evolve toward intelligence and spiritual lucidity. In this cosmos he permitted the two spirits, the "good" and the "evil," to compete even in the very making of the creatures.

In the long early ages the spirits struggled over the evolution of the innumerable species. The "good" spirit worked to produce creatures more highly organized, more individual, more delicately related to the environment, more skilled in action, more comprehensively and vividly aware of their world, of themselves, and of other selves. The "evil" spirit tried to thwart this enterprise.

The organs and tissues of every species manifested throughout their structure the conflict of the two spirits. Sometimes the "evil" spirit contrived seemingly unimportant but insidious and lethal features for a creature's undoing. Its nature would include some special liability to harbour parasites, some weakness of digestive machinery, some instability of nervous organization. In other cases the "evil" spirit would equip some lower species with special weapons for the destruction of the pioneers of evolution, so that they should succumb, either to some new disease, or to plagues of the vermin of this particular cosmos, or to the more brutish of their own kind.

A still more ingenious plan the evil spirit sometimes used with great effect. When the "good" spirit had hit upon some promising device, and from small beginnings had worked up in its favoured species some new organic structure or mode of behaviour, the evil spirit would contrive that the process of evolution should continue long after it had reached perfect adjustment to the creature's needs. Teeth would grow so large that eating became excessively difficult, protective shells so heavy that they hampered locomotion, horns so curved that they pressed upon the brain, the impulse to individuality so imperious that it destroyed society, or the social impulse so obsessive that individuality was crushed.

Thus in world after world of this cosmos, which greatly surpassed all earlier creations in complexity, almost every species came sooner or later to grief. But in some worlds a single species reached the "human" level of intelligence and of spiritual sensibility. Such a combination of powers ought to have secured it from all possible attack. But both intelligence and spiritual sensibility were most skilfully perverted by the "evil" spirit. For though by nature they were complementary, they could be brought into conflict; or else one or both could be exaggerated so as to become as lethal as the extravagant horns and teeth of earlier kinds. Thus intelligence, which led on the one hand to the mastery of physical force and on the other to intellectual subtlety, might, if divorced from spiritual sensibility, cause disaster. The mastery of physical force often produced a mania for power, and the dissection of society into two alien classes, the powerful and the enslaved. Intellectual subtlety might produce a mania for analysis and abstraction, with blindness to all that intellect could not expound. Yet sensibility itself, when it rejected intellectual criticism and the claims of daily life, would be smothered in dreams.

2. MATURE CREATING

According to the myth that my mind conceived when the supreme moment of my cosmical experience had passed, the Star Maker at length entered into a state of rapt meditation in which his own nature suffered a revolutionary change. So at least I judged from the great change that now came over his creative activity.

After he had reviewed with new eyes all his earlier works, dismissing each, as it seemed to me, with mingled respect and impatience, he discovered in himself a new and pregnant conception.

The cosmos which he now created was that which contains the readers and the writer of this book. In its making he used, but with more cunning art, many of the principles which had already served him in earlier creations; and he wove them together to form a more subtle and more capacious unity than ever before.

It seemed to me, in my fantasy, that he approached this new enterprise in a new mood. Each earlier cosmos appeared to have been fashioned with conscious will to embody certain principles, physical, biological, psychological. As has already been reported, there often appeared a conflict between his intellectual purpose and the raw nature which he had evoked for his creature out of the depth of his own obscure being. This time, however, he dealt more sensitively with the medium of his creation. The crude spiritual "material" which he objectified from his own hidden depth for the formation of his new creature was moulded to his still tentative purpose with more sympathetic intelligence, with more respect for its nature and its potentiality, though with detachment from its more extravagant demands.

To speak thus of the universal creative spirit is almost childishly anthropomorphic. For the life of such a spirit, if it exists at all, must be utterly different from human mentality, and utterly inconceivable to man. Nevertheless, since this childish symbolism did force itself upon me, I record it. In spite of its crudity, perhaps it does contain some genuine reflection of the truth, however distorted.

In the new creation there occurred a strange kind of discrepancy between the Star Maker's own time and the time proper to the cosmos itself. Hitherto, though he could detach himself from the cosmical time when the cosmical history had completed itself, and observe all the cosmical ages as present, he could not actually create the later phases of a cosmos before he had created the earlier. In his new creation he was not thus limited.

Thus although this new cosmos was my own cosmos, I regarded it from a surprising angle of vision. No longer did it appear as a familiar sequence of historical events beginning with the initial physical explosion and advancing to the final death. I saw it now not from within the flux of the cosmical time but quite otherwise. I watched the fashioning of the cosmos in the time proper to the Star Maker; and the sequence of the Star Maker's creative acts was very different from the sequence of historical events.

First he conceived from the depth of his own being a something, neither mind nor matter, but rich in potentiality, and in suggestive traits, gleams, hints for his creative imagination. Over this fine substance for a long while he pondered. It was a medium in which the one and the many demanded to be most subtly dependent upon one another; in which all parts and all characters must pervade and be pervaded by all other parts and all other characters; in which each thing must seemingly be but an influence in all other things; and yet the whole must be no other than the sum of all its parts, and each part an all-pervading determination of the whole. It was a cosmical substance in which any individual spirit must be, mysteriously, at once an absolute self and a mere figment of the whole.

This most subtle medium the Star Maker now rough-hewed into the general form of a cosmos. Thus he fashioned a still indeterminate space-time, as yet quite ungeometrized; an amorphous physicality with no clear quality or direction, no intricacy of physical laws; a more distinctly conceived vital trend and epic adventure of mentality; and a surprisingly definite climax and crown of spiritual lucidity. This last, though its situation in the cosmical time was for the most part late, was given a certain precision of outline earlier in the sequence of creative work than any other factor in the cosmos. And it seemed to me that this was so because the initial substance itself so clearly exposed its own potentiality for some such spiritual form. Thus it was that the Star Maker at first almost neglected the physical minutiae of his work, neglected also the earlier ages of cosmical history, and devoted his skill at first almost entirely to shaping the spiritual climax of the whole creature.

Not till he had blocked in unmistakably the most awakened phase of the cosmical spirit did he trace any of the variegated psychological trends which, in the cosmical time, should lead up to it. Not till he had given outline to the incredibly diverse themes of mental growth did he give attention fully to constructing the biological evolutions and the physical and geometrical intricacy which could best evoke the more subtle potentialities of his still rough-hewn cosmical spirit.

But, as he geometrized, he also intermittently turned again to modify and elucidate the spiritual climax itself. Not till the physical and geometrical form of the cosmos was almost completely fashioned could he endow the spiritual climax with fully concrete individuality.

While he was still working upon the detail of the countless, poignant individual lives, upon the fortunes of men, of ichthyoids, of nautiloids, and the rest, I became convinced that his attitude to his creatures was very different from what it had been for any other cosmos. For he was neither cold to them nor yet simply in love with them. In love with them, indeed, he still was; but he had seemingly outgrown all desire to save them from the consequences of their finitude and from the cruel impact of the environment. He loved them without pity. For he saw that their distinctive virtue lay in their finitude, their minute particularity, their tortured balance between dullness and lucidity; and that to save them from these would be to annihilate them.

When he had given the last touches to all the cosmical ages from the supreme moment back to the initial explosion and on to the final death, the Star Maker contemplated his work. And he saw that it was good.

As he lovingly, though critically, reviewed our cosmos in all its infinite diversity and in its brief moment of lucidity, I felt that he was suddenly filled with reverence for the creature that he had made, or that he had ushered out of his own secret depth by a kind of divine self-midwifery. He knew that this creature, though imperfect, though a mere creature, a mere figment of his own creative power, was yet in a manner more real than himself. For beside this concrete splendour what was he but a mere abstract potency of creation? Moreover in another respect the thing that he had made was his superior, and his teacher. For as he contemplated this the loveliest and subtlest of all his works with exultation, even with awe, its impact upon him changed him, clarifying and deepening his will. As he discriminated its virtue and its weakness, his own perception and his own skill matured. So at least it seemed to my bewildered, awe-stricken mind.

Thus, little by little, it came about, as so often before, that the Star Maker outgrew his creature. Increasingly he frowned upon the loveliness that he still cherished. Then, seemingly with a conflict of reverence and impatience, he set our cosmos in its place among his other works.

Once more he sank into deep meditation. Once more the creative urge possessed him.

Of the many creations which followed I must perforce say almost nothing, for in most respects they lay beyond my mental reach. I could not have any cognizance of them save in so far as they contained, along with much that was inconceivable, some features that were but fantastic embodiments of principles which I had already encountered. Thus all their most vital novelty escaped me.

I can, indeed, say of all these creations that, like our own cosmos, they were immensely capacious, immensely subtle; and that, in some alien manner or other, every one of them had both a physical and a mental aspect; though in many the physical, however crucial to the spirit's growth, was more transparent, more patently phantasmal than in our own cosmos. In some cases this was true equally of the mental, for the beings were often far less deceived by the opacity of their individual mental processes, and more sensitive to their underlying unity.

I can say too that in all these creations the goal which, as it seemed to me, the Star Maker sought to realize was richness, delicacy, depth and harmoniousness of being. But what these words in detail mean I should find it hard to say. It seemed to me that in some cases, as in our own cosmos, he pursued this end by means of an evolutionary process crowned by an awakened cosmical mind, which strove to gather into its own awareness the whole wealth of the cosmical existence, and by creative action to increase it. But in many cases this goal was achieved with incomparably greater economy of effort and suffering on the part of the creatures, and without the huge dead loss of utterly wasted, ineffective lives which is to us so heart-rending. Yet in other creations suffering seemed at least as grave and widespread as in our own cosmos.

In his maturity the Star Maker conceived many strange forms of time. For instance, some of the later creations were designed with two or more temporal dimensions, and the lives of the creatures were temporal sequences in one or other dimension of the temporal "area" or "volume." These beings experienced their cosmos in a very odd manner. Living for a brief period along one dimension, each perceived at every moment of its life a simultaneous vista which, though of course fragmentary and obscure, was actually a view of a whole unique "transverse" cosmical evolution in the other dimension. In some cases a creature had an active life in every temporal dimension of the cosmos. The divine skill which arranged the whole temporal "volume" in such a manner that all the infinite spontaneous acts of all the creatures should fit together to produce a coherent system of transverse evolutions far surpassed even the ingenuity of the earlier experiment in "pre-established harmony."

In other creations a creature was given only one life, but this was a "zig-zag line," alternating from one temporal dimension to another according to the quality of the choices that the creature made. Strong or moral choices led in one temporal direction, weak or immoral choices in another.

In one inconceivably complex cosmos, whenever a creature was faced with several possible courses of action, it took them all, thereby creating many distinct temporal dimensions and distinct histories of the cosmos. Since in every evolutionary sequence of the cosmos there were very many creatures, and each was constantly faced with many possible courses, and the combinations of all their courses were innumerable, an infinity of distinct universes exfoliated from every moment of every temporal sequence in this cosmos.

In some creations each being had sensory perception of the whole physical cosmos from many spatial points of view, or even from every possible point of view. In the latter case, of course, the perception of every mind was identical in spatial range, but it varied from mind to mind in respect of penetration or insight. This depended on the mental calibre and disposition of particular minds. Sometimes these beings had not only omnipresent perception but omnipresent volition. They could take action in every region of space, though with varying precision and vigour according to their mental calibre. In a manner they were disembodied spirits, striving over the physical cosmos like chess-players, or like Greek gods over the Trojan Plain.

In other creations, though there was indeed a physical aspect, there was nothing corresponding to the familiar systematic physical universe. The physical experience of the beings was wholly determined by their mutual impact on one another. Each flooded its fellows with sensory "images," the quality and sequence of which were determined according to psychological laws of the impact of mind on mind.

In other creations the processes of perception, memory, intellection, and even desire and feeling were so different from ours as to constitute in fact a mentality of an entirely different order. Of these minds, though I seemed to catch remote echoes of them, I cannot say anything.

Or rather, though I cannot speak of the alien psychical modes of these beings, one very striking fact about them I can record. However incomprehensible their basic mental fibres and the patterns into which these were woven, in one respect all these beings came fleetingly within my comprehension. However foreign to me their lives, in one respect they were my kin. For all these cosmical creatures, senior to me, and more richly endowed, constantly faced existence in the manner that I myself still haltingly strove to learn. Even in pain and grief, even in the very act of moral striving and of white-hot pity, they met fate's issue with joy. Perhaps the most surprising and heartening fact that emerged from all my cosmical and hypercosmical experience was this kinship and mutual intelligibility of the most alien beings in respect of the pure spiritual experience. But I was soon to discover that in this connection I had still much to learn.

3. THE ULTIMATE COSMOS AND THE ETERNAL SPIRIT

In vain my fatigued, my tortured attention strained to follow the increasingly subtle creations which, according to my dream, the Star Maker conceived. Cosmos after cosmos issued from his fervent imagination, each one with a distinctive spirit infinitely diversified, each in its fullest attainment more awakened than the last; but each one less comprehensible to me.

At length, so my dream, my myth, declared, the Star Maker created his ultimate and most subtle cosmos, for which all others were but tentative preparations. Of this final creature I can say only that it embraced within its own organic texture the essences of all its predecessors; and far more besides. It was like the last movement of a symphony, which may embrace, by the significance of its themes, the essence of the earlier movements; and far more besides.

This metaphor extravagantly understates the subtlety and complexity of the ultimate cosmos. I was gradually forced to believe that its relation to each earlier cosmos was approximately that of our own cosmos to a human being, nay to a single physical atom. Every cosmos that I had hitherto observed now turned out to be but a single example of a myriadfold class, like a biological species, or the class of all the atoms of a single element. The internal life of each "atomic" cosmos had seemingly the same kind of relevance (and the same kind of irrelevance) to the life of the ultimate cosmos as the events within a brain cell, or in one of its atoms, to the life of a human mind. Yet in spite of this huge discrepancy I seemed to sense throughout the whole dizzying hierarchy of creations a striking identity of spirit. In all, the goal was conceived, in the end, to include community and the lucid and creative mind.

I strained my fainting intelligence to capture something of the form of the ultimate cosmos. With mingled admiration and protest I haltingly glimpsed the final subtleties of world and flesh and spirit, and of the community of those most diverse and individual beings, awakened to full self-knowledge and mutual insight. But as I strove to hear more inwardly into that music of concrete spirits in countless worlds, I caught echoes not merely of joys unspeakable, but of griefs inconsolable. For some of these ultimate beings not only suffered, but suffered in darkness. Though gifted with full power of insight, their power was barren. The vision was withheld from them. They suffered as lesser spirits would never suffer. Such intensity of harsh experience was intolerable to me, the frail spirit of a lowly cosmos. In an agony of horror and pity I despairingly stopped the ears of my mind. In my littleness I cried out against my maker that no glory of the eternal and absolute could redeem such agony in the creatures. Even if the misery that I had glimpsed was in fact but a few dark strands woven into the golden tapestry to enrich it, and all the rest was bliss, yet such desolation of awakened spirits, I cried, ought not, ought never to be. By what diabolical malice, I demanded, were these glorious beings not merely tortured but deprived of the supreme consolation, the ecstasy of contemplation and praise which is the birthright of all fully awakened spirits?

There had been a time when I myself, as the communal mind of a lowly cosmos, had looked upon the frustration and sorrow of my little members with equanimity, conscious that the suffering of these drowsy beings was no great price to pay for the lucidity that I myself contributed to reality. But the suffering individuals within the ultimate cosmos, though in comparison with the hosts of happy creatures they were few, were beings, it seemed to me, of my own, cosmical, mental stature, not the frail, shadowy existences that had contributed their dull griefs to my making. And this I could not endure.

Yet obscurely I saw that the ultimate cosmos was nevertheless lovely, and perfectly formed; and that every frustration and agony within it, however cruel to the sufferer, issued finally, without any miscarriage in the enhanced lucidity of the cosmical spirit itself. In this sense at least no individual tragedy was vain.

But this was nothing. And now, as through tears of compassion and hot protest, I seemed to see the spirit of the ultimate and perfected cosmos face her maker. In her, it seemed, compassion and indignation were subdued by praise. And the Star Maker, that dark power and lucid intelligence, found in the concrete loveliness of his creature the fulfilment of desire. And in the mutual joy of the Star Maker and the ultimate cosmos was conceived, most strangely, the absolute spirit itself, in which all times are present and all being is comprised; for the spirit which was the issue of this union confronted my reeling intelligence as being at once the ground and the issue of all temporal and finite things.

But to me this mystical and remote perfection was nothing. In pity of the ultimate tortured beings, in human shame and rage, I scorned my birthright of ecstasy in that inhuman perfection, and yearned back to my lowly cosmos, to my own human and floundering world, there to stand shoulder to shoulder with my own half animal kind against the powers of darkness; yes, and against the indifferent, the ruthless, the invincible tyrant whose mere thoughts are sentient and tortured worlds.

Then, in the very act of this defiant gesture, as I slammed and bolted the door of the little dark cell of my separate self, my walls were all shattered and crushed inwards by the pressure of irresistible light, and my naked vision was once more seared by lucidity beyond its endurance.

Once more? No. I had but reverted in my interpretative dream to the identical moment of illumination, closed by blindness, when I had seemed to spread wing to meet the Star Maker, and was struck down by terrible light. But now I conceived more clearly what it was that had overwhelmed me.

I was indeed confronted by the Star Maker, but the Star Maker was now revealed as more than the creative and therefore finite spirit. He now appeared as the eternal and perfect spirit which comprises all things and all times, and contemplates timelessly the infinitely diverse host which it comprises. The illumination which flooded in on me and struck me down to blind worship was a glimmer, so it seemed to me, of the eternal spirit's own all-penetrating experience.

It was with anguish and horror, and yet with acquiescence, even with praise, that I felt or seemed to feel something of the eternal spirit's temper as it apprehended in one intuitive and timeless vision all our lives. Here was no pity, no proffer of salvation, no kindly aid. Or here were all pity and all love, but mastered by a frosty ecstasy. Our broken lives, our loves, our follies, our betrayals, our forlorn and gallant defences, were one and all calmly anatomized, assessed, and placed. True, they were one and all lived through with complete understanding, with insight and full sympathy, even with passion. But sympathy was not ultimate in the temper of the eternal spirit; contemplation was. Love was not absolute; contemplation was. And though there was love, there was also hate comprised within the spirit's temper, for there was cruel delight in the contemplation of every horror, and glee in the downfall of the virtuous. All passions, it seemed, were comprised within the spirit's temper; but mastered, icily gripped within the cold, clear, crystal ecstasy of contemplation.

That this should be the upshot of all our lives, this scientist's, no, artist's, keen appraisal! And yet I worshipped!

But this was not the worst. For in saying that the spirit's temper was contemplation, I imputed to it a finite human experience, and an emotion; thereby comforting myself, even though with cold comfort. But in truth the eternal spirit was ineffable. Nothing whatever could be truly said about it. Even to name it "spirit" was perhaps to say more than was justified. Yet to deny it that name would be no less mistaken; for whatever it was, it was more, not less, than spirit, more, not less, than any possible human meaning of that word. And from the human level, even from the level of a cosmical mind, this "more," obscurely and agonizingly glimpsed, was a dread mystery, compelling adoration.

CHAPTER XVI

EPILOGUE: BACK TO EARTH

I WOKE on the hill. The street lamps of our suburb outshone the stars. The reverberation of the clock's stroke was followed by eleven strokes more. I singled out our window. A surge of joy, of wild joy, swept me like a wave. Then peace.

The littleness, but the intensity, of earthly events! Gone, abolished in an instant, was the hypercosmical reality, the wild fountain of creations, and all the spray of worlds. Vanished, transmuted into fantasy, and into sublime irrelevance.

The littleness, but the intensity, of this whole grain of rock, with its film of ocean and of air, and its discontinuous, variegated, tremulous film of life; of the shadowy hills, of the sea, vague, horizonless; of the pulsating, cepheid, lighthouse; of the clanking railway trucks. My hand caressed the pleasant harshness of the heather.

Vanished, the hypercosmical apparition. Not such as I had dreamed must the real be, but infinitely more subtle, more dread, more excellent. And infinitely nearer home.

Yet, however false the vision in detail of structure, even perhaps in its whole form, in temper surely it was relevant; in temper perhaps it was even true. The real itself, surely, had impelled me to conceive that image, false in every theme and facet, yet in spirit true.

The stars wanly trembled above the street lamps. Great suns? Or feeble sparks in the night sky? Suns, it was vaguely rumoured. Lights at least to steer by, and to beckon the mind from the terrestrial flurry; but piercing the heart with their cold spears.

Sitting there on the heather, on our planetary grain, I shrank from the abysses that opened up on every side, and in the future. The silent darkness, the featureless unknown, were more dread than all the terrors that imagination had mustered. Peering, the mind could see nothing sure, nothing in all human experience to be grasped as certain, except uncertainty itself; nothing but obscurity gendered by a thick haze of theories. Man's science was a mere mist of numbers; his philosophy but a fog of words. His very perception of this rocky grain and all its wonders was but a shifting and a lying apparition. Even oneself, that seeming-central fact, was a mere phantom, so deceptive, that the most honest of men must question his own honesty, so insubstantial that he must even doubt his very existence. And our loyalties! so self-deceiving, so mis-informed and mis-conceived. So savagely pursued and hate-warped! Our very loves, and these in full and generous intimacy, must be condemned as unseeing, self-regarding, and self-gratulatory.

And yet? I singled out our window. We had been happy together! We had found, or we had created, our little treasure of community. This was the one rock in all the welter of experience. This, not the astronomical and hypercosmical immensity, nor even the planetary grain, this, this alone, was the solid ground of existence.

On every side was confusion, a rising storm, great waves already drenching our rock. And all around, in the dark welter, faces and appealing hands, half-seen and vanishing.

And the future? Black with the rising storm of this world's madness, though shot through with flashes of a new and violent hope, the hope of a sane, a reasonable, a happier world. Between our time and that future, what horror lay in store? Oppressors would not meekly give way. And we two, accustomed only to security and mildness, were fit only for a kindly world; wherein, none being tormented, none turns desperate. We were adapted only to fair weather, for the practice of the friendly but not too difficult, not heroical virtues, in a society both secure and just. Instead, we found ourselves in an age of titanic conflict, when the relentless powers of darkness and the ruthless because desperate powers of light were coming to grips for a death struggle in the world's torn heart, when grave choices must be made in crisis after crisis, and no simple or familiar principles were adequate.

Beyond our estuary a red growth of fire sprang from a foundry. At hand, the dark forms of the gorse lent mystery to the suburb's foot-worn moor.

In imagination I saw, behind our own hill's top, the further and unseen hills. I saw the plains and woods and all the fields, each with its myriads of particular blades. I saw the whole land curving down from me, over the planet's shoulder. The villages were strung together on a mesh of roads, steel lines, and humming wires. Mist-drops on a cobweb. Here and there a town displayed itself as an expanse of light, a nebulous luminosity, sprinkled with stars.

Beyond the plains, London, neon-lit, seething, was a microscope-slide drawn from foul water, and crowded with nosing animalcules. Animalcules! In the stars' view, no doubt, these creatures were mere vermin; yet each to itself, and sometimes one to another, was more real than all the stars.

Gazing beyond London, imagination detected the dim stretch of the Channel, and then the whole of Europe, a patch-work of tillage and sleeping industrialism. Beyond poplared Normandy spread Paris, with the towers of Notre-Dame tipped slightly, by reason of Earth's curvature. Further on, the Spanish night was ablaze with the murder of cities. Away to the left lay Germany, with its forests and factories, its music, its steel helmets. In cathedral squares I seemed to see the young men ranked together in thousands, exalted, possessed, saluting the flood-lit Führer. In Italy too, land of memories and illusions, the mob's idol spell-bound the young.

Far left-wards again, Russia, an appreciably convex segment of our globe, snow-pale in the darkness, spread out under the stars and cloud-tracts. Inevitably I saw the spires of the Kremlin, confronting the Red Square. There Lenin lay, victorious. Far off, at the foot of the Urals, imagination detected the ruddy plumes and smoke-pall of Magnetostroy. Beyond the hills there gleamed a hint of dawn; for day, at my midnight, was already pouring westward across Asia, overtaking with its advancing front of gold and rose the tiny smoke-caterpillar of the Trans-Siberian Express. To the north, the iron-hard Arctic oppressed the exiles in their camps. Far southward lay the rich valleys and plains that once cradled our species. But there I now saw railway lines ruled across the snow. In every village Asiatic children were waking to another schoolday, and to the legend of Lenin. South again the Himalayas, snow-clad from waist to crest, looked over the rabble of their foot-hills into crowded India. I saw the dancing cotton plants, and the wheat, and the sacred river that bore the waters of Kamet past ricefields and crocodile-shallows, past Calcutta with its shipping and its offices, down·to the sea. From my midnight I looked into China. The morning sun glanced from the flooded fields and gilded the ancestral graves. The Yang Tse, a gleaming, crumpled thread, rushed through its gorge. Beyond the Korean ranges, and across the sea, stood Fujiyama, extinct and formal. Around it a volcanic population welled and seethed in that narrow land, like lava in a crater. Already it spilled over Asia a flood of armies and of trade.

Imagination withdrew and turned to Africa. I saw the man-made thread of water that joins West to East; then minarets, pyramids, the ever-waiting Sphinx. Ancient Memphis itself now echoed with the rumour of Magnetostroy. Far southward, black men slept beside the great lakes. Elephants trampled the crops. Further still, where Dutch and English profit by the Negro millions, those hosts were stirred by vague dreams of freedom.

Peering beyond the whole bulge of Africa, beyond cloud-spread Table

Mountain, I saw the Southern Ocean, black with storms, and then the ice-cliffs with their seals and penguins, and the high snow-fields of the one unpeopled continent. Imagination faced the midnight sun, crossed the Pole, and passed Erebus, vomiting hot lava down his ermine. Northward it sped over the summer sea, past New Zealand, that freer but less conscious Britain, to Australia, where clear-eyed horsemen collect their flocks.

Still peering eastward from my hill, I saw the Pacific, strewn with islands; and then the Americas, where the descendants of Europe long ago mastered the descendants of Asia, through priority in the use of guns, and the arrogance that guns breed. Beside the further ocean, north and south, lay the old New World; the River Plate and Rio, the New England cities, radiating centre of the old new style of life and thought. New York, dark against the afternoon sun, was a cluster of tall crystals, a Stonehenge of modern megaliths. Round these, like fishes nibbling at the feet of waders, the great liners crowded. Out at sea also I saw them, and the plunging freighters, forging through the sunset, port holes and decks aglow. Stokers sweated at furnaces, look-out men in crow's-nests shivered, dance music, issuing from opened doors, was drowned by the wind.

The whole planet, the whole rock-grain, with its busy swarms, I now saw as an arena where two cosmical antagonists, two spirits, were already preparing for a critical struggle, already assuming terrestrial and local guise, and coming to grips in our half-awakened minds. In city upon city, in village after village, and in innumerable lonely farmsteads, cottages, hovels, shacks, huts, in all the crevices where human creatures were intent on their little comforts and triumphs and escapes, the great struggle of our age was brewing.

One antagonist appeared as the will to dare for the sake of the new, the longed for, the reasonable and joyful, world, in which every man and woman may have scope to live fully, and live in service of mankind. The other seemed essentially the myopic fear of the unknown; or was it more sinister? Was it the cunning will for private mastery, which fomented for its own ends the archaic, reason-hating, and vindictive, passion of the tribe.

It seemed that in the coming storm all the dearest things must be destroyed. All private happiness, all loving, all creative work in art, science, and philosophy, all intellectual scrutiny and speculative imagination, and all creative social building; all, indeed, that man should normally live for, seemed folly and mockery and mere self-indulgence in the presence of public calamity. But if we failed to preserve them, when would they live again?

How to face such an age? How to muster courage, being capable only of homely virtues? How to do this, yet preserve the mind's integrity, never to let the struggle destroy in one's own heart what one tried to serve in the world, the spirit's integrity?

Two lights for guidance. The first, our little glowing atom of community, with all that it signifies. The second, the cold light of the stars, symbol of the hypercosmical reality, with its crystal ecstasy. Strange that in this light, in which even the dearest love is frostily assessed, and even the possible defeat of our half-waking world is contemplated without remission of praise, the human crisis does not lose but gains significance. Strange, that it seems more, not less, urgent to play some part in this struggle, this brief effort of animalcules striving to win for their race some increase of lucidity before the ultimate darkness.

THE END

A Note On Magnitude

IMMENSITY is not itself a good thing. A living man is worth more than a lifeless galaxy. But immensity has indirect importance through its facilitation of mental richness and diversity. Things are of course only large and small in relation to one another. To say that a cosmos is large is only to say that, in relation to it, some of its constituents are small. To say that its career is long is merely to say that many happenings are contained within it. But though the spatial and temporal immensity of a cosmos have no intrinsic merit, they are the ground for psychical luxuriance, which we value. Physical immensity opens up the possibility of vast physical complexity, and this offers scope for complex minded organisms. This is at any rate true of a cosmos like ours in which mind is conditioned by the physical.

The probable size of our cosmos may be very roughly conceived by means of the following analogy, adapted from one given in W. J. Luyten's *The Pageant of the Stars*. Let Wales represent the size of our galaxy, say 100,000 light years. This is said to be surrounded by a system of seven much smaller sub-galaxies and globular clusters, all lying within a diameter of 1,000,000 light years. In our model, they would spread far into the Atlantic and into Europe. Other such systems would lie throughout space at average intervals represented by the distance from Wales to North America. On the same scale the remotest galaxy visible through the great 100-inch telescope, some 500,000,000 light years distant, would lie 60,000 miles off, or a quarter of the distance to the moon. The forthcoming 200-inch telescope will doubtless have a far greater range. The total extent of the cosmos would be represented in this model by a volume about 11,000,000 miles across, or one-eighth the distance from the earth to the sun. The distance between the sun and the nearest star (4.5 light years) would be about thirteen feet. A light year itself would be rather less than three feet. The average speed of stellar motion (20 miles a second) is represented by a rate of about four inches in 100 years. The earth's orbit is one-thousandth of an inch in diameter; the sun's diameter is six-millionths of an inch; the earth is reduced to a grain one-twentieth of a millionth of an inch across.

435

Time Scale 1

Note.—Every item on this scale is placed where it is solely to illustrate the fictitious story of this book. Many scientists would deny that man can be so far from the birth of the stars as I have found it convenient to suppose.

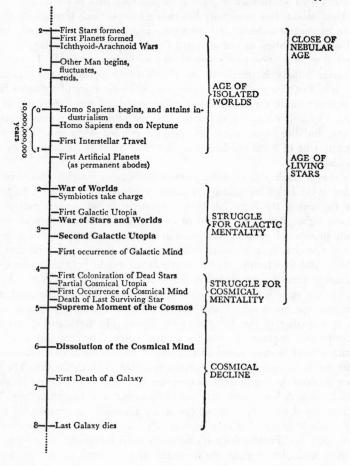

2 —	First Stars formed	
	First Planets formed	CLOSE OF
	Ichthyoid-Arachnoid Wars	NEBULAR
	Other Man begins,	AGE
1 —	fluctuates,	
	ends.	
		AGE OF
		ISOLATED
0 —	Homo Sapiens begins, and attains industrialism	WORLDS
	Homo Sapiens ends on Neptune	
	First Interstellar Travel	
1 —	First Artificial Planets (as permanent abodes)	AGE OF LIVING STARS
2 —	War of Worlds	
	Symbiotics take charge	
	First Galactic Utopia	STRUGGLE
	War of Stars and Worlds	FOR GALACTIC
3 —	Second Galactic Utopia	MENTALITY
	First occurrence of Galactic Mind	
4 —	First Colonization of Dead Stars	
	Partial Cosmical Utopia	STRUGGLE FOR
	First Occurrence of Cosmical Mind	COSMICAL
	Death of Last Surviving Star	MENTALITY
5 —	Supreme Moment of the Cosmos	
6 —	Dissolution of the Cosmical Mind	
		COSMICAL
	First Death of a Galaxy	DECLINE
7 —		
8 —	Last Galaxy dies	

10,000,000,000 years

Time Scale 2

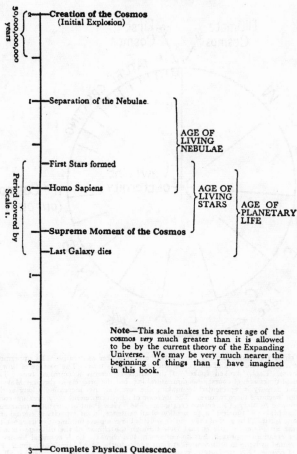

Creation of the Cosmos
(Initial Explosion)

50,000,000,000 years

Separation of the Nebulae.

AGE OF
LIVING
NEBULAE

First Stars formed

Homo Sapiens

AGE OF
LIVING
STARS

AGE OF
PLANETARY
LIFE

Supreme Moment of the Cosmos

Last Galaxy dies

Period covered by Scale 1.

Note—This scale makes the present age of the cosmos *very* much greater than it is allowed to be by the current theory of the Expanding Universe. We may be very much nearer the beginning of things than I have imagined in this book.

Complete Physical Quiescence

Time Scale 3

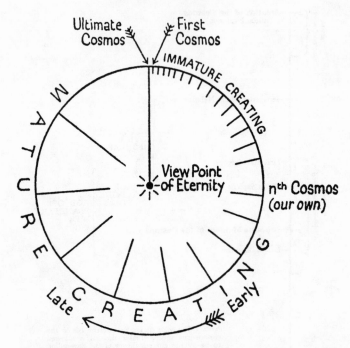

The circle represents the time proper to the Star Maker as creative. Its uppermost point is the beginning and the end of the Star Maker's time. The passage of time is clockwise. Each ' broken spoke ' of the wheel represents a cosmical time. The cosmical times are, of course, incommensurable ; but the progress in the Star Maker's creative activity is represented by making the cosmical lines increasingly long as the creation becomes more mature. The increase of length represents the increasing complexity and subtlety of successive creations. The ' View Point of Eternity ' represents the Star Maker's ' timeless ' apprehension of all existence, in his capacity of eternal and absolute spirit. The goal of the creative spirit is the complete fulfilment of its capacity, and the attainment of the eternal view through the climax of the ultimate cosmos. Earlier creations approach, but do not reach, this climax. Each cosmical history is represented as lying in a dimension at right angles to the Star Maker's own time. He can, of course, ' live through ' a cosmical history, but he can also apprehend it all at once. Some of the cosmical histories might have been represented by circles, since the times of some are cyclic. Others might have been areas, since they have more than one temporal dimension. I have only represented a few of the infinite number of creations.

A CATALOGUE OF SELECTED DOVER BOOKS
IN ALL FIELDS OF INTEREST

A CATALOGUE OF SELECTED DOVER BOOKS
IN ALL FIELDS OF INTEREST

AMERICA'S OLD MASTERS, James T. Flexner. Four men emerged unexpectedly from provincial 18th century America to leadership in European art: Benjamin West, J. S. Copley, C. R. Peale, Gilbert Stuart. Brilliant coverage of lives and contributions. Revised, 1967 edition. 69 plates. 365pp. of text.

21806-6 Paperbound $3.00

FIRST FLOWERS OF OUR WILDERNESS: AMERICAN PAINTING, THE COLONIAL PERIOD, James T. Flexner. Painters, and regional painting traditions from earliest Colonial times up to the emergence of Copley, West and Peale Sr., Foster, Gustavus Hesselius, Feke, John Smibert and many anonymous painters in the primitive manner. Engaging presentation, with 162 illustrations. xxii + 368pp.

22180-6 Paperbound $3.50

THE LIGHT OF DISTANT SKIES: AMERICAN PAINTING, 1760-1835, James T. Flexner. The great generation of early American painters goes to Europe to learn and to teach: West, Copley, Gilbert Stuart and others. Allston, Trumbull, Morse; also contemporary American painters—primitives, derivatives, academics—who remained in America. 102 illustrations. xiii + 306pp.

22179-2 Paperbound $3.50

A HISTORY OF THE RISE AND PROGRESS OF THE ARTS OF DESIGN IN THE UNITED STATES, William Dunlap. Much the richest mine of information on early American painters, sculptors, architects, engravers, miniaturists, etc. The only source of information for scores of artists, the major primary source for many others. Unabridged reprint of rare original 1834 edition, with new introduction by James T. Flexner, and 394 new illustrations. Edited by Rita Weiss. 6⅝ x 9⅝.

21695-0, 21696-9, 21697-7 Three volumes, Paperbound $15.00

EPOCHS OF CHINESE AND JAPANESE ART, Ernest F. Fenollosa. From primitive Chinese art to the 20th century, thorough history, explanation of every important art period and form, including Japanese woodcuts; main stress on China and Japan, but Tibet, Korea also included. Still unexcelled for its detailed, rich coverage of cultural background, aesthetic elements, diffusion studies, particularly of the historical period. 2nd, 1913 edition. 242 illustrations. lii + 439pp. of text.

20364-6, 20365-4 Two volumes, Paperbound $6.00

THE GENTLE ART OF MAKING ENEMIES, James A. M. Whistler. Greatest wit of his day deflates Oscar Wilde, Ruskin, Swinburne; strikes back at inane critics, exhibitions, art journalism; aesthetics of impressionist revolution in most striking form. Highly readable classic by great painter. Reproduction of edition designed by Whistler. Introduction by Alfred Werner. xxxvi + 334pp.

21875-9 Paperbound $3.00

VISUAL ILLUSIONS: THEIR CAUSES, CHARACTERISTICS, AND APPLICATIONS, Matthew Luckiesh. Thorough description and discussion of optical illusion, geometric and perspective, particularly; size and shape distortions, illusions of color, of motion; natural illusions; use of illusion in art and magic, industry, etc. Most useful today with op art, also for classical art. Scores of effects illustrated. Introduction by William H. Ittleson. 100 illustrations. xxi + 252pp.

21530-X Paperbound $2.00

A HANDBOOK OF ANATOMY FOR ART STUDENTS, Arthur Thomson. Thorough, virtually exhaustive coverage of skeletal structure, musculature, etc. Full text, supplemented by anatomical diagrams and drawings and by photographs of undraped figures. Unique in its comparison of male and female forms, pointing out differences of contour, texture, form. 211 figures, 40 drawings, 86 photographs. xx + 459pp. 5⅜ x 8⅜.

21163-0 Paperbound $3.50

150 MASTERPIECES OF DRAWING, Selected by Anthony Toney. Full page reproductions of drawings from the early 16th to the end of the 18th century, all beautifully reproduced: Rembrandt, Michelangelo, Dürer, Fragonard, Urs, Graf, Wouwerman, many others. First-rate browsing book, model book for artists. xviii + 150pp. 8⅜ x 11¼.

21032-4 Paperbound $2.50

THE LATER WORK OF AUBREY BEARDSLEY, Aubrey Beardsley. Exotic, erotic, ironic masterpieces in full maturity: Comedy Ballet, Venus and Tannhauser, Pierrot, Lysistrata, Rape of the Lock, Savoy material, Ali Baba, Volpone, etc. This material revolutionized the art world, and is still powerful, fresh, brilliant. With *The Early Work,* all Beardsley's finest work. 174 plates, 2 in color. xiv + 176pp. 8⅛ x 11.

21817-1 Paperbound $3.00

DRAWINGS OF REMBRANDT, Rembrandt van Rijn. Complete reproduction of fabulously rare edition by Lippmann and Hofstede de Groot, completely reedited, updated, improved by Prof. Seymour Slive, Fogg Museum. Portraits, Biblical sketches, landscapes, Oriental types, nudes, episodes from classical mythology—All Rembrandt's fertile genius. Also selection of drawings by his pupils and followers. "Stunning volumes," *Saturday Review.* 550 illustrations. lxxviii + 552pp. 9⅛ x 12¼.

21485-0, 21486-9 Two volumes, Paperbound $10.00

THE DISASTERS OF WAR, Francisco Goya. One of the masterpieces of Western civilization—83 etchings that record Goya's shattering, bitter reaction to the Napoleonic war that swept through Spain after the insurrection of 1808 and to war in general. Reprint of the first edition, with three additional plates from Boston's Museum of Fine Arts. All plates facsimile size. Introduction by Philip Hofer, Fogg Museum. v + 97pp. 9⅜ x 8¼.

21872-4 Paperbound $2.00

GRAPHIC WORKS OF ODILON REDON. Largest collection of Redon's graphic works ever assembled: 172 lithographs, 28 etchings and engravings, 9 drawings. These include some of his most famous works. All the plates from *Odilon Redon: oeuvre graphique complet,* plus additional plates. New introduction and caption translations by Alfred Werner. 209 illustrations. xxvii + 209pp. 9⅛ x 12¼.

21966-8 Paperbound $4.50

DESIGN BY ACCIDENT; A BOOK OF "ACCIDENTAL EFFECTS" FOR ARTISTS AND DESIGNERS, James F. O'Brien. Create your own unique, striking, imaginative effects by "controlled accident" interaction of materials: paints and lacquers, oil and water based paints, splatter, crackling materials, shatter, similar items. Everything you do will be different; first book on this limitless art, so useful to both fine artist and commercial artist. Full instructions. 192 plates showing "accidents," 8 in color. viii + 215pp. 8⅜ x 11¼. 21942-9 Paperbound $3.75

THE BOOK OF SIGNS, Rudolf Koch. Famed German type designer draws 493 beautiful symbols: religious, mystical, alchemical, imperial, property marks, runes, etc. Remarkable fusion of traditional and modern. Good for suggestions of timelessness, smartness, modernity. Text. vi + 104pp. 6⅛ x 9¼.
20162-7 Paperbound $1.25

HISTORY OF INDIAN AND INDONESIAN ART, Ananda K. Coomaraswamy. An unabridged republication of one of the finest books by a great scholar in Eastern art. Rich in descriptive material, history, social backgrounds; Sunga reliefs, Rajput paintings, Gupta temples, Burmese frescoes, textiles, jewelry, sculpture, etc. 400 photos. viii + 423pp. 6⅜ x 9¾. 21436-2 Paperbound $5.00

PRIMITIVE ART, Franz Boas. America's foremost anthropologist surveys textiles, ceramics, woodcarving, basketry, metalwork, etc.; patterns, technology, creation of symbols, style origins. All areas of world, but very full on Northwest Coast Indians. More than 350 illustrations of baskets, boxes, totem poles, weapons, etc. 378 pp.
20025-6 Paperbound $3.00

THE GENTLEMAN AND CABINET MAKER'S DIRECTOR, Thomas Chippendale. Full reprint (third edition, 1762) of most influential furniture book of all time, by master cabinetmaker. 200 plates, illustrating chairs, sofas, mirrors, tables, cabinets, plus 24 photographs of surviving pieces. Biographical introduction by N. Bienenstock. vi + 249pp. 9⅞ x 12¾. 21601-2 Paperbound $4.00

AMERICAN ANTIQUE FURNITURE, Edgar G. Miller, Jr. The basic coverage of all American furniture before 1840. Individual chapters cover type of furniture— clocks, tables, sideboards, etc.—chronologically, with inexhaustible wealth of data. More than 2100 photographs, all identified, commented on. Essential to all early American collectors. Introduction by H. E. Keyes. vi + 1106pp. 7⅞ x 10¾.
21599-7, 21600-4 Two volumes, Paperbound $11.00

PENNSYLVANIA DUTCH AMERICAN FOLK ART, Henry J. Kauffman. 279 photos, 28 drawings of tulipware, Fraktur script, painted tinware, toys, flowered furniture, quilts, samplers, hex signs, house interiors, etc. Full descriptive text. Excellent for tourist, rewarding for designer, collector. Map. 146pp. 7⅞ x 10¾.
21205-X Paperbound $2.50

EARLY NEW ENGLAND GRAVESTONE RUBBINGS, Edmund V. Gillon, Jr. 43 photographs, 226 carefully reproduced rubbings show heavily symbolic, sometimes macabre early gravestones, up to early 19th century. Remarkable early American primitive art, occasionally strikingly beautiful; always powerful. Text. xxvi + 207pp. 8⅜ x 11¼. 21380-3 Paperbound $3.50

ALPHABETS AND ORNAMENTS, Ernst Lehner. Well-known pictorial source for decorative alphabets, script examples, cartouches, frames, decorative title pages, calligraphic initials, borders, similar material. 14th to 19th century, mostly European. Useful in almost any graphic arts designing, varied styles. 750 illustrations. 256pp. 7 x 10.   21905-4 Paperbound $4.00

PAINTING: A CREATIVE APPROACH, Norman Colquhoun. For the beginner simple guide provides an instructive approach to painting: major stumbling blocks for beginner; overcoming them, technical points; paints and pigments; oil painting; watercolor and other media and color. New section on "plastic" paints. Glossary. Formerly *Paint Your Own Pictures*. 221pp.   22000-1 Paperbound $1.75

THE ENJOYMENT AND USE OF COLOR, Walter Sargent. Explanation of the relations between colors themselves and between colors in nature and art, including hundreds of little-known facts about color values, intensities, effects of high and low illumination, complementary colors. Many practical hints for painters, references to great masters. 7 color plates, 29 illustrations. x + 274pp.
20944-X Paperbound $2.75

THE NOTEBOOKS OF LEONARDO DA VINCI, compiled and edited by Jean Paul Richter. 1566 extracts from original manuscripts reveal the full range of Leonardo's versatile genius: all his writings on painting, sculpture, architecture, anatomy, astronomy, geography, topography, physiology, mining, music, etc., in both Italian and English, with 186 plates of manuscript pages and more than 500 additional drawings. Includes studies for the Last Supper, the lost Sforza monument, and other works. Total of xlvii + 866pp. $7\frac{7}{8}$ x $10\frac{3}{4}$.
22572-0, 22573-9 Two volumes, Paperbound $11.00

MONTGOMERY WARD CATALOGUE OF 1895. Tea gowns, yards of flannel and pillow-case lace, stereoscopes, books of gospel hymns, the New Improved Singer Sewing Machine, side saddles, milk skimmers, straight-edged razors, high-button shoes, spittoons, and on and on . . . listing some 25,000 items, practically all illustrated. Essential to the shoppers of the 1890's, it is our truest record of the spirit of the period. Unaltered reprint of Issue No. 57, Spring and Summer 1895. Introduction by Boris Emmet. Innumerable illustrations. xiii + 624pp. $8\frac{1}{2}$ x $11\frac{5}{8}$.
22377-9 Paperbound $6.95

THE CRYSTAL PALACE EXHIBITION ILLUSTRATED CATALOGUE (LONDON, 1851). One of the wonders of the modern world—the Crystal Palace Exhibition in which all the nations of the civilized world exhibited their achievements in the arts and sciences—presented in an equally important illustrated catalogue. More than 1700 items pictured with accompanying text—ceramics, textiles, cast-iron work, carpets, pianos, sleds, razors, wall-papers, billiard tables, beehives, silverware and hundreds of other artifacts—represent the focal point of Victorian culture in the Western World. Probably the largest collection of Victorian decorative art ever assembled—indispensable for antiquarians and designers. Unabridged republication of the Art-Journal Catalogue of the Great Exhibition of 1851, with all terminal essays. New introduction by John Gloag, F.S.A. xxxiv + 426pp. 9 x 12.
22503-8 Paperbound $5.00

A HISTORY OF COSTUME, Carl Köhler. Definitive history, based on surviving pieces of clothing primarily, and paintings, statues, etc. secondarily. Highly readable text, supplemented by 594 illustrations of costumes of the ancient Mediterranean peoples, Greece and Rome, the Teutonic prehistoric period; costumes of the Middle Ages, Renaissance, Baroque, 18th and 19th centuries. Clear, measured patterns are provided for many clothing articles. Approach is practical throughout. Enlarged by Emma von Sichart. 464pp.   21030-8 Paperbound $3.50

ORIENTAL RUGS, ANTIQUE AND MODERN, Walter A. Hawley. A complete and authoritative treatise on the Oriental rug—where they are made, by whom and how, designs and symbols, characteristics in detail of the six major groups, how to distinguish them and how to buy them. Detailed technical data is provided on periods, weaves, warps, wefts, textures, sides, ends and knots, although no technical background is required for an understanding. 11 color plates, 80 halftones, 4 maps. vi + 320pp. 6⅛ x 9⅛.   22366-3 Paperbound $5.00

TEN BOOKS ON ARCHITECTURE, Vitruvius. By any standards the most important book on architecture ever written. Early Roman discussion of aesthetics of building, construction methods, orders, sites, and every other aspect of architecture has inspired, instructed architecture for about 2,000 years. Stands behind Palladio, Michelangelo, Bramante, Wren, countless others. Definitive Morris H. Morgan translation. 68 illustrations. xii + 331pp.   20645-9 Paperbound $3.00

THE FOUR BOOKS OF ARCHITECTURE, Andrea Palladio. Translated into every major Western European language in the two centuries following its publication in 1570, this has been one of the most influential books in the history of architecture. Complete reprint of the 1738 Isaac Ware edition. New introduction by Adolf Placzek, Columbia Univ. 216 plates. xxii + 110pp. of text. 9½ x 12¾.
                          21308-0 Clothbound $12.50

STICKS AND STONES: A STUDY OF AMERICAN ARCHITECTURE AND CIVILIZATION, Lewis Mumford. One of the great classics of American cultural history. American architecture from the medieval-inspired earliest forms to the early 20th century; evolution of structure and style, and reciprocal influences on environment. 21 photographic illustrations. 238pp.   20202-X Paperbound $2.00

THE AMERICAN BUILDER'S COMPANION, Asher Benjamin. The most widely used early 19th century architectural style and source book, for colonial up into Greek Revival periods. Extensive development of geometry of carpentering, construction of sashes, frames, doors, stairs; plans and elevations of domestic and other buildings. Hundreds of thousands of houses were built according to this book, now invaluable to historians, architects, restorers, etc. 1827 edition. 59 plates. 114pp. 7⅞ x 10¾.
                          22236-5 Paperbound $3.50

DUTCH HOUSES IN THE HUDSON VALLEY BEFORE 1776, Helen Wilkinson Reynolds. The standard survey of the Dutch colonial house and outbuildings, with constructional features, decoration, and local history associated with individual homesteads. Introduction by Franklin D. Roosevelt. Map. 150 illustrations. 469pp. 6⅝ x 9¼.   21469-9 Paperbound $5.00

THE ARCHITECTURE OF COUNTRY HOUSES, Andrew J. Downing. Together with Vaux's *Villas and Cottages* this is the basic book for Hudson River Gothic architecture of the middle Victorian period. Full, sound discussions of general aspects of housing, architecture, style, decoration, furnishing, together with scores of detailed house plans, illustrations of specific buildings, accompanied by full text. Perhaps the most influential single American architectural book. 1850 edition. Introduction by J. Stewart Johnson. 321 figures, 34 architectural designs. xvi + 560pp.

22003-6 Paperbound $4.00

LOST EXAMPLES OF COLONIAL ARCHITECTURE, John Mead Howells. Full-page photographs of buildings that have disappeared or been so altered as to be denatured, including many designed by major early American architects. 245 plates. xvii + 248pp. 7⅞ x 10¾.

21143-6 Paperbound $3.50

DOMESTIC ARCHITECTURE OF THE AMERICAN COLONIES AND OF THE EARLY REPUBLIC, Fiske Kimball. Foremost architect and restorer of Williamsburg and Monticello covers nearly 200 homes between 1620-1825. Architectural details, construction, style features, special fixtures, floor plans, etc. Generally considered finest work in its area. 219 illustrations of houses, doorways, windows, capital mantels. xx + 314pp. 7⅞ x 10¾.

21743-4 Paperbound $4.00

EARLY AMERICAN ROOMS: 1650-1858, edited by Russell Hawes Kettell. Tour of 12 rooms, each representative of a different era in American history and each furnished, decorated, designed and occupied in the style of the era. 72 plans and elevations, 8-page color section, etc., show fabrics, wall papers, arrangements, etc. Full descriptive text. xvii + 200pp. of text. 8⅜ x 11¼.

21633-0 Paperbound $5.00

THE FITZWILLIAM VIRGINAL BOOK, edited by J. Fuller Maitland and W. B. Squire. Full modern printing of famous early 17th-century ms. volume of 300 works by Morley, Byrd, Bull, Gibbons, etc. For piano or other modern keyboard instrument; easy to read format. xxxvi + 938pp. 8⅜ x 11.

21068-5, 21069-3 Two volumes, Paperbound $10.00

KEYBOARD MUSIC, Johann Sebastian Bach. Bach Gesellschaft edition. A rich selection of Bach's masterpieces for the harpsichord: the six English Suites, six French Suites, the six Partitas (Clavierübung part I), the Goldberg Variations (Clavierübung part IV), the fifteen Two-Part Inventions and the fifteen Three-Part Sinfonias. Clearly reproduced on large sheets with ample margins; eminently playable. vi + 312pp. 8⅛ x 11.

22360-4 Paperbound $5.00

THE MUSIC OF BACH: AN INTRODUCTION, Charles Sanford Terry. A fine, nontechnical introduction to Bach's music, both instrumental and vocal. Covers organ music, chamber music, passion music, other types. Analyzes themes, developments, innovations. x + 114pp.

21075-8 Paperbound $1.50

BEETHOVEN AND HIS NINE SYMPHONIES, Sir George Grove. Noted British musicologist provides best history, analysis, commentary on symphonies. Very thorough, rigorously accurate; necessary to both advanced student and amateur music lover. 436 musical passages. vii + 407 pp.

20334-4 Paperbound $2.75

JOHANN SEBASTIAN BACH, Philipp Spitta. One of the great classics of musicology, this definitive analysis of Bach's music (and life) has never been surpassed. Lucid, nontechnical analyses of hundreds of pieces (30 pages devoted to St. Matthew Passion, 26 to B Minor Mass). Also includes major analysis of 18th-century music. 450 musical examples. 40-page musical supplement. Total of xx + 1799pp.

(EUK) 22278-0, 22279-9 Two volumes, Clothbound $17.50

MOZART AND HIS PIANO CONCERTOS, Cuthbert Girdlestone. The only full-length study of an important area of Mozart's creativity. Provides detailed analyses of all 23 concertos, traces inspirational sources. 417 musical examples. Second edition. 509pp.

21271-8 Paperbound $3.50

THE PERFECT WAGNERITE: A COMMENTARY ON THE NIBLUNG'S RING, George Bernard Shaw. Brilliant and still relevant criticism in remarkable essays on Wagner's Ring cycle, Shaw's ideas on political and social ideology behind the plots, role of Leitmotifs, vocal requisites, etc. Prefaces. xxi + 136pp.

(USO) 21707-8 Paperbound $1.75

DON GIOVANNI, W. A. Mozart. Complete libretto, modern English translation; biographies of composer and librettist; accounts of early performances and critical reaction. Lavishly illustrated. All the material you need to understand and appreciate this great work. Dover Opera Guide and Libretto Series; translated and introduced by Ellen Bleiler. 92 illustrations. 209pp.

21134-7 Paperbound $2.00

BASIC ELECTRICITY, U. S. Bureau of Naval Personel. Originally a training course, best non-technical coverage of basic theory of electricity and its applications. Fundamental concepts, batteries, circuits, conductors and wiring techniques, AC and DC, inductance and capacitance, generators, motors, transformers, magnetic amplifiers, synchros, servomechanisms, etc. Also covers blue-prints, electrical diagrams, etc. Many questions, with answers. 349 illustrations. x + 448pp. 6½ x 9¼.

20973-3 Paperbound $3.50

REPRODUCTION OF SOUND, Edgar Villchur. Thorough coverage for laymen of high fidelity systems, reproducing systems in general, needles, amplifiers, preamps, loudspeakers, feedback, explaining physical background. "A rare talent for making technicalities vividly comprehensible," R. Darrell, *High Fidelity*. 69 figures. iv + 92pp.

21515-6 Paperbound $1.35

HEAR ME TALKIN' TO YA: THE STORY OF JAZZ AS TOLD BY THE MEN WHO MADE IT, Nat Shapiro and Nat Hentoff. Louis Armstrong, Fats Waller, Jo Jones, Clarence Williams, Billy Holiday, Duke Ellington, Jelly Roll Morton and dozens of other jazz greats tell how it was in Chicago's South Side, New Orleans, depression Harlem and the modern West Coast as jazz was born and grew. xvi + 429pp.

21726-4 Paperbound $3.00

FABLES OF AESOP, translated by Sir Roger L'Estrange. A reproduction of the very rare 1931 Paris edition; a selection of the most interesting fables, together with 50 imaginative drawings by Alexander Calder. v + 128pp. 6½x9¼.

21780-9 Paperbound $1.50

AGAINST THE GRAIN (A REBOURS), Joris K. Huysmans. Filled with weird images, evidences of a bizarre imagination, exotic experiments with hallucinatory drugs, rich tastes and smells and the diversions of its sybarite hero Duc Jean des Esseintes, this classic novel pushed 19th-century literary decadence to its limits. Full unabridged edition. Do not confuse this with abridged editions generally sold. Introduction by Havelock Ellis. xlix + 206pp.   22190-3 Paperbound $2.50

VARIORUM SHAKESPEARE: HAMLET. Edited by Horace H. Furness; a landmark of American scholarship. Exhaustive footnotes and appendices treat all doubtful words and phrases, as well as suggested critical emendations throughout the play's history. First volume contains editor's own text, collated with all Quartos and Folios. Second volume contains full first Quarto, translations of Shakespeare's sources (Belleforest, and Saxo Grammaticus), Der Bestrafte Brudermord, and many essays on critical and historical points of interest by major authorities of past and present. Includes details of staging and costuming over the years. By far the best edition available for serious students of Shakespeare. Total of xx + 905pp.
21004-9, 21005-7, 2 volumes, Paperbound $7.00

A LIFE OF WILLIAM SHAKESPEARE, Sir Sidney Lee. This is the standard life of Shakespeare, summarizing everything known about Shakespeare and his plays. Incredibly rich in material, broad in coverage, clear and judicious, it has served thousands as the best introduction to Shakespeare. 1931 edition. 9 plates. xxix + 792pp.   21967-4 Paperbound $3.75

MASTERS OF THE DRAMA, John Gassner. Most comprehensive history of the drama in print, covering every tradition from Greeks to modern Europe and America, including India, Far East, etc. Covers more than 800 dramatists, 2000 plays, with biographical material, plot summaries, theatre history, criticism, etc. "Best of its kind in English," *New Republic*. 77 illustrations. xxii + 890pp.
20100-7 Clothbound $10.00

THE EVOLUTION OF THE ENGLISH LANGUAGE, George McKnight. The growth of English, from the 14th century to the present. Unusual, non-technical account presents basic information in very interesting form: sound shifts, change in grammar and syntax, vocabulary growth, similar topics. Abundantly illustrated with quotations. Formerly *Modern English in the Making*. xii + 590pp.
21932-1 Paperbound $3.50

AN ETYMOLOGICAL DICTIONARY OF MODERN ENGLISH, Ernest Weekley. Fullest, richest work of its sort, by foremost British lexicographer. Detailed word histories, including many colloquial and archaic words; extensive quotations. Do not confuse this with the Concise Etymological Dictionary, which is much abridged. Total of xxvii + 830pp. 6½ x 9¼.
21873-2, 21874-0 Two volumes, Paperbound $7.90

FLATLAND: A ROMANCE OF MANY DIMENSIONS, E. A. Abbott. Classic of science-fiction explores ramifications of life in a two-dimensional world, and what happens when a three-dimensional being intrudes. Amusing reading, but also useful as introduction to thought about hyperspace. Introduction by Banesh Hoffmann. 16 illustrations. xx + 103pp.   20001-9 Paperbound $1.00

POEMS OF ANNE BRADSTREET, edited with an introduction by Robert Hutchinson. A new selection of poems by America's first poet and perhaps the first significant woman poet in the English language. 48 poems display her development in works of considerable variety—love poems, domestic poems, religious meditations, formal elegies, "quaternions," etc. Notes, bibliography. viii + 222pp.

22160-1 Paperbound $2.50

THREE GOTHIC NOVELS: THE CASTLE OF OTRANTO BY HORACE WALPOLE; VATHEK BY WILLIAM BECKFORD; THE VAMPYRE BY JOHN POLIDORI, WITH FRAGMENT OF A NOVEL BY LORD BYRON, edited by E. F. Bleiler. The first Gothic novel, by Walpole; the finest Oriental tale in English, by Beckford; powerful Romantic supernatural story in versions by Polidori and Byron. All extremely important in history of literature; all still exciting, packed with supernatural thrills, ghosts, haunted castles, magic, etc. xl + 291pp.

21232-7 Paperbound $2.50

THE BEST TALES OF HOFFMANN, E. T. A. Hoffmann. 10 of Hoffmann's most important stories, in modern re-editings of standard translations: Nutcracker and the King of Mice, Signor Formica, Automata, The Sandman, Rath Krespel, The Golden Flowerpot, Master Martin the Cooper, The Mines of Falun, The King's Betrothed, A New Year's Eve Adventure. 7 illustrations by Hoffmann. Edited by E. F. Bleiler. xxxix + 419pp. 21793-0 Paperbound $3.00

GHOST AND HORROR STORIES OF AMBROSE BIERCE, Ambrose Bierce. 23 strikingly modern stories of the horrors latent in the human mind: The Eyes of the Panther, The Damned Thing, An Occurrence at Owl Creek Bridge, An Inhabitant of Carcosa, etc., plus the dream-essay, Visions of the Night. Edited by E. F. Bleiler. xxii + 199pp. 20767-6 Paperbound $1.50

BEST GHOST STORIES OF J. S. LEFANU, J. Sheridan LeFanu. Finest stories by Victorian master often considered greatest supernatural writer of all. Carmilla, Green Tea, The Haunted Baronet, The Familiar, and 12 others. Most never before available in the U. S. A. Edited by E. F. Bleiler. 8 illustrations from Victorian publications. xvii + 467pp. 20415-4 Paperbound $3.00

MATHEMATICAL FOUNDATIONS OF INFORMATION THEORY, A. I. Khinchin. Comprehensive introduction to work of Shannon, McMillan, Feinstein and Khinchin, placing these investigations on a rigorous mathematical basis. Covers entropy concept in probability theory, uniqueness theorem, Shannon's inequality, ergodic sources, the E property, martingale concept, noise, Feinstein's fundamental lemma, Shanon's first and second theorems. Translated by R. A. Silverman and M. D. Friedman. iii + 120pp. 60434-9 Paperbound $2.00

SEVEN SCIENCE FICTION NOVELS, H. G. Wells. The standard collection of the great novels. Complete, unabridged. *First Men in the Moon, Island of Dr. Moreau, War of the Worlds, Food of the Gods, Invisible Man, Time Machine, In the Days of the Comet.* Not only science fiction fans, but every educated person owes it to himself to read these novels. 1015pp. (USO) 20264-X Clothbound $6.00

LAST AND FIRST MEN AND STAR MAKER, TWO SCIENCE FICTION NOVELS, Olaf Stapledon. Greatest future histories in science fiction. In the first, human intelligence is the "hero," through strange paths of evolution, interplanetary invasions, incredible technologies, near extinctions and reemergences. Star Maker describes the quest of a band of star rovers for intelligence itself, through time and space: weird inhuman civilizations, crustacean minds, symbiotic worlds, etc. Complete, unabridged. v + 438pp. (USO) 21962-3 Paperbound $2.50

THREE PROPHETIC NOVELS, H. G. WELLS. Stages of a consistently planned future for mankind. *When the Sleeper Wakes,* and *A Story of the Days to Come,* anticipate *Brave New World* and *1984,* in the 21st Century; *The Time Machine,* only complete version in print, shows farther future and the end of mankind. All show Wells's greatest gifts as storyteller and novelist. Edited by E. F. Bleiler. x + 335pp. (USO) 20605-X Paperbound $2.50

THE DEVIL'S DICTIONARY, Ambrose Bierce. America's own Oscar Wilde— Ambrose Bierce—offers his barbed iconoclastic wisdom in over 1,000 definitions hailed by H. L. Mencken as "some of the most gorgeous witticisms in the English language." 145pp. 20487-1 Paperbound $1.25

MAX AND MORITZ, Wilhelm Busch. Great children's classic, father of comic strip, of two bad boys, Max and Moritz. Also Ker and Plunk (Plisch und Plumm), Cat and Mouse, Deceitful Henry, Ice-Peter, The Boy and the Pipe, and five other pieces. Original German, with English translation. Edited by H. Arthur Klein; translations by various hands and H. Arthur Klein. vi + 216pp. 20181-3 Paperbound $2.00

PIGS IS PIGS AND OTHER FAVORITES, Ellis Parker Butler. The title story is one of the best humor short stories, as Mike Flannery obfuscates biology and English. Also included, That Pup of Murchison's, The Great American Pie Company, and Perkins of Portland. 14 illustrations. v + 109pp. 21532-6 Paperbound $1.25

THE PETERKIN PAPERS, Lucretia P. Hale. It takes genius to be as stupidly mad as the Peterkins, as they decide to become wise, celebrate the "Fourth," keep a cow, and otherwise strain the resources of the Lady from Philadelphia. Basic book of American humor. 153 illustrations. 219pp. 20794-3 Paperbound $2.00

PERRAULT'S FAIRY TALES, translated by A. E. Johnson and S. R. Littlewood, with 34 full-page illustrations by Gustave Doré. All the original Perrault stories— Cinderella, Sleeping Beauty, Bluebeard, Little Red Riding Hood, Puss in Boots, Tom Thumb, etc.—with their witty verse morals and the magnificent illustrations of Doré. One of the five or six great books of European fairy tales. viii + 117pp. 8⅛ x 11. 22311-6 Paperbound $2.00

OLD HUNGARIAN FAIRY TALES, Baroness Orczy. Favorites translated and adapted by author of the *Scarlet Pimpernel.* Eight fairy tales include "The Suitors of Princess Fire-Fly," "The Twin Hunchbacks," "Mr. Cuttlefish's Love Story," and "The Enchanted Cat." This little volume of magic and adventure will captivate children as it has for generations. 90 drawings by Montagu Barstow. 96pp. (USO) 22293-4 Paperbound $1.95

THE RED FAIRY BOOK, Andrew Lang. Lang's color fairy books have long been children's favorites. This volume includes Rapunzel, Jack and the Bean-stalk and 35 other stories, familiar and unfamiliar. 4 plates, 93 illustrations x + 367pp.
21673-X Paperbound $2.50

THE BLUE FAIRY BOOK, Andrew Lang. Lang's tales come from all countries and all times. Here are 37 tales from Grimm, the Arabian Nights, Greek Mythology, and other fascinating sources. 8 plates, 130 illustrations. xi + 390pp.
21437-0 Paperbound $2.50

HOUSEHOLD STORIES BY THE BROTHERS GRIMM. Classic English-language edition of the well-known tales — Rumpelstiltskin, Snow White, Hansel and Gretel, The Twelve Brothers, Faithful John, Rapunzel, Tom Thumb (52 stories in all). Translated into simple, straightforward English by Lucy Crane. Ornamented with headpieces, vignettes, elaborate decorative initials and a dozen full-page illustrations by Walter Crane. x + 269pp.
21080-4 Paperbound **$2.00**

THE MERRY ADVENTURES OF ROBIN HOOD, Howard Pyle. The finest modern versions of the traditional ballads and tales about the great English outlaw. Howard Pyle's complete prose version, with every word, every illustration of the first edition. Do not confuse this facsimile of the original (1883) with modern editions that change text or illustrations. 23 plates plus many page decorations. xxii + 296pp.
22043-5 Paperbound $2.50

THE STORY OF KING ARTHUR AND HIS KNIGHTS, Howard Pyle. The finest children's version of the life of King Arthur; brilliantly retold by Pyle, with 48 of his most imaginative illustrations. xviii + 313pp. 6⅛ x 9¼.
21445-1 Paperbound $2.50

THE WONDERFUL WIZARD OF OZ, L. Frank Baum. America's finest children's book in facsimile of first edition with all Denslow illustrations in full color. The edition a child should have. Introduction by Martin Gardner. 23 color plates, scores of drawings. iv + 267pp.
20691-2 Paperbound $2.50

THE MARVELOUS LAND OF OZ, L. Frank Baum. The second Oz book, every bit as imaginative as the Wizard. The hero is a boy named Tip, but the Scarecrow and the Tin Woodman are back, as is the Oz magic. 16 color plates, 120 drawings by John R. Neill. 287pp.
20692-0 Paperbound $2.50

THE MAGICAL MONARCH OF MO, L. Frank Baum. Remarkable adventures in a land even stranger than Oz. The best of Baum's books not in the Oz series. 15 color plates and dozens of drawings by Frank Verbeck. xviii + 237pp.
21892-9 Paperbound $2.25

THE BAD CHILD'S BOOK OF BEASTS, MORE BEASTS FOR WORSE CHILDREN, A MORAL ALPHABET, Hilaire Belloc. Three complete humor classics in one volume. Be kind to the frog, and do not call him names . . . and 28 other whimsical animals. Familiar favorites and some not so well known. Illustrated by Basil Blackwell. 156pp.
(USO) 20749-8 Paperbound $1.50

EAST O' THE SUN AND WEST O' THE MOON, George W. Dasent. Considered the best of all translations of these Norwegian folk tales, this collection has been enjoyed by generations of children (and folklorists too). Includes True and Untrue, Why the Sea is Salt, East O' the Sun and West O' the Moon, Why the Bear is Stumpy-Tailed, Boots and the Troll, The Cock and the Hen, Rich Peter the Pedlar, and 52 more. The only edition with all 59 tales. 77 illustrations by Erik Werenskiold and Theodor Kittelsen. xv + 418pp. 22521-6 Paperbound $3.50

GOOPS AND HOW TO BE THEM, Gelett Burgess. Classic of tongue-in-cheek humor, masquerading as etiquette book. 87 verses, twice as many cartoons, show mischievous Goops as they demonstrate to children virtues of table manners, neatness, courtesy, etc. Favorite for generations. viii + 88pp. 6½ x 9¼.
22233-0 Paperbound $1.25

ALICE'S ADVENTURES UNDER GROUND, Lewis Carroll. The first version, quite different from the final Alice in Wonderland, printed out by Carroll himself with his own illustrations. Complete facsimile of the "million dollar" manuscript Carroll gave to Alice Liddell in 1864. Introduction by Martin Gardner. viii + 96pp. Title and dedication pages in color. 21482-6 Paperbound $1.25

THE BROWNIES, THEIR BOOK, Palmer Cox. Small as mice, cunning as foxes, exuberant and full of mischief, the Brownies go to the zoo, toy shop, seashore, circus, etc., in 24 verse adventures and 266 illustrations. Long a favorite, since their first appearance in St. Nicholas Magazine. xi + 144pp. 6⅝ x 9¼.
21265-3 Paperbound $1.75

SONGS OF CHILDHOOD, Walter De La Mare. Published (under the pseudonym Walter Ramal) when De La Mare was only 29, this charming collection has long been a favorite children's book. A facsimile of the first edition in paper, the 47 poems capture the simplicity of the nursery rhyme and the ballad, including such lyrics as I Met Eve, Tartary, The Silver Penny. vii + 106pp. (USO) 21972-0 Paperbound $1.25

THE COMPLETE NONSENSE OF EDWARD LEAR, Edward Lear. The finest 19th-century humorist-cartoonist in full: all nonsense limericks, zany alphabets, Owl and Pussycat, songs, nonsense botany, and more than 500 illustrations by Lear himself. Edited by Holbrook Jackson. xxix + 287pp. (USO) 20167-8 Paperbound $2.00

BILLY WHISKERS: THE AUTOBIOGRAPHY OF A GOAT, Frances Trego Montgomery. A favorite of children since the early 20th century, here are the escapades of that rambunctious, irresistible and mischievous goat—Billy Whiskers. Much in the spirit of Peck's Bad Boy, this is a book that children never tire of reading or hearing. All the original familiar illustrations by W. H. Fry are included: 6 color plates, 18 black and white drawings. 159pp. 22345-0 Paperbound $2.00

MOTHER GOOSE MELODIES. Faithful republication of the fabulously rare Munroe and Francis "copyright 1833" Boston edition—the most important Mother Goose collection, usually referred to as the "original." Familiar rhymes plus many rare ones, with wonderful old woodcut illustrations. Edited by E. F. Bleiler. 128pp. 4½ x 6⅜. 22577-1 Paperbound $1.00

TWO LITTLE SAVAGES; BEING THE ADVENTURES OF TWO BOYS WHO LIVED AS INDIANS AND WHAT THEY LEARNED, Ernest Thompson Seton. Great classic of nature and boyhood provides a vast range of woodlore in most palatable form, a genuinely entertaining story. Two farm boys build a teepee in woods and live in it for a month, working out Indian solutions to living problems, star lore, birds and animals, plants, etc. 293 illustrations. vii + 286pp.

20985-7 Paperbound $2.50

PETER PIPER'S PRACTICAL PRINCIPLES OF PLAIN & PERFECT PRONUNCIATION. Alliterative jingles and tongue-twisters of surprising charm, that made their first appearance in America about 1830. Republished in full with the spirited woodcut illustrations from this earliest American edition. 32pp. $4\frac{1}{2}$ x $6\frac{3}{8}$.

22560-7 Paperbound $1.00

SCIENCE EXPERIMENTS AND AMUSEMENTS FOR CHILDREN, Charles Vivian. 73 easy experiments, requiring only materials found at home or easily available, such as candles, coins, steel wool, etc.; illustrate basic phenomena like vacuum, simple chemical reaction, etc. All safe. Modern, well-planned. Formerly *Science Games for Children.* 102 photos, numerous drawings. 96pp. $6\frac{1}{8}$ x $9\frac{1}{4}$.

21856-2 Paperbound $1.25

AN INTRODUCTION TO CHESS MOVES AND TACTICS SIMPLY EXPLAINED, Leonard Barden. Informal intermediate introduction, quite strong in explaining reasons for moves. Covers basic material, tactics, important openings, traps, positional play in middle game, end game. Attempts to isolate patterns and recurrent configurations. Formerly *Chess.* 58 figures. 102pp.   (USO) 21210-6 Paperbound $1.25

LASKER'S MANUAL OF CHESS, Dr. Emanuel Lasker. Lasker was not only one of the five great World Champions, he was also one of the ablest expositors, theorists, and analysts. In many ways, his Manual, permeated with his philosophy of battle, filled with keen insights, is one of the greatest works ever written on chess. Filled with analyzed games by the great players. A single-volume library that will profit almost any chess player, beginner or master. 308 diagrams. xli x 349pp.

20640-8 Paperbound $2.75

THE MASTER BOOK OF MATHEMATICAL RECREATIONS, Fred Schuh. In opinion of many the finest work ever prepared on mathematical puzzles, stunts, recreations; exhaustively thorough explanations of mathematics involved, analysis of effects, citation of puzzles and games. Mathematics involved is elementary. Translated by F. Göbel. 194 figures. xxiv + 430pp.   22134-2 Paperbound $3.50

MATHEMATICS, MAGIC AND MYSTERY, Martin Gardner. Puzzle editor for Scientific American explains mathematics behind various mystifying tricks: card tricks, stage "mind reading," coin and match tricks, counting out games, geometric dissections, etc. Probability sets, theory of numbers clearly explained. Also provides more than 400 tricks, guaranteed to work, that you can do. 135 illustrations. xii + 176pp.

20335-2 Paperbound $1.75

MATHEMATICAL PUZZLES FOR BEGINNERS AND ENTHUSIASTS, Geoffrey Mott-Smith. 189 puzzles from easy to difficult—involving arithmetic, logic, algebra, properties of digits, probability, etc.—for enjoyment and mental stimulus. Explanation of mathematical principles behind the puzzles. 135 illustrations. viii + 248pp.

20198-8 Paperbound $1.75

PAPER FOLDING FOR BEGINNERS, William D. Murray and Francis J. Rigney. Easiest book on the market, clearest instructions on making interesting, beautiful origami. Sail boats, cups, roosters, frogs that move legs, bonbon boxes, standing birds, etc. 40 projects; more than 275 diagrams and photographs. 94pp.

20713-7 Paperbound $1.00

TRICKS AND GAMES ON THE POOL TABLE, Fred Herrmann. 79 tricks and games— some solitaires, some for two or more players, some competitive games—to entertain you between formal games. Mystifying shots and throws, unusual caroms, tricks involving such props as cork, coins, a hat, etc. Formerly *Fun on the Pool Table*. 77 figures. 95pp.

21814-7 Paperbound $1.25

HAND SHADOWS TO BE THROWN UPON THE WALL: A SERIES OF NOVEL AND AMUSING FIGURES FORMED BY THE HAND, Henry Bursill. Delightful picturebook from great-grandfather's day shows how to make 18 different hand shadows: a bird that flies, duck that quacks, dog that wags his tail, camel, goose, deer, boy, turtle, etc. Only book of its sort. vi + 33pp. 6½ x 9¼.

21779-5 Paperbound $1.00

WHITTLING AND WOODCARVING, E. J. Tangerman. 18th printing of best book on market. "If you can cut a potato you can carve" toys and puzzles, chains, chessmen, caricatures, masks, frames, woodcut blocks, surface patterns, much more. Information on tools, woods, techniques. Also goes into serious wood sculpture from Middle Ages to present, East and West. 464 photos, figures. x + 293pp.

20965-2 Paperbound $2.00

HISTORY OF PHILOSOPHY, Julián Marias. Possibly the clearest, most easily followed, best planned, most useful one-volume history of philosophy on the market; neither skimpy nor overfull. Full details on system of every major philosopher and dozens of less important thinkers from pre-Socratics up to Existentialism and later. Strong on many European figures usually omitted. Has gone through dozens of editions in Europe. 1966 edition, translated by Stanley Appelbaum and Clarence Strowbridge. xviii + 505pp.

21739-6 Paperbound $3.50

YOGA: A SCIENTIFIC EVALUATION, Kovoor T. Behanan. Scientific but non-technical study of physiological results of yoga exercises; done under auspices of Yale U. Relations to Indian thought, to psychoanalysis, etc. 16 photos. xxiii + 270pp.

20505-3 Paperbound $2.50

Prices subject to change without notice.
Available at your book dealer or write for free catalogue to Dept. GI, Dover Publications, Inc., 180 Varick St., N. Y., N. Y. 10014. Dover publishes more than 150 books each year on science, elementary and advanced mathematics, biology, music, art, literary history, social sciences and other areas.